Fire of the Jidaan

By Whit McClendon

**Complete in One Volume
(previously published as
three separate titles in the
Fire of the Jidaan Trilogy)**

Copyrights

First Printing, Rolling Scroll Publishing

(Fire of the Jidaan Omnibus)
Copyright © August 2018 by Whit McClendon

Mage's Burden Copyright © 2014 by Whit McClendon
Gart's Road Copyright © 2015 by Whit McClendon
A Mage Awakens Copyright © 2016 by Whit McClendon

ISBN-13: 978-1-7326300-2-4
ISBN-10: 1-7326300-2-X

Cover by: Lauria
Copyediting: Michelle McClish
Published by: Rolling Scroll Publishing, Katy, TX
Website: www.jidaan.com

**To join my mailing list to be notified when a new novel is published, go to
http://www.whitmcclendon.com**

**You can also Like my Facebook page!
http://www.facebook.com/fireofthejidaan/**

MAGE'S BURDEN

Book 1 of the Fire of the Jidaan Trilogy

Whit McClendon

Rolling Scroll Publishing

Mage's Burden

Book One of the Fire of the Jidaan Trilogy

By Whit McClendon

Chapter 1

Zothar's breath was coming in ragged gasps, and white spots were dancing before his eyes, but the terrified little man ran on. Although the moon was full, her silvery light seldom filtered down through the vast canopy overhead, and Zothar blindly stumbled again and again in the darkness, frantically tearing his way through the thick vegetation. The taste of blood was in his mouth, and his hands, face, and arms were scored with deep cuts from the unseen branches and sticks that slapped and scratched him as he ran. *Far better that than the blades of the dark-skinned ones!* The thought blossomed in Zothar's mind for only an instant before the toe of his boot caught on something, sending him headlong to the ground. *SSNAP!* The pain of Zothar's newly broken wrist shocked him so badly that he could not breathe for a moment. Curling his body around his injured arm, Zothar tried to regain control of himself. The haze of agony that now emanated from his injury dwarfed the cuts and scratches he had sustained in his narrow escape, and it was all he could do to make himself breathe through the pain.

It had been only blind luck that had saved him. He had been relieving himself in the bushes when the Tballa had attacked his caravan, and he had been able to race into the jungle while his workers and bearers had been mercilessly butchered.

Zothar rolled slowly to a kneeling position, still protecting his injured wrist, and grimaced as he peered back into the jungle, searching for any sign of the grim-faced Tballa. Moments passed, and Zothar saw nothing.

"Yawa! Yawala butu!" Zothar's head jerked in the direction of the shout as fear exploded anew within him. *Sweet Goddess, they're almost upon me!* Turning to run, he tripped again and slammed to the ground, sending fiery bursts of agony up his arm as he scrambled to escape.

Seconds later, a gnarled man, black as oily midnight, materialized in the darkness where Zothar had been only moments before. He squatted there and looked at the ground, scratching his scarred chin absently as he did so.

More shouts answered the first, and suddenly the jungle was alive with voices as the Tballa warriors converged on the old tracker. There were twenty warriors in all, and as one they hushed to hear the Elder's findings.

Frowning, Baho cast his eyes over the trampled grass and broken fronds of fern. He snorted to himself, scornful of their quarry's pitiful flight. *A baby could follow this stupid man!* The Elder peered into the foliage ahead, and the warriors waited.

Even with the constant chirping and rustling sounds of the jungle, they could still distinguish the racket of Zothar's hurried passage from somewhere ahead and east of them. A single gesture from the tracker, and deadly smiles split the faces of the warriors as they melted into the jungle, eagerly anticipating the capture, torture, and eventual grisly death of another unwanted intruder.

The pain in Zothar's fractured wrist had lessened. For that, at least, he was thankful, even though it was badly swollen. He was far beyond his body's natural limits now, and shock and pain had blended all of his hurts into a dull haze of general agony. Suddenly, the clutching arms of the jungle fell away, and Zothar stumbled into a wide clearing. Illuminated brightly by the moon's glow, thick stalks of knee-high grass waved gently in the breeze, and Zothar ran forward, grateful to be free of the grasping foliage.

Almost directly ahead of him, Zothar could see a group of dark, shadowy objects. As he moved closer, he could see that they were massive boulders, strewn across one edge of the clearing as if by the careless hand of a god. The central stone dwarfed the others, and as Zothar peered through the dark at the huge, reddish monolith, a deep sense of foreboding washed over him. Gritting his teeth against the pain of his injuries and the odd sense of dread that lingered about the stone, Zothar staggered towards the rocks with the last of his strength, the cold knot of fear in his soul driving him forward. However slim the chance might be, he hoped he could find some cranny in which to hide himself until the Tballa had gone.

The tall grass ended abruptly as he neared the stones, and Zothar stumbled again in his haste. Pain flared anew in his broken wrist as he slammed to the naked earth on his knees, and his vision blurred with tears of agony and terror. Even so, he scrambled doggedly towards the rocks and moved behind one of the larger chunks of rubble, keeping his back to the huge red boulder. From this poor cover, he turned to look back at the edges of the jungle, hoping that he had somehow lost the angry warriors.

But Zothar's luck was quickly running out. He could hear their shouts, their angry voices sounding among the trees. Suddenly, the entire group of warriors emerged into the meadow from various points along the tree line. As Zothar watched them gathering together, he prayed feverishly to the Goddess to hide him from the dark-skinned natives, promising a huge donation, and to attend temple services much more often in the future. He tried to slow his frantic breathing, hoping the warriors wouldn't hear his fatigued gasps from across the clearing.

One of the warriors suddenly screamed a warcry and burst into a run, heading straight for the stones. The other Tballa immediately followed suit, bellowing their bloodcurdling whoops of victory as they, too, caught sight of Zothar cowering behind his rock.

Panic suddenly robbed Zothar of his senses. He stared wide-eyed at the warriors racing towards him, gliding through the high grass like an ebony flood, armed to the teeth with spears, hatchets, and bows and arrows.

The Tballan warriors raced on toward the terrified merchant until the lead warrior saw the border of dead grass and skidded unexpectedly to a stop a mere stone's throw from Zothar's hiding place. Frantically, he turned and waved the others to a halt, fear newly evident in his voice. The resultant shouts of outrage were immediate.

Zothar stared in disbelief as the leader addressed his shouting men, gesturing wildly. He spoke rapidly in their singsong, clicking tongue and pointed several times to the rocks and the surrounding area. As he did so, their demeanor changed. Anger and bloodlust quickly gave way to fear. All the warriors fell silent, save one.

The huge warrior pushed his way to the front, and his fellows gave way. He was easily the largest man Zothar had ever seen. His scars were many, and the leader's words had apparently not fazed him one bit. He began to yell at him, obviously wishing to continue the pursuit. He shouted mightily at the smaller man, gesturing violently with his hatchet toward the cowering merchant. The leader stood his ground and shook his head several times, making negating gestures towards the rocks. The other natives began muttering amongst themselves while the two men argued.

Zothar was perplexed at the situation, but thankful that he still lived. Apparently, the Tballa had some reason for not coming any closer to his hiding place, but the brutish, hulking warrior did not seem to care what the smaller man said. As Zothar watched the natives argue at the edge of the dead grass, he backed away from the smaller boulder. His questing right hand met the larger stone's surface and found it surprisingly cold. Zothar kept his eyes on the bickering natives as he flattened himself against the chill monolith and began to slide along its frigid surface, hoping to make it to the other side where he could slip unnoticed into the jungle beyond. The argument in the meadow escalated.

The cold from the massive stone chilled Zothar, eliciting a shiver in spite of the hot, muggy night. As he moved, Zothar slid his uninjured hand along the stone, feeling his rings of silver and gold lightly scoring the surface of the rock.

Thump. Zothar felt more than heard the sound, a deep and resounding impact of some sort that terrified him. He froze in place, his eyes darting frantically as he tried to ascertain its source.

The muscled warrior was getting more furious by the minute, but his adversary stood firm. The huge native finally screamed in fury, and raised his hatchet to cleave the elder's skull before resuming his attack on the merchant. Before he could strike, a burst of scarlet radiance exploded from the great boulder. The warrior stopped in mid-strike, his eyes wide as he saw the glowing red mist boil forth from the rock, enveloping the struggling form of the ragged little merchant. It lifted him from his hiding place on serpentine arms of nothingness. Zothar's screams pierced the night as he frantically tried to free himself. The other Tballa turned and fled at no small speed, leaving the brutish warrior, hatchet upraised, staring at the writhing crimson blaze.

The nebulous mass lifted Zothar and positioned him directly above the top of the huge boulder. CRACK!! The great stone split down the middle as if struck with a massive chisel, and a blast of cold wind emanated from within. In spite of his fear, the warrior stepped closer to the stone and hurled his weapon at the swirling radiance. Instantly, a scarlet tendril of mist snapped out to intercept the spinning hatchet, freezing it in flight. The hatchet then exploded, sending a deadly shower of metal and wooden fragments hurtling towards the quaking warrior. He screamed and covered his face with his arms as flying splinters lacerated his body. Wounded, he turned at last to flee, the merchant's screams and the explosion of his weapon ringing in his ears.

From his place within the roiling mist above the rock, Zothar watched the warrior turn and sprint for the jungle. He saw another crimson tendril snake out to capture the warrior before he had taken five running strides. He heard the man scream in terror as he was borne into the air on the freezing grip of the mist.

As the warrior was brought closer, Zothar saw his frantic struggles suddenly cease; his muscled body hung limply in the clutching embrace of the mist. Horrified, Zothar watched as the body began to shrivel in upon itself, drying up and shrinking until only an empty husk remained. The mist pulsed brightly for a moment, as if strengthened. The desiccated shell of the warrior dropped out of sight to the ground, and Zothar screamed anew, fearing a similar end.

You. A dry, rasping voice scraped along the edges of Zothar's mind. *You have freed me! At last, at long last, I am FREE!*

"Who are you?" Zothar shouted, still struggling to free himself from the icy coils.

I? the voice grated silently. *I am he who shall rule this world. I am Mordak.*

It took but a moment for Zothar to remember where he had heard that name, and a fear greater than anything he had ever known blossomed in his heart. That name had terrified him as a child, just as it had every other child he had known. A man bearing that name had once used dark powers to slaughter thousands upon thousands, and had committed such atrocities that his name was reviled even now, two thousand years after his fabled defeat at the hands of a northern Mage. The stories that his father had told him had given him nightmares long ago, but this nightmare was real, and there would be no waking from it.

The mist tightened its icy grip as it spilled out of the boulder, forming a twisting maelstrom around Zothar. It quickly began to seep into his body, searing him with its freezing caress. As Zothar's mind began to fade, he caught fleeting glimpses of the twisted madness that was Mordak. Better to die now, he thought as his life ebbed from him, than live to see Mordak arise. Contemptuous laughter followed him into the abyss.

Chapter 2

Deep within the caverns of the Heartstrong Mountains, Brunar suddenly opened his grey eyes. Flinging back the covers, the Mage quickly sat up in bed, swung his legs over the side, and rubbed his face with one graceful hand while he tried to get his bearings. Carefully, he tested his stiff legs, and then stood to stretch himself and shake off the thick grogginess that plagued him. He looked around at the stone walls of the chamber, letting his eyes wander where they might. There were no doors that he could see and three of the rough walls were bare. Shelves were carved directly into the rock of the remaining wall, and these held neatly folded blankets, clothes, and other mundane items.

In one corner, there squatted a great, ponderous desk. It was covered with parchments, scrolls, quills, inkwells, and huge books with placemarkers sticking out of them, all neatly arranged. Above it, he spied the small glowing globe that provided a subdued illumination for the room. It hung in space with no visible means of support, shining merrily. Brunar silently blinked at it.

At first, he could not exactly remember how the hovering lamp had gotten there. For all he knew, this was the room of a stranger. Brunar squeezed his eyes shut and took a deep, cleansing breath, held it for a moment, and then slowly let it out.

When his eyes opened once again, they fell on a small gem that rested on the corner of his desk. It was glowing an ugly red. Moving as quickly as his unsteady legs could carry him, Brunar made his way to the desk where he could now recall having studied and written of so many subjects over so many years. He picked up the shining gem, and found it cold. Despair took him for a moment then, and he sighed a deep, pained sigh.

"This cannot be! He...he was imprisoned with the most powerful spell! And only white gold could have unlocked it. How could that have happened?" Horrified, he gazed at the gem in his hand as he contemplated the possibilities. Then his slender fingers clenched around it in a grip of iron. "No matter. It doesn't matter how it happened, only that it has occurred."

Although his fatigue was deep, and his bones ached painfully, Brunar steeled himself against the despair that had momentarily taken him. Quietly, he spoke a Word of power, and when he unclenched his fist, the gem's light had vanished, having served its purpose. It had been magickally linked to the wards placed upon Mordak's prison back in the time of the Banishing, and set to alert Brunar should the unthinkable happen, and Mordak somehow break free. Brunar opened a drawer in the huge desk and dropped the gem into it, wishing that he'd never seen its scarlet gleam.

Spreading both hands on his desk, Brunar leaned forward and settled his weight heavily on it. He remembered the evil of the Dark One, Mordak, trapped in Triagga over two thousand years ago. Brunar's weathered face hardened as his memories returned him to that heart-rending time. He had lost four Guardians in that final battle, four beloved friends. They had died defending him. Despite such a shattering loss, the remaining Guardians had rallied to weaken Mordak enough that Brunar could recover and attack, sealing the Evil One's essence within an ancient stone. That feat in itself had nearly destroyed Brunar, requiring every trace of power he had possessed.

Somehow, after two thousand years of imprisonment, Mordak was again free to corrupt and destroy.

Brunar became aware of the knotty ache between his shoulders, and he leaned back and tried to shrug the stiffness away. Staying alive this long had come at a price, and Brunar's ten year longsleep had been interrupted by the alarm. For every hundred and fifty years of life, Brunar was forced into a deep, rejuvenating longsleep for ten years, lest he finally grow old and die. A quick glance at the astrolabe told Brunar that he still had eight years to go before his magickal sleep was to end, and the many aches and pains of his body made it seem as though he had slept for only moments. With so little rest, the Mage was painfully aware that his full strength would be denied him.

Weakened though he was, he knew he had to try to find out what had happened. Turning from the desk, Brunar moved to the shelves and retrieved a jagged crystal about the size of a man's head, and placed it on the floor in the center of the room. Chanting as he stepped away from the crystal, Brunar spoke the Words that would send his mystical Sight out from the mountains, south to Triagga and towards the ancient stones of Mordak's prison. Images, indistinct at first, but increasing in clarity, began to form in the empty space above the crystal. The green blanket of jungle trees appeared, and Brunar's Sight moved rapidly over the vast canopy, searching for the massive, ruddy stone.

Brunar gasped as he suddenly sensed the presence of the Dark One himself, a malignant evil that festered like a raging sickness deep within the jungle's heart. Cold laughter echoed in his mind, and a searing pain stabbed into Brunar's forehead. The

Mage cried out and dropped to one knee, struggling to see through the pain.

Fool! You're already too late! My day is coming, and this time, your Guardians will be helpless against me!

Brunar felt the magickal pulse before it struck, and managed to throw his arms over his face and enable his shield as his scrying crystal exploded under the force of Mordak's magick. The deadly shards ricocheted from him, shattering against the unyielding stone walls and embedding themselves in the wood of the desk.

Brunar slumped to the floor, exhausted. He lay there for several heartbeats before cursing his weakness and staggering back to his feet. He knew the only way Mordak would have had the strength to attack so quickly was for him to have killed and absorbed the lifeforce of the first people he could find. Centuries of imprisonment within the warded stone should have weakened the sorcerer, and most likely driven him beyond madness, as well. But it seemed that he was formidable again already. No one was safe.

Thousands upon thousands of innocents had suffered unspeakable horrors under his evil rule so long ago, and it seemed certain that Mordak would attempt to reestablish those dark times as soon as his power was fully renewed. After this episode, Brunar knew that he would never be able to kill Mordak alone. The sorcerer was already too strong, while he had only just awakened. If Mordak was willing to absorb the lifeforce of others, he would rise in strength far faster than Brunar, and his hatred and madness would eventually grant him an evil power that would be difficult to match.

Only the combined force of all seven of the protectors, the Mage and six Guardians, could hope to put an end to Mordak. Brunar knew what he had to do. Those possessed of the power, those descended from the first Guardians, had to be found and trained until they reached their full potential. Then the battle could begin in earnest.

"And this time, we won't be so easy on you, Evil One." The Mage's voice was still dry and cracked from disuse, yet another sign of his weakness. Brunar went to the shelves again, this time bringing out a small box which he carried to the desk and placed there. He passed one hand over it, and its runes flashed in response. He opened it to find a small chunk of cooked beef, a piece of cheese, bread, grapes, and a stoppered flask of water, fresh as the day he had placed them inside. Once the small meal was finished, Brunar replaced the box and turned to the eastern wall of his sleeping chamber. As he approached, the wall simply disappeared and he stepped through the opening into the darkened, echoing Hall of Jidaana.

From his doorway in the southwestern corner of the vast chamber, Brunar walked quickly to the center of the room, willing the larger globelights here to awaken. They sprang to life high in the corners and center of the lofty ceiling, brightly illuminating the room that Brunar had known intimately for centuries.

The vaulted ceiling was fifty feet above him, supported by eight wide stone columns evenly spaced around the massive room. The chamber was eighty yards long and half that distance wide. Sometimes, Brunar wondered what massive receptions might have taken place here before he had been called to the ancient, forgotten mountain keep.

The floor was polished stone, thickly coated now with a pale layer of dust. In spite of the severity of the situation, Brunar raised an eyebrow at this and allowed himself a ghost of a grin. *Good help is hard to find these days,* he thought, making a mental note to clean the hall later on. For the time being, it would have to wait.

Along the long north and south walls yawned the doorways that led to the Guardians' private quarters, as well as larger openings that led to the other parts of the Hall. The sturdy wooden doors stood open now as they had for centuries, as if anticipating the arrival of their new tenants.

At the far end of the Hall was a much larger doorway than those of the residence chambers, opening into a wide corridor that led to the outside. It was dark now, but when the massive eastern gates at the end of the tunnel were thrown open at dawn, the entire chamber would be awash in the blazing light of morning. Many a beautiful sunrise had crested the eastern peaks to shine into the Keep and greet the Mage in the past.

Brunar turned to his left and saw the western wall of the chamber, the sight of it filling him with hope. Displayed there as they had been for centuries were the six short-hafted spears that were the Jidaan. He strode up to the steps of the dais and mounted them, keeping his eyes on the beautifully crafted blades on the wall, drinking in the sight of the weapons that had armed the Guardians for time immemorial. Long ago, the world had seen these spears not as instruments of bloodshed, but instead as keepers of peace and goodwill. He noted that not one of the slim blades showed the least sign of use-they gleamed in the globelight as if newly forged.

Five feet long they were, and their single-edged blades made up one third of each weapon's length. At first glance, the blades were similar to common butcher knives, save for a short, blunt parrying spur on their thick spines. However, closer inspection would show the fine inscriptions of golden Weya runes running along the blades, and the incredible keenness of the weapons. Their edges were razor sharp, and would always be so, just as their hafts would never hold a nick or cut.

Clutched in the finely-wrought pommel of each spear was a jewel, a different gem for each weapon. These represented the Gift each Jidaan would bestow on its user. Sapphire, onyx, opal, diamond, ruby, and emerald gems sparkled and danced, one stone within each pommel's unbreakable grip. Brunar often gazed at these weapons and marveled at the sheer power that the Weya Lormages of old had somehow harnessed to create them. Now, they stood side by side in their places on the wall, waiting.

Brunar walked over to the leftmost spear, the ruby-handled weapon. He took a moment to steady himself, and then he reached out with one slender hand and slipped his fingers around its wooden shaft.

"Bringer of the Gift of Power, who hast thou Chosen?"

The ruby in the weapon's pommel flared a brilliant, clear scarlet as it was awakened after two millennia. It thrummed in the Mage's hands, and Brunar opened his mind to its power. A sense of incredible potency and great strength washed over Brunar, and was gone. Brunar felt himself move, though he knew that his body would remain in its place, and watched the Hall of Jidaana fade around him to be replaced by a wooded glen still cloaked in the shadowy folds of dawn.

A cool stream coursed lazily through the center of the small valley. Brunar could hear the birds trading songs in the leafy treetops overhead as the sky began to brighten with the first hints of sunrise. The stream opened out into the gently dancing waters of a small lake to Brunar's left, and the dense foliage of the forest beyond provided shade at the lakeshore. He could see ducks swimming in the water on the far side of the lake, quacking contentedly. The land was calm and peaceful, and the leaves in the trees waved as a breeze blew across the mere's rippling waters.

Suddenly, Brunar heard a booming voice bellowing with laughter. He turned toward the sound and saw a massive fellow just within the boundaries of the forest struggling with what looked to be the trunk of a rather large tree. He appeared to be having trouble carrying the thing, but he seemed to be enjoying himself in spite of his enormous burden. Brunar saw a small cabin set back away from the lapping shores of the lake, and surmised that this was the huge man's home. What purpose the felled tree might serve, he had no idea.

As a flock of birds erupted from the trees above the large man, Brunar willed his essence towards the small cabin at the lakeshore, and the huge laughing fellow beyond.

Chapter 3

The tree trunk must have weighed more than thirty-five stone, but that was of little concern to Bjarke. He had wrestled bears twice that size and had always managed to teach them a thing or two before sending them running off into the woods. Bjarke was just having a little trouble finding a good way to lift the thing. He had trimmed it well, so it had no limbs to grip, and it was too long to roll effectively through the forest. But now he had to find a way to carry it back to the cabin, if he were going to be able to cut it into smaller pieces for building.

He finally decided to do what any good man carrying a massive timber through the forest would do. He picked it up near the middle, heaved it up onto his right shoulder, and began to walk briskly down the wooded slope towards his cabin at the lakeside.

He had been doing fine until he heard a commotion in the trees above him. He glanced up to see a pair of squirrels bickering over an acorn, and saw them start to chase each other around the treetops. He was beginning to chuckle softly at their antics when he slipped on a small stone and slammed one end of the trunk he carried into a tree in front of him. This brought forth even more laughter from the huge man as he shuffled and twisted to regain his balance. Turning, he managed to strike another tree with the opposite end of his burden. The birds above suddenly erupted from their perches atop the trees, startled by the ruckus below.

The sight of the beautiful blue birds winging towards a safer and quieter haven did the bearish man in. He dropped the ponderous trunk with a resounding thud before falling in a heap on top of it. The peals of booming laughter pouring forth from him were easily loud enough to shake the leaves on the trees.

"Oh, what a sight I must have been!" Bjarke said aloud to himself, wiping tears from his eyes as his mirth finally subsided. "It's not every day one enjoys a dance with a tree so pretty as this!" He slapped the fallen log and began to stand. "I'm terribly sorry to have disturbed you up there," he called to the now absent birds. "Maybe next time I won't get so tickled!"

He knew very well that he got tickled at least twenty times a day. Anyone looking for the mighty Bjarke need only wander in this direction, listen, and let the massive fellow's laughter guide them to his home. Bjarke noted that the thick braid that usually confined his ruddy hair behind him had come undone during his dance with the enormous log, and his usually neat beard had somehow become full of leaves and tiny twigs as well. He chuckled once more at himself for becoming such a mess as he sat back down on the fallen log and picked the debris from his beard. When he was satisfied that his thick whiskers no longer resembled a brush pile, he began to rebraid his hair.

As his fingers worked, Bjarke hummed a little tune, enjoying the coolness and solitude of another early morning in his valley. He loved seeing the dappled, grey shadows that were just starting to appear on the rich earth before him at this time of day. They brought back so many childhood memories, especially those of playing hide-and-seek with his parents in these woods.

He grinned as he remembered his hulking father, Bekkoran, blundering noisily through the shrubbery, laughing all the while and pretending that he had no idea where his son might be. Since Bjarke had inherited his father's solid muscular build and towering height, it had been increasingly difficult to find decent hidey-holes large enough to accommodate his stout young body. Bjarke had then resorted to stealth, and managed to fool his father many times by sneaking around him.

Bjarke laughed to himself as he remembered the time he had hidden atop the cabin's stone chimney to escape his father's playful searching. Bekkoran had roamed the nearby woods, laughing and calling for his son. He had known that if he could get close to Bjarke, the sturdy boy's barely-stifled giggling would betray him and the chase back to the cabin would begin.

Bjarke would have won that day, but for his mother's lighting the fire for the morning meal. Bekkoran had by then given up on the woods, and had started searching near the cabin. In fact, he ended up standing just below Bjarke's unsteady perch. It had been all the youngster could do to stay silent, his hands clamped over his mouth, just in case.

As Bekkoran had stood there, perplexed and scratching his mane of brown hair, Bjarke had felt as though he might burst trying to contain his laughter. His father was so close, but still oblivious to his new hiding place.

Suddenly, the chimney had belched smoke, soot, and heat right up into Bjarke's rear end. He had let out a yell of surprise and jumped from the chimney directly onto his startled father, sending them both sprawling onto the grass.

Bekkoran had desperately tried to scold his son, but was laughing too hard at the sight before him to do so. The poor boy was hopping around trying to put out the fire he imagined was burning in his britches. And then Diedre, Bekkoran's wife, had come barreling around the corner to see what all the commotion was about. She saw her soot-covered son hopping about, slapping at his seat, and her husband lying flat on his back with grass in his hair and obviously trying to stifle a large case of giggles.

"Excuse me, boys, but did I miss something?" Bjarke's mother had asked innocently, sending them all into gales of mirth.

Yes, Bjarke's had been a happy life, filled with the simple pleasures of life outdoors, away from the cramped confines of the cities Bekkoran had so detested. His father had always seemed to have time for a story or two, no matter what chores he probably should have been doing right then. Bekkoran caught no end of scolding from Diedre when she found her husband and son seated behind the cabin, laughing at some tale or other. But more often than not, they would all share the end of the tale together. Bekkoran and Diedre had taught Bjarke that life was good. In their simple point of view, why be sad when being happy was more enjoyable? Bjarke smiled at the thought as he neared the end of his braid.

After his parents had passed, Bjarke had stayed in the little cabin by the lake, cherishing the good memories it gave him. He had turned into a massive fellow, not quite seven feet in height, and well over twenty-one stone. But for all his size and strength, he was as kind and joyful as a man could be. His deep brown eyes were the color of earth, and twinkled quite merrily in their nest of laugh lines in his sunbrowned face. Bjarke smiled at any provocation, and, of course, a laugh was usually quick to follow.

The forest around Bjarke was quiet, save for the sounds of the soft wind and the birds. The few that he had not frightened away chirruped happily overhead. He finally finished braiding his hair and stood, preparing to shoulder his load once more.

As he studied the fallen timber, Bjarke slowly became aware of a faint radiance that appeared to emanate from a space just before the doorway to his cabin. He turned towards his home, trying to gain a better view of the strange brightness that seemed to sparkle in the growing light of the morning.

The pale blue glow was approximately the size of a man, and appeared to contain a small but brilliant trace of crimson deep within it, near to the ground. The glow began to move away from the cabin and towards the relative darkness of the forest in which Bjarke stood.

The huge man's usually smiling face adopted an uncommon expression of concern as he studied the brightness approaching him. The glow passed unswerving through the trunks and branches before it, as if it were naught but a phantom. Bjarke poised himself to attack or flee.

Hold, friend Bjarke. A misty voice touched the man's mind. *There is no need for fear. I am an ally.*

"What trickery is this? A light with no torch and a voice with no body? And how is it that you know my name?" Bjarke showed no signs of relaxing.

Ah, yes. I forgot that you could not see me as yet. I beg your pardon, mighty one. One moment please. The amorphous glow began to dim somewhat. A moment later, it had coalesced into the shape of a striking, white-robed man holding before him a short-hafted, long-bladed spear. The gem held tightly within its ghostly pommel glowed brightly with scarlet luminescence. Bjarke studied the features of the spectre before him, noting the man's chiseled face and short, dark hair, shot through at the temples with silver. The smaller man's eyes were grey as stone, and they seemed to penetrate deep into Bjarke's very being. Intense as they were, they betrayed no sense of malice, only urgency. Still, Bjarke remained wary.

I am Brunar, the Mage, and the world has need of you. The spectre stood rock-still, gazing intently up at the much larger man. *I bear with me the Jidaan of Rhu; he was the strongest of the Guardians of old. The time has come for you to take his place and bear this weapon in his stead. The Jidaan, itself, brought me to you and told me your name.* The faded image of the Mage gestured slightly with the unusual spear, and a sparkle of light glinted off its razor edge.

A powerful evil has arisen, a vile sorcerer by the name of Mordak. In times past, he nearly destroyed the world, yet we bested him. We had thought him gone forever.

However, the Evil One again threatens all life on this world, and only a few hold the power to stop him. You, Bjarke, are one of those few. I call on you to accept your destiny. I call on you to become a Guardian and aid me in ridding the world of Mordak's evil once and for all. The apparition's eyes burned deeply into those of the giant forester.

Bjarke's face lost all trace of its usual mirth as he considered what he had just been told. Guardians? Mordak? Those names writhed back in the farthest corners of his mind, trying to find their way to the front where he might examine them. He vaguely recalled hearing those names during his youth, when his beloved parents would tell him stories of a time long past, a bleak time when the evil sorcerer had almost taken over the world, only to be vanquished in the end by the valiant warriors of the mountains.

The few times his father had told him the darker tales of Mordak, his mother had always protested. Bekkoran had continued anyway, insisting that the boy must understand that although great good exists in the world, so too, does evil.

"But I thought those were just hearthtales, legends to be told by the fire," Bjarke thought aloud.

Nay, mighty one. They are very real. The evil that is Mordak did indeed come very close to dominating and enslaving this world some two thousand years agone. Only the combined strength of all six of the Guardians routed him at the last.

"But then, what have I to do with the Guardians? I certainly am no wizard. I know I'm strong, but I don't even know how to fight...I am really quite ordinary." Bjarke scratched his beard thoughtfully as he looked down at the image of the Mage.

You have much to do with the Guardians, Bjarke. Rhu was a great warrior, possessed of strength beyond measure. At times, I thought there was no end to it. You do resemble him a bit, you know, though you are a hair's breadth taller. Rhu was your ancestor. You are directly descended from Rhu Bearsheart, most likely from father to son, and so on. You have the power within you, as your father did, and his father before him, all the way back to Rhu. This is why you are as strong as you are. Even so, there are also many other abilities that must be explored.

Bjarke's face went completely blank as he sat heavily on the fallen log. He had always considered his strength as simply a part of himself. He gave it as much thought as he might give to breathing. And as he had so little contact with other people, he had nothing to compare his strength to.

What you are is special, Bjarke. There are few like you on this world. The power is not always passed along as it was in your family. It is your destiny to become a protector, for unless you and your brethren can come together now to meet and destroy Mordak, this world is lost. No other hope exists.

"You said that there are others like me. Who are they?" Bjarke's steady gaze returned to meet the steely eyes of the Mage.

In truth, I know not, Brunar replied. *I did not know that you were Chosen until the Jidaan brought me here to meet you. It will be the same for the others. Each weapon will bear me to its Chosen as well, so that I may bring those warriors to their destiny.*

"Let's say that I believe you, Mage. What must I do?" Bjarke looked up at the shining apparition. His eyes held no small amount of doubt, but the tone of his voice betrayed his interest.

You must make ready to come with me, friend Bjarke. I know that leaving this beautiful valley pains you, but take heed: if we cannot stop the Evil One, he will destroy all things of light and beauty in his quest for power. Nothing will be spared. Bjarke's expression paled slightly as he imagined his valley as a dead thing, a barren hollow in the mountains. *Such is Mordak's way.*

However, I would have you believe in me fully before following me into this war. I will return in four days to take you to our Keep in the Heartstrong Mountains in the west. In the meantime, you will see what has gone before, and what you will face in the future. I wish you to understand the full extent of your potential for power, as well as your responsibility. Even so, none can be forced to wield the Jidaan. But then, none that have been Chosen have ever refused the honor.

The shining form of the Mage raised his left hand. The big man saw the bluish glow intensify around Brunar's slender fingers and then he felt something brush at his mind, stirring up memories long forgotten. Still other, far older images began to emerge from the depths of Bjarke's subconscious mind but were still too indistinct to be made sense of. Bjarke shook his head to clear it. He glared at the Mage and growled, "What have you just done to me?" Bjarke rubbed the back of his head with one massive paw.

Fear not. The Mage lowered his hand. *I have only passed on to you a sort of record of what passed before. You will dream, and in your dreams, the past will become clear to you. Your own talent makes this possible, mine only helps it along. It is one of the gifts you possess.*

"Do all of these Guardians have such talents?" Bjarke asked, awed that he might actually have magickal ability within him. "I mean, how am I supposed to use these gifts?"

I will teach you much in that respect. The training will also bring your other gifts to light, for you must use all of your powers if you hope to defeat Mordak.

"I have not agreed to go with you yet, wizard." Bjarke stood and shook his head once more in another attempt to wrestle the stirring memories into some semblance of order. "I just don't know what to think about all this."

You cannot be forced to be one of us. But I remind you, without all of us working together, there is little hope. I will return in the morning of the fourth day to hear your decision. Be ready, strong one. In time, your might will be sorely needed, and we must begin as soon as possible.

Fare thee well, Bjarke. Brunar bowed slightly to the towering man before him. Bjarke bowed in return, respectful of the obviously powerful magician. He saw the scarlet pommel of the spear Brunar held flare to brightness, and then the shining image of the Mage was gone as if it had never been.

Bjarke stared at the spot where the smaller man had appeared to be standing a moment before, and noted the lack of footprints. "Maybe I hit my thick skull on my log when I fell," he said to the trees around him. "That would certainly explain all this." And yet, the memories that stirred in his mind refuted that possibility.

Bjarke decided it was time for some breakfast. The thought occurred to him that his quiet cabin and a meal - a huge meal - would help him to sort this thing out. Forgetting completely about the heavy log, Bjarke walked towards his home to ponder the turn that his fate had suddenly taken.

Chapter 4

Subaa peered into the dense foliage of the jungle, trying to pierce the thick morning fog that enshrouded all. Behind him, he could just detect the sounds of his tribe's bustling movement as they mobilized for a hasty retreat at the urgent behest of the tribal Elder, Baho. Baho and his small warband had come screaming into the small cluster of huts just minutes before, frantically calling for all to come and listen. Subaa remembered the frightened little man's eyes bulging in the firelight as he recounted the awakening of the Demon of the Stones. No one in the village had hesitated for an instant once the tale had been told. They had rushed to their huts to gather their few possessions, preparing to run towards the dawn until the sun rode high in the sky, its blessed light hopefully dispelling the evil spirit.

Subaa jumped at a sound to his left, a quick scraping of claws on wood. The young warrior raised his spear and crept toward the sound, his bare feet making no noise on the thick earth beneath him. The quiet chirruping of the jungle insects embraced him as he moved, covering any sounds his careful steps might have otherwise made. He was terrified, but he did not falter. He had been left behind to cover the retreat, and he would do so, no matter what harm might come to him. To do otherwise would cast shame upon his spirit, and his trip to the hereafter would be a rough one.

Sweating now, he focused on a large tree a few yards away. As the pale light of dawn began to reach into the curtain of fog, he could just make out the trunk of the tree and the thick vegetation at its base. Whatever had made the noise was there in the concealing leaves. He raised his spear to strike, and a screeching monkey burst out of the shrubs to hurtle up the trunk of the tree.

A startled scream escaped the young warrior's lips as he jumped away from the tree. He watched the monkey disappear into the dense canopy of limbs overhead and hurled a curse at its nimble form. His nerves were frayed to the breaking point, and the monkey was not helping his disposition. Subaa breathed deeply to calm himself and resumed his watch, hoping that he would see nothing until he was called to join the evacuation.

As his watchful eyes continued to scan the jungle before him, Subaa worriedly tried to recall the tales of the Demon, hoping to remember some clue that would help him battle the creature if it appeared. In his fright, all he could recall was that the evil spirit had been entrapped within the cursed stone eons ago by the gods. He could remember nothing of its appearance aside from Baho's description. Beyond that, he knew only that it used evil magick and was powerful beyond imagining. Based on the elder's tale, Subaa believed this to be quite true. In spite of his fear, the young man continued his watch.

Moments later, a sudden stillness seized the area, and Subaa sucked a hissing breath in between his teeth. The insects of the jungle had fallen silent, and the hairs on the back of the warrior's neck began to stand on end. Terrified, Subaa crouched and prepared to launch his spear at anything that moved. His eyes darted about, searching.

A flash of crimson to his right attracted his attention. His eyes widened as the flash appeared again, and brighter. Just then, the voice of one of the tribal warriors sounded from the camp, calling Subaa from his post. Two other voices joined in the call, but Subaa heard them not, for his eyes were riveted on the scarlet radiance that grew as it approached him. His arm remained cocked to throw his weapon, but it seemed stiff, frozen. Subaa's mouth opened in a soundless scream as the radiance became a man, a man soundlessly gliding across the jungle floor towards him, held aloft by a roiling nimbus of magick.

His mind numbed in terror, Subaa recognized the man that Baho had described, a small man with short curly hair that was black as jet. A black moustache and goatee touched the lower portion of the Demon's swarthy face, and his clothing was slashed and tattered, as Baho had said. The eyes of the Demon were gone. In their sockets, there boiled a seething magma of magick most foul. Subaa knew that his death was even now reaching a slender hand to claim him, and he could not even cry out.

The Evil One's outstretched hand alighted on the trembling warrior's forehead. Subaa saw the Demon's face split in a malevolent grin as the hand gently caressed his brow. The young warrior tried to break free, tried to stab his spear into the Demon's chest, but he could not. He could only watch as the Demon threw his head back and laughed.

Enjoying the newfound freedom that the merchant's body had afforded him, Mordak savored the powerful essence of the helpless man before him. He could nearly taste the strength and vitality of the young warrior, and the sweet tang of fear made it all the more exciting for the sorcerer. Shaking with anticipation, Mordak's hand surged with scarlet as he sent a stream of frigid magick into the body of the young man. The warrior began to convulse, his eyes widening in agony as the foul coldness began to blossom within him, a cold so intense that it began to burn.

The pain became unbearable, and still the cold fire grew, sapping the warrior's strength and life. As Subaa looked deeply into the seething roil of the Vile One's molten eyes, a frantic scream finally burst from his lips, a cry of utter horror and despair. Subaa had seen an evil in those eyes that seemed as old as time itself.

Mordak began to withdraw his energy, bringing with it the life and strength of the motionless warrior before him. The scarlet radiance surrounding the sorcerer grew perceptibly brighter as the captive Tballa shriveled and shrank in upon himself, his scream dying away as his essence was torn from him to mingle with Mordak's evil soul.

When the warrior was naught but an empty shell, Mordak dropped the shapeless remains to the earth. He breathed deeply as he felt the young man's strength added to his own. The essence was strong, but it would not last. He needed more life, more essence, if he was to survive for long. There was yet much to be done.

Invoking his Sight, Mordak searched for the voices he had heard moments before. Instantly, he caught sight of three more warriors, racing through the jungle towards the cluster of huts, shouting in fear. Beyond them, he saw the village itself and the other natives scrambling into the jungle, clutching their few belongings. Apparently, the three nearest had witnessed their companion's demise and were attempting to warn the others and escape.

Mordak laughed again, a sound of stone grating on stone. He knew they would not get far. With a thought, he began to glide through the trees once more, faster now, gaining on the fleeing little men before him.

Meanwhile, the warriors had reached the village and were frantically shoving the stragglers into the jungle. One young mother, Kulia, had fallen with her baby just on the far side of the camp. Two of the warriors sprinted past, unseeing, but the last, Panu, scooped up the baby and hurriedly helped the young woman to her feet. One backward glance showed the approaching red glare to be entering the far side of the village, a small man at the center of the silent blaze. The stout warrior propelled the frightened woman into the jungle ahead of him, and yelled at her to run. He clasped the baby to his chest and sprinted beside her, urging her on, almost dragging her by one arm in his attempts to save them both.

They continued a few yards more, looking ahead and seeing no sign of their tribesmen, when the air suddenly turned cold, and the Demon's magick washed over them. They tried to continue their flight, but tendrils of misty redness shot past them into the jungle. The pair skidded to a halt among the scarlet tentacles, watching them spear hungrily into the vegetation ahead. The baby had not made a sound. The warrior dropped quickly to the ground, covering the baby with his body, and started to drag Kulia down as well.

Before she could move, a tendril snaked around her waist from behind and bore her screaming into the air. She struggled mightily, but could not free herself from the misty arm. Her cries grew frantic as she was snatched backwards through the jungle. Answering wails of fear came from farther up ahead as the other arms began to return, bearing their captives quickly back towards the red brightness behind the prone warrior. Panu counted the captives as their struggling bodies were carried overhead and noted that no one from his tribe had escaped.

As the last of the vaporous tendrils carried their writhing burdens back towards the camp, Panu quickly shoved the baby under some sheltering fronds of fern that grew near him, hoping that the child would escape their own hideous fate. The baby looked at him uncomprehendingly as its small body was covered with leaves. It gripped the young warrior's finger in one small fist for a moment, and then closed its eyes and somehow managed to drift off to sleep.

Panu, an old and seasoned veteran of the tribal wars, stood and turned to face his fate with honor. The scarlet radiance immediately enveloped him as it had the others, and yanked him back toward the village.

As he was carried roughly out of the jungle, he shuddered as he saw what had become of his tribe. All of them, men, women, and children, were being held several feet above the ground in the clutches of the red glow that emanated from the creature they had feared for centuries, the thing they called The Demon.

The evil being was holding his captives aloft in a rough semicircle around himself, and apparently had killed half of the men and women already. Their shriveled bodies hung motionless in the red glow, while others howled and struggled until their lives were sucked away from them in a chill rush. One by one, they died, and with each death, the Demon's eyes glowed more brightly.

As the evil magick brought Panu to his place in the deadly gathering, he saw that he was to be last in line, just after Kulia, whose baby he had just hidden. She screamed as the others were killed, and when she saw Panu's stout body borne through the air to hover beside her, she frantically tried to reach him. He stretched his arm to the limit, but her extended fingers were just beyond his reach. The Demon had begun to laugh again, and the shouts of the few remaining tribesmen faded, dying as the tribe of Tballa died.

As the man next to Kulia died and the cold brightness grew, the sorcerer's glowing eyes fastened on her. His laughing stopped for a moment, but the cruel smile remained on his lips.

I believe you have forgotten something. Kulia's screams went silent, so startled was she at hearing this thing speak to her in her own language. No, the Demon had not spoken, but she had heard him all the same. His evil smile widened, exposing a few gleaming teeth. *Might this be yours?*

Kulia's eyes flew wide and she screamed anew as her baby dropped from the sky to hover in front of her, carried by another arm of scarlet. His tiny brown eyes were wide with fear, and tears were streaming down his face.

The Demon absorbed the baby's energy in an instant, and then slowly let the tiny corpse drift towards Kulia. Her wails ceased as the still form of her baby drew near. She gazed at her dead child for a moment, and then quickly drew the small knife at her belt, defiantly intending to stab herself before the Demon took her.

Her hand halted just as the tip of the blade entered her skin. Held motionless, she looked back at the demon that controlled her. His curling, evil smile widened as he watched her strain to kill herself. While her hand was motionless, her head was not. In a final burst of pent-up fear and rage, she spat at the little man before her, and cursed him until he finally stole her life with his frigid fire.

Mordak had enjoyed this last display of defiance from the girl. Her spirit had still been vital and strong when he had absorbed it; the taste of it had been sweet. Almost as an afterthought, he killed the last Tballa warrior, and Panu's life force flowed into him.

Filled with stolen strength, Mordak turned from the empty shells that had once been humans, and dismissed the corpses from his attention. The empty husks that had once been human dropped to the ground, where they stirred small clouds of dust that moved gently in the sudden quiet. The red glow of power snaked back into Mordak at his command.

The life energies he had absorbed coursed through the body that had once belonged to the spice merchant. The power of over twenty people had become too much for such a small form to contain, and the swarthy skin had begun to peel and split, sending trickles of blood flowing down his arms and torso. Mordak looked at himself and decided that this frame had served its purpose. He had gained more than enough power to change himself to a more suitable form and continue the trek to his ancient home on the rocky plains, far to the east. With over two hundred leagues to travel, he decided on an appropriate shape, and willed a change.

His eyes glowed fiery red as his body began to reshape itself. Loud pops sounded as his bones began to lengthen and reform. The torn skin remolded itself and stretched, taking on a much darker, tougher texture. Mordak crouched as small leathery wings split the skin of his back, tearing through the ragged material of his shirt, expanding and spreading behind him. The wings grew as his hands and feet became grasping claws with wickedly curved talons. His lower jaw pushed outward, the teeth stretching to become razor sharp fangs. Only the burning scarlet of his eyes remained constant.

When Mordak stood erect, his new body was easily two feet taller than the old one had been. Where the form of the little merchant had been only moments before, a hideous winged monstrosity now stood, its evil eyes piercing the early morning gloom with scarlet luminescence.

The Mordak-thing turned and uttered a horrendous shriek. It flapped its massive wings, and the resulting wind picked up the shriveled corpses and flung them into the jungle on swirling eddies of dust. With a leap it became airborne. As it rose above the dense jungle canopy, the morning sun struck it fully for the first time.

RRRRAAAWWWW! It screeched defiantly at the brightness, and its flaming eyes squinted shut. The sunlight was quite unwelcome. The night was much more to the sorcerer's liking. Eastward it flew, shrieking now and then to let the world know that Mordak had returned.

Chapter 5

Brunar released the ruby-pommeled weapon as his spirit returned from the wooded glen of Bjarke, and once again found himself standing atop the dais in the Hall. Brunar mused that the large, bearish man he had just met was much more jolly than Rhu ever had been, but Bjarke had every bit as much potential for power as his ancestor. The great strength that Brunar had seen him use was obviously a manifestation of magick, and though he was already incredibly strong, Brunar knew that he would see Bjarke become far stronger.

Slightly dizzy from his etheric journey, Brunar carefully walked down the steps of the dais that surrounded the wall-mounted Jidaan. He still had much to do, and even though the burden of the trip had fallen mostly on the enchanted weapon, it had still taken its toll on the weakened Mage. Brunar smiled a bitter smile as he walked across the dust-laden floor of the Hall, remembering when his power had been a thousand times greater than it was now. He knew that he would be able to regain a measure of his previous strength through meditation. However, this was little comfort against the fact that Mordak would be taking human lives to rebuild his own power, and in so doing, would become much stronger in far less time.

As he approached the darkened tunnel at the front of the Hall, the Mage willed the unseen doors at the far end of the shadowy corridor to open. He felt the magick within him stirring, and then, with a ponderous creaking, the huge doors slowly swung apart. A bright column of sunlight appeared and widened, dispelling the darkness that had previously dominated the wide chamber, and a cool breeze wafted in to stir up the layers of dust on the floor. When the doors were fully open, the morning sun streamed in, illuminating the ornate stone carvings that lined the walls of the huge passageway. The carvings depicted battles of long ago, and the forgotten warriors of another age.

Brunar passed the intricate artistry of the carvings without a sideways glance. Centuries past, he had taken it upon himself to begin the painstaking work of chiseling out the expansive scenes, and had only finished them a few decades ago. He knew every inch by heart.

Invigorated by the fresh air, the Mage walked briskly into the courtyard that stood beyond the open doors. At this altitude, the wind was a bit chill even in summer, and snow could be found atop the surrounding mountains year round. Now, the cold of early Spring was bracing, and the Mage enjoyed the sensation as he always had. His breath plumed in a misty cloud as he strode across the small, natural plateau that served as an entryway to the Hall of Jidaana.

The courtyard was a stone's throw in diameter, and was articulated by a waist-high retaining wall that encircled it and a stone archway at the opposite end that denoted the trail that wound down through the mountains and away from the Keep. Built as it was, directly into the mountain's heart, the courtyard was but one of many places from which a person could look out over the range and revel in the rugged beauty of the land.

Brunar moved to the northern railing and placed his hands on its chilled surface. Centuries of weather had worn the stone smooth, and the Mage gripped it firmly as he scanned the snow-covered crags that towered above and around him. He had long since discovered that it was easier for him to become one with the magick of the world if he were actually standing in it, experiencing the joys of the elements. He had seen enough of the cities, those places where both humanity and nature were often forgotten.

He could feel his power deep within his body. Brunar removed one hand from the wall and placed it on his belly, just beneath his navel. He could best feel the sensation of his magick there, swirling and moving within him. The Mage gazed at the white-capped peaks for a few moments more, then closed his eyes against the majestic splendor of the mountains. He focused his attention inward, towards the very center of his being.

Quiet moments passed as he sought out his core, his center of energy, from within. He felt his awareness sinking deeper as he began his effort to rebuild the well of power that had dwindled during his last waking century. It had taken decades of study for Brunar to master this method of recuperation. He knew that he would spend the next few nights in this state, building his strength for the arduous days ahead. Though he could not even begin to reach the level of power that his longsleeps could afford him, Brunar would still be formidable. For now, he only needed a bit more of his energy to return before he could contact anyone else, and he set himself to work.

Brunar saw the center of his power as a sphere of blue fire, a small, concentrated mass of magick embedded deep within him. He was startled to see its pale color, the hue of a summer sky. Never before had he been so weak, but then, he had never been awakened so early in his slumber. Plunging into the task of regaining his might, the Mage imagined himself within the sphere, inside the swirling azure clouds of magick. From there, he encouraged it to grow, to build upon itself. Reaching out, he sought the living energy of the land. For a moment, Brunar felt that he was floating in an ocean of constantly eddying currents, waves, and swells of power. Tapping into a nearby current, he began to gently add to his own strength.

The spherical center of Brunar's magick answered him immediately with a pulse of brighter blue, and streaks of deeper color began to appear. Brunar smiled as he felt the first touches of his former potency begin to move within him. He knew it would take time, and he knew better than to try and rush this process. Patiently, he guided the smallest amount of earth magick into himself, and watched as the pulsing hue slowly changed from the weak bluish color to a more potent violet.

When his magickal center glowed a deep, shimmering purple, Brunar reopened his eyes and noted with shock that the sun had risen on towards midday. The meditation had taken far longer than he had hoped, still another sign of Brunar's weakness. He regretted the delay, but he knew that it could not be helped. The time had been well spent, and he felt his power swelling within him.

Brunar released his hold on the railing and strode purposefully back through the tunnel and into the Hall beyond, coming once again into the presence of the spears, the Jidaan.

With a decidedly springier step, he mounted the stairs again to stand before the six gleaming weapons. The ruby-pommeled spear glimmered deep within its jewel, as if knowing that its new Chosen would soon arrive. Brunar stepped up to the next weapon, the spear with a fiery diamond clasped in its pommel. He grasped it as he had the first and uttered the ritual words.

"Bringer of the Gift of Healing, who is thy Chosen? Show me that I may seek and unite thee."

The diamond held in the weapon's pommel sparkled, bursting with crystalline light. The vibrations of the spear moved up the Mage's arm and into his body, carrying a sweet wave of health and vitality into Brunar's very soul. As before, Brunar felt his journey begin as his shade, his spirit, left the Hall of Jidaana and traveled towards an unknown warrior-to-be.

Chapter 6

Norby staggered into the waiting area of the Rowook Home and tried to focus his vision. He was not really sure why he had come here, but figured he should make the best of it.

"Weena! Weeeeeennaaaa! I've come to take you awaaay, milady!" He slurred loudly, struggling to maintain his balance. He called for her once more, and felt better upon seeing her rush towards him from a nearby doorway. His vision swam as the white-clad Sister of Rowann approached him, and then he finally succumbed to his dizziness and collapsed, trembling, to the cold floor.

"Ian! Come here and help me!" Weena called for assistance. Ian was a strapping young fellow who helped out in the Home, most often by carrying heavy things and moving the sick and injured that could not move themselves. Almost instantly, Ian appeared from the opposite door of the small room.

"I see Norby is paying us another visit," observed the lad through the sandy hair that always flopped across his face. He stepped over to the kneeling priestess as she tended the moaning man on the floor. "What, is he drunk again? That's three times this week already!" The youth worked his arms under the sweating man and gently picked him up. Norby was a small fellow, and lifting him was no trouble for Ian.

Sister Weena gestured for Ian to move the semiconscious man onto an unoccupied cot in the larger room near the back of the Home. "Yes, I know, Ian. One of these days I hope to Rowann that he will learn that drinking so much is just not good for him. Put him there for now and I'll see that he's comfortable."

Her brow furrowed as she watched Ian lay her new patient down on the little cot. "He should be fine after he sleeps for a bit. Funny though, I don't remember him ever getting so bad off so early in the day before." She bent to check him more closely and heard him start to mumble a rather bawdy tavern limerick.

"Well, he did win that bet with the Farmen brothers about that horse race over in Oakleaf. Maybe he just started celebrating a bit early, eh?" Ian ran a hand through his already tousled hair and shrugged. "Anyway, I'll be in the back with Alyssa. She needed me to move some barrels or something."

"Thank you, Ian." Sister Weena looked up from her mumbling patient, a smile lighting the corners of her eyes. "I'll call you if I need you in here again."

Ian walked out the back door and the priestess turned to Norby once more. He was still trembling and sweating. He moaned about the world spinning, and then he was silent.

"It seems that you have had a bit too much yet again, Mister Norby. You'll feel better after you've slept it off." Something about the old man's plight bothered her. She paused to consider it, and found herself frustrated that she couldn't put her finger on the problem.

"Norby again?" A childlike voice whispered just below Sister Weena's shoulder, startling her.

The older woman turned to find Alyssa, the director of the Rowook Home, standing behind her. She was a tiny woman, and although she was nearing twenty-five years of age, she would never see the far side of five feet in height. Her auburn hair was swept back in a tight, matronly bun, but her liquid brown eyes gave her a childlike quality that was echoed in her musical voice. She was a beautiful young woman, to be sure. In spite of her age and diminutive stature, all of the Sisters of Rowann acknowledged her as their mentor and leader, for her powers of healing surpassed anything the sisters had ever seen.

Weena remembered when, as a seven-year-old orphan living in the nearby mission of Rowann, Alyssa had wandered into the tiny sickroom and began attending to the few patients that had been staying there. One farmer had been fevered and very ill, and somehow, she had immediately known that it was due to an infected wound in his foot, a small puncture that had festered. None of the other healers had caught it. She had expressed such compassion and talent that she had been schooled in the arts of healing by the good Sisters, and over the last several years had become the best of them all.

Alyssa had always seemed to know where it hurt, why it hurt, and what would make it feel better. . .sometimes against the better judgment of the older sisters. But in the end, the tiny woman had always proved to be correct. The people of the nearby villages and townships of the Shadowed Forest loved her hugely, and they had even come together to build this structure so that Alyssa and the priestesses could better help the sick and injured.

Sister Weena recovered quickly from her momentary shock. Alyssa could move as silently as a soft breeze and tended to startle those who were not expecting her. "Yes, Alyssa, it seems that he has already had his fill this day. He should be fine after a nap." The priestess stood and moved aside so that her mentor could examine the trembling patient.

Alyssa stepped closer to the cot and sat gently upon it, rolling up the sleeves of her blouse as she did so. She reached a tiny hand out to touch the man's sweating brow. A frown creased her pretty face and she moved her hand to rest on his sternum. "That's odd. I don't smell any liquor on him at all. Do you?" She moved it down to his stomach and stopped there, pressing gently against him. Her eyes lost focus for a moment, then she quickly turned to Sister Weena.

"Weena, get me a cup of sugar water, please. Make it strong! Quickly now!" Sister Weena looked down at Alyssa uncomprehendingly for a moment, but then bolted to the kitchen for the mixture. The tiny woman returned her gaze to Norby, the trembling man still just barely conscious.

"Rest easy, Norby. I know what's wrong." She felt sad for the little man. His youngest son had died suddenly not a year ago, and with his wife dead and other sons already married and gone, he had taken to drinking a bit to ease the pain and loneliness. This time, it was not the drink that had brought him here, though none but Alyssa could have known it.

She knew that he would be fine after taking the sugar water, and she instinctively allowed a feeling of warm reassurance to flow from her body into his. He relaxed a bit, then Sister Weena returned in a rustle of white skirts, bearing a large mug in hand.

"Thank you, Weena. Help me give this to him, please." The priestess helped move Norby to a sitting position, and Alyssa helped him to drink. He made a face at the sweetness of the brew, but he drank it all the same and reached his hands up to hold the mug himself.

The trembling gradually stopped, and his breathing slowed to a more relaxed rhythm. Coherence returned to his eyes, and he turned to look at his benefactors. "Well, hullo, ladies. Sorry to be such a bother, but I'm not feelin' verra well." He continued to sip at his drink, his hands now steady.

"Hello to you too, Norby. Be sure to drink all of that sugar water, and you'll be on your way to being all right again." Alyssa smiled as Norby flashed a small, shy grin at her and drank a bit more from his mug.

"Ordinarily, I'd be a drinking verra different stuff, but not this time. I've not had a drop in the last three days." Norby sipped at his drink as he talked. "I started feelin' like I'd been on a tear wi' th' boys at th' inn, but since I had no', I knew it hadda be somethin' else altogether, so I came here. I dinna recall actually gettin' here, but I'm awful glad I made it." He finished his drink and handed the mug back to Sister Weena as he leaned weakly back in his cot.

"We're glad too, Norby. You rest now, and I'll be back later to tell you what you need to do to keep this from happening again." Alyssa gave his hand a squeeze as she stood up. She saw his face begin to darken and she laughed. "Don't worry, you don't have the plague or anything terrible like that. You just need to watch what you eat from now on."

Norby did not like the sound of that very much either, even though he really had not been eating much at all lately. His ale had seemed food enough. Still, whatever Alyssa said was law as far as Norby was concerned, and he gave her a wink and settled down to rest. Alyssa gestured quietly for Weena to follow her.

Sister Weena and Alyssa left another sister to watch over Norby and the few other patients and walked out the front door and around to the beautiful garden that lay beyond the south side of the building. The spring air was crisp and clean, and the noon sunshine made everything look vibrant and alive. At this time of year, the lands of the Shadowed Forest were beautiful beyond compare. The surrounding trees, just beginning to show their bright new leaves, and the flowers that bloomed in the soft meadows scattered throughout the forest made the region one of the prettiest in the land. Alyssa loved it here.

"What was wrong with him?" Sister Weena asked as they both sat on a stone bench at the center of the garden. "I thought he was just drunk again!" Weena clasped her hands tightly before her in anxiety. She had never been prone to mistakes in the past, and this incident had frightened her badly.

Alyssa smiled sweetly as she looked at the fretting Weena. She paused for a moment before she spoke, as if searching for words. "Something inside him has stopped working, I think. I really cannot be sure what, but it seems that he needed sugar more than anything just then. I'm not sure why a lack of sugar could have such an effect on a person, but that seemed to be the cause of his behavior."

"And what if he had not gotten it?" Weena asked coldly. The priestess's eyes had become hard as flint. "He could have died, couldn't he?"

Alyssa's eyes lowered for an instant before returning to lock their gentle gaze on the priestess. "Yes, I think that he could have. But the fact is that he did not die, and chances are that he won't for a very long time." She reached a tiny hand and took her friend's larger, timeworn hand in hers. "Weena, I know that you did the best you could with Norby. This...sugar-sickness is not something we have seen around here until only just now. You could not have known that it was sugar that he needed instead of sleep."

Sister Weena's eyes remained distant and cold. Alyssa continued, "I heard him come through the door, and when he bellowed about taking you away with him, I thought he was drunk as well. I mean, he's normally very shy, isn't he?"

Weena turned her head away for a moment, as if embarrassed, but then she turned her face back to the tiny woman next to her and offered a demure smile. Alyssa grinned at the display. The whole town knew of the growing affection between the usually bashful widower and the stern priestess.

"Well, he can be bold sometimes." Sister Weena actually started to blush. "I admit, he has talked sweetly to me in the past and asked me to run away with him and find a little kingdom for two once or twice, but that was always in playful jest. This time it seemed that his ale had given him quite a bit more courage." The two women laughed, and Alyssa knew that Weena would be all right.

"Weena, I think we had better take very good care of that fellow in there, so that when he finally does summon up the courage to take you away from all this, he will be able to do it properly. In the meantime, let's be sure to record this incident in the journals." Alyssa had founded the library of medical journals in the rear of the Rowook Home, and all known illnesses and their effective treatments were written down for future reference. Rowook Home boasted of the largest medical library in the land, and its store of information was constantly growing.

With a quick word of thanks and a comforting hug, Sister Weena stood and walked briskly back towards the front of the Home so that she could continue tending her patients. Alyssa stayed on the bench, basking in the warm sunshine.

She remembered touching Norby with the thought that he was drunk. The sense of wrongness of that thought had assailed her as soon as her fingers had lighted on his damp forehead. As she had sat next to him, it had seemed as if she had somehow joined with him for a time. She had *felt* what he needed. Later, she had given him a feeling of reassurance as effectively as she would give him the sugar brew minutes later. The feeling had emanated from her without her knowing exactly how it happened. In a sense, she had simply wished for him to relax and be calm, and he had done just that.

She had used her talents hundreds upon hundreds of times over the years, sometimes even saving those who had seemed doomed beyond all hope. Alyssa had helped so many, save an unfortunate few who were beyond even her ability. These skills had always been hers, and though she did not understand where they might have come from, she thanked the Goddess every day for them.

Alyssa. A melodic, rich voice came from behind the bench on which the tiny woman sat. She turned with a start to see the glowing form of a striking man standing a few feet away, holding a short spear in one hand. He was wreathed in a purplish glow, and he stood proudly, a man both confident and strong. The weapon's pommel sparkled as a fiery diamond blazed within.

With a gasp, she jumped up from the bench and stepped quickly away from him. She thought about running, but then realized that he had called her name. Puzzlement overrode her fear, and she asked, "Who are you? What do you want here?"

There is no need for alarm, my dear. Brunar's renewed strength had allowed him to appear in a much more solid form than the misty ghost that had visited Bjarke earlier. *Please allow me to introduce myself.* The Mage executed a courtly bow before the tiny healer. Her wary eyes tracked his every move.

I am Brunar, the Mage, and I have come to ask for your assistance in ridding the world of an evil far worse than any illness or plague you might have imagined.

"Brunar?" Alyssa's eyes opened wide in surprise. "The Protector?"

A faint smile crossed the lips of the Mage. *Yes, I have been called that a time or two.* He walked slowly towards the tiny woman, passing through the stone bench between them. *Are we remembered?*

Alyssa forgot her fear as the Mage came closer to her and she could see him more clearly. "Why, yes. The Sisters of Rowann have kept the tales of Brunar and the Guardians alive for centuries. They have passed them down for generations, and I grew up in their mission not far from here." She remembered his earlier comment and grew cautious once more. "What do you mean when you say that you need my assistance? I am a healer. Does someone need my help?"

Indeed, my lady. Brunar gazed intently down into her pixie face, beautiful and determined. *The entire world is now in need of your services, those that only you can provide as a healer, and as a Guardian. The weapon I bear is to be yours, and you must come with me to the Keep for training. Foul Mordak has escaped.* The Mage's face echoed the pain that emerged in his voice.

Alyssa's intake of breath indicated that she had an idea of the Vile One's power. "Mordak has escaped? But, I thought he was entombed forever! At least, that's what the stories say. What could have happened to release him?"

Brunar's expression hardened further, and his grey eyes looked away from her. *I know not. Since there is no such thing as a foolproof enchantment, any number of things might have occurred. The stone that held him was unbreakable, and far enough away from humans that contact was unlikely. The few natives of the region had regarded that particular area as cursed long before we trapped the Evil One there, and Mordak's entombment only reinforced their fear of the place. It is doubtful that they released him.*

The Mage returned his gaze to the beautiful woman standing near him. *In any case, the time has come for the Guardians to wield their Jidaan once more.* He held forward the short spear in both hands, displaying it to Alyssa. *I bring with me the Jidaan of Willen, he who was your ancestor. In his time, he was a healer such as you, though not nearly as well known as you seem to be. It is no surprise to me that you have followed a similar path as he.*

The young woman let her eyes wander over the weapon that the Mage offered her. Its diamond sparkled as if the sun's rays were being refracted into a million beautiful shards of light.

Alyssa reached out to take the dazzling weapon. Her eyes widened as her fingers passed through the spear's handle as if it were made of light, and nothing more. Brunar allowed himself the briefest of chuckles.

No, Alyssa, you can't take it from me just yet. You see, at the moment, I am still in the Keep in the Heartstrong Mountains. What you see is a projection of my essence, carried here by the power of the Jidaan so that I might offer you what is to be your destiny.

"My . . . destiny?" Alyssa quietly answered. "Have I been Chosen, then?" Her eyes locked onto Brunar's, waiting for the answer.

A stern nod from Brunar punctuated his response. *Yes, little one. You have indeed.*

Several different emotions flashed across Alyssa's face as she absorbed the news that she was to be one of the fabled few, a

Guardian. The last emotion to cross, uncertainty, stayed longer than the rest.

"What must I do?" the young woman asked.

You must leave here and come with me, Alyssa. You and the other five Guardians must gather in the Hall of Jidaana to accept the charge of protecting this world. You must then become versed in the ways of the magick which you possess, and learn to use the power of your Jidaan. Only when we have all learned to work as one may we hope to best Mordak.

Alyssa nodded. "I think I understand." She looked up at the glimmering Mage, and stood with her feet braced slightly apart, her chin jutting in a gesture of determination. "I must first see that the Home is prepared for my absence, but then I will gladly go with you."

I am happy to see that you understand how desperately we need you. When the sun rises four days from now, wait for me here, and I will transport you to the Keep. Until then, take care, Alyssa. He offered a bow to the tiny woman.

Alyssa bowed deeply to the Mage, and then turned to walk quickly around to the front of the Rowook Home. Brunar could hear her calling loudly for the sisters of Rowann to gather in the waiting area, and he smiled. She had not curtsied, as custom usually dictated, and Brunar liked that immensely. Alyssa would be interesting. She seemed to possess far greater strength than her diminutive stature might suggest.

Brunar noticed for the first time the laughter of the children that played in the street just before the unseen entrance to the Home. His smile widened for an instant as he observed their unbridled joy and happiness. The figure of Willen, the Guardian who had wielded the diamond-pommeled *Jidaan* so long ago, came unbidden to his mind. Willen had loved children and had enjoyed playing with them at every opportunity. Brunar's smile vanished as he remembered how Willen had changed after killing his first enemy soldier, one who had been hardly more than a boy. The happiness had gone from Willen after that, leaving him a grim and stormy young man.

As he willed himself back to the Hall of Jidaana, and the diamond pommel flared to brightness, Brunar hoped that Alyssa was tougher than poor Willen had been. The loss of laughter in him had been a sad thing, indeed.

Chapter 7

It was nearing mid-afternoon, and the lack of wind made the spring sun seem more akin to one of summer. Gart found a dry spot on his damp tunic and wiped it across his stinging eyes. When he could see again, he resumed the task of loading the remains of his crop into his sturdy cart, his wiry muscles working tirelessly. The last two days had been unusually lucrative in the markets of New Caldea, and nearly all of Gart's vegetables had been sold. Now, as he packed the empty baskets into the cart in preparation for the five-day trip home, he could almost be happy again. He had managed to make a good deal of profit this season, and Gennie would be proud.

Someone tapped him twice on the shoulder. "You there! Have you paid the taxes - Ye Gods!" As Gart turned his icy blue eyes on the stranger, he could see that he had already startled the slightly larger man. Gart's wicked facial scars had a tendency to frighten people.

The burly man standing before the young farmer was dressed in rusty chain mail and held a gaudy plumed helmet under his left arm. His hair fell to his shoulders in greasy black ringlets, and Gart noticed that the fellow was missing a tooth or two. Gart's eyes blazed from beneath his pale blonde bangs as he watched the fellow swiftly regain his composure.

"I said," the man continued, "have you paid the taxes on the goods you sold? No one leaves New Caldea without paying the sales tax to the Duke, not even someone as 'handsome' as you." The man smiled at his own joke, and dropped his right hand to the ornate but well-worn sword he carried at his belt.

Gart said nothing, his eyes boring up into those of the local tax collector. The man was becoming impatient, and that was just fine. Gart was a slender man, but the vicious scars that ravaged the right side of his face lent him a sinister aspect that had caused many children to run screaming to their mothers. As a farmer, his lithe body was burned brown by the sun and his sinewy muscles were like iron from the constant work.

It was his eyes, however, that really lent a chill to those who locked gazes with him. Those eyes held no humor, no joy. . .only a cold blue fire locked deep within. Something had scoured the happiness from him long ago, and those sapphirine blue eyes shone out at the world with their cobalt light. None who saw him ever forgot them.

Gart looked at the fellow that had just insulted him, as so many idiots before this one had done. As his anger grew, he felt the power rise within him, begging for release. The seasonal trip had already given Gart enough ridicule, enough gasps at his scarred face to last him a lifetime, just as it did every season. He had had enough of the insults from just beyond reach, the taunting from the street youths that passed his booth in the market. This ignorant fool was the last he would tolerate on this particular visit.

In a voice laden with fury, Gart spoke, "I paid the required taxes just yesterday. I'll thank you to leave me alone. Go back to whatever kennel you just crawled out of." His blue eyes watched the tax man's smile die on his stubbled face and turn into a grimace of rage.

The man drew his sword with a snarl and pointed it menacingly at Gart's face. The tax man was not used to being insulted, and now there was hell to pay.

"You'll be coming with me. Now, you ugly bastard!"

CHANG!! Without warning, Gart's left hand had lashed out and swatted at the man's naked blade, sending it spinning from his fingers to fly end over end and land in the street. The jarring impact numbed the bigger man's arm to the shoulder, and he started to backpedal in an attempt to recover his balance and get away from the scarred madman. Fear crossed his face as he saw the young man moving towards him, far too quickly for him to evade.

With an audible snarl of rage, Gart stepped smoothly in and slammed his right palm directly into the man's mail clad chest.

The tax collector flew backwards towards the inn as if kicked by a horse, crashing through the inn's wooden door and leaving only a few splintered boards in his wake. An outcry rose from within, and a little balding fellow with an apron came rushing out of the shattered door to see what had happened. When he saw Gart standing like a furious statue, fists clenched and scars aflame with anger, the innkeeper paled and hurriedly stepped back inside his establishment, tripping over the tax man's fallen helm as he went.

Gart watched the man go and tried desperately to rein in the power he had just released. This unnatural ability, this power to move things and strike with great strength, was getting stronger, and it was all he could do to bring it back under control again. He hated himself for using it almost as much as he hated the cursed scars on his face. The damned mongrel dog that had attacked him as a child had doomed him to a lifetime of scorn and contempt.

Still fighting to control his unearthly power, he threw his few remaining baskets into his cart and jumped into the seat. He could hear the city guards heading this way, and it was best if he left in a hurry. He snapped the reins at his faithful cart horses and shouted for them to move. The team bolted up the road away from the inn, and a few strolling men and women had to jump out of the way to avoid being run down by the furious man with the torn face and the fiery blue eyes. The cart jolted and jerked over the dirt road, but its speed did not wane.

Gart looked over his shoulder at the shrinking inn and saw the guardsmen just arriving at the establishment, and the balding little man pointing in his direction. There was enough distance between them, though, that Gart did not fear the city watch. The edge of the city was already drawing near, and he would be far up the road before they could take after him. He was certain the tax man had not been badly injured. At least, that was what he hoped.

"Blast!" Gart thought. "There goes another marketplace!" Gart had been attacked in a few towns in the past few, usually by thugs who insisted on tormenting him until he was forced to defend himself. This would not have been such a problem, but when Gart defended himself, he was frequently far too enraged to control the power within him, and he always ended up being feared and ridiculed in those towns.

He fumed at the fates that had brought this about as his team galloped past the signs marking the outer boundaries of the town, and then raced along the road that split the grassy plain beyond. Nothing was ever easy for him.

A short time later, Gart turned in his seat to see that no one pursued him, then finally slowed the horses to a walk. They had done well, and he would rest them soon.

The sounds of swift water breaking over rocks reached his ears, and he looked up to see the sparkling blue of the Corris River up ahead of him. As the road approached the river, it forked to run directly alongside the flowing waterway in either direction, and Gart took his team on the eastward fork towards home. He knew that the city guardsmen would never follow him this far out of town.

Gennie! Five days from now he would be home, and his beloved Gennie would be there waiting with their beautiful daughter, Rheann. A smile crept onto his lips, not really knowing what to do there. He loved his dear Gennie more than anything in this world. He remembered her laughing brown eyes, sparkling in the morning sun as she waved goodbye to him days ago. There had been a touch of sadness in those warm, loving eyes when he had last seen them. She always hated to see him go, but she knew that the trip was necessary.

From the moment they had met, Gennie had seemed to know that Gart would be her husband. Though the darkness of a tormented and painful life might never be dispelled completely, she was the light that pushed his darkness back. Her laughter was the only thing that had the capability to make him smile in return. She had always loved him completely. Once, in a fit of rage and shame, Gart had asked her about his torn face.

"How can you even look at a man with a face like this? How could you possibly ever love me?" he had screamed, angry tears flowing down the ragged trails of his scars.

Answering tears had run down her own cheeks as she had come to him, placed one gentle hand directly on the damaged side of his face and told him that she saw no scars at all.

"Gart, when I see you, I see YOU. All that you are is far greater than any scars...to me, you are beautiful." Gart's heart of stone had cracked in two then. He had clasped her tightly to him, and they had been married the following week.

Since then, life had actually been good to Gart. He farmed the land in the small village in which they lived, and Gennie made his life worth living. Happiness, so long an unremembered dream, seemed almost possible. And when Rheann had come into the world with her mother's lustrous raven hair and her father's blue eyes, Gart had been so full of joy, he had actually laughed. He remembered holding his baby daughter and feeling love for her blossom in his heart, momentarily shutting his darkness away completely.

The memory faded then, and Gart's smile fell away from a face unaccustomed to holding such an expression. The darkness and the rage were still there, but for now, memories of his family brought him as close to happy as he could be until he held them in his arms once again, the incident with the tax collector forgotten. The dry, dusty miles made their way under the wagon's wheels with dogged determination, and Gart leaned back in his seat as the sun shone down from its lofty perch in the heavens.

Several miles later, the horses started to whicker, and they suddenly became skittish. Gart pulled on the reins and tried to calm them. They continued to whinny and pull at their traces until Gart jumped down from his seat. He stepped forward to stroke their noses and whisper quiet words to them. When he finally calmed them to stillness, he began checking their harnesses to see if something was pinching or poking them.

I am sorry to have startled your horses, Gart. Gart spun and saw a man standing beside the road, a striking man with dark hair, streaked through at the temples with silver. The man held a spear in his right hand, but held it in a non-threatening position with the gleaming blade pointing skyward. An emerald gem glistened brightly within its pommel. *I must speak with you.*

Gart crouched and pulled a small knife from his tunic. He held his left arm before him, concealing the movements of his knife hand. Quietly, Gart spoke. "Who are you?" He stepped away from the horses, keeping the stranger in front of him.

You may as well put that knife away, Gart. You cannot harm me with it. What you see before you is just a shadow of my physical self, a shade brought to you by the weapon I hold. The man briefly held out his spear. *I am Brunar, the Mage, and the time has come for the Guardians to gather once more.*

Gart stopped moving, but did not abandon his fighters crouch. "And just what, Brunar, is a Guardian?" Gart's eyes blazed as he tried to gauge this man's intent. The stranger did not seem agitated or dangerous, yet he carried a sense of great power. Gart noticed that the man seemed to be emitting a faint violet glow of some sort, but since people simply do not glow, Gart figured that his vision must be playing tricks on him.

A Guardian is a Protector of this land. There are six, one for each of the Jidaan created eons ago to ward against those who would use dark magick to overcome the world. Each chooses its bearer, and only those who have the use of the magick within them can be chosen. The Mage saw Gart's eyes narrow at the mention of the innate well of power possessed by all Guardians.

These six Chosen become trained in the use of their extraordinary abilities, and in the use of their Jidaan. I carry with me the Jidaan of Lillia. It grants its wielder the Gift of Storms, and its power is devastating. It is difficult to control, and its Chosen must be up to the task. The Mage presented the weapon for Gart to see. Its pommel gem burned brightly in the golden afternoon light, emitting a constant fire of deep green.

"I see." Gart had not relaxed in the least. This man with the spear was obviously crazy, and was one to be dealt with carefully. Gart surreptitiously switched his knife to a throwing grip, and kept his penetrating gaze locked on the Mage. "So just what has all of this got to do with me? I've never heard of you or of these mystic warriors." He stood on the balls of his feet, poised for action.

All of this, as you put it, has quite a bit to do with you. The Jidaan I carry has Chosen you. I know that you have the power in you. Gart's eyes betrayed his sudden nervousness. *The heart of the matter is this: a great evil, once thought locked away forever, has managed to escape his prison and now stands to threaten us all.* Gart noticed that although the man's lips were moving, he was not actually hearing the words in the usual sense. The words were more in his mind than in his ears.

Only the Guardians have a hope of destroying this monster. The armies of the land will not be able to stand against him once he gathers his sorcerous might. Only we can stop him, and only if you and the others come together as a team and master your powers. You must agree to come with me, Gart.

Brunar was not altogether surprised to see the knife hurtling towards him. It flashed wickedly as it turned end over end in its flight, speeding unerringly towards Brunar's chest. The Mage paid it no attention, choosing instead to watch Gart's mouth drop open in disbelief as the dagger passed through his body as if through a cloud.

You cannot hurt me, Gart. As I told you before, my physical self is far from here. Now please stop this. You must understand, the fate of the world hangs in the balance. You must come, and must learn to use your magick or we may not be able to beat the Evil One this time.

Gart's disbelief turned to anger. He knew that the power in him was unnatural, possibly even evil. His parents had told him so when he was just a child. If this man wanted him to learn to use it, he must be evil as well. Even so, he could still feel himself reaching out to the dagger that pierced the earth behind the glowing figure, trying to move it and return it to his hand.

He beat down the magick welling within him, clamping down on it with his rage. "I'll not come with you, Brunar, or whatever you said your name was. Powers like that are evil, and I've been trying to purge myself of mine since I was a boy. Now leave...me...ALONE!" Gart screamed this last, hating himself for his power, and hating Brunar even more for trying to bewitch him into using it. He turned and leapt up into the seat of his cart and grabbed the reins. With a yell, he snapped them at his two horses, and the cart bolted forward, leaving the Mage at the side of the road behind him.

I know this is a shock, but I implore you to think about this! The Mage's words echoed in Gart's mind, unaffected by the widening gap between them. *Entire armies of ordinary men were slaughtered by the Evil One in ages past.* The cart did not slow. *Thousands upon thousands of innocent people were killed before the Guardians bested Mordak. It is up to us to fight him again, or more innocents will die! Gart, wait! WAIT!*

Gart urged his horses on, trying to shut the Mage out of his mind. He shook his head once, then concentrated on keeping the Mage's pleas from reaching him. Silence returned to Gart's thoughts as he somehow managed to form a barrier against the man's words. As the cart rocketed up the dirt road, he turned in his lurching seat and looked over his shoulder. He saw no sign of the now silent Mage. Gart turned back to the road ahead and saw the white robed man standing some twenty yards in front of the cart horses, the glowing spear held loosely at his side. A snarl escaped Gart's scarred lips, and he whipped the horses to a gallop. The cart threatened to come apart beneath him, yet Gart did not slow. He meant to ride this fool into the dust of the road.

The horses thundered down on the silent Mage, yet he did not move aside. Brunar, his chin held high, his grey eyes burning, watched the racing horses until they were nearly upon him, and then he raised his left hand and pointed to the animals. A purple flash came from his outstretched fingers, and the horses skidded to a stop as surely as if they had suddenly encountered a solid wall. Another flash, and the young man in the wagon flinched as if he had been struck a blow to the head. Gart raised one hand to his forehead before grasping the reins again.

Brunar lowered his hand, his eyes still burning as he watched Gart's anger rise. The Mage walked quickly around to his left until he was even with the small wagon, still a good twenty feet from him. The blonde man's scars were livid with rage as he tried to whip the horses into movement once more, screaming viciously at the immobile beasts. When he saw that they would not move, he turned his twin points of icy blue back to the Mage.

Power is not evil, Gart, no more than a hammer is evil. It is a tool. It is the user that defines whether it is used for good, or for darker purposes. Gart stood up in his cart, his breath coming in great ragged gasps as his fury grew. The power inside him seemed to writhe and grow of its own accord, aching for release.

"I told you, Mage, I will not go with you!" Gart shouted, trying desperately to control himself, and failing. "My place is with my family, so LEAVE ME ALONE!"

The power came exploding out of him, lashing out at the robed figure of the Mage. Dust and debris from the road shot through Brunar's form as Gart's power hurtled towards him. A large stone directly behind the Mage shattered with a thunderclap, pulverized into rubble that was then carried on the shrieking gale that emanated from the raging young man in the wagon.

Through it all, Brunar stood unperturbed. Nothing Gart could do here could harm his physical form, safe as it was, hundreds of miles away in the mountains. Even so, the Mage was surprised by the power he felt radiating from the scarred young man. *So much anger!* Brunar thought to himself as the blast raged around him. *I must be careful with this one, else I risk much in training him. But then, without training he could become even more dangerous.* Brunar waited for the young man to finish his onslaught.

Gart's world had narrowed until he could see only the white-robed form of the Mage before him. Gart sent forth his power in a crushing wave, hoping to smash the man that tormented him. He had seen the boulder shatter and its pieces join other, smaller bits of rubble and hurtle away from him, carried on the current of his power. He watched the Mage stand in the path of the blast, untouched. Gart sent more of his magick, and still more, hating himself for using the unnatural force within him, but glad to have something to use against this insane fool. The Mage never moved.

Finally, Gart collapsed heavily back into the seat of the cart, gasping for breath. He had loosed every bit of his unnatural power at Brunar in an attempt to destroy him, but he had failed. His exhaustion had left him bereft of the fury that had fueled him, and he sat, breathing heavily and resting his head on the back of the hard wooden seat, trying to regain enough strength to stand.

Impressive. Brunar's voice gently stroked the younger man's mind. *That was quite a display for one so unschooled in the use of his magick. Even so, there is much you will learn before you become a Guardian.* Gart turned his head slowly to look into the Mage's grey eyes.

"I told you before, I'm not going anywhere with you. I belong with my family." Gart's ice blue eyes showed that his anger yet smoldered deep within, but his fatigue kept him from shouting. "I want no part of you or the Guardians. Leave me alone." Gart turned his head away from the Mage to stare up into the cloudless blue sky. The only sound was that of Gart's labored breathing.

The Mage walked slowly up to the cart until he was standing within arm's reach of the exhausted young man. For a moment, he said nothing. He silently stared at the wicked scars that were visible on Gart's face from this side. Finally, he spoke.

I cannot force you to come with me. That would be a violation of the very principles that we fight for. Brunar saw the young man turn his head back to him, and noted that although the angry blue fire in his eyes still burned, now those eyes held a hint of curiosity as well. *You must join us willingly, or not at all.* Brunar's shoulders seemed to slump just a little. He looked at the spear he carried and then back to the reclining Gart.

All right, then. I will leave you. However, mark me well, Gart. This weapon I bear is yours. Brunar jabbed a finger at the young man. *None but you can wield it, and none but you can help us defeat the evil that has come again. Mordak is out there, and he will stop at nothing until he either dominates this world or destroys it.* Gart watched the grim set of Brunar's features and said nothing, allowing the strength to slowly return to his weary limbs.

A day will come when you see the folly of denying your destiny. But until then, you may go. Take this with you. The Mage held out his left hand and a tiny shimmering glow appeared, hovering like a purple cloud just above his outstretched palm. The blazing emerald held within the spear that Brunar carried flashed brighter, and the smaller glow in the Mage's hand began to take on a deep green color, identical to that of the shining gem in the spear.

Gart leaned forward, curious in spite of himself. He saw the glow above Brunar's hand gain solidity, and form into a gem about the size of his thumbnail, radiant with green sparkles. This drifted gently into Brunar's open palm. As Gart watched, the glow subsided and then disappeared, leaving only an occasional emerald gleam to flash across the jewel's faceted surface.

The Mage held the gem, easily worth more money than Gart had ever seen in his lifetime, up to the light, as if testing it for color. He then let it rest again in his open palm, and extended it to Gart.

"What is that?" Gart said, eyeing the Mage warily.

This is your means of reaching us, should you see the importance of being Chosen. Take it. Brunar pushed his palm closer to the young man above him.

Gart eyed the stone for a moment, and then surprised himself by reaching out to accept it. As his fingertips closed about the emerald, he noticed that he did not feel the Mage's palm beneath it. He shrugged to himself, and took a close look at the stone. It certainly was unusual, and quite beautiful. Gart thought of his wife, Gennie. She had never possessed anything so pretty.

He turned back to the Mage and abruptly nodded once, his mouth set in a thin line. If he could get a smile from his wife for this little trinket, then it would be worthwhile.

Should you change your mind, hold the stone and call to me with your spirit. I will hear, and the Jidaan and I will come for you. Brunar stepped away from the cart, keeping his eyes on the angry young man. The farmer carefully put the tiny gem in a pocket in his tunic, and grabbed the reins once again.

Please hurry, Gart. We need you.

Gart turned from the Mage and snapped the reins curtly at the horses, urging them to a walk. The cart drew slowly away from Brunar, dust rising from its turning wheels.

Brunar watched it until he was certain that it would not be turning back, and then turned away. Despair washed over him for the first time. Never had he faced a problem such as this. Such power! In a novice, that could be dangerous beyond reckoning. He hoped the young man would change his mind soon, before Mordak came into his full powers. If not, the others would have to move without the Gift of Storms, and their effectiveness as a whole would be significantly diminished. Never before had anyone refused the call to be a Guardian.

Brunar gazed at the dusty remnants of the shattered boulder at the roadside, marveling at the power it had taken to pulverize it.

Such a waste. Soon after, the Mage vanished from the road, and a warm wind began to blow across the land.

Chapter 8

The sun was nearing the western horizon, and the shadows down below were stretching towards the coming night. Mordak flew on. His great flapping wings were more suited to gliding on the air currents than great speed, but he was making good progress towards his holt in the northeast.

RAAAWWWWWW! Mordak's cry split the air above the edges of Triagga. Below him, he could see the green carpet of the dense jungle canopy, breaking here and there as he neared the waving grasslands that separated the jungle from the naked, jutting peaks ahead. Those peaks burst from the earth below like fangs, and were easily as sharp.

Once beyond the Teeth of Triagga, Mordak knew he would pass over more of the gently rolling grasslands before encountering the River Elde. Night would be fallen by then, and he could fly lower to the ground without being seen. He felt his energy coursing through him, burning with cold fire. The lives he had taken would easily sustain him for the second half of the journey, when he would pass the river and traverse the rich farmland beyond. Then would come the barren plains of Gorran, littered with massive boulders and stone formations. Deep within those inhospitable plains lay the foul sorcerer's holt, a massive fist of stone raised defiantly against the sky. A hideous chuckle scraped from Mordak's mutated throat as he laughed at the irony of breaking free of a prison of stone only to seek haven in a fortress of the same.

It had been quite a while since Mordak had seen this place, built eons ago as a refuge in case his primary home on the roaming island came to ruin. The Guardians had long since destroyed that larger keep, but none save Mordak knew of the second, more remote hiding place that he now approached. Once there, the sorcerer would find the means to commune with his vile god, Balroth.

The powerfully evil presence would be pleased that Mordak had escaped. Mordak hoped the god would show him a way to increase his powers, to gain an advantage over the Mage. Then again, he might take his life for the fleeting amusement it would bring. However, Mordak had always been the most powerful of the mighty Balroth's servants, and the Daemon-God had been generous in the past.

As twilight fell, Mordak's scarlet eyes glowed like hot coals in the face of the beast, and he flapped his membranous wings to gain speed as he approached the jagged mountain range ahead. *Guardians, bah! They will bow before me just as the rest of the world will! It will be that or death for those bothersome fools. Then there shall be no one to stop me!*

The beast flew onward, gliding now and then on the air currents, a nightmare given shape.

Chapter 9

Nessar slipped into the darkened tavern and was immediately assailed by the odors of roasted meat, spilled ale, and the rather distinctive aroma of the clientele. This was a rough and ready bunch that included mercenaries, cutthroats and thieves as well as a few of the less noble members of the City Watch. It took only a moment for the aging thief's eyes to adjust to the dim light, and then he walked smoothly to his customary table at the back of the common room. He seated himself in one of the three rickety wooden chairs that surrounded the small circular table, and positioned himself so that he could survey the entire room at a glance. He tensed when he saw a serving girl approach him, but relaxed as he recognized her as one of the usual workers.

"Something for you, Ness?" The girl was about seventeen, but looked far older than her years. Life in Rualtha was rough, indeed. Her face held a quiet frown as she waited for a reply from the wiry, silver-haired man seated before her.

"Rita, you must get prettier each time I see you." Nessar enjoyed the smile this brought from the girl. "I think I'll just have an ale, and another one of those beautiful smiles of yours for the time being." He gave her a crooked grin, and winked slyly at her.

"Why, thank you, sir!" A surprised giggle escaped her. This oldster's comments were not at all rude and suggestive as her usual customers were, and she enjoyed his playful compliments. "I'll have both for you right away!" The smile remained on her face as she bustled towards the bar for his ale. Nessar had not been in here for quite some time, but he remembered that Rita had always been pretty when she smiled.

She came back in a moment and left the ale on the table in front of Nessar. He tipped her generously, eliciting another winning smile from the girl, and then he was alone again. He sipped at his drink and found that the Rusty Dagger had not changed its brew since his last visit, and he was pleased. Slowly, he sat back and relaxed for the first time in weeks. Being head of the Thieves Guild in the port city of Rualtha was difficult at the best of times, and these were not the best of times.

The old man had seen sixty-odd years in this city, and spent far more of them as a thief than he cared to admit. Actually, he had been a thief ever since his parents were killed in the poor quarter of the city, and he had been left on his own at the tender age of six.

Sometimes, he allowed himself to wish that he, too, had been killed by the ragged band of thugs that had accosted his mother and father. Then he would not have had to endure the horrors of life in the deadly back streets of Rualtha. He had learned to survive along with the other street boys, eating whatever he could scavenge from the rubbish bins and sleeping wherever he could find shelter from the rain. Those first years were the worst, and he lived on the brink of starvation until he grew old enough to steal effectively.

He seemed to have a knack for thievery, and managed to avoid even the most watchful eyes. His skills grew daily, and the Thieves Guild eventually took an interest in his abilities. At the age of ten, his talent for stealth and sleight-of-hand had bettered that of experienced thieves twice his age. He had been marked early on by the Guild's leaders for advancement.

Nessar sighed as he downed another draught of ale. He had gotten advancement, all right. Now he was the head of the Guild, and a more quarrelsome, petty and argumentative bunch of bandits he had never seen. Some threatened to take over, not quieting until Nessar demonstrated that neither his mind, nor his fighting skill had suffered for his advanced age. These demonstrations usually proved deadly. He had already killed three of the more unruly troublemakers this month. While his predecessors always seemed to relish that kind of thing, he hated it. He killed to survive, yes, but taking a man's life just because he wanted to take Nessar's position didn't sit well with him. It seemed nothing but a waste.

Though things were quiet now, soon enough some of the more ambitious members of the Guild would begin calling for him to abdicate his post. Nessar looked at the aged hand that held the glass of ale. There was no sign of palsy or shaking there, and in fact, it looked quite strong. Still, sixty is awfully old for a thief, and he felt that he would have to move on soon, lest he be forcibly removed by a younger, stronger man.

"Something on your mind, thief?" The feminine voice came from the stairs to Nessar's right, bringing him to full readiness. "And by the way, you might want to put that dagger away before people get the wrong idea." Nessar saw the young woman step towards him, her chain mail and weapons gleaming even in the dimness of the tavern. He knew the voice as well as his own, and upon seeing Kiran, he smiled and resheathed the dagger that had flown almost miraculously into his hand.

"Well, you mercenaries shouldn't go around startling old men like that. My heart could have stopped, and then where would you be?" He stood and stepped around the table to embrace the smiling woman, a head or so shorter than he. He gestured for her to sit with him. Kiran pulled a chair around to face the door, nearly side by side with Nessar's, and slid into it with uncanny grace as Nessar resumed his seat.

Nessar saw that she was dressed in her usual fashion. Tight-fitting black breeks hugged her legs until they disappeared into her soft boots, and her flowing white shirt was tucked smartly into a pair of black gauntlets. Nessar smiled to himself, knowing that beneath those gloves, her shirt was bound at the forearms by tight leather wrist guards. Although obviously of an older style, Kiran's weapons were clean and well-kept, and he knew without checking that her sword and daggers were of the finest balance and quality; they were also razor sharp. She was the only female mercenary in Rualtha, possibly the entire western Realm, and she was counted the best fighter, male or female, by more than a few. She was also one of the few who knew Nessar for the Guildmaster that he was.

"It's good to see you again!" Kiran smiled at her friend, her pale green eyes twinkling in the dim light as she squeezed one of his hands on the tabletop. "I haven't seen you about the town for months now. Is everything all right in the Guild? I heard there has been some unrest in the ranks." Removing her tight gauntlets, she motioned to Rita for an ale as she secured her gloves in her belt.

"It could definitely be better." Nessar's smile had dwindled, leaving his lined face looking tired and worn. He ran a hand through his thinning hair. "Some of them still want me out, Kiran. They think that an old man like me is useless in my position. I think the new fellow, Jared, is behind most of this, but even without him, the general feeling is that I'm washed up."

"That's ridiculous!" Kiran retorted. "Not one of them has a tenth of your experience running things. They don't have a clue as to what being Guildmaster really means." She brushed a stray lock of dark brown hair from her face and tucked it fiercely behind her ear. "Not only that, but your street skills are still better than any of theirs. If they're saying you've lost your touch just to discredit you, they're blind...or they are listening to that *Jared*. I think I might have to pay him a little visit." Kiran cracked her knuckles loudly as if ready to get right to work.

Nessar shook his head and laid a gentle hand on her armored shoulder. "No, Kiran. Even without Jared stirring things up, I've been hearing this kind of thing for some time now. I know that I can't head the Guild forever, and I suppose the time has come." He shook his head wearily. "Maybe I need to face the fact that I am just an old man who has outlived his usefulness." He looked into Kiran's eyes and saw her outrage as she clenched her fists on the scarred tabletop.

Her angry reply was interrupted when a giant man ambled over to their table, followed by two more imposing fellows. They smelled strongly of dirt and sweat. Judging by the number of weapons they carried, the trio looked to be mercenaries, probably guards of one of the many caravans that traveled to and from Rualtha. Nessar and Kiran caught each other's gaze and the thief made an all but imperceptible gesture. *I'll handle this.* Kiran dropped her right hand to the hilt of her dagger anyway.

"Pardon me, there, Gramps, but you and your ladyfriend are sittin' at our table," the giant rumbled down at the seated pair. He was a massive bald fellow with a jagged scar running across one cheek. A large axe dangled from a thong at his belt, and one of his huge hands rested pointedly on its handle. The man's bushy eyebrows and mustache twitched as he waited for a response from the old geezer.

Nessar responded with courtly poise and a smile. "I'm terribly sorry, sir. If only we had known that these seats were reserved we would certainly have found other accommodations." One of the thug's eyebrows went up in surprise. The thief pushed back his chair to stand, but a huge boot planted itself in his chest and Nessar found himself seated again. He quickly grabbed Kiran's knee under the table, keeping her from attacking the brute.

Thumping his boot back on the floor, baldy continued. "No, it's too late for that now, old man. You see, now that you've sat in our chairs, you've got to pay our fee before you can leave." The giant's two companions grinned hugely. Apparently, they had seen this particular play before.

"And if I don't pay?" Nessar asked quietly, brushing the dirt from his tunic and smiling absently.

A wicked grin cracked the face of the burly giant, showing a gap or two in the teeth that gleamed from under the wide mustache. "Then you get to meet my friend here." The man deftly pulled his axe from its resting place and hefted it in one meaty hand. Its edge was filled with nicks and notches, yet Nessar could see its sharpness. He looked from the weapon to the two ruffians behind the giant and saw that they were snickering loudly to one another. The giant brought the edge close to the thief's face and leaned in to speak. "You wouldn't like to meet my friend, I can tell you that."

Looking directly into the huge man's dull brown eyes, Nessar dropped his polite manner and let a harsh coldness seep into his own eyes. His smile suddenly turned from a good-natured grin to a grim, tight line turned up only at one corner. Quiet as death, Nessar spoke.

"No, I don't think we would. I suppose we'll have to avoid that, now won't we?"

Surprise dawned in the thug's eyes as the old man's fingers shot out and struck him just below his breastbone, taking the wind from him in an instant. The giant started to fall forward but Nessar jumped from his seat as if to help an old friend who had suddenly taken ill. Nessar plucked the axe from the man's loosening fingers and leaned it against the wall just beyond the gasping man's reach. The remaining two ruffians stopped laughing abruptly as their leader sat woodenly in the old man's chair, his eyes bulging in pain. Nessar started to fan the seated man. "My, my, that ale certainly does pack a punch, doesn't it Kiran?"

Kiran stood and stepped around the table towards the two thugs, who blanched at the mention of her name. She wore a predatory grin as she eyed the two brigands.

"Why yes, it does! You know, I think these two fellows ought to have some. It might calm them down a bit." She flexed her fingers and rested her right hand lazily on the pommel of her sword. The two men were larger than Kiran, but they had heard of this madwoman with a blade. She was not known for her politeness...and often left few survivors. The men had begun to sweat in the thick heat of the dark tavern. One of them drew his sword, and all eyes turned to the two men and the woman squaring off in the back.

The thief continued to fan the seated giant, as if truly concerned for his welfare. Nessar spoke quietly to Kiran. "If you're going to take them, do it now. I've called far too much attention to myself as it is. I'll meet you in a half hour. You know where I'll be." The big man started to rise, still white with pain, but the old thief helped him back to his seat with another surreptitious blow to his midsection.

Kiran nodded, keeping her eyes on the two desperate toughs before her. She knew that Nessar would be gone when she finished with these two, and she also knew exactly where he intended to meet her. She stood, relaxed and calm as the other man pulled his weapon and the pair began to circle her. She felt the tension mount as they crept on either side of her, and instinctively knew that her legs would be the first target.

Suddenly, the man to her left aimed a wide slash to her legs as a high attack whistled in from her right. *Typical*, she thought. With blinding speed, she whipped her sword from its scabbard and parried the low attack, even as she ducked the blade that slashed for her head. Her small but stone-like fist slammed into the first man's face, sending a spray of blood and teeth to the dirt floor. He staggered back a few steps, holding his shattered mouth. A solid kick to the lower leg knocked the rightmost attacker from his feet an instant later.

"How dare you attack a lady?" Kiran bellowed in her most unladylike manner, and turned to the standing thug to her left. Bleeding from a mashed face, the man screamed in rage and aimed two quick slashes to Kiran's side. She parried them without effort, and caught an overhead slash on her guard. Before he could pull back, she slammed her left palm sharply upwards, into his elbow. It dislocated with a loud snap, and his weapon clattered to the ground.

"It's high time someone taught you boys some manners!" Still holding the man's ruined elbow, Kiran quickly bashed him in the face again, but this time with the curved guard of her sword. The ruffian slumped to the ground, bleeding and unconscious.

Catlike, she hopped over the prostrate fellow to see the other thug regain his feet and pick up his weapon, limping. He eyed her warily. He knew what she could do, but was undaunted.

"Are you ready for me, big man?" Kiran smiled sweetly, almost seductively. She saw his eyes widen, and watched the sweat run down his face to drip on the floor. She pointed her blade directly at his face. "Do you want some of this? Well then, you shall have it!"

She leapt in and attacked with a blinding overhead cut meant to cleave her adversary from skull to chest, but he managed a hasty block, and their blades rang together in the still of the tavern. She continued her assault with a furious series of slashes and thrusts, each parried less strongly than the last by the tiring thug. Fear spread across his dirty face as her pace escalated, and he felt her blade dig in here and there as his defenses weakened.

She paused for an instant, feinted once with her blade and watched his frantic parry meet only empty air. Kiran whirled and kicked him solidly in the side of the head. Like his partner, he fell straight to the floor, bleeding from a score of cuts and slashes.

Kiran turned and checked the first attacker and saw that he was still just as unconscious as the second. She wiped her blade on one of the sleeping bandits before resheathing it; its shiny surface had been moistened by only a bit of blood on the tip. She stepped back over to the table she and Nessar had shared, and saw the burly fellow slumped over in his seat, one huge hand wrapped around Nessar's ale mug. She chuckled to herself. These fellows were strictly small time, and now that they posed no threat to anyone, there was no need to kill them. Maybe next time, Kiran thought. For now, they would live, and possibly learn not to pick on people they did not know.

The graceful warrior wheeled and strode up to the bar, stepping over one of her former attackers in the process. "Terribly sorry for the trouble, Stefan. I hope this will cover it." She tossed a few gold coins over the counter to the owner as she headed for the door.

The little fellow caught them and made them vanish with practiced ease. "No problem, Kiran. Those guys have been making trouble in here for quite a while. I ought to be paying you! I'll have them dragged outside and call the Guards." He cracked a grin and waved at the swordswoman as she walked quickly out of the Rusty Dagger and into the dusky evening beyond.

Outside, Kiran walked a few streets over from the tavern, then ducked into a little smithy. She nodded to the owner, a short but well-muscled man smudged all over with grit from his forge, then passed into a back room. The room was quite small, having only enough space for a bed, a small table, and a chest in one corner. The single window was smudged and dirty, and nothing could be seen through its musty glass. A lantern was on the desk, and she lit it before closing the door behind her.

She sat on the bed for a moment and listened to the sounds of the forge as she rubbed her neck. She had slept on it awkwardly the night before, and the skirmish had aggravated it somewhat.

Stretching out on the small bed, Kiran let the wheezing of the bellows and the clanging of the smith's worn hammer lull her, relaxing her as it always had. This little room had always been a haven for her, for the smith was a trusted friend, and many was the time that she had stayed here for a brief rest. Nessar would be along in good time, so she need not worry about him.

Kiran was a light sleeper and knew she would wake instantly if anyone entered the room, so she decided to catch a quick nap while she waited. Her eyelids fell shut and her breathing slowed as she relaxed.

Some minutes later, a familiar voice broke the silence. "Kiran, I've told you to lock the door when you come here." She sat up in a flash, her dagger already poised for combat. When she saw Nessar seated on the chest in the corner, smiling broadly with his hands behind his head and his ankles crossed before him, she put her weapon away and cursed softly.

"I did lock it, you sneak." Kiran watched him raise an eyebrow at the remark. "It never fails. You are the only person I've ever known that can creep up on me. Even when I'm sleeping, no one else can do that." Kiran turned and placed her feet on the floor and looked at him. The thief's smug expression made her laugh, in spite of the faint twinge of consternation she felt at being unable to detect his approach. It was a game they played, and Nessar had always won. "And you think that you haven't got your skills anymore. Pah! You're just as good as you ever were, and you know it, you old scoundrel!"

The smile stayed on Nessar's face, but a sadness flowed into his eyes as he spoke. "Well, maybe I still have some of it, Kiran. Maybe."

A new voice, rich and strong, interrupted the mercenary's reply. *Maybe you still have all of it, Old One, and you just don't believe in yourself anymore.* Kiran rose instantly, dagger in hand once again, searching for the source of the voice. Nessar stayed still and quiet, waiting.

A silent purple radiance exploded in the empty corner of the room, blinding them for a heartbeat. When their vision cleared, a man had appeared before them, a man radiating power and strength, his stone grey eyes boring into those of the thief. In the crook of his arm he held two short spears, both beautiful and deadly. One pommel glowed with a cobalt blue fire while the pommel of the other was black, darker than the deepest night. It actually seemed to absorb the dim light in the room.

"You have only a few seconds before I dispatch you, wizard," Kiran warned. "Who are you and what do you want?" Her eyes narrowed as she calculated the brief distance between them and the attack she would use. Strangely, she felt that something was missing. She felt disconnected from this adversary, as if she were facing empty space rather than a real opponent. She tried to refocus herself on him, and prepared to lunge.

The stranger's majestic face turned to her and the strength in his eyes gave Kiran pause. This man was dangerous, no matter that he held his weapons in a position ill-suited for combat. The white-robed man looked at her for a moment before speaking again. *Kiran, I see that you are a fighter and, unless I am a pitiful judge of character, rather a good one.* His praise met silence as the mercenary realized that his words did not echo in the small room as theirs had.

The stranger turned back to the thief, still seated on the chest in the corner. *And Nessar, thief extraordinaire. Both of you have more talent within you than you have ever dreamed. I am Brunar, the Mage, and I am here on a mission of great urgency. You both are needed. Your skills will be quite necessary in the near future.*

"You mean you have a job for Ness and me?" Kiran's mercenary nature asserted itself. "Just what kind of work will we be doing and at what price?" She glanced at Nessar and saw that he had been shaken by something that this Brunar had said, but the prospect of a new job had piqued her interest, and she paid the thief no attention.

The Mage chuckled gravely, a small smile playing at the corners of his silent mouth. *No Kiran, it is not a job offer that I have come to give you. It is your destiny. I take it that neither of you has ever heard of me or of the Guardians?* Kiran shook her head while Nessar remained still. The Mage scowled. *I realize that our last battle was over two thousand years ago, but I had hoped that more would remember us.* He sighed. *In any event, let me explain.*

The Mage picked up the ebony-pommeled spear in his left hand and offered it to Nessar. The thief had remained silent throughout the visit, and his eyes cautiously flicked from Brunar to the weapon. His gaze lingered on the gleaming blade and the stout oaken haft. When he saw the midnight stone in the ornate pommel, his eyes narrowed and he leaned closer to gain a better view of the inky blot clutched within the metalwork.

This, Nessar, is the Jidaan of Reynor. It brings with it the Gift of Stealth, something a man in your present position could well appreciate. The weapon has a few other abilities, foremost among them, the ability to show me the person it has Chosen to wield it.

Nessar's eyes rose to meet those of the Mage. "Chosen?"

Yes, Chosen. The power within you marks you as a Guardian, a Protector of this world. Haven't you ever wondered why you are such a successful thief? Nessar made no reply. *Your innate powers have manifested themselves in certain skills that you may have taken for granted all these years. Your dexterity, your coordination, your very powers of concentration all stem from the magick you were born with, powers that you have not even begun to tap.*

Nessar stared again at the ebony gem that pulsed darkly in the weapon's pommel. "So this weapon chose me to wield it, and become a Guardian? Then, why now? Why not thirty years ago when I might have been of some use to someone?" His angry eyes bored into those of the Mage as his voice rose. "I'm just a dried up old man! I don't intend to spend my last days trying to be some kind of wizard-warrior, not for you or for anyone else!" Brunar's eyes hardened at this.

"Nessar, wait!" Kiran interjected. "At least hear him out. He wouldn't have come to us if he didn't think we could handle whatever he wants us to do, and I want to hear the rest of this." The Mage lowered the spear in his left hand and turned to the mercenary on his right.

"Now, where do I fit in? Am I supposed to have some magickal powers, too?" She had not lowered the dagger, but seemed less like a cat about to pounce than she had before. She was eyeing the blazing sapphire in the second weapon.

Kiran, you are indeed destined to become one of us. Your obvious fighting skills come from your, as you put it, 'magickal powers'. And when you are fully trained, the powers that now lie dormant within you will make your present talents seem insignificant in comparison. The Jidaan of Durok has chosen you as its wielder, and it brings with it the Gift of Warding.

Kiran made a face at that. "Warding? Like a shield?"

Brunar nodded once. *Just so, Kiran. However, there is far more to it than that. I shall teach you what I can.*

Looking back at the angry thief, the Mage continued. *The Jidaan do not choose unwisely. You must learn to control your powers, to use them to the best of your ability. You must also learn to use the Gifts that the weapons give you, for the task we face is most difficult, and without them, it may be insurmountable.*

"And just what massive task are we supposed to accomplish?" Kiran sheathed her dagger and folded her arms across her mail-clad chest. "Are we supposed to save the world or something?" She laughed at her own joke, until she saw that the expression of the Mage had not altered in the slightest. Her laugh died in the still of the small room.

Possibly, Kiran. Possibly. An ancient evil has only just awakened. This evil attempted to enslave this world once before, and very nearly succeeded. It has come again.

"Mordak." Nessar's voice interrupted the Mage's explanation, and Brunar turned surprised eyes back to the thief, followed closely by Kiran's openmouthed stare. With a wave of his hand, Nessar dismissed the pair's shocked expressions. "Yes, yes, I know all about it. I may be old, but I do still remember things I've heard and read over the years, and that chapter in our history is one that I studied closely some time ago. If I remember correctly, you lost a few of your precious Guardians trying to put him down. Why should I go traipsing off into battle against the likes of him? He could destroy us with a thought!"

If you know the history, Nessar, then you know that the peace of the last 2000 years came about as a direct result of our intervention. No one else on this world can combat him, and he knows it. If we do nothing, it will only be a matter of time before he renews his quest for domination.

Kiran spoke up. "Let me get this straight. You want us to go with you, learn about magickal powers that we've always had but never knew about, use these magickal weapons to fight this Mordak fellow, and save the world."

The Mage could not repress a slight grin. *Yes, Kiran, I believe that you have the gist of it. Will you come?* He watched her eyes drop again to the sparkling sapphirine gem in the Jidaan of Durok.

Kiran made a face as she seemed to turn over the question in her mind. Finally, she made a short nod to herself and replied, "Hels, yes, I will. I probably won't get paid, but it sounds a lot more interesting than guarding some fool merchant caravan on a boring trail to market." She turned to her friend. "Ness? This is your chance to leave those grumbling idiot thieves to themselves! Come on, what have you got to lose?"

"Well for starters, how about my life?" Nessar stood to stretch his long legs. He stared long and hard at the white-robed man before him. The old thief's eyes stayed strong for a moment longer, then dropped away as if he had just surrendered something. "But then, that's almost done with anyway, isn't it?" He sighed and looked at Kiran. "I suppose I ought to go along, if only to see that you don't get into trouble. All right, Brunar, just when do we leave and what do we need to take with us?"

Brunar nodded at the thief, accepting the man's reluctance. *I will return for you in the morning, four days from now. Take with you what you will, but we have ample supplies back in the mountains, and I think that you will find everything else you might require to be there.*

"Mountains? Which mountains? The nearest are several weeks away from here," Kiran observed. She hated long journeys, an odd dislike for a mercenary. She much preferred to be fighting right here and right now, wherever here and now might be at the moment.

"He means the Heartstrong Mountains, Kiran. Unless my memory is failing, the Keep is somewhere on the western coast, high in those mountains where they reach the sea." Nessar stepped closer to the Mage. "But somehow, I don't think that a long trip will be necessary, will it, Brunar?"

Brunar was pleased. It seemed that Nessar had, indeed, read the chronicles of the last war. The Mage smiled. *I thought that you knew much more of us than you let on, Nessar.* Brunar then turned to Kiran. *He is quite correct. By the time I come for you, I will have regained enough of my energy to use the Jidaan to transport you two back to the Keep in an instant. It saves wear and tear on the horses, you know.*

Meet me here when the time comes, and I will take you to your destiny. Until then, fare thee well Nessar and Kiran.

The room again flared with the silent purple flash, mingled with bright blue and black, and the Mage and his two short spears had gone, leaving the mercenary and thief alone.

Kiran's excited face turned to Nessar. "This promises to be quite interesting, don't you think?"

The old thief laid a hand on his friend's shoulder. Sometimes he felt that she was his daughter instead of just a friend, so strong were his protective feelings for the girl. He knew that she could handle herself quite well, but, like a true father, he never stopped worrying about her.

"Kiran, I have much to tell you about the Guardians and Brunar and Mordak. At least, I'll tell you what I remember, and the rest will be up to the Mage. If the stories I read are even halfway true, and Mordak is risen, then we are in for the fight of our lives, little one."

Kiran suggested that they talk over dinner, and Nessar agreed. He even offered to pay for the meal with the gold he had lifted from the ruffian with the axe.

Chapter 10

Layton raced down the moonlit mountain path, mindful of the stray rocks that littered the narrow roadway. Although he had been running for the better part of an hour at a blistering pace, his breathing was even and steady. He ran quietly for a young man loaded down with a sword, hand axe, long dagger, and a pair of forklike eastern weapons known as sai.

The youth rounded a corner, hugging the cliff wall to his right, and picked up speed as the path sloped sharply away from him. The King's garrison at River Pass had been rather quiet of late, and when the captain had learned from a captured spy that the Prince's traveling party would be ambushed at midnight as they traveled up the mountain road towards the garrison, Ranger Squad had been mobilized to attempt a rescue. Layton had been thrilled to be a Ranger at that moment.

A boyish grin struck his face as he loped along. His commander had been quite surprised (and furious) to see Layton wave farewell and burst away from the rest of the squad as they saddled their horses, then dash down the path into the night. Doubtless, they thought he was a deserter or some other type of rogue. No, Layton just knew that he alone would be able to reach the ambush site in time to forestall some of the destruction and possibly save the Prince. The horses had to take the winding road down the mountain, but Layton had no such limitations, and he chose a somewhat quicker route. His path led straight down the craggy side of the mountain.

At times the young man traveled at breakneck speed down inclines that bordered on the vertical, but his uncanny acrobatic ability led him down the mountainside without incident. He made his way from rock to rock, slope to slope with the sure-footed grace of a mountain goat, and when he finally met the road ahead of the ambush site, he sprinted down it, hoping that he could reach the Prince before the fighting started.

He knew the contours of the road fairly well, and he noted that the ambush site indicated by the spy was only a few minutes away. Any other man would be exhausted at this point, racing full tilt for more than an hour down a treacherous mountainside by moonlight, but not Layton. Thanks to his mother, he had been trained in several of the fighting arts of the Easterners by the very masters themselves. That training, years of intense physical conditioning, had left him with endurance and energy that far surpassed those of even his most athletic comrades in the King's army.

His earliest memories included holding a tiny wooden sword in both hands and whacking himself in the head with it while his mother laughed and tried to show him how to hold it properly. She had been his guiding force, his mentor, and his taskmaster, and he had loved her. Under her watchful, caring eyes, he had learned all that the powerful Eastern masters had to offer, and had become a warrior without equal. The masters had sought to teach him that his less-than-average height and slight build were not hindrances, that he needed only that which he already possessed to excel. They had succeeded beyond their wildest dreams.

Early in his training, he had found his ki, that mystical energy that the Easterners believed was possessed by all people. However, only a select, disciplined few could cultivate it until it became a weapon unto itself. Over time, the masters had taught him to find his ki, to build it, and then channel it through his arms and legs until his blows could shatter stone. His coordination and skill with weapons rivaled that of even the old legendary masters. By the time he had left the East to take his place in his own part of the world, he had earned the respect and admiration of his teachers, a feat made even more remarkable due to his age: just over seventeen summers.

That was two years past, and since then, he had fought all over the Realm. Though he had not tried to do so, his reputation had grown until it was much greater and heroic than the image he held of himself. He was simply trying to protect others by fighting where they could not, using his skills for the greater good as best he knew how. And now, he had the chance to protect the Prince. The half-smile that always appeared on his face when he exerted himself widened at the thought.

Bringing his mind back to the present, he scanned the road ahead, watching for holes and loose stones. As he neared the site of the battle that would soon take place, he felt the first hints of fatigue begin to caress his churning thigh muscles. Reaching within himself, he focused on his ki, and channeled a tiny bit of it coursing down into his legs. As renewed strength surged through him, he crested a slight rise and saw several torches on the road below him not half a league away. He knew that the road between the Prince and himself passed into a small canyon before emerging to skirt the larger mountain once more. The ambush would occur in moments.

He gauged the distance and realized that the traveling party would pass into the canyon and be attacked before he could arrive. He swore softly to himself and picked up his pace. In spite of his determination, Layton smiled faintly as he raced onward.

Below, he saw the torches disappear into the canyon. Moments later, the sounds of battle reached his ears. The clang of steel on steel and the harsh screams of the wounded echoed up from the skirmish as Layton raced into the near end of the canyon, drawing his short, curved sword as he ran.

The youth rounded two sharp bends in the canyon and skidded suddenly to a halt as he found himself at the edge of a small but frenzied battle. The Prince's guardsmen, dressed in the royal blue of the King, had rallied to defend three men astride horses. Fifty or so masked warriors, garbed in close-fitting black robes and masks, harried the guardsmen on all sides. Layton could see a young man ahorse in the center of the protective formation. The lad was the spitting image of his sire, King Tespan, and was obviously furious at not being able to join in the fight, restrained as he was by his two advisers on either side of him. The Prince's face flushed crimson in the flickering torchlight, and he held his sword at the ready. The battle raged between the guards and the shadowy attackers, but the assassins had been efficient, and they now outnumbered the guardsmen four to one.

Layton took five running steps and flung himself into the battle, quickly cutting down two of the assassins before they knew what had happened. Another of the renegades turned and engaged the sandy-haired youth, only to find himself dying from a massive stomach wound a moment later. Layton was in his element now, and the strident clashing of swords was as music to him. Still wearing a faint smile, he wove a path of death through the assassins, felling his opponents with his darting, slashing sword and devastating kicks at every turn.

As more of the shadowy renegades became aware of the newcomer's whirling blade, the thick of the battle shifted from the guardsmen to the constantly leaping, twisting young man that had seemingly appeared from nowhere to wreak havoc upon their ranks.

The guardsmen managed to dispatch their immediate attackers, and then fell on their opponents with renewed vigor. The tide of the battle began to turn.

Layton fought like a whirlwind in the midst of the swarm until his sword shattered near the hilt as he blocked a swinging axe. After flinging the broken weapon into the shrouded face of his nearest adversary, he leaped into the air, somersaulting out of reach of the nearest swords. When he touched lightly to the ground once more, the three-pronged sai had found their way into his deadly hands. Without pause, he began laying about himself with the weapons, shattering his opponents' blades and limbs in the process. The flipping strikes and vicious thrusts of the foreign weapons were unknown to the renegades, and some fell back from the youthful Weaponsmaster only to be cut down by the guardsmen from behind.

Moments later, the battle was ended and the bodies of the dead littered the dusty road. Alone, Layton had accounted for more than thirty-five of the fallen assassins. He stood in their midst, holding his sai at the ready, searching for another opponent. Finding none, he relaxed, allowing the detached smile to leave his lips as he briefly took note of the dead. A look of sorrow washed quickly across his features. Layton hated to see such a waste of life, but he had done this before, and would do so again.

He knelt to clean his weapons on the black tunic of one of the bodies and started to hum a tune under his breath. He put the sai away and began searching for a suitable replacement for his broken sword. Gradually, his mood lightened as he picked through the blades, gauging each weapon's worthiness. Layton knew that he had served the Crown well, and was feeling quite exhilarated from the battle.

The nearest guardsmen, still panting from their exertions, eyed each other, not knowing what to make of this young man with his flashing weapons and unearthly skill. The senior officer that remained from the decimated ranks of the Prince's retinue cleared his throat and approached the green-eyed young man. Layton had just found a wonderfully balanced saber, and was testing its edge with his thumb.

"Ho there!" the guardsman managed, keeping his distance as the younger man strapped the new scabbard onto his baldric. "Name yourself before the Prince!"

The young man quickly sheathed his new blade and snapped to perfect attention.

"Sir, my name is Layton, sir!" He slapped his right fist over his heart in salute. "I am enlisted in the Ranger Squad at the River Pass garrison. I ran ahead of the group to offer my assistance. The rest of my squad should be along soon, sir!" A jaunty grin appeared on his boyish face.

Bewildered, the soldier returned Layton's salute. The tired man turned and strode towards the approaching Prince and his advisers. As the four men met and exchanged words, Layton straightened his dusty uniform and offered cheery remarks to the other guardsmen, who had been talking amongst themselves. They seemed awed by him, but some returned his greetings. His abilities were well known, if not believed by the general populace of the King's army.

The Prince finished his conference with the senior officers and strode regally to Layton. "*You* are Layton, the Weaponsmaster?" Prince Keston asked the young man standing among the dead, a man only slightly older than himself.

Kneeling, fist over heart, Layton replied, "Yes, Your Highness. How may I serve thee?" He raised his eyes to the Prince, and showed that his joyful expression had not dimmed in the least.

"It seems that you already have. The throne thanks you for your assistance. Upon looking at you, I must say that you don't have the look of someone whose name is revered at training halls and armories throughout the kingdom as that of a man with no equal." Prince Keston looked his benefactor up and down for a moment before continuing, "I thought you would be taller." He gestured for the youth to stand.

Layton laughed at that as he rose. "Stature is in the heart, more than in the height, my Lord. I have other gifts that tend to make up for that particular lack." The Prince and several of the guardsmen joined in the tired laughter.

"Yes, I have seen those gifts, and I heartily agree with you." Prince Keston liked this young man. He would have to speak to his father, the King, about him. "How did you know to aid us?"

At that moment, one of the soldiers unmasked one of the dead assassins, and called to the senior officer. "These are not men of the Realm, sir! They seem to be Briggen, the whole lot of them." The soldier referred to a tribe of nomads from the north that had been making war on the Kingdom for some time.

Layton agreed and told the Prince about the captive spy back at the garrison.

"After all the peace treaties, and all the goodwill gestures, this is what we get?" The Prince shook his head. "We had hoped for peace, but it seems that they prefer the suffering of war."

"My Lord, I would scout the surrounding area for more of these assassins," Layton volunteered. "The Rangers should be here very soon, and I would rest easier knowing that you are safe."

Prince Keston nodded and dismissed Layton to search the benighted canyon for any stray assassins. The nimble warrior trotted off into the darkness bearing a new sword at his back.

After making two sweeping surveys of the adjacent area, Layton had found no trace of any additional enemies. Apparently, the Briggen had expended the whole of their force on the attack in the canyon. The young warrior stepped onto an outcropping of stone and looked down into the canyon. He saw that the Ranger Squad had arrived and was tending to the wounded, and making ready to move Prince Keston to the garrison.

Alone in the moonlight, he raised his eyes to the gleaming stars above. Layton had always loved the beauty of the night sky. He thought of the men he had just killed, their spirits rising to the heavens.

He did not relish the killing, as many soldiers did. Instead, he found joy in the combat itself, in using his abilities to the fullest. There was a harmony within the movements of battle, and Layton's body, mind, and spirit all worked in unison so that he might hear its song. And though he was loyal to the crown, and thoroughly enjoyed fighting in the King's army, he always offered a brief prayer for his fallen opponents. After all, they were loyal to someone, somewhere. They might have families and loved ones back home, and most likely truly believed in the cause for which they had fought. Unfortunately, their destiny had led them to Layton, and so they could not help but fall.

Layton said his silent prayer for the deceased and stood quietly for a moment, breathing in the chill night air. Just as he was about to make his way back down to rejoin the others, a flash of violet light exploded behind him. He drew his sword in an instant, and turned to face the direction of the flash.

Several yards from him, Layton saw a white-robed figure standing still, bathed in moonlight and cloaked in a faint purple glow. In his right hand the stranger held a short spear the likes of which Layton had never seen, its pommel radiant with swirling opalfire. Little could be made of the man's features in the darkness, but the pale moonlight and the writhing light from the weapon showed a majestic, stern face and short dark hair with twin shocks of silver in the temples.

Recognition flooded the young warrior, and he dropped quickly to one knee, sword still clenched in his trembling fist. His eyes found the darkened ground in front him, and he uttered in disbelief, "Brunar!"

You know of me? The wordless reply echoed within Layton's mind.

"Yes, Great One." The words were filled with awe, as if spoken to a god. "I know of you and of the weapon you bear." Layton's mother had taken special care to teach her son of the Guardians and their leader. Layton had never even wondered why she had done so, but at this moment, he was glad she had. "Tell me, powerful Mage. Have I been Chosen?"

Layton's eyes lifted to gaze at the mystical figure before him. Brunar had taken several steps and was now only a few feet away from the kneeling young man.

Yes, Weaponsmaster. The Jidaan of Dani has Chosen you. You seem to know much of us, and yet you kneel. Why?

Layton swallowed before answering. Here before him was a figure of legend, a powerful sorcerer of ancient times, a man who had seen and fought the evil of the Vile One himself. "Mighty Brunar, I am but a humble soldier, and you are Brunar, the Mage. I cannot help but kneel in your presence, Great One." Layton's eyes dropped from those of the Mage once more.

Brunar was silent for a brief moment before replying with a hint of a smile. *As much as this might appeal to my ego, I must tell you that this kneeling and calling me 'Great One', and 'Mighty Brunar' are simply unnecessary. Now get up from there and let us speak as equals. I may be the leader of the Guardians, but each one is most important, and none is more important than the others.*

Layton continued to look at the ground for a moment longer, then tentatively stood and focused directly on the stern Mage. He still seemed uncertain, but Brunar had gotten his point across, and the youthful warrior would get used to the familiarity.

Brunar spoke again. *Each of us brings a different power, a different viewpoint to the team, and each of us is indispensable. The power we can attain by working together far surpasses anything that any of us might achieve alone.* He gestured with his gleaming weapon towards the canyon. *I saw the battle below. It seems that you have already mastered much in the way of combat. You have already learned to use your magick?*

Layton looked puzzled. "Magick? Sir, I know nothing of magick. My masters told me that my *ki* was exceptionally strong, but I'm no Mage." He sheathed his sword with a deft motion.

Brunar nodded in understanding. *Ah, yes. I know something of the arts you have studied, though not nearly as* much as you. *The power that you mention has many names, and can be used in many, many different ways. In the East, it has long been used primarily for combat and longevity, while in other places, it is used, well. . .differently. It is my task to teach you those ways, and it appears that you already have a solid foundation upon which to build.*

Brunar gestured toward the valley below. *The movements that you used down there were very effective, but a far cry from what I might have used. Your style is incredibly energetic and acrobatic. We that do not possess such outstanding physical skill use a more efficient method of hand to hand combat, something that requires a little less jumping.*

Layton was suddenly intrigued. "Oh? What style? Could you show me something of it?" He was as eager as a puppy to learn something new, and in his excitement, he forgot for a moment that he was speaking to the Mighty Brunar.

The Mage smiled. This was exactly the reaction he had hoped for. *Layton, I think that you have much to learn, but not of fighting. After watching you down there, I think you may be teaching us.*

Brunar's smile widened as he watched the emotions play on Layton's face. The young man was struggling with the idea that he might actually be training the Guardians, the fabled heroes who had once saved the world. Simply being Chosen was more honor than Layton had ever hoped to gain in this life, but this was beyond belief. Looking into the younger man's eyes, Brunar knew that he had found a most worthy Guardian.

Then a frown crawled onto Layton's face. "Wait a minute. Why have you come for me? The last time the Guardians were called was over two thousand years ago to battle Mordak. What has happened? Why must new Guardians be Chosen?"

Brunar's smile vanished as he explained Mordak's release. Layton listened intently, nodding as he recognized portions of the tale from the legends that his mother had imparted to him. Though long-lived, the Guardians had not been Mages, and had passed away centuries ago. Since then, the Guardians had not been needed.

So you see, it is vital for those who have been Chosen to come with me for training, to learn to use their abilities and master the Jidaan. The coming battle with Mordak will require all of our skills and talents.

Layton was quiet for a time after the Mage finished. "I gladly accept your call to arms, Brunar, and I will not fail you. I will learn that which you would teach me, and if I can help the

team in any way, I will do so. The sorcerer must be stopped."
Layton saluted the Mage then, standing at attention and looking
directly into his eyes. The youth saw approval there, and a hint of
gladness underneath the somber grey that resided in the eyes of
Brunar.

*You are only the second of six to embrace your destiny
so enthusiastically. I only hope that your attitude rubs off on
some of the others.* Brunar smiled wistfully at the thought of Gart
and Nessar's reluctance.

"Shouldn't we inform the King?" Layton asked suddenly.
"I mean, the Prince himself is in the canyon below, and if
Mordak is loose, then shouldn't we let him know? He could begin
raising the army, preparing defenses against whatever Mordak
may have in store for the Realms!"

Brunar nodded his assent. *Yes, leave that to me. I intend
to pay a visit to the King during the daylight hours. He will be
informed, and I am certain that the army will begin to prepare
for the battles soon enough. But until we know where Mordak is
and what his first targets are, there is nowhere for them to go.
It would do no good to march off to war when you haven't a
clue as to where that war is to be waged. Until he reveals
himself, all we can do is train and prepare as best we can.*

Layton nodded. "I understand, Brunar. As I have said, I
will do everything I can to help."

*Good! Be prepared to come with me in the morning
three days from now. I will come for you then, and your
training, and that of the others, will commence. Until then, fare
thee well, Layton.* Brunar turned and took a few steps in the
direction he had come.

Layton watched him go, and suddenly his eyes fell on the
opal jewel that blazed in the pommel of the *Jidaan* that Brunar
carried.

"Brunar, wait! Which Gift does the Jidaan of Dani bring?
I've forgotten that part!"

Just as the purple fire flashed, and the Mage disappeared
within its silent caress, Layton heard the reply: *It brings the Gift
of Gates, Weaponsmaster.*

Then the young man was alone under the stars once
more. For a moment, he stared at the spot where Brunar had
stood. The sounds from the canyon below drifted up to him, the
clip-clopping of hooves letting him know that the Prince and
soldiers were on the move up the mountain once again. The
young warrior began his descent, dodging left and right as he
navigated the sloping, rocky terrain.

He wondered briefly what the other Guardians would be like. Becoming a member of such a legendary group of heroes was an honor unparalleled, and he looked forward to meeting the others. In any case, the Evil One must be stopped, and the sooner the better. Layton relished the chance to help rid the world of such a vile being. A joyful smile flashed to his face, unseen in the darkness, as he clambered down towards the soldiers below.

Chapter 11

The dawn was yet hours away, and a chill wind blew across the desolate earth, stirring huge eddies of dust as it howled and moaned on its way to the horizon. The reddish dirt of the rocky ground swirled skyward, filling the air with a ruddy haze. The light of the moon was as blood on the vast waste below, flowing over the rocks and hardpacked earth of the Gorran Plain, illuminating everything with its dull scarlet glow.

For leagues in all directions, the desert sprawled like a dead thing. Nothing grew here, save the hardest of creatures, those who could endure the chilly nights and the scorching days. It was only fitting that Mordak had chosen this barren, lonely land for his retreat. Eons ago, he had created a stronghold here, a refuge, sealed against the passage of time and against the prying eyes of men. Only fools would come this far into the Gorran, and they would find only death awaiting them.

A hideous shriek rent the night as Mordak's mutated form neared his ancient holt. His molten eyes burned more dimly now, the flight of the last full day and night having drained much of his stolen vitality, but still they surveyed the bleak wasteland beneath him with a potent scarlet glare. Those flaring eyes scanned the Gorran Plain, searching for the home they had last seen so long ago, when his power had nearly reigned supreme on this world.

Another raucous scream tore from his fanged snout as he made out a looming shape on the horizon, a massive pile of rock that stood as a silent sentinel, watching the windblown plains around it. The winged monstrosity caught the cold currents of the blowing wind and picked up speed as it approached the hulking formation, as if the very wind were aiding its wicked flight.

Down through the reddish, shifting haze the monster sped. Its clawed feet reached for the earth near the base of the huge rock that was shaped like a giant clenched fist raised against the bloody moon. It touched down with a screech, its curved claws digging into the dense, stonelike earth beneath. Quickly folding its wings against the blowing gale, the creature shuffled into a hollow at the base of the great stone, a shelter from the wind.

The eyes of the beast smoldered fiery red as its bones began to pop and crack. Skin crawled and shifted, shrinking in upon itself as the change began, the repulsive sounds carried away on the wind. The beast's wings were swallowed up into its back, and the curved, wicked talons pulled back into hands and feet that rapidly took on a more human appearance. The crimson eyes of the creature squeezed shut as it knelt, hunched over, its quivering form wracked with the blinding agony of the change.

The howling wind took no notice of the naked shape that knelt before the massive fist of stone. It reached around the sheltering walls of the hollow in which the figure waited, grinding the reddish sand and grit into his pale skin, whipping his curly mane of silver hair about his leonine head. Eventually, the popping noises ceased, and the huddled form stopped shaking, the searing pain of his metamorphosis ended at last.

The man that finally stood was far different from the little merchant whose body he had appropriated earlier. This impressive figure was well over six feet in height, and his leanly muscled frame was held with dignity and grace. Even unclothed as he was, he carried himself as if he were regally dressed, in a way befitting his stature. His face was strong and noble, a deep cleft residing proudly in his jutting chin. His aquiline nose would have given him rather a handsome, striking countenance, had the scorching scarlet of his eyes not revealed the twisted madness and evil power that resided within him.

This was the form that Mordak employed most often, as it was his original human form, and easiest to maintain. He looked down at his hands, strong hands that had been used in countless incantations, sacrifices, and forbidden rituals. Many had died under the power of those graceful fingers, and he flexed them with glee. The sensations of wearing the semblance of his own body again after what seemed an eternity in that cursed prison stone were welcome. He made two powerful fists and smiled at the physical strength that this form afforded him.

Still, his internal powers were weak after the flight, and he set about the business of entering his ancient retreat. He stepped further into the hollow, and found a narrow crevice leading deeper into the bowels of the rock. He followed the constricting passage as it wound through the stone, gradually sloping downward, leaving the ruddy moonlight behind. The howl of the wind lessened as he drew farther away from the opening, and the heavy silence of ages fell upon him. He continued downward, the crimson glow of his pupilless eyes showing him the way.

Minutes later, the narrow, winding passage leveled out and opened into a tall cavern. The bloody glow of Mordak's eyes revealed a massive pair of doors that were embedded deep into one wall of the chamber. The doors were fully fifteen feet tall and five across, forming a huge, imposing portal in the stone. As the sorcerer stepped into the cavity, he noticed a moldering skull decaying atop a dusty pile of nearly disintegrated bones. Ancient chain mail, and other traces of rotted clothing remained, mixed in among the few recognizable human remnants on the floor.

Mordak's majestic face twisted into a leer as he stepped forward to lay his right hand on the joining of the two doors. It was icy to his touch, and he knew that the wards he had placed here eons ago were still in effect, keeping the unwary from trespassing within. Such an unwary traveler lay at his feet, and a low grating laugh rasped from Mordak's throat as he thought of how surprised this unknown intruder must have been when his body had begun to fall apart as he touched the door. Mordak hoped that he had suffered unbearably before dying.

A word in a foul language that was ancient thousands of years ago echoed in the room, and the doors shuddered at Mordak's command. They strained against the stiffness of over two thousand years, and finally broke the seal of time, creaking open before the grinning sorcerer. The portal beyond was black as pitch, and into this yawning space walked the naked madman, his evil laughter trailing behind him.

Chapter 12

Gart gasped as he sat bolt upright in bed. Sweat was running down his face and chest in rivers, and he struggled to control his breathing. He quickly glanced down at his wife, Gennie, only to see that she still slept peacefully next to him. His ragged respiration slowed enough for him to listen for the baby in the cradle across the room, but she had remained asleep also, and with any luck would stay that way for a few more hours.

The young man peeled back the coverlet and silently slid out of bed, careful not to disturb his Gennie. He padded across the room to check on Rheann, and though the dream had disturbed him, her beautiful face still brought a smile to his scarred face. He marveled that any living thing could be so wonderful. Her soft breathing sounded like music to him, and for a few moments, he lost himself in his love for his two-year-old baby daughter.

Suddenly, remnants of the dream that had woke him pushed their way to the forefront of his mind, shutting out his daughter for a moment. Gart's face clouded immediately, and he turned from the crib. The dreams had come every night since he had been met on the road by that Brunar. And every night, they had become more vivid, more real than any dreams that he had ever experienced in his life. At times, they seemed like actual memories rather than the random ravings of a sleeping mind, and that is what bothered him the most.

He slipped on his shirt, trousers, and boots, and tiptoed to the door of their small cottage. He turned back to see that no one had wakened while he had dressed, then he eased the stout wooden door open and slipped noiselessly outside. The door swung shut, and Gart relaxed as the cool night air caressed his body, seemingly turning his sweat to ice for a moment as the breeze fanned his garments.

He started along the path that led away from their small dwelling, walking towards Overlook Hill. It was the highest spot in the village of Tiller's Grove and afforded the best available view of the surrounding countryside. Rich farmland abounded for miles until it was swallowed up by the desolate reddish waste of the Gorran Plains. He had walked this path many times before, but this was the first time since his arrival from New Caldea three days ago.

The moon shone down over the gently rolling hills and their swaying grasses, illuminating the scattered trees that resided here and there, lighting Gart's way as he strode towards his old roost. Gart drank in the crisp predawn air as if it were a potion that could dispel the specters of his dreams. His scarred face twisted into a vicious frown as he reflected on his night visions as he approached the Hill.

As a boy, Gart had come here whenever he needed to be alone. The other children of the village had never been very tactful after his scarring, and their constant teasing had instilled in him a need for solitude at a very early age. Many times, his mother had come to take him home long after dark.

As he crested the hill, the dream caught his attention again. He sat down as he had as a child, legs folded beneath him. His icy blue eyes were focused eastward in the general direction of the Plains as he tried to make sense of things.

He had been a woman in the dreams, of that much he was certain. He had never seen himself, but the voice he heard issuing from his own mouth had been distinctly feminine. Whenever he looked down at the slender hands that he seemed to be using, he had seen that they carried the weapon the Mage had insisted was meant for him. In the dream he could feel the comforting weight of the spear as if it were real. He could see every detail of its razor edge; it was nearly as long as some short swords he had seen. The emerald gem embedded within its pommel had winked up at him, constantly glimmering and shining from its metal resting place, and the smooth, dark wood of the haft was solid under his grip. He had felt that the weapon was a part of him, an extension of his body and his mind.

In this latest dream, he had been fighting several creatures. A shiver went up Gart's spine as he recalled the way the things had shambled towards him from the darkened, mist-covered forest that his dream-self had been traveling through. They had seemed to be men, but men who had been turned into mindless puppets, their flesh rotting from their bones even as they stumbled towards him. Behind their dead eyes, he could see something, a distant glimmer of crimson that seemed to be the source of their bloodlust.

He had seen his weapon burst into radiant emerald fire as he began hacking his way through the creatures. As the things had died, he heard his dream-self sobbing, crying as her blade sundered the reaching arms of the monsters from their bodies. The anguish that stabbed through the woman's heart touched Gart also, though it did not diminish the woman's fighting skill. Gart caught glimpses of long black hair as his dream-self twisted and fought, raven-like tresses that swirled about her face as she battled.

As more of the things ambled out of the forest, she quickly became surrounded. Still the spear whipped out, lopping off heads and arms, cleaving the rotten legs of the creatures like twigs, but they came on, heedless of the damage done by the whirling blade.

There were too many of them. The fight became desperate, and Gart felt his heart hammering in his breast as his dream-self unleashed a burst of blinding speed, momentarily clearing a space around herself with the razor-edged spear. For an instant, she was free of the dead, grasping hands that sought her.

She thrust her weapon above her head, and Gart heard her voice ring out as she invoked the power of her Jidaan. He felt the familiar force swelling within himself, but, as in the previous dreams, it had been different from his own. The sheer might of this woman dwarfed his own, and yet it was focused, controlled into a tight, intense current of energy within her. It sought out the upheld weapon and found it. Emerald light exploded from the Jidaan's pommelgem as her power coursed into it.

Gart had felt the intense current flowing through the Jidaan, building, growing within the verdant heart of the blazing emerald gem. It seemed to gather there for an instant longer, and then it had shot through the handle of the weapon to emerge from the blade in a brilliant display of energy that stirred a leafy whirlwind around his dream-self. Gart had watched the flare light up the night sky and had not been immune to the woman's exultation, even as the dead things renewed their relentless attack and closed in for their final deadly embrace.

The surge of power ceased, and for a moment the only sound was that of the wooden, dragging steps of the monsters. Then the combatants had been rocked as a deafening crash of thunder had threatened to split the world apart. In that instant, great, jagged bursts of lightning had speared down into the midst of the milling creatures, and the night sky had flared brighter than day. When the destruction had ceased, the creatures had all been destroyed by the blazing bolts from the sky, their bodies charred beyond recognition where they had not been blown completely apart. The thunder had died and echoes had rolled out over the benighted land.

The glowing of the pommelgem diminished immediately as its power was spent, and his feminine dream-self had lowered the weapon to her side. Gart had noticed that the surge of magick brought with it a wonderfully rich, loamy smell, reminiscent of growing things, that subsided when the Jidaan was quiescent. All was silent save the gentle breeze that rustled the leaves in the trees, and the distant rumblings of remembered thunder. Gart had heard her breathing heavily in the stillness, and once again felt her anguish as she looked on the dead. These had been men once, and now they were so much less than that.

As she had surveyed the carnage around her, tears drying on her cheeks, the hairs on the back of her neck had suddenly stood, and a chill had shot down her spine like the kiss of an icy knife. She had sensed something . . . a presence. A misty nothingness that could not be seen, but had substance nonetheless, an unseen wraith. Her eyes had widened as she began to perceive it more clearly. Frightened, she had peered into the night in an attempt to find this thing, pulling her weapon to a ready position. Then, it had touched her mind, and Gart heard her gasp in fear and recognition as the entity made itself known, whispering vile threats and evil promises. Its icy touch had tried to enslave her, capture her, and she had fought back with all of her might, the internal battle wringing a tortured cry from her lips. As she had struggled to repulse the foul force that gripped her, Gart had caught a glimpse of evil, and he had been afraid. He had heard a name slip between the woman's clenched teeth. Mordak.

Gart had awoken then, panicked and sweating. Now he sat peering out at the coming sunrise. Since the first dream three nights ago, he had become well acquainted with the female that wielded the spear with such proficiency, and he had come to recognize a few of the powers that the weapon held. The dream that had awoken him this night had been the most frightening yet, and the evil presence that battled with his dream-self had seemed to follow him into waking. He imagined that he could still feel the icy touch of its clutches on his will and mind, no matter that it was all an insane illusion brought about by that Mage.

Now, as he sat under the dying stars, Gart turned his mind back to Brunar. *That Mage has done this,* he thought, his luminous blue eyes boring into the east. *He did something to me to convince me to follow him.*

Rage began to build in the young man as he thought of Brunar's outstretched fingers flashing violet, of the blow that he had somehow felt inside his skull. *He did something to my mind, and now invades my dreams with fantasies and visions. He is trying to trick me. If I ever see him again, I will kill him for this intrusion.*

Gart felt his power swell within him, so different from the focused potence of his female dream-self, and yet he knew it was the same. He crushed it beneath the formidable strength of his will, bending his anger to the task of restraining the roiling energy within him, rather than fueling it.

When he had himself under control once more, his thoughts turned back to his family, still sleeping back at their cottage. He would have to go back soon, or Gennie would awaken and be worried that he had gone.

Gart spent a few more minutes gazing out at the eastern horizon until the first hint of dawn began to creep into the sky, slowly dispelling the darkness as the morning gently crested the distant flatlands. He watched until the stars disappeared and the faraway, reddish clouds over the Gorran Plains glowed pink with the waking light of the sun. He then stood and strode resolutely back down the path to rejoin his wife and child.

"One day, Mage," Gart muttered just under his breath. "There will be a reckoning, and you will pay."

Chapter 13

Mordak laughed as he dragged the screaming young woman to the black altar that lay deep within the huge caverns of his subterranean lair. The strength in his great hands held her bleeding wrists in a grip of iron, and her frantic struggles aided her not. He slammed her back up against the cold, unyielding stone, and the wind came out of her lungs in a rush, momentarily silencing her.

It had been easy for him to swoop down and snatch this girl from her place at the lake as she did her washing. The shape of the winged horror had been most useful in finding a suitable subject for the necessary ritual, and the memory of her screams as she had looked up and seen his curved, clutching talons reaching for her pleased him immensely.

Now, the moon was near its zenith, and the time was almost upon them for the Ritual to take place. A vile grin split Mordak's evil face, and his scarlet eyes seemed to burn more brightly.

The girl was young, only sixteen or so, and her hair had been pale blonde before her abduction. Now it was matted with drying blood, evidence of the tortures she had endured after the flying creature had brought her here, deep within the massive fist of stone. Her beautiful face was now strained with horror, and her body was bloody and bruised from Mordak's vile pleasures. Her blue eyes were wide as she gasped for breath, searching for an escape, trying not to look at the foul man before her. Her gaze flicked towards him involuntarily, and she saw the burning eyes of a demon glaring only inches from her own. In seeing those eyes and the wicked grin, Pattye knew that her time on this world was rapidly coming to a close, and she wished that the end would be quick. Somehow, she didn't think Mordak would grant that luxury.

As she regained her breath, Mordak suddenly released her wrists and turned from her, leaving her standing unshackled next to the ancient altar. He strode quickly towards a cluttered table that crouched against one wall, his blood-spattered black robe gently brushing the stone floor as he moved.

As he reached for a small wooden chest, its worn surface carved in alien runes that seemed to writhe within the wood, Pattye gathered her strength and rushed on wobbly legs towards the passageway that led to the upper door. For a moment, she thought she might just make it.

"Stop." Mordak's rich voice reverberated in the vast chamber. Pattye jerked to a stop as if she had reached the end of a tether. A moan escaped her as she tried in vain to move her arms and legs. They no longer obeyed her wishes, and tears slid down her bloodstained cheeks as her final hope of escape was denied her.

"Return." Mordak had not yet turned to face her, yet his command pierced deeply into her exhausted body. She felt her legs shuffle beneath her until she was facing the altar once again. Pattye then walked slowly back to her previous position and stood next to the great black stone that dominated the chamber. Her traitorous body awaited the sorcerer's next command, and all she could do was cry.

At the table, Mordak ran his hands over the smooth black surface of the box. It was over a foot long, half that wide, and half a foot deep. It was bound in burnished gold, and carried about it the weight of ages. The runes that were carved in the ebony wood were those of an ancient language that Mordak and few others could still translate after so many millennia. He ran his strong fingers over the symbols from left to right and whispered the foul words that they represented. Each rune glowed briefly as he passed his fingers over it, and when he had touched them all, he removed his hands from the box.

It opened without a sound, revealing the slender dagger held captive within. Its blade was needle sharp, and curved slightly like the undulations of a snake in motion. The handle was curiously shaped, rounded with finger impressions facing towards the blade rather than the straight cylindrical hilt possessed by most daggers.

Mordak removed the knife from its case and carried it in both hands to where the young woman stood, quivering in fright. He grinned to see that tears still coursed down her face, though she made no noise. Her terror had finally stolen her voice.

"Ascend the altar, and lie down." The sorcerer's voice carried a hint of dark laughter within its melodic command. Pattye walked around to the far side of the rectangular block and mounted its rough steps. The altar was as high as Mordak's waist, and she looked down at him as her bare, battered feet navigated the sloped surface of the block. From this vantage point, she could see that the altar was angled down from where her feet would be, and she also saw that the surface near the lower end of the stone was deeply stained. She tried not to think anymore as she turned and lay on the stone, shackled by the force of Mordak's sorcerous will. The rock of the altar was icy cold, and Pattye shivered as she squeezed her eyes shut.

Mordak positioned himself at the head of the altar, still holding the dagger in both hands in front of himself. He leaned over the face of the helpless young woman and raised his hands upward. The dagger rested on his outstretched palms, glinting in the flickering torchlight. He had performed this ritual many times, yet this time it would be different. There was no turning back once he had begun.

The sorcerer's scarlet eyes closed, and he began the incantation that would bring him before his Lord, the mighty Balroth. Words that had never been meant for human utterance grated from his throat, and a stillness fell over the room. The chanting continued, rising slowly in intensity and volume. Mordak shifted his hands and held the dagger in a two-handed grip, holding it as it had been made to be held, its waving, needle-like blade facing directly towards his own vile heart.

*"Agga t'hothnu Krual Balroth . . .*Hail, Mighty Balroth. I bring thee two gifts this day, that thou may one day take thy rightful place over all. Grant me audience, for thy servant is in need. As tribute, I give thee this life."

The dagger rose slightly and arced down into the sternum of the young woman. Her scream was loud and brief, for Mordak's aim was true and her life's blood spurted from a pierced heart. Twin channels had been carved into the altar's surface, and the blood flowed downwards along them until it poured into a collecting basin at the bottom of the squat, ebony pedestal.

Grinning fanatically through a face covered in the young woman's blood, Mordak completed the chant. "And with this life, as the second gift I would also give thee mine own!" He wrenched the dagger from the young woman and plunged it deep into his own breast, his cruel smile never wavering as the crossguard slammed against his sternum.

The slim blade burst his heart, completing the ritual. Suddenly, what remained of Mordak's soul was yanked from his body to hurtle forward at blinding speed. As his shade shot into a lightless, crushing abyss, he looked back to see his body frozen in time, both hands still clutching the strange dagger hilt that protruded from his chest. As the scene faded in the distance between worlds, Mordak noted that the flames in the wall torches flickered not, another sign that, for his body at least, time stood still.

The evil spirit of Mordak sped through the icy void, rushing through a dimension of total darkness and cold. The blackness pressed in at him, slowing his passage, but he slipped through the clinging dark, escaping its clutches. He would have laughed then, had he a voice in his astral state. This place held no terrors for him. He *knew* this world, just as he had known many others.

All around him were points of light, each a very different color and size. Some were quite far away, looking like multicolored stars in a moonless night, while others were much nearer and more distinct. Each of these was a doorway, a threshold that led to another dimension of time and place. No one had ever been to them all, for the number of different worlds that could be reached from this netherworld was said to be infinite. There were many ways to reach the abyss through which Mordak traveled, yet he had always needed a human sacrifice to enter, or else the particular doorway he searched for would be denied him.

Ahead, a pale greenish light filtered through the murk, acting as a beacon for the traveling shade. This was the portal Mordak sought. He willed himself towards the dull, grey-green glow, for he knew that his Master lay beyond it. As he moved, the pressure around him escalated, as if trying to crush his intruding spirit. As his shade neared the doorway to the demesne of Balroth, he started to feel the pain that moving through this world caused, and was taken aback. Never before had his powers sunk to this low level. Usually, the trip from world to world was easily made, but this time the evil sorcerer was not certain that he would survive the journey. But then, if he did not receive the aid he sought, he was dead anyway.

The greenish glow grew closer, and Mordak strained towards it, willing his spirit to move faster in an attempt to leave the dense blackness behind him. It seemed an eternity, yet at last the evil shade came upon the glow, a massive circular opening in the very fabric of the void. The doorway shimmered as though it were behind a waterfall, and the pale verdant light wavered as it reached out into the blackness, only to be swallowed up by the abyss.

Mordak's astral self streaked through the opening, and the crushing pressure of the traveling dimension vanished as if it had never been. He found himself looking at a vast, roiling ocean from above. The sky was dim and shifting, the same murky grey-green that had beckoned him in the abyss. The brackish waters below rolled ceaselessly, crashing in great waves on the rocky beach of an island that rested not far from his position. Mordak willed himself towards the center of the island, his anticipation growing as he neared his goal.

The craggy surface of the island was barren and lifeless, and a chill wind blew over the rocks, bringing a mournful moaning sound to the dank, salty air. Ahead, Mordak could see a single flattened space amidst the jagged stones and boulders. It was here that he would meet his Lord and Master, Balroth. The spirit drifted to the edge of the roughly circular area and held there for a moment. Mordak gathered his strength within himself. His god would either grant him powers enough to begin his quest for domination, or he would simply keep his soul forever as a plaything. In that case, his body would fall to the ground back in his holt, dead from the self-inflicted dagger wound. Dealing with a Daemon-God was chancy at best, and Mordak knew it.

When he felt himself ready, he passed through the unseen boundary that separated the circle from its surroundings and set a foot down on the black, sandy soil within. He concentrated on maintaining this illusion of a body, for any lapse might offend the vile Balroth, and the sorcerer's life would be forfeit. He could smell the foulness of the moist, salty air, and he listened to the sorrowful whine of the wind over the rocks. The sound brought a smile to his face. The ethereal form of Mordak knelt in the soil and waited for his deity to arrive.

The sorcerer had been here many times before, offering tribute to the powerful Daemon-God. However, he had never before come to this desolate place with a request such as the one he brought this time. He hoped that his centuries of worship and tribute would stand him in good stead, and that his Master was feeling generous.

Mordak. The voice was deep and beautiful, filled with hints of music and power. Mordak quickly cast his face downward, lest he offend Balroth by looking directly at him. *It seems that thou left me only yesterday. What can it be that brings thee back so soon to this place?*

The sorcerer detected a touch of annoyance in the voice that spoke from somewhere before him. Keeping his eyes downward, he answered strongly, "Mighty Balroth, in our trifling little world, time travels at a much more rapid pace than it does for one of your great eminence."

I suppose it does, doesn't it? Soft laughter echoed in the circle. *Speak, and ask of me what thou will. If I am of a mood today, I will grant thy request. If not, then thy soul shall dwell with me forever. The pretty one thou sent me was quite enjoyable, so I mayhap I will listen to thee.*

Mordak considered his reply for the briefest of moments, then requested that which he craved. "Master, I have awakened from a long sleep, and my strength grows dim. Grant me the tiniest sliver of thine own power, a hint of the vast might that flows through thee, and I will strive to open the gate to our world. I know that domination over it was denied you eons ago, but I may be able to create a pathway through which you could reach us and claim your destiny!" Mordak had no intention of loosing this Daemon on the world, but Balroth did not know that.

When no reply was immediately forthcoming, the dark mage became nervous. He eyed the ground uneasily as the mournful wind suddenly died, leaving an oppressive silence hanging over the clearing in the rocks. Mordak steeled himself for whatever might come. Death-or unimaginable power-lay only seconds away.

The melodic voice of Balroth broke the silence, an undercurrent of steel lacing the musical words.

Thine offer sounds promising. The kneeling sorcerer barely managed to stifle a grin.

Thy world has always been mine, though I have lacked the means to claim it. Mordak felt the awesome power of his god as an almost tangible force around him. He was staggered by the vast energy he felt surrounding his phantasmic form.

Couldst thou open such a gate, I would at last rule supreme on Talwynn, as I was meant to. Yes...that would please me. Thunder cracked mightily in the distance, heralding the return of the foul, gusting wind. The shrieking blast quickly rose to a gale, sending great clouds of dust swirling across the clearing. The lightning from the coming storm began to strike repeatedly, its whiplike reports resounding through the darkened sky.

So be it. Thy request is granted.

Mordak's evil heart leapt with joy. His illusory body almost quivered with excitement, yet the sorcerer managed to contain himself and maintain his subservient posture.

Stand, loyal Mordak. I offer thee a tiny hint of my own strength. Beware, lest it burn thee beyond recall. Mordak stood, keeping his eyes towards the blackened soil. *Look on me, servant, and know the true meaning of power!*

The sorcerer started in surprise. Never before had he been allowed to lay eyes on his wrathful god, and the opportunity was unexpected. Slowly, Mordak turned his crimson eyes upward, towards the source of the beautiful voice, and gazed full upon the face of Evil. He saw exactly what he had thought he would see, a vision taken directly from the ancient scrolls he had held in secrecy for ages.

Balroth appeared as a normal man, a man even smaller than most. He wore his golden hair in a long braid that hung over one slender shoulder. His clean-shaven face was that of a youth, certainly not more than twenty. He was garbed in a simple robe of black that mirrored Mordak's own, belted at the waist with a red cord.

However, even Mordak was not prepared for the sheer power, the fathomless evil that shimmered from his Lord's youthful form in palpable waves. The Daemon-God's eyes were inky pools of pure jet, and those eyes showed the hate, the lust, and the madness that swirled within the form of Balroth, the Destroyer.

Even considering his own madness, Mordak nearly had to turn away from his god, so overwhelmed was he by Balroth's irresistible might. Somehow, he kept his scarlet eyes on the figure as it raised one elegant hand and gestured for him to come closer. Before he could will his illusory self forward, he found himself drawn swiftly towards the mighty being, pulled by the Daemon's power.

One slim hand reached towards Mordak's furrowed brow, and the sorcerer saw his Master smirk. *Enjoy thy new potency, dark one. I shall look forward to our meeting upon Talwynn. But remember: thy pitiful soul now belongs to me. And thy destiny is forever decided.*

The hand touched Mordak's forehead and the sorcerer felt power surge through him, scorching his spirit, surpassing anything he had ever known. Even as he struggled to control this massive influx of magick, he knew that his quest could now come to pass. The Guardians would be destroyed, and the world would be his! A cry of triumph escaped him, and he saw the smirk of his Master's face break into a grin. *Oh yes, sorcerer, thou art mine. Go now, and bring me to thy world.*

The smiling, evil face of Balroth vanished instantly, and Mordak found himself back in the caverns of his underground holt once again. The dagger was still embedded in his sternum, blood spurting from the wound. He contemptuously withdrew the dagger from himself, then sealed the wound in his chest with a thought. The cut closed itself and left no trace of ever having existed. Mordak took the time to clean the magickal blade on the tattered raiment of the dead girl on the altar, then returned the ancient weapon to its resting place in the box.

Mordak then placed his fingers to his temples, and concentrated. He sent his astral Sight up and out of his home, out over the Gorran Plains and into the lands beyond, and smiled at the ease of this exercise. His powers had been magnified twenty-fold, and the Guardians were now out of their league.

"Oh, yes! Those spear-bearing buffoons are in for quite a surprise this time!" His laughter echoed in the cavernous chamber as his sorcerous vision showed him a small village to the west, a perfect place to test his new powers and gain soldiers for his army. And then there were the vicious Krell of the Gorran, ferocious and tribal humanoids with a taste for flesh. With such immense sorcerous might as this, he could easily sway them to war on the humans again. His scarlet eyes flared brightly now, burning in his skull like twin bloody suns as his murderous chuckles followed him out of the chamber. *Even a Daemon-God can be a fool!* Mordak thought.

But beyond the vast gulf of time and space, Balroth smiled as well.

Chapter 14

As the sun heaved itself slowly over the eastern mountains, all within the Keep was in readiness. After so many centuries, the Hall of Jidaana would be put to use once more. Brunar checked over the six cells that would house the new Guardians while they endured their training, making sure that the few supplies the new tenants would require were prepared and ready for their arrival.

Each cell was identical to the others in its arrangement. Each held a bed, a desk, a few shelves carved into the stone of the walls, and a private area for the students to attend to their bodily needs. The shelves held a variety of texts Brunar had selected for each Guardian. All the books were ancient and in perfect condition due to a simple preservative spell. The leather-bound tomes contained the knowledge of many renowned scholars and mages, as well as several epic works of fiction. Brunar was quite proud of the enormous library he kept within the Hall, feeling as he did that the training of a Guardian was not singularly physical, nor did the training rely solely on magick. Intelligence and knowledge were two of the most powerful weapons a person could ever have.

Brunar walked to the north wall near the entrance and strode into the easternmost of the four openings that resided there, heading for the supply rooms and kitchen. He wandered about for a time, noting that enough food had been stocked, and checking the general readiness of the place. He knew he had already checked everything when he brought supplies back from his recent foray into the nearby town of Tamaransett. His rechecking of the Keep's facilities was nothing more than the result of a bit of nerves. *Even Mages get nervous at times like this,* he thought to himself with a laugh.

Brunar paused in his route for a moment, then realized the time was upon him. The morning was just underway on this, the fourth day, and those who would join him were waiting in their prospective homes. All save Gart, Brunar amended.

Willing the massive eastern doors open, Brunar walked into the morning sunlight that washed over the pale stone of the courtyard. He stationed himself in the very center of the small plateau, and stood braced against the chilling wind that whistled briskly over the rocks. Reaching deep within himself, Brunar delved into the core of magick he had built since his awakening and probed the vast distances separating him from his new students, seeking the telltale signs of the magick they bore. Back in the Hall, all six of the Jidaan came to life, aiding him in his search. Once his power was augmented by the powerful, mystical weapons, he quickly located those he sought, and set about bringing them to the Keep.

A few words in an ancient tongue escaped Brunar's lips, and he reached out towards the courtyard with one elegant hand. Brunar could feel the Jidaans' answering pulses of energy from deep within the Keep. The force from the ancient weapons coursed into him, joining with his own and empowering him for the task at hand. The Mage affected a single deft motion, no more than a smooth downward shrug of his hand, and magick poured from his outstretched fingers, deep violet swirls of power snaking from him.

The eddies of violet coalesced into four vaguely rectangular shapes, evenly spaced in a semicircle around the Mage. Abruptly, the purple hue vanished from the rectangles, and in the place of the swirling clouds lay visions of four very distant places as their respective doorways had suddenly been opened. In those four newly opened rifts, Brunar saw each of the new Guardians in poses of waiting.

Layton was on Brunar's leftmost, seated upon a stone with weapons aplenty slung across his back and a large leather pouch across his knees. Though Brunar could not be certain because of the blowing winds that surrounded him, the young fighter appeared to be whistling to pass the time, apparently enjoying the morning sun in the mountains near River Pass. In the next doorway was Alyssa, standing in the garden where Brunar had last seen her. An even larger pack than Layton's was at her feet, and she appeared to be reassuring several of the priestesses of Rowann that stood nearby.

The next gate showed the front of the cabin in the wooded glen that Bjarke called home, but the burly man was nowhere in sight. As Brunar watched, the door of the cottage suddenly jerked open, and the giant fairly fell out of the opening, trying unsuccessfully to juggle a small knapsack, put on one large boot, and shut the door at the same time. He looked in a terrible rush, and managed to fall to the ground in a tumble. The Mage noted the grim look on his face. It seemed the visions Brunar had left Bjarke with had shown the big man more than enough to bring him to the mountain. The Mage nodded to himself and looked to the next portal.

Nessar and Kiran stood in that opening, talking to one another in the small room in back of the smithy's shop. They seemed to be deep in conversation. The packs on their backs and the extra weapons strapped in various places to Kiran's body conveyed their continued acceptance of their involvement in this crisis, and Brunar gave a small sigh of relief.

All seemed ready to begin their training, and none had apparently had second thoughts. None, that is, save Gart. A frown creased Brunar's brow as that thought struck him again, but he let it pass.

"Chosen." His words cut through the wind of the mountains, and he knew they would be heard clearly by those on the other sides of the gates he had constructed. Each of the Guardians snapped to alertness and looked about them, searching for the unseen source of the voice. Bjarke finally managed to stand up and compose himself at the sound of Brunar's call.

"The time has arrived for you to accept your destiny. Come." Brunar opened the gates fully, and for the first time the others could see the gates from their side. Each of them saw a doorway hanging in thin air, through which a cold wind blew and the Mage stood only a few steps away.

Layton leaped through the opening as soon as it appeared, closely followed by Alyssa, the tiny woman having to drag her ponderous bundle through the portal. The two looked around themselves in wonder, and Alyssa looked back through the magickal rift. She found Sister Weena standing just at the threshold of the opening, tears running down her face.

Alyssa took a moment to reach out and touch Weena's face, telling her to be strong and run the hospital well. The dour priestess snuffled but smiled at last, stepping away from the gate to rejoin the other sisters who watched from a distance. Alyssa turned from her gate to see a female garbed for battle step through the portal farthest from her.

Kiran was followed closely by Nessar, who shivered in the sudden blasts of cold wind that buffeted the mountaintop. Kiran looked around in wide-eyed wonder at the rifts in space that hung near her, and the people that stood before them. A smallish fighter, a tiny woman with an enormous pack, and after a moment's pause, the biggest man Kiran had ever seen finally made up his mind to step through his gate.

"Cripes!" Kiran's voice was low. "He's huge!"

Alyssa's eyes also widened as the hulking man stepped through his portal, clutching his knapsack to his chest, a look of sad intensity etched on his open face. The giant stood quite still, but saw the small woman to his right and managed a small nod in her direction. She smiled and nodded back before turning to face the Mage standing in the center of the rough semicircle of gates.

Brunar stood unmoving in the blowing wind, and then, with a curt gesture, he closed the rifts, causing them to simply vanish. Now they were alone with the Mage on the mountain, and the only sound was that of the ever-present wind.

"It will be warmer inside. If you please?" Brunar indicated the huge doors at the end of the courtyard, and Layton led the group into the mountain. They walked quickly, single-file through the great doorway, Brunar at the last, and the massive doors swung silently shut behind them.

The group had settled their bundles against one wall of the echoing Hall of Jidaana, and now stood at the foot of the dais that led to the gleaming weapons that had Chosen them. As Brunar turned to address the group, some looked on with wonder in their faces, while other faces reflected caution. Bjarke looked especially grim, not at all his usual self. It seemed his countenance had not been made to hold such an intense expression, and it was beginning to pain him. Alyssa stood next to him and noted his nervousness. She could almost feel his tension as if it were her own. In response, she reached up as high as she could and patted him companionably on the back. He looked down at her, his face still pale, and mustered a smile for the tiny woman that sought to comfort him. He relaxed a bit, and returned his eyes to the Mage at the foot of the dais.

Brunar addressed the group. "Welcome, Guardians. It has been long since those like you last walked the floor of this hall. In case any of you have forgotten, let me refresh your memory." The Mage eyed each visage before him, slowly reacquainting himself with their features. The group watched as he began to pace before the raised platform. At last, he spoke.

"You all know why you are here. Mordak has broken free of the stone in which your forbears and I imprisoned him many years ago. I had thought him locked away forever, but somehow, he has escaped." His grey eyes moved from face to face. "Alone, I cannot hope to battle him. In our last encounter, his madness gave him strength to surpass my own, and his evil, his rage, made him unpredictable. The battle that ended his bid for domination cost many lives, including those of some of your predecessors."

Brunar caught the glances that darted between Nessar and Kiran, and noted that Alyssa seemed to hang on every word.

He remembered that the young healer had been in the company of the Priestesses of Rowann, and to them, Brunar the Mage was a figure of legend. He made a mental note to try harder to put her at ease. His glance flicked to Layton, and saw him watching and listening with a look of acute interest. Bjarke looked as if he were carved from stone.

"I hope we can stop Mordak before he regains his powers. He has remained entombed in that stone in a state of limbo for over a hundred generations, with nothing to sustain him save his own hatred of us, and of mankind."

"And now we come to you." Brunar swept his gaze over the group. "I explained to each of you that you are special . . . different. Each of you has untapped magick within you. It is an innate well of power that sets you apart from the rest of humanity. The weapons behind me were created to seek out those like you, so that you may wield them in defense of our world. They serve as a focus for your own magick, as well as having magick of their own."

Brunar turned and gestured towards the short spears. Their pommelgems twinkled brightly, as if in anticipation. "Each of these has Chosen one of you to bear it. You will find, I think, that the Gifts they bring will suit each of you. The Jidaan have always Chosen wisely."

"What are these gifts, exactly?" Kiran spoke at last, her voice echoing slightly in the cavernous chamber. She looked up at the Mage, her tough, brash exterior momentarily giving way to the eager, inquisitive girl that lay buried beneath.

"The Gift that you shall receive, Kiran, is the Gift of Warding." He pointed to the blue pommeled spear.

Kiran scowled as if disgusted. "Warding? What good is that in a fight? What about fire, or lightning, or something strong like that? If we are going to confront some powerful wizard, I, for one, would like something to help me take the fight to him!" She looked at the Mage, frowning.

The Mage's face froze, and a faint glint of purple flashed from the depths of his eyes and then vanished. Kiran saw the display, and held herself still.

"Kiran, only when you have fully mastered the power of your Jidaan will you truly know what a formidable force has been entrusted to you. I suggest you set about learning how to use it before you decide how feeble it is. For instance, let me ask you this. Have you ever used a shield in combat?" Brunar waited expectantly for her reply.

Kiran cocked her head to one side and lifted an eyebrow. "Well, of course!"

A sly smile appeared on Brunar's lips. "Ever bash anyone in the face with it?"

Kiran opened her mouth to answer, froze, and then saw the Mage's point. She closed her mouth.

Brunar continued, addressing the whole group. "The method of crafting these weapons is long since lost to us, and the sheer amount of energy within each one is difficult to comprehend. Even so, the creators of the weapons realized that there would be a need for more than just Power, and so imbued the other weapons with more subtle, but no less powerful Gifts. Those which have Chosen you are: Stealth, Gates, Healing, and Warding." Brunar gestured to each weapon as he named them, leaving only one unmentioned.

Bjarke's rumbling voice echoed in the chamber. "And what of the emerald spear? What is its Gift?"

Silence descended on them for a moment as Brunar's gaze went to the emerald Jidaan.

"That is the Jidaan of Storms. It could be argued that it is the most dangerous, and most powerful magickal relic on Talwynn. However, the strength of any of the Jidaan's Gifts is limited by the strength of the user, by the limits of their endurance and skill. This is why I must train you all, and prepare your bodies for the trials ahead."

The Mage looked at each of his new pupils as he spoke, and tried to see into them. Do they understand the depth of their power? Do they even begin to know the terrible weight of the responsibility they share? If he had been alone, Brunar would have sighed heavily, but now was not the time for such weakness. He continued to speak.

"As I was saying before, these weapons serve as a focus for the magick that you each possess. They will help you become aware of your own power, and they will also help you learn to tap into it and use it. You must learn to use your talents properly, or else you will be nothing more than a soldier with a magickal spear, and without mastery of your own magick, you will be unable to control the vast might of the Jidaan. The most powerful Gifts of the spears will be lost to you."

Brunar turned and mounted the dais. "Now then, each of you step up here, and be Chosen." Brunar waited for his students to follow. "Bjarke, you are first."

Bjarke hesitated for a moment, then mounted the steps and stood next to the Mage, facing the Jidaan. The weapon's gem flashed, deep glints of scarlet playing within the pommel's ornate clutches. Bjarke took two steps towards the weapon and reached a massive hand towards the haft. All was still in the cavernous Hall, and the others were holding their breath as Bjarke's fingers closed over the smooth handle.

As his hand touched the weapon, the gem flashed brilliantly, its light surrounding him, caressing him. He gasped as he felt its power join with his own, a feeling of unstoppable strength and energy flowing through his entire being. It was like nothing he had ever felt before in his life.

"The Jidaan of Rhu welcomes you, Bjarke." Brunar spoke gladly from behind the big man, but Bjarke hardly heard. His mind was filled with dancing images, fleeting visions of a beautiful world that far surpassed the quaint valley in which he had lived. It was as if the weapon were saying 'This is what we fight for. This is as it should be. This is your destiny, Chosen.' Tears streamed down his face as scenes of agonizing beauty continued for a moment to flash before his mind's eye, and then ceased.

"The Jidaan of Rhu is no more. It is now the Jidaan of Bjarke." The big man heard the words of the Mage as if from a distance.

The glowing of his gem diminished to a gentle glimmer, and Bjarke came back to himself. His heart was pounding, and his breathing was labored, so intense had his vision been. He found that he was now holding the weapon in his right hand, and its weight was comforting. He also noticed a stirring deep within himself, in the very core of his body. Turning, Bjarke looked down at the Mage, unspoken questions in his huge eyes.

"The stirring you feel is your own magick, Bjarke. As I said, the Jidaan helps you find your power so that you can learn to use it." Brunar reached up to place a hand on the giant's shoulder.

"Welcome, Guardian." An uncertain smile appeared on Bjarke's open face at Brunar's words.

"Tell me Mage," Bjarke asked quietly. "The visions I just had. Were they real?"

"I know not." Brunar answered firmly. "I have never been a Chosen." Turning to address the group, he continued. "The Weya used exceedingly powerful magick to create the Jidaan. Some even say that they invested part of their souls into the weapons so that they might better understand us. I do know that whatever you experience during your Choosing may not mean a thing to anyone else. You must comprehend their meaning for yourselves, for no one else could fully understand that which is only yours. I also know that the Jidaan do not lie." Bjarke nodded and stepped down from the dais, a look of wonder still playing across his face.

Layton came up next, followed by Alyssa, Nessar, and then Kiran following warily at the last. Layton stepped up to the weapon he knew to be his own and grasped it firmly, eliciting from it a burst of opalfire similar to the ruby light that had enveloped Bjarke. The young man gasped as he was Chosen by the Jidaan of Dani, and he began to smile.

Alyssa watched him for a moment as his Choosing continued and Brunar voiced the passing of the weapon to a new wielder, and then looked to Bjarke. His face now held a much more jubilant expression, which seemed perfectly at home on his bearded face. The giant smiled a great smile at her and motioned her forward.

"Go on, little one! This is as it should be." His smile was infectious, and she stepped over to her own weapon, the diamond-pommeled Jidaan of Willen, and reached a slender hand up to clutch it and make it her own.

As the tiny healer was enveloped by the crystalline, sparkling light, Kiran and Nessar positioned themselves before their own weapons, the ebony-pommeled and sapphire-pommeled Jidaan. Kiran looked at Nessar with one eyebrow upraised.

"Well? What do you think about this?" Kiran quietly asked her lifelong friend. She saw him shrug his narrow shoulders at her with a half-smile on his worn face.

"Let's get on with it." He replied as he reached out to clutch his spear with slender fingers. The burst of inky blackness that shot from the pommel of his weapon was unsettling to Kiran. Where the other Jidaan had illuminated their Chosen, Nessar was apparently being smothered by the power of his own weapon, and now stood completely cloaked in the swirling black tendrils emanating from the Jidaan of Reynor.

Before Kiran could make a move towards him, Nessar's voice called to her from somewhere within the blackness. "I'm all right, Kiran." She detected a tremor in his voice she had never heard before. "Sweet Goddess above, I think I'm all right. It . . . it's warm in here." Nessar's voice faded into silence.

Uncertain now, she looked to the Mage. He gestured to the weapon on the wall in front of her. "Please, Kiran."

She looked back at the cloaked form of her best friend and made her decision. She reached out and grabbed her weapon from the wall. As soon as her hand made contact with the haft, the sapphirine blue light enveloped her, and the visions came. Resistance drained from her as her own Choosing commenced and the Jidaan of Durok welcomed her to the ranks of the Guardians.

Soon, they stood before Brunar. Each was hefting their new weapon, getting the feel of their Jidaan. Kiran had tears freely streaming from her eyes, a fact that bothered her to no end. Nessar had a touch of remembered youth in his step, and a gleam in his eyes that had long been absent. Layton looked much as he had before, save the new weapon he bore, and if it were at all possible, a slightly higher level of enthusiasm. Bjarke and Alyssa had begun speaking to each other quietly, since they seemed to be the only ones who had obviously never carried a weapon of any kind, and presently, Bjarke's booming laughter filled the hall for the first time. It would definitely not be the last.

Though they did not all know each other's names by heart, and knew not at all how to use their Gifts, all were filled with purpose. Their Jidaan had bonded with each of them, and showed them what they needed to see. Now they were as one, each warrior part of a team destined, hopefully, to save their world.

One Jidaan was left unclaimed on the wall. Layton looked at it as Brunar led them down the stairs and towards the center of the chamber. Its emerald gem gently glistened, as if it slumbered patiently while awaiting its owner. He wondered what kind of person would refuse the call of Brunar. For a moment, he felt sad for him or her, then dropped the matter from his mind.

Chapter 15

Toying with his bow, Trevan squinted out over the rolling hills and into the arid, scarlet wastes beyond. The sun had not been climbing the sky for long, yet already he could see the waves of heat beginning to rise from the farthest reaches of the Gorran Plain before him. The stout little man spat to one side and then resumed his watch, glad to be this close to the river rather than out there in the desolate hardpan.

Some twenty yards behind him, Lucanos was rounding up the other four members of their party and packing the horses for the day's travel. With luck, they would reach the next small town by sundown tomorrow. Once there, they could rest and replenish their supplies. Lucanos bellowed for the others to hustle up and get moving. After the long days of traveling northward from the edges of the southern jungle, he was looking forward to their next stop with eagerness.

"Get a move on, you dogs!" Lucanos laughed as he playfully launched a kick at one slow moving comrade. "I'd see us in that village upriver by tomorrow's darkfall, but we'll never make it if we keep lollygagging around here!" His men laughed as the recipient of the kick made a raucous hooting noise and began rushing comically about, hurriedly packing his meager supplies. "One of these days we might even make it to Bos Aldas!" The mention of their goal, the royal city far to the North, brought a light chorus of cheers from the men.

Lucanos was the leader of this small band of mercenaries, mostly by default. The men did not mind doing what he said because he was a likable fellow, and because he had been the best fighter on this side of Triagga's Teeth. He was not an overly large man, but his strength was evident in his panther-like movements, and his dexterity was amazing. These traits, coupled with his extensive mercenary experience, had kept him alive quite handily thus far.

Seeing that the breaking of camp was going smoothly, Lucanos stepped over to the river to slake his thirst and fill his waterskin before beginning the day's journey. He produced a thong from his belt pouch and tied his thick, black mane into a ponytail that hung well down his back. As he stepped one boot into the clear water of the river and plunged his waterskin beneath its surface, he saw his reflection mirrored in the settling water. Looking back at him were a pair of large green eyes, with more than a few laughlines at the corners. Those lines softened an otherwise stern face, but his ready grin and jaunty mustache softened it even more. His striking visage had led many a tavern wench astray, as had his laugh and his playful manner. For a mercenary, Lucanos was a surprisingly good-natured man. He raised the waterskin to his lips for a time, refilled it, then capped it as he made his way back to his horse.

"Hey, Lucanos!" Trevan hollered from his post. "Maybe this time you'll leave a few women for the rest of us, eh?" The group laughed merrily in the morning sun.

"Trevan, I've told you before that you'd have much better luck if you'd try being nice to some of those women, rather than trying to impress them with your belching skills." Lucanos placed his waterskin on his horse as the group laughed again. He then checked his armor, a motley collection of chainmail, boiled leather, and even a few more exotic pieces of armor obtained from their last job in the small outpost nestled in Triagga's Teeth. "Anyway, pay attention over there. You're supposed to be on watch, remember?"

Trevan spat again, but smiled as he turned back to watch the Plains. "That Lucanos is a good man," he said quietly to no one in particular. "A bit uppity perhaps, but a good man to have around in a fight." He continued smiling until his scanning eyes saw something out in the desert waste that had not been there a short time before.

From the deepest part of the Gorran Plain, a man appeared. Trevan frowned. Men did not live in the Gorran, and those that traveled it in the daytime tended to die young. Nevertheless, a dark shape roughly the size of a man continued to glide across the reddish earth of the Plain about a mile away, and it was moving directly towards Trevan.

Trevan considered alerting the company, but it was only one man after all. If he could not handle one man with his trusty bow and his trustier belt axe, Trevan figured he was not fit to live anyway. He spat once more, then melted into the scraggly brush, intending to accost the man before he got too close to the others.

Back at the camp, all was nearly ready. Lucanos and the other four rogues had finished loading up, and in moments, all was in place for the journey. Lucanos surveyed the mounts and bellowed, "All right, you scoundrel Trevan, get your arse in here and let's mount up!" One of the mercenaries swung up onto his horse, and another prepared to do the same. The remaining two were still checking their tack.

"Trevan! I said get over here, you little squat!" The other men, who had been laughing and joking before, fell silent as

Trevan did not immediately return. Lucanos turned and looked in the direction of the rock the man had been using as a watch post. His green eyes scanned the sparse vegetation for signs of the stout fellow, yet Trevan was nowhere to be seen. A sense of wrongness touched Lucanos, and he reacted instantly.

"Ben, Jash, come with me. You two stay with the horses." Lucanos pulled his great two-handed sword from his back, and suddenly the others knew this might be serious. This man's intuition had saved them many times over in the jungle, and they were not about to doubt him now. With a rasp of sword on scabbard, the two he had indicated were armed and ready, and the lout atop his horse immediately unlimbered his crossbow. The last rushed to pull his own bow from his horse as Lucanos led his two companions in the direction that Trevan had been only minutes before. The raucous calling of the waterbirds and the gentle rushing of the river were the only sounds as the three warriors crept across the thin grass, searching for their comrade.

Lucanos swept his eyes carefully around him, his massive sword held ready for work. They came upon the rock where Trevan had last been sitting, and Lucanos saw the faint signs of the little man's recent passage. The big man knelt to read the tracks more closely, and noted that they led east, towards the Gorran Plains. A frown creased his face as he pondered that.

Turning to his two comrades, he spoke just above a whisper. "Trevan went that way," he pointed east. "He must have seen something. Spread out, and be careful."

Ben and Jash nodded, and silently resumed their search, weapons ready. Lucanos began to follow the light impressions of Trevan's booted feet in the grass, following the trail around the few bushes and stubby trees that littered the land near the river. He dodged quietly among the ruddy boulders that lay as if strewn about by some great giant of old.

Faint rustling noises from either side reached the mercenary's sharp ears, and he almost smiled at the slight ineptitude of his companions. He had managed to teach them quite a bit during their time together, yet the concept of stealth continued to elude the rowdy fellows. Lucanos returned intently to the task at hand, and continued to track his wayward companion.

Rounding a good-sized bush, Lucanos suddenly saw Trevan standing quietly, facing way from him, about twenty yards ahead. He stood at the rough division that separated the stony, reddish earth of the Plains from the more fertile grounds of the riverbed. Trevan held his powerful bow loosely in his left hand, but he made no move.

"Trevan!" Lucanos hissed between his teeth. "What is it? Did you see something?"

The sentry did not reply. He simply stood facing the plains.

Lowering his sword, Lucanos strode over to him and laid a hand on his shoulder. "What now, are you deaf? What's going on?"

Slowly, Trevan's face turned towards Lucanos, revealing eyes that had gone wide and staring. The pupils had shrunken to pinpricks around irises that had begun to take on a bloody tint. Trevan showed no signs of recognition as his red gaze fell on Lucanos, who sucked in his breath as he stumbled back from the man, yanking his hand from Trevan's shoulder as if it were on fire.

Lucanos knew that something had gone dreadfully wrong. The brief touch of Trevan's shoulder was cold as ice. He whipped his sword before him and prepared to cut down his former companion should the need arise.

Silently, Trevan turned with slow, shuffling steps to face Lucanos just as Ben and Jash rumbled into the clearing. They started to utter greetings, but their words froze on their lips as they saw this was not the Trevan they had known. They readied their swords and waited for a command from Lucanos.

Suddenly, Trevan's face began to writhe and contort. Soundless, he seemed to struggle mightily against something within himself. Finally, he spoke, the words grinding from his tortured throat.

"Kill . . . me."

Ben's face paled visibly as the words washed over them like a chill wind. Jash tightened his grip on his sword and waited. Lucanos hefted his blade, but moved no closer. "Have you lost your mind, man? What's happened? Tell me!"

Again the words grated haltingly from Trevan's throat. "Kill . . . me. He . . . comes!" Trevan began to tremble with the effort of speaking.

His face a mask of intensity, Lucanos yelled, "Who comes, Trevan? Answer me!"

Trevan took a shaky step forward, hunching over in apparent agony. "Please! K-kill me! He comes! Mordak!"

Neither Ben nor Jash recognized the name, but Lucanos went pale. Before he could move, Trevan convulsed. One final shudder passed through the little man, and Lucanos watched as blood welled up in Trevan's left eye to spill down his pain-stricken face in a crimson tear. The expression of agony left his face then, leaving it witless and slack. Trevan woodenly pulled his body erect, and somehow, Lucanos realized that what stood before them was no longer Trevan.

The thing dropped its bow to the ground and pulled the hand axe from its belt. Lucanos hesitated for only a moment, then sprang forward to impale the advancing figure with his great sword. The honed point of the blade slammed through the thing's stomach with ease and instantly jutted out of its back. Before Lucanos could free his weapon, the creature dealt him a smashing backhanded blow to the head, sending him reeling to the dust, leaving his sword lodged firmly in the body of the still-standing horror.

While Lucanos lay dazed, Ben and Jash quickly flanked the thing and began to strike frenzied blows to the creature's arms and legs. Ignoring the great cuts that began to appear on its limbs, as well as the sword still jutting from its middle, the creature twisted around to face Jash. Before the mercenary could react, the thing had sent his axe hurtling towards him with deadly accuracy. With a horrendous scream, Jash went down, trying in vain to pull the heavy axe from his chest. Ben stabbed and slashed, opening up even more wounds on the creature as it turned to face him. When Ben saw the malevolent grin that suddenly widened in Trevan's dead face, he wailed in despair, but did not slow his onslaught.

In an instant, the dead thing's hand shot out to grasp the startled man's neck. As the cold fingers began to crush the chainmail links deeply into the skin beneath, Ben struggled, still trying to slash the creature with his sword. As the creature's grip tightened, Ben's face began to turn red, and his frantic struggles lessened. Ben looked into the brutish face and saw the wide, bloody, staring eyes and the vicious grin. The world began to darken as the life was choked out of him.

Then the gripping hand was suddenly gone, and Ben collapsed, gasping, to the ground. When his vision cleared, he looked up to see Lucanos grappling with the shorter creature, and losing. Each held the other at the right wrist while straining for a better position. Inch by tortuous inch, Lucanos was forced down to one knee under the unrelenting pressure of the dead thing. As the creature bent towards the kneeling mercenary, Lucanos suddenly went down on his back and rolled, flipping the monster well over and away from him to land with a jarring thump several yards away, dislodging the great sword from its body. Lucanos was up in a flash, and now had time to unsheathe his poniard. The thing got up and returned to the attack once more.

"Enough of this!" A great, slashing bolt of scarlet magick slammed into Lucanos' right side, sending him hurtling into the panicked Ben. They collided and fell. Maniacal laughter pealed out, chilling the two downed men. Lucanos was first to his feet, and he yanked Ben up as well.

Standing before them was a tall, majestic looking man in a black robe bordered in crimson. His silver hair flew in the breeze, and his laughter betrayed his madness. The thing that had been Trevan ambled to his side, ignoring the gaping wounds that had been inflicted upon it.

Lucanos watched the newcomer's glowing scarlet eyes, and struggled to accept what he saw. He knew this man, though only from old tales that had scared him as a youth. He quickly whispered to Ben, urging him to run and find the others. Ben did not even take the time to nod, but turned and sprinted away from the ominous stranger as fast as he possibly could.

"Really? You think you can run from me?" The stranger pointed one finger at the fleeing figure. Lucanos watched in horror as a tongue of scarlet magick boiled from the man's extended hand, stretching past him towards the retreating Ben. Ben's scream a moment later was proof that the stranger's spell had been effective. The black-clad man beckoned, and the tendril of magick carried Ben's struggling form back to him. The sorcerer laughed again and held Ben in the air, clutched in a swirling miasma of energy. Ben screamed as the misty coils began to tighten.

"Truly, you did not think to escape me?" Bones began to pop, and Ben's screams reached a new, terror-stricken pitch.

"No!" Lucanos shouted at the regal madman before him. "Release him! Let him go, by Rowann, or I'll . . ."

"Or you'll what, master of mercenaries? Lop off my head? Hmmmmm?" The sorcerer's smug smile infuriated Lucanos, but as long as Ben was held captive, nothing could be done. "I hardly think that you are up to the task." A loud snap echoed in the still morning air and Ben's screams abruptly ceased as he lost consciousness. "My, he wasn't as tough as he looked. Oh well."

With the air of a petulant child that has lost interest in a broken toy, the sorcerer released the crippled, unmoving form of Ben, letting the man fall heavily to the ground. Lucanos rushed to his aid and crouched beside his friend, checking for signs of life. Upon examination, Ben was only unconscious, but he would never walk ably again.

The madman's voice interrupted Lucanos' observations. "I have need of soldiers, and though I've definitely seen better, I believe that your men will serve quite well."

"And what of me, Mordak?" Lucanos snarled the name, not taking his eyes from his fallen comrade.

A note of surprise crept into Mordak's voice. "Why sir, I am impressed. Most think me a legend long gone, and yet you recognized me! How marvelous!" Lucanos still did not look at the foul being, but at least he knew that his hunch had been correct. Trevan had uttered Mordak's name before he became that. . . thing. Now that he knew what he was dealing with, he settled on one final effort.

Mordak approached the crouching mercenary, the travesty of a man that had been Trevan following close behind. The sorcerer stopped a few feet away from the pair of mercenaries.

"What I have in store for you is a great honor indeed! You are to be my Champion. You will lead my armies across this land, and will be my right hand." He looked down at the big man, who still gazed at his injured companion. "Won't that be wonderful?"

Slowly, Lucanos began to stand.

"Actually, I'd rather die."

Moving with the feline grace and quickness that were his trademarks, Lucanos sprang at the sorcerer and plunged his silver boot dagger deep into the sorcerer's stomach. A look of astonishment crossed the features of the vile Mordak just before he bent in agony. Lucanos stepped back and kicked the bending sorcerer full in the face, sending him sprawling back to collapse in the dirt at Lucanos' feet.

As Mordak writhed in pain, trying to withdraw the dagger, Lucanos stepped over to him, careful to stay out of his reach.

"A Tballa shaman gave me that silver dagger. He said that it was ancient beyond all things and had the power to destroy evil." The big man watched as Mordak went limp and a trickle of blood emerged from his lips. The pale form of Trevan collapsed as well, apparently dead for good.

"Consider yourself destroyed, Evil One."

Lucanos watched the sorcerer for a few moments to be sure he was dead, then reached down to withdraw the ancient dagger. His fingers stopped a few inches from the smooth, carven bone handle of the silver-bladed knife, and then he thought better of removing it. It seemed to be doing its job well enough where it was, and removing it might be a bad idea.

Turning away from the body, he went back to Ben, who was starting to make groaning noises as he regained consciousness.

"Hey, Ben," Lucanos whispered as he gently slapped the reclining man's face. "We've got to get you out of here. It's safe now; the Evil One is dead!" Slowly, Ben's eyes opened, and Lucanos saw that they now were tinted deep scarlet as Trevan's had been. A wicked grin stretched across Ben's face as he grabbed Lucanos' throat with an icy grip, and a familiar voice spoke behind them.

"Really, Lucanos, you should know better than to believe anything some ignorant Tballa wizard might tell you!" Mordak's laugh sent a cold stab of fear into Lucanos as he struggled to be free of Ben's grip. Suddenly, a smashing blow struck the mercenary in the back of his head, causing black motes to dance before his eyes. He almost collapsed, but more cold hands grabbed him and hauled him to his feet. Lucanos groggily looked around at his captors to see that they were the two soldiers he had left with the horses. Their crimson eyes and cold bodies attested to the fact that they were under Mordak's control.

The two dragged Lucanos in front of the sorcerer, and forced him to his knees before the black-robed figure. Mordak toyed with the dagger that had been so recently embedded in his innards.

"Soon you will realize that my power is much greater than any magickal trinket that might exist on this world." Mordak held the dagger in his palm, and as Lucanos watched, it began to melt and drip as if it were made of nothing more than ice. The smug smile returned to the sorcerer's face. He looked down at the mercenary that now began to strain against the unyielding grip of his captors. Soon, the futile struggles ceased and Lucanos again raised his fierce green eyes to his tormentor, piercing him with their gaze.

"I'll do nothing for you, you bastard! I'm stronger than these louts! You can't take over my mind, and I'll kill myself at the first opportunity if I can't escape!" Proudly, Lucanos stared at the man who would subvert him, turn him into something less than a man.

"Well, we can't be having that, now can we?" Mordak smiled, showing white, even teeth. "No, I have something better in mind for you. My Champion must be ruthless beyond all else.

Stronger, more vicious than even you can possibly imagine. And deadly. Very, very deadly to those who would oppose me."

"Well it sounds like you'll need someone else for that job. I've been bested before, and I am certainly no Champion!" Lucanos began to pull away from the cold, grasping hands that held him fast.

"Oh, I know that already. In your present form you would be of little more use to me than these brutes." A gleeful chuckle escaped Mordak's curling lips. "However, after watching you work, I think you have quite a lot of potential. Yes indeed, I believe that you'll do quite nicely. I think you might just be strong enough to survive the bonding process!"

Lucanos stopped struggling as he tried to make sense of the Mordak's words. "What do you mean, bonding process?"

"I'm going to bond a daemon into you. If you survive, you will be my Champion, whether you like it or not!" Stepping back from the kneeling captive, Mordak spread his arms. Crimson energies began to boil around his outstretched hands and he began to speak in a foul, ancient language that jarred Lucanos' senses.

A tiny sphere of deepest scarlet appeared in the air between them, little more than an inch in diameter. Slowly, as Mordak chanted, it grew, swirling about itself, streaked here and there with darkest black.

Lucanos was awed by the power he felt gathering in the air around him. Thoughts of escape were forgotten as he felt the sheer strength of the magick that emanated from the sorcerer. He watched as the sphere grew larger, and larger still, until it was about three feet wide. It hung there in space, spinning, its scarlet and ebony energies playing about it and making the hairs stand on Lucanos' neck.

Mordak uttered a final harsh word and clapped his hands. The sphere seemed to bulge outward, and then collapse into itself, leaving a three foot hole in space. The two men that held Lucanos suddenly dragged him closer so that he could look into it. It appeared to be a window into nothingness, a doorway into some vast, fathomless abyss. A cold wind moaned from the aperture, drying the sweat on the mercenary's face.

"Look into the doorway, Lucanos, and see your fate!" Mordak laughed again, that gleeful, maddened laugh. Lucanos searched the blackness before him and saw nothing. But then...there! Deep in the darkness, something moved, as if a world away.

As Lucanos watched, something approached the doorway...something monstrous. Waves of palpable evil smashed into Lucanos, heralding the arrival of some vile being.

The last thing Lucanos saw before he was consumed by the ancient and evil presence from the doorway was Mordak's eyes, his blood red, smoldering eyes. Then the bonding, and the horror, began in earnest.

At the last, Lucanos screamed.

Chapter 16

Brunar led the little group throughout the Keep, showing the new warriors most of what the mountain palace had to offer. The massive library, with its countless shelves of books on many subjects made Alyssa gasp, and even Nessar's interest was pricked by some of the older volumes. Layton and Kiran had nearly burst into a jig when they saw the racks upon racks of swords, daggers, bows, and several more exotic weapons in the armory.

From here, Brunar issued each warrior a specially fitted leather scabbard, a sturdy device that managed to hold the Jidaan out of the way on the wearer's back. It still allowed for a quick unsheathing of the weapon, as Layton demonstrated only moments after donning the thing.

Later, as they passed through the kitchens and dining areas, Bjarke's stomach emitted a growl that brought laughter from all of them, and Brunar promised that lunch was on its way.

Much was left unseen, for the halls, chambers, and caverns that twisted throughout the mountains were extensive. It would have taken months to explore them fully, and there yet remained many deep, unknown chambers and passages that even Brunar had not traversed. Brunar had taken the time to draw up several maps of the Keep, and instructed his students to refer to them often. Eventually, the tour ended back in the Hall of Jidaana, and the group gathered around Brunar once again.

"I have shown you only a small part of what is yours, and you must understand that it all belongs to each of you. The weapons, the books, the gold in the treasury, all of it is at your disposal." At the mention of the treasury, Brunar noticed Nessar and Kiran suddenly poring over their maps.

"There is more gold in there than you two could possibly dream of getting through those doors, so stop worrying about it; you'll always have access to any finances you might need." Brunar cast a baleful eye on the thief and mercenary. Kiran put away her map and looked at the floor, a faint flush seeping into her cheeks while Nessar snorted in derision.

"Really, Mage! Accusing us of planning to steal that gold is hardly complimentary." Nessar actually did a good job of looking wounded, but Brunar laughed.

"Nessar, why would you wish to steal that which is already yours?" Brunar delighted in the surprise that stole over the eld thief's face at that comment.

Addressing the group again, Brunar continued, "Much of the wealth that fills our treasury has been there for so long that its origin is lost. The are chests of gold and jewels in there that lay unopened for centuries before I arrived here, and that was nearly two thousand years ago. More recently, we received a large donation from the grateful King Valerius when we first bested Mordak. We really had no need of it, but he was most insistent that we take it. Now we use it to fund the endeavors that require such monetary support. And as Guardians, it is all yours. The responsibility you carry is worth ten times what lies on the floor in that particular cave, so let us not concern ourselves with money from here on."

Alyssa could not keep still any longer. "What about the library, Brunar? I've never seen so many books in my life! Are there medical texts in there too?" The eagerness shone forth from her blue eyes, making Brunar smile again.

"Ah, I'm glad you asked! I've worked very hard to fill those shelves, traveling far and wide in search of books I found of value. Some of them are irreplaceable, whereas others are quite common. And yes, there are quite a few medical texts in there that would be of great interest to you." Brunar laid a hand on her shoulder. "I think I know where you will be spending what little spare time you have, neh?"

The group laughed again, and Brunar swept his gaze over the new warriors before him. "All right then. It is almost time for the midday meal, so get settled in your rooms and then meet me in the dining hall in half an hour. You will notice that each room has a gem affixed directly above the doorway-they match the gems in your Jidaan, and so show you which room is yours."

All eyes turned to the wall above the doorways and saw the gems that mirrored their own winking back at them. Kiran quickly found her room on the north wall nearest the main entrance.

"Do those gems have power too?" she asked of the Mage.

"Not at all, Kiran. They are just signposts. Hurry along then, for we have much to discuss."

With that, Brunar turned and strode in the direction of the kitchens, leaving the group to settle themselves in their new dwellings. Everyone walked quickly over to the wall where their belongings lay and gathered up their packs and bundles.

Alyssa was delighted to find that her own room was next to Bjarke's on the south wall. She had taken an immediate liking to the big fellow, and he to her. He carried her massive pack into her room for her before heading to his own cell.

"Good Gourds, little one, what have you got in here? This pack is nigh bigger than you are!" He carried the pack lightly on his right shoulder and clutched his sheathed weapon and his own leather knapsack in his left hand.

Motioning for him to put the pack down in the one empty corner of the small room, Alyssa laughed as she replied, "Those are medical supplies. I'm a healer, remember?" She pulled the stool away from the carven desk in the other corner and sat down. Surveying the room, she saw that there were bookshelves carved into the stone on the eastern wall. They stood empty at the moment, but she knew that she would quickly fill them with texts from the library.

Setting the pack gently down in the corner, Bjarke laughed, the sound buoyant and lively in the small room. "Actually, I did not remember because I did not know in the first place." He turned and bowed elaborately to the tiny woman.

"I am Bjarke, O mighty healer! And I am most pleased to meet such a beautiful and obviously talented woman."

Alyssa laughed and curtsied to the giant. "And I am Alyssa, O towering giant. Thank you, and I am pleased to meet you as well!"

Their laughter found Kiran and Nessar across the great hall, and Kiran nudged her companion in the ribs as they walked to their own rooms.

"What do you think of all this, Ness? I mean, are you feeling the same thing I am?" She looked up into his grey eyes and saw the shine there.

"I'm not sure. What I felt back there was . . . wonderful." His face still held a faint flush, as if the excitement of the Choosing had not yet ebbed completely from him. "I know that I'm probably kidding myself," his eyes dropped to the floor. "I'm too old to save the world. But after what I just experienced...I feel like I have to try." Kiran saw his eyes return to her own, and in them was a softness that she could not remember ever seeing there before.

"What did you see back there?" she asked, wondering what could have affected him so.

Nessar hesitated before answering. He looked away for a moment and drew a breath. "I'd rather not say just yet, Kiran. I want some time to dwell on what I saw before I decide what it means, but I'll tell you something," he turned back to her and gently cupped her chin in one strong, slender hand, "it was worth the trip." Nessar planted a quick, fatherly kiss on her forehead and then walked into his room and quietly closed the door, leaving Kiran aghast behind him.

She looked at the closed door for a moment, then turned to see Layton walk into the room farthest to her left, whistling a merry tune as he went. She remembered how fluidly he had whipped his opalfire weapon from its new sheath, as if he had made both weapon and sheath himself. A frown creased her face as she tried to remember where she had heard his name before. With a shrug she decided it would come to her at some point, and that she would have to show him a thing or two about weaponry. He had seemed pretty knowledgeable with the Jidaan, but she knew a thing or two about blades herself. She decided to have a talk with him later about his technique. After all, he *was* just a boy, and he might want some advice from a battle-seasoned mercenary.

Nodding to herself, she walked into her room and surveyed its contents: a desk and stool in one corner, a firm bed opposite, and a door that led to a privy in the back of the chamber. She had stayed in much worse in her day, and these accommodations were not half bad. She found a trunk under the bed and began to unload the contents of her backpack into it, wondering how long they would be residing within the mountain.

A short time later, the group assembled in the dining hall. The smells of roast beef, cooked vegetables, and hot bread wafted through the air, bringing another growl from Bjarke's apparently empty stomach. The large, circular table was filled with platters of food. Six of the seven places were set, and each of the new warriors wondered briefly about the single empty chair at the table, but did not dwell overlong on it. Before anyone could sit down, Brunar swept in through a side door and motioned for them to have a seat.

As they seated themselves, Brunar walked to the chair nearest him and stood behind it. "Guardians, again, thank you for answering the call. Soon, we will all embark on a great journey-a journey of discovery and danger." The Mage looked around at the new faces surrounding him. They looked back at him with a mixture of eagerness and not a little wariness. They knew of the dire threat that Mordak posed, but they seemed prepared to meet it.

"For now, let us eat and get to know one another." He smiled and sat down, grabbing a steaming hot roll from a nearby platter as he did so, and the meal commenced.

The new companions spoke to each other tentatively at first, but as time wore on, they came to be acquainted. Bjarke was easily the merriest of the group, laughing at everyone's jokes with equal enthusiasm. Nessar's dry wit livened up the conversation at times, and everyone eventually discovered that Layton could be rather easily embarrassed, though he took no offense. That he was seated between the two females of the group may have had more to do with that fact than anything that was said at the time. Brunar actually said very little, though he did much to pull the others into the conversation.

After more than an hour of talking and eating, Brunar stood and asked that everyone help to clear the table. "Each of us is as important as the others, so we all must help things move along around here," he quipped as he carried a few empty platters and dishes to the kitchens. The washing basin was large enough to accommodate all of the warriors at once, and the dishwashing took only minutes.

When the cleaning was finished, Brunar bade them return to their seats at the table, but asked them to sit a few feet away from the edge.

"Now then," his voice lost the bantering tone it had held during the meal and tightened into the voice of a leader, "I will show you what happened before, and we will discuss a few things."

Brunar stepped over to the wall and depressed a tiny stud thereon. The sound of a mechanism engaging clicked somewhere deep within the stone, and the table began to slowly sink into the floor, rotating slightly as it did so. When it reached the level of the seated warriors' knees, another loud click was heard, and the table's descent ceased.

Brunar uttered a quiet word and motioned towards the table with one hand. Gasps escaped a few of those seated around, for one side of the table disappeared to be replaced with what appeared to be an ocean viewed from far above. The transition continued down the table away from Brunar as a tiny coastline came into view, and the land scrolled down, mountains jutting from one side of the land to the other, no more than half a foot high. Rivers could be seen, as could lakes and forests. Soon the map covered the entire table, from the deep green jungles of Triagga to the south to the oceans on the north and the west, and the dark reddish wastes of the Gorran Plain to the east. A thick ribbon of blue cut the map nearly in twain as the river it represented flowed south from the Heartstrong Mountains to split into two branches near the middle of the continent: the

Corris River traveling west, and the River Triagga flowing southward into the jungle. Cities could be seen on the surface of the land below. The royal city of Bos Aldas on the sea just north of the Heartstrong Mountains, Rualtha on the western coast of the continent at the mouth of the Corris River, and other smaller communities were scattered here and there across the land.

Layton carefully put his hand into the reddish portion of the map nearest him. His fingers passed through the surface of the flat plains of Gorran, then stopped as they reached the unyielding wood underneath. He looked up to see the Mage return to his place near the table.

"What you see is a map of our land. One day's ride is about this much," Brunar held one thumb and forefinger about an inch apart, denoting the scale of the map.

Bjarke was the first of the Guardians to speak.

"How can this be? This looks real. I've seen the land from mountaintops before, and this," he gestured to the map, "is astounding!"

"One of my talents as a Mage, Bjarke, is the ability to create complex illusions. This map is one of the more useful ones." Brunar allowed each person to gaze at it for a moment longer so they could get their bearings. To this end, he uttered another word, gestured once more towards the map, and words in golden, flowing script appeared across the surface of the land, denoting the different regions, along with a rather ornate North arrow that resided in the ocean to the west.

"There now, I think that will help us a bit. Let us begin."

The warriors leaned in as close to the illusion as they dared, listening intently.

"You stand within the Hall of Jidaana, also known as Guardians Keep. It is here." A bright purple glint appeared high in the Heartstrong Mountains to the west, near the spot where the stone-grey peaks marched into the sea.

"But we were in Rualtha!" blurted Kiran. "That's way down here!" She pointed to the port city, far south of the purple spark.

"Indeed, Kiran. My abilities do not stop at illusions, you know. What brought you all here was a gate or a rift. It is a doorway of sorts, allowing people and objects to go from one place to another." Brunar watched Layton's eyes rise quickly from the map.

"A gate? Isn't that the power of my Jidaan, Brunar?" Layton's eyes were alight at the possibility that the power of the Mage was so great.

"Yes, Layton, it is. There are other ways to create such Gates, but they are far more complicated and difficult to construct. Your Jidaan empowered me to open multiple Gates at far greater distances than I could ever hope to reach on my own. I was further aided by the other Jidaan, each of which is strongly linked to one of you. They added their own power to my spell. Without their assistance, I couldn't have brought even one of you here so easily, much less all of you from such different and faraway places. Now that you have been Chosen, its power is yours alone to wield, and you must explore its many possibilities during your training." Brunar turned his attention back to the map.

"As I was saying, we are here. The Evil One known as Mordak was last imprisoned here just about two thousand years ago." The Mage indicated a point deep within the western reaches of the jungles of Triagga and a scarlet blot appeared in that location. "Four days past, I was wrenched out of sleep by a great magickal disturbance from this region. I sent my Sight down that way to investigate, and sure enough, I sensed the presence of Mordak. Before I could locate him exactly, he sensed my own presence and shielded his essence from me. I know not where he is now."

Pain was evident on the Mage's face, and Alyssa felt his regret. Before she could speak, Brunar continued.

"What I will show you now is a picture of the land as I knew it two thousand years ago, before Mordak began his first quest for power."

A gesture from the Mage caused the map to ripple and change. The crimson spot in Triagga disappeared, but the purple glint remained steady and strong. The river twisted for a time and settled into a slightly different path than its present route. The Twilight Forest that rested between Rualtha and the Hall of Jidaana swarmed over the land to the east, crossing the river and even reaching into the Gorran Plains before losing its grip on the reddish sands. The mountains remained unchanged, but the coastline was different, extending further into the ocean.

"And now you will see what happened after the war with Mordak and his minions was ended." Another gesture, and the land changed again. Great portions of the Twilight Forest lay blackened and charred, apparently from a sweeping fire. Smoke actually rose from different places on the map, only to disappear after reaching a height of a foot or so. They could see that the cities had been shattered, and even from their lofty vantage point they could see the wreckage and burnt debris floating in the harbors of the port cities of Rualtha and Bos Aldas, the former being worse off.

They were all shocked at the devastation they saw before them. Alyssa had shivered when she had seen the Twilight Forest in its former glory, but shudders of a different kind crawled up her spine as she surveyed the damage that Mordak and his fanatical hordes had caused.

Nessar broke the stunned silence. "How exactly did you stop Mordak last time?"

Brunar pointed to the spot on the map that had held the scarlet blot, and it resurfaced. "We found him there. He and part of his army had been headed down the coast from Rualtha to Ghal Spir. We attacked them before they could reach the southern port, and managed to decimate their ranks. Many broke and ran, and those we spared. Mordak retreated into the jungle, and we followed after. Here is where he turned to fight." The pained look had returned to Brunar's face.

"Here is where four of us died at his hands." Brunar let the fact sink in. Only three of those gathered around that table had ever risked their lives in combat. Two had never fought another living soul. The Mage wanted them to know what they faced.

"Who died?" Brunar turned to answer Alyssa's question and was pleased to note that her face was filled with determination rather than fear.

"Willen, Lillia, Reynor, and Rhu died in that jungle. They bore the Jidaan of Healing, Storms, Stealth, and Power. And they were all good friends. We would prevent such losses this time around. We would also like to spare our lands such devastation, not to mention the thousands of innocent people that live here." A wave of his hand transformed the map to the present day's topography.

"As I said, I know not where he his. He should still be weak from his imprisonment, yet he will forcibly absorb the life and energy from anyone he meets until he is comfortable again."

"Well then, how are we supposed to find him? If you can't find him with your magick, and we are not trained in the least just now, how are we supposed to fight someone we cannot even lay our hands on?" It was Layton who had spoken this time, and the others nodded in agreement.

Brunar looked around and spoke to them all. "There are other ways that I may use to find him. I have spent the last two millennia gathering information about the uses of this world's magick, and until I have exhausted them all, we have a great chance of finding him before he causes some catastrophe. If not, then we must wait until we receive news of his whereabouts."

"I take it that you have informants in the cities?" Nessar scratched his chin as he spoke.

"Yes, I have friends in many places throughout the land, and I have left them the means to contact us." Brunar uttered another word and chopped his hand at the table; the map vanished. The Mage rose and depressed the wall stud again, returning the table to its original position.

"Also, the Weya will be looking for him, and they will send word when they have learned something." Brunar awaited the usual expressions of disbelief, and he was not disappointed. All around the table, mouths gaped in astonishment. The Weya were reputed to be nothing more than fairy tales, elves from the storybooks. Only Bjarke did not look surprised.

"You mean to tell me that the Weya really do exist?" Kiran's jaw seemed to hang as she grappled with her surprise.

Brunar smiled. "Who do you think built this place and created the weapons that you all carry? The Weya have existed since the dawn of time, and they are intelligent, powerful creatures that care very much for this world. Thousands of years past, their strongest Lormages easily hollowed out this mountain, using powers that I can barely fathom, and they also instilled your weapons with magick."

Nessar spoke up. "Yes, but if they are so powerful, then why don't they take care of Mordak themselves? It seems to me that they wouldn't have any trouble with the likes of one rogue sorcerer."

Brunar paced a bit as he spoke. "I'm afraid the Lormages of the Weya are not what they once were. Eons ago, that handful of benign wizards commanded powers that bordered on being godlike, but even those precious few were not immortal. They each disappeared over the centuries, claimed by we know not what. None of those Masters remain. Our modern Weya are powerful indeed, but they still only command a fraction of their former power."

Kiran snorted. "Great. The most powerful mages on Talwynn have gone soft, leaving us to do the dirty work." Her tone dripped with sarcasm, yet Brunar remained unruffled.

Brunar raised an eyebrow at Kiran. "Soft they are not, Kiran, but yes, I'd give my left foot to have even one of the old Lormages to aid us...I could manage with a limp or a pegleg, I'm sure." Brunar addressed the group again. "However, that may be why they created this place and our weapons: they may have known that the need for such would outlast their ability to meet it, so they left what tools they could so that we might rise in defense of our world and be able to use their magick against such villains as Mordak."

Layton offered tentatively, "But the Weya Lormages of today will still help us, won't they, Brunar? We need all the help we can get." The others murmured their agreement.

"Yes, Layton. Although their most powerful magick is lost, they will use everything that is currently at their disposal to aid our cause. They are the best forest rangers that the land has ever seen, and their knowledge of life and nature is second to none. They still use many forms of magick, and they have certain other abilities that they will not hesitate to use to aid us. I'm sure that you will agree they are formidable allies. Weya messengers will arrive when they have news of Mordak's minions or the Vile One himself."

Bjarke's gravelly voice rumbled across the room. "I've met Weya before. A pair of them stopped at my lake to fill their waterskins a few years ago. They are wondrous creatures, and they move as gracefully as anything I have ever seen." Bjarke's eyes shone with happiness at the memory, and the others looked at him with gentle envy that he had actually seen legends given life. "They left me with the impression that they desired to be seen. If they had not, I surely would not have found them. They were very cordial and friendly, but they left rather quickly. They said they were on their way to a gathering or something."

Brunar nodded. "If it was in early spring, midsummer, early autumn, or midwinter, then they were on their way to their Assembly. That is when they celebrate the turning of the seasons, paying homage to the Goddess Rowann." Bjarke nodded in assent, and replied that it was, indeed, midsummer when he had seen them. Brunar continued. "In any event, they will send word when they become aware of anything that might have to do with Mordak."

"What about the King? Has he been warned?" Layton sat back in his chair as he considered the situation.

Brunar nodded as he answered. "Yes, Layton. I spoke to him two days past." A wry grin surfaced on the Mage's face. "At first, he was hesitant to take me very seriously. After a time, however, I managed to persuade him that the threat was very real." No Guardian doubted for a moment that Brunar had convinced the King that Mordak was a force to be reckoned with, and not just a hearthtale.

Brunar continued. "He is presently mustering his army, quietly, so as to avoid alarming the populace. Until Mordak strikes, we cannot be certain where he is, so sending the masses into panic would only aid the Evil One's plans, whatever they may be. The King will have sent messengers to the other large cities to warn them as well."

"So what do we do in the meantime?" Bjarke rose from his chair, towering over the Mage.

A gleam appeared in Brunar's eyes as he smiled again.

"You will learn the ways of the magick you possess, and learn the power of the Jidaan. You all must become proficient in the use of both if you hope to survive. First, you will undergo extensive physical conditioning. You must make your body as strong as possible so that you may make the best use of your power, and the physical training will also aid you in combat. You will learn our way of fighting in addition to those to which you may already be accustomed." Brunar inclined his head toward the two fighters in the group.

"Using your magick must become an automatic reaction, something you do without thought. It will take some time, but this is most important. Lastly, you will learn to use the Gifts of your Jidaan. I assure you that it will be most interesting."

Brunar rubbed his hands together and said briskly, "Your training will commence this very day, so meet me in the central hall just outside your rooms in one hour. In the meantime, feel free to do as you please. Alyssa, the library is that way, and for those of you who love sharpened objects, the armory is in that direction. Be careful not to stray from the mapped areas. There are places deep within the mountain that even I have never seen, and I don't want to have to waste time finding you."

Predictably, Alyssa trotted off towards the library, and the two mercenaries wandered off to find the armory. Bjarke pulled his map from his pouch and carefully unfolded it. He perused it for a moment, then nodded to himself before setting off towards some private destination. Nessar alone remained in the dining room with Brunar.

"I'd like to ask you something, if I may." Nessar strode to where Brunar was standing. The Mage gestured for the thief to walk with him, and the pair headed out towards the main hall and Brunar's chambers.

"Absolutely, Nessar. What would you like to know?"

"Well, I've noticed, as I am sure the others have, that there is one weapon remaining on that wall, and that a cell and a chair have remained empty. Where is the last Guardian?" He watched Brunar's face for a sign but got none.

"A young man named Gart is the remaining Chosen. He has not yet decided to join us." With a wave of his hand, Brunar created a floating image of Gart's face for the old thief.

Nessar examined the young man's stern, scarred features and nodded. "I see. What power does his weapon bring?"

"Gart is to be given the Gift of Storms. It is a powerful Gift, and it grieves me terribly that he is not here to accept it." A wave of Brunar's hand dismissed the illusion.

"Well, what if he doesn't come? I mean, will we just go on without him?" Nessar sounded like a man exploring his options.

"Yes, that is what we will do if we must. No one else may use his Jidaan but he. It has Chosen him, and will not choose another while he lives." The pair stepped from the corridor into the spacious Hall of Jidaana.

"Why is he not with us? I mean, I'm an ornery old bastard, cynical as can be, yet I'm here. Even I could see how important this all is, even if I probably don't mean much in the way of sheer strength to this team. Doesn't this fellow know what kind of trouble is headed this way?"

Brunar heaved a sigh, and stopped walking. He turned to face the thief and fell silent for a few moments before he spoke.

"Each man has a world to live in, Nessar. Gart's world consists of his wife, his child, and his little plot of land. Right now, he does not acknowledge the danger because it doesn't seem real to him, doesn't affect his world. Also, I think he has some scars that run very deep in him, much deeper than those that mark his face. That, more than anything, keeps him from being here. However, the Jidaan have always Chosen wisely, and I'm sure that he will be along soon. I just hope he comes in time for me to train him so that he doesn't endanger himself." *Or us,* Brunar added silently.

Nessar accepted the information with another nod, then strode towards his chamber. Brunar walked past the dais, towards the west wall where his room lay, and his thoughts turned to the lone weapon that remained. He hoped that Gart would, indeed, arrive in time to learn all that he needed.

An hour later, the group had assembled in the main hall, each eyeing his or her new spear with interest. Brunar was nowhere to be seen at first, but presently he appeared. The Mage had changed from his white robe into something better suited for physical exercise. His roomy black breeks were tucked into a pair of knee-high, soft leather boots that made almost no sound as he strode across the floor, and the sleeves of his flowing purple shirt were pulled firmly back to his elbows, exposing a surprisingly strong pair of forearms. He was still adjusting the few buttons on the front his shirt, even as he walked. Nearing the group, he quickly tightened the deep scarlet sash at his waist. Alyssa thought he looked rather like a pirate. She bit her lip to keep from laughing, but Kiran also seemed to be stifling a chuckle.

Brunar had just settled the sash to his liking when he found himself in the midst of his students. Glancing around at their faces, he was gladdened to see that they were in good spirits, though the two women were a bit red in the face for some reason.

"All right, then, let us begin. Would you please stand back just a bit?" Brunar gestured for the group to step away from him, forming a large circle with himself in the middle.

"Good. Now then, I will show you a bit of what you will learn. Some of you are already good fighters, and some of you are not. Hand-to-hand fighting is only a part of what you will need to master, but we must start somewhere." The Mage turned to Layton. "Layton, kind sir, would you please attack me to the best of your ability? No weapons yet, if you please."

"Sir?" Layton's eyes widened in surprise and his mouth hung open just a fraction. Attacking a Mage was generally not considered to be a good idea. Then again, if Brunar did not use his magick to defend himself, Layton doubted that the Mage would survive against his full-force attack.

"You heard me, boy. I know of your reputation as a canny fighter, but humor me and attack this feeble old man anyway. I'll not blast you with magick, if that's what frightens you." Brunar stood quietly in the center of the open space, arms folded at his chest.

The mention of fear embarrassed the youth just enough to goad him into action. He handed his opal-pommeled weapon to Nessar, then turned his attention back to the Mage. A dreamy half-smile appeared on Layton's handsome face, and Brunar suddenly sensed the youth's magick flare powerfully to life. Layton took two steps towards the Mage, and launched a blinding kick at the older man's midsection. Brunar intercepted the kick and almost gently guided it up and away from himself, sending Layton flailing through the air in total surprise.

Layton recovered in midflight, twisting his body towards the ancient floor until he landed on his feet with the lithe grace of an acrobat. Without pause, he leapt to the attack once more, this time with his fists.

The Mage deflected the next three whirlwind strikes with similar ease. Suddenly, the Mage's right hand snaked past Layton's guard to deftly tap him on the chest, just as the lad prepared to unleash another crushing blow.

A flash of violet burst on the young man's sternum, flinging the youth hard to the floor. The seemingly gentle touch of the Mage's fingers had sent the breath exploding from Layton's lungs, reminding him of his old days with the Eastern Masters.

Brunar watched him for signs of anger, but the lad's calm smile never wavered. He stood and struck a relaxed fighting crouch. Slowly, he stalked closer to the Mage, his eyes focused on the older man's chest.

Layton feinted once, twice, and a third time, each time searching the Mage's reactions for an opening. His next move was a lightning fast punch to Brunar's head. As Brunar moved to catch the incoming fist, the punch disappeared, and Brunar saw the low footsweep almost too late. Brunar had to smile at the boy's dynamic style as he lightly jumped over Layton's tripping technique.

As he rose from the floor, Layton lunged again, his hands blurring as they moved. Slipping inside Brunar's guard, Layton thrust his rigid, spearing fingers towards Brunar's vulnerable throat. The Mage somehow caught the younger man's fingers, twisting them sharply in such a way that Layton could not help but be thrown to the ground, or else risk a broken hand. Layton swiftly got to his feet and moved in for another attack.

Brunar deflected the next two punches easily, but the third, a short uppercut to the body, actually slipped through the Mage's guard. Layton's fist slammed into an unseen barrier, and the lad jumped back, holding his bruised fist. Alyssa quickly stepped over to him and asked to see the injured hand.

"Thank you, Layton, I've taken quite enough of a beating for the moment." Brunar smiled at the young fighter.

"You're welcome, Great One," Layton replied almost shyly as Alyssa examined his knuckles. She was surprised to find that she could vividly *feel* the hand beneath her testing fingers, much more so than she had been able to do before the Choosing. The strength and vitality she felt in Layton's fingers and hand were formidable. She pronounced him to be generally unharmed, then returned to her place with a sidelong glance at the Mage. She knew that this enhanced health-sense was probably part of the magick of which the Mage spoke, and wondered anew what else awaited her.

Brunar turned towards the rest of the group. Kiran and Nessar were talking quietly to each other, no doubt discussing technique. The others were watching intently, waiting for an explanation.

"What you have seen is a small part of all you will learn. The art that I employed against your comrade is called Tinn Quan. It is an art that allows you to use your opponents' powers against them, and also allows you to conserve your magick. It art uses precise, powerful strikes that utilize the power within you to best effect, coupled with graceful intercepting techniques similar to those you just saw."

"But he hit you at the last," Kiran observed, arms folded across her chest. This Tinn Quan doesn't seem to be foolproof, now does it?"

Brunar smiled just a bit. "Indeed, Kiran. An art is only as good as its practitioner, you know. But notice that Layton did not exactly hit me. He hit my shield. I have a habit of unconsciously erecting a magickal barrier around myself when combat commences. As you can see, it can be quite effective at protecting you from some attacks."

"You mean that we can each create a shield that can protect us from any attack?" Nessar spoke skeptically.

"No, not from any attack. And the shield is only as strong as you are. It takes time to learn to control your magick to the degree that holding a shield automatically will require, and time is a luxury that we cannot particularly afford. However, we will do the best we can, so we will spend some time today in discovering what kind fighting ability you each have, and we shall go on from there."

Alyssa's quiet voice emerged from her place in the circle. "I thought we were to fight with these." She held her Jidaan before her in both tiny hands. "Why must we learn this Tinn Quan? Not that I mind, of course."

Before Brunar could answer, Layton spoke with a sad smile. "Have you ever tried to fight someone with a blade . . .and not hurt them badly?"

A puzzled look crossed Alyssa's lovely features as she shook her head. "I've never fought at all. Usually, I'm the one putting people back together afterwards."

Layton nodded. "I see. Well let me tell you, it's a lot less damaging to knock someone out with your fists or feet, rather than gut them like a fish. I'm assuming we will not kill unless we must, though there'll be ample chance of that."

Brunar nodded his agreement. "You have the right of it, Layton." He addressed the group again. "We shall avoid rather than check, check rather than hurt, hurt rather than maim, and maim rather than kill. All life on this world is precious, and cannot be replaced. We kill when we have to, without hesitation. But if a solid chop to the neck can render an enemy unconscious, and that alone will serve your purpose, then it is enough. Besides, there will be times when you may be in close quarters, and unable to use your Jidaan. Though your magick will help you, the knowledge of such hand-to-hand fighting evens the odds considerably."

The next hour or so was spent in mock combat, with each of the new Guardians attacking the Mage so that he could ascertain their skill level. Alyssa had no fighting experience whatsoever, but she was a fairly nimble woman, and determined to learn everything that was presented to her. Brunar saw much potential in her, and made several mental notes as to the specialization of her training.

Nessar was next. The oldster was nowhere near as agile or strong as the younger warriors, yet the life of a thief had seen him fight for his life more times than he could remember. For a man in his sixties, his blows carried quite a bit of authority. However, many of his nastier tricks would not work on the Mage, suited as they were for silent assassinations and furtive attacks. Brunar sensed the thief's magick flare to life several times during their encounter, and the Mage smiled broadly as he told Nessar that he was making progress already. The Choosing had awakened all of the new Guardians' magick, but some were slower to tap into it than others. Nessar stepped away from the Mage feeling somewhat satisfied that he had given a good account of himself, but knowing that there was much to do.

The huge forester was next in line, and for all his massive size and strength, Bjarke was about as effective in combat as a pillow. Time and again, Brunar evaded his clumsy attempts to grapple him, and the few punches that Bjarke threw were nowhere near their intended target. Their encounter ended with Bjarke on the floor after having lost his balance trying the same kick that Layton had performed earlier. He hit the floor with a tremendous, jarring thump, and Alyssa started to rush to his side, fearful that he had broken a rib or two. But then Bjarke's booming laughter echoed throughout the vast chamber, and the other warriors laughed with him, glad that he was uninjured.

Brunar extended a hand to the fallen man. "I can tell that you have led a peaceful life, Bjarke."

Laughing still, Bjarke grasped the offered hand and rose quickly to his feet. "Outside of wrestling a bear or two, I've never fought another person in my life. This is all new to me!"

For a moment, Brunar's smile faded. It seemed such a shame to him that this peaceful, joyful man should be thrust into the waiting war. But then, he thought, if not for him and the others like him, many would suffer unspeakable harm. Bjarke knew the danger was coming, and Brunar hoped that the forester would be prepared. Brunar patted the giant man on the back and sent him away while Kiran came close by for her turn.

Although she lacked Layton's flawless skill and focused strength, Kiran's empathy served her quite well. Though she greatly preferred fighting with a sword, she was by no means a stranger to unarmed combat. She did not score on the Mage as Layton had, but she came much closer than had any of the others. Brunar twisted and ducked away from Kiran's punches and kicks, seemingly impossible to lay a hand on. Suddenly, the mercenary had to defend herself as the Mage began some offensive strikes of his own.

As she attacked and parried, she noticed that she was far more aware of her perceptions, sensing where and how Brunar would move often an instant before he did so. There was an odd feeling that stirred deep within her, a growing warmth at her core where the Mage had said her magick rested. On a hunch, she imagined some of that energy flowing into her legs as she prepared to attack Brunar with a jumping kick. To her surprise, she hurtled upwards, rising over ten feet in the air before she started her rapid descent. She braced for impact, but Brunar gestured with one hand, and her fall slowed until she stepped gently to the polished stone floor as if she were stepping off a staircase. Her eyes were alight with questions as she stared at the Mage.

Before she could begin, Brunar blurted excitedly, "Wonderful! Simply wonderful! I assume this has never happened to you before?" Brunar was quite animated as he walked quickly over to Kiran. The others gathered a bit closer to hear.

"No, Mage, I usually don't make a habit out of leaping over my assailants. What exactly did I do?"

"You did what you were supposed to do. You tapped into your magick. It can be used to empower your movements, to give you strength and stamina. You must have channeled it into your legs for it to have such an effect."

Kiran looked down at her legs as if they were not her own. "Well, something like that. I thought I felt something inside me, as you said we would. I wanted to jump as high as I could, and I sort of imagined that power moving into my legs." She looked apprehensively back to the Mage. "You can help me control this, can't you?"

"That, my dear, is exactly what we are here to do." He thumped her heartily on the back and addressed everyone.

"Feel the magick within yourselves. It swirls here," he placed one hand over his stomach, just below his navel. The others mirrored his action. "Become aware of it, and channel it into your muscles. In this way, we become stronger and faster than most people dream possible. This is one of the most important skills you must master, and as I said earlier, it must become second nature to you. There are other exercises that will help you to do this, and the meditations we will practice will help you become far more in tune with your power."

Brunar watched their faces as they dwelled on this for a moment: Nessar and Kiran nodded slowly to themselves; Bjarke stood motionless with one hand still pressed to his midsection, his eyes glazed in concentration; Layton was watching the Mage intently, simply absorbing every word that Brunar said; Alyssa was quietly trying to imitate some of the fighting motions that both Layton and Kiran had used.

Kiran spoke again. "You said we have always had this magick within us. What did the Choosing do that makes me able to use it like this?"

Brunar nodded sagely as he replied, "Your Jidaan have simply made you aware of your power. It was always there, but you may never have known what it was, or even that you had it at all. The Jidaan just brought it to your attention so that you could better make use of it."

"What of me?" Nessar spoke up from the back of the group. "I just don't feel that much stronger or faster. How can I use it?"

A knowing gleam appeared in the Mage's eye as he answered the thief. "While we fought just now, I felt your power flare several times." Nessar's eyes widened at this.

"You mean I used it? Without knowing it?"

"Indeed, Nessar. I noticed that it tended to come into play when you were preparing for a particularly accurate strike, such as those finger jabs you aimed at my nerve centers. I am certain you were using your magick to guide your hand. I can tell you that if those strikes had landed, they would have been quite lethal."

Nessar began to stammer an apology. He had definitely not intended to kill anyone, and he did not think that his blows had really had that much strength behind them. To discover that his power was working in that manner was a bit of a shock to the thief. Brunar quieted him with a wave, and congratulated him for his progress.

"There is much to learn, for all of you." Brunar noticed more than one pair of eyes shift towards Layton, who seemed oblivious to the fact.

"Even you, Layton." Everyone laughed good-naturedly as Layton grinned and blushed to the tips of his ears.

"Guardians, there is more to this than just the enhancement of your physical abilities. I will teach you how to move objects without touching them, to send your thoughts to each other, and to do many other things that may never have occurred to you. In any case, I believe that I have discovered what I need about your individual fighting abilities, and we will move on to the physical training. The war with Mordak will be difficult to say the least, and we must be strong."

The mention of Mordak brought the lingering laughter to a stop. They all knew why they were there, and the name of the Evil One reminded everyone of the dread task ahead.

A quiet voice spoke up then. "What about the Gifts of the Jidaan, Brunar? How are we going to learn to use them? I mean, we know what they are, but how do they work?" Alyssa was looking up at the Mage with determined eyes.

Brunar smiled only slightly as he replied. "The Gifts of the Jidaan take a toll on their Chosen. This is one of the reasons that we must first make our bodies strong, little one. Otherwise, a single, simple use of your Gift might leave you unconscious; that's how powerful they are. As you know, Bjarke's Jidaan brings Power. Sheer strength, most often in concussive blasts of magick. In the distant past, I saw Rhu nearly level mountains with the power he carried. However, in the beginning, he took care to restrain himself, lest he leave himself senseless after releasing more energy than even his strong body could handle."

"Rest assured, Alyssa, that I will teach you how to endure the use of your Gift as soon as possible." Alyssa and the other Guardians digested this, and a sour look of impatience crossed Kiran's face, only leaving when an elbow from Nessar struck her lightly in her ribs. Brunar saw the exchange and continued. "And that goes for all of you. You each have an idea of what your Gift does. As your bodies and magick get stronger, you will find opportunities within your training to use those Gifts, and I will guide you. There will also be times when you will feel the Jidaan calling to you, suggesting that you invoke its Gift for a particular purpose. Do not fear this. Instead, just follow your instincts, and see what happens."

"But until then, we have some work to do, so sheathe your weapons and follow me!" Brunar turned and trotted towards the massive front gates, willing them open as he ran.

Layton was the first to follow. He deftly dropped his Jidaan into its scabbard on his back, then took a few lengthy strides until he was only a yard or so behind the Mage. Kiran, not to be outdone, quickly followed the pair, though she had problems getting her weapon into its proper position in its scabbard. Bjarke and Alyssa wrestled their Jidaan into their resting places and gamely trotted after. Nessar came last, grumbling something about making an old man run until he remembered that the Mage was over two thousand years old. He harumphed at the thought.

"Well, Mages are a different case altogether!" he commented loudly as he followed his fellows out to the courtyard, out into the daylight as they began the most rigorous training that any of them, save Layton, had ever dreamed possible.

The next several days saw all of the new Guardians training most of the daylight hours, and sometimes into the night. They all practiced together at first, tentatively encouraging each other through the demanding calisthenics, the mountain climbing, the running, and the combat techniques. They knew that they could receive word of Mordak's whereabouts at any moment, so they trained hard and tried to absorb as much information as they could.

Much of their time was spent in a chamber almost as big as the main hall, but where the Hall was empty of all but majestic columns, carvings and the dais, this large room held many of the training implements that were familiar to the two fighters, and several that were not. Man-sized wooden targets that already had many deep stabs and slashes gouged into their rough surfaces attested to the fact that the previous Guardians had taken their training seriously. Among those were hanging bags of several sizes that were used to build strength in hand-to-hand combat. They were filled with rags, sand, or small stones. Layton had long since burst one of the stone-filled bags with a powerful kick, while Alyssa was still pounding away on the rag-filled bags with an iron-willed determination. The others were working with the sandbags, strengthening their punches and kicks and using their magick to enhance that practice.

It was here that the group learned the ways of fighting with the fabled Jidaan. Though Layton seemed at home with any weapon, the short-handled spear took longer for the others to get used to. Kiran was constantly heard mumbling, "Couldn't have been a magickal sword, or even a magickal axe. Noooooooooooo, it had to be a magick *spear*!"

Without the three foot long handle, Kiran thought, *this blade would make a decent short sword, but this extra length of wood is only making things difficult.* So far, she had attempted to use it like a sword on a stick, and that was just not working very well. Brunar offered several well-placed instructions that helped her more than she cared to admit, but learning the ways of battle with a foreign weapon still took longer than she would have liked. Sweating and frustrated, Kiran would usually cut her eyes towards the youngest of the group, Layton. She frowned continually at him. He always seemed to learn things faster than she, which bothered her to no end.

Though he had long ago been schooled in the use of various Eastern weapons, and though many of them had large blades on longer handles, the Jidaan was altogether different. Layton's eyes shone as he moved and danced with the weapon. He had started slowly, getting the feel of its balance as he gently parried and offered tentative thrusts and cuts to imaginary opponents. He had been taught that each weapon had a unique personality. To use that weapon well, a fighter must become acquainted with that personality, and use it in a way that complemented its own temperament.

Layton stepped up the pace of his motions as he became more comfortable with his Jidaan. He instinctively found the parries and attacks that the weapon liked best. Other weapons he had used, such as the *kwan dao*, the 7-ring-long-handled-broadsword, and the shorter-handled sheung dao that was closest in general form to the Jidaan, had all been effective for him in the past, but they were slow and clumsy compared to the weapon he now held.

Where the 7-ring was ponderous and slow, the Jidaan was as quick as lightning, and was equally effective at short range or long. Where the *sheung dao* was unwieldy due to a bad balance point, the Jidaan was ready and willing to attack from all angles.

Layton soon found that the jeweled pommel offered several vicious striking capabilities as a bludgeon. It was when he began the whirlwind motions, striking with both razor-edged blade and unyielding pommel, that the Jidaan began to sing in his hands. He felt the magick in the Jidaan as a dull vibration that was answered by the magick he carried within himself, and Layton wielded his weapon as if he had been created solely for the purpose of using it. He spun, thrust, and parried in a blur of precise and deadly beauty as he lost himself within the motion.

The others, especially Bjarke and Alyssa, looked at their Jidaan in a more skeptical fashion. Although the Choosing had bonded them to their weapons and made them more aware of their own magick, it had done little for their fighting skills. And yet, they were more than willing to learn. In anyone other than Guardians, training of this nature would have taken years.

But soon, Brunar noticed that even the nonfighters were gaining proficiency with their weapons. Clumsy hacks and wayward slashes and pokes slowly became precise cuts and well-timed thrusts. Layton was always assisting the others, lending helpful advice where it seemed most needed. Bjarke and Alyssa especially were grateful for his help. All of Layton's life had been spent learning how to use exotic weapons such as this, and he had a quiet tone and an easy manner of teaching that everyone naturally accepted. Even Kiran sometimes took his advice.

It turned out that Nessar had once been part of the castle guard in Rualtha, where he had gained a tiny bit of experience with a similar weapon; the familiarity of it helped him learn quickly. He took no end of ribbing from Kiran about that, but he would only say that he had been 'in disguise' at the time.

After teaching them as a group for several days, Brunar began to specialize their training, attuning their regimens to their specific abilities, or lack thereof. Bjarke was easily the strongest of all of the Guardians, yet he lacked stamina and coordination. Brunar took care to tailor the big man's exercises so that they made him build those weaker attributes while still increasing his great strength.

Alyssa was a strong-willed soul. Though she was the smallest and the weakest of the Guardians, she easily carried enough grit and determination for them all. She suffered through the strength-building exercises and pushed herself unmercifully during the endurance runs and shorter sprints. By leaps and bounds, she began to see progress, both in her physical condition and in the use of her magick to aid her movements. She also approached Kiran, asking the mercenary to teach her some additional fighting techniques. Kiran had heartily agreed, and afterwards, the Hall of Jidaana often reverberated with the whistling of their blades as they practiced their movements, or the sounds of unarmed combat as the two women sparred.

It was more difficult at first for Nessar. Though he was still in good physical condition, he simply could not believe that the magick he carried was as powerful as everyone else's. For the first week, he tended to lag behind when the group went for an endurance run through the lower parts of the mountains, and did not put as much effort into the climbing and other exercises as the others did.

Late in the third week of training, Brunar led the group along a mountain trail that hugged one of the largest peaks, skirting the mountainside in an ever-rising spiral. The path was quite steep, and the sheer drop on the right side of the path was daunting for all. Yet Brunar loped up the trail as if he gave no thought to the looming chasm that lay only a few feet away. As usual, Layton followed the Mage closely, followed by Kiran, Bjarke, and Alyssa. Nessar came following at some distance, the pain of his exertions showing plainly on his weathered face.

At times, the other Guardians had taken to calling out to one another, urging each other on. Their encouraging cries rebounded from the surrounding peaks, leaving playful echoes in their wakes. Nessar heard his fellows up ahead, but was so far behind them that he did not bother to reply. *They are young,* he thought. *They have the strength for this sort of thing. I'll get there when I get there.*

Then Nessar heard footsteps on the path above and in front of him. He looked up through stinging eyes to see Layton lagging behind the others. Nessar frowned. He knew of the young man's reputation, and had seen the boy's talents firsthand in the last few weeks. The fact that Layton seemed so perfect in his abilities before he had even arrived here galled Nessar somewhat, and he had to fight against resenting the lad. In the face of Layton's ability to use his magick so adeptly, Nessar just could not see how he, himself, could be useful. Even the ebony Jidaan Nessar carried did not seem too impressive to him, especially since he had not yet learned to use its Gift.

Layton slowed until he was running even with the thief, jogging between him and the edge of the path. The youth ran smoothly, with no hint of effort, and Nessar slowed a little more, as if to magnify the difference in their gait. They ran in silence for a time, and then Nessar looked over to see that Layton had been staring at him, apparently for some time.

"Having trouble, Nessar?" Layton spoke easily, as if they were seated comfortably back in their chambers.

Nessar's sweaty face puckered as he scowled in the lad's direction.

"No, I'm just fine, thank you," Nessar managed to reply between heaving breaths. He saw that the lad was running perilously close to the trail's edge. "You'd better watch yourself. That drop would kill you."

"Look," Layton said, ignoring the comment. "I know that you can feel the magick. It kind of twirls and moves in a little ball just under your stomach. Can you feel it?"

"Yes, I can feel it!" Nessar snapped. "Why don't you . . ." Just then, he stumbled on a stone in the narrow path, and collided with Layton, shoving him towards the edge. Fighting for his balance, Layton tried to remain on the path, and failed. He started to tip outward, towards the bottom of the canyon hundreds of feet below.

Seeing the lad start to fall, Nessar lashed out with one long-fingered hand and grabbed hold of Layton's left wrist. The force of Layton's full weight jerked the thief down to the ground, towards the very brink, and Nessar strained to keep his grip on Layton's wrist while desperately trying to keep himself from going over as well. Lying on his stomach at the edge of the path, Nessar groaned in pain. His shoulder seemed as though it were being ripped from its socket. The mountain's face was nearly vertical here, and Nessar could see that Layton had nothing to grab onto. The only thing that kept the lad from plunging to his death was the thief's tenuous grip.

Through teeth tightly clenched, Nessar spoke. "Climb! I can't hold you!" He looked down into Layton's eyes, and was shocked to see that the young fighter was making no effort to save himself. He did not even grasp Nessar's thin wrist with his left hand, and his free hand was simply held at his side. He actually seemed quite calm.

"No. Use your magick to pull me up." Layton's words were soft, but they infuriated the thief.

"Are you MAD, boy? I haven't the strength! Help me!" Veins bulged at Nessar's temple and throat, throbbing with the effort of keeping Layton from plunging to his death.

"Listen to me. Feel the magick. Dig into it, and use it to pull me up." Layton still made no move to save himself.

Nessar's hold started to slip, and his narrow shoulders quivered with the strain. "I can't! I can't do it! I'm losing my grip!"

"Then I will die." Layton kept his eyes on the thief, maintaining his placid expression. It was as if he had already accepted his impending death.

Nessar uttered a wordless cry as his fingers began to lose their hold. This young fool would die, and it would be no one's fault but the thief's. Nessar frantically tried to think of another way to save him.

Just as he was certain that he could hold on no longer, Nessar found the magick within him. In panic, he delved deeply into it, and suddenly felt it racing through his arm towards his clutching hand. Nessar's old, slender fingers clenched tightly, digging into the skin of Layton's wrist, and a muffled grunt escaped the dangling fighter.

Breathing easier now, Nessar pulled against Layton's weight. Slowly, inch by terrible inch, Nessar lifted until he got his legs under himself to apply more leverage. Within moments, Layton stood on the trail, brushing the dust from himself with his right hand. Nessar looked at his own hand as if it should belong to someone else.

Layton was the first to speak. "You see? With your magick, your strength is far greater than it was. It's the same for all of us, Nessar. All you have to do is use it and learn what you can do with it."

Nessar replied by slapping the young fighter in the face. Layton stoically absorbed the blow and waited for the thief to speak.

"You could have died just now. If I had dropped you, even your skills couldn't have saved you. Everyone else is too far up the trail to even know what happened. Why in the Hels did you do this?" Nessar's anger reddened his worn face.

Layton carefully placed his right hand on Nessar's shoulder and replied quietly, "Brunar says that we are Guardians, and that means that we are as family. We must learn to trust in one another. I did not expect to be pitched over a cliff when I came back here to run with you, Nessar, but when it happened, I trusted you to save me. You can expect the same from me. We are all in this together."

Nessar found that his own piercing gaze was met with nothing more or less than Layton's calm sincerity. Nessar could not help but see in his eyes that he was telling the truth. A sigh escaped the older man, taking much of his anger with it, and all was silent on the trail for a few moments as Nessar gathered his thoughts.

"Well don't do that again! I might not be able to save you next time!" Nessar was still angry, but he knew the boy was right. He knew he had to learn to trust.

Layton smiled his great wide smile at the older man. "Come on, Grampy, we need to catch up to the others."

Smiling broadly over one shoulder, Layton burst into a sprint and raced away from Nessar as the thief's mouth flopped open in rage at the gibe.

"I'll show you 'Grampy', you little snot-rat!" Nessar heaved his long legs into motion and began to pick up speed, his pace much quicker than it had previously been. Layton laughed and called back for the older man to continue using his magick, urging him to run faster still.

Though he was quite upset at the young upstart for his teasing, and he continued to hurl threats of great pain and doom towards the younger man up the trail, Nessar was beginning to think that maybe, just maybe, the little snot-rat wasn't so bad after all.

Chapter 17

The setting sun turned the western sky into a wash of orange and red, as if a painter had gently smeared the most beautiful colors he could find across the heavens. Gennie smiled in the direction of the slowly descending sun as she basked in the ebbing warmth that caressed her upturned face. She lived for moments like this, when she felt that the sky had been colored just for her. She stood at the western edge of the village, still gazing at the sunset over the thick woodland. Gart would be coming from those woods at any moment, bearing his usual gift of venison for the festival feast. The thicket that followed the nearby river's southward path was teeming with game, so it was unusual that Gart would take this long, but Gart was Gart. He would arrive when he chose, and not before.

Behind Gennie, the sounds of the annual festival continued with mirth and joy, and the cheering of the crowd brought her back to herself. She felt someone tugging at her skirt, and looked down into the petulant little face of her only daughter, Rheann. She had her father's icy blue eyes, but instead of Gart's coldness, the girl's eyes twinkled with glee. Otherwise, her flowing black hair and pretty face mirrored Gennie's own. Gennie bent, scooped up her daughter, and began to walk towards the festival in town.

As she walked, carrying two-year old Rheann comfortably on her hip, Gennie played the tickling game with the girl. Gennie would make faces at her daughter, trying to entice her to giggle. If Rheann did, she was tickled soundly in her ribs. It was a game they both enjoyed, and they played it until they neared the crowd of people that surrounded the town square, where the traditional contest of bagatt was loudly underway.

From the sidelines, Gennie watched a tanned, muscular fellow named Tabor stretch out with his bagatta stick and pluck the ball from the air as it passed over his head. In the same motion, he spun and twisted, barely dodging an opposing player's attempt to knock him down. Using a special rocking motion to keep the small sphere settled in the hand-woven net at the end of his three-foot-long stick, he sprinted down the dusty playing field, leaving the defending players behind him as he searched for an open man on his own team to whom he could pass the ball.

He swore to himself as he saw that his teammates were closely guarded by their green-clad opponents from Tiller's

Grove, and he could hear the pounding footsteps of the defenders rapidly approaching from the rear. He had to either pass the ball to someone else or try to get close enough to the goal, a large lean-to constructed of wood and fabric, to try and hurl the ball past the burly goalguard for a score. The goalguard, Lowen, was well known as one of the best bagatt players around. Few points had ever made it past his small, brightly-painted shield and stick, and he usually preferred to block those with his body.

Bagatt had been played in this region for centuries, and was an important part of the town's festival culture. The sport involved a tremendous amount of body-checking, elbow-throwing, stick-knocking, and an occasional fight, but it was enjoyed by all. Only the toughest men in the community played the game, and they played it well.

Tabor picked up speed and apparently decided on a one-man frontal assault on the goal, since the other defenders were still behind him, and the only defenders on that side of the field had to stay with their own assigned attackers. He motioned for his teammates to back away from the goal so he would have some room to maneuver, and he bore down on Lowen, making ready to hurl the sphere towards the guard's feet in the hopes that he would not be able to block its flight.

The crowd watched the unfolding drama from the sides of the playing field, and they hooted and yelled as the lone player raced towards his target, preparing to take the shot that might win the game. The annual festival had been created only one hundred fifty years before, and the bagatt game, with its blend of brute strength and finesse, had always been one of the most favored events of the gathering. The people of Tiller's Grove had won last year, even though the festival was held at the neighboring town, High Rock. This year, the festival and its game were being held in Tiller's Grove, and the visitors from the Rock were determined not to lose again. The rivalry was a great one, yet it retained the high spirit of camaraderie between the sister towns that had begun the festival in the first place.

The lively spectators were careful to stay clear of the game's boundaries. Behind the crowd and encircling the entire game was a ring of food vendors, each loudly proclaiming their wares to be the most wonderful in the land. Smells from their carts wafted through the air, assailing everyone with the aromas of beef, pies, and many other treats. These dishes were merely meant to whet the crowd's appetite for the huge SpringDay Feast to be held soon after the bagatt contest ended, and each year's feast seemed better than the last. Laughter and cheering rose from all sides as the strolling jugglers and illusionists entertained those who lacked interest in the game. Though they were all farmers for the rest of the year, the performers nevertheless gave impressive performances. SpringDay gave them the chance to show off their usually undisplayed talents, and they enjoyed it immensely.

Evening was rapidly approaching, but the twilight had no dimming effect on the brightly dyed pennants that waved in the breeze. The riot of colors was just wild enough to lend the proper atmosphere to the yearly festival without being irredeemably gaudy, and the mood of the hundred or so festival-goers seemed especially joyful. Gennie could feel their high spirits almost matching her own.

As twilight flowed gently into night, Gennie saw torches being lit and placed in sconces on the fronts of the buildings that flanked the town square. As she surveyed the scene around her, she noticed with alarm that Rheann was not standing next to her as she had been a moment ago. Gennie looked frantically about for a moment, then spotted the little girl only a few yards away, running shakily towards the food and pastry carts.

Rheann let out a high-pitched giggle and ran as fast as her stubby, two-year-old legs could carry her. She could hear her mother close behind, urging her to stop, but the little girl paid no heed. Rheann knew that her Mommy would catch her eventually, but the milling crowd of legs before her made this game more interesting than usual. She laughed again, and promptly tripped over a small rock in the dirt, smacking her forehead rather soundly on the ground as she fell.

"Rheann!" Gennie rushed to her fallen daughter's side and picked her up. The child's face was dirty, and turning a peculiar shade of red as she fought the tears that wanted to come out.

"By Rowann, girl, you are going to have to stop running away from Mommy every chance you get!" Gennie brushed the dirt from the girl's dress and tried to calm her down. It was a beautiful red fabric that Gart had brought from New Caldea only three weeks before, and was Rheann's new favorite. Rheann finally seemed to decide that she would survive her latest tumble, and immediately shifted her interest to a passing juggler. The girl's bright blue eyes twinkled merrily, and she laughed as the young boy deftly kept four brightly colored clubs aloft. The performer heard her laughter and turned to face the beautiful young woman with an equally pretty little girl in her arms.

Brushing a stray lock of Rheann's hair from the girl's eyes, Gennie smiled at the juggler, aa young man from Tiller's Grove named Erin. He was usually a stable boy, but in keeping with festival tradition, today he was one of the finest performers in the land. Or at least, in the town. Rheann clapped her little hands with glee as the lad effortlessly twirled the clubs in the air, guiding them in ever more intricate patterns. Suddenly, he threw all four of the clubs high into the air, did a curt backflip, and caught the clubs one by one as they returned to earth. Finished with his act, Erin's face broke into a wide grin, and he bowed to the pair with a flourish.

Gennie laughed at Erin's bow, pleased with such a grandiose ending to his act, and shifted Rheann to her hip so that she could pull one of the small bead tokens from her festival purse and give it to the lad.

"Thanks be to you, Gennie. Er, I mean 'Milady'," Erin corrected himself. He blushed slightly at the mistake. During the festival, all performers were to pretend they were nothing more than traveling entertainers who knew none of the townspeople personally. The common folk brought with them five homemade festival beads, which were given as tokens of approval to any performers that were deemed exceptional. The performer with the most beads at festival's end would receive the coveted title of 'SpringDay's Victorious'. Competition was fierce but good-natured, and though Erin was not very experienced, he had improved his juggling ten-fold since last year. Gennie hoped he would win the award.

Gennie fished out a token and gave it to Rheann, who happily dropped it into the lad's outstretched palm. "Think nothing of it, kind sir. I hope you win today!" She smiled and winked, and the young man bowed once more before turning away to continue his performances.

Just then, Rheann pointed towards the cart that held the small assortment of pies and sweets, and began to plead for Gennie to take her there. Gennie complied. The cheers from the crowd around the bagatt game seemed to echo those in her heart, for this had been a good day. Gart would be along soon and that would make things even better, so maybe a little celebratory snack would be in order. She felt sure that Rheann would not complain.

Gennie wished Gart enjoyed the annual festival as much as she did. She understood that her husband had little liking for great crowds of people, mostly because his scars always caused others to stare. Also, Gart had been more reticent than usual lately. He was not particularly social in any event, but he had been spending a lot of time on his hill and in the forest since his return from New Caldea.

As she walked towards the cart, she reached up to finger the tiny emerald gem that he had given her upon his arrival. He never had told her much about it, only that he had found it during his ride home. She wondered briefly if it had anything to do with his recent sullenness. But then she shrugged to herself. Gart's childhood had been a difficult one, and periods of moodiness like this were not uncommon with him. Before Gennie could muse on his behavior any further, Rheann began to squirm and fidget in her eagerness as they neared the display of sweets.

"Wigglewort!" she chided her daughter. Rheann laughed then, a high, sparkling sound of pure joy that could only come from a young child's heart. For a moment, Gennie forgot the dourness of her husband and let her own heart answer that of her daughter, and the pair giggled together.

As she reached the cart, a movement behind it caught Gennie's eye. She glanced towards the buildings that lay beyond the cart, a simple marketshop and a smithy, and saw a man on horseback pass behind the structures. He was only in view for a moment through the alleyway before the building obscured her vision, but she noticed something odd about the rider.

Ignoring Rheann's protests at leaving the cart with no treats in hand, Gennie nodded to the smiling woman tending the pies, and excused herself to have a closer look. The little shops that surrounded the town square were set several feet away from each other, so there was ample room for Gennie to walk between them as she moved slowly towards the rear of the buildings. As she left the torchlight behind her, she stopped a moment to let her eyes adjust to the deepening gloom before continuing. Before she could take another step, the man she had seen appeared from around the corner ahead. He had apparently left his horse behind the building, and now strode towards her with a slow, methodical step. He made no sound.

Rheann started to cry as the man approached, now about thirty feet away. Twenty-five.

"Hello? Who's there? Are you new to our Festival?" Gennie asked, trying to hush Rheann's tears. The stranger, shrouded in darkness, said nothing. He was twenty feet away, and Gennie felt a chill caress her spine. Rheann's cries got louder.

"Can I help you? Are you lost?" Gennie heard a slight tremor in her voice, and took a small step backwards as the shadowy man advanced, now fifteen feet away.

"Who are you?" Gennie asked as she stared into the dark, searching the inky blackness of the man's features. She finally noticed the man's eyes, two glaring red spots in the rider's face. They burned dully with a hideous scarlet gleam, and Gennie's heart went cold. He was only ten feet away now.

A quiet grunt of fear escaped her lips, and Gennie turned and sprinted back towards the light of the festival, bouncing Rheann painfully on her hip. She looked back once to see the stranger stepping out of the alleyway and into the torchlight. He was a bedraggled, bearded man that looked as though he had ridden for days without rest. His torn garments hung loosely on his slender frame, almost as if his body had shrunken within the clothes. His face held no expression, save the crimson evil that glowed faintly from his empty eye sockets, and his skin was pale, even in the torchlight. At that moment, other riders stepped out from the other alleyways along the street, and Gennie felt terror for the first time. Their eyes all glowed scarlet.

Gennie screamed as the horrific riders drew their swords, axes, and daggers, and continued their plodding march towards the crowd. Heads turned in the festival, and as the townspeople saw what was advancing on them, other screams echoed through the night. Carts were abandoned in haste as their owners saw the shambling figures moving slowly towards them, and those men and women hurried to join the safety of the crowd. The musicians fell silent, and the festivities stopped as all eyes turned towards the pallid newcomers. More of the ashen-faced riders began to emerge from the alleyways, steadily advancing.

Several women, Gennie foremost among them, began moving towards the center of the throng, and the mass of people roiled again as the bagatt players shouldered their way towards the front of the group. To a man, these were the toughest that the two cities could muster, and the closest thing to a militia that either of the two possessed. Tabor, the biggest of all, gripped his stick firmly in his right hand. It was no match for a sword, but the three-foot long shaft was made of hardened wood, and the wooden basket used for catching the bagatt ball was nearly as hard as metal. It would serve, if need be. The other players readied their sticks as well. There seemed to be about thirty of the riders, still flowing from the shadowy recesses of the alleyways.

"Ho there! Who are you?" Tabor yelled across the steadily declining distance that separated the eerie riders from the cluster of frightened villagers. Silence was the only response. The breeze shifted, and a vile, dead smell of corruption swept over the gathering, causing many to gag and retch.

Ignoring the stench, Tabor stepped towards the nearest rider. From within the crowd, Gennie shuddered as she clutched Rheann close to her, trying to calm her baby's terrified cries. Gennie watched as the barrel-chested Tabor stopped only a few yards from the rider, the very one she had seen. Tabor spoke again, menace now creeping into his voice. This time, Gennie couldn't hear what Tabor said, but the response was horribly clear.

Without a sound, the haggard rider raised his sword and slashed at Tabor, a vicious overhand cut that Tabor only just managed to block with his stick. Braced firmly in both of Tabor's strong hands, the stick sent a shower of splinters to the ground as it cracked, but it did not break. Tabor wrenched it free and jammed its small end into the face of his scarlet-eyed assailant. He was rewarded with a sickening crunch as bones shattered and the stranger's face began to lose shape. The rider staggered and fell to the ground, still clutching his sword. The crimson glow faded from the thing's eyes almost immediately, and it lay where it fell.

A weak cheer went up from the crowd as Tabor turned and yelled to his teammates.

"Fight them! They fall like any other men!" Tabor stepped quickly towards another rider and felled him with a great two-handed swing of his stick. As the rider went down, nineteen of the strongest men in two villages screamed a wordless cry of fury and broke from the ranks of the crowd. The battle was quickly joined, sticks cracking into the brittle bones of the foul horrors that came from the shadows. Tabor was like a whirlwind, swinging his heavy stick about like a wand until it finally cracked to pieces across the skull of a rider.

The crowd watched in fearful anticipation. They knew not where these riders had come from, nor why they were here, but the stench of evil was in the air, wafting over the crowd like a wind of death. Deep in their hearts, the townspeople knew these men had to be stopped.

The battle continued, the torches casting horrid shadows on the ground as the men battled with the silent newcomers. The only sounds were the crunch of stick on bone, and, as the men picked up weapons from the hands of fallen riders, the sickening sound of sword on flesh. Players continued to fell rider after rider, until soon, only the men remained standing. Several of the players from both towns had died fighting the foul attackers, but the townsmen were victorious. They raised their sticks and appropriated weapons, and they cheered. Astonished at the brutality of it all, the crowd nevertheless responded in kind. Dead riders lay about the town square, as did the few townsmen who had fallen. But for now, victory was theirs.

Tabor, though, did not cheer. He was kneeling down beside one of the corpses, examining it thoroughly. Covering his nose and mouth with a strip of cloth that had been serving as his headband, Tabor leaned towards the corpse, noticing that no blood flowed from its wounds. The thing's skull was caved in on one side, no doubt from a wicked bash from a stick, but nothing was coming out of the wound at all. It seemed as though the rider had nothing inside him but muscle and bone. The gaping eyesockets were dry and barren, containing no hint of the hideous gleam that had animated them previously.

Before Tabor could examine the rider further, something happened. The light breeze that had been blowing gently throughout the evening faded into nothingness, and then the very feel of the air *changed*. It was as if the air had become taut as a bowstring, and the sense of death that the riders had brought with them seemed to intensify.

The crowd's cheering abruptly ceased as they realized the danger had not ended with the fall of the riders. Silence descended on the people. Gennie saw Tabor leap to his feet, a rider's broadsword in his hands, his eyes searching the shadows for a new threat.

Hoofbeats sounded to the north, and the sound sent a rush of fear stabbing into the hearts of every man, woman and child gathered in the square. Gennie whirled to find the source of the dreaded sound, her eyes wide with terror.

"Look! Look there!" One man held out a shaking arm, pointing into the darkness as Tabor rushed through the mob in the direction of the man's voice. He emerged on the other side of the throng to see a huge man riding towards them from the darkness of the north.

If the eyes of the riders had been evil, the twin fires that pierced the night from the face of this gigantic figure were a hundred times more so. They were the eyes of a massive serpent, shining brightly, a deep, rancid yellow. Every man and woman in the crowd stood in shock as the rider came near enough for them all to see his eyes.

With a deep, bone-chilling laugh, the rider reined in his mount, keeping himself just out of range of the torchlight that illuminated the exhausted crowd. His eyes, demon's eyes, glared in from the night at the mass of townsfolk, and his power was evident even in the darkness. His massive body, sheltered by the shadows, moved with unearthly grace as he dismounted. Not once did he take his ghastly eyes from the frightened faces of the crowd, and not once did he blink.

Gennie watched the man grip the reins of his huge horse to keep it from shying. A cold drop of icy sweat slithered down her spine as she saw that this man looked to be around seven feet tall, and was heavily muscled. But for all his bulk, his movements were lithe and effortless, with more than a hint of feline quickness.

The voice that issued forth from the shadowed figure was deep and strong, and surprisingly melodic. Its music held a tantalizing, almost seductive quality, and as he spoke, the crowd collectively held its breath to hear better.

"I see you've met my friends," the massive stranger commented, still not stepping into the light.

Tabor shouted at the shadow-wrapped figure.

"Step out where I can see you! But if those were your friends, then you'd better come no closer than that, else you'll receive the same welcome that they did!"

Several of the players at Tabor's side nodded in grim agreement as they clutched the weapons stripped from the riders' corpses. Some other men of the town had now picked up weapons and stood alongside the bloodied bagatt players.

A deep, rumbling laugh met the threat, and Gennie distinctly heard a faint hissing sound from the man. A terrified murmur arose from the crowd as they, too, heard the unnatural sound.

"I'm afraid you don't understand your situation. You seem to believe that you are in a position to discuss your fate." The serpent-eyed man laughed again, sending more chills racing the length of Tabor's sturdy spine.

"Our fate?" Tabor asked. He took two steps towards the hulking figure at the edge of the firelight. "Just what do you think you will have to do with our fate?"

The cold hissing sound came again, and now Gennie realized the sound was not coming from the huge man, but instead from the shadows around him. Gennie watched Tabor peer into the darkness, apparently trying to identify the source of the menacing sounds just as she had been. But then, Gennie found her eyes returning to the twin fires that blazed in the massive stranger's shrouded face.

"Why, I have everything to do with your fate. Yours, and that of everyone here. Please allow me to introduce myself." His voice held the crowd in thrall. No one among them could move as the towering fellow finally stepped into the firelight, pulling his reluctant horse behind him. As he hove into view, the light finally reached his gargantuan body. The gathered townsfolk's blood ran cold and more than one jaw dropped in utter amazement as the massive man finally revealed himself.

He was indeed just over seven feet tall, and looked to be close to three hundred pounds of rippling muscle. The shimmering torchlight did nothing to dim the evil yellow fire that shone from his slitted eyes. Oddly, around those eyes was a strongly handsome face, made even more so by the suggestive grin that appeared beneath a tightly trimmed, dashing black mustache. Luxuriant black hair cascaded down over his shoulders, almost shining blue in the reflection of the firelight. His huge body was covered by an odd collection of armor, including plates, leather, and swatches of chainmail. In the shifting light of the fire, Gennie could see the corded muscles playing beneath the swarthy skin of the man's bare forearms as he reached for the great sword that hung from his belt, a sword that a strong man might just be able to wield with two hands.

Gennie watched the giant as he whipped the gleaming blade from its scabbard in one deft motion and held it loosely in his right hand as if it weighed nothing at all. Her eyes quickly turned to Tabor. She noted that he had lost his determined expression, only to have it replaced with one of fear. Looking back to the enormous figure, she felt the same icy grip of fear clutching at her own heart. How could we stand against such obvious power? Such evil?

"I am Jor Dayne," the great figure spoke again, his resonant voice captivating the crowd before him, "and I have come at the behest of the Dark One, Mordak. He is my master, and by his order, you must be sacrificed." The handsome face of Jor Dayne suddenly split into an impossibly wide grin, displaying a mouth filled with needle-sharp teeth.

Before anyone in the crowd could react, Gennie finally saw the source of the hissing sounds she had been hearing. The darkness began to take on substance, and the hissing became an angry yammering as strange, hunched shapes began to emerge from the shadows beyond Jor Dayne. Nightmares had suddenly taken shape, and the very earth beneath their clawed feet seemed to rebel at their evil touch.

Through a growing haze of fear, Gennie watched as a few of the stooped things, each no more than five feet tall, stepped reluctantly into the light. Their bloodlust radiated from bulbous eyes as black as jet. The things were thin, but whipcord muscles bunched and moved beneath the mottled green and black skin that covered their horrid bodies. Each hand held only three fingers and a thumb, and the digits were horribly elongated, ending in gleaming razors of bone. They gazed at the stunned crowd with inhuman intensity, and Gennie saw one wolf-like snout split into a savage grin that revealed great fangs, dripping with venom. A sound began, a dead, hollow clicking sound that Gennie identified as the noise made by the things as they tapped their claws together in anticipation of a slaughter.

"Gholans! Those are *Gholans!"* a shaking voice whispered somewhere behind Gennie. Terrified whispers took up the name, realizing what it was that was about to take their lives in a frenzy of gore and death. Fighting to gain a grip on her terror, Gennie clutched a quiet Rheann in a fierce hug as she remembered the stories of the Gholans that she had heard as a child.

Frightening hearthtales, stories to make children mind their manners and go to bed early-these had been the tales of the bloodthirsty Gholans, an evil race of hateful beings that had existed in the ancient past. Gennie remembered her mother telling her of these wicked creatures that had lived deep within the darkest caves, in the farthest reaches of the northern ice swamps, and in places so foul that mankind stayed far from them. They ate human flesh, killed each other for sport, and some said that they worshipped a god even more foul than Balroth.

Yet these things were no hearthtale. They were real. Gennie could smell their gagging, reptilian stench that made her skin crawl with revulsion. Their unintelligible gibbering struck a chord deep within her, and threatened to paralyze her with fright. They continued to materialize from the fabric of the darkness until *scores* of them stood revealed in the firelight. Their black eyes held no remorse, no pity. Only death.

Gennie fought her fear as she watched the deadly Gholans stalking closer to the crowd, pausing only a few short yards away from Tabor and his naked blade. Her heart pounded in her throat as she watched the burly farmer overcome his own terror. With a mighty yell, Tabor raised his sword and rushed the three Gholans nearest himself. His cry was echoed by his fellows, and the lot of them attacked the horde of hideous creatures.

Tabor's first swing lopped off the ugly head of the first Gholan, but the other two moved almost faster than thought as they darted inside Tabor's sword range and slashed his naked midsection with their wicked talons. Scarlet slashes appeared on Tabor's muscular body as if by magick, and he fell to one knee. Instantly, he was covered with slashing, biting Gholans, and the rending, tearing noises suddenly sickened Gennie more than anything else had in her life.

The battlecries of the other farmers turned immediately to similar screams of agony as they met opponents who moved faster than anything they had ever seen, and whose razor-sharp claws killed with every vicious swipe. The ground was literally swarming with the monsters, and they threatened to engulf the defenders in a wave of death.

Gennie watched the slaughter for only a moment, then she turned and began to thrust her way through the throng. As the stench of their terror threatened to overcome her, she pushed forward. All fear for herself had vanished with the attack of the Gholans, and one thought now occupied her mind: Rheann must be saved. She broke into a run as she cleared the edge of the crowd, and her flight spurred the frightened townspeople into motion as they finally found the strength to flee the destruction. Gennie made for the southernmost building, a large common barn and stable. People were all around her, fleeing as fast as they were able.

Rheann's cries had ceased, and Gennie stole a moment in her rush to look at her daughter only to find her wide-eyed and staring, gazing at nothing as they hurried to safety. A scream just a few yards away and off to her left drew her attention. She glanced in that direction and saw something that horrified her again, nearly pushing her mind to the breaking point. The young juggler, Erin, was being throttled by one of the riders who had been 'dead' only moments before. Gennie heard a sharp crack as his neck snapped in the steely grip of the rider, and the boy's cry was abruptly cut off.

The rider's eyes, again glowing scarlet in the night, betrayed no emotion as he cast aside Erin's corpse and looked around for new prey. Other riders had awakened, and were now wreaking havoc among the terrified folk of the two villages.

Just then, Gennie slammed into the barn door, nearly knocking herself down as she did so. At the sound, the nearest rider's head turned in her direction, and he started to move towards her. Gennie's free hand fumbled at the large latch for an eternity before she managed to get it open, and she slipped quickly inside and engaged the flimsy lock just as something slammed heavily into the door from the other side.

The dreadful screams of the others being butchered outside assaulted her as she turned toward the dark interior of the barn. Her mind worked furiously as she hugged her silent daughter tightly to her breast, searching for a way to save them both. A loud hammering commenced on the door of the barn. Gennie whirled at the sound only to see that the old wood was already beginning to splinter under the onslaught.

Outside the barn, men, women, and children lay dying and dead, their blood sprayed in great scarlet rivulets across the dusty ground. The fighting men of both villages had been killed within the first frenzied moments of combat, and now the reanimated riders mingled with the repulsive and malevolent Gholans, killing every human they could find. Fires set by the riders made the shadows dance wildly as buildings were consumed by hungry flames. Screams from within told of a few unfortunate people who had thought themselves safe behind those locked doors, now burning alive in flaming prisons.

Some who tried to escape into the night found themselves attacked from behind by the lightning-fast Gholans, and many others met their doom at the hands of the corrupt, scarlet-eyed riders. Jor Dayne had mounted his horse and was riding about, killing the terrified townspeople with great, cleaving slashes of his massive blade. His hideous yet beautiful laughter filled the air as the number of dead mounted, and his blade bled crimson to its hilt. The screams of the dying sang in his black heart.

Spinning his horse about, he saw three riders engaged in an attempt to batter down a door to an old barn. It was not yet ablaze, but Jor Dayne decided on a more direct approach. Grinning savagely, he spurred his horse toward the structure, already savoring the impending deaths of those inside.

Gart shifted the deer's carcass on his shoulders as he walked, redistributing the load. His feet followed a tiny path through the thick vegetation of the forest, tracing a little known trail of his that led to the town that lay just a mile or so away. Darkness had fallen, yet his easy stride never wavered as he steadily picked his way through the foliage.

He carried the extra weight without much thought; his life as a farmer had hardened him to such labors. His left hand steadied the deer draped across his back and he held his powerful longbow easily in his right. The quiver of arrows that bumped against his hip as he walked held a full load of twenty clothyard shafts, and he had not lost a single arrow during his hunt. In truth, Gart had only needed one shot to kill the animal, but he had allowed the hunt to last long past the point of necessity so that he could ponder the dreams again. They had been especially vivid the last few nights, the powerful images flitting across his sleeping awareness and leaving their marks for him to examine in the light of day.

Looking up, Gart saw the light from the festival. A frown creased his scarred features for a moment, but then a grin appeared upon his face as if by mistake as he thought about his Gennie. He knew that she would be having a wonderful time at the festival by now, and he silently berated himself for not arriving sooner. She was so tolerant of his moods, to let him slip away for hours at a time so that he could try and come to terms with his dreams. Yes, Gart knew that Gennie was a treasure. Her love was unconditional and true, something he never thought he would find in this world. He quickened his pace a bit as he thought of his bride. Seeing her beautiful face always had the power to cheer him, and the thought of his sweet little daughter, Rheann, made him smile even more.

Drawing closer to the edge of the forest, Gart began to hear the noises of the crowd, the yelling that seemed to indicate that the bagatt game had not yet ended. Gart's frown returned. He had never heard of a game lasting so long after dark.

He stopped on the path, listening, looking at the glowing light of the festival torches over the trees. The crowd's noise seemed...odd. He closed his eyes and focused on the sounds, trying to decipher the garbled voices from afar.

Without warning, a vision more powerful than any of his dreams smashed into him with almost tangible force, paralyzing him, and he knew that somehow, he was seeing through someone else's eyes. He saw a pair of old wooden doors shatter under the force of a massive horseman, heard himself screaming in terror so absolute that it held him immobile. The horseman reined in his mount, and Gart saw his eyes, flaming yellow serpent eyes that burned into his own. One great hand reached for him, and he heard himself scream again. Then the vision was gone.

Gart gasped as his paralysis lifted and he found himself still deep inside the forest. The scream from his vision still rang in his ears. In an instant, he realized that the scream had followed him from within, but now he recognized it. It was Gennie.

In one fluid motion, Gart dropped the carcass from his shoulders and exploded into a run, hurling himself through the forest towards the town. He became a pale blur, moving swiftly through the darkness. Gart reached deep within himself, pushing his body to its limits and beyond as he raced at breakneck speed through the grasping trees.

The screams grew louder as he drew closer to the town, and Gart saw the trees before him start to thin out as he neared the forest's edge. A tiny part of his mind registered the fact that the light he had taken for festival torches now obviously came from many, much larger fires. The smell of smoke reached his nostrils then, accompanied by the awful stench of burning flesh.

As Gart burst free of the forest, he picked up speed over the flat ground that separated the trees from the town, now only a quarter of a mile away. The fire's source could now be clearly seen as all of the buildings blazed furiously, sending flames and thick, black smoke high into the night sky. Still racing, his feet pounding against the dusty earth, Gart pulled an arrow from his quiver and set it to string.

He could now see the small shapes darting about in the dancing light of the flames, inhuman shapes that were tearing into the thirty or so humans that remained alive. Gart snarled as he watched the townspeople screaming and flailing ineffectually at the slashing creatures, only to see gouts of their own blood pour from mortal wounds. Gart also marked several other targets, corrupt men with glowing scarlet eyes. Lastly, he began to look for the huge horseman he had seen in the vision. His rage began to boil within him, and he knew that he would not be able to control his terrible magick for very long.

As Gart reached the edge of town, he saw several of the hideous little beings turn and race towards him with frightening speed. Still in a full run, Gart pulled his bow to anchor point and loosed. Before the first foul thing fell to earth, an arrow protruding from one of its eyes, Gart had already nocked another shaft, and he let that one fly as well.

Within the space of a few heartbeats, Gart felled six of the wicked creatures, and their fellows checked their headlong attack as if sensing that he was not easy prey. They began to circle him cautiously, and more of the foul monsters joined the trap with each passing moment.

Gart skidded to a stop and began to loose arrows as fast as he could put them to string. His right hand was a blur as he whipped arrow after arrow at the inhumanly quick Gholans. For all their speed, the monsters were helpless against the flying death that slammed into their hideous bodies. After loosing a few arrows at the foul-smelling men that aided in the slaughter, Gart realized they seemed to have little effect on them, save for knocking them down. He did not even take the time to swear to himself at this revelation. Instead, he turned his attention solely to the ugly monsters that now surged towards him, brandishing their talons and gnashing teeth. These, Gart knew he could kill.

As he aimed, loosed, nocked, and aimed again, Gart searched the night for the horseman, and for Gennie. He could see the barn doors, hanging in shards from bent hinges, and he saw movement within. Gart shifted his stance to face the ragged opening, obviously the portal he had seen in the vision, but for now he could only try to kill as many of the attacking Gholans as he could.

Never tiring, Gart continued to launch his deadly shafts, thankful that he had a full quiver that day. However, his store of arrows rapidly depleted, and suddenly, they were gone. Fully a score of the beasts had died, but there yet remained a small army of them, and they began to tighten their circle around Gart, clicking their claws in anticipation of their next victim.

Feeling the magick welling up inside himself, Gart gripped his great ash bow in both hands and prepared to use it as a bludgeon. A flash of memory burst in his mind for only an instant, and he remembered his dreams. The woman, his dream-self, had faced odds like this, but she had used her infernal magick to save herself. Fury ripped across Gart's scarred face as he clamped down on his power, pushing it deep into himself where he would not be tempted to use it. Magick was evil, and he knew that if he used it against these demons, he would be no better than they.

The first Gholans darted in, feinting at Gart's legs. Gart swung his heavy bow at the retreating monsters and realized too late that it had been a ruse. Searing pain erupted across his back and shoulders as another creature landed on him and slashed viciously with its razor-sharp talons.

With his left hand, Gart reached up and snatched the brute from his back, gripping it tightly by one bony ankle. It reeled and thrashed in his grip, but Gart's anger lent him strength, and he began to swing the vile creature about, using its very body as a weapon against its brethren.

The other beasts slashed and bit at the hapless Gholan in Gart's fierce grip, until it was an unrecognizable hunk of gory meat. This Gart threw away, and he then began swinging his bow at the frenzied monsters again. On all sides, the great bow smashed into the creatures, killing them by ones and twos.

Gart could feel his magick singing within him, trying desperately to wriggle free of the bonds he had placed on it, but he threw more shackles on his power until he held it firmly once again. For an eternity he fought, battering his foes until his forearms were soaked to the elbows in thick Gholan ichor, and still the little monsters attacked from all sides.

At that moment, the great rider came galloping out of the barn, dragging Gennie, his dear Gennie, by her hair. Her face was bloody and bruised. At the sight of his terrified wife being handled so, Gart's rage consumed him. He barely heard the evil giant's laughter.

As if at a signal, the Gholans made way for the huge warrior and his captive, completely disengaging from their attack on Gart. But Gart took no notice of the Gholans. The rage at seeing his Gennie held so was almost blinding, and Gart gave himself to his fury.

Yet unseen by the massive horseman, Gart burst into action, springing to the nearest Gholan body that held one of his arrows. With a terrible rip, he yanked the gory shaft from the monster and set it to string, intending to take the rider from his seat with one shot.

Gart's stomach clenched in revulsion as he heard the rider's cruel laughter, coupled with his wife's screams of pain. The magick that had been trying to free itself writhed and heaved within him, threatening to explode from him, but somehow, Gart reined in his power, straining his body to the breaking point. For an instant, he felt that his magick would tear him apart. Then he fettered the roiling power within himself one last time, though it threatened to break its bonds at any moment.

With shaking hands, he aimed at the horrific rider and loosed. For an instant, Gart thought his shot sped true, but his aim had been off. The arrow struck a glancing blow and was deflected by a patch of plate armor on the great monster's shoulder. The laugh that had been continuously floating on the heated night air ceased instantly, and burning yellow eyes turned to focus on Gart. Gart trembled with rage bordering on madness, and with power contained in a vessel about to burst.

Through a haze of fury, Gart watched his wife being held a foot off the ground by her blood-streaked hair, at the mercy of a huge Daemon. His questing hands found another arrow near him, and he wrenched it free of its fleshy prison. Gart nocked it quickly as he saw his wife's tears carving wet furrows down her bloody cheeks. Her screams tore into his heart. He had to end this madness now.

"My, but you're a feisty one!" Jor Dayne's lovely, hideous voice reached Gart's ears, and the young farmer forced himself to breathe deeply to calm himself as he aimed. "And valiant as well! 'Tis a shame that you will die just as this thing here will." The giant shook Gennie for emphasis, and a pained cry escaped her lips.

Gart's teeth bared as a naked, unfathomable hatred showed on his brutally scarred face. He sighted carefully on the giant's vulnerable throat, but then the massive brute used his sword hand to pull aside his own breastplate, giving Gart a clear shot at his heart.

"You wish to try again? Here then, have at it! Jor Dayne fears nothing, and least of all do I fear such a pitiful fool as you!"

But before Gart could loose, a powerful blow was struck to the side of his head. His final arrow suddenly stood quivering in the dirt only a few feet away. Gart reeled with the force of the blow, and went down to one knee. He tried to look around, but only had time to see a pair of booted feet as a rider struck him again, sending him towards a spinning darkness. He fell facedown onto the hard-packed earth, fighting desperately to retain consciousness.

"Ignorant fool!" Jor Dayne's words filtered through Gart's mind, taking hold only tenuously through a mist of pain and rage. "It is useless to fight us! In the end, you will all kneel to my master, Mordak, or you shall die like the pitiful creatures you are!" The laugh, Jor Dayne's cold, bloodthirsty laugh, echoed again through the night.

Gart's strong hands clutched and clawed the earth hard enough to crack his fingernails as he tried to crawl in the direction of the cursed Daemon, towards his wife's screams. Blood from a scalp wound ran into his eyes as he sought to raise his head. He saw the horseman smoothly dismount from his horse, still holding Gennie aloft, her hair clutched tightly in his left hand. She had passed the point of exhaustion, and now hung limply, her tears mingling with blood and spattering the dusty earth below. Jor Dayne readied his sword for a final thrust.

Gart's bloody fingers closed on the broken handle of a bagatt stick, lying forgotten in the dirt. A burly, scarlet-eyed rider stepped close, sword-hand upraised, ready to deliver the final blow. Desperately, Gart kicked out at the rider's feet, tripping him. The bulky creature toppled towards Gart, who swung the weighty handle with all of his failing might, connecting with the side of the rider's skull with a sickening crack as it fell. The downward arc of the falling sword shifted just enough to glance off of Gart's already battered skull, instead of cleaving it. As the ruddy light left the twice-dead rider's eyes, its body collapsed atop Gart's feebly struggling form.

"Gennie . . ."

Gart whispered his beloved's name as the breath was knocked out of him, stealing his awareness at last. Gennie's agonized scream followed him into that cold dark place, and then Gart knew no more.

Chapter 18

Pain ripped through Gart's throbbing head, and he slowly opened one eye. He could not see much through the red haze of agony that engulfed him, and he realized he could barely breathe because of the crushing weight that held him down. Straining muscles he never knew he possessed, he managed to roll the weight off of himself and sit up. Smoke drifted lazily through the air, obscuring much from view, but dawn appeared to be less than half an hour away. For a moment, he tried to remember just how he came to be lying in the dirt, but the memory eluded him. Wincing, he pushed himself up to a kneeling position and noticed that his hands and forearms were coated with a sticky, brownish substance. He absently wiped his hands on his shirt and then looked around, still comprehending little of what he saw. Silent moments passed until the dawn slowly illuminated the horrible scene of gore and death that surrounded him.

Scores of bodies lay before him, all torn, bludgeoned or slashed to pieces. The blood of men and monsters mingled, changing the dusty earth to a red-brown muck beneath the still forms that lay everywhere. Gart saw many of the monsters had his own arrows lodged firmly in their bodies, and then the memory of the night before finally returned to him.

He remembered Gennie, held by her hair by that monstrosity that called himself Jor Dayne. Gart's stomach clenched as he remembered her screams, and then it convulsed sharply, sending the remnants of his last meal to the ground in a rush.

With a strangled cry, he lurched into motion, the awful memory of his wife's pain goading him into action. Gart called Gennie's name again and again, his rasping voice falling flat in the pre-dawn stillness.

His booted feet quickly became mired in gore and mud as he searched the bodies for any sign of his wife. He avoided the Gholans, somehow afraid that they might not be truly dead, but his well-aimed arrows had been quite enough to kill them. Gart noted with horror that many of the dead humans had a chewed aspect, and he knew without a doubt that the Gholans had fed well last night. Though it sent bolts of searing pain lancing through his head, Gart hurried his search.

Scanning the area where he had last seen the dire horseman attack his wife, Gart at first found nothing but the bodies of others. He recognized many of the blank, empty faces as men and women of his own town. Tears began to slide down his scarred cheeks as he stepped from one to another, in each face finding only the horror of a death borne by the hands of a massive daemon and his minions.

Gart paused alongside the body of a farmer that he knew. Old Jacob's eyes held an odd look of surprise, as if he had been astonished to see his belly ripped open by Gholan talons. More bodies had been piled about Jacob's corpse, and this pile drew Gart's attention. He began to pull the bodies away so that he might see those underneath, and then he saw one fragile hand poking out from the jumble of bloody limbs. It was a hand that had held his own countless times.

With a scream, Gart frantically wrenched the remaining corpses away from Gennie and threw them aside. She lay on her back, her beautiful face staring upwards into the growing light of a new dawn. Gart carefully cradled her in his trembling arms as new tears slipped across the ragged terrain of his face.

Gart tried to tell himself that she looked as if she were only asleep. He smoothed her matted hair and cleaned her blood-spattered face as best he could with his fingers. He tried not to look at the horrible sword wound that gaped in the center of her chest. Quickly, Gart's composure began to crumble, and soon he was sobbing uncontrollably as he rocked his wife's body in his arms. His tears fell like rain, landing upon Gennie's upturned face, washing some of the sticky blood away.

For an eternity, Gart held her. He remembered her unconditional love, the sweet music of her laugh. Gennie had been the only one to offer him understanding, trust, and affection. Since childhood, Gart's heart lay behind thick walls of anger and mistrust. He had built them as a child to keep himself safe from a cruel home and a crueler world, but Gennie had seen past it all. Gennie had effortlessly glided past those defenses and somehow seen Gart as he could have been, should have been, as he wanted to be...kind, noble, and full of laughter. She had made him believe that one day, the real Gart would emerge from behind those walls. And now it was all gone, taken by a monster with one vicious thrust of an unholy blade. Gennie was gone.

He threw his head back and sobbed in pain and anger, howling his grief into the sky. Gart's hoarse screams rose up to meet the rising sun, telling of an agony far worse than any of his physical wounds. He fell into the abyss, wondering how he could go on, why he should bother to keep breathing and living without Gennie.

With a gasp, Gart whipped his head towards the burning remains of the barn. His voice rasped out, "Rheann! Rheann, baby, I'm here!" As quickly as he could, he gently laid Gennie back on the ground and staggered to his feet, still calling for his little girl . Gennie had last been in the barn, Rheann must have been with her there, Gart reasoned. Even as the thought crossed his mind his heart sank, for the barn was a fiery ruin; nothing could have survived within.

His unsteady feet brought him as close to the barn as the remaining flames would allow. The heat began to sear the battered skin of his face and hands long before he reached what was left of the big barn doors, and Gart fell to his knees in agony. Just then, the giant timbers of the walls finally gave way, collapsing and expelling waves of heat, flames, and smoke that drove Gart stumbling away from the wreckage on his hands and knees. As he hastily crawled away from the fire, his hand closed upon something soft and he reflexively clutched at it. When he was outside the fire's reach, he brought it up to his stinging eyes and found that it was a tiny shoe. He knew that shoe. He had made it with his own two hands, had made it for his darling little daughter. And there was blood on the side of it.

Gart sat up and gazed numbly at the shoe, dazed and frozen in place. First Gennie, and now Rheann. They had been perfect, so wonderfully alive only hours before, and now they were as dust. Gone forever. He would never hear their laughter again, and most likely, his own was gone as well. He cried again, sobbing quietly as he gazed at the shoe and remembered Rheann's smile, her laugh, her voice, and how her little arms would squeeze his neck so hard when she would hug him.

Suddenly, Gart fell silent, bowing his head, and he sat in silence for a time. Slowly, Gart felt his love for Gennie and Rheann being pushed away, shoved into a deep, darkened corner of himself. The black grief that had nearly overwhelmed him faded away, and in its place blossomed something new, a powerful, driving passion that whirled and danced upon the fine line between sanity and madness. His body seemed to pulse with it, and slowly, it brought him back from the depths of despair.

It was hate. Pure and uncontrollable hate grew in him and turned his already-tortured soul to ice. Gart's tormented stomach knotted painfully as his hatred grew. The sheer power of it sickened him, and yet it was sweet. Although his bitterness felt strong enough to split him in twain, Gart knew that it would also keep him alive.

"Jor Dayne..." Gart's voice strained through the tight line of his mouth. "That was his name. Jor Dayne. And his master was Mordak. I'll find them both, and they'll pay for this. Yes...they'll pay." His hatred burned within him, causing his magick to swirl and roil within him like a thing alive. A lifetime of restraint suddenly crumbled under the strength of his rage, and Gart embraced his power for the first time. Reaching into himself, Gart felt his power swell, and he encouraged it to new heights until he thought he would burst. But he did not. Somehow, Gart's passion helped him to maintain control over his foul magick. Looking inward, he started to explore it, and he felt its reach, its strength.

Gart got to his feet and dropped the tiny shoe. He slowly raised his arms and pointed both hands at the burning remains of the barn, his daughter's tomb, and released his power in a dizzying rush. The magick reached the charred timbers that still stood, and smashed them aside like matchsticks, scattering burning debris in all directions. Fiery buildings on either side of the barn collapsed as Gart's power shook their smoldering foundations, driving clouds of dark smoke up into the already sooty air. A grim, deadly smile slowly spread across his face as he saw the damage that he was now capable of inflicting.

With this magick, he knew he would destroy Jor Dayne. So, too, would Mordak fall.

Gart quickly shut off the flow of his power, and then he looked at Gennie once more. His icy eyes traveled the length of her silent, unmoving body, and he noticed that one of her delicate hands was held in a tight fist.

He walked to her body and gently lifted her clenched hand so that he could examine it. Gart pried her slim fingers apart, only to find the gleaming emerald gem that he had given her-the same gem that the Mage had given him. She had painstakingly replaced the stone from her only other necklace with the green gem, and had secured it around her neck with a flourish, twirling and laughing with delight. She had adored the gift, and had never been separated from it. Now the sight of it filled Gart with loathing for the Mage, and with another pang of grief for his beloved. He took the necklace from her palm and tied it firmly behind his neck so that it dangled in the hollow of his throat.

Looking over his shoulder at the debris of the barn, Gart saw that it burned still, with flames higher than himself still dancing among the old timbers. He couldn't leave Gennie behind, lying in the sun for the crows. He knelt down and carefully gathered her in his arms. Moving slowly, Gart walked towards the barn, pressing his cheek to her forehead and whispering quiet words of love and sorrow. Gradually, the heat became almost too much for him to bear, and he stopped, clutching Gennie tightly for just a few moments more. Tears flowed freely down his cheeks one last time, carving furrows through the soot and ash on his battered face.

Searching within himself for the power, he found it eager to answer his call. He imagined Gennie rising out of his arms and he felt her weight lift away as she floated before him, her body shimmering in the heat. He sent her higher, and higher still. Gart moved her until she floated over the center of the shattered barn, then quickly lowered her into the flames so he would not see her burn. His gaze fell to the tiny shoe that lay in the dirt, and with a flick of his power, sent it into the flames after her.

The sun slowly rose further, giving the world its gift of heat and light for another day. Gart moved among the silent corpses, savagely ripping free arrow after gore-covered arrow. He filled his quiver with his own arrows as well as any other undamaged shafts he managed to find, though those were few. He found a good sword under one of the foul-smelling men that lay decapitated there, and relieved the dead fiend of his scabbard as well. He looked briefly for a horse, but found none. All had been taken by the evil ones, or left dead in their traces as food for the vile Gholans.

When he had gathered as much edible food as he could find and loaded it into an old pack, Gart searched for the tracks of the foul marauders. He found them following the road that led to the north, which he knew would turn westward towards New Caldea, and farther west, towards distant Laro. Without looking back, Gart strode quickly towards the forest on a northwesterly path, leaving his old life behind him, hoping the shortcut would bring him face to face with his quarry as soon as possible. Ghostly, mocking images of Jor Dayne filled his mind, and he started to make plans-brutal plans. Vengeance would be slow and painful, Gart decided, and onward he walked.

Thus occupied, Gart was completely oblivious to the three tiny figures that emerged from the forest to the west. They moved silently, making no more noise than the vague whisper of a breeze. They watched Gart's retreating figure disappear into the forest, and then they began to move about the carnage.

They were four to five feet tall, and though they shared the stature of the Gholans, they were as different from the vile swamp-dwellers as day was to night.

Their bodies were clad in simple greenish tunics, and yet the pattern almost seemed to shift as they moved, being equally difficult to see in grass or forest. Tight sashes of the same color as the tunics belted their waists, and these bulged with hidden objects nestled comfortably within. Knives of stunning workmanship hung at their hips, and each figure carried an oddly-shaped short bow that curved sharply away from the archer.

Their flesh was pale and clean, and it seemed to shine in the morning light. Where the Gholans' eyes were bulbs of pure jet, the eyes of the newcomers were more humanlike, and they glittered with intelligence. Like tilted jewels, they sparkled in the sun, and tears ran freely over their beautifully sculpted faces as they took note of the dead.

Normally choosing to live apart from men-to the extent that most thought them nothing more than a fable-these were the Weya. An ancient race, they lived in the deepest forests, the highest mountains, and many places nearly unreachable by man. There was even said to be a Weya stronghold deep beneath the ocean, but only the Weya and the fish knew for certain.

So long-lived that they seemed immortal, the Weya had existed long before the earliest memory of mankind, and had seen the rise and fall of empires long since vanished from the faded memory of man. Exquisite craftsmen, they created works of astounding beauty and function, and their knowledge of nature and the elements was unparalleled. It was said that the Weya knew magick, and they could use it to turn unsuspecting travelers into crows and snakes, but this was far from true. They did, indeed, have power, but it was the power of life that they revered.

What men would call magick was left to the few Weya Lormages that followed that path of power and responsibility. Lormages were respected in Weya society, and held in high esteem, for to them was left the charge of shielding the Weya dwelling places from the prying eyes of man. A man could travel directly through the center of a thriving Weya encampment and never know because of the gentle, persuasive arts of the Lormages. This is how they most often used their abilities. The more powerful, destructive magick took its toll on their small bodies, sapping even near-immortals of life and energy.

Otherwise, the Lormages used their talents to nurture, to grow, and to heal.

These three Weya were rangers and hunters. They had roved far from their village, and had been drawn to the site of the massacre by the deep sense of wrongness that had assailed them even from over a day's ride away. Such terror and death had created echoes in the ether that had left many Weya restless and agitated. These had set out in search of the disturbance, and were sickened to their core when they found it.

The Weya had little contact with humankind, seeing the younger race as children lacking in knowledge, patience, and experience. They disliked how warlike humans could easily be, but Weya also saw in them a great capacity for good, and it was this trait that the Weya loved.

To see them so, hacked to pieces by a butchering, remorseless enemy, wrenched the hearts of the rangers. All three cried unashamedly as they surveyed the still bodies of men, women, and children that had seen their last festival. They also examined the dead Gholans, mortal enemies of the Weya, and noted the vast number of them that littered the field.

Weya hated the Gholans because they were undeniably evil. They corrupted everything they touched, and scarred the very land they lived upon. Gholans hated everything around them, and considered the killing of Weya children to be a delicious thrill. Wars of necessity had been fought with those creatures until the Weya had finally driven them into their swamps and caves, scattered them until they no longer posed a threat to Weya or men.

But the sheer number of them here indicated that some force had united them, and the Weya rangers realized the dire possibilities that such a thing suggested. The bodies of the foul-smelling men had nearly crumbled into dust, and this spoke of magick used to ill effect. The largest male bent to examine one, and estimated that it had been dead for at least two weeks. However, it had apparently fought yesterday, and had only fallen when it had been partially decapitated by a lucky sword stroke. The magick necessary to achieve such evil manipulation of the dead could only have been wielded by one wicked person: Mordak.

The bowmaster of this hunt, Tian by name, turned his gleaming emerald eyes to his wife, and a wordless communication passed between them. Krisa nodded to her mate and turned towards the forest. She broke into a trot that slowly accelerated into a Weya long-run, a pace that would carry her the forty or so miles to their traveling village long before the sun reached its zenith at noon. She would be utterly spent upon arriving, but she would be able to carry news of these baleful tidings. The Lormages would know what to do.

Tian turned to the remaining Weya, a younger male, and spoke in the quiet, elegant tongue of his ancestors.

"Stay here and await the others. Krisa's news will have more of us here by nightfall, and I'd rather they not fall into some Gholan trap. See to the dead as best you can, but remain watchful." A scowl crossed the younger Weya's face, and Tian lay one hand on his friend's shoulder. He knew that the youth, only ninety years old, would not wish to stay.

Tian continued, pointing in the direction that the human had gone. "I must follow that man and divine his purposes. If he knows where these evil ones went, then I must find out what he knows so that I may alert our elders. Your task here is equally important. Perform with honor, young Rask."

Surprised, Rask swelled with pride at the request, worded in such a way that it indicated Tian's implicit trust in him to do his duty well. He nodded, then moved away to begin his labors of moving the dead into the fiery remains of one of the shattered buildings, sending the souls of the dead to the stars on the rising flames.

Tian watched his young friend work for a moment, grateful to know that the dead would no longer lay sprawled under the sun. Their bodies would be treated with dignity at the last. A deep feeling of foreboding came over him, and he knew this would be a scene repeated in the future.

With a wave to Rask, Tian turned northwesterly towards the forest where the wounded human had headed not long before. He started off at an easy trot, angling towards the woods so he could remain unseen from the road. He would catch up to the blonde human soon enough.

Chapter 19

Alyssa crawled quickly through the narrow, horizontal passage that led to the next phase of the obstacle course. She had sheathed her Jidaan and had a long knife in her right hand. If one of Brunar's stuffed targets had come at her just then, she would have stabbed it, exactly as she had been taught to, but none came. She looked at the crack of faint, flickering light ahead that was her destination. Somewhere behind her, a muffled thud and a grunt informed her that the others were close behind. She quickened her pace, trying to remain as silent as possible, just as Brunar had instructed her before this training session had begun.

Pain began to creep into her muscles as she moved, the deep, burning ache of a long day of training finally catching up with her. Alyssa had already negotiated at least eight different chambers during this exercise, and each was more difficult than the last, especially for one of her stature. The first chamber had held a sheer wall that must have been at least a hundred feet in height, and no decent handholds to speak of. Alyssa remembered the pang of envy that had struck her as she had watched Layton scale that wall like a lizard, but she and the others had followed soon after, climbing only a little less swiftly.

A smile spread across Alyssa's face as she recalled having the mighty Layton come to her quarters one short week ago. It was late evening, and she had been sitting on her bed, experimenting with her newly heightened awareness, when she had *felt* Layton's approach. Before he had even knocked on her half-opened door, she had known that he was in great pain, and she had hurried to usher him into the room for examination.

Layton had sat on her bed and held his left forearm out for her inspection, and Alyssa had noted the purpling finger marks encircling the wrist. As she bent to probe the injury, she had commented to the young fighter, "Well, this wrist is broken, to say the least. Exactly what happened?"

Layton had blushed slightly as he recounted the events that had transpired up on the mountain trail with Nessar. Alyssa's eyes widened as she heard the abbreviated tale of Layton's attempt to help the thief use his abilities. His bravery was obvious, but he had downplayed his own role in the episode, focusing instead on Nessar's rising to the task at hand.

"And you waited until NOW to come and see me? You idiot! Next time, come to me immediately, or I'll leave you to tend to it yourself!" Layton had the good sense to look ashamed under the verbal assault from the diminutive woman. She had continued, more gently though. "That was an awful risk you took," Alyssa had chided the young fighter. "You could have been killed."

Layton's shy smile had answered her, and he replied, "Well, it's not like I planned to end up dangling off the side of a cliff, but I'm glad of the results. Nessar is too important to us for him to lose heart. It seemed he didn't believe he could really do the things that the rest of us could. I've had my arse handed to me by several men his age while I was training, so I know Nessar is far more capable than he thinks he is, especially with his magick. I just wanted to help him, that's all. He wouldn't be here if he weren't Destined to be here."

Suddenly, a mock-stern expression appeared on Layton's face, and he lowered his voice in a perfect imitation of Brunar. "'The Jidaan have always Chosen wisely!'" Surprised, Alyssa laughed out loud, inadvertently jolting Layton's injured wrist in the process.

As Layton's breath hissed through his teeth in sudden pain, Alyssa quickly apologized and went back to examining his injury. "Sorry about that. Good Goddess, Layton, you sounded just like him!"

Layton's smile returned. "Well, I do my best. Anyway, I believe Brunar. The Jidaan are a force more powerful than any I've ever heard of, and I don't doubt the dark-pommeled one Chose the right person when it Chose Nessar. He has a mind like a bear trap, and his experience probably outstrips everyone here except for Brunar. In his profession, you just don't live as long as he has unless you have some real talent somewhere."

Alyssa frowned. "His *profession*. Hmph. I didn't like the idea of having a thief among us. It made me feel really awkward around him when I first found out."

Layton cocked his head to one side. He wasn't very good at reading people, but since coming to the Keep, it seemed he was a bit more perceptive about the thoughts and feelings of others. Brunar had said that many things would change in them when their magick fully awakened, so he figured his new perceptiveness just came with the territory. Now he sensed that Alyssa had more to say. "And now?" he leaned forward to hear.

Alyssa continued to probe his injury for a bit longer, but then looked up at him with bewildered eyes. "Well, it's different now. I've always been able to tell things about people, especially when it came to their hurts and ills, but also about their...character. I guess that's as good a word for it as any. The only thieves I ever saw in the Rowook Home struck me as good-for-nothings the moment I came near them. A few of them were rotten to the core, and didn't care who knew it. They'd steal from their own family if they could get away with it. But Nessar is...well, different."

A faraway look crossed over Alyssa's face as she tried to put her perceptions of the past few weeks into words. "There is something extremely good, even noble, in him. It's kind of like a big warm spot in the middle of a block of old snow. He never shows it, of course. But I have to agree with you. I think he was Chosen wisely." Her gaze returned to Layton's face, noting how quickly he shifted his own away from hers as a hint of a blush crept up his neck. Apparently, he had been gawking at her while she spoke.

"Er, well, yes. That's what I think too." *Good recovery, Layton.* Alyssa smiled as he regained his composure. He continued more steadily. "Though, I don't think I can see into people quite like you can. All I know is that we were *all* Chosen wisely. Every one of us has a Destiny that brought us here, and his is just as important as the rest of ours. If there is anything I can do to help any of us fulfill those destinies, then I'll do it." There was a calm resolve in his voice, an unbreakable solidity, and Alyssa's keen perception felt that it came from his very heart. She was startled to find such strength in one so young, but the more she learned of Layton, the more she came to expect it.

"Well, I don't doubt that for a minute, my good man. Now let's see what I can do with this wrist." With that, she bent to her work.

After a deep breath, she had sent her awareness into Layton's broken arm, grimacing as she felt the pulped edges of bone where the forearm had been crushed as if in a vise. It had taken much less time than it once would have for her to feel the extent of the damage. Alyssa noted once again how vast the difference was between her previous ability and her newly burgeoning powers.

Without removing her awareness from Layton's arm, Alyssa instinctively reached one tiny hand towards the corner, where stood her Jidaan. As if in answer, the diamond pommel sprang to life, sending crystal shards of light dancing about the room. Using her newfound powers, she reached out with her magick and grasped the weapon. It answered her summons and smoothly floated across the short space to her waiting hand. When her fingers closed about the wooden haft, she instinctively called upon its Gift.

She had heard Layton gasp as power thrummed through them both, coursing from the glittering spear and into Layton's smashed arm. Alyssa had guided that power directly into the injury without knowing exactly how she had done so. Heat had blossomed within the bones, a healing, soothing warmth that had taken away the pain in moments, leaving only a feeling of strength and wholeness in Layton's arm.

The sparkling light from Alyssa's Jidaan had suddenly winked out, leaving the room in relative darkness compared to the dazzling crystalline flare. Alyssa's eyes were alight with triumph when she raised her gaze to meet Layton's. She had found him looking at his arm with a wide-eyed expression of wonder on his face. "Feel better?" she had asked.

For a moment, Layton did not speak. He flexed his hand this way and that, and stared at the smooth, unbruised skin of his forearm.

"I don't know what to say." His eyes found hers again as a huge smile appeared on his face. "I guess I'll start with 'thank you'! Yes, it feels better than ever!"

Alyssa beamed at her handiwork and then walked to the corner to put away her Jidaan. "Good. Don't go breaking it again this week, all right?"

They had chatted about the nature of the magick for a while longer before Layton hopped from her bed, bade her goodnight, and then trotted off towards his own chambers. Alyssa then sat down on her bed, breathing heavily. Sweat had beaded her brow, and she wiped at it with a sleeve as she lay down. Brunar had warned that invoking the Gift of the Jidaan was demanding in the extreme. That had been the first time Alyssa had actually healed someone with it, and indeed, it had felt like she had been running up a steep incline while carrying Bjarke upon her shoulders.

Now, as Alyssa crawled through the darkness towards the opening fifty feet ahead, she wondered again just how she would apply her healing Gift if she was going to be fighting all the time. Of course, she would be able to heal otherwise mortal injuries at any moment, but as far as actively hurting the enemy was concerned, her Gift was useless.

Brunar had been most inventive in training his new Guardians. Cunningly constructed dummies, traps, obstacles, and other unique training implements had been their opponents and teachers every day. The others had only just started learning how to use their weapons' gifts to aid them in battle. Brunar tended to teach them separately, so Alyssa had seen little of the others' Gifts. From talking with them, she had surmised the obvious, that Bjarke's gift of Power seemed to be the most useful in combat. His shining ruby magick was capable of moving great objects and shattering even unyielding stone. But Alyssa could only rely on her fighting skills and her own personal magick...unless she wanted to heal an enemy to death.

Alyssa smiled at the irony of that thought. She was amazed, sometimes, to hear herself thinking of causing pain and death to anyone, even the foul creatures of Mordak. But her healer's nature was strong and sure, and she knew that some infections had to be cut out to save the patient. If that could be achieved by combat, so be it.

As she neared the opening, she paused for a moment to catch her breath. The pain in her body was becoming more than just a distraction, and she realized she had better tend to it before moving into the next chamber. She reached within herself, to her own magick, and sent its energy flowing through her cramped muscles to relieve herself of the pain that had begun to throb in her legs. Layton had taught her how to do that, and Alyssa silently thanked him for the lesson as the fatigue seeped from her as if it had never existed.

Relieved, Alyssa peered out of the opening in an attempt to see what lay in the chamber beyond. She could see little past the passageway's end, but a vast sense of openness, of huge, looming space seemed to touch the edge of her senses, and the quiet lapping of water on stone drifted to her ears. Cautiously, she pulled herself as close to the outlet as she dared and looked about.

Peering outward, she saw that the crawlway in which she rested opened at a spot three feet above a stony beach, and stretching out before her lay a vast underground lake of surprising dark beauty. Alyssa's eyes opened wide as she scanned the enormous cavern, absorbing the silent majesty of the vast chamber. Her eyes were drawn to the glowing lichens that covered the steep walls of stone, each tiny plant radiating a different color of the rainbow in muted luminescence. The wash of pale colors reflected off the ebony waters of the lake, whose depths Alyssa could not even begin to gauge. It seemed to absorb light almost as efficiently as Nessar's Jidaan did, and only the wavering flicker of a single torch, firmly ensconced in the opposite wall, kept the chamber illuminated enough for Alyssa to see.

A hundred feet away and directly across from Alyssa's vantage point, another small patch of land sat between the water and the sheer walls of the cavern, another opening leading deeper into the bedrock of the mountain beyond the small beach. Everywhere else, the water lapped directly against the stone of the cave walls, so Alyssa knew that the beach on the far side of the lake was her next destination. As she slipped silently out of the passage and stepped down onto the crushed stone beneath, Alyssa saw that a pattern of wide stepping stones traced a pathway across the water to the opposite beach, thus confirming her assumption. She put her knife back in its sheath and held her Jidaan before her, waiting.

Suddenly, a gurgle in the water to her left caught her attention, and Alyssa snapped to full readiness. Already today, the young healer had been forced to fight against several wooden contraptions, built to move almost like real opponents, and Alyssa bore scrapes and bruises from those confrontations. Taking a deep breath to steady herself, Alyssa reached out with her senses again to discern the source of the noise.

She remembered Brunar saying they would be tested many times by his machines, but he also mentioned that they were not alone in this mountain. The sounds of disturbed water moved closer, and the hairs on the back of her neck abruptly stood. Fear touched her for the first time that day.

A cold reptilian consciousness swept across her mind, and Alyssa realized that whatever was drawing nearer was neither an illusion nor a wooden dummy. She crouched, peering into the dimness in search of whatever shared this chamber with her.

Suddenly, a flat, viperous head reared from the water, and Alyssa turned to face the threat. It was a snake, and its glassy eyes fastened on her own, holding her in place. Its forked tongue flicked out at her once, twice, as if testing her scent. Though it was bigger than any snake she had ever seen, the reptile's size was not what frightened her. Instead, it was the wide, flaring hood that spread out silently around its head, the unmistakable mark of the fabled water cobra.

Alyssa's eyes narrowed in concentration as she shut her fear away and forced her mind to work. She had only read about such creatures. They were thought to have vanished from the world hundreds of years ago. The only thing she knew for sure was that the water cobra was said to be one of the most dangerous living things ever encountered. They struck faster than thought, and even a small dose of their venom was supposed to be able to kill fifty men. No cure had ever been described in the old texts that Alyssa had seen, and its victims were always reputed to have died in madness and agony.

The snake's head swayed gently from side to side, and Alyssa found herself moving almost imperceptibly in time with its motion. Her eyes fastened on those of the snake, and time began to lose its meaning. As she gazed into its eyes, the danger of her situation began to slip away from her. Alyssa started to feel drowsy as she watched the snake drift closer to her. It was only a few yards away, and after a moment, she thought she could hear its thoughts. Faint whispers caressed her, and suddenly she wanted nothing more than to hear them, to understand them. If the snake would only come a bit closer, she thought she might grasp their meaning. Closer.

Suddenly, a rock came hurtling out of the darkness behind her to strike the serpent squarely on the nose. The cobra jerked its head back and hissed ferociously, but then another rock pelted it, harder than the first, and the massive snake instantly vanished beneath the dark waters of the lake. The spell broken, Alyssa jerked backwards with a gasp. She rubbed her eyes with both hands, and then realized she had dropped her Jidaan.

Alyssa turned to see Bjarke standing behind her, holding another stone in his right hand, his face a mask of determination. She shook her head to clear it of the serpent's hypnosis and smiled her thanks at the bearish man, blushing as she did so. His wide grin answered hers, and Bjarke pocketed the stone, keeping an eye on the murky waters of the lake.

Alyssa picked up her Jidaan and turned her attention to the stepping stones that led into the lake, remaining watchful for any sign of motion in the water. The stones were each roughly a foot square, and large enough to negotiate without effort. They were situated about four feet apart, enough that Alyssa had to stretch to reach the next one. As she set her weight on the first stone, Alyssa tensed, expecting the snake to attack at any moment. When nothing occurred, she relaxed a bit and stepped to the next one. As she made ready to step to the third stone, a voice rang in her mind.

Nay, lass! Look overhead!

For a moment Alyssa was confused, but she turned to see Bjarke looking sternly at her. He had not spoken, but instead had used the mindspeech that Brunar had taught them.

What is it? Alyssa *spoke* back. *The way out is there!* She pointed one finger towards the opposite shore.

Another smile sprang forth from the reddish growth of beard on Bjarke's face as he *spoke* again, *I know that, wee one, but I think that if you look directly upwards, you'll understand!*

Alyssa picked up one eyebrow at the comment, then looked up to see what appeared to be a large netted bundle hanging a score of feet above her. It was silent, but squirming violently. Alyssa squinted in the darkness until she saw that it was none other than Layton, caught handily in one of Brunar's traps. She bit her lip to keep from laughing as she noticed one hand poking through the netting in an unbelievably awkward position. Layton wiggled his fingers at her in greeting, then continued his futile escape attempts.

Nessar and Kiran had arrived by the time Alyssa stepped carefully back to the stony beach, and the four *spoke* to each other for a few moments, deciding on a course of action. Apparently, the trap somehow dulled Layton's power to use the mindspeech, else they would have heard him long ago. It also seemed to keep him from using his Jidaan properly, or he would have created a magickal gate to get himself out of the trap.

Soon, it was decided that Nessar would examine the next few stepping stones. Kiran suggested that Bjarke could throw Alyssa up to the net, where she might be able to cut Layton down. As Nessar stepped out onto the second stone to examine the next in the watery pathway, Bjarke formed a cup with his hands for the tiny healer. After firmly couching her Jidaan in its scabbard, Alyssa put her foot into the offered hands and nodded that she was ready.

With almost no effort, Bjarke stood to his full height and sent Alyssa somersaulting through the air. Using the new skills that Brunar and Layton had taught her over the past few weeks, she managed to land squarely, if heavily, on the netted bundle and heard a muffled grunt from its captive. Moving carefully, she tried to put her feet in places that did not squash the man inside. Now that she was close to him, Alyssa found that she could hear his thoughts.

Thanks for the help! This thing caught me napping. It looked like a clean shot to the other shore. Layton's embarrassed smile could barely be seen through the tight netting, but Alyssa could sense his chagrin. She anchored herself on the thick rope that held the trap and went to work.

Just hold on to one of the upper ropes, or you'll be in for a dunking when I get you loose! Alyssa pulled her dagger and began working on the topmost cords of the netting. The sharp knife sliced easily through a few select cords, and soon a large portion of the trap fell away, leaving Layton dangling from a firm one-handed grip on the supporting rope.

The young man grasped the hand of his rescuer and lowered her until he could swing her towards the shoreline, being careful to avoid Nessar as he stood beneath them, examining the next stepping stone.

After one good swing for momentum, Alyssa landed lightly as a cat on the stony beach, and Layton followed a moment later. Bjarke was grinning from ear to ear, and Layton threw a stormy look at him. That only made the big man's grin grow even more, causing Layton to throw up his hands in mock disgust. They all turned as Nessar returned to the beach after examining the next stones, and they listened intently as he outlined the traps that Brunar had set for them.

Each stone had been rigged in a similar fashion to the one that had snared Layton, and it appeared that the traps were somehow able to cut off their mindspeech, presumably to prevent the captives from calling for help.

Ness, is there some way to get around the traps? Kiran's silent question echoed in the minds of all five Guardians. *They seem so simple. What can we do?*

It's a simple trap, alright, Nessar addressed the entire group. *The problem is that there is no way around it. Every stone from there,* Nessar pointed to the fourth stone in the path, *all the way to the other side is rigged, and from what I can tell, there is no other path across the water. I poked my Jidaan down in there to check the depth, and I couldn't feel the bottom. I'd swim it, but those water cobras are deadly, and it's a far swim even for the fastest of us.*

Layton's eager mindvoice cut into the silent conversation. *Could we climb these walls and make it across the ceiling?*

Sorry, Layton, but my climbing skills are not what yours might be, Bjarke's voice replied quickly. The big man stepped to the cavern wall nearest him and ran his thick fingers down its surface. Grimacing, he looked at the slippery grime that came off on his fingertips, glowing faintly in the darkness. *Besides, this odd growth on the walls makes the stone very slick. I don't think a spider could crawl up here.* Bjarke's reply brought nods from the others.

Well, we can't stop now, Kiran's voice suggested. *What about your Jidaan, Layton. Why don't you just Gate us to the other side?*

Layton shook his head, *Brunar told me not to. He said that we needed to learn not to use our Jidaan at every step of the way. We'd exhaust ourselves needlessly, and we'd not be able to use their Gifts when we most needed them.*

That sneaky Mage! Kiran fiercely tucked a wayward strand of hair behind her ear. *Seems like he's thought of everything. Hmph! Well, let's keep looking until we find something. He'll skin us alive if we can't get out of this, and there's got to be a way, Jidaan or no Jidaan.* All eyes turned towards the dark waters of the lake that kept them from their goal. In several places, the waters rippled as long, sinewy shapes swam just beneath the surface, but no more water cobras showed themselves.

Nessar's mindvoice called their attention back to the shore. *If the lad might allow me to finish?*

Layton's face registered surprise, then embarrassment as he realized that he had cut off Nessar's explanation earlier.

As I was saying, there doesn't seem to be a way around the traps. So we'll have to just go through them. After I spring the traps, of course. Nessar turned and picked up an armful of fist-sized stones. *Keep an eye out for those blasted snakes; they give me the creeps.* The old thief carefully stepped out to the third stepping stone while the others spread out across the beach, watching for the massive serpents.

Nessar took aim and easily bounced the first rock off of the nearest stone that was known to be trapped, and a net exploded out of the water to gather in a sodden bundle at the roof of the cavern. Stepping out to the now-safe stone, he took aim again.

"Ness, behind you! SNAKE!" Kiran's shouted warning came almost too late as a hugely hooded cobra rose smoothly out of the water behind the old thief. Nessar turned to see the snake rearing over him. A look of naked horror flashed across his lined face...and he simply vanished.

The snake twitched for a moment, searching for its target. Then, faster than an eyeblink, it struck downwards towards where Nessar had been, only to bounce smartly off of a bluish haze that suddenly materialized before it. It hissed angrily and shook its head, one broken fang drizzling a greenish sludge that spitted and smoked where it hit the water. It turned, searching for something else to strike, and found Kiran standing on the nearest stepping stone.

Her face already pale from holding her Ward over Nessar's invisible body, she swung her Jidaan in a vicious sideways slash even as the snake opened its mouth wide to strike. The weapon's keen edge cut cleanly through the snake's thick body, and Kiran ducked out of the way as the creature's severed head fell heavily into the water beside her. The resulting splash and the thrashing of the snake's decapitated body sent great gouts of water over her, drenching her through, but she took no notice. Her use of her Gift to shield Nessar and the following attack on the snake had exhausted her, and she dropped wearily to one knee on her tiny island of stone. As she fought a wave of dizziness, a pair of gnarled hands steadied her. Visible once more, Nessar kept her from sliding into the cold water.

"Easy girl, we've got you," Nessar's raspy voice calmed her. More hands gently supported her until she could stand. She looked up to see Layton standing next to her, and the others eyeing her cautiously from behind him.

"Quickly, let's get you across before another comes!" Layton carefully nudged her towards the next stepping stone, and received an elbow to the ribs in response. "Oof!"

"I can make it across; I'm fine!" Kiran yanked her arm from Layton's supporting grip and nearly fell into the water, but Nessar's firm grasp saved her. The old thief could not keep the chuckle out of his tired voice as he guided her along the stones.

"Yes, yes, you've the strength of ten...watch your step. Hold on, let me finish with these traps." Somehow, Nessar had kept hold of his stones and quickly tossed them onto the remaining traps, springing them to the ceiling. Moments later, he guided Kiran's shaky steps onto the solid ground of the opposite shore. Directly behind them, the remaining Guardians quickly followed, keeping wary eyes out for more serpents. Soon, the group stood near the opening of the new passage, safely away from the water's edge. Kiran and Nessar leaned heavily on each other, exhausted from the use of their Gifts.

Suddenly, Brunar's voice echoed from farther down the passageway. It was closely followed by the Mage himself.

"What's taking you so long over there? Don't tell me you can't get past a few snakes and..." Brunar stopped short as he came upon his students, standing in a knot just outside the passage. His formerly stern expression turned to one of approval as he noted their progress. "Well, well, I see that you've made it past my slithery friends. Good!

"Friends? Those 'friends' of yours could have killed us all! Their bite is deathly poisonous, and would have eaten through us like acid had they bitten us!" Although still spent, Kiran was more than a little agitated at the presence of the huge reptiles. She never had liked snakes, and these had been the largest and most dangerous that she'd ever encountered.

Brunar turned and looked at her. "Why yes, Kiran, that's quite true. Those are the most venomous serpents known to mankind. But even so, it doesn't seem to have deterred you...any of you." He looked from one face to another and was actually pleased to see puzzlement on more than one. Turning back to Kiran, he said, "I mean, none of you gave up on your goal, am I correct?"

"Well...no." It was Nessar who spoke. "We didn't think that was an option."

A smile turned up the corners of Brunar's bearded face. "It wasn't. But you didn't know that. And yet, you persevered, fought through traps and terrifying creatures to reach your destination, and managed to do it by working together. I am pleased."

Brunar prepared to say something else, but he suddenly stopped, then looked away as if listening. He stayed that way for a heartbeat, then two.

Alarmed, Kiran's weary voice broke the sudden silence. "Brunar? Are you all right? You were telling us how wonderful we were...?" As flippant as she was, her fellow Guardians could feel her concern.

Then, as quickly as he had detached himself from them, Brunar returned. "Yes, Kiran I'm fine. We have visitors."

A collective grunt of surprise escaped the five Guardians. Then they all started talking at once, their voices overlapping. Brunar hushed them with a gesture and then pointed at Layton.

"Layton, make a gate and take us to the main chamber. No, wait, make six gates. You need the practice."

Thrilled to be able to practice the use of his weapon's special ability, Layton's face broke into an excited smile even as he moved. The youth stepped away from his fellows and unsheathed his Jidaan. Concentrating, he willed its Gift to life, and a brilliant, opalescent light burst from its pommel. Six squares of light, no bigger than a handspan, appeared in the air in front of him. These grew until each was the size of a doorway, and then Layton began to move the first one towards Bjarke.

Brunar knew that each gate had a counterpart somewhere in the world. The first gate was an entrance, and the other was its exit. In passing through one, a person could travel hundreds of miles in a moment if the wielder were strong enough to hold them open at that distance. However, handling more than one pair of gates was difficult, as was moving them about, and at such an early stage in his training, Layton would be doing well even to get them all to the main chamber from here. Two thousand years ago, Brunar had seen Dani move a score of gates no bigger than a handspan at blinding speed to intercept a horde of arrows in flight and redirect them so that they struck Mordak's attacking army head-on. She had been highly skilled, indeed.

"Layton, move them all at once. You must become proficient in using many gates at the same time, otherwise you won't be using your powers to the fullest." Brunar watched the one moving gate suddenly stop and hover in midair as Layton heard his teacher's command.

Layton, his face brilliantly lit by his weapon, nodded his assent. At first, nothing happened. Layton's gaze was focused on a spot a few feet in front of him, and intense concentration was scrawled across his boyish face. Moments passed, and the shining doorways still hung motionless in the air. Layton's face began to contort with the effort.

Suddenly, Layton's grimace was replaced by his usual, dreamy smile. Then all six of the magickal gates moved to engulf the five Guardians and the Mage, their opalescent light washing across their faces. In the brief moment before they were moved by the magick, Brunar saw their expressions range from Bjarke's awed surprise to Nessar's calm stoicism. Then the magick took them. In an instant, they all stood on the dais where they had first accepted their weapons, and the light from Layton's weapon vanished. Through the power of Layton's Jidaan, they had traveled several hundred yards through the rock of the mountains without even taking a step. Sweat beaded on Layton's brow, and he surreptitiously wiped his sleeve across his forehead, breathing heavily. The strain of using any Jidaan's Gift was exhausting, and Layton was just beginning to build the strength to use his more often.

It took a moment for everyone's eyes to adjust from the faint, flickering illumination of the cavern to the bright light of the magick, and then finally to the warm light of the main hall. However, it did not take long for the group to see that they were not alone in the cavern. Before them stood three small figures, none even so tall as the tiny Alyssa.

There were two males and a female, and they all bore similar features: bright, sparkling eyes of stunning color, shoulder-length hair, and garments made of an elusive greenish color that threatened to blend with the natural color of the stone that surrounded them. They stood proudly before the steps of the dais. The female was striking, with hair of jet and eyes of deepest emerald, and she stood slightly in front of her two male companions. The two could have been brothers, so alike did they seem; the only difference was that honey-brown hair fell to the shoulders of one, while his twin kept his darker brown hair tied off in back.

The swords that the two males wore were carried in plain scabbards on their backs, but Layton's eyes widened at the workmanship of the weapons themselves. Sheathed as they were, only the hilts and grips were visible, but the simple and elegant artistry that was evident in those pieces alone was astonishing. Layton knew weapons, and he could easily tell that these would be perfectly formed for the small hands of their wielders. He ached to get a better look at them.

In a voice that carried as music upon a summer breeze, the female began to speak. "Mighty Brunar, I am Moihra, ValElder of the Weya. My companions, Cohl and Ginn, and I have come to alert you to a great evil." Her chin was raised high, and strength radiated from her every movement. But the smoothness with which she moved made her seem more like a small jungle cat than an elf. Her grace made Alyssa feel downright boyish, and all of the men present felt a powerful attraction for the lithe Weya leader. Layton's cheeks reddened as her presence suddenly hit him with an almost physical force, and Bjarke nervously cleared his throat.

Brunar bowed deeply, then started down the steps to meet the visitors. "My lady, I have been awaiting your arrival. We are aware of the evil of which you speak, but not of its recent doings." The Guardians followed Brunar's example, bowing deeply to the Weya, and moving down the stairs as well. "Please, tell us what you have learned."

The darker-haired male spoke up. "Are these the Guardians then?" A note of uncertainty was evident in the Weya's voice, and Kiran bristled at it. *Of course we're the Guardians! Who else would we be?* But before she could open her mouth to retort, Brunar replied for them all.

"Indeed, Ginn. They are but newly Chosen. The ones you knew are long since departed from us."

From deep within Ginn's saphirrine eyes, there emerged a look of longing, of gentle sorrow. However, only the barest hint of regret seeped into his voice as he replied. "Ah, yes. I tend to forget that you are not quite so long-lived as we. I had hoped to see Dani again. She was...a treasure." For a moment, Ginn's attention seemed to wander, but then he quickly returned to the conversation.

ValElder Moihra fixed a cold stare on the Mage as she spoke. "Newly Chosen? Brunar, I hope they come to know their abilities well. We fear that Mordak will cause ruination and sorrow far worse than that which we suffered from him so many years ago." Her musical voice was grave, and the power of her words sank into the hearts of the Guardians.

"Worse? Mordak devastated the Realm last time. In what way could it be worse?" Brunar's eyes betrayed nothing, but his heart filled with trepidation at the thought of the destruction and death that had occurred so long ago. The possibility of it being greater this time appalled him.

"A fortnight ago, our scouts found an entire village decimated. Actually, it appeared to be a gathering of two villages, and it seemed that not a soul was spared. However, there were very few actual bodies to be found." A heartbeat of silence descended as Moihra took a breath before continuing. Sadness gathered in her voice when next she spoke. "There were signs of reanimation, Brunar."

The pain in the Weyas' eyes and hearts was all too clear to the Guardians. Weya had a profound respect for life and death. Since their kind so seldom died, it was a great tragedy when a Weya actually did pass away. Yet they also believed that the deceased would move on to another stage of existence, a brighter, more wondrous life than those left behind could even fathom. Reanimation, the calling back of a soul to its body solely for the purpose of controlling the dead flesh, was to the Weya as abhorrent a practice as could be found in the world. The soul would be helpless within its own body. It could only experience the horror of what its body was made to do, and do nothing to stop itself.

Brunar was visibly stricken by the news. His mouth gaped and for a moment or two, he stood speechless.

"So soon!" he finally whispered. "Goddess! To be able to reanimate the dead so soon after his escape. I had hoped he would remain weak for a time longer..." A haunted look appeared around the edges of his eyes, making him seem older by a score of years.

Kiran spoke up from behind the Mage. "You mean that Mordak can actually use the dead as his soldiers?" No fear was evident in her voice, but the underlying current of dread was felt by all the Guardians through the tenuous link of empathy they all shared. The depths of Mordak's evil were only now becoming real to them.

Turning so he could address all of his students, Brunar quickly steadied himself before replying.

"Yes, Kiran, he can. However, in the past, it took him years to build the power that is necessary for him to perform this atrocity. In the previous conflict, he only used the dead near the end, when he knew that his time was growing short, and only after he had gathered enough strength to do it. He had less than a hundred reanimates, and it was amazing he could have even that many. It takes tremendous power to do this, and for him to accomplish such a feat already. . ." the words hung in the air like a warning.

"There's no telling what he might be capable of." Bjarke's rumbling voice arose at last. "Let's get moving. This fiend must be stopped."

The others nodded their assent, and all eyes turned back to the Weya visitors. Moihra, Ginn, and Cohl saw that the faces of the Guardians were firm with determination, rather than fear. They nodded, a hint of new respect lighting their own jeweled eyes. The thought that these humans may yet have been rightly Chosen crossed the minds of the Weya.

Brunar addressed the ValElder once again, "ValElder, please show me where this happened. And clear a space for me, if you would be so kind." He gestured for the group to step away from him a bit so that he had room to work his magick.

The Weya did as they were asked, stepping back a few paces so that Brunar had a clear view of the floor in front of them. With a word and a gesture, he transformed the empty space into the same three-dimensional model of the land he had used earlier in the Guardians' dining room. He then added the script and north arrow as well as the purple spot that denoted their present location.

"We are here." Brunar pointed at the purple blot. "Where was the village that your people found?"

Stepping forward, the third Weya carefully examined the map. As he looked over it, Moihra spoke to Brunar again. "Cohl was one of those who went to view the dead. He can locate the place better than I."

After only a moment's perusal, Cohl pulled his sword silently from its scabbard at his back, and used it to point to the place on the map that he had visited. Light flowed along the blade's slender length like water, and Layton whistled softly at the sight of the Weya-made sword.

After years of handling weapons of all sorts, from all methods of manufacture, Layton had thought he had seen the best. But the slim sword that rested in Cohl's firm grip far surpassed anything he had ever seen, even in the farthest parts of fabled Huanjin in the East. The blade was thin and light, yet stronger than any metal forged by Mankind, and even from a few yards away, the keenness of its edge was evident.

Surreptitiously stepping a pace back from the other Guardians, Layton quietly unsheathed his Jidaan and looked at its blade, noticing for the first time that Weya sword and Jidaan were nearly identical in composition. Only their shape and balance were unalike. The golden runes that decorated his own blade were of a more archaic, flowing style that differed slightly from those he had fleetingly seen on Cohl's.

"Here," Cohl's voice was deep and rich, belying his size. "It was at this place you have marked as 'Tiller's Grove'."

Brunar nodded as he fixed the location in his mind. "How many? Could you tell which direction the Vile One's minions were headed?"

Cohl gestured with his sword as he spoke, "They seemed to move north and then west, along the road to Laro. Since it was such a large gathering, the tracks were difficult to read, but it appeared that at least fifty humans were in on the initial attack. Three hundred or so more were gathered in the town, and the majority of them left the site afterward, either ahorse or on foot. There were also at least five hundred Gholans in attendance as well, though nearly a third of those were killed by bowshot." He resheathed his sword in one smooth motion.

"Gholans? You mean Gholans really exist?" All eyes turned to Alyssa, whose surprise was evident. Everyone had heard of the evil creatures, but they were thought of as only hearthtales, myths. But then again, Alyssa thought, here she stood, wielding a magickal weapon and talking to the legendary Weya. She suddenly resolved to be a lot more open-minded about such things in the future.

Brunar took a moment to nod at Alyssa before reaching up to tug on his beard as he mulled this new development over. "Gholans. This is an ill thing, indeed. Those creatures have been isolated from humans for centuries." The Weya nodded. Brunar looked to Cohl for his next question. "Is there anything else you remember that might aid us?"

Cohl shook his head slowly. "We saw only the remains of the dead and the tracks made by the marauders. Some of the human bodies had already been long dead, apparently reanimated by the sorcerer, and then killed with more finality in the battle. It is certain that many of those who died at the village were reanimated to fight for Mordak, for that is his way. He uses the humans against themselves. The tracks spoke of humans, Gholans, and horses leaving the village, and many of the human tracks were laced with drying blood."

Though Cohl had been very still during his report, there was a palpable feeling that he wished to be in motion, eagerly moving towards a confrontation with the foul soldiers of Mordak. It was a feeling that they all shared.

"The only sizeable town between that village and the city of Laro is New Caldea. By now the reavers will certainly have overrun them, as well as anyone else they have run across, absorbing their people into Mordak's army. Depending on their speed, we might be able to get to Laro ahead of them and help Duke Gensen's army to ward off the attack, if that is their destination."

"Might?" Nessar's voice grated, making Brunar's head swivel to see him. "What do you mean, 'might'? With that gate thing of Layton's, and your powers, couldn't you just take us there...like that?" A curt snap of his fingers indicated Nessar's idea of speed.

Brunar's weighty gaze hid the fact that he was pleased his students were starting to trust each other's abilities. The magick was still so new to them all, at times they forgot that many possibilities were open to them. Even when they did think along those lines, they still tended to be hesitant, and that would have to change. Brunar felt that it would, in time.

However, the possibilities in this situation were few. "No, Nessar. The effort of transporting us all the way to Laro is far beyond Layton's meager experience and strength." Layton started to protest, but the Mage shushed him with a gesture. "Lad, I saw you sweating from the exertion of just getting us up here from the caverns below. I think that a trip of even a few leagues would leave you incapacitated for at least a week." Layton reluctantly nodded to his mentor. Even one league was too far just now.

Nessar was tapping his foot in impatience. "Well, if he can't do it, what about you? After all, you're the one who got us here, and we were way down in Rualtha! Can't you do the same to get us to Laro?"

"No, the Gates that brought you here were wrought by the Jidaan, not by me. I was but a conduit for their power, and that can be done but once. I can only use those Gates to unite the Jidaan with their Chosen, and that is all. We will have to ride to the coast and secure passage on a ship bound for Laro, and we must move with all speed."

The Mage's gaze traveled over his students, those who had been Chosen by magick beyond his understanding to protect the world he so cherished. The time for action had come unbidden, and he prayed to the Goddess Rowann above that he had taught them enough in their short time in the Keep, enough to defeat Mordak...enough to keep them alive.

"Guardians, we can stay here no longer. We will spend one last night in the Keep, and then we will set out at dawn tomorrow. Pack what you wish, and be ready to move out one half-hour after the morning meal. Our horses are quartered near the lowermost entrance, and you can start loading their packs tonight. We will head down the Southern Road out of the mountains to Tamaransett, and we'll spend the night there at an inn I know. The next day will see us to the port at Cohen. I've a ship in mind that will take us where we need to go from there."

For a moment, no one moved, and Brunar's words faded into gentle echoes within the great Hall until they vanished altogether. After weeks of training, each Guardian still felt as though they had only just begun to learn the ways of their magick, the powers of their Jidaan. They hardly felt like the legendary Guardians of whom fables were still told and written, and the weight of their responsibility was heavy upon their shoulders.

Nessar's gravelly voice spoke up. "So it's off to sea we go, eh?" He laid a hand on Kiran's shoulder, knowing that although she complained constantly about any time she had ever spent aboard a ship, she had secretly loved it as well. "I suppose *somebody'd* better bring her oil if she wants to keep wearing that stupid, heavy chainmail." He turned and quickly strode towards his cell, knowing exactly what would follow.

Kiran whirled towards Nessar's retreating form, her mouth gaping in outrage.

"I'll have you know that this chainmail has seen me through more fights and scrapes than you could count on fingers and toes, you old . . ." Kiran's energy was evident as she trotted to catch up with her old friend, determined to get the last word in.

Brunar watched them go for a moment before turning to the largest Guardian. "Bjarke, I have several packs of supplies in the first storeroom. Would you mind taking them to the stables, please? You should be able to get them all in one trip, my sizeable friend."

Bjarke smiled broadly as he bowed slightly to his teacher. "Don't worry, Mage. After some of the things you've made me carry over the last few weeks, some packs of gear will be no problem whatsoever. Let me just grab a few things of my own on the way, sir." He started towards his own quarters, following Alyssa and Layton as they, too, hurried off to load their own traveling packs.

Brunar then turned his attention to his guests.

"ValElder Moihra, I would be honored if you, Cohl, and Ginn would accompany me to my chambers. I can offer you rest and refreshment there, if you so desire."

A brilliant, relieved smile from the strikingly beautiful Weya leader made her answer apparent.

"You honor us, good Mage. Though we are a hardy race, and are quite capable, my companions and I have traveled over a hundred miles since dawn, and are sorely in need of even the briefest respite."

Ginn's weary smile echoed Moihra's as they followed the Mage towards his chamber. "Aye, sir. A solid night's sleep will be most welcome. The ValElder sets a fast pace, and we are most grateful for your hospitality."

Only Cohl was silent, and he did not smile. The offer of food and a night's rest was no less welcome, but the dead he had seen, so remorselessly butchered by Mordak's minions, were still fresh in his memory. Even the usually merry Weya could carry grief in their hearts, and Cohl's heart was heavy with it.

Chapter 20

As the dying scarlet sun lost its grip on the world, the evening sky ran with blazing color. As Gart crested a hill, he glanced briefly at the wondrous display that spread across the heavens, but the glory of the sunset held no beauty for him. He saw only the color of blood. Shrugging his heavy pack up higher on his back, Gart dropped his gaze from the crimson sky to the lush forest below him. Since emerging from his shortcut and regaining the road days ago, the trail he had been following had continued to lead him ever westward, taking the same route towards New Caldea that he had traveled just a month or so before. Now, looking down on the vast forest from his high vantage point, he could see the road below cutting like a crease into the blanket of green. For leagues in all directions, the lush, slumbering forest was undisturbed, except for the road and a sparkling blue lake that shimmered through the trees a fair distance northwest of where Gart stood.

He had been hiking rapidly since before dawn, and he would continue until well after the mid of night, his progress no longer impeded by the thick growth of the forest. So it had been for the last several days, always moving, always following the tracks of the murderous forces of Jor Dayne. When his stomach growled loudly enough to penetrate the haze of pain and rage that drove Gart onward, he simply pulled his rations from his pack and ate them without slowing his pace. He only stopped each night when the blinding fatigue of his muscles and mind finally overcame him, and he fell to the ground, unconscious. Upon awakening, Gart always cursed his need for sleep, scant though it was. He knew that every hour he spent in slumber widened the gap between himself and those who had murdered his Gennie and Rheann, but in the corner of his mind that retained a trace of practicality, he also knew that his battered body needed rest. It would do him no good to come upon the vile slayers only to drop from exhaustion before he could gain his revenge. Sleep was nothing more than a necessary evil, something to be endured only so that he could continue his pursuit.

Gart had long since stopped wishing he had found a horse. Back at the Grove, it had only taken a few moments of searching for him to discover that all of the horses had been taken, save an unfortunate few that appeared to have been partially eaten. Running was also lost to him, for his quarry had at least a full night's headstart, and he would do naught but wear himself out before making any real progress. Instead, he had settled into a groundeating pace that was just short of a trot, enough to tax every muscle and fiber of his being, but bearable over the long, lonely hours of his solitary trek.

Eventually, he would catch them. And they would pay.

The night began to gently unfold its cool, velvety cloak about the ancient forest as Gart followed the hard-packed road that had been worn into the earth centuries before. This was the deepest part of the wood, and on either side of the lone, weary traveler, the gathering darkness made the spaces between the trees look like doorways to other worlds. Massive trees loomed like quiet sentinels on either side of the path, stretching their majestic branches across the road's corridor towards each other to merge with the branches from those directly opposite, forming a leafy canopy that left only a few, scattered windows to the darkening sky above.

One icy blue eye searched the horizon for any sign of a camp, but if his enemies were immediately ahead of him as the tracks indicated, they were either too well hidden, or were yet too far away to be seen from the hill. Gart's other eye had been swollen shut for the first few days, but seemed to be slowly returning to its normal state. For now, one eye was all he needed.

As the young man started down the gently sloping incline, he pulled a bulging waterskin to his lips. Tepid water coursed down his chin as he drank his fill, making tracks in the road dust that had covered his scarred face.

Gradually, the forest came alive with the sounds of its many night creatures. Gart listened with only half an ear. He had been in and around forests all his life, though he had never spent any time in this particular part of the land, and he was no stranger to such noises. Soon, the melody of the evening insects played loudly in the background, nearly drowning out his weary footsteps. And onward Gart walked, drawing nearer to his enemies by the moment, planning his painful vengeance all the while.

He could feel his magick flowing through him as he moved. Since he had embraced it for the first time, back at Tiller's Grove, he had finally allowed himself to practice with it, to get accustomed to it. To *use* it. Gart practiced picking up things from the side of the road with his magick-stones, sticks, and the like. He had managed to gain much more control over it than he had ever attempted in the past. He had learned to pick up small stones, move them through the air at his command, slamming them into larger stones. The smallest ones, he had learned to crush in a sudden flex of magick, although the strain of such had cost him blinding pain behind his eyes and a trickle of blood from his nostrils. Even so, many of the boulders he had passed on the sides of the road now bore the scars of Gart's practice. All the while, Gart held an image of Jor Dayne in the forefront of his mind. Each stone he pulverized was a part of the evil rider, each twig he snapped with his powerful magick was another bone in the huge monster's body.

*If only I had learned to use this power sooner. . .*Gart crushed that thought every time it surfaced. He had done everything he could to save Gennie, had he not? *It had all happened so quickly, and . . .*again, Gart wrestled his exhausted mind into order, hating himself for having the magick, and hating himself even more for not using it to save his Gennie. *No matter,* Gart shrugged to himself. *Justice will be done, magick or no.*

The shadows slowly deepened as night brought its full weight to bear on the great forest. Gart's weariness had grown appreciably since the sun had left the sky, but his hatred gave him strength, and he continued onward. He guessed that he could continue for at least another two hours before collapsing for the night, and he pulled his waterskin up for another drink.

As he brought the unstoppered end to his lips, the sounds of the forest insects ceased altogether. A thrill ran through him, but he did not pause. He continued walking at the same pace and dropped the waterskin back to its customary position, striving to look as if he were oblivious to anything but putting one foot before the other. However, his good eye began to carefully scan the darkened woods on either side of him, searching for any sign of the attack that was certain to come. One hand strayed to the unfamiliar sword that hung on his hip. His bow would be useless if they attacked him here in the confined space of the narrow road, so he nonchalantly unslung it and began using it as a walking staff that he could drop in an instant to make room for his desperate swordplay.

As Gart loosened his sword in its scabbard, he also reached into himself to ready the magick. It churned and moved within him, eager to escape. Gart doubted that Jor Dayne was near, but he would take some of the foul ones here and now. Most likely, this would be a rear guard of some kind.

Stealthy shuffling sounds came from the road several yards behind him, yet he did not look back. The noises did not sound like booted feet, so he prepared himself to battle the hideous creatures he had seen at the Grove, the Gholans. He kept his eyes forward as he waited for them to spring their trap so that he could spring his own. A fierce glee raged through him at the prospect of avenging his wife on these monstrosities.

The shuffling sounds drew closer along with a reptilian stench, skittering up behind him, only a few yards away. Gart calculated the distance, and guessed that ten more steps would put them in proper position for him to turn and fight. The unseen attackers came closer, and Gart could suddenly hear the sounds of their wicked talons clicking in unholy delight at the prospect of tearing another unsuspecting traveler to shreds. Their awful, swamplike smell wrinkled Gart's nostrils. Only three steps more. Two. One.

Gart dropped his bow, unsheathed his sword, whirled, and slashed all in one fluid motion, cleaving two of the foremost monsters in twain. Yet behind them, Gart saw not a few, not a score, but nearly *fifty* of the vicious Gholans swarming to the attack. Unleashing his rage, Gart bellowed a war-cry as he slashed and cut with unbridled ferocity, splashing brown Gholan blood in every direction. Still, they came onward, the sheer force of their numbers forcing Gart back.

Bleeding now from several small wounds, Gart prepared to unleash his magick. As he hacked and slashed, it boiled within him, aching for release. When he could stand the strain no longer, he lowered his arms to his sides and threw his head back. Seeing their prey drop his defenses, the Gholans attacked with renewed frenzy, only to have their very bones shattered within them by the clenching force of Gart's might. Gart extended a hand towards the screaming mass of little monsters and guided his magick to pummel, crush, and break each Gholan in turn, the dead falling in heaps to the bloody road. Hideous screams of dying Gholans rent the night, and still Gart threw more power after them.

The rearmost Gholans tried to escape to the trees, but the magick found them ere they reached safety. Massive trunks were severed like twigs as Gart's ferocious power quested for the retreating Gholans, searched for them, and found them. Broken and splintered, a few of the great trees fell towards the road, crashing into their brethren across the way and leaning heavily on them for support. Gholans died as the magick found them, their repulsive bodies crushed by a force they never even saw.

When the screams had stopped, Gart shut off the flow of his magick, and dropped like a marionette whose strings had been cut. His breath came in ragged gasps, and every muscle in his body burned as if molten rock had been poured within them. Bright lights danced before Gart's eyes, and his head spun wildly as he tried to shake off the raging dizziness and nausea, the effects of releasing so much of his magick while so exhausted. Slowly, he pushed himself to his hands and knees, still panting from the exertion. Blood pounded in his ears, drowning out all other sounds of the night.

Massive beads of sweat dropped from his forehead to splatter in the dust of the road, and Gart watched them fall as he slowly regained his senses. He looked up the road, in the direction he had been traveling before the monsters had attacked, and his eyes widened as he saw several darkened shadows approaching. They bore no torches, but enough moonlight filtered through the trees to show five horsemen trotting towards him, roughly a hundred yards away, malignant power burning in their crimson eyes. With cold, strong hands, they held their unwilling mounts in control as they skittered and shied from the horde of Gholans that ran alongside them, teeth gnashing at the sight of Gart's battered form in the road before them. Gart could hear their maddened chittering, and their wicked talons played the music of death for him. Farther away, Gart could see a few larger, shambling forms, moving purposefully at the sides of the road, away from the few shafts of moonlight. He could not even guess what horrors those shadows might represent.

One of the riders carried a bow, and as he nocked arrow to string, Gart desperately tried to gather his magick for another attack. A faint stirring within him was the only answer that came, and Gart knew in a heartbeat that he was finished. He would never be able to avenge his wife and daughter.

Rage took him then, rage at not finding Jor Dayne, at not making him pay for what he had done to Gennie and Rheann. The magick flared weakly, and Gart tried to fan it, to build it to fighting strength, but the effort brought a wave of nausea that made the darkened world tilt before his eyes.

An arrow struck the dirt scant inches from Gart's hand on the road, sending showers of dirt into his face. Gart flinched, then looked up at his attackers. They would be on him in another few moments, and Gart decided to die fighting. Wearily, Gart forced his drained body to stand. His bloody sword was almost too heavy to lift, but he held it shakily before him, hoping that he could at least take a few more Gholans to the grave with him.

The next arrow took him in the shoulder, forcefully knocking him back to the ground, his blood spraying into the dirt of the road. He felt for the arrow, but only found the gory hole where it had punched through him. Mordak's foul minions were close enough now that Gart could smell the putrid breath of the Gholans, mingled with the strong sweat of the horses. Fighting against the agony that threatened to render him senseless, he pushed up to one knee, determined to die on his feet. The foremost rider had nocked another arrow, and it was just then that he let it fly. As if in a dream, Gart watched the shaft hurtling through the air towards him. Time seemed to slow until Gart could almost see the bolt's broad, sharpened head spinning as it closed the distance between them. This time, Gart knew, the rider's aim was true, and the shaft would bury itself in his face.

In that instant, Gart delved deeper into himself than ever, searching for the faint traces of magick within him. With the last strength of his failing body, he found the dregs of his power, reached out with it, and touched the speeding arrow ever so slightly. It did not stop, or veer from its path more than a few inches, but in the end, Gart succeeded. The shaft slammed into the side of his forehead, glanced off the thick bone of his skull, and buried itself into a tree at the side of the road.

Gart's blood flew again. Yet another gash opened in the tracery of scars on the right side of his torn face, and he fell backwards, unconscious, before his body settled into the dust. The Gholans yowled with glee as they saw their prey go down, and they finally broke from their keepers, rushing forward to taste of his blood and tear his prone body to ribbons. Suddenly... THWOK! TWHOK! THWOK! Three arrows pierced the bodies of the first Gholans, heaving their dead forms back into their fellows, throwing them into confusion.

A hail of arrows started flying from the trees near where Gart lay in the road, and out stepped a shining Weya, his short, powerful bow loosing bolt after deadly bolt into the milling horde of monstrosities. Every shot sped true, and several of his arrows pierced two Gholans each, so closely packed were the monsters in their rush to reach their prey. A grim look of determination was etched into Tian's face, and his bow sang a song of death for the hideous creatures in the road.

One of the riders saw the small Weya's attack, and uttered an awful, drawling shriek at the frenzied Gholans. Though furious beyond reason, the snarling, spitting Gholans obeyed his wordless command. With evil fleetness, the remaining horde split in two, each half melting into the depths of the ancient forest on either side of the road, the riders following after. In a short moment, the roadway was clear, save for the bleeding form of Gart, and Tian, his bow still at the ready.

Moving with inhuman speed, Tian unnocked his arrow and slapped it home in his belt quiver, even as he laid his bow down on the ground. He grabbed the senseless man, heaved his inert body over his shoulder, and grabbed his bow up again as he bolted into the forest on the north side of the road.

When he had picked Gart up, Tian had seen that the farmer was still bleeding from several wounds. They were not mortal injuries, but certain death was only yards away as the Gholans tried to close their trap. Gholans could easily follow a blood trail, and Tian knew there was no time to stanch the man's wounds. He had to reach safety as quickly as possible if both of them were to live.

Bloodcurdling yowls assailed Tian's ears as he rushed through the thick growth of the forest. He was strong as a Weya could be, and if need be, he could carry the unconscious man for a fair distance. But the pursuit was close behind. Tian's mind raced as he searched for a haven, a place he could rest and hide the wounded farmer.

As his feet moved swiftly and silently across the forest floor, Tian realized that the Lake of Whispered Sorrows was near. If he could reach it, there was the slightest chance that She who dwelled there could aid the wounded man. It was a risky choice, for She did not aid all who entered her domain, but facing the Gholans was not a preferable alternative.

Tian changed direction slightly, angling to the northeast, heading for the nearest shore of the lake. As he ran, he heard the wheezing yowls of the Gholans and the wordless raging of the riders as they tried to maneuver their unwilling mounts through the dense woodland. Tian's legs began to burn as he picked up his pace, but he ignored the ache and ran on. The furious howls of their pursuers told him that the Gholans had found the blood trail and were now following them. Tian silently prayed to Rowann that his legs would not fail him.

Several painful minutes passed, and just as Tian thought he could not carry the weight of the man on his shoulder one step further, he felt a change in the air, a blessed, damp coolness. The sounds of chirruping frogs and distant waterfowl reached his sensitive ears. Squinting, his jewel-like eyes searched beyond the trees nearest him, and he saw the dense forest begin to thin out. He dodged between a few more towering trees, through a stand of bushes and then skidded abruptly to a stop on the shore of the widest, most crystalline lake he had ever seen. The rising moon was reflected brilliantly in its mirrorlike surface, and Tian stood quietly for a moment, panting, drinking in air laden with the clean purity of the Lake. It soothed him, and yet he could feel the faint hint of sadness that seemed to rise from the lake on the mist that covered it here and there.

The lake was beautiful beyond any description that Tian had ever heard of it. As he stood for no more than a few heartbeats, gazing at the starlit waters of the lake, the hint of sadness quickly became more urgent, more immediate. After only a moment of standing on the shore, the faint sense of loss became as real as if it had come from the Weya's own heart. It seeped into Tian, filling him with many emotions: sorrow, loss, love, regret. The sweating Weya sighed as he let the aura of the lake wash over him, and he abruptly decided that the name was well-chosen.

A shriek ripped from the throats of the approaching Gholans as they closed in on their quarry, jerking Tian back to the task at hand. Tian knew that he had slowed in the last few hundred yards, and also that the vile creatures were closing in on his own scent and that of the bleeding man on his shoulder. Dropping his bow, Tian gently eased the man to the lakeshore and pulled his limp body into a sitting position. Reaching one hand into the nearby lake, Tian splashed water on the man's face, cleaning it, the bracing coldness bringing the unconscious man briefly to his senses. One blue eye opened and tried dizzily to fix on the strong, elegant features of the Weya that held him up.

"Friend, listen to me. Listen!" Tian's musical voice was strained with urgency, but beautiful nonetheless. Gart's newly bloodied face was still slack and senseless, but his one open eye managed to focus on the small fellow that now fiercely gripped the front of his ragged shirt. His attention was lazily drawn to the tilted, gemstone eyes of this small stranger, as well as to the upturned ears. Before he could think on these oddities, the fellow spoke again.

"There is magick in you. I have seen and felt it." The deep emerald eyes of the Weya bored into the icy blue eye that Gart groggily held open.

"This place is ancient, and powerful. There is one here who may help such as you, if your heart is pure." Gart almost tried to snort at this. Pure heart, indeed. But Tian would have none of it. He shook Gart briefly, harshly, to regain his complete attention. As he did so, he heard their pursuers crashing through the underbrush only yards away, grunting to each other in their guttural tongue. They were still hidden by the tightly-bunched bushes, but not for much longer.

"Shush! The foul ones are near. Give the Lady RaeLynn no offense, and She may be kind. Go, and Rowann be with you!"

Without another word, Tian stood up and grabbed Gart by his collar and belt, and with unbelievable strength for one so small, pitched the bigger man headlong into the cool, mirrorlike waters of the lake. He disappeared instantly into surprisingly deep water, and not a ripple marked his passing.

Moments later, a small group of snarling Gholans snuffled at the ground where Tian and Gart had been. The strong, clean scent of the Weya agitated the fell creatures, and they snarled and snapped at each other in anger as they realized that their prey had vanished. The healthy, misty air was repellent to the Gholans, and they were especially loath to even touch the clear, sparkling waters of the Lake. Snarling, they split up to search the edges of the vast tarn, never knowing that Tian was only a few feet above them, hidden safely in the boughs of a massive, sheltering oak.

Tian waited for more than an hour before he allowed himself to move once again. By then, all sounds of pursuit had disappeared completely. Still wary, the Weya dropped lightly to the ground, landing silently on the balls of his feet, holding an arrow nocked to string at the ready.

He crept to the edge of the lake and peered into it. Only the smooth reflection of his own smudged face greeted him, framed by the overhanging limbs of the oak above, and the glowing stars that peeked through the branches. The music of the forest's night insects had begun again, and their melody continued under the twinkling light of the stars.

Chapter 21

Cool, comforting darkness surrounded Gart as soon as his body plunged beneath the surface. The instant he was immersed in the water, he was seized in a silent rush, an irresistible force that drew him rapidly into the velvety embrace of the Lake of Whispered Sorrows. Gart could feel himself moving, his body pulled easily by the great swirling currents that surrounded him, drawing him deeper into the lightless abyss that seemed to yawn open beneath him. Oddly, the water's touch was gentle on his skin, soothing his hurts and easing the pain of his many gashes and wounds. Moments passed as Gart allowed himself to be moved, allowed the water to caress the exhaustion from his fatigued muscles.

He was surprised to discover that he was calm, at ease. The rage that had fueled him for days had diminished, pushed far back into a corner of his mind. Gart could still feel it there, a seemingly solid core of anger deep within him, but with it tucked away, he was almost able to enjoy the newfound serenity that the lake had given him. Rather than being afraid of the unfathomable darkness that surrounded him, Gart relaxed completely, succumbing to the sensation of being cradled in safety, surrounded by the sheltering vastness of the lake. It nearly lulled him into a doze, but Gart managed to retain awareness, such as it was after what he had been through in the last several days.

A few thoughts surfaced in Gart's mind. Foremost among them was the fact that though he had taken a deep breath just before he had hit the water, it astonished him that he was not yet gasping for air. It seemed he had been here for quite some time, and he knew that he would need to breathe soon. However, the cool water erased any ache that his chest might have been harboring, and he felt as though he could hold his breath forever. Downward he drifted, flowing silently with the currents.

Faintly, ever so faintly, a light began to grow in the distance. Gart squinted against the invisible currents that washed over his face, but all he could see was a growing brightness, a hazy luminance that seemed to beckon him. Still relaxed, he let the waters carry him forward and downward, calmly accepting whatever might lay ahead. On an impulse, he closed his eyes.

For a moment, the inky blackness behind his closed lids mirrored that of the lake around him. But then he felt the brightness surge forward to claim him, bringing with it a gentle warmth, and a feeling of. . .sorrow? Love? Pain? Joy? Gart felt the emotions as acutely as if they were his own, but somehow, he knew they were not. They overlapped each other as they fought for prominence in his mind and heart, and in the space of a few moments, Gart knew the giddy, heartpounding joy of newfound love, as well as a wrenching, bone-deep pain, a loss so dear as to rival his own. He nearly cried out, overwhelmed by the sheer force of emotion. Then, as suddenly as it began, the torrent of sensations ceased, to be gently replaced by a single, warm feeling. Love. Gart felt clearly that the love was tempered with sadness, but it swept over him and made him whole.

A face appeared in his mind's eye. It was the face of a woman, blond hair flowing about her in golden waves. Eyes of deepest sapphire gazed from a face that could have been sculpted by a master of masters, had he been trying to capture the very essence of beauty. Suddenly, her eyes narrowed, and Gart felt a powerful concern seep into the love that poured from her. A warning? The thought disappeared as soon as it had arrived. Gart shuddered under that gaze, feeling unworthy of her compassion. He ached to speak to her, but mere words felt insufficient.

Thou hast suffered. Her words were felt, rather than heard, but the voice in his mind pierced his heart with sweet agony. If he could, he would have given all for this nameless apparition. His quest was meaningless. Only she mattered, and being here with her. Nothing else was real.

In answer, Gart's tiny core of rage pulsed for a moment, surging against its bonds. With it came a tiny thread of the smoldering magick that was slowly rebuilding itself deep within Gart's body. Though he was weak, Gart recognized that feeble awakening for what it was, and latched onto it with grim determination. He tried to fan the flame that stirred in him, to build it high enough to lend him strength. He failed. It responded briefly to his summons, but then slept once more.

But the effort gave Gart a focus, something to help bring him back from the brink of losing himself in the painfully wonderful swirl of feelings that buffeted him. Releasing his tenuous hold on his magick, Gart realized that there was an ancient power here. It would not do for him to forget himself in this place. Gart tried to relax again, but stayed wary. He answered her by thinking, *Yes, I have, Goddess. And there is more that I must do.*

A silent hint of laughter, delicate as the tinkling of tiny bells, reached him in response. *No Goddess am I, though of her I know much.* Then, relief flooded over him in a wave, and the lovely face beamed at him in a heartbreakingly beautiful smile. *To jest with me shows that thou art strong. Overwhelmed are most of those few who come here. And all I wish to do is help.* Her regret washed briefly over him, but it was quickly replaced with joy, as well as an eagerness that startled him.

Sleep will shelter thee for a time. Thy hurts are many, and deep. I will do what I can for them, and then I would speak with thee. I would aid thee in thy quest, for thy path is a long and dangerous one. There is much thou should know before moving on. Gart felt her concern again, deep and foreboding. But before he could protest, he felt his consciousness drifting on gentle waves, slipping away from him as he eased into slumber.

Chapter 22

Gart floated, weightless. He had lost track of how long he had been here, wherever here might be. Of his body, he felt nothing, but it did not concern him much. Fortunately, he could not feel the wounds he had taken, either. Attempts to raise his hands to touch his face were fruitless, as if he had no hands or arms to begin with. He let himself drift. It was nice here.

Abruptly, he realized that he could see, but what he saw was not at all what he had expected. Though Gart still felt as if he were floating, he seemed to be inside a hall in a grand palace, the floors tiled in stunningly white marble. The vaulted ceiling above him was higher than any building he had ever seen, much less from the inside. All around were tapestries of the finest weave and fabric, and the furnishings were exquisitely carved from exotic woods that had certainly come from faraway lands.

Gart seemed to be alone in the vast room, but suddenly the huge doors at one end swung inward, admitting a single man. The silent figure shut the door quickly behind himself and began pacing in one corner of the chamber.

Gart tried to shut his eyes against the odd sights, but found again that he had no control of such things. There was nothing he could do but watch the events playing out before him.

The man walked hurriedly towards the center of the room. Gart noted that the short, square-cut beard jutting from his weathered face held a single streak of white that elegantly offset its pure blackness. Not heavily muscled, the man nevertheless moved with a wolfish grace, his brown eyes staring at nothing as he began to pace the massive flagstones.

Gart could see that he was still a young man, though his handsome face was lined and brown from the sun. The stranger rested one hand casually on the pommel of the sword on his hip, and from the way he held himself, it was plain that he was familiar with its use. That, and the badge of rank on his right shoulder, was more than enough to mark this man as a knight of some sort, though he wore no armor here in the palace of Caldea.

Gart tried to frown, but could not. Caldea? How had he known that? The only place he knew of by that name was New Caldea, which was near the lake that he now was supposedly floating in, and it had no palace. Before he could wonder further, one of the tapestries billowed outward for a moment before yielding up a young woman dressed in yellow silk. She hurried out from behind it to throw herself into the arms of the young knight. Her flowing golden locks swirled about them both as they embraced. It seemed that Gart's heart pounded in tandem with theirs as he sensed the raw passion generated by their two bodies.

Though he could not hear what was being said, he knew suddenly that the young man was Sir Cord of Nalan, a poor but valiant knight only recently raised to his station. As soon as the girl's face came into view once again, he realized with a start that it was the same face that he had seen in the lake, though somehow different, and full of the fire and uncertainty of youth. It was the Princess RaeLynn of Caldea, daughter of King Nikolas and heir to the throne of the forest kingdom.

It was clear that they were madly in love, and equally clear that they were fearful of being found. They appeared to speak quietly for a short time while Gart watched, and then they embraced fiercely once more, ending with a fiery kiss that at once embarrassed Gart for watching, yet pulled his gaze more strongly than ever.

Reluctantly, the lovers parted. The Princess blew Cord a kiss from behind the tapestry, where a hidden passage surely awaited, and then he slipped quickly out the door. Gart knew somehow that the next time they met they would be on their way from Caldea, headed towards a future neither had anticipated, but a future in which they would be together. Caldean custom forbade the Princess to marry any but a Lord chosen by the King himself. No lowly knight would ever be allowed to court, much less marry, a full princess of the blood. Apparently, both Cord and RaeLynn were willing to forego their titles and their privileges if only they could be together.

Gart wondered what that must be like, to willingly give up all you had ever known for love. But then, thinking of Gennie, he found it easy to believe that Cord would do just that. The Princess was the most beautiful woman he had ever seen, next to Gennie, and Gart somehow knew that she was loved throughout Caldea not only for her beauty, but for her kind and loving nature. She counciled mercy when others would not, and her quiet insistence over the last several years had brought many boons to the people of Caldea that some of the Lords had thought madness. But after seeing the results, even they could not help but be pleased. She was loved by many, noble and common alike, and revered as no Caldean princess had ever been before.

All this swept through Gart's mind in an instant, and before he could learn any more, another man emerged from behind a different tapestry in the room. He was only of middling height, but built strong as a wild bull. A golden circlet sat on his temples, a simple affair that held his pale blonde hair from his face. His eyes were the same deep blue as RaeLynn's had been, but where hers had conveyed love and compassion, his were hard and unyielding as glass. Still as a statue, the only motion came from the muscles of his jaws as they bunched in fury, and from strong hands that clenched and unclenched mindlessly at his sides. He was nearly shaking with rage.

The light in his eyes told of madness held carefully in check. 'Mad King Nikolas' this must be, Gart thought. His new store of information confirmed that this was, indeed, the King of Caldea, destined to lose his kingdom somehow, though Gart could not yet see how that would come about.

Then the images of the room in the palace swam before him, swirling in a liquid run of color until all was dark. Then, just as quickly, the swirling took him to a different place. Things slowly took shape before his eyes, and this time it was a beautiful lakeshore he saw.

It was night, but the half-moon above was bright, sending its silvery light down to dance and sparkle upon the waters. A cool wind blew through the trees, gently tugging at their leafy branches, making them sway in time to an unheard melody. Gart could see a small boat pulled up on the shore, nearly hidden in the reeds. Movement in the darkness attracted his attention and he felt himself drifting towards the boat.

As he drew closer, he was able to make out two cloaked and hooded figures loading parcels into the boat. A shimmering lock of hair fell from the shadows of one hood, glistening silvery-gold in the moon's glow, and Gart instantly knew it to be the Princess. She was pacing, looking back into the woods every few seconds. Gart guessed that the castle lay in that direction.

The larger figure, Sir Cord, loaded the last of the parcels into the boat, then turned to his beloved and took both of her hands in his. The hood kept Gart from seeing the man's face, but he knew that he was giving words of love and courage to his fair princess. They were to begin a new life, a life of hardship and struggle, but a life that would see them together forever. Her hooded head bowed as Sir Cord spoke to her, but only for a moment. She squared her shoulders, picked her head up, and nodded firmly to her love. Sir Cord put his big hands around her waist, and effortlessly lifted her into the boat. She settled in, and he pushed the craft away from the shore before jumping in himself.

Gart could easily see that they were running away. Leaving under nearly any other circumstances would have called unwanted attention to themselves, thus making their escape impossible. In the dead of night, cloaked and hooded, Sir Cord and his love, the Princess RaeLynn, were eloping.

They planned to cross the lake and head towards the river to the south. Horses awaited them at a small cote just downriver, where they would leave the water and make their way overland to the small city of Laro. Once there, they would procure more supplies for their journey, then head into the mountains beyond. The trip through the dense forest was a more difficult one than was necessary, especially since there were larger cities to the north that were far closer, but Cord knew that King Nikolas would expect them to go that way. He would never expect them to go to Laro.

The small boat was moving across the water then, Cord skillfully rowing the craft. They glided smoothly over the surface, leaving little wake behind them, and the pair headed southward, directly towards the large island that sat in the center of the lake. Gart's presence followed them, keeping them in sight until they were within a stone's throw of the island, the cool breezes at their backs making their cloaks gently billow about them both.

Gart's view of the Lake shifted abruptly then. His vision swam for but a moment, and then he was seeing the shadowy boat from a new vantage point that was farther south, but on the same shore that Cord and RaeLynn had just left. Here, many rocks jutted from the shallow water near the Lake's edge, and upon these stood a single figure, still as the stone upon which he stood. Shrouded in shadows, a glint of gold at the figure's brow immediately revealed that King Nikolas had been waiting, silently watching all under the light of the half-moon.

He watched them enter the tiny bay created by the horseshoe-shaped island, where it appeared they would dock. Gart was taken aback by the sudden surge of hatred that washed over him, as if Nikolas' stout body simply could not hold such a vast store of rage within its meager confines. Again, Gart sensed the slender thread of madness that was cunningly interwoven into the thoughts and emotions of the King, and he sensed it growing with every passing moment. The gnarled, powerful hands of the King clenched, shook, and relaxed in a steady rhythm, but otherwise, he simply stood and watched the cloaked pair in the boat.

Gart watched the King's eyes follow the craft as it entered the small bay and headed for the shore. In silence,

Nikolas saw Cord bound out of the boat and drag it up onto the narrow beach, pulling it far enough out of the water so that RaeLynn could step onto dry ground. For a moment, they disappeared into the surrounding foliage, but it seemed that Nikolas knew where they were headed.

In a sheltered grove of trees atop the highest hill on the island lay a circle of massive stones, each far larger than a man. At each of the four corners of the compass stood a pair of stones with a third placed as a capstone. At other intervals stood single stones, all as dark and unfathomable as the others. They all appeared to be as old as time, these brooding monoliths. The peculiar dark granite of the stones could not be found at all in the surrounding lands, not even as far as the sea to the west or the mountains far to the north. Their origins were a mystery, but the place held power, just the same.

This all came to Gart just as the other knowledge had, and with it the understanding that Cord and RaeLynn had docked on the island to visit the ancient circle and call to the Goddess to witness their handfasting. And then, wed in the eyes of the Goddess, the couple would depart once more, heading for the south side of the Lake and the Corris River beyond.

But not if King Nikolas had anything to say about it. Moving silently as a ghost, the King stepped down to the water's edge and entered it, wading out into the deepening chill. When it became deep enough, Nikolas started to swim for the island, using smooth, powerful strokes to pull himself quietly through the water. Gart could feel the malice that surrounded the King, as if it were pouring from him in waves. His madness seemed to roil around him like the smoke from a fire that burned within, smoldering slowly, but growing hotter with each passing moment.

Suddenly, Gart's vision swam again. It seemed to Gart that some time had passed within the vision, though he couldn't say just how much. When his sight cleared, he was again looking at the young lovers, standing amidst the great stones that formed an ancient circle. They were facing each other, hands clasped together under a loose binding of silken ribbon. Their eyes danced and sparkled in the light of the tiny fire they had built nearby and their lips moved in unison as they chanted a prayer of hope and love to the Goddess. Gart wanted to scream at them, to warn them that death was coming at the hands of a mad King, but he could not. He could only suffer as the power of their young, strong emotions washed over him, engulfing him with warmth and love as they finished their chant. The silvery light of the half-moon washed everything in a pale silver glow, and Cord and RaeLynn kissed each other as a husband and wife, each heart filled to overflowing with hope and promise, eyes filled with tears of gentle joy, bound hands clasped between them.

A knife buried itself to the hilt in Cord's back then, thrown with unerring precision and the weight of hatred and madness behind it. Cord's eyes flew wide and his mouth fell open in a silent scream as he pitched forward into RaeLynn's arms. She struggled to keep him upright, but his weight was too much for her, and he slipped from her clutching hands to fall heavily in the dirt at her feet. She saw the dagger embedded in Cord's back and recognized all too easily the intricate craftsmanship of the handle, work that could only have been commissioned by a King, and she knew in an instant that their doom was upon them.

Gart wanted to scream as he watched Cord take his last, painful breaths as RaeLynn knelt close to him, her face right next to his. Tears of pain crisscrossed Cord's face as he spoke one last time to his love, and then he was gone. His great hand, always filled with strength and tenderness, fell limply from her own. Never again would it caress her cheek as he looked into her eyes and spoke with no words, saying everything in a glance.

Great, wracking sobs took her then, and grief beyond measure flowed from her in waves that threatened to engulf Gart's consciousness completely. He knew that feeling all too well, and reliving it again was nearly more than he could bear. But somehow, he held on. He watched the girl cry for only a moment, then Gart saw her reach out and grip the dagger in her husband's back with both hands and wrench it free. Still crying, but moving with purpose, RaeLynn untangled the silken handfasting ribbon from Cord's lifeless hands and from her own.

Gart moved closer, and in the pale moonlight he could see that the ribbon had been sewn with symbols, not fancy or gaudy, but somehow sincere and elegant. Gart realized that those symbols had been sewn by Cord himself, with his own and RaeLynn's sigils on it. It was now also stained with blood.

RaeLynn quickly tied it around the dagger, wrapping it firmly and knotting it about the weapon's short quillons. Her lips moved as she tied, and continued moving even as she turned and flung the dagger into the trees farthest away from where she knew her father would be standing. It flipped end over end, glinting in the moonlight, and disappeared into the great trunks of the island's forest. Gart felt hope rushing from her, hope that the Goddess would hear her prayer and let the dagger be found by friendly hands. She then turned to meet her father as he strode into the circle of stones, still dripping from the lake.

Another blade was in his hand, and the light in his eyes told of madness finally loosed, all traces of humanity burned away by its raging fires. Gart watched him in horror, wishing again that he could be heard. *No more!* he screamed in his mind. *Please! I beg you, show me no more of this! I can't bear it!*

Silence was his only reply. Gart could only scream soundlessly as King Nikolas calmly walked up to his only daughter, gently placed his left hand on her shoulder, and then viciously jammed his dagger up under her ribcage and into her heart.

After that, Gart simply watched, his mind still numb from the tumultuous roil of emotions that had assaulted him during the visions. He watched in silence as the King dragged the two corpses away from the stone circle and towards a rocky cliff that dropped into the still waters of the lake below. Cord went first, weighted by a few head-sized stones tied firmly into his jacket, and then RaeLynn followed. Gart could not believe the nonchalance with which the King disposed of the body of his only daughter. He was sure that if he could hear, he would hear Nikolas humming a tune as he heaved her encumbered body over the side, giving her to the lake forever.

King Nikolas turned and walked back towards the stone circle, intent on finding his other dagger, but Gart's field of vision remained focused on the water where the two bodies had plunged into the dark waters. Gart saw nothing but the moonlight glistening on the surface.

But then, from deep within the lake, much deeper than Gart had guessed the water could have been so close to the island, a tiny spark of light appeared. The light grew, as if it was moving towards the surface, yet Gart could make out no shape below. Soon, the aura was strong enough to actually breach the surface of the water, sending rays of dancing light up and into the clear night sky above.

Then, as if it had never been, the light vanished.

Gart did not understand much of this, but something occurred to him immediately. Earlier, he had learned from Nikolas' mind that this was a powerful and ancient place, but there was more. Gart suddenly felt certain that Nikolas did not even know the half of it. The magick in this place did not reside only in the standing stones, as most thought. Instead, the power was everywhere, and every tree, stone, and drop of water in the Lake was saturated with old magick. That power had awakened to claim RaeLynn and Cord on behalf of the Goddess whose world this was.

Gart's viewpoint drifted upwards, away from the island and into the darkened sky. He could see the moon's reflection, the face of the Goddess as some called it, dancing in bright sparkles upon the black surface of the Lake. A peculiar sense of connection washed over Gart's mind, as if he were momentarily linked to everything below him, joined with the very energy of life that pulsed through the veins of the entire world. He was dwarfed by it all.

Then, Gart's vision faded into inky blackness. Along with the fading came the knowledge that although the King had searched for hours, he had never found the incriminating dagger, the longknife yet stained with Cord's blood and tied round with a silken ribbon. . .but the Weya had.

Called from afar by the shudderings and echoes of the powerful magick that had awakened to claim the Princess, the Weya arrived only days later. One of the Lormages had keenly felt the disturbance, and had quickly found the blade as if he had known all along where it had lain. Lormagus Kinleaf had then used the old magick to scry the happenings within the circle, and the small party of Weya had witnessed the murders much as Gart had. Tears had been shed as the horrible vision played out before the Weya's jewel-like eyes.

The Weya had quickly passed word of the deed to the people of Caldea, and the Caldeans, enraged beyond reason and thirsting for justice, had risen up to depose the mad King in the year following RaeLynn's death.

After that, the forest kingdom of Caldea had been left to rot where it stood, its inhabitants fearing that the palace and city would be cursed by the madness of a King who would murder his only daughter. The people scattered into the forest, many going as far away as Laro to the southwest, some heading east, and many heading north to other cities and to the mountains far beyond them. In time, a new city was founded, though far to the west of the ruins of old Caldea, and descendants of those who had left that cursed city had named their settlement New Caldea in honor of the memory of the Princess and of the grand Caldea that once had been.

Floating in the gentle dark, Gart waited. The loss of the intense emotions that had accompanied the visions had left him feeling hollow and weak. Slowly, he gathered himself and looked for a reference point, something to cling to that would bring him back to himself. The power of what he had just seen and felt had marked him, and he knew it.

What troubled him the most was the sense of oneness, the *joining* he had felt with the vast lifeforce of the world. It had been deeply comforting and exhilarating, yet frightening as well.

He turned it over in his mind, examining his perceptions thoroughly. He had sensed sharp pinpricks of anger, shame, hatred, and other painful emotions throughout the world, from so many faraway, unseen places. Gart recognized those hurts as easily as he recognized his own. But those stings had been easily overpowered by the sense of belonging, acceptance, and quiet strength that had filled him as he had touched, so briefly, the lifesblood of the world. So peaceful, so strong. This was the magick of life, and the swirling magick that resided within his own soul was both borne of it and part of it.

As that thought started across his mind, Gart jerked away from it as though it were a viper. He rebelled against that thought, knowing that if he were to accept it, he would lose himself in it forever.

It's not true! Gart screamed in silence. *I don't believe it! I'll not become a puppet of yours or anyone else's!* His spirit lashed out as he raged, but there was nothing to hit, nothing to hit it with. He thrashed again, vehemently denying the last part of the vision.

It was all too much, this *oneness*. He was only one man, a single tortured soul. He would not believe that such a living web of magick truly existed in the world, or that his unholy power was a good thing, a natural thing. Unholy or not, he would use it against Jor Dayne, but he would not be convinced that it was such a wonder as he had seen and felt in the vision. His power was for killing, and that was that.

Searching for an escape, Gart looked inward and found the core of rage that he had carried with him all his life. It had been nearly shut away by RaeLynn's magick, but it was still there. He reached out to it with his questing mind, only to be seared with a numbing cold that threatened to burn him inside out. Furious, Gart waited a few moments before trying again.

Tentatively, Gart reached within himself once more, this time trying to gently probe the ward that RaeLynn had placed around his rage, the source of his power. Instinctively, he felt for a crack, a hole, anything that would let him reach his magick, and without knowing exactly how, he found it. The protective ward peeled away and Gart's coiled rage sat before his mind's eye like a perfect sphere of deepest ice.

He made ready to plunge into it, to immerse himself in the blinding rage that had fueled him for as long as he could remember and reawaken the smoldering fire that had been brought to blazing fury by Gennie's death.

But then the warm embrace of the Lady RaeLynn washed over him, shielding him from himself again, carrying him away from the pain and the anger. A tranquil peace settled over him as her beautiful face appeared again in his mind's eye. Her emotions swept across him and he felt her shock and surprise at the dispelling of her ward. She redoubled it and then pulsed with something akin to pride. This puzzled Gart, and he ceased to fight. It almost seemed that she was glad he had found his way through her ward, and he did not know what to make of that.

Although he knew that she had once more shut him away from the wellspring of his own power, Gart decided that he was no longer angry with her. She was obviously a being of tremendous strength, and he had never felt the least bit of malice, deceit, or guile from her. Although he deeply resented the loss of his newfound ability, he chose to see what she had to say. He formed the words in his mind as he had before and tried to sound defiant.

Why have you shown me this? What good is it going to do me? And why the Hels have you shielded me from my power?

Initially, only silence answered him. The feelings that Gart had been constantly receiving from her lessened briefly, as if she were pulling them back into herself. The absence of her was startling, and a chill started to creep in around the edges of Gart's consciousness. Nevertheless, he held firm. The rage was still there, and he felt he could get to it if he chose to do so, but he had to admit again that the Lady RaeLynn seemed to mean him no harm. He waited.

Suddenly, her velvety voice brushed against the jagged corners of his mind.

I have shielded thee from thyself, farmer, because I am trying to heal thee somewhat. Use of thy power weakens thee, and thou didst come to me in a most grievously injured state. Fight me not, and I will do what I am able, that thou may yet live another day.

Gart was surprised at that. He knew that any use of his power drained him, but he had been unaware of her attempts to heal his wounds. Grudgingly, he resolved not to fight her again. There was still much to be done, and any healing that she could give would be welcome.

From what I have seen in thy mind of Gennie, she was a rare and wonderful woman. 'Twas a tragedy that she was taken.

Startled at the mention of his wife's name, Gart replied with stony silence. Shielded from his rage, he felt the only other emotion that had been driving him for days. The relentless grief came back to him in a flood, untainted by anger or hate.

That thou loved her dearly is beyond question . . .and too, thy memories speak volumes of her boundless love for thee.

But heed: many others died as she did. Many others. Dost thou not think that they loved someone as did thee? Didst they not have someone loving them just as much?

Stricken, Gart did not reply.

The silken voice continued its gentle, insistent caress. *Many have known despair, I among them. Hast thou not thought that the reason I feel thy pain so acutely might be because it mirrors mine own? I shared my pain with thee so that thou might see that thou are not alone.*

For an instant, Gart tried to understand, tried to take her words to heart. But his grief was too deep, too raw yet to be eased by the compassionate words of the Lady RaeLynn.

I still don't understand what you want from me, Lady. I will not rest until I have avenged her. What else is there for me but that? Nothing else matters.

The briefest flicker of anger struck deep within Gart's soul. It was clean and bright, the righteous anger of a princess eternally young and pure. Next to it, Gart's familiar rage suddenly felt like a mottled, slimy lump that now shamed him.

Does even the smallest release of thy pain escape thee? A simple sharing? Or dost thou somehow use thine hate and anger to keep thyself alive? Thou will burn through thine own heart long ere the Slayer lies within thy feeble grasp! And thy death will count as nothing!

Impassively, Gart floated and listened. He did not like what he had heard, but he liked even less the fact that the Lady RaeLynn was making sense. Even with his newfound magick, Gart had nearly been killed on the road before even getting close to Jor Dayne. But what other way was there? Jor Dayne and his ilk must pay, but how could he bring it about without walking into his own doom?

Well, I suppose you're going to tell me what I should be doing instead? Gart's sarcastic tone was far greater coming directly from his mind than he could ever have achieved with his voice alone. His biting remark brought a surprising pang of grief from RaeLynn, and Gart instantly regretted having made it. As her hurt washed over him, he waited for her to speak once more.

Nay, Gart. Only thou can choose thy path, be it for good or ill. I only wish to remind thee that of the many possible courses thou might follow, many of those will cause others to suffer as have thee . . .and Gennie. Should thou continue to hunt the Slayer alone, thy pain will soon end for thee in this life. This much I can see. And after thou art gone, Gennie will be just as dead, and thousands will follow her.

I can only suggest that there are other paths that thou should explore before throwing thyself headlong into the grasp of the Slayer. And I can set thee on one of these.

Gart turned her words over in his mind. She knew that he would pursue the Slayer, no matter what. It sounded like she was offering him a more feasible plan. In his current position, he finally decided that it would be foolish to turn away such assistance. He would have revenge for his Gennie. He would see the Slayer die. But if Lady RaeLynn could help him find a better way to achieve that end, then so be it.

Looking into the beautiful face of an ancient princess, Gart nodded his acceptance.

Chapter 23

The morning meal had long since ended, and the time for departure was only a quarter of an hour distant. In his sparsely decorated chamber, Layton stood before the weapons rack he had constructed since arriving here at the Hall. A wide variety of swords, daggers, flails, whips, throwing implements, and assorted other weapons were carefully arranged there. All had been thoroughly tested by Layton for particular balance, heft, and ease of use. He had personally handled every single weapon in the armory, and had pared his choices down to these twenty or so.

He picked up each weapon, testing them again in attempt to choose a few to take with him. He noticed that he could feel their imperfections much more readily than before. A sword he had previously considered perfect was now a trifle imbalanced. It was the same for a small hand axe he had especially liked, though he would probably take it with him anyway. After going through them all, and discovering many new shortcomings in each, Layton stood away from the rack and drew his Jidaan. Its opalfire flared in response to his touch, and in a sudden blur of motion, he wove the blade about himself in an intricate pattern that he had learned from an Eastern spear-master long ago. The blade sliced through the air with an audible hiss, and yet another imaginary opponent fell before its flashing might. Layton ceased his motions as suddenly as he had begun them, as he had found the answer to his puzzle.

Holding his Jidaan in front of him, he looked on it with awe and a new appreciation. The weapon was perfectly made. *Perfectly*. He had become so accustomed to its flawless balance, the unbroken smoothness of the haft, and the comforting feel of its potent weight in his hands that any other weapon just felt inferior by comparison.

The lad performed a few more parries and cuts with his weapon, a gentle smile upon his face as always, and then resheathed it in one fluid motion. His choices were much easier after that. The small, broad-bladed axe had earned a place at his side, as well as several daggers and throwing stars that could be secreted about his person. The sai that he had brought with him were a foregone conclusion. They had been with him since he had been almost too small to wield them, and though he never intended to use them instead of his Jidaan, he just could not see himself without them.

Once his weapons were suitably arrayed, he left his cell and headed straight for the storerooms to add a few more necessities to his supplies. He intended to be prepared for anything.

After stopping briefly in her own cell to grab her huge pack, Alyssa headed straight for the small infirmary to pick up a few of the rarer unguents and herbs that she had only seen here at the Hall of Jidaana. Although her Jidaan had granted her the power to heal most any wound or sickness, Alyssa knew that her strength would not suffice to aid hundreds or thousands of injured soldiers. If an attack on Laro was imminent, she knew that times would be dire, indeed, and the local healers would need every bit of aid she could provide.

After her healing of Layton, Alyssa had learned in no uncertain terms why Brunar had said they must be strong of body so that they might control the vast might of the Jidaan. Endure was the word Alyssa would probably have chosen afterwards. Using her weapon's Gift had left her drained for quite a few hours, and she now totally understood Brunar's comment that the sheer power of the Gifts were limited to the strength of the users. If Layton's injury had been more serious, she might have nearly rendered herself unconscious with the power of the healing, and she knew it.

Since then, she had attacked her strengthening exercises with iron determination. Now, after only a few short weeks of training, augmented and accelerated by her own innate magick, her body had grown stronger than she had ever imagined possible. She still had a long way to go, she thought, but she felt capable of handling herself as a Guardian, and that she would not let the rest of her comrades down.

In the infirmary, she filled her prodigious pack with various medicines and poultice ingredients, along with many bandages and notes on the uses of the rarer medicines. Then she was off in a flash to her own chamber to add some of her personal things to her bundle. As she walked, she reflected on the fact that she had been a healer for as long as she could remember. It was a title she had taken seriously, and as a Guardian possessed of the healing Jidaan, she was probably the most capable healer in the entire world. And now, there was to be war the likes of which the Goddess Rowann herself might not have seen. Thoughts of the sheer number of wounded, the devastation of which Mordak was capable, swirled in her mind and she began to wrestle with the weight of that awesome responsibility.

Moments later, just as she entered the vast Hall of Jidaana, that weight came crashing down on her all at once. Visions of mobs of dead and dying people threatened to overwhelm her, and she stopped in the middle of the stone floor as she searched for the strength to bear what she knew would be coming. She was so small, and she was only one woman, no matter what Gifts she possessed, or what weapons she carried. *What if I can't handle it?* she thought.

But then she felt the magick flowing from her sheathed Jidaan, and felt the answering swell of power from deep within herself. Reaching out with her senses, she felt the others in their own chambers, readying themselves for the journey. She gently touched each of them with her magick, only to feel their presence, but not alert them to hers. She was not alone. These competent, powerful warriors were with her, and she was with them. Drawing herself to her full height, she took a deep breath and found the calm center inside herself. "The Jidaan have always Chosen wisely," was what Brunar had said. Feeling the power within her, and the unspoken support from her fellow Guardians, she was finally able to agree.

The tiny knapsack that Bjarke had brought with him to the Hall was far too limited for the extended journey that surely lay ahead. However, Bjarke was loath to part with it. Instead of leaving it behind, he rolled it into a tight little bundle and tucked it away into one pocket of the larger rucksack he had gotten from the storage chamber. This accomplished, he began to transfer the few things he had brought with him into the larger sack.

He had rarely carried much with him, even when he had been known to travel throughout the forests near his home for days at a time. He knew how to live off the land, and so needed little in the way of supplies. But the few things he always carried then were with him now. His dagger, some strong twine, fishhooks, extra clothing, waterskins, and such were the main things he needed, along with a cunningly-made hammock. Though he knew he would have little time for rest in the coming days, he felt somehow comforted to have it with him, so into the bundle it went. The big man then walked over to the desk beside the bed and chose four books to go alongside his other supplies.

The first was blank, save for the first several pages that he had written himself. Bjarke did not know if the others had journals in their chambers, but he felt an odd and powerful urge to write in his, so he added it to his pack.

Another was a history of the last war with Mordak, written by Brunar himself. Bjarke had only read the first several chapters, but already he had learned that their foe was evil beyond anything he had ever imagined. By reading this tome, Bjarke hoped to gain more knowledge of their enemy, so that he could combat him more effectively. Though a peaceful man at heart, Bjarke was more than capable of using every resource at his disposal to destroy the Evil One so that thousands of innocents might escape harm.

The last two books were Weya storybooks, translated by Brunar. The gentle beings had fascinated Bjarke since he had seen them years ago at his lake, and the fables they had written soothed him and filled him with childlike wonder. Bjarke figured there would be days ahead when those healing stories would probably help keep him sane. Fastening the strings on his rucksack, Bjarke sat on the bed to gather his thoughts for a few minutes before meeting the others.

He looked down at his hands, such huge, powerful hands, and realized that they had never before caused anyone harm. For the briefest of moments, Bjarke envisioned those hands and arms soaked to the elbows in blood of creatures most foul, those evil minions of Mordak, and an icy chill crawled up his spine. But the warmth of his magick, deep in the center of his being, as well as the answering thrum of power from his great Jidaan, kept him from shivering. He knew that his path was the right one, however dangerous or frightening it might be.

In another chamber, Kiran checked her backpack fastenings and made certain they were secure. She had long since been ready to embark, filling her pack as she always had. As a mercenary, she had been traveling more often than not, and it was second nature to her. She had left the outermost pockets empty, as those were the ones she tended to put food into, and as soon as she finished her final preparations in her chamber, she would be off to the kitchens to load up.

After checking her weapons again, she sat on the bed for a moment. After much struggling and experimentation, Kiran had found a way to wear her Jidaan so that it paralleled her side when she moved and did not interfere with her movements. It was still not quite as readily accessible as the others had theirs, but this was of little consequence to Kiran. Even though the weapon was well-made beyond belief, she just could not leave her sword behind, and in fact, would probably prefer to use her own blade instead of the fabled spear that she carried.

She had only seldom invoked the gift of her Jidaan, but even so, she could still feel the magick of the weapon as it sat in its scabbard. She had guessed that she could still invoke its gift even if she was not actually holding it, as long as she was close to it, and the idea of fighting with her own sword while keeping her Jidaan sheathed appealed to her.

For a moment, she thought about her new allies, the supposedly mighty Guardians. A frown creased her face briefly as she thought of the young soldier, Layton. Throughout their training, she had taken every opportunity to pick at him in an attempt to goad him into a friendly sparring match, but he had deflected her jibes with an embarrassed, self-deprecating comment and a smile, and had continued whatever he was doing. She knew he was good, but *how* good? She was still unconvinced that this mere lad was the great and mighty Weaponsmaster she had heard of. Kiran shook her head in mock frustration. She figured she would find out soon enough just what kind of fighter he was when the real battle started.

Of the huge man Bjarke, and the tiny Alyssa, she had great reservations. She liked them both well enough, that much was certain. But she was worried for them. The big man was strong, of course, and his Jidaan gave him access to untold power. But, he had never once been in a battle. Not even a single fight in a tavern! And it was the same for the healer. At some point, she had probably even bandaged a few people that Kiran had damaged in the first place. They had been working hard, and were now trained in at least the rudimentary fighting skills of Tinn Quan, as well as the techniques she herself had taught them. There was whatever Layton had taught them, as well. But when the real combat began, how soon would it be before someone bested them?

Kiran made up her mind then and there to try and help them as much as she could. They were all in this together, after all, and hers was the power of Warding. Not that she had any idea how it worked. However, Kiran resolved to use it to best effect where she could to keep them safe.

With one last look around at her unadorned chamber walls, she shrugged on her backpack and went in search of her old friend, Nessar. She expected to find him in his chamber, but he was not there. His pack was leaning on the wall next to his door, apparently ready for travel, but the old thief was nowhere in sight.

Sticking her head into the open door of Bjarke's chamber across the way, she asked if the big man had seen Nessar, and he pointed out towards the gates of the hall.

"I think he stepped outside the doors and into the courtyard, Kiran. I haven't seen him since." He paused for a moment before he continued. "Kiran, is there anything you need? Can I help you get ready or anything?"

For a moment, Kiran thought he might be making some sort of inept pass at her, but he was not blushing in the least, and Kiran could somehow feel that this huge forester was simply trying to help. She smiled and looked, really looked at Bjarke for what seemed like the first time. Even sitting on the bed as he was, the immensity of him was what struck her. She could see the powerful, oaken muscles of his shoulders and arms, hardened by the recent training. Whenever he moved, he did so with surprising grace and fluidity, far more than he had shown upon first arriving in the Hall. She had seen this man throw stones nearly as big as herself while training under Brunar's watchful gaze, and suddenly, Kiran rethought her vow to keep such a careful watch out for this man's safety. Standing this close to him, she could feel and sense his power, and realized that he would be much more formidable an ally than she had first thought. He would need no looking after. A genuine affection for the big man erupted from her hardened heart, and she realized that she would look after him anyway, just because she cared.

Embarrassed by her sudden rush of feelings, she shook her head.

"No, thank you, Bjarke. I just wanted to check on Ness before we left."

A big grin appeared in the depths of Bjarke's beard, and a knowing gleam shone in his eyes. "He's a good friend of yours, isn't he?"

Kiran sighed. Ness was more than that to her. He had been more like a father to her for more years than she could remember.

"Indeed he is, BigBear. He's probably the closest friend I've ever had in my life. As a mercenary, I traveled a lot, and never made many friends. But he's always been there for me when I needed him."

Bjarke nodded, still smiling. Like the others, his magick had expanded his feelings of empathy so that he, too, could feel what others were feeling. The rush of emotions in Kiran had not gone unnoticed.

"Well, just so you know, I'm here if you need me."

Kiran's faint blush lessened, and she smiled at her large comrade.

"I'll keep that in mind. You just watch yourself in the days ahead, you hear? And don't trip if I'm walking in front of you. You'd squash me flat." With that, she left his doorway to find Nessar, and Bjarke's laughter boomed out of his chamber.

Outside in the courtyard, Nessar was kneeling before a small statue of the goddess Rowann. The light from the rising sun had not yet found the courtyard, but Nessar paid no attention to the dark. His head was up, and his left hand was held just in front of his chest, fingers pointed upward in a ritual prayer. His other hand was clasped tightly to his Jidaan and he made no sound. Nessar was doing something he had not done in over thirty-five years; he was praying to the Mother Goddess. The expression of complete serenity looked entirely new to his worn face, but it seemed welcome there. His magick swirled within him, and as peace flooded into his body, Nessar found that he had more control over that magick than he had ever imagined.

Nessar had been out in the cold wind for quite awhile, but inside the circle he had drawn around himself in the snow, he was warm and comfortable. He concentrated, and for a brief, shining moment, he was aware of the vast wonder of the world that he lived in. In that moment, he had felt in touch with a great and powerful...*something*. As the sun's rays finally alighted on Nessar's craggy face, showering it with warmth, he opened his eyes, lifted his gaze to the smiling, beautiful face on the statue, and thought simply: *Thank you.*

He had sensed Kiran long before she actually stepped through the partially open gates, and had almost smiled as he "saw" her jaw drop in disbelief. He remained quiet for a few moments longer, finishing his silent prayer, and then he stood. Taking a deep, cleansing breath, he turned to the woman who might as well have been his daughter, and at that moment he felt like a man of only thirty years again. A smile burst across his features, chasing away the somber expression he usually carried. He had to admit that it felt good to smile.

Kiran's mouth had remained open until he had closed the distance between them, and Nessar's smile widened.

"Is your jaw all right, or are you setting a trap for horseflies?"

Kiran closed her mouth, then opened it again, but the words still would not come out. Eventually, her voice made itself available once more.

"Were you just doing what I think you were doing?" Utter astonishment was evident on her striking features.

The old thief allowed a chuckle to escape him. "Yes, Kiran, I was praying just now. I know that's something you're not accustomed to seeing me do."

"Not accustomed? You've said ever since I've known you that people who pray are weak! And idiotic! And...and foolish! What in the world has gotten into you?" Her mouth dropped open again, and Nessar nearly burst out laughing.

Most of his life had been spent as a coldly pragmatic man, only believing in what he could see, touch, and hear. That was one of the reasons he felt that he had survived as long as he had. As a thief, and eventually as a leader of thieves, his life had required a cold, hard reasoning, and that left no time for belief in anything at all that had to be taken on faith.

But the Choosing had changed that for him. Indeed, the entire course of his life had changed the moment he had laid hands on his Jidaan. Things just felt different now. New worlds had opened to him as a result of his innate magick blazing into prominence. His senses had been widened to an extent that continued to amaze him, and many things he had taken for granted now became new and wonderful as when he was young. Sights, smells, even the very currents of the breezes held new meaning for him.

"Kiran, I don't think I have time to explain myself just now. We'll be leaving in a matter of minutes." Kiran started to protest, but Nessar's gnarled hands on her shoulders gently stilled her. "Hang on, now! I'll explain everything when the time presents itself. For now, just remember that I am a 60-something-year-old thief whose life has been given new meaning, and new purpose. Will that hold you for a while?" His crafty smile did nothing whatsoever to reassure her, and she said as much.

"What I think, old-timer, is that your old age is catching up with you. And in the worst possible moment! Here we are, getting ready to traipse off to war, sail on some rickety ship for weeks, and then head into a battle the likes of which has not been fought for over two thousand years, probably fighting Gholans, Drakes, Killiths, reanimated dead men, and, and. . ." Kiran's voice trailed off into silence, and she frowned. "On second thought, say a little one for me, would you? Every little bit helps."

At that, Nessar really laughed. He whooped and howled, filled with a boyish glee that he had not felt since he was a child. Nessar looked through teary eyes to see Kiran finally chuckling with him and he embraced her, pulling her tightly to him. Still laughing, he hugged the daughter that he wished was his in name, as well as in spirit.

"Come on, then. It's time we stuck our head in the panther's mouth. Have you finished getting your stuff together?" Nessar released her as they started to walk, keeping his arm still comfortably around Kiran's shoulders, and hers around his, though she had to stretch a bit to reach him. Together they reentered the gates and found the others standing outside their chambers, checking over their individual travel packs. Brunar and the Weya had not yet emerged from the Mage's chambers, where they had been in council since breakfast had ended, so Kiran and Nessar walked over to join the others with smiles on their faces.

Chapter 24

Mordak smiled in the midst of the swirling sandstorm as it howled furiously around him. The reddish sand obscured even the blazing sun above, and nothing else was visible through the tempest. The storm wasn't a bad one, but nothing could touch him now, even if the winds had been ten times as violent. He wore his power like a cloak, and its scarlet folds kept even a single grain of sand from touching him. Mordak stood upon a jagged rise of stone, unmoved by the winds.

The sorcerer had traveled deep into the western reaches of the Gorran, searching for the elusive tribe of nomadic creatures that called themselves the Krell. Using his astral sight, he had located them long ago and had called them to this place, a deep valley that sat like a massive gash in the surface of the Gorran Plains. The Krell were a vicious, bloodthirsty race, and cannibalism was known to them. That they survived this deep in the wastes of the Gorran was a testament to their strength, and Mordak knew that for all his power, he still needed them.

Ages ago, the Krell had followed Mordak into battle. He had fooled them with false promises and sweeping lies. Mordak had known that the Krell worshipped Balroth, though they knew him by a different name, and that many a screaming sacrifice had died at the hands of Krell shamen so that the bloodthirsty god might be appeased. Mordak had persuaded them that he was the emissary of that dark being, and that they would inherit the very world if they would only follow him.

Follow him they did, to the near destruction of the entire western continent. It had only been when Mordak was defeated by the Guardians near Ghal Spir that the Krell had finally realized that they had been duped. Their rage at his treachery had been so great that those Krell nearest the battle had flung themselves at the remaining army of the Realm, ensuring their deaths. Krell who had been farther away gnashed their teeth in anger as word of Mordak's demise reached them. The war was over for them, and all who were able eventually made their way back to the Gorran Plains, carrying with them the hatred of the False One, the Betrayer, Mordak. Hatred of the sorcerer grew until now he was a figure of legend, reviled by all Krell for all time.

The storm started to abate, and Mordak waited. As the winds slowly subsided, the sorcerer reached out with his mind and touched the daemon-man that called itself Jor Dayne.

Mordak's Champion responded instantly, and a wordless communication passed between them. Mordak's smile widened. Everything was moving according to plan. Apparently, the attack on the village gathering had been a success. Those bodies that could still be used had been assimilated into the small army of riders and Gholans that now moved steadily towards Laro. They still had weeks to travel, and even when they reached their destination, they would have to wait for Mordak and his Krell to arrive. But then, Mordak's powers would speed the travel of the Krell, and Jor Dayne would be gathering new recruits while they traveled. By the time the two armies joined at Laro, they should be more than a match for the Duke's men . . . and then there were those *other* surprises that were on their way. A cruel smile crawled across the sorcerer's face at the thought.

Once Laro was taken and its people absorbed into Mordak's horde, the march towards the capitol city of Bos Aldas could begin, as well as the attack on the city closest to Laro, the port of Rualtha. It would not be long before the entire western continent would be under Mordak's rule. And it would only be the beginning.

The reddish clouds of stinging sand began to dissipate, and Mordak started to see the valley floor beneath him for the first time. At first, it seemed that the entire floor of the valley was moving somehow, rolling and undulating with the fierce winds. Moments later, the winds died completely, and Mordak saw that the valley was not moving at all.

Apparently, the visions he had sent had been well received by the Krell shamen, and his instructions had been heeded. The motion he had seen was the subtle movement of thousands upon thousands of Krell, more than he had ever dreamed existed, standing in quiet expectation. A wicked grin split his face as he gazed out over the multitude of vicious, feral warriors. He had no idea they were so many! He could barely contain his swelling mirth.

Taking a few moments more to be sure that all was in readiness, the vile sorcerer prepared to take command of the Krell, much as he had so long ago. Mordak himself may have been a hated figure to them, but through his vile arts, it was not Mordak who stepped farther out onto the rock and into their view . . . it was Balroth himself.

If Mordak had any doubt as to the strength of the illusion he had just cast, it was removed in an instant as the massive throng moved as one, dropping to both knees to honor him. A thrumming mantra reached his ears as the Krell began to chant their god's name in unison, and Mordak could feel the stone beneath him vibrating with the strength of their combined voices. Behind the false face of Balroth, Mordak chuckled with mad glee.

Chapter 25

Nightfall settled over the grassy plains just north of the Corris River, and the wains had finally been pulled to a stop beside the road. It was a small group of wagons, well-made and sturdy, for those who rode them were all carpenters.

Johan stood watching his charges share their supper as they talked animatedly amongst themselves. Johan's sons and their families bustled about, moving with brisk efficiency. As the family patriarch, he had naturally been elected as the leader of this little group, though he had protested mightily, saying that he "didn't know a thing about leaderin'," but they had persisted. Actually, it had not been all that bad. Everyone did what they knew they ought to be doing, and he had said next to nothing the whole trip.

Johan smiled to himself, pulling a knife from his belt and laying it to a small piece of wood that he had been carving on for the last day or so. He liked the feel of the wood under his stout fingers, as well as the sweet odor of it as the knife worked magic under his expert direction. Johan watched with interest as an image of his wife appeared in the wood, amazingly detailed and lifelike in his hands.

He hummed a little tune to himself as he leaned against one of the wain wheels, looking up every so often to keep an eye on the children that were old enough to get into trouble. Seeing that everything was still all right, Johan would nod and go back to his carving. Things were going well enough so far on their migration to the southern province, and if all went as planned, they would be in the town of Shaded Tree by eventide two days hence. By all accounts, there was lots of work down there for a family of carpenters.

A few minutes later, a faint humming noise reached Johan's ears over the laughing of his family. Stilling the knife, he stood away from the wain, trying to identify the sound. After a moment, Johan likened it to the buzzing of bees, swarming somewhere beyond the firelight. With a stern frown, he walked past the circle of diners and headed towards the knee-high grass of the open plain, looking for the source of the noise. If there was a colony of bees or hornets out here, it was up to Johan to find out where they were so the youngsters could be warned to stay clear until their departure, and maybe turn up some honey for the trip.

Several yards away from the camp, Johan stopped and searched the deepening darkness for any sign of the insects. There was nothing but the starry sky above and the inky, unbroken dark of the plain before him. His eyes scanned the knife's edge of a horizon that separated the two. The humming grew louder, and then louder still. Johan's eyebrows rose in alarm as he felt his skin begin to vibrate with the intensity of the sound, and his scalp prickled as his close-cropped hair tried to stand on end. He retreated a step, then another.

Without warning, a great scarlet slash appeared on the ground several yards away from Johan. North to south it flared, fully half a mile in each direction, and Johan's terrified face glowed crimson as if it were covered in blood. Horrified, Johan could only watch as the line of light began to expand, stretching upward until it was twice as tall as he, a great wall of bloody power. The pressure and sound intensified, beating against him until Johan was forced to his knees, hands clapped over his ears to shield himself from its potency.

Suddenly, the surface of the wall disintegrated, leaving a long, empty rectangle of light that hung in the air, motionless and terrible. Johan struggled to comprehend the meaning of what he was seeing. Never in his most horrible nightmares had he imagined anything like this. Trying desperately to overcome his fear, Johan squinted into the ruddy light, trying to see into the space behind the rectangle. He knew he should be able to see the horizon beyond it, but inside the blazing outline of scarlet, all was dark.

Then, the ground beneath his knees began to rumble, a very different sound than the intense hum of the light. Johan's wide-eyed gaze was held to the space before him as he tried in vain to pierce the veil of darkness within the light. Before he could place this new sound, its origin was abruptly made clear.

All at once, hundreds upon hundreds of figures poured from the ebony portal. They moved quickly, and in the darkness, Johan had trouble seeing exactly who they were. Glints of metal caught Johan's eyes, and he realized they were all carrying spears, axes, or knives of some sort. The figures moved with a feline grace that frightened him. In the demonic gleam of the wall of power, Johan could see the long, stringy hair that each figure kept pulled back and tied, lending a horrifying skull-like aspect to their shadowy faces. Bracelets and armbands of sharpened bone rattled and clanked eerily as their wearers walked purposefully forward on naked feet.

The men before him marched closer, their combined steps pounding the earth below. Johan tried to get to his feet so that he could attempt to speak with them. A frenzied howl erupted from the nearest figures as he moved to one knee and made to stand, and the terrible shapes surged towards him.

Before Johan could rise from his other knee, an axe came flying out of the swarm and buried itself in his chest with a sickening, wet thump, knocking him to the ground. He lay there, disbelieving, as bloodthirsty shrieks surrounded him, and he felt the hideous presence of his slayers next to him. Johan glimpsed a horrible face that pressed close to his own, yammering in an unintelligible tongue. A grinning mouth filled with teeth that were filed to needle-sharp points flashed for a moment only to be replaced by another demonic face, and another. They were all around him then, yowling and laughing in their madness. One stepped forward, put a sandaled foot on Johan's shoulder and wrenched the axe from his chest with a great spray of blood. Johan watched helplessly as the axe-wielder held his dripping weapon aloft and yelled triumphantly. He was instantly answered by thousands of howling voices.

Vaguely, he heard the awful screams of his doomed family a few yards away. Johan tried not to think of what was happening to them as he breathed his last, gurgling breath. As the light faded from his eyes, the odd thought crossed his mind that this leaderin' business was not for him after all. Mercifully, the carpenter was gone before the Krell began to divide up his bloody carcass for an impromptu meal.

Minutes passed, and it seemed there was no end to the flowing horde of Krell that marched through the scarlet rift in space. They had covered a score of miles in mere moments with the use of Mordak's power, and at this pace, they would join their undead brethren near Laro in only a few short weeks. The Krell were wildly aroused, overcome with the religious ecstasy that came from directly serving their foul god.

Not in two thousand years had the Krell made war on the humans, and the very thought of killing and maiming and consuming their enemies was enough to charge them with inhuman energy. They would continue their trek long into the night until exhaustion finally forced them to sleep. A few hours later, they would rise and continue onward, swarming across the grasslands that covered the next few hundred miles until Mordak created another rift for them.

As the last of the Krell passed through the demonic light of the rift, it instantly closed and blinked out of existence, leaving a great, scorched scar upon the earth. Mordak was using Balroth's power now, and it was not of this world. The very earth rebelled and screamed at its touch.

As one, the thousands of Krell turned their eyes skyward and searched for the crimson blot of power that they knew would be there. They shouted their joy at being led into battle by their god, flying high overhead. They raised their weapons in salute, and their battle cries echoed in the clear night.

Looking down upon his horde, Mordak smiled. The wind whipped through his flowing grey hair, and the sensation thrilled him. No longer did he have to change to the form of the flying beast in order to soar the skies. Now, he could simply float unaided upon his stolen magick, easily keeping pace with his army below as well as maintaining the illusion of Balroth. Thinking of how unprepared the city of Laro would be against his force of undead riders, Gholans, and Krell, Mordak laughed to himself with glee. He would see the walls of Laro smeared with blood, and savor the wails of the dying. And he hoped that the Mage would be there to die as well.

GART'S ROAD

Book 2 of the Fire of the Jidaan Trilogy

Whit McClendon

Rolling Scroll Publishing

Gart's Road

Book Two of the Fire of the Jidaan Trilogy

By Whit McClendon

Prologue

A strangely chill wind blew across the jungle of Triagga, and the rustling of the millions of thick leaves sounded oddly like waves upon the faraway ocean. The Augenan were restless tonight, and the fierce, copper-furred warriors gripped their spears and clubs tightly as they watched and listened for an attack that never came. For weeks now, there had been whispers of something evil on the horizon, a horror that none could name, but one that all of the gorilla-creatures could feel, nonetheless. Even though peace had reigned since the ascension of mighty Ch'shok to the throne, the patrols had been doubled, and the fiercest among them, the Na'tam warriors, had been spread throughout the jungle for miles around to protect the greatest of the Augenan tree-cities, Neronda. In the wake of the wind, many warriors turned quickly to look behind them, startled by nothing they could see, feeling the unfamiliar touch of fear upon their hearts.

Far above the jungle floor, in the highest chambers of Neronda, Ch'shok sat and pulled absently at the copper ornaments that adorned his reddish beard as he contemplated. They were the sign of his high office, as were the ornate copper armbands that barely encircled his massive biceps, and he never seemed to get used to them. He had been a warrior, not a leader, but as the sole heir of the last Augenan chief, Wo'kandor, he had been compelled to challenge for leadership of the tribe. He would have died before dishonoring the memory of his father by failing to compete, and after several days of trial by combat, he had easily won the right to wield the Tugan as chief, just as he had been afraid he would. Despite what he thought of himself, he had to admit that his people seemed to thrive under his firm but fair rule.

Then things had started to change.

His people had begun to squabble among themselves over trivial things, and a peculiar anxiety had fallen over his tribe. Fights broke out where no quarrel had been before, and his people had fallen into a constant state of unease. Ch'shok itched to find the source of this amorphous ill that now festered in the Augenan, but there was nothing he could clearly put his gnarled finger on, and the inability to do so much as discover the problem had him frustrated and grievously worried. It had the stink of magick about it, and he liked it not.

Ch'shok looked around at the thickly woven branches that formed his chamber. He wondered anew how the woodguiders had managed to coax the massive trees to grow in such a way, making hundreds of structures throughout the treetops nearly invisible from the ground. His gaze wandered upwards to the woven leaves that made up the ceiling of his room, and again he marveled. They kept much of the rain out, but still allowed air to circulate. With a snort, Ch'shok thought of how much he would rather be on patrol with his border guards, out in the thick of the jungle. He chuckled at himself and rubbed a leathery finger over a tracery of white lines that crisscrossed the back of one thick hand. They were a reminder of his last border patrol, when his group had been attacked by a renegade Tballa band.

At least with those puny humans, I could see what I was fighting. Ch'shok longed to pick up the Tugan, the huge, double-bitted axe that had become his to wield as High Chieftan, and smash it into the foe...whatever that foe might be. Frustrated, he clenched his formidable hands into a pair of tight fists.

Rustling and a babble of voices reached Ch'shok's ears. He picked up his head to fasten his steely gaze upon the doorway. Moments later, the dark-furred head of K'won, his second-in-command, popped into view. Fear and urgency were plain upon his wrinkled face, his wide nostrils flaring in alarm.

"My Chief! Come quickly! The Seer calls for you, and she's screaming, and . . .great Donda, she's lost her mind!"

"Has the healer been fetched?"

"Yes, my chief! But she says that there is little to be done for her! Please, sire, come quickly!"

In a startlingly smooth motion for one so huge, Ch'shok bolted from his seat and grabbed the shining axe from its place against the bark-covered wall on his way out the door. He leaped past the startled officer, straight out into the waiting arms of the jungle below, using his free hand and both feet with equal ease as he traveled the branches and vines as one born to do so. K'won followed as quickly as he could, but he knew that Ch'shok would easily outdistance him, even burdened as he was with the Tugan. In moments, K'won saw Ch'shok's mighty back, its reddish fur shot through with silver, vanish in a rustle of foliage ahead of him.

As Ch'shok swung, climbed, and jumped through the jungle, he gradually became aware of a faint screaming up ahead, muffled by the trees. A low murmur of other voices also reached his ears, but the howls of Renelda, the Seer, set his fur on edge.

It sounded like she was being rent limb from limb. He hooted deep within his chest to let whomever was assembled at the Seer's lodge know that he was near. Answering hoots from his warriors were quick in coming, and when Ch'shok dropped to the jungle floor, twelve of his warriors, Na'tam all, had already assembled in ranks and formed a pathway to the Seer's door.

Ch'shok nodded to the officer present, who dipped his head and held out one hand in deference to his leader as he rested his weight on the knuckles of his other hand. Ch'shok grunted in acknowledgement and rapidly scraped his hand along N'briah's outstretched palm, and the smaller gorilla quickly stepped aside. From inside the lodge, a massive and ancient tree that had long ago been rendered hollow within, another gut-wrenching scream tore the air. Ch'shok noted the brief flash of fear in his officer's eyes. Ch'shok knew N'briah, to be a steadfast and powerful warrior, the victor in countless battles and skirmishes, and it did his heart good to know that such a fearless warrior could feel the same nervousness as he. He clapped the smaller Aug on the shoulder before walking the path to the Seer's quarters. Taking a deep breath, Ch'shok ducked his head to get through the door and went inside.

The first thing he noticed was that the Seer was tied down upon her bed of leaves. Apparently, the Healer had asked the warriors to bring in four large stones, and had carefully bound Renelda's wrists and ankles to them. Although they had been well-padded, blood still soaked the ropes where Renelda's struggles had abraded her skin.

Her fur was matted with sweat, and her wide nostrils were flaring as she snorted and coughed in obvious distress. Deep, bloody furrows ran down the length of her wrinkled face, as if one of the jungle beasts had clawed her. She continued to pull weakly at her bonds, paying no heed to the damage they caused to her fragile flesh. Her eyes were wide and staring, with no hint of understanding within.

Jarjen, the healer, knelt by her side, wiping a damp cloth across the old Augenan's brow. The look of fright and concern on Jarjen's face told Ch'shok that the situation was worse than he thought.

Jarjen looked up from the Seer to the huge chief as he stepped inside. Rising from her place on the floor next to the Seer's thick bed of leaves, she wiped one furry hand across her sweating brow as she approached him, and then bowed quickly to her chief.

Ch'shok spoke first.

"What ails her?"

"My chief, I know not. One of the warriors fetched me, saying only that Renelda was screaming. When I arrived, she was on her knees, there," Jarjen pointed to a spot in the middle of the floor. "She was moaning and crying, and she had already clawed at her own face. It was all we could do to subdue and restrain her as we have."

Jarjen was silent for a moment, frustrated at her inability to find any conceivable cause for Renelda's affliction.

"She's been calling for you, my chief. That's the only thing she's said that makes any sense to me."

Ch'shok blinked once at the Healer, then nodded grimly. Looking back to the moaning form on the floor, Ch'shok *huff*ed, a short, determined sound in the still of the lodge. Still holding the Tugan, he stepped forward and knelt by the tortured Healer's side, leaning over so she could hear him.

"Renelda. I am here."

At the sound of Ch'shok's deep, rumbling voice, Renelda sucked in a breath and jerked her head towards him. Comprehension dawned in her tired, frightened eyes, and she started to cry.

"My chief! Thank the Donda you have come! Now, I can end my suffering!"

Ch'shok frowned.

"Why do you suffer so, Renelda? What is it?"

Renelda's eyes widened in fear and she started to shake her head.

"The Sight! I have seen it, and it is horrible! I cannot bear it any longer!"

"What? What have you seen, Renelda? You must tell me!" Ch'shok carefully placed one massive hand on Renelda's shoulder to calm her, and was surprised to find that it was solid as rock, her muscles clenched tight in terror. Renelda continued to cry.

"My chief! Baulotha is come!"

Ch'shok sucked air in through his teeth even as he heard Jarjen gasp behind him. A cold knot of dread blossomed deep within him, and he took a deep breath to calm himself before continuing.

"Renelda, this cannot be! Baulotha was banished eons agone! The gods have forbidden him to return!"

The Seer moaned, a long, low wail of despair that sank the hearts of those who heard it. She turned her face away from Ch'shok for a moment, as if gathering strength. When she turned back to him, a new determination blazed forth from her eyes.

"Listen well, for my time is short! Baulotha can yet be stopped! I have Seen it! There is one to the north, a human, who cloaks himself with Baulotha's power. Even now, he brings death to humans and Augenan alike. You must gather the Fist, and take them to the humancity they call Laro. Aid the humans in their fight against this foul pretender, and the Prophecy will soon be fulfilled!"

Ch'shok's eyes flew wide at her words. He glanced down to the Tugan yet clutched in his powerful fist and gazed at it as if for the first time. Made eons ago of an unknown metal, the great axe had been handed down throughout time to each and every Augenan High Chieftan. Along with the axe came the legend, a Prophecy, that the massive weapon would one day be used by an Augenan warrior to strike a blow against the evil god Baulotha. Could the Seer be right? Could that fabled time have arrived?

A faint sigh brought Ch'shok's gaze back to the Seer only to see that the light had gone from her eyes. With her message delivered, she had gone to rest, at last. Ch'shok clenched his teeth in sadness and anger. He had known Renelda all his life, and though she had been ancient when he had been a young Aug, he had somehow assumed that she would live forever. Seeing her die like this, in fear and torment, filled him with rage. Ch'shok placed his wide hand upon her damp face and spoke softly.

"May the Lady Donda guide your way, Renelda. And may she watch over us all."

He stood and looked over his shoulder at Jarjen. He could see the tears that rolled down her face, and he wished he could take more time to comfort her. But if the Seer's words were true, there was much to be done.

He took a moment to squeeze Jarjen's shoulder in sympathy and shared loss, but then he squared his shoulders and stepped out of the lodge and became High Chieftan once more. Drawing himself to his full height, towering over most of his Na'tam warriors by a head or more, his voice was loud and strong throughout the benighted jungle.

"Gather the Fist. I want the entire force of a thousand warriors ready to move at dawn. We must leave for a mancity on the morrow. And may the Lady Donda guide our steps, for Baulotha draws nigh."

Chapter 1

Gart awakened to the feeling of warm sunshine on one side of his face. He raised his head and warily looked around, trying to remember where he was and how he had arrived wherever 'here' happened to be. He found himself on the shore of a beautiful lake, resting comfortably on the soft grasses near the water's edge. His pack was nearby, and he noticed that it no longer had the slack, empty look that it had taken on after days of dogged, arduous travel.

And with that thought, it all came back to him. He remembered the laughing demon that had reft him of his Gennie, the hours upon hours of pursuit, and his miserable defeat on the road. It all came flashing back to him in an instant, along with the memory of a rage so intense that it had threatened to burn him alive. That rage kindled again within him, but it burned lower now, no longer blinding him with its ferocious intensity. Gart turned to sit up and slowly scooted backwards until he could feel the rough bark of a massive, sheltering oak tree at his back. He leaned against it, enjoying its comforting solidity, and rubbed one callused hand across his eyes as he tried to remember what had happened after the road.

Gart remembered the battle, joined after several days of solitary, dogged pursuit. He had come upon the band of marauding riders and Gholans on the road, and although he had slain at least fifty of the hideous little brutes, he had nearly died then and there. Beyond that, he knew little. He knew he had been knocked senseless for a time, but he also vaguely recalled being carried through the forest, seeing a pair of feet moving at blinding speed as someone hauled him away to safety. But who had saved him?

Gart closed his eyes and a face finally came into view. It was a handsome face, at once ageless and youthful, with tilted eyes of emerald green. Gart sucked in a breath. A Weya! A Weya had saved him! The reclusive creatures were not unknown to Gart but he had never troubled himself with them, or ever even seen one. By all accounts, they were a noble people, far more so than most humans Gart had ever met. After this episode, Gart had to agree that their reputation was well earned. He hoped that his unknown savior was well, and wished a silent thanks to him.

Leaning back and stretching his arms out as far as they would go, Gart noticed that he felt amazingly fit after such an ordeal. To his grim surprise, nothing hurt. Wincing as he suddenly remembered the two arrows he had taken, Gart pulled open his shirt and explored his left shoulder where the first arrow had punched through. Gart's mouth dropped open as he discovered only a pale scar. His right hand flew to a spot high on his forehead only to find another barely discernible scar marking the second arrow's passage. Gart let out a low whistle of admiration for whatever healing arts that little elf had possessed. The fellow must have . . .

Another wave of remembrance crashed against the folds of his mind, bringing visions of a beautiful face, a goddess, a spirit with an achingly lovely voice. Gart's eyes went wide as he recalled her. *Her name was RaeLynn,* he thought. *She was the Lady of the Lake of...of Whispered Sorrows.* She had tried to ease his anguish, his pain.

A path, Gart thought to himself as his icy heart quickened its beat. *She was going to show me a path that would lead me to the one who killed my family...Jor Dayne.* Gart's gaze leapt out over the surface of the lake before him, catching the dancing shards of sunlight that reflected from the breeze-blown water. He frowned, trying to remember the exact words they had exchanged at the last.

Thou hast long since met one who offered thee such a path, and yet thou refused, she had said. There had been a hint of reproach nestled within the silent beauty of her voice, but Gart had ignored it.

You mean that Mage. His scorn had been evident. Gart held no love for Brunar. He yet felt that the Mage had invaded his life, his privacy, and even his dreams. He had flatly refused the summons Brunar had brought him.

Suddenly, the Lady RaeLynn's voice had become louder, her anger battering him from all sides as her comely face loomed larger before him. He had not been prepared for the intensity of her response to his contempt.

Aye, 'that Mage!' Thou show disdain for one who has often risked death for the sake of the whole world, one who has devoted himself wholly to the preservation of all. Heed me, selfish farmer, there are those who see beyond their own pain, and choose to act with honor so that hundreds, thousands might be aided! It would do thee well to follow such an example! If he called you, he had good reason to do so!

Taken aback, Gart had simply nodded, not wishing to anger her further. Apparently, that Mage was more than he had appeared to be. Still, Gart was not cowed. He cared nothing for the Mage, but if Brunar could offer Gart the revenge he sought, then so be it.

I see. So then, I should use the stone to contact him? I should follow him? Gart had thought of the strange and beautiful emerald that had passed from the Mage's spectral hands into his own. Brunar had instructed Gart to hold it and call to him should he change his mind.

Moments passed, and she had made no answer. Straining his patience to the breaking point, Gart had managed to keep silent until she spoke again.

Nay. It would do thee no good to join him now, for he has traveled far since you last spoke. However, it is the weapon he offered to thee that will aid thee in thy quest.

Gart had been confused for a moment. He had been about to protest that he had no idea what she meant when the sudden realization came to him.

That spear? Is that what you mean?

A lovely smile had crossed her face, and he had felt her assent.

Indeed. It is a formidable token of power. That spear is meant for thee alone, and in thy hands, it is a most powerful weapon. Thou must go where he bade thee go, and accept it. With it, and only with it, canst thou possibly achieve thine ends.

Gart had no idea where he was supposed to go, and had said as much.

There are those who will help thee on thy way. I will help thee as well. When thou dost awaken, simply follow the path to the North. It is said that the weapon thou dost seek resides in the western region of the Heartstrong Mountains, in the Hall of Jidaana. It is a great castle wherein the Mage dwells. Find into the largest peak...there, you must go.

Vague impressions and tales of the mountain range far to the north swam through Gart's mind. He had never seen a map, but had heard travelers mention those mountains. *If that is where I can find the means to kill Jor Dayne, then I'll do as you say. And I thank you for all you've done.*

That was the last thing that he remembered. And now, he appeared to be on the shore of that same lake. Gart watched the water in silence for a time, wondering about the spirit that resided within. It had been she who had healed him, he knew, not the Weya. And she had helped him to cool his rage enough to let him think clearly. The burning hatred for the one called Jor Dayne was still there, but now it simply resided deeper inside him, not so close to the surface. He closed his eyes and curtly offered her his thanks, just as he had to the Weya who had rescued him from the creatures on the road.

After a few moments of silence, Gart turned and pawed through his pack. As soon as he opened the flap of the knapsack, the sweet smell of food made his mouth water and his stomach gurgle loudly. He was startled to find a loaf of honeyed bread, dried meat, and even some small apples all carefully arranged inside. Gart pulled off a small hunk of the bread and ate it, savoring its sweet, nutty flavor. A full waterskin lay next to the pack and he drank from it, enjoying the coolness of the water on his throat. Not the most varied fare, but to Gart, it was ambrosia.

After finishing his meal, Gart repacked his gear and hoisted the pack onto his back. He lamented the loss of his sword and his bow, but still had a longknife at his belt as well as the reassuring weight of the few silver coins that he habitually carried in his belt pouch. He could probably buy a sword in the next town he ran across. His quiver had been on the ground next to his pack, and though it had been full before the attack, it was nearly empty now. Gart supposed that being slung over a Weya's back and hauled through the forest like a sack of grain had something to do with those lost arrows. Though he had no bow, he strapped the quiver on anyway. If he could lay his hands on just about any bow at all, those few arrows would come in handy.

Checking the position of the midmorning sun, he started to skirt the lake, looking for any sign of a trail or path heading to the north. As he rounded the eastern edge of the lake, Gart saw that a large area on the northwestern shore appeared to have been cleared and covered with small stones and gravel. A small pier jutted out into the water and a faded rowboat floated there, tied to the dock. Relief flooded through him at the sight of a pebbled pathway leading into the forest from the shore, and Gart made for the wide trail. He saw no other signs of people about, though at first glance, the dock and boat seemed well-kept.

Soon, Gart's feet were crunching in the gravel and he was headed up the path, alert for signs that anyone might be nearby. The sun was shining merrily down, though it did little to warm him, and he shivered in the cool air. Still, the birds were singing in the trees on all sides, and the forest had an almost palpable feeling of peace and security. Gart allowed himself to enjoy the sweet, thick scent of the forest, but never once did he take his mind from his goal. He would follow the Lady RaeLynn's instructions and find the mountains in the north, however long that might take. He would overcome whatever obstacles stood between himself and the odd-looking weapon that the Mage had offered him, and then he would hunt down and destroy Jor Dayne. Beyond that, nothing else mattered.

He had no idea how that spear would help him, but the Mage had said something about storms. If Gart's dreams were to be believed, the spear could somehow call down lightning at the very least. Though uncertain as to whether his dreams had been real visions of the past or just some kind of trickery from the Mage, Gart had been told to follow his heart. Using a magickal spear to kill a demon-monster like Jor Dayne seemed like a better idea than anything he had come up with so far.

As he walked, Gart began to experiment with his magick just as he had done before the Gholans attacked. Stones of various sizes and shapes rose, danced in the air, and then dropped back to the ground as he passed. Though his grim purpose had not changed, and his heart still burned with suppressed fury, the Lady had eased his pain enough so that he could breathe again, and could see the need to test his magick in other ways besides just pulverizing things. The stones twisted and whirled through the air around him as Gart continued up the road, estimating the many weeks of travel ahead of him.

Chapter 2

Kiran leaned against the railing and relaxed into the ship's steady swaying as the *Damsel* cut cleanly through the gentle waves. She licked the salty spray from her lips and took yet another deep breath. She had always enjoyed the smell of the ocean, and today was no different. The sun rode high in a clear blue sky, and its warmth was welcome on her shoulders and arms, bare as they were for the moment. Most of the armor and weapons had been stored inside the cabin to avoid the ever-present danger of rust, but the Jidaan suffered not, and remained at her side.

Gathering her hair into a ponytail, Kiran turned to check on her comrades. She knew without looking that Nessar was in the small lookout perch high on the mainmast. She heard a chuckle from somewhere up there as the ship swayed to one side, and she had to laugh in return. Though he was long out of boyhood, Nessar still found a child's joy in riding in the crow's nest of a ship whenever he had the chance, and the captain, a grizzled but respectable ruffian, had been more than happy to let him take a turn at high watch.

Kiran's eyes absently wandered across the deck and found a great hulking form hugging the railing several yards away. Bjarke had not taken to the sea quite so well as the others, and was still heaving his breakfast over the side. As always, Alyssa was next to him, reaching high to pat his back and reassuring him that he'd be fine after a while. The greenish tinge to his face would have been quite alarming had they not been at sea where such ailments were common among landlubbers. A few moments later, Alyssa guided the ailing Bjarke towards the door to the passenger cabins, trying her best to keep him upright.

The trip down from the mountains had been uneventful, and after a restful night in Tamaransett, they had loaded their horses and followed the road westward towards the modest seaport of Cohen. It had taken almost no time at all to secure passage southward toward Rualtha. Brunar had just walked them right up the dock to the *Damsel* and started yelling for Terrence, the captain, to show himself. Moments later, a fuzzy head of greying hair had leaned over the side, and insults the likes of which even Kiran had never heard came raining down on the little company.

To their surprise, Brunar had hurled back as good as he got, and soon both men were laughing. They all boarded the ship soon after, and were pleased to see a sturdy, clean vessel, complete with a small crew of barefooted sailors climbing like monkeys in the rigging above.

As it turned out, Terrence had known Brunar for years. When questioned, Brunar had simply said, "You don't think I spent *all* of my time up in the Keep, now do you? I did get out now and then."

Terrence had guffawed at that, and gave Brunar a hearty slap on the back. "Aye! And there's more'n one tavern maid in Cohen that pines away for 'im every time 'e goes back up there!"

"He's only joking. Really." Brunar turned a stern stare towards his companions, looking into five pairs of surprised eyes. They had all burst out laughing at that.

Kiran smiled at the memory of the shared laughter at Brunar's expense. That was two weeks past, and the seas had been smooth and the wind steady ever since they had shoved off.

As was his wont, Brunar stood next to the Captain as he steered his vessel, both staring across the undulating ocean with looks of admiration and respect. The Mage had chosen to doff his traveling shirt in the manner of many of the sailors, and Kiran was surprised to note that, while still a slender man, Brunar was well-muscled and strong.

"Not bad for a two-thousand-year-old," she heard herself say aloud as she felt a smirk turn up one corner of her mouth.

After another few moments, Kiran decided she had loitered around long enough, and made her way towards the rear of the ship to find Layton and the Weya. She had heard of the legendary fighting ability of the normally peaceful creatures and figured that if Layton was anywhere, it would be near them. That boy was just obsessed with fighting arts, and if there were any to be learned, Layton was always first in line.

This observation was borne out immediately when Kiran rounded a corner and heard a solid thump nearby. The force of the blow made the boards beneath her feet quiver for an instant, and Kiran moved towards the sound, curious now as to what could have made such an impact.

A small crowd of sailors were clustered around something, and Kiran pushed through them to see what was going on in their midst. She burst out laughing when she saw Layton sprawled out on the deck, facedown and gasping like a fish, held there by one of the Weya. Ginn, the smaller of ValElder Moihra's two companions, effortlessly held Layton's right hand bent at a painful angle while only using a one-handed thumb-and-midfinger grip. Layton tried to struggle, but the tiniest pressure from Ginn had Layton tapping the deck fast and hard in the time-honored signal for surrender. Immediately, Ginn released his captive and helped him up.

"Goddess, Layton, if I'd have known that they were going to be throwing you around like that, I'd have paid to watch!"

Seeing Layton's familiar blush start to creep up his neck was too much for Kiran to take, and laughter forced her to abruptly sit down on the deck, folding her legs up under her. The sailors' laughter joined hers, as well as the sparkling mirth of the Weya. Cohl and Moihra were nearby, their jewel-like eyes shining in the midday sunshine.

Running one hand through his sweaty hair, Layton turned to her, a chagrined smile on his boyish face.

"Well, believe me, it wasn't exactly what I had planned. Ginn has been kind enough to show me something of their fighting arts, and let me tell you, he is amazing."

Ginn's hands instantly went up to protest. "While 'tis true that I am a fair warrior, no Master am I. However, <the art> is known to all of us, and I am honored that Layton wishes me to share it with him."

"So you're going to teach him, then?" Kiran's eyebrow went up. Though she had not spent the same kind of time in training that Layton had, fighting was still her business, and she bristled at the thought that the Weya might be teaching him and not her. She had as much right to learn from them as he.

"Indeed. We would never refuse such a request from a Guardian. Would you, too, wish to learn our <art>?" Ginn's gleaming eyes, an unsettling shade of deep blue, gazed at her with a hint of hopefulness. Kiran's own eyes narrowed warily for a moment before she replied.

"You're sure you don't mind teaching a woman?" A thread of challenge wove into her words before she could catch herself. She quickly stood up and awaited his response.

Ginn blinked once, then looked over his shoulder at Moihra and Cohl. They were silent, yet Kiran felt something pass between them, a faint flow of energy that barely caught her senses. Kiran listened intently, but if they were using mindspeech, it was of a sort beyond her grasp.

Ginn's head swiveled back towards her. He cocked his head to one side in a puzzled gesture.

"Why, of course not. Is there some reason I should mind? You wish to learn. I wish to share. That is reason enough, is it not?"

Kiran stayed silent for a moment. How could she begin to explain the number of times she'd had to fight for her life simply because some idiot was offended that a woman would dare wear a sword and strut around 'pretending to be a warrior'? As far as she knew, it was a man's world, and she was an oddity because she wasn't barefoot, wearing an apron, and herding children about. Brunar's simple belief in her capabilities and his lack of chauvinism had been an unexpected, but wholly welcome surprise. Now it seemed that he was not the only one with his head on straight.

With a firm nod, she allowed her smile to return in full force.

"It is. Now, where do we start?"

A smile of dazzling brilliance answered her, and Ginn gestured for her to come forward. Moihra moved to continue working with Layton, and the sailors that had surrounded them bade them well as they scattered to tend to their various duties on the ship. As much as they would have liked to stay and watch their passengers at their practice, they knew that a ship did not sail itself, and their fierce pride in the *Damsel* drew them back to their tasks.

While Moihra continued showing Layton various joint manipulating techniques, Ginn took a different approach with Kiran. Nearly a foot shorter than she, Ginn nevertheless guided her with grace and authority. He bade her extend her arms before her, and he stood opposite, his arms extended as well, his wrists touching hers.

"Relax, and follow my movement. Do not lose contact with me, and do not tense. Just follow." Ginn began a circular motion with his hands, and Kiran dutifully imitated his movements, instinctively following his circles with her own. Soon she relaxed, and their combined hands wove lazy circles between them. Moments passed, and the sounds of distant seabirds, shushing waves, and the creaking of the ship lulled Kiran into a calm, but ready state. Though she had no idea what they were doing, or how she could fight with it, she found that she was enjoying herself immensely.

As they moved, their bodies swaying with the gentle rolling of the *Damsel*, Kiran felt a shift in Ginn's pattern. His speed remained the same, but the Weya began to make subtle attempts to invade her space. She instinctively countered, continuing to maintain contact with Ginn's arms. She felt his approval as he gradually accelerated their pace and added more force to his movements. Kiran continued to counter. She found that as long as she stayed relaxed and acted on her instinct and empathy, she could feel his 'attacks' and respond to them appropriately. Gradually, their speed increased, and Kiran began to slip in a few attacks of her own.

Ginn smiled as he saw Kiran's responses to his motions. She learned quickly when she wasn't trying too hard. He accelerated his attacks again, and Kiran followed. Soon, their hands were whipping through the air, each trying to break through the other's guard. Their hands and arms whirled, neither gaining ground over the other. Suddenly, Kiran's left fist connected firmly with Ginn's rock-hard stomach, though she held back enough that it failed to injure him in the slightest. She jumped back, triumphant.

"Ha! Gotcha that time!" She blew at a few strands of hair that had come loose to dangle in her eyes. Ginn's laughter pleased her.

"Indeed, Kiran! You learn well. Though I should caution you that this is just a beginning. It will take far more time for you to gain anything resembling proficiency in our way."

"Oh really? I took everything you threw at me, Ginn. And wasn't *I* the one who landed a strike first?" Kiran made a show of checking the shine on her fingernails.

"You certainly were, and I am mightily pleased. You are still slow, by our standards, but I can see Brunar's influence in your movements. Practice will help." Ginn was nodding thoughtfully, happy to be able to offer guidance.

"SLOW? Are you kidding? I'm faster than you think! Come on, try me!" Kiran had never backed down from any sort of challenge, and this seemed like a challenge to her, albeit a polite, roundabout one. She moved back into her usual fighting stance and raised her fists into a ready position. Her weight shifted to the balls of her feet and she prepared herself.

Ginn's smile spread widely across his alabaster face, and his eyes twinkled with delight. To him, this was all fun and sharing. Though he knew that humans tended to be overly concerned about their pride, he gave it no thought here. She was a Guardian, after all, and probably not given to such failings.

"Certainly! I'll be most happy to demonstrate my meaning."

He placed his hands behind his back and walked forward a few steps until he was within easy reach of anything Kiran wished to throw at him.

"I'm going to tap you upon your forehead, stomach, and forehead again, in that order. Please block my attempts. Are you ready?" In spite of his huge smile, Ginn appeared calm and motionless, looking for all the world as if he might fall into a deep, happy sleep if he merely closed his eyes.

Kiran set herself, took a deep breath and let half of it out, then nodded. *T-t-tap!* Three firm taps of Ginn's fingertips upon her forehead, stomach, and forehead again, left her flailing ineffectually as she tried to block attacks that had already landed with blinding speed. Ginn was standing just as he had been, with the same shining smile.

Astonishment crossed Kiran's face only a moment before frustration clenched it into an angry scowl. But before she could say a word, another great jarring thump vibrated the boards beneath her feet and she turned to see Layton on the deck again, this time being held by Valelder Moihra. Layton's face was pressed hard into the unyielding wood. Moihra sat with one knee firmly on the back of his neck even as she held Layton's left arm in a vicious hammerlock.

The beautiful Weya leaned down so that her prone opponent could hear her better. "Your left side remained undefended that time. Do you see my meaning, young one?"

"Ow. Just now, all I can see is the deck, milady."

Kiran's anger dissipated completely. If that was the best that Layton could do against a Weya, then she must not be doing too terribly herself. A sigh escaped her, and she shook her head.

"Laytie, honey, I've told you before never to underestimate a lady!"

A muffled grunt was the only response until Moihra allowed Layton to rise. His face retained the faint imprint of a knothole in the wood of the deck, and he rubbed his left shoulder in an attempt to regain feeling in it. A blush was creeping up his neck from Kiran's use of her pet name for him. It embarrassed him to no end but, quite frankly, he was also starting to like it.

A pair of grey eyes watched as the pair laughed and continued their impromptu training session with the Weya. After a few moments, Brunar nodded to himself. He was pleased that his Guardians continued to train. There was still so very much they needed to know, and the more time they spent in training of any sort, the better their chance for survival would be. Brunar walked back to his position next to the captain of the vessel and relished the sensations that washed over him: the sun's warmth, the smells of the ocean, the sounds of the wind and waves. It had been many years since he had been on a ship, and then it had been with a much younger Terrence.

Long ago, Brunar had been making a trip down south to Ghal Spir to check on some obscure bit of magickal curiosity, and had run across a smart and rascally young sailor. Terrence and Brunar had become fast friends, and when Terrence had managed to acquire the *Damsel* in a particularly cutthroat game of cards, Brunar had stepped in to protect him from the *Damsel's* rather irate previous owner. In return, Terrence had promised to take Brunar anywhere he wished to go. Over the intervening years, they had traveled up and down the coast of the Realm together, and to many of the islands to the west. They had spent the last few days catching up on old times, and now had settled into long periods of comfortable silence as they gazed towards the distant horizon.

As Brunar resumed his post, Terrence spoke.

"So, this Mordak, 'e be a mean one, eh?"

A bitter smile crossed the now sun-browned face of the Mage. He nodded slowly as he replied.

"Indeed he is, Terrence. You know I've battled him before, and that I've seen what he can do."

Nodding, Terrence leaned over to spit unerringly into a large spittoon that sat nearby. No one spit over the side into the ocean on Terrence's ship, lest it offend the Goddess, or one of her special folk. Terrence figured that vomiting was allowed, as it was something that oftentimes could not be helped, and the Goddess would surely understand. He resumed his chewing as well as his conversation.

"Aye. I've heard the legends, and I've heard yer tales. Known ye for a long time, have I, and ye know that I trust ye like no other . . .though there be some that'd never trust one that ne'er ages as ye." A snaggle-toothed grin and a friendly elbow to the ribs caught Brunar simultaneously.

Brunar took the ribbing with good nature. As a Mage, his longevity resulted from his cultivation of the magick within him, and also due to his long periods of rejuvenating sleep. Terrence was well aware of both.

"What I be wonderin'," Terrence continued out of one side of his mouth, "is just how do ye plan to take 'im this time? These young 'uns...they be ready for the likes of 'im?"

For a few moments, the only sounds were those of the sails flapping in the wind, the swelling of the waves, and the creaking of the *Damsel*. Brunar continued to scan the horizon as he enjoyed the salty tang of the air and the sweet breeze that ruffled his dark hair. He let the sea calm him, let that calmness seep down into his very bones. Times ahead would not allow for many such moments, and Brunar wanted to savor this one.

"There are many things I do not know for certain, Terrence. I know not where the Foul One is just now, only where he is probably heading. I know naught of the numbers he brings with him, or of the nature of the corruption he has conjured this time. And I know little of his true plans, other than his wont to quest for power over all. But one thing that I have learned over the last score of centuries is that the Jidaan will always choose their wielders wisely. And I also know that we will oppose Mordak unto the very last breath we have within us. I pray to Rowann that these things will be enough."

Again the grizzled sailor nodded, and thoughtfully sent another gout of spittle into its waiting vessel.

"Wull, then. Guess I'll jest say that whate'er ye need from me, I be good for it. The *Damsel*, her men, and me'll get ye all as far as we're able, and we'll see what ye need from there on, aye?"

"Aye, Terrence. And our deepest thanks for it." Brunar clapped his friend on the back. Allies were hard to find. Friends like Terrence were rarer still. The Mage wandered forward to the upper deck's railing and leaned upon it, still taking in the joys of the open sea.

Below decks, Bjarke's face was still tinged with green, though he had improved after sending the disagreeable contents of his prodigious stomach over the side of the ship. He lay quietly in his bunk with his feet sticking out over the end of the bed. Alyssa sat next to him and applied a damp cloth to his sweating brow, humming a faint tune as she did so.

Next to the massive Bjarke, Alyssa felt positively tiny. She had been worried for him earlier, but her senses told her that he was a victim of nothing more than simple seasickness and would be fine. She had given him some herbs to quell his lurching stomach as well as an additional draught that would calm him enough to let him sleep. Now, his breathing was deep and even, and she found herself staring at his wide, bearded face.

Life in the outdoors had tanned him deeply, and the laugh lines around his eyes were many. She had never met anyone so big and strong, and yet possessed of such a kind and jovial manner. He treated everyone around him with respect and deference in spite of his strength and size, and his childlike delight in the simple wonders of life never failed to move her. Alyssa had to admit that being near the huge forester filled her with a joy that she found difficult to describe.

As he slept, she let her eyes travel over him, taking in the corded muscle of his exposed forearms and the sheer size of his hands. If it weren't for her own magick and the recent training she had undergone, she doubted that she would have been able to move so much as one of his arms by herself.

Alyssa laid aside the cloth she had been using and dried her hands. A few strands of damp hair seemed to tickle Bjarke, and he wrinkled his nose in his sleep. Gently, she brushed the hair away from his face, her touch lingering for a moment. A smile appeared on the slumbering giant's face, and he moved slightly towards her tiny hand. Alyssa bit her lip and froze, but then relaxed as Bjarke settled back into slumber. Sighing softly, she carefully withdrew her hand. A few moments later, she tiptoed out of the cabin, leaving Bjarke to his quiet and happy dreams.

The little ship sailed on without incident. The weather was perfect, the sea was gentle, and they made good time. Crisp southerly winds pushed the *Damsel* along at a fast pace, and Brunar was pleased. The Guardians busied themselves as best they might, given they would be at sea for at least another three weeks before reaching the port of Rualtha. Brunar continued to train them in the uses of both magick and combat skills, with the Weya adding their own <art> to the mix.

In the silence of the predawn hours, Brunar's shadowy figure could barely be discerned near the prow of the ship. With the wind in his face and the wide ocean before him, Brunar spent many of those early morning hours in meditation, rebuilding his store of magick. Since awakening early those months ago, he had continued his practice each morning, gaining more strength each day. He knew that there was no way he could be at his best without his long mystical sleep, but even so, his meditations fanned the potent fire within him until he knew that he would be able to deal with all but the most dire of threats. Brunar hoped it would be enough.

Days went by without mishap, and the crew of the *Damsel* sang boisterously at every opportunity, enjoying the beautiful weather as only sailors could. Kiran sang along loudly, and even taught them a bawdy tune they had never heard before.

Each morning, Brunar thanked the Goddess Rowann for the shining sunrise and for the bright, sunny day that followed. He knew that the peace they shared was only temporary, and that soon the battle would be joined in earnest.

Chapter 3

Gart stood at the top of a small rise, his mouth hanging open in disbelief.

He had followed the path out of the forest some time ago, and now the afternoon sun hung low in the sky. The great majesty of the ancient forest that had surrounded the lake had eventually given way to gently rolling grasslands filled with the sweet smells of wildflowers. The fields of tall, waving grasses and brilliantly colored blossoms had lulled Gart into an almost pleasant state as he had walked, and he had nearly managed to enjoy the beautiful landscapes that lay all around him. A vague sense of unease had plagued him, though, and he could not say why.

He had never traveled in this part of the country before, and so he did not expect anything to be familiar, but something just felt *wrong*. Nevertheless, he continued his journey, alert for anything out of the ordinary.

The path had eventually led to a wide road that headed almost directly north, and it was this that Gart still followed. He figured that he had a pretty good idea of his location, given the circumstances. He knew that he had followed the road along the Corris River until his attack, and then the Weya had most likely taken him to the Lake of Whispered Sorrows, which was somewhere to the north. So by now, he should be nearly a day's journey north of the Corris River Road.

But then Gart had topped a hill that was a bit higher than any he had passed this day, and now he was struggling to believe his eyes.

For the first time in his life, Gart was looking at mountains. Not hills, not mounds, not big piles of dirt...mountains. They were still far enough away that it would take him weeks to reach on foot, but they were there, looming in the distance like the backbone of the world. Many of the peaks disappeared into the clouds, and Gart could just see the snow that permanently covered the highest slopes.

From the western horizon, the dark gray peaks silently marched across the landscape until they faded from sight far to the east, forming an immense wall of impenetrable stone. Gart stared in wonder and shock at the sight, trying to make sense of it.

In his time, Gart had traveled as far west as the city of Laro, as far north along the Elde River as the smaller city of

Pemberton, and there had even been one long trip into the south, but there had been no mountains anywhere near those places. Certainly none were within a day's march of the Corris River Road. Gart rubbed his forehead briskly, wondering if that last arrow had done more of its work than he had thought.

Although it was yet an hour or more before dusk, Gart decided that it was a good time for a rest. Just ahead and to one side of the road stood a lone tree, its sheltering arms shading a goodly patch of ground. Gart walked briskly towards it and relished the sudden coolness that washed over him as he stepped out of the late afternoon sun and into the deepening shadows that the old tree seemed to gather beneath its branches.

As he removed his pack and set it down, a loud gurgle erupted from his stomach and Gart realized that it had been some time since he had last eaten. Kneeling, he rooted around in the bag until he found one of the small, sweet apples that had been mysteriously placed there. Gart sat heavily, leaned back against the rough bark of the tree, and then took a great, crunching bite from his fruit. Chewing noisily, he tilted his head a bit so that he could see the cloud-shrouded mountains as he considered the impossibility of their very existence.

The fact that the image of the mountains before him did not waver or fade as he silently watched them gradually brought him to the realization that they were real. As such, they had probably been real for quite some time and had not just sprung up this morning. He knew, without a doubt, that there were not, nor had there ever been, any mountains this close to the Corris River. And that would mean, since he was sitting there staring at some mighty impressive peaks, that he was nowhere near that river anymore.

An icy stab of fear and anger plunged into his stomach as he realized that he had somehow been *sent* far away from the Lake, far from where he had last seen the murderer, Jor Dayne. His anger rose higher at the thought of how many miles now separated him from the monster he had sworn to destroy. Gart heard a crunching sound and then cast his eyes downward to see his own strong fingers slowly wrapping themselves around the fragile remains of the apple, squeezing.

A moment passed, then another, Gart's shaking left hand still clenched around the dripping fruit. Then Gart sighed. The way to revenge lay before him, not behind. The Lady had set him on the right path, he was certain of it. If she had sent him northward, then she had done him a great service by taking him closer to the weapon that could vanquish the Slayer.

If Gart was actually in the Northlands, then she had taken weeks upon weeks from his voyage. He would probably never fully understand how she had done it, but he decided to be grateful for the help. She had told him what to do and helped him on his way, and now it was left to him to follow the path. He would claim his revenge.

Gart opened his hand to see that his apple now bore deep indentations where his fingers had tightened upon it, but was still edible. Switching it to his other hand so he could wipe his left on his breeches, he took another bite. It was sweet, just as before. His eyes wandered back to the mountains as he finished eating, taking in the vastness and harsh beauty of the range. If those were the Heartstrong Mountains, then all he had to do was find out where the Mage had been trying to take him. The spear would most certainly be there.

Gart recalled his short meeting with the Mage on the dusty road from New Caldea. Brunar had wanted him to go along and join 'others'. That was a surprising thought...that there might be others like him. He wondered who they might be. He could not remember if Brunar had mentioned how many of them there were supposed to be or what they would really be doing if they chose to come with him. The Mage had only said that they were supposed to work together to fight against the great evil that had reawakened.

Brunar had also mentioned the same name that the foul Slayer, Jor Dayne, had uttered when Gart had last seen him. Mordak. Gart nodded absently to himself as he chewed. It seemed that he and Brunar shared a common foe. If Mordak was behind Jor Dayne's attack on Tiller's Grove, as the Slayer had claimed, then he would certainly have to die as well.

Gart nodded to himself again as he made his short list of targets. Yes, Mordak had many lives to pay for. By now, it was certain that more had fallen victim to Jor Dayne, his vile Riders, and the nightmarish Gholans that traveled with him, and all had been sent by Mordak. They would all be made to pay for their murderous deeds.

Minutes later, Gart finished the apple and tossed its core away from the tree. He got to his feet and shouldered his pack, looking off towards the mountains as he did so. Gart's cold blue stare searched the whole of the Heartstrong Mountains, slowly moving from horizon to horizon, looking for anything that might aid him in his quest. His weapon was out there somewhere, the instrument of his vengeance. All he had to do was find it. He suddenly had a vague feeling about the western mountains, and decided to head in that direction.

What was that saying about a needle and a haystack? Gart thought to himself as he stepped away from the shady embrace of the tree and marked one of the largest western peaks to use as a guide. Satisfied with his choice, he strode with purpose and energy. At his throat, a gentle gleam of emerald went unnoticed.

Chapter 4

Terrence spit expertly into a nearby spittoon and turned his squinting eye back to the precious spyglass he held.

"What think ye, Brunar?"

The Mage stood next to Terrence on the starboard side of the ship, leaning against the railing as they both stared westward. Their eyes were focused far beyond the edge of the tall shadow of the *Damsel* that stretched away from the rising sun.

Brunar was silent for a moment. He closed his eyes, placed his fingers to his temples and sent his astral vision upward and westward, searching.

The day had dawned much as the others had, clear and bright, driving away the faint chill of late spring that still came with the eventide. The weather had been growing subtly warmer as they had traveled, heralding a hot summer to come, but the nights were still cool on the sea. Brunar had met the dawn as he had each day since boarding the *Damsel*, sitting cross-legged in the bow of the boat, meditating deeply. He had already been there for over an hour when the alarm had come.

One young sailor, near the end of his turn at high watch, had spied something to the west that had made the hairs on the back of his neck stand on end. In seconds, he had monkeyed down from the crow's nest and rushed to find the captain.

Now every hand was on deck, silently staring out across the water, straining to locate whatever might be out there. No one was certain what had been seen, least of all, the sailor who had seen it. A sea monster? Pirates? Something worse? No one could say.

Nessar's gravelly voice rumbled across the deck.

"Brunar? What is it? What's going on?" Nessar made his way up to the captain and the motionless Mage, rubbing the sleep from his eyes as he walked. Kiran was at his side, and they walked to the rail to stand next to Layton, Bjarke, and Alyssa, who had already taken posts there. Nessar watched as Brunar returned to himself, opened his grey eyes, and dropped his hands back to his sides.

When Brunar turned to the old thief, he wore an unaccustomed look of confusion on his bearded face. He scowled as he replied, speaking to them all.

"Truth be told, I know not. It appears to be a great black spot upon the water, larger by far than the *Damsel*. It appears to be some type of oil."

Kiran stifled a yawn. "Oil? Well that's a relief. Let's go back to bed."

Brunar shook his head once, his lips compressed into a thin line.

"No, Kiran, it wasn't oil. As I neared it, I sensed in it some kind of life. Whatever it is, it is most definitely a living thing, but I could sense little more than that. If it is a creature, it's one that I've never seen before." Brunar left unvoiced the vague impression he had received from the blot, a strange sense of intensity that he could not yet put into words.

Just then, the Weya made their way to the rail. Valelder Moihra's face was stern as she climbed as high as she could and peered across the water. She looked out at the gentle waves for only a moment, then turned to Ginn and spoke quietly to him in their melodic language. Ginn nodded, then hurried to the mainmast and climbed towards the crow's nest, moving with amazing agility.

Turning back to the waves, Moihra spoke, her melodic voice somehow carrying to everyone.

"If what Brunar says is true, we may have a serious problem. I have sent Ginn to confirm my suspicions, but I feel that we should change our course, nonetheless. Captain, we need to put some distance between us and yon spot, and we need to do it with all speed. Turn to the southeast, if you please."

Without questioning or even raising a grizzled eyebrow, Terrence turned over his shoulder and barked the orders that would turn them sharply towards the distant coast. Instantly, the men of the *Damsel* swarmed about, performing their tasks with flawless precision as the helmsman spun the wheel to change their course.

The ship smoothly angled more to the east, making the Guardians sway in unison as the *Damsel* moved beneath their feet. Within seconds, she had altered course and settled back into a gentle, steady rhythm.

When Terrence turned back to Brunar, the Mage nodded approvingly and both men turned to look to the west once more. Pressing closer, the Guardians added their gaze to those of the two men and the Weya. It seemed that more than one Guardian held their breath as they waited to hear the news.

From above, Ginn's voice rang out in Weya, clear and strong in the early morning air. Moihra grimaced and waved one graceful hand to summon him down from his lofty perch. Though she had hoped for anything but this, Ginn had only confirmed her fears. She turned her back to the waves, and spoke only loudly enough that Brunar and his Guardians could hear.

"The thing that the watchman sighted this morning is called a Shipsbane. It has also been called an Ooze and a Black Water Wraith. Though we have walked and sailed this world for millennia, we still know very little of them, what they are or where they came from. They are exceedingly rare, a fact for which we are thankful. All we know is that they live in the oceans, resemble large patches of black, oily water, and they appear to be drawn to ships that pass nearby. Their method of life is beyond us."

Kiran folded her arms and cocked her head to one side. A world-weary half-grin slid across her face as she spoke.

"I take it that these things eat ships, or something to that effect?"

"Yes, Kiran, they are surpassingly good at that. We know not what draws them. By all accounts, they attack passing ships, swarming up from the waterline and coating every exposed surface. Its very body acts like an acid, dissolving everything it touches, including wood, metal, flesh, and bone. A ship attacked by such a beast will be crippled in minutes, and completely consumed within an hour. And that includes the entire crew. Diving off the ship or taking to the sea in a longboat only delays death, for the beast will quickly finish the ship and then come after anything else in the water. I am hoping that we changed course soon enough to escape its notice."

Nessar spoke up from his place next to Kiran. As it always did whenever the oldster addressed the leader of the Weya, Nessar's voice was filled with respect and deference, in spite of his alarm.

"I've lived in a seaport all my life, Valelder, and I've never heard of one of these things. Why is that?"

A wry smile appeared on Moihra's lovely face. "Because they work so quickly that there are usually no survivors to report what happened to them. Ages ago, friends of the Weya asked some of us to investigate the disappearance of several ships in a particular group of islands not far from here. The lack of any trace whatsoever of the ships led some to believe that magick was involved, so naturally, our friends sought us out, thinking that we would know the way of it. Those of us who chose to explore the mystery found absolutely nothing for years upon years. However, we are a patient people, and we eventually managed to glean this much lore of the creature from a handful of survivors over the centuries."

Bjarke cleared his throat and took a deep breath before speaking. He was feeling much better, but still feared that he might yet vomit at any moment. "So this. . . blot. It is a creature, then?"

A quick nod from Moihra answered him. "It acts as such, although we have never been able to directly observe one to find out."

Terrence snorted at that.

"Respectfully speakin', Mum, but 'ere be yer chance ter see one up close and personal-like, so be takin' notes in case Brunar can wizard us away from 'ere. Might come in 'andy later on."

In spite of the danger, Moihra laughed. Her light, tinkling mirth lightened the hearts of those who heard it; it was a welcome sound.

Layton leaned back from the rail as he spoke. "So what do we do if it sees us? Will it chase us? How do we fight something like that?"

The Valelder nodded again. "If we have already managed to pass it by without alerting it to our presence, then we should be safe. However, if it did sense us, it will most certainly pursue. As for fighting it, we may as well be fighting the water itself, for all the good it would do."

Her answer unnerved Layton. He had never met anything that he could not best in actual combat, and he was at a loss for what to do.

Before she could elaborate further, a shout from the crow's nest alerted them. The sailor on watch pointed towards the ships wake, a good distance behind them. Brunar stepped toward the rear of the boat as he followed the watchman's direction. Everyone followed him closely enough to hear him mutter, "I can see it. It comes."

Gathering at the rear of the ship, the Guardians peered out at the open sea behind them, searching for the creature that Brunar had already seen. It took only moments for the Shipsbane to become visible to them all.

Still quite a distance away, the creature appeared as a darkening of the water, like the shadow of a dense cloud upon the ocean. But this was no shadow, and it was rapidly skimming across the surface of the water, steadily gaining on the fleeing ship. Parts of its inky body would rise and fall above the water, as if looking for its prey.

Suddenly, the Mage was in motion, barking orders. "Stand back, everyone! Bjarke, ready yourself to use your Gift.

With luck, we can persuade the beast that we are not to be trifled with." Brunar motioned for Bjarke to step forward. Although yet unsteady, Bjarke stood with Jidaan firmly in hand and ready for action, his jaws were tightly clenched against his nausea.

Placing a steadying hand upon Bjarke's beefy shoulder, Brunar instructed the larger man. "Let's hope this works. You can see the beast now?" Bjarke nodded. "Good. Call your power and send a blast of magick into the water just ahead of the beast. We'll see if we can frighten it away."

Concern etched the newly-tanned features of the Mage as he surveyed the swaying form of his most powerful warrior. The sickness had not yet left him, and for all Bjarke's seemingly endless strength, Brunar could feel the tremors of weakness radiating from Bjarke's massive form.

Softly he added, "It need not be your most tremendous blast, Bjarke. Save your strength, for we may have need of you again soon." Without another word, Brunar removed his hand from the big man's shoulder. He stepped back to leave Bjarke alone at the railing, peering out at the oncoming beast.

For a few seconds, all was silent, save the whipping of the sails and the crash of the waves against the boat. Bjarke took a deep breath and let it out. Then another. He took one more, longer than the first, and then he began to hum. The sonorous rumble came from deep within him, his way of calling to his Jidaan, asking its power to awaken.

The ruby pommel of his weapon flared brilliantly to life in answer to his summons. Bjarke's eyes were intent on the approaching shadow of the beast, and the light from his Jidaan was reflected in them.

Kiran felt the deck beneath her booted feet begin to quiver as Bjarke's power began to build.

"What in the world . . .?" Kiran heard Nessar's startled voice just over her shoulder. It suddenly occurred to her that in all the time they had trained at the Keep, they had never seen Bjarke fully unleash his Gift. Bjarke and the Mage had always trained outside where the power of Bjarke's Jidaan would not undermine the strength of the caves and passageways within the mountain. Now, she could feel the sheer potency of Bjarke's power thrumming through every part of the ship.

Bjarke swayed gently as he gathered his power. Still humming, the gentle giant removed his left hand from his Jidaan and reached towards the ocean, towards the monster that threatened them.

The dazzling ruby fire that blazed within the Jidaan's pommel intensified until Kiran had to shade her eyes. It was like gazing into a small, crimson sun. The blaze finally became too much to be contained within the gem, and its magick flowed along the entire length of the weapon in Bjarke's mighty right hand, enveloping it. Still it grew. The giant's humming got louder as he continued to gather the Jidaan's Gift of Power.

Just when it seemed that Bjarke would explode with ruby magick, he made a sound like a sharp cough. The power that had built in his Jidaan instantly flowed through his body at his command. Using his will to guide it as Brunar had taught him, Bjarke easily channeled the Gift, and a massive gout of scarlet force erupted along his outstretched left arm and surged towards the distant creature, roiling through the air with incredible intensity. Though the questing crimson power was well above the agitated surface of the water, it still ripped its own wake into an ocean already split open by the passing of the ship.

Before his magick could even reach its mark, Bjarke collapsed, leaning heavily on the rail and trying desperately to maintain his footing. The strain of channeling so much power was plain on Bjarke's pale face, and a low groan escaped him as he tried not to fall to the salty wet boards of the deck. Ill though he was, Bjarke still maintained a firm grip on his Jidaan. Alyssa, Nessar, and Kiran were at his side in an instant, helping him away from the rail, looking for a place where they could set him down to rest more comfortably.

Just then, Bjarke's magick hit the water a few yards ahead of the oncoming creature. The resulting explosion of seawater dwarfed the ship, sending a great burst of water in all directions. The Guardians held their breath as their eyes lighted on the ebon spots of dark water within the towering geyser, surely pieces of the beast caught in the eruption. High in the air the black droplets went, spreading apart from each other and losing cohesion from the force of the blast.

Instantly, a raucous cheer went up from the crew of the ship. Many fists rose high in exultation at their victory over the Shipsbane, and a few sailors broke into a rowdy jig. But the Weya cheered not. Their eyes stayed on the far-flung droplets of jet-black ooze as they rose in the air, slowed, then began to plummet back towards the surface of the water with the rest of the spray. It was their far-seeing jewel-like eyes that first saw that the droplets of darkest black were beginning to search each other out, to join with one another, even as they fell from the sky.

Ginn's firm voice cut through the celebration of the sailors. "'Ware! It reforms itself and comes for us anew!" He pointed one finger out towards the place where the Weya had seen the reforming beast reenter the water. The noise of the sailors died at once, and all eyes turned again to the sea. White-knuckled, the Mage peered intensely at the spot where he had seen the dark droplets fall.

For a moment, there was nothing save the settling of the ocean as it swallowed the aftermath of Bjarke's great blast. Then, from just beyond the ship's wake, a black, shapeless *something* reared up out of the water. It had no head, arms, or tail; it was a great inky glob of a beast. Without a sound, it surged towards the boat, merging instantly with the surface of the water and slithering towards its prey at horrifying speed.

Brunar felt the intensity of the beast quicken as it neared them. A focused sense of wrongness reached the Mage, and he knew that he had to learn more. Reaching out with his senses, Brunar filtered out everything but the unidentifiable feeling that he had touched earlier, and was finally rewarded.

The beast was furious. Its consciousness was alien, far unlike anything Brunar's mind had ever touched before. The Mage winced at the peculiar feel of the monster's thoughts, vague impressions that he could make little sense of. The only thing of which he was certain was that something within the beast raged with a strength far beyond that of any creature Brunar had ever encountered. In touching that inhuman rage, Brunar knew without a doubt that the beast would not stop, could not stop, until it had taken the *Damsel* and all aboard her. The Mage knew also that his own power could not sway this creature where the potent might of Bjarke's Jidaan was ineffective. Another way must be found.

Brunar turned to Layton, whose young face was settled into a frown as he looked towards the onrushing death that pursued them.

"Layton, let us try your Gift. If you can catch that creature in one of your Gates, it is possible that we can transport it far enough away that we can escape."

Without a word, Layton turned and unsheathed his weapon. Brunar had noticed that the lad always preferred to have his Jidaan at battle readiness when he called to it. Old habits die hard, Brunar thought.

Layton did not hum as Bjarke had done. Instead, he simply took a breath, exhaled, and then willed his Jidaan to brilliant life. As his pommel gem flashed its opalescent fire,

Layton's face took on the dreamy half-smile that he assumed when fighting. Without a hint of effort, he asked, "Where should I put the second gate, Brunar?"

"If you can, place it directly behind us as far away as possible, and face it away from us. Hopefully, that will disorient it and give us time to run." Brunar watched his pupil nod once, then tilt his chin upwards a fraction as he prepared to create the Gates.

Out in the sea, several yards before the onrushing creature, a bright, opalescent square burst into being. It was more than big enough for the beast to pass through, and far beyond that first gate flashed its counterpart, the portal that would expel the monster in the opposite direction. Only seconds separated the dark ooze from the first gate, and it did not slow. Brunar and all of those watching held their breath again as they awaited the outcome.

Moving through the sea like quicksilver on a stone floor, the deadly creature raced right up to the Gate. . .and flowed around and under it, appearing on the nearer side of the glowing portal. It was undeterred in its pursuit.

Winded now, Layton let the gates dissolve into nothingness as he turned worried eyes towards the Mage. Perspiration dripped from his brow and stung his eyes. With a grunt of dissatisfaction, Layton resheathed his Jidaan.

Brunar clenched his teeth in frustration, but only for a second. "We have to get this ship out of here. I can show you a way, but you'll have to use your Gift again, and move the entire ship to safety. I know you're tired, but I don't see an alternative."

"I understand. I'll do my best." Layton's fist went to his heart and he bowed his head a fraction, as was his custom. Inwardly, he tried to marshal his strength. The Gates he had just created and dropped had been far less than half the height of the ship, though at least as wide. Although his powers had vastly increased throughout his training, he and the other Guardians were still exhausted by the use of their Jidaan's Gifts. That kind of stamina was much harder to build. "I don't think I have the strength to take us very far from here, Brunar. I might only be able to open one more set of gates this size before I'm spent, and it won't take us far enough away. The creature will surely catch us."

"I know. You'll only need to move us once, Layton, and hopefully it will be enough." Brunar nodded and took the young warrior's arm in a firm grip. Looking upwards towards the crow's nest, Brunar said, "Jump when I jump," and Layton nodded his assent. The Mage flexed his knees and spoke two short, arcane words that pricked the ears of the Weya. Layton jumped as instructed, and instead of a mere hop, the pair suddenly left the deck as they jumped up, up, up, gaining speed as they floated through the air towards the lookout perch. In moments, they had alighted within the small space. Brunar released Layton's arm so they could both grip the handholds and rails provided for that purpose.

After scanning the approaching coastline for only a moment, Brunar turned back to the young Guardian.

"Listen. We haven't much time. I need you to Gate me to that tall spire of rock, the one just there." He pointed, and Layton's gaze followed his teacher's direction.

As they neared the rocky shore, they could see great fingers of rock jutting out of the ocean, forming tall, steep islands that walled off parts of the coast from the open sea. There were many sheltered inlets and lagoons, and Layton guessed that Brunar intended for him to send the ship to one of them. He marked the high peak that Brunar had indicated, and nodded.

"Gate me there, and then prepare to create another Gate for the ship. From that vantage point, I can guide you and show you exactly where to take the Damsel. I'm betting there's a cove back there that's hidden from the open sea, and from the creature as well. We can hide there until it leaves us. Understand?"

Layton nodded as he pulled his Jidaan from its sheath. The pitch and sway of the ship was far more pronounced at that great height, so he firmly gripped the railing with his other hand. He had some doubts about Brunar's plan, but his trust in the Mage was total, and he discarded them.

Brunar held still for a moment as he spoke to the captain, quickly trying to explain his strategy. Terrence's gruff voice answered loudly from below.

"Whatever you're goin' ter do up there, just do it, ye blasted wizard! Goddess above, we're running out o' time!"

Brunar smiled at his friend's usual bluntness and then nodded to Layton. "Send me there, and listen for my call."

Layton took a deep breath and opened a Gate for his teacher. Upon the tall spire, the Gate's opalfire twin appeared as well. Brunar stepped through the portal and onto the dark, rough stone. It took an instant for him to adjust to the fact that the stone was solid beneath his feet and did not move as the ship had, but then he stood firm again.

Turning, he immediately saw the ship cutting through the ocean, heading diagonally towards the coastline. In seconds, it raced by, the beast not far behind. He could see that the dark blot of the Shipsbane was quickly closing the distance. From his new vantage point, Brunar saw how truly big the beast was, bigger than he had thought.

He turned away from the ocean, looking down into the lagoon far below him. What he saw made him swear aloud.

The inlet was more than large enough for the ship to coast to a stop after being suddenly Gated into it. It was also concealed in such a way that the ship could hide there safely until the beast left the area. But there were complications.

The tall pillars of stone that had helpfully sheltered the little bay from the open sea had also hidden a line of jagged rocks, a squat and deadly jetty that rose an arms length above the surface of the water, bisecting the narrow channel. Neither of the two resulting pools were quite long enough in themselves to be of use.

Time was growing short, and Brunar knew it. There wouldn't be enough room to stop or even slow the ship once it hurtled into the hidden grotto. Another way had to be found. Looking over the lagoon below and then back at the ship to gauge its speed, Brunar made his decision. He prayed to Rowann that his calculations were correct. Gathering his magick, he stepped from the spire and plummeted towards the distant rocks below, ignoring the sharp ledges and jutting protrusions that flashed past him as he fell.

Brunar chanted a short spell as he neared the rocky base of the spire, and his descent slowed until he touched down gently upon an outcropping. The Mage wasted no time, and quickly picked his way across the slippery rocks until he gained the beach. As he had fallen, he had spotted a huge, flat stone on the narrow shoreline. He needed a firm base upon which to stand if his new plan were to succeed, and that rock looked like it would work. He sprinted for the stone, hoping it would suit his purpose.

As soon as his booted feet touched the wide stone, Brunar instantly knew that it would be more than sufficient. He keenly felt the deep strength of the boulder, and knew that the vast majority of it was buried beneath the white sands. The exposed plane of rock was only a tiny fraction of the whole, and it would hold him well for what he intended to do.

The Mage settled himself into position in the middle of the flat stone, bending his knees slightly as he prepared to cast his spell.

Back aboard the *Damsel*, Terrence bellowed commands to his crew, and all hands prepared for whatever might come. On the deck, Bjarke was back on his feet, dark circles of exhaustion under his eyes from the combined stress of the seasickness and the strenuous use of his Gift. Alyssa, Kiran, and Nessar stood next to him, keeping their eyes on the approaching horror behind them. Without words, the Weya finally left their places and rushed towards the rigging, lending their firm, strong hands to the readying of the ship.

In the crow's nest, Layton concentrated on the task before him. He needed to build the two gates, one for the ship to enter and one in the lagoon for the ship to exit, and then quickly close them before the beast could pass through as well. If he waited too long to close the portals, then the creature would follow them into the cove, and they would surely perish. If he shut the Gates too early, he risked clipping the ship in half. Goddess willing, the hidden lagoon would shield them from the creature, and they could at least hope to escape with their lives. Layton took another deep breath to steady his racing heart as he waited for Brunar's call.

Moments later, Brunar's voice echoed in Layton's mind, followed by a view from the Mage's own eyes. Shocked at the vision, Layton's mouth fell open and he started to voice his objections.

Brunar, the rocks. . .! Layton's fear and uncertainty bled through the mental connection he shared with the Mage, only to be answered by Brunar's firm resolve.

Leave them to me, Guardian. Now use your Gift.

For an instant, Layton grimaced at the hint of reproach nestled within Brunar's words. He had reacted like a frightened child at the sight of the rocks, not as a warrior-born, and certainly not as a Guardian. Ashamed, he strove to remember his training, the years of harsh discipline he had endured in the East, and then drew upon it to calm his spirit. The almost supernatural focus that his old training afforded him returned almost at once, and he banished all thoughts except for the task before him.

At peace once more, Layton invoked his Gift.

Layton's Jidaan eagerly answered his summons, flaring brightly in his hands. Directly within the path of the ship, a great shining square of opalfire suddenly blinked to life. Thousands of colors played within its boundaries, dancing and spinning in the magick's silent embrace. Following the view from Brunar's eyes, Layton also opened the twin of this gate in the nearest end of the lagoon. A half-smile played across his tired face as he guided the huge portals, holding them in position with perfect control.

Many of the sailors gasped in astonishment at the huge opalescent doorway they approached, but they stayed where they were, proving themselves to be the stalwart crew that Terrence knew and trusted. The *Damsel* rushed upon the Gate, reached it . . .and suddenly hurtled into the lagoon, fiercely churning the still, blue water.

With a silent thump of power, Layton slammed the gates shut behind them, leaving the hungry, raging creature to search an empty ocean. He whirled to scan the frothing water behind them to be sure that he had closed the gate in time and was relieved to see that he had succeeded. His blood sang in his ears and his vision blurred with sudden exhaustion. Layton willed himself to stay on his feet, but he could tell that the toll of using his Gift on such a massive scale had nearly been too much.

Turning his attention forward, Layton wondered vaguely about the sudden shouting that arose from sailors in the rigging. He realized that they were getting their first look at the jagged rocks that lay in their path. Scant seconds remained until the ship would meet its doom upon them. Hoping that Brunar knew his business, Layton hurriedly sheathed his weapon and clutched the railing in front of him.

Sailors were yelling frantically at each other as they scurried about their tasks, and Terrence's strident voice overpowered them all. The Captain shouted orders, trying to make adjustments that would aid the ship before she slammed into the jetty, but he knew that it was already far too late. The helmsman spun the wheel with all his might, but everyone could see that it would not be enough. Some of them might survive, but certainly not all. The crew and passengers of the *Damsel* braced for impact.

Suddenly, the voice of the Mage rang out over the cove. Strange and beautiful words of magick carried easily to the *Damsel* as the Mage sang his powerful plea to the ship, the water, and the wind. Frightened eyes turned to see Brunar standing tall upon a massive stone on the beach, arms outstretched, a pure violet fire blazing furiously around him. The craggy rocks ahead jutted from the bottom of the lagoon like vicious claws, waiting to rip out the valiant ship's underbelly. Unflinching, Brunar continued his chant as they rushed towards the deadly barrier.

With a great popping of canvas, the sails suddenly strained at their masts, filled near to bursting with a great gust of wind that knocked more than one sailor unsteadily to the deck as the gale pushed the hurtling ship even faster. The Damsel lurched forward in her headlong flight as the wind embraced her. . .embraced her, and lifted her.

"Hold on, ye bastards!" Terrence yelled to his crew as he grabbed a nearby railing. He prayed to Rowann fervently-though with a great smattering of foul language-that his beloved ship would survive. He figured that the Goddess would forgive his vulgarity, given the circumstance.

Brunar's chant escalated, as did the gale, but he could not yet see if it would be enough. His song pleaded for the ship to rise, for the water to swell upwards and push the ship over the obstacle. Even as the churning waters rose beneath the ship, surging away from the beach as they were called to lift the rushing vessel, Brunar prayed.

The Damsel rose higher, and higher still upon the water and wind and magick that drove her. But it was not enough.

The ship jerked in midflight as its vulnerable hull was viciously raked open by the rocks, dislodging a handful of sailors from the rigging. The rending and cracking of wood filled the air, and shards of the hull began to fall away from the ship as it cleared the reef.

"HANG ON!" Brunar's disembodied voice, louder than thunder, called from all sides as the ship rode the huge wave of water and wind into the lagoon beyond the jetty. The ship sagged deeply into the water, her already battered hull slamming into the submerged rocks that were hidden there. A great *SNAP!* was felt and heard by every crewman and passenger on the ship as the keel gave way, and the impact loosened the grips of more unlucky sailors, flinging them about like ragdolls.

The ship quickly heaved herself upwards again, but it was painfully clear that she was already taking on water.

Standing upon his boulder on the beach, Brunar abruptly changed his song as he beseeched the wind to change its direction slightly, to lift and carry the ship even as she moved forward. He knew that he had to get her to the shallower water if there were to be any hope of saving her. Blazing violet magick radiated from the powerful Mage as he cast his spell, again asking the elements for their assistance. They heard him, and responded.

The sails snapped forwards and upwards again as the wind answered Brunar's plea. The masts groaned at the abuse, but held strong. The *Damsel* lurched forward, angling towards the beach, dragging lower and lower into the water as her belly filled. Sailors swung painfully from their tethers in the rigging with rope burns on hands and waists.

Pulling against the water in her hold, the *Damsel* slid sluggishly through the cove. As she approached the far side, the damaged hull scraped bottom again, and the ship rode up in the water as the wind drove her firmly into a sandbar at the edge of the lagoon. The sails went limp as the Mage-summoned wind dissipated, and all was quiet.

Chapter 5

Beneath the sweeping branches of a majestic oak tree, a short distance from the narrow path he had been following for days, Gart sat looking at his right hand. He had only built a tiny cooking fire, and the day's light was waning quickly. He squinted in the gentle twilight to better see the muscles and tendons of his hand and forearm as he slowly clenched and unclenched his fist, turning it this way and that. His hand had been badly slashed and torn during his battle with the vicious Gholans a few nights ago. Had so little time passed? Gart shook his head. Being under the water, if that was truly where he had been, had left him with a vague sense of timelessness, and he could not tell for certain whether he had been with the spirit of the Lady RaeLynn for a few hours or for days upon end.

He shrugged to himself, looking at the unbroken skin on his hand and forearm. However long he had been with her, it had obviously done him some good. The wounds taken during the battle against the monster Jor Dayne and his undead riders and filthy Gholans had been healed completely, leaving naught but the faintest of scars where deep, painful wounds had been. She had somehow healed him and then sent him on his way.

Gart raised his eyes to the faraway mountains, still visible in the dying light, their massive, looming shapes lending an impression of immovable solidity that Gart found somehow comforting. Miles upon miles she had borne him, somehow depositing him on the shore of a lake that was far closer to the Heartstrong Mountains than her own had been. Closer to the stronghold of that Mage, Brunar, and to the odd weapon that was meant for Gart's hand alone.

A quiver of anger rippled through Gart's body at the thought of the Mage that had invaded his dreams with haunting images, and his hands clenched into fists. The visions of a woman who wielded a long-bladed spear as though it were a part of her own body still came to him, shocking him awake in the night. But although he deeply resented the Mage's intrusion, he had decided to take the advice of the Lady RaeLynn. In order to kill Jor Dayne, Gart would need the weapon that Brunar had called a Jidaan. Without it, the Lady RaeLynn had said that Gart would never succeed in his quest for revenge.

Gart planned to succeed or die trying. Jor Dayne had murdered his wife, Gennie, and his baby daughter Rheann. No death, no matter how slow or painful, would serve as just punishment for that, but Gart planned to see justice done. He would see the life drain from the monster's body, crushed and broken under Gart's magick and the strange power of the Jidaan.

He had been examining the dreams closely, letting himself feel every nuance of his dream-self's emotions and actions. Again and again he had felt his dream-self awaken the fire within the weapon, calling down rain, lightning, and even the very wind to do her bidding. After so many nights of dreaming and watching and feeling, Gart was beginning to understand. He almost knew how to call to the weapon and awaken its Gift, and once he knew how to do that, nothing could stop him. Soon, the weapon would be his, and Gart smiled at the thought of bringing the fury of the elements down upon Jor Dayne and his evil master, Mordak.

Nodding absently to himself, he picked up the knife that lay on the ground next to him and reached for the sturdy branch he had found just before settling down for the night. It was not so long as he was tall, but was nearly a handsbreadth thick at the thickest part, and he had liked the feel of it in his hands. He had already whittled the bark from its rough surface. He now began the laborious process of shaping it to his purpose, slimming the middle, rounding one end while flattening the other, and testing it for balance every so often. Gart's eyes, icy blue even in the warm glow of the tiny fire, narrowed in concentration as he strove to recreate something he had only seen in a dream.

Chapter 6

A rough breeze whipped around the sheltering rocks of the lagoon, and it snapped and ruffled the pennants and limp sails of the stricken *Damsel*. She lay fully mired in the sand at the lagoon's edge, tilted off to one side. Her belly was open to the sky above. She was badly wounded, and it would be a long while before she would sail the seas again.

During her short, bucking ride, several barrels and crates had been dislodged from their lashings on deck and now floated in the lagoon, mingling with the broken shards of the ship. Four unfortunate sailors had been pulled from among those bobbing items, all dead. The wheezing wind did little to cheer those who had survived.

Brunar surveyed the scene from atop a tall promontory of stone, his cold grey eyes more tired now than anyone alive had ever seen them. The effort of calling the wind and water to aid the ship had nearly rendered him senseless. As soon as he had seen that the ship had run aground and would move no more, Brunar had promptly collapsed atop the great boulder that had supported him during his casting. His entire body was weary and sore. The magick he had expended was taking a far greater toll on him than he had hoped it might, but he dare not let his Guardians know it. While they aided the crew and helped the injured, Brunar tried to slow his breathing and gather strength enough to continue.

He watched silently as Terrence's crew carried supplies from the heavily damaged ship to the shore. The lifeless bodies of the crewmates they had pulled from the water had been laid carefully in the shade of the trees at the edge of the beach and covered with a canvas. As tough and seasoned as these men were, more than a few had cheeks that were wet with tears. Terrence had been nearly silent since the ship had run aground, save to direct his men to their tasks. Although he did not blame Brunar for the fate of his ship, the loss of his men and the damage to the *Damsel* had hit him hard.

Brunar knew that the ship could be repaired, but not in time for them to reach Rualtha and Laro beyond it. Even his magick was not able to mend such damage as had been done to the brave little ship in such short order.

The hull had been holed, of that there was no doubt, and the keel was broken. Indeed, the sound of its demise had filled the air when the ship had dragged the bottom beyond the jetty.

Brunar guessed that some of the huge, U-shaped ribs and their tie-plates inside of the ship had been broken or damaged as well. If they were lucky, the keelson would still be intact, but somehow, Brunar doubted that they would be so fortunate.

They had managed to save the ship from total destruction, but the damage had been massive nonetheless, and there was little to be done with her until she was repaired. She was beached in a coastal lagoon, surrounded by tall cliffs of stone, and badly wrecked. It was beyond Brunar's power to move her again without her own momentum aiding him, and although Layton could use his Gates to easily move the ship back out to the open sea, it was useless to do so until the repairs were made. They would have to move on without the ship.

A distant *whump!* erupted from somewhere behind Brunar. He turned his gaze in that direction and noticed movement a score of yards or so into the dense forest beyond the narrow beach. A large tree was just beginning to fall. As its thickly-leafed top quickly disappeared into the canopy and headed for the earth, Brunar could hear Bjarke's deep voice bellowing for any and all to clear the way.

In spite of the pain he felt at the deaths of the brave sailors, Brunar had to smile a little bit at the sound. Bjarke's illness had literally vanished the moment he had his feet back on land. With renewed vigor, he had set about aiding the injured and hauling supplies from the stricken ship like a man possessed. His prodigious strength had obviously returned, as the big man had single-handedly carried massive crates from the ship that usually needed three or four men to move.

Many of the horses had been saved, though a few had been sorely injured and had to be put down, much to everyone's dismay. Bjarke had been the only one able to calm the frightened beasts until they could be safely removed from the ship.

Alyssa, Valelder Moihra, and Ginn tended the injured on shore once all those in need of care had been moved from the ship. Bjarke and Cohl had gone into the forest seeking wood for the repairs that would eventually be made to the *Damsel*, though the Guardians would be long gone before she would be seaworthy again. Brunar knew that Cohl would have said brief prayers of thanks to the trees before Bjarke used powerful swings of his blazing Jidaan to fell them.

A ripple passed across Brunar's senses and he turned to his right once again. An instant later, one of Layton's gates appeared, man-sized this time, and the sandy-haired youth stepped through it. It disappeared, leaving Layton facing the

Mage. The strain of the recent uses of his Gift was evident in the slump of his shoulders and the drops of sweat that coursed down his face. Where neither a long run in the mountains nor a prolonged battle could faze him, using his Jidaan still drained him mightily, leaving a bone-deep weariness behind.

Emotions swirled from the younger man as would steam from a teakettle. Brunar did not have to see the drawn, tired look of Layton's face to know that he blamed himself for the ship's plight and for the deaths of the sailors, as it had been his Gate that had taken them into the lagoon. Brunar also knew that it had been their only chance. To try to evade the Shipsbane on the open sea would have most certainly cost the ship as well as the lives of the entire crew, and there had not been time for them to find a better cove. The loss of the four brave sailors and the ship was tragic, but it was far better than the loss of all.

Brunar reached out and squeezed Layton's shoulder in a silent gesture of understanding. As was his wont, Layton slapped a fist over his heart and bowed his head briefly to show his respect for his teacher, but left his eyes downcast. Brunar sighed. It would take time for the lad to understand. The Mage hoped that what little time they had would be enough.

Brunar spoke first. "Where is Nessar?" Once the Guardians had regained their composure following the wreck, he had sent Layton and the old thief to scout their position in case there might be renegades about. "Are we alone here? What have you found?"

"Sir, I have found no sign of any danger nearby. There is an ancient ruin a few miles to the east of here. There is a stable and a few outbuildings that are reasonably intact, and part of the main keep seems to be undamaged as well. It would shelter us far better than anything we could make here." He spent a few minutes describing the layout of the ruin, the remains of what had apparently been a grand castle at one time, now fallen into disrepair.

Brunar nodded at this. The land, though wooded, would not hinder them terribly, and the ruin would most likely be the best place to take stock of their situation and ready themselves for the journey overland to Laro. They could not afford to wait too long.

"And Nessar?" Brunar repeated.

Layton blinked and remembered that Brunar had asked about the thief. "Oh, yes! He and Kiran moved towards the southeast while I went northeast. They should be returning at any time now."

Brunar nodded at that. Once the supplies from the ship were all safely ashore, they could make ready for the trip through the forest and towards the ancient keep. They had plenty of time to make it there before nightfall, if they so chose. Something tugged at the back of the Mage's mind, something that made Brunar turn to Layton.

"Layton, did you see anything. . .strange about those ruins? Anything at all?" Brunar knew that the question sounded odd as soon as he uttered it. He had no idea what he was looking for, and if Layton had seen something, he most certainly would have mentioned it already.

"Strange? No sir. Just stone buildings, falling down here and there. It looked as though the place has been unused for ages, but I couldn't say why that might be." The lad thought for a moment longer before continuing. "Is there anything particular that I should watch for, sir?"

Brunar sighed and shook his head. "Well, castles rise and fall for any number of peculiar reasons, lad. I'm trying to remember if I've heard of one in this area that might have been well-known once and then deserted. For the life of me, though, I'm drawing a blank. I'll have to ask the Weya. Perchance they know something of it."

Layton agreed and then set off at a trot along the steep path that Brunar had used to mount the tall outcropping on which they stood. Tired though he was, the brief rest had helped him recover somewhat. Brunar watched him go, marveling at the young man's stamina. "Ah, the young," Brunar allowed himself a bit of a grin as the thought crossed his mind, smiling more at the fact that *everyone* was young to him, save the Weya, of course.

He turned his face to the open sea and resumed his wakeful meditation. He gauged that another quarter-hour or so would bring him enough strength to be more useful to the *Damsel's* stricken crew, and then he could rest again when night came.

The minutes passed slowly, and a small measure of Brunar's dwindling strength began to return to him. When the bone-deep weariness had finally faded, Brunar took a deep, cleansing breath. For now, at least, he was strong once more. Not for the first time since his awakening, Brunar thought that it was just like Mordak to be rude enough to rouse him early from his long, much-needed slumber, leaving the Mage so vulnerable and weak.

The thought of the foul one made Brunar turn away from the ocean to face southeast. His gaze wandered over the lush forest that bordered the rocky coastline, and he squinted into the distance at the rolling sway of the land. It undulated like a thick carpet of emerald green that covered leagues upon leagues. The sky above was a clear, beautiful blue, a smooth ocean upon which a few majestic cloud-ships silently sailed, watching over the land from above. There was no sign from here that such a malevolent evil as Mordak was abroad.

Feeling stronger, Brunar closed his eyes and Searched for Mordak, using his magick to look only for a faint trace of the madman that lurked somewhere out there. He did not want to betray his location with a more powerful sending, but he knew that his spell, the weakest of Searches, might suffice to find the foul sorcerer.

Without warning, a sharp pain pierced Brunar's mind, and the world faded into a red haze. Struggling to keep his balance, Brunar still fell heavily to the rocks on which he stood, skinning his knees and cutting his palms in the process. A deep, melodic laugh rang in Brunar's mind as he quickly regained control of himself and climbed back to his feet, wiping his bloody hands on his breeches. In spite of the pain in his head, Brunar tried to trace the sending, to locate the source of the attack, but it was gone. The foul one had struck quickly, then vanished.

Wiping tears of pain from his eyes, Brunar steadied himself. It had seemed to be a directionless attack, one only designed to strike a searcher, but not necessarily to locate him. Even in his pain, Brunar marveled at the effectiveness of the ward. He doubted if he could duplicate such a thing at this point.

Turning back towards the beach, Brunar noticed that Bjarke had laid the great tree trunks against the hull of the ship just so, making a perfect ramp to the Damsel. Sailors were still hauling supplies from the vessel and carrying them up the beach, where they piled them in a shady spot. Of Nessar and Kiran, there was no sign, but Layton had said that they would be back soon, and he could always Call to them if he chose. The lad himself was among the haulers, as was Bjarke.

Alyssa was still tending to several wounded sailors that had been carefully lain down in the shade below, and while Brunar watched, he saw and felt her will her Jidaan to life. The crystalline sparkle was dazzling, even from where the Mage stood. Someone had apparently been hurt badly enough that Alyssa deemed it necessary to heal him.

Brunar was glad to see her use that Gift. If Mordak was strong enough to cast such a powerful ward as the Mage had just encountered, there would be a great need for her healing powers in the very near future. Her strength would only increase with the practice. Indeed, there would be a great need for all of the Guardians' powers. Brunar hoped, as he had every day since awakening, that their combined strength would be enough to thwart Mordak's growing might.

Stepping carefully, lest he lose his footing yet again, Brunar started to make his way down the path to the beach. It was not yet midday, and there was much to be done.

Nessar and Kiran walked through the dense forest, listening to the unfamiliar sounds of its secretive life. They heard a distant thump every so often that they recognized as Bjarke's power, but otherwise heard only the rustling of the leaves overhead and the many little sounds of the forest. Sunlight streamed through the green, leafy canopy that sheltered them, making dappled shadows that danced all around, and a gentle breeze cooled their damp faces as they walked.

"Goddess, Ness, it almost seems like the forest is breathing, doesn't it?" Walking along beside her friend, Kiran's eyes nervously darted from one shadow to the next, searching for the source of her unease.

Nessar laughed. "Well, in a way, it is. Everything here is alive, and I think that we're just feeling that more acutely than we might have before."

Kiran raised an eyebrow as she cast a derisive glance at the old thief. "For a thief, you certainly sound like you think you know what you're talking about. Care to enlighten me further?"

He laughed again. "I'm not exactly an authority on this kind of thing, but I'll tell you what I think and you can take it or leave it." Abruptly, Nessar switched to the mindspeech that Brunar had taught them. *Can you hear me, little one?*

Kiran snorted and *spoke* back. *Well of course I can. I was there during that lesson, remember?*

Right. Nessar smiled as they walked, still watching around him for anything that might be interesting or dangerous, but he saw nothing. *Well, it's like that, I suppose. Before we started really using our magick, we could only hear and see the same things that everyone else does. But now, we can see or hear more than that. If we open our minds, there's a lot that we can learn just by feeling it. You told me once that you could feel what your opponents were going to do before they did it, right?*

Kiran nodded even as she answered. *Right. I just thought I was good at guessing what they were thinking, but according to Brunar, it's the magick, isn't it? I really do connect with them somehow.*

Yep. What you're feeling here in the forest is just an amplified version of that. You're in touch with everything here that's alive, if only in a small way. And there's an awful lot of living going on in here, even if we can't see it.

Kiran suddenly rapped Nessar on the shoulder, a good-natured little punch. He had known it was coming, but took it anyway.

"So when did you start going all mystical on me, old man? I thought you were the world's biggest skeptic."

Nessar laughed loudly at that, enjoying the sound of it in his ears. When his mirth subsided, he turned and planted a loud, fatherly kiss on Kiran's forehead.

"Egads, woman! If being transported across the Realm by a Mage to take up a magickal weapon and fight an evil sorcerer isn't enough to erode my skepticism just a bit, then I don't have a clue what would!"

Kiran made a show of wiping her forehead, but her grin betrayed her true feelings for the old man. "Come on, Grampy. We'd better be getting back to the beach before too long. It doesn't seem like there's much over this way to worry about anyway."

"I'll agree with you there, little girl." Nessar turned to head back the way they'd come, and Kiran suddenly laid her shoulder into him, slamming him down into the leafy earth. Without a word, she started dragging him behind the nearest tree.

"What in the nineteen Hels. . .!" Nessar ended his curse as soon as he saw the arrow quivering in the tree above him, right about where his head had been only an instant before. "Oh Goddess. This could be bad."

"Will you hurry up and get back here!" Kiran had already drawn her Jidaan and laid it on the ground beside her. She was pulling a pair of throwing daggers from her belt when Nessar scrambled around to join her.

Another arrow struck the tree, lower this time, and they heard another hiss past them on one side. A loud, masculine voice reached them.

"Hey back there! It's all right; we won't shoot you. Just come out with your hands up and we can all be nice!" Rowdy laughter followed, and Kiran counted at least four other voices besides the first.

Kiran and Nessar glanced at each other behind the shelter of the tree. *Is he kidding? He just did his best to feather us!* Kiran's mindvoice had more than a hint of amusement in it.

Nessar suppressed a smile. He had sensed excitement in Kiran's speech. She had been training for months and was about to see what she could do. Truthfully speaking, Nessar was excited as well. *Here, let me see what he wants. We might be able to have some fun with this. After all, we're the mighty Guardians, aren't we?* He winked at Kiran and she nodded back with a grin.

In a voice far more shaken and scared than Nessar had ever been, he yelled out, "Please! P-please! Don't shoot us! What do you want?" Nessar looked back at Kiran quickly.

How's that? Scared enough?

Kiran put a hand to her mouth to stifle her laughter. *It was perfect! Let's see what they say!*

It did not take long for the first voice to reply.

"Oh, we don't really want much, just the girl." The voices laughed again, louder this time. "She looked real pretty! Just send her out with her hands up, old man, and we'll let you leave with your life!"

Kiran's smile died. They had just made a rather massive mistake. It was most likely that this would not end without bloodshed, and as far as Kiran was concerned, the more, the better. She felt a hand on her arm and turned to look into Nessar's calm eyes.

Easy, Kiran. Let's do this the smart way, eh? Nessar had felt her tense and had known that she had come close to stepping out on the attack at the ruffian's words. From experience, he knew that she had a very simple plan of action where rapists were concerned: kill them. Quickly, slowly, it did not matter so long as they were killed. Kiran preferred slowly.

Her eyes blazed with fury but the hand on her arm calmed her somewhat. After a moment, she *spoke.*

All right then. I assume you have a plan?

A wink accompanied Nessar's response. *I do.* He silently outlined his plan to her and she considered it for only a moment before accepting.

Instantly, Nessar pulled a worn leather sap from somewhere and hefted it in a gnarled hand. The mischievous gleam in his eye told Kiran that this dull brown piece of weighted leather had been used many times before. Holding the sap at the ready, Nessar got his feet under him, closed his eyes, and invoked his Gift.

The stone of his sheathed Jidaan suddenly came to life, though it did not flare brightly as the others did. Instead, the solid outlines of its dark stone seemed to blur, leaving an unearthly, lightless void, a fathomless abyss clutched within the delicately-wrought steel of the pommel. A moment later, Nessar simply vanished.

Kiran had never seen him do this from so close by. She caught herself reaching out a hand to feel the place he'd been seconds before only to find him gone, as if he had never existed. The loud voice called again, and more laughter followed, bringing her back to the task at hand.

"Hey back there! You too scared to talk? Just send out the girl and we'll let you be on your way!"

Following Nessar's plan, Kiran replied in as sheepish a voice as she could stomach.

"You. . .you promise you won't hurt my father?"

Much laughter greeted that before the leader shushed the rest to silence. In a mocking voice, he called, "Why, of course, little girlie! We'll just let him go, and we'll even give him some money for the trip! We just want to visit with you for a while, that's all!"

Kiran replaced her throwing daggers in their sheaths then reached for her Jidaan. She remembered how awkward it used to feel in her hands, but now it somehow seemed right. Kiran stood to her full height behind the shelter of the tree and affected the little girl voice again.

"You promise?"

"Absolutely!" They laughed again. A wicked smile crossed Kiran's face when she thought how quickly that laughter would soon cease. She readied herself to play her part and stepped out from behind the tree, prepared to invoke her Gift of Warding at any moment.

As she had guessed, there were five of them, ragged and dirty to a man. Two of them held longbows, and Kiran knew that they would be the first to fall. Behind them stood another pair of thugs, armed with knives, and little else. The largest man stood in the rear, and it was obvious that he was the leader of this little troupe. He wore a sword on his hip, and his clothes were the least dirty and torn. He still had most of his teeth, as well. A thick scar ran down his left arm to the elbow, and Kiran thought about adding a matching scar to his other arm.

Kiran walked with her head held high and made no attempt to quell the anger that glowed on her face alongside a contemptuous smirk. Uncertainty dawned in the eyes of the bandits. This was not the girl-child they had expected. This woman was garbed as a warrior, with a warrior's stride and confidence. Their laughter ceased abruptly as their eyes were drawn to her beauty, and to the gleaming spear that she carried with ease.

"Well, well. Five big strong men against one defenseless little girl. How do you manage such bravery in the face of such overwhelming odds?" Kiran strolled slowly towards them, reaching out with her senses. She could feel their uneasiness now, far clearer than she ever had in the past. If she concentrated, she could almost feel their hearts thumping within their chests, racing with fear and nervousness. As she caressed their being with her own consciousness, she knew them for what they were: cowards, all. But even cowards could be dangerous.

The leader angrily pushed his way to the front. "Who are you? Where's the old man? I'm warning you, these lads'll feather you if I say so!" He craned his neck to search for Nessar.

"If I were you, I'd stop worrying about my 'father' and start worrying about *me*." Kiran's voice was firm and strong. There was no trace of the girlish fear the men had heard earlier. "We can do this nicely, or we can do it more roughly. I'm hoping that you decide to fight. . .I need the exercise."

The men exchanged nervous looks, but their leader threw back his head and laughed heartily. Kiran's smile widened. This was exactly what she had hoped for.

"Have you lost your mind, girlie? Look around! There's five of us, with longbows, and you've only got that stupid spear! What's to keep us from taking you down?" He let his eyes travel over her, lingering on the swells and curves that Kiran's armor could not hide.

Kiran ignored his lascivious gaze. She had been well-inured to such things long ago. Her eagerness for battle swelled within her, but she forced herself to wait.

"Well, first of all, you might rethink that bit about there being five of you."

Whump! Whap! The two bowmen crumpled to the ground, their weapons falling from nerveless fingers. Their comrades stared in shock, mouths and eyes wide in disbelief. The girl had made no move at all, and yet the two men had fallen like stones, large goose-eggs already forming on the backs of their skulls. Their leader drew his sword as they fell, but had no idea where to use it.

"Would you like to give up now, or do I need to take out the rest of you? I'm a bit of a Witch, you know. There's sooooo much more that I could do to you, if I choose. So what'll it be?" The question hung heavily in the gentle quiet of the forest.

The two men with knives promptly turned and started to run. Before they had even begun their sprint, they, too, were felled. *Thap! Whap!* Suddenly, their leader stood alone, shock still plain upon his grimy face. Fear followed soon after.

Turning bloodshot eyes towards Kiran, he paled as he saw her start to move. She had a sly, curling smile as she sauntered towards him, and her eyes were locked upon his, fiercely holding his gaze. She moved with a feline grace that now frightened him beyond words. His men had never had a chance against such a Witch, and he was terrified. He tried to hold his sword up, to point it at her throat, but her gaze seemed to sap the strength of his very soul, and the sword trembled in his grip.

"So, what shall I do to you, hmmm?" Kiran's smile widened, and the bandit's sword shook. She could tell that he was almost ready to panic and run. "Shall I boil your blood? Or turn you into a frog, perhaps? Or maybe I'll just roast the flesh from your bones while you stand there and. . ."

A groan and a thump jerked the bandit's gaze away from Kiran. A few feet away, Nessar lay facedown on the soft floor of the forest, his leather sap still in his hand. His clothes were drenched through with sweat, and it was clear that he was unconscious.

It took only an instant for the bandit to realize that he had been had. The old man had clearly used magick to get so close to them unseen, but the woman was no more a Witch than he. He whirled back to her, ready to fight, but it was already far too late.

Sensing his realization, Kiran moved faster than she ever had in her life, past his outstretched sword and inside his guard. A lightning-fast elbow smash to the face brought the last bandit down in a heap at Kiran's feet, unconscious. Without slowing, she moved to Nessar's side.

"Ness! Nessar! Are you alright? Can you hear me?" Kiran rolled her oldest friend over on his back and listened for his breathing. She checked to see that the blood was still thumping along in his neck, and was relieved to find that he seemed intact. She tried to give him some water and brushed a few strands of graying hair from his damp face while she waited for him to awaken.

Moments later, she was rewarded.

"Huh? Whuzzat? Who. . .?" Nessar tried to rise up on his elbows, but Kiran quickly pushed him back down.

"Just hang on, you old coot. I think you wore yourself out that time. Just take it easy for a minute, eh?" Amazingly, Nessar did not protest. He sipped at Kiran's waterskin for a few more minutes before trying to get up again. Still keeping a watchful eye on their sleeping attackers, Kiran helped him to his feet.

"Sweet Goddess, that was something else!" Nessar shook his head in disbelief, still allowing Kiran to help him stand. He was more tired than he had ever been in his life, but somehow, he was invigorated as well. "It was incredible! But I feel like I could sleep for a week."

"Well, you knew that using it for so long would wear you out, old man! You've used your Gift before, I've seen you!"

Nessar slowly shook his head. "Not like that, not for so long. I held it for as long as I could, but I think I finally just passed out." He turned to look at her. "You've used yours more often than I have, right?"

Kiran averted her eyes slightly as she spoke. "Yeah, well, I have, but not really that often. I've been too busy learning how to fight with the stupid thing to worry about the magick stuff. I'm a rank amateur when it comes to anything other than hack, slash, thrust, and parry."

Nessar shook his head once more to clear it, standing on his own at last. His head was still swimming, but he was slowly coming back to himself. "Woman, you need to learn how to use that Gift of Warding. It might come in handy later, don't you think? I mean, we are headed for a war." A hint of sarcasm was evident in his voice.

Kiran walked over to one of the prone bandits. He had started to stir, so she kicked him solidly in the head. He lay still once more.

"Yeah, well, I'll get to it. We just hadn't gotten to that point yet when the Weya showed up. How many times had you practiced yours, eh?"

Nessar scratched his head, then bent to the unconscious leader of the ragged little band. He pulled a small coil of rawhide from somewhere and cut a piece of it to bind the smelly brigand's hands tightly behind his back.

"Not nearly enough, yet...I guess you have a point. Brunar had only just started showing me how to use mine when the Weya came to get us. This was my second time to use it, and I held it for as long as I could. I could tell that I'm getting stronger with it, though." He cut a piece of rawhide and tossed it to Kiran, who deftly caught it and started binding.

Blowing a stray lock of hair from her face as she worked, Kiran agreed. "Yeah, I know you're right. I think I had a good idea of how to use it if that one had tried to attack me, but then I already knew eighteen different ways to take him out without using the Gift." She threw a frowning glance at the unconscious leader.

Nessar bound another pair of hands, and then another. "Well, be sure to bother Brunar about it when we get back. If things are going to get as bad as I think they are, we'll need every bit of power and magick we can muster, and that certainly includes you, baby girl."

Kiran smiled at his use of his pet name for her. He seldom used it anymore, for she had always given him holy Hel when he had used to call her that. She had to admit that she liked it this time.

"You're right as always, Gramps. Now let's get these bastards back to the camp. We'll let Brunar decide what to do with them."

Chapter 7

Gart had wandered far from the path, following his nose into the woods. He had been walking along, thinking about how best he could kill the slayer, Jor Dayne, and suddenly the smell of freshly baked bread caught his attention. The first hint of it made his mouth water, and although his thoughts were dark, the smell brought him back to the present. He loved fresh bread, and Gennie used to bake him a loaf anytime he requested one so that he didn't have to go to the town baker, who was always surly towards Gart. As the smell filled his nostrils, he decided that his pack was getting lighter all the time. If there were a settlement nearby, he could at least replenish his supplies, and maybe buy a hunk of that bread.

Pushing through a layer of low-hanging branches, Gart emerged at the top of a high overlook where he could see the forest spread out below him. There were no signs of humans anywhere-no smoke from cooking fires, no buildings, nothing at all but the lush greenery of the forest as far as he could see. It was early, and the air was still cool from the passing night. Gart took a deep breath, inhaling the delicious smell, wondering where it was coming from. He took a few steps forward to peer over the edge of the cliff to see if, by chance, there might be a dwelling at the base below.

Suddenly, the loose rock beneath his feet gave way and Gart slid out into space, frantically pinwheeling his arms in a vain attempt to regain his balance. For a few sickening moments, Gart fell, and then he impacted on his back with a loud splat that knocked the wind out of him. Clenching the thick mud in between his fingers, Gart struggled for a few moments before finally managing a relieved gasp as air found its way back into his lungs. He sat up, his head still ringing from the abrupt landing, and saw that he had fallen into a large pool of mud and water, covered over in places with lily pads and tall water grasses. From somewhere up above, a flow of water cascaded down the side of the steep bluff, creating a marsh with a small lake at the cliff's base. Gradually, his head stopped throbbing; he didn't feel anything broken or otherwise damaged. Cursing his luck, he turned to find his way to the edge of the bog. Spying the nearest bank, he pulled off his sodden pack and threw it as far from the water's edge as he could. His walking stick had fallen clear of the mud, and was lying in the grass nearby.

As his head cleared, Gart noticed that the smell he had followed was now intensely strong around him, so stong that he thought he should have been sitting in a bakery rather than stuck in the mud in a marsh. Instead of being a good smell, it was so thick that it almost made him nauseous. The scent was so out of place there in the bog that Gart instinctively knew something was not right. He turned over on his belly so that he could crawl out of the clutching mud and found that he was sinking deeper with every movement. He could feel his legs held tightly by the cloying muck, and knew that if he didn't escape soon, he never would.

Moving slowly, he managed to spread himself out as much on top of the mud as he could, slowing his descent. Mud was in his eyes, his mouth, and completely coating his body, but he ignored it as he set his sights on a jutting tree root just a few feet away. If he could just reach it, he knew he could pull himself out. Inch by torturous inch, Gart worked his way towards the root, taking slow, deep breaths in spite of the bready stench that surrounded him. Moments later, Gart stretched his right arm out as far as he could, straining mightily, and wrapped his slippery fingers around the exposed root. It was a tenuous hold at best, but he knew that he could use it to escape the muck.

Just then, a loud, burbling hiss froze him in place. Slowly, Gart turned his head in the direction of the sound and saw only an area filled with tall grasses and weeds. The hiss came again, and the grasses started swaying as something moved through the brackish water beneath. Whatever it was, it was big. Gart quickly turned his attention back to the tree root. Straining to reach, he tried to get a better grip and pull himself far enough to grab the root with his other hand, but his legs had sunk farther into the sucking mud, and it was all he could do to keep his one-handed hold.

Beneath the water, something slithered around Gart's right leg and wrapped itself tightly there. The pain was instantaneous; what felt like scores of sharp daggers jabbed themselves into his leg everywhere the serpentine thing touched. He cried out and frantically kicked his legs at the unseen creature that had snared him, but more snakelike arms reached him and grabbed his other leg. Both of Gart's legs felt like they were on fire. He struggled furiously, and managed to keep his slippery hold on the root. The tentacles began a slow and steady pull that felt like they were stripping his flesh from his bones. Gart knew that he had only moments before he would be dragged under the water. Anger came then, washing over him in a wave, lending him strength.

Using his free hand, Gart felt under the water and mud for the handle of his longknife. His searching fingers finally found the hilt and he carefully drew it from its sheath, thankful it had not been lost in the fall. As he drew it, the creature's head finally broke the surface, and Gart grimaced at the sight of it.

The head alone was nearly the height of a man, the rest of its huge bulk yet hidden under the mud and water. The creature was covered in mottled brown and black, heavily warty skin. It had massive golden eyes like a frog on either side of its pulsating head, and three hard ridges ran down its snout and over its eyes. Its impossibly wide mouth opened fully to display an alarming array of backward pointing, razor-sharp teeth and a questing tongue with barbs on the end, wiggling about as it tested the air. The creature hissed again as it worked its way closer to its prey and the thick, yeasty stink emanating from it intensified. Gart gagged as the smell, one he had thought so inviting before, now clogged his nose and throat. Crazily, he wished he had more mud in his nostrils to keep out the stench.

Gart reached down and laid the edge of the knife on one of the trapping tentacles on his leg and began to saw through it. The creature hissed in pain, and its tongue reached out, whipping through the air at Gart. He pulled his arm out of the mud to slash at the barbed tongue, but it lashed out and wrapped around his wrist before he could cut it. The pain was far worse than that of his legs, like acid being poured onto his wrist, and he screamed as his hand opened and the longknife dropped harmlessly into the mud next to him and began to sink. The creature hissed again, eager for its next meal.

In desperation, Gart awakened his magick. Reaching into the mud, he quickly found the sinking knife and pulled it out of the mire, holding it aloft where it floated, glinting in the sunshine. Quickly, Gart slashed the knife through the creature's tongue, severing it. The beast roared and hissed in pain, retracting its wounded tongue into its mouth and rocking side to side. The tentacles holding Gart's legs squeezed tighter and pulled harder, almost blinding him with intense pain. Struggling to maintain his grip on the tree root, Gart concentrated on keeping the knife in the air. The creature hissed again, and Gart saw his chance.

Manipulating the knife with his magick, Gart whipped it through the air at the creature's open mouth, embedding the long blade deep into the back of the monster's throat with a sickening, wet sound. The creature thrashed violently, its tentacles yanking Gart's hand off of the tree root at last and pulling him deep into the muck. Gart caught a fraction of a breath as he was pulled under the surface. He frantically tried to claw his way back towards the tree, his lungs already on fire. Furious, Gart fought with all his might against the inexorable, agonizing pull of the beast, certain that he was only moments from death. Suddenly, the tentacles unwrapped themselves from his torn legs and slithered away, unseen beneath the surface.

Energized by his newfound freedom, Gart exploded out of the water, gasping in a huge breath of air. Moving as fast as he could, he made his way towards the nearest bank. Behind him, the creature hissed and howled in agony, and pulled itself back into the deeper water, back into the shelter of the reeds and lilly pads, taking Gart's only weapon with it. Gart finally managed to grasp the root with both hands and pull himself onto drier ground. He crawled until his body was completely free of the muck and then his strength abruptly gave out. He collapsed facedown and panting, still covered in mud and grime from head to toe.

He stayed there for a time, lying on a soft cushion of grass, listening for any further sounds from the creature. None came, and Gart finally rolled over with a heavy sigh and found himself staring up into the leaves of a great oak tree. The sunlight played through the branches, leaving dappled shadows everywhere he looked. The cooling breeze washed away the thick, cloying scent that had drawn Gart-and likely many others-into the pit. The birds were singing, and had he not just escaped a gruesome and agonizing death, he might have found it pleasant. Instead, he was furious.

His legs and wrist were afire where the beast's tentacles and tongue had cut him, and Gart was concerned that his strength was not returning as fast as he thought it might. He swore under his breath, and considered going after the beast to finish the job. He thought better of it when he finally sat up and instantly became nauseated. Turning quickly to one side, Gart heaved what little remained of his breakfast into the grass. When he was sure that there was nothing more to bring up, he sat back once again to recover. His wrist was burning more each passing minute, and Gart tried to examine the wound, but it was difficult to see clearly through all the mud. Looking around, Gart spotted his backpack and walking stick, and slowly got to his feet to collect them. Spells of dizziness came and went as he moved, and he knew that something was wrong.

Keeping a wary eye on the marshy area where he had last seen the frog-like creature, Gart leaned heavily on his walking stick as he picked his way towards the tiny waterfall that cascaded down the side of the cliff. Dropping his pack nearby, he immersed himself in the brisk flow, allowing the water to cleanse him of the mud and filth that had covered him. He paid special attention to the slender gashes at his wrist and the many small cuts and punctures on his legs. He wished he had a clean cloth or shirt for a bandage, but most of the wounds had stopped bleeding, so he just left them alone. Gart didn't like the look of them, though; many were already beginning to turn red at the edges.

Stepping away from the waterfall, Gart surveyed the cliffs above. He knew that the road he had been following was not far from where he had fallen. Thankfully, the cliffs were no more than forty or fifty feet at the highest point. He had never done a lot of rock climbing, growing up in the forest as he had, but climbing into the tallest trees had often been an escape from the taunting of the older kids during his youth. He knew that he had to reach the road to continue his journey north, so there was no way around it. Carefully scanning the stone wall in front of him, Gart searched out the easiest way up.

After lashing his walking stick to his pack, Gart slipped his arms into it and settled it more comfortably on his shoulders. Still dizzy, he found a spot on the rockface with good hand and footholds, and started to climb. It took only moments for sweat to start pouring down his face. His breathing became labored after only a few feet, and Gart's nausea came and went in vicious waves.

I'll bet there was some kind of venom in the tentacles, he thought. *Just what I need.* Anger rose in him, frustration at feeling so weak and frail. He had a job to do. Jor Dayne and his master Mordak needed to be killed, and all of this was doing nothing but slowing Gart's quest for justice. Anger turned to rage, and Gart quickened his pace, pushing himself towards the top as fast as he could go without being reckless. He was still dripping from the waterfall, and he had to slow down to keep his wet boots from slipping off the tiny ledges and protrusions that barely held his weight as he climbed. The dizziness and nausea intensified as he picked his way up the cliff, and Gart repeatedly pressed his face to the cool stone and tried to catch his breath. The rage he felt at his predicament started to make room for a new emotion, that of desperation.

Up, he thought angrily, trying to shake it off. *Just got to keep moving up. I'm not far, now. I can do this. I've GOT to do this.* Gart's stomach heaved, though it had nothing left to give, and the dizziness hit him again. Gritting his teeth against the awful spinning sensation, he waited until his equilibrium returned, then doggedly started up again. Inch by tortuous inch, Gart scaled the face of the cliff, his muscles shaking from the exertion.

With each movement, he felt his strength failing. Rage flowed through him still, lending a last bit of resilience to weakening muscles. Even that had its limit, and Gart could feel the end approaching. Looking up, he could see the edge of the cliff, still twenty feet away. It was too far. Gart realized he would either make it to the top or die trying, so he figured he should get on with it. He searched above him for a new handhold and found none. He knew he could hold where he was for only a short time; he had to move. Spying a solid-looking outcrop a few feet up and to his right, he decided he had to make a jump for it. If he stayed, he would die when his hold finally slipped. If he missed the jump, he would die then, too. Anger and frustration raged within him as he gathered his strength, and he pushed off with everything he had, reaching both hands for the outcrop.

It wasn't there.

Panic rushed through him as his hands closed on empty air. His eyes told him that his aim had been true, but an instant later, his body bounced at an unexpected angle off a stone wall and then slammed into the floor of a small cave that had not been there an instant before. Gart lay there, panting heavily, clenched around the nausea and exhaustion that wracked his body. Every breath kicked up a small cloud of dust in the tiny cave, and Gart coughed as he lay there, dimly aware that he had survived. Slowly, a measure of strength returned to his battered limbs, and he sat up.

The roof of the cave was no more than a foot above his head, and slightly wider than a doorway. Looking out, he could see the forest spreading out below him. Sliding on his belly, Gart inched his way to the opening and hung his head out over the edge. Below, he could see the bog where he had fought the frog-like creature. Thankfully, there was no sign of it. Craning his neck to look upwards, he was astonished to see no visible sign of the cave entrance above him, only the blank face of the cliff. Moving carefully, he raised his hand to his face and saw it emerge from the rock next to him, passing effortlessly through the illusory stone. Sliding himself carefully back away from the entrance, Gart realized that some kind of magick - an illusion - hid the cave from outside eyes. Resting his back against the wall, he allowed his breathing to return to normal, fighting the occasional stomach cramps and nausea that hit him with increasing frequency. Looking for the first time deeper into the cave, Gart was astonished to see an armored figure sitting cross-legged in the middle of the passage. The afternoon sun hit the entrance at a slant, leaving the silent figure in shadow, but there was more than light enough for him to see that it was ancient and leathery, a dessicated shell. Moving slowly, he crawled towards it to get a closer look.

Even in death, the mummified sentinel was big, Gart guessed nearly seven feet in height. Black metal greaves protected its legs, and the remains of leather sandals clung to its skeletal feet. A leather kilt with similar metal plates covered the figure's lower body, and an ornate breastplate mimicked an impressively muscular physique. Overlapping plates covered the right arm all the way to the wrist. The bony hand was lost in the smooth, round basket hilt of a black short sword that lay across the mummy's kilted thighs, while the left arm bore a small oval shield with a sharpened outside edge. It wore a smooth helmet with a horizontal slit for the eyes, and a raised metal band that encircled the brow. The band was adorned with a single rune that was clear to the eye, but Gart could not guess its meaning. The lower part of the helmet was pushed forward to resemble a fanged snout of some sort. Gart peered into the eyeslit and saw only the hollows of an empty skull staring back at him. Looking past the silent guard, he saw that the cave continued deeper into the rock, sloping gently downwards as it flowed into complete darkness.

Gart briefly examined the figure again, then sat heavily back against the stone wall as fatigue washed over him. Digging in his pack, Gart found his waterskin and drank half of it, knowing that his body would need the water. Even that simple motion exhausted him. After packing the skin away, he was pleased to discover that his tinderbox had remained dry. He pulled it out, and looked around for something that would burn. Checking over the mummy, he unbuckled the armor and found the tattered remnants of an undertunic beneath it. Although he knew that the mummy was naught but bones and armor, Gart still felt oddly reverent towards it, and tried to disturb the body as little as possible as he gathered fuel for a small fire.

Carefully wrapping the longer strips of ancient cloth around the end of his walking stick, he set to work with flint and steel. Sparks flew easily, and the flames caught in the cloth, illuminating the cavern and showing Gart that the cave led steadily downward. Not far away, the naturally rough walls of the cave gave way to carefully smoothed stone. Stowing his few supplies and shouldering his pack, Gart picked up the blazing brand and slowly got to his feet. Although he was exhausted and feeling worse by the moment, the mystery of the cave was too much for him to ignore. As an afterthought, Gart knelt by the mummy once more and carefully dislodged the sword from its clutching hand and thrust the empty scabbard through his belt.

Holding the sword at the ready and torch lighting the way, Gart followed the passage for a few yards, where it then angled somewhat to his left. Just past the corner, Gart noted a shelf sticking out of the wall near the ceiling, only a handsbreadth wide. It seemed to have a shallow depression in the center, and it followed the wall deeply into whatever awaited in the dark. Putting his sword aside for a moment, Gart reached a hand up to check it and his fingers came away slick with oil. On a hunch, Gart lifted his burning torch up high and carefully touched it to the top of the shelf.

Fire burst up from the shallow trough, flowing rapidly down the shelf along the entire length of the corridor, throwing bright, flickering light across the passage. It continued until it reached a pair of enormous wooden doors, closed tightly and banded with iron. Gart walked up and examined them carefully. Sliding his sword into its scabbard, he carefully ran his hand over the thick, ancient wood. It felt as solid as the surrounding stone. He coughed a few times and fought off another wave of chills as he leaned his torch against one of the walls. He let his hands drift down to the two sturdy handles. He pushed weakly at the doors and they resisted. He pushed again and this time, they creaked forward an inch until they fetched up against solid resistance. His hands still on the handles, Gart sensed that the doors were held firm by a locking bar on the other side.

Concentrating his energy, he dug deep within himself and wakened his magick. Closing his eyes, he tried to focus it into a small probe. A wry smile crossed his scarred face as he thought of the frog monster that had wounded him. *Thanks for the inspiration, you ugly beast.* Sweating and shaking, Gart imagined his magick flowing out of himself like one of the tentacles the creature had used on him. He visualized a slender, questing stalk growing from his body and sent it easing through the doors, his awareness along with it. Although he could see nothing, a torrent of sensations assaulted him, and he gradually began to sift through the impressions coming back along the tendril of magick, slowly putting them in order. Silent moments passed as he sensed and felt the grain of the wood on the opposite side of the doors, the contrasting smoothness of the iron bands that bound the formidable doors together, and the solid wooden beam that held them firmly closed.

Gart took several deep breaths to steady himself and braced his booted feet on the stone floor, one hand on the rightmost door. Focusing on the locking bar on the other side of the portal, he *pushed*. At first, nothing happened. Gart squeezed his other hand into a tight fist, grunting as he poured what little strength he had left into his magick. He was rewarded with a scraping noise from the opposite side, and the sense of something long held in place finally giving way. Nearly exhausted, Gart nevertheless kept pushing. The bar slowly moved upwards, scraping itself free. Gart grunted and threw one last push at the bar, finally shoving it up and out of the ancient brackets that had held it firmly for centuries. It thumped heavily to the stone floor beyond the entrance just as Gart collapsed, exhausted, his damp body pushing the doors open as he fell across the threshold. The ancient seal broken, Gart felt a subtle hiss of air pass over his body as it rushed inside.

Utterly spent, his body wracked with fatigue, fever, and vicious stomach cramps, Gart fell spinning into a dark abyss even as he came to rest on the ancient stone of the unknown chamber. The darkness claimed him and he passed into a place somewhere between sleep and wakefulness, where nothing seemed real. The pain from his wounds drifted away, and he felt them only as faint annoyances at the edge of his awareness.

For a time, Gart lay on the cold stone, shivering and clutching himself tightly as he battled the sickness. Suddenly, his perception shifted and he could see his own body on the floor before him, curled around his pain and fever. He raised his hands to look at them and saw himself as a transparent apparition, fading in and out of sight with the flickering of the flames that still burned above him. Turning his attention back to his own body, he examined himself. The wounds on his legs were not easily visible through his torn trousers, but there were ample bloodstains to show that the damage had been substantial. His left wrist lay exposed and Gart was alarmed to see how inflamed the gashes had become. On instinct, he reached out his ghostly hand to touch the cuts and was rewarded with a strong feeling of wrongness emanating from the wounds. Gart recoiled from them at first, but then probed them again, getting a better sense of the injuries. The wounds themselves were superficial, but whatever venom had been in the creature's tongue and tentacles was leaching the strength from his body. It would kill him soon if he did nothing.

Gradually, Gart became aware of his own magick surging within him, moving almost on its own, as though it were eager to be released. Intrigued, Gart reached out towards his tortured flesh and his magick gushed forth, pouring from his ethereal form and into his fleshly body. His physical self convulsed, but Gart continued on instinct, allowing his magick to scour the venom from his wounds. The wrist wounds were cleansed in moments, and he turned his attention to his battered legs. The strain of focusing his will caused his vision to blur, but he doggedly continued. The damage there was worse but he purged that venom as well. As the last of the poison vanished, Gart's exhaustion finally overrode his determination, and his focus fell apart. The world went completely dark.

Time passed, and Gart slept soundly, finally free of fever. When at last he woke, the only light in the cavern was from the low flames in the shelf overhead, the sun having set long past. Gart sat up with a groan. He felt as though he'd been beaten thoroughly by a gang wielding sticks. His makeshift torch had burned out, and he grabbed the stick and brushed the remains of the charred cloth from the end of it. He was pleased to see that it was not damaged by the fire, and made a mental note to whittle it down soon, shaping it more like the weapon he saw in his dreams. He pulled his pack from his back and drank thirstily from the waterskin. He ate as much as his battered stomach could handle before putting it away, and then he leaned back against the stone wall and rested a while longer. He felt his strength returning as he sat there.

In truth, he was baffled by his improvement. He vaguely recalled a dream in which he had seen his own body and done *something* to himself, but the longer he was awake, the more distant it seemed. He knew that he had used his magick to open the door, though, and it still lay partially ajar before him.

"Well, let's see what's back here, then," Gart spoke the words aloud, and heard them echo in the chamber beyond. From the sound of it, it was big. He stepped through the opening he had created and saw the locking bar on the floor. Pushing it aside with his foot, he opened the doors fully, noting that the corridor continued forward a short way before widening into a darkened space of unknown dimensions. Another shelf ran along the wall past the doors, so Gart gathered a few remnants of the ancient tunic from the floor and set one alight in the flames of the previous shelf. He carried the flaming fabric carefully past the doors and reached up to gently place it into the new shelf. Flames ignited immediately and flowed along the wall towards the unknown cavern. Gart shifted his walking stick into his left hand and drew the black-bladed short sword with his right, keeping his eyes on the chamber ahead as he carefully walked towards the opening.

As the fire sped around the shelf in the wall, it brought light to a room cast into darkness eons ago. Gart stood in awe as he took it all in. The chamber was completely round, more than thirty feet across, and its smooth domed ceiling was easily twenty feet above the flagstones of the floor. The only sounds were the crackle of the flames and Gart's excited breathing, but his eyes were instantly drawn to the ornate fountain before him, not quite in the center of the room. It was a beautiful sculpture, at its heart a series of shining stones, the bottommost being the largest. All were balanced carefully to make a spiral tower twice as tall as Gart, supported by the most beautiful sculptures of handsome men and women that Gart had ever seen, each only a foot or so tall. Their muscular arms held the stones aloft, several of the figures standing on each other's shoulders to reach the higher stones.

Something about the figures tugged at Gart's mind, but he could not put his finger on what it was, and he resolved to think on it. Empty stone benches were set in rows near Gart's entrance, apparently arranged so that viewers could lounge and take in the majesty of the fountain. As beautiful and impressive as it was, Gart's eyes only lingered there for a moment before being drawn to more figures arrayed on the far side of it.

Gart walked slowly, sword at the ready and staying close to the wall on his left, keeping his eyes on the kneeling shapes. There were twenty of them, and at first, he thought they were statues as well. As he drew closer, he saw that they were not made of stone at all, but were bodies, mummified just as the outer guard had been. Where the guard's clothing had rotted away from being exposed to the outside air, these figures were completely and splendidly clothed and armored, their tunics and footwear still in fine, if dusty, condition. The outside guard's helmet had been almost unadorned, but the black metal helmets on these warriors sported bright golden crests from front to back. Each stylized, snouted face guard was unique, and each carried the same rune as the first guard's helmet, though these were inlaid with gold. Capes of dark green trimmed in gold fell from their armored shoulders, and there were boots on their feet. They knelt on one knee, arranged in rows facing the wall opposite the entrance Gart had walked through.

Keeping his eyes on the kneeling figures, Gart kept moving around the edge of the room. He sensed no danger, no furtive movements, but he had never seen anything like this and thought it wise to take care. There had been tales aplenty of ancient heroes fighting bloodthirsty demons, of course, but he had no idea what these people represented or who they might have been. The room had the feel of something both ancient and highly important, and it occurred to Gart that he should watch his steps closely.

As he approached the far side of the room, a raised platform came into view, and it was this that the kneeling warriors faced. Or rather, what was upon the platform. Gart stopped in his tracks for a moment to get a good look.

The throne had to be at least eight feet tall, and the figure seated upon it would likely have been equally tall when standing. It was clad in a robe of forest green and brown, edged in gold, its leathery, skeletal arms jutting out of the sleeves on the armrests of the huge chair. It had on a wide belt with a gold buckle, again inscribed with the rune Gart had seen. The enormous figure had shoulder-length, dark hair, held back by a golden torque on the being's forehead. Its great head lolled to one side in death, but even so, Gart could see that it was not human. The sunken, desiccated face looked like a cross between a man and a dog, its facial bones pushed forward into a snout. Fangs were visible where the lips had pulled apart over the centuries. Gart looked back at the kneeling soldiers with their peculiar helmets and frowned. He decided they were likely not decorations at all, but simply forged to fit their canine faces. Casting a look back at the fountain, he finally noticed that the smaller figures also had the same features.

"Well, you don't see things like this every day..." Gart spoke the words quietly, but aloud. Hearing another voice, even his own, seemed to help him stay grounded in such a surreal place. Dog-warriors? He had never heard the like. And the figure upon the throne was obviously a king or leader of some kind, yet he had never heard a single tale or legend regarding these beings. He wondered just how long they had been down here, in the dark and silence. Gart let his eyes roam the edges of the room and saw what looked like a stack of crates and bags to one side of the throne. Supplies? Tribute, perhaps? One of the bags had split open, and the glint of gold caught Gart's attention.

Keeping a watchful eye on the mummified figures, he moved carefully over to the pile.

Kneeling quickly, Gart placed his sword and stick on the ground and dug out his money pouch. It only had a few coins in the bottom, the money he had been able to gather before leaving Tiller's Grove. He scooped up a few handfuls and added the shining coins to the pouch until it was full. He tied it securely and tucked it away in his pack, then hid a few more coins for emergencies. There was enough gold in one of the split open bags to ransom a king, but Gart could only carry so much, and being too free with gold would only make him a target. A ruby slipped out of the bag and Gart picked it up. It was the size of his thumb. Holding it high, he watched it sparkle in the firelight. He thought to himself how much Gennie would have loved it. *Then again,* he thought, *she was just as happy with that wooden horse I carved for her. She loved that silly thing, and it looked more like a pig than a horse.* Anger rolled over him again and he clenched the ruby tightly in his fist, squeezing it as hard as he could. For a moment, he raged inwardly at the loss of his Gennie, and again at the loss of his baby daughter. He should be home with them, not hundreds of miles away in an unknown cavern. They should still be alive, not ashes in the burned out shell of a barn.

Finally, he sighed. He could not long sustain the anger in his weakened state, and the effort left him exhausted and panting, reminding him that he had yet to fully recover from his battle with the creature in the bog. He opened his fist to see the ruby, completely unharmed. He was about to toss it back on the pile of loose coins and gems on the floor, but decided to keep it instead. It was small, therefore easily hidden, worth a fortune, and might come in handy at some point. He tucked it away in his pack, wrapped in a scrap of the ancient tunic that had escaped the flames.

Gart stood to leave when something on the throne caught his attention. He squinted into the flickering light and peered at the right hand of the large figure seated there. The leathery hand was curled tightly around a piece of white wood about the length of Gart's forearm. It was carved in a spiral that ended in a sharp point at the smaller end. Gart thought of the stories he had heard as a child, and realized that it looked like the horn of the fabled unicorn.

Still staring at it, he realized that he was standing on the dais next to the throne. He didn't remember climbing the steps, and although that thought vaguely concerned him, he kept his eyes on the wand. The curves were so beautifully carved and the grain of the pale wood flowed in graceful swirls from one end to the other. Gart's hand suddenly felt very empty. He could almost feel the weight of it in his grip. He knew that it would fit his hand perfectly, as though it were made just for him. There was power in that wand - immense power. With it in his hands, he could have everything he ever wanted. Wealth, power, fame, it could all be his, if only he would reach out and grasp it. Just reach out and pick it up. His hand rose from his side and moved towards the wand, and Gart saw his fingers shaking with need.

No. The voice was quiet, barely heard in Gart's mind. His hand froze in midair above the wand, only inches away. Gart suddenly felt a drop of sweat crawl down his face and he grimaced at the voice.

"It's mine. I want it." His voice had an edge to it, and Gart felt oddly separate from the sound, as though it were not his own.

No. The voice repeated itself, quietly but firmly.

Gart started to feel desperate. "I can do anything with it. Anything! I can bring back Gennie, Rheann, I can have everything I want!" His body started trembling. He wanted, with all his being, to reach out and grasp the wand, yet something was holding him back.

NO. The voice was louder, and Gart finally recognized it as his own. Something was very, very wrong here, and a part of him knew it. Slowly, carefully, he clenched his fist above the wand, fighting his urge to snatch the piece of wood from the desiccated hand that held it. He tried to step backwards, but his feet would not obey. Anger rose in him and he tried again to move away from the throne, away from the accursed wand, and again he did not move.

A low growl started in his throat as he struggled to make his body follow his commands. He strained against the unseen force that had lured him and now held him against his will. Within him, his magick awoke and started coiling, growing, searching for release. Finally, Gart clenched every muscle in his body and *pushed*. The massive throne scraped a few inches as Gart's magick thrust against it, and Gart jerked backwards as if yanked by a giant, unseen hand.

He landed on his back on the cold floor and although he tried to roll out of the impact, he still hit hard on his elbows and tailbone. Gart scrambled to his feet as quickly as he could, staring at the huge robed figure that now leaned away from him in its throne. The push had shifted it in its seat, its head flopping from one side to the other as it settled. Its right hand had fallen into its lap, but Gart could still see the curlicue wand there, beckoning him. He squeezed his eyes tightly shut and shook his head. Furious, he realized that the thing had tried to control him, to possess him. He thought about trying to destroy it, but that would mean getting close to it again, and he wasn't willing to risk that. In the end, Gart decided to leave well enough alone. He picked up the sword and walking stick and resettled his pack on his back so that he could be on his way. The sooner he left this strange and silent place, the better he would feel.

Moving carefully, Gart made his way back out of the chamber to the wooden doors. Once outside, he pulled them closed and used his magick to lift the heavy bar back into place. It took more out of him than he liked, but he did not feel right until the way was barred once more. A strong desire to be away from the ancient chamber further motivated him.

Although tired, enough of his strength had returned that he felt he could climb the remaining distance to the top of the cliff. He retraced his original steps and moved quickly past the seated guard to the cave entrance. Looking out, he could see that the night still held sway over the land, but the light of morning was brightening the sky in the east. He figured he could start the climb soon. He sat near the entrance to wait, keeping an eye on the doors. Although he was eager to leave the cave, he would need the light to see during the climb. In the growing light, he looked over the silent guard again, this time noticing a long dagger at its belt. Careful not to disturb the body more than necessary, he gently pulled it from its scabbard. He could see that it was of the same light, strong material as the black sword, and razor sharp. He decided that it couldn't hurt to take it along as well, since the bog beast still had his own knife. Minutes passed, and the sun peeked over the horizon, shedding its light over the forest. Gart gathered his things to leave. He was stronger after the short rest, and wanted to waste as little time as possible.

Carefully leaning out of the cave entrance, he found solid handholds immediately. Within moments, he had climbed up the cliff face and heaved himself over the top. He got to his feet and stood for a moment, looking down at the cliff. There was no sign of the cave he had just left, and truth be told, he doubted that he'd be able to find it again. Not that he wanted to; no, he just wanted to get as far from the cave as possible. The smell of fresh bread wafted to him then and he recoiled, snorting to clear his nostrils.

That was enough for Gart. He spun and marched back the way he had come the day before, eager to find the road and get back to his quest. Somewhere up the road, he knew he'd find a settlement of enough size that he could get some food and a few other things before continuing his search for the Mage.

Deep beneath his feet, within the domed chamber, everything was still once more. The flickering fire was diminishing as the ancient oil burned low in the stone shelf, and all was quiet as it had been for millennia. At the top of the fountain, a single drop of water gathered. It sat there for some minutes, growing slowly, ever so slowly. At long last, it slid down the first, tiny level of the dry fountain, evaporating almost instantly as it spread itself along the stone. Hours passed. Nothing moved. Then another drop began the slow struggle to free itself from the ancient depths of the fountain. And the fire burned lower.

Chapter 8

It took the rest of that day and all of the next for the crew to get all of the supplies and animals to the shelter of the ruined castle. They settled into the courtyard, surrounded by the crumbling outer wall, and briefly explored the remaining structures of gray stone. The roofs had fallen in at many places in the main keep, but several of the outer buildings were still sturdy and would shelter them from whatever weather might arise. Brunar and Terrence seemed to be everywhere, directing, guiding, and pitching in at every turn.

Kiran and Nessar's grumbling captives were brought before Brunar, who simply ordered them stripped of their weapons and escorted far from the camp. As an added safeguard, Brunar had Bjarke step forward and bend one of their swords into a knot before their eyes, stating that he would be glad to do the same to each of them if they decided to come back and cause the least bit of trouble. Kiran was not at all happy to see them let off so easily, but there were really no accommodations for prisoners. The ruffians were more than happy to leave in haste after Bjarke's display of strength, and a few of Terrence's hardened sailors volunteered to see them safely away.

The castle that Layton had found was obviously quite ancient, and what few clues might have remained about its former occupants had likely been looted long ago. Brunar walked the halls with the Weya, and though they were many centuries old, none of the three had heard of this particular castle in their travels. The Weya took a liking to the place almost immediately, pointing out oddly-shaped turrets and octagonal courtyards that were scattered throughout the castle grounds. When asked why, they simply said that they were similar to others they had seen in the distant past and left it at that.

Once Brunar was certain that there were no surprises in the old castle, and that Terrence and his crew would be safe there, he began preparations for departure. The march overland to Laro would take them nearly a month with no delays, even with Layton's use of Gates, and there was no guarantee that they would reach the city before Mordak's murderous horde arrived. At the dawn of the fifth day following the destruction of the *Damsel*, Brunar and the Guardians said farewell to Terrence and his crew. The group set off, angling southeast towards the distant city. By then, the crew was already hard at work repairing the Damsel, and the sounds of sawing and hammering slowly faded in the distance as the leagues rolled by beneath the hooves of the sturdy horses.

The forest was an old one, the trees tall, majestic, and widely spaced, affording the group easy travel under their sheltering branches. Layton's Gates were limited to his line of sight or places he had actually been, so it would be days before they reached the wide open plains beyond the forest where they would be useful. In the meantime, everyone rode easily along, enjoying the sounds and smells of the woodlands. Everyone, save Bjarke, who still found riding a horse to be somewhat more difficult than expected. The trip down from the mountains to the port city of Cohen had done little to improve Bjarke's riding skill.

"Just relax, big fellow! Let the horse do the work; you just keep your balance and guide it with the reins and your knees." Nessar periodically offered advice to the floundering Bjarke, whose flapping elbows and pained expression made his lack of horsemanship obvious. Grunts and groans were usually the replies, but eventually, Bjarke managed to find a rhythm that worked for him.

"I don't recall taking...oof!...lessons on this ..oomph!...particular subject!" Laughter answered him, and talk then turned to the journey ahead. Although the mission they faced was grim, the sky above the leafy branches o'erhead was clearest blue and the wind in the trees sang its own sweet song, easing the travel for all.

A routine was established: waking, eating, riding, resting, eating, riding again, then stopping to make camp as darkness began to creep over the land each night. Lessons always continued even as the moon rose, and while Brunar held forth on the wonders of magick, the Weya taught the skills of their own <art>, and discussed the lore of life, leaf, and love. Alyssa was instinctively drawn to the Weya and their healing ways, and spent much of her time jotting down recipes for poultices and herbal medicines in her already battered journal. The days passed quickly and the nights without incident, and the forest eventually began to thin and give way to the grassy plains beyond.

As the last of the trees vanished behind the plodding horses, and the gently rolling hills spread out before them, Brunar called over his shoulder from his place at the head of the traveling column. "Layton! Please join us up here!"

Hooves suddenly pounded the earth as Layton spurred his horse forward to join Brunar where he rode with the Weya on ponies on either side of him.

"Yes sir?"

"It's time we put your Gift to use again. We need to be moving along."

Eager to be helpful, Layton put both his reins in one hand and unsheathed his Jidaan with the other, a dreamy little smile already appearing on his face.

Chapter 9

In the darkest part of the forest, there was a place that the sunlight seemed to avoid. The trees there were stunted and twisted, and the grass yellowish and wan. Mud and slime made travel treacherous there, and even the animals shied clear of it, feeling, perhaps, the evil that lurked within. A ponderous hillock of stone lay amidst the decaying growth, rising far above the ragged trees that surrounded it. A great hole gaped at its base, a yawning opening leading from shade into complete darkness. A faint, viperous stench floated from within.

Squelching sounds of clawed feet mashing the noisome mud and snarling words in a horrid, guttural language flushed animals from their hiding places. Twenty Gholans made their way through the forest, squabbling, gnashing teeth, and growling all the while. One was larger than the rest and wore a dirty red sash across one shoulder. With him in the lead, the ghastly little creatures easily found their way to the hillock, for they knew the feel of their own evil kin.

It had been slumbering here for at least a century, slowly leaching the life force from the surrounding lands in lieu of live prey. However, Mordak had decreed that such beasts were needed...and all evil beasts would heed the call of the Vile One. It was time for this one, and others like it, to wake.

"Gaaaahhhh! Tarik! Uk kak tu noma!" The leader slapped the nearest of his fellows, gaining his attention, and pointed to the dank hole in the base of the hill.

"Fak umu nakk!" Tarik, the second Gholan, defiantly slashed his claws at the first, who then instantly felled him with a clenched, bony fist. Two quick steps brought the leader to stand with one foot firmly on Tarik's neck, pinning him to the ground.

"Sama tu! Kak tu NOMA!" The leader barked as he pointed one grimy claw at the entrance, making it clear that the smaller one was going in there, like it or not. Removing his foot from Tarik's throat, the lead Gholan kicked the downed beast in the ribs. Skittering away from the next kick, Tarik scrambled up, wiping brownish-black blood from his ragged mouth as he snarled a reply. He turned warily towards the tunnel opening, knowing that he would be slashed to bits for refusing to enter. Quietly, the little monster crept towards the line that divided the shadow from the sunlight, and then vanished into the dark.

Silent minutes passed, and the squad of Gholans milled restlessly as they waited. Suddenly, a terrified screech erupted from the depths of the tunnel. It lasted only a moment before being abruptly cut off, followed immediately by a low rumble that shook the ground beneath the Gholans' bony feet. The rumble grew louder by the moment, turning into a terrifying roar that shook the wilted leaves from the trees on all sides. Frightened yowls erupted from the little creatures as they scattered, sprinting away from the opening in all directions, leaving the lead Gholan to stand his ground before the cavern's entrance.

The overwhelming sound died away, leaving a heavy silence. Gholans peeked out from behind rocks and trees, but did not venture forth.

Massive footsteps from within the darkness heralded the approach of the Killith, and suddenly two enormous yellow eyes shone from beyond the failing of the light. A great blast of fetid air kicked up clouds of dust from within the entrance-the throaty growl of a beast awakened. Crunching, chewing sounds from the unseen creature told of the fate of the lone Gholan that had awakened it.

"Senn tama kuk! Baant! Baant!!" The leader howled into the cave. The eyes blinked in response, and the chewing stopped as it paused to consider the lead Gholan's words. "Hakama man tusoo...Mordak bala saam!"

At the sound of the vile wizard's name, the Killith snorted once, then one hugely-muscled paw reached out into the sunlight. Its scaly hide was black and mottled gray, glistening in the light. Curved talons as long as daggers gouged the earth as the paw flexed, pulling the bulk of the beast into the light, and the other paw followed, clutching the headless remains of the hapless Tarik in its grasping claws like a broken toy. It was like a giant, scaled panther, though no true panther had such an impossibly wide mouth filled with row after row of needle-sharp teeth, or a head the size of a small wagon. Its face was scarred and battered from centuries of battles with its own kind and other fell creatures, and iron muscles bunched and moved as it craned its serpentine neck to mark the Gholans who cowered in the wood nearby.

The lead Gholan's smoldering scarlet eyes locked on the baleful yellow eyes of the Killith, and an understanding was reached. Mordak called. The Killith would come.

With a snort, the Gholan leader turned on his heel and started back through the muck towards the cleaner parts of the forest. The massive Killith followed behind, shouldering trees out of the way as necessary, and pausing now and again to take a bite of his Gholan snack. The other creatures gave the beast a wide berth, but followed apace on all sides.

Southerly they fared, planning to join with other foul folk along the way, bringing a dreadful fate to the people of Laro.

Chapter 10

The smell of cooking meat reached Gart long before he came in sight of the village, making his mouth water. He had been following the road for three days after escaping the bog monster and his supplies had given out. After all the traveling, the smell of meat was heavenly, and his stomach responded with a low growl. Gart thought of the bread smell that the bog monster had used to lure him. He almost chuckled as he hoped that the meat he smelled was actually meat, and not some other awful beast.

Gart shifted his walking stick to his other hand and checked the full pouch at his belt. At least he knew that he'd be able to buy anything he needed. The afternoon sun shone down through the trees of the forest, making dappled shadows on the road, and birdsong drifted in the air. It was a pleasant day, and here and there, Gart managed to actually enjoy the walk. Whenever he found himself doing so, he scowled and remembered why he was walking in the first place. Gennie was gone. Rheann was gone. Everyone he had ever known was gone, and Gart was set on his course. It just felt wrong to be having any emotions other than anger, rage, and determination. Gart pledged with every step that, one way or another, his family would be avenged.

It was hard to maintain that furious intensity, though. He had walked miles upon miles, seeing naught but beautiful countryside, hearing wind in the trees and the sweet songs of birds overhead. Once, a deer had burst onto the trail ahead of him, and Gart was so taken by its beauty that he had only stood and watched it go on about its business. All around him was peace and tranquility.

At times, his rage boiled near the surface. Gennie and Rheann would have loved to travel roads like this with him and enjoy the sights, but they were gone, and that fact hurt him to his core every time his mind lingered on it. His pace would increase, and he would stab the butt of his walking stick into the ground harshly with every other step. Forward, always moving forward, Gart trudged towards his destiny and thought about what a hateful place the world was to allow such things to happen to innocent people.

Other times, though, the long walk and fresh air worked on him. They allowed him a kind of warm numbness that hid the anger for a while, and Gart occasionally found a semblance of peace without realizing it. At such times he continued on, ever forward, but his mind wandered away from the blackness and despair that had dogged him for so long.

Often, the face of the Lady of the Lake returned to him. He remembered her kindness, her understanding. She had sent him a long way towards his goal, and healed him as well. That had been a surprise to Gart. In his experience, the world was a cold, hard place where no one did anything without hope of something in return. Even so, she had helped him, though she had nothing to gain. Not only that, but the unknown Weya had saved him from the Gholans on the road and most certainly risked death himself to carry Gart away from danger. Why? Gart had never even seen Weya before, much less known this particular one. Why had he gone to the trouble of a dangerous rescue?

Gart shook his head and grudgingly had to admit that although there was evil out there--absolute, overpowering evil-- there was apparently good out there as well. Gennie was part of that. She had seen him for what he truly was and for what he could be; she had cared for him in spite of his surly attitude and gruffness. She had been happy, loving, and kind. Gart took a deep breath, held it, and let it out. A shaft of sunlight made its way through the trees and caressed his face for a while as he walked, warming him. The birds overhead continued their sweet songs, oblivious to the man who walked the path beneath them. For the first time in a long time, Gart felt good.

The feeling was still with him as he followed the road out of the trees and caught sight of the town just outside the forest. Even from there, Gart could see folks bustling around, moving between the few wood and stone buildings, loading carts, carrying bundles, and just getting on with their lives.

There was some commotion to his right, shouting, and a yelp of pain from a dog. Gart quickly turned, startled, to see two running men, one with a sword, the other with a hand axe, yelling at the top of their lungs as they ran. The object of their chase was the biggest dog Gart had ever seen, and his eyes widened at the sight of it. Standing, it would be about as tall as Gart's waist, and although it was worn and battle-scarred, its strength was still evident as it ran. The beast, a mastiff by the look of it, was carrying the remains of what looked like a turkey in its mouth, to the extreme displeasure of its pursuers. One man threw a rock with his free hand, bouncing it off the creature's flank. It brought another pained yelp from the beast, but it ran on. It had a hitch in its gait, but even so, it easily outdistanced the two struggling men and disappeared into the surrounding forest. The two men cursed it with what breath they had remaining after their sprint, and they were close enough for Gart to hear their wheezing conversation.

"Blasted monster...somebody oughta feather that beast! He's a menace! If only I had a bow...didn't it kill that farmer and his wife?" the first man managed to get out between deep breaths.

The other was bent over, hands on knees. "That's what I heard...and the kid, too." He slowly straightened up. "We should gather up some men and hunt it down."

"Right! Maybe after lunch...yeah...maybe after that. We need more men, though. That thing is bigger than your mother-in-law, and even meaner!" He slapped his companion on the shoulder and they both laughed as they started back the way they came. At the mention of lunch, Gart's stomach growled rather loudly and he started looking for an inn or tavern, anywhere he could get some food.

Almost immediately, Gart spotted what looked like a general store, complete with a round little man wearing an apron and sweeping the steps of his establishment. He was bald, save for a brownish fringe of frizzy hair that ringed his shiny pate, and clean-shaven. He swept with the air of one who had swept the same area thousands of times, and knew he was good at it. As Gart got closer, he could hear the man whistling a tune as he worked.

Gart walked right up to the steps and called ahead, already steeling himself for the man's response to his face. "Hello there! I'm passing through and my pack's just about empty. I could stand to eat, and get more supplies. I have money. What's available?"

The fellow stopped sweeping and looked down at Gart. He squinted at his face for a moment before leaning back and pulling a dirty rag from his pocket. "Whew!" the man said amiably as he mopped the sweat from his face and the top of his balding head. "Nice day, ain't it? A little warm, though. Summer's coming, seems like." He looked Gart up and down for a moment. "There's a tavern up ahead, but I have a pot of stew and some good bread inside...some folks would rather eat here in peace than go where the trouble always seems to start. That suit you, stranger?"

Gart couldn't believe it. It was the first time he'd ever come to a new place where he had not been immediately accosted because of his scars. Before he realized it, he found himself touching his own face to be sure they were still there, and was suddenly embarrassed.

"Oh, I see your face just fine, sonny...it just don't bother me none. Everybody's got scars somewhere, just some is more visible than others, is all. Lots of folks 'round here fought in the Hillsdown Skirmishes a few years back and got far worse than that. What did that, if I might ask?"

Gart was taken aback to be talking about his scars so openly. He had been teased mercilessly about them ever since childhood, and they had been the source of so much of his anger and frustration for so long that talking about them this way was disconcerting. "A...a dog. I was only two years old."

The man let out a low whistle. "Helluva thing, that...lucky you kept the eye and ear! Anyhow, come in and we'll get you fed and see what you need for your travels after. I'm no fancy cook, but my stew is good enough, I'd wager." With a slight waddle to his walk, the man turned and disappeared into his store, leaving Gart gawking after. "Well? Come on in, then! I'm Geordie, by the way..." The store owner's voice trailed off as he disappeared inside. A moment later, Gart finally climbed the few steps and ventured in after him.

The smell of beef stew was thick in the place, and Gart's mouth watered instantly upon entering. It was a cozy little shop with baskets of vegetables on tables in orderly rows and shelves of other goods lining the walls. Off to one side sat a few small tables with accompanying chairs, cheap, but sturdy and serviceable. Gart walked to the nearest table, laid his nearly empty pack on it and leaned his makeshift wooden Jidaan against it within easy reach. It still looked more like a stick than the weapon he had seen in his dreams, but he was getting closer. He then sank gratefully into the closest chair with a sigh. After uncounted miles of walking, Gart was deeply grateful to be able to sit and eat something that he hadn't had to kill and cook for himself. A waist-high wall and a small bar separated the store area from the kitchen, and Gart could see Geordie as he ladled a thick stew into a wooden bowl. Gart smiled...it was a big bowl. Geordie efficiently sliced a large piece of bread from a huge loaf and added a mug of something to the platter, then ambled back into the store.

"Here you go, sir. I hope you enjoy it! There's plenty in the pot, so just holler if you need more. I'm going to get back to work on my bookkeeping, so just sing out if you need anything else. We'll settle up when you're ready." Geordie unloaded the food on the table and then tossed the empty platter behind the bar. Without another word, he seated himself at a desk near the entrance and quickly busied himself with a stack of papers, leaving Gart to enjoy his meal in peace.

Gart gently shook his head as he picked up a spoon. Geordie seemed to know what his customers liked, and Gart had to admit that a quiet, relaxing lunch would be awfully enjoyable at that point. He looked into the mug and was pleased to see a frothy ale looking back at him. After taking a deep drink, Gart dug into the stew, and it was not long at all before he was asking for another bowl. Geordie quickly supplied it, and Gart ate his fill, enjoying the change of pace from days of walking.

Once sated, Gart handed his dishes over to Geordie, and then began to fill his pack with necessities for the trail. As he picked up the few things he knew he would need, he heard horses outside the store. A quick look out of the front window revealed an old wagon pulled by two horses and driven by a young lad not yet into his teens. Gart watched as the skinny kid jumped down and checked the horses. Small and bony as a bird, the lad wore a wide brimmed hat much too large for him, and his worn trousers had been patched so much that there was almost more patch than original material. He was painfully thin, and judging by the way his eyes darted this way and that, nervous.

"Come on, move it, brat!" The wagon's other occupant was an older burly fellow, with a thatch of gray, unruly hair that matched his beard. His nose had obviously been broken more than once, and there were more teeth missing than present. The man's stomach was straining the limits of his belt, but the forearms that emerged from the rolled up sleeves of his dirty shirt were corded with old muscle. "Stop fussing with those blasted horses, they'll keep! Get your bony arse over there and unload the wagon before I skin you alive!"

"Y-Yes, sir, Mr. Jack!" The boy hurried to the back of the wagon and started working to undo the straps that held the cargo, several rolls of colored cloth, in place. The straps were tightly knotted, and his small hands appeared to be having trouble with them.

"Damn it boy, hurry up! I've got things to do!" Mr. Jack jumped down from the wagon and strolled around to where they boy had redoubled his efforts. "Move it! Get those bolts of cloth inside!" The boy frantically worked at the knots, looking panicked.

Gart walked over to Geordie's desk, leaned his walking stick nearby and began laying out his purchases, keeping one eye on the newcomers outside. Geordie stood with a sigh and started jotting down the prices of Gart's supplies. Turning back to the little store owner, Gart said, "What's the story with those two?"

Geordie sighed again and scratched his shiny head. "That there is Mr. Jack Badenauer. He used to be a rich merchant around here."

Gart volunteered, "But not anymore?"

"No, he's still got money, but not nearly what he once did. He started drinking somewhere along the way and turned mean. Folks stopped wanting to deal with him, so they buy their cloth elsewhere. It's still good cloth that he brings in, though, so I still buy some, but I don't much care for the man, myself. The boy's name is Will. His father died in the Skirmishes, and his mother has been hard-pressed to keep food on the table. She does what she can, and Will found a job working for Mr. Jack. I'd hire the boy myself, but I don't want trouble from Jack. He'd just as soon beat a man to death as look at him."

Still listening to the man outside berating the child, Gart could see the fear in Geordie's eyes, as well as the shame. Gart shook his head and reminded himself that it was none of his affair, and tried to focus on the items in front of him, making sure that he had everything he would need for the miles ahead.

The yelling outside got louder, and the boy's voice pleaded in defense. Gart tried to shut out the sound. He had supplies to buy and a mission to fulfill. He looked at the grocer and saw that he would no longer meet Gart's eyes. The rotund little man had apparently been through this all before and had not liked it then, either. As Jack's voice got louder and more abusive, Gart's icy blue eyes narrowed in anger. The boy was still just a kid, not nearly old enough to shave. He didn't deserve this. As the yelling outside continued, it was suddenly punctuated by a hard slap and a cry from the boy. Loud enough for all to hear, Jack bellowed, "You're worthless! Just like your mother! Not worth spit, either of you!" And old Mr. Jack started laughing.

Gart froze.

Suddenly, Gart was taken back many years, when the baker back in Tiller's Grove had thought he had stolen a newly-baked loaf. He hadn't, but that apparently didn't matter to the old baker. In spite of his protests of innocence, the baker had called him an ugly, lying little brat. Then, he had slapped Gart full across the face, splitting his lip and making his ears ring...and then he laughed. That laugh had held the same scorn as Jack's, with a cruel, mocking edge that Gart understood all too well. Gart hated that kind of laugh. Outside, he heard another slap, and still another, and then more laughter. Through the window, Gart saw Will fall on his backside, Jack looming over him.

"Excuse me, I'll be right back." Gart turned towards the door.

"Yes sir...I wouldn't do that, though. Like I said, Jack is not a nice man, and he's liable to hurt you if you interfere." Concern laced the grocer's words, as well as a certain resignation. Geordie's gaze dropped to the sword at Gart's waist, then back to the icy blue of his eyes. He shook his head. Jack was a big, strong man, and although Gart carried a sword, was far more slender. This was bound to end badly.

Gart turned and cracked a tiny, grim smile at the grocer. "I'm pretty sure I can take care of myself, but thanks." Geordie had no idea of the iron control that Gart was using to keep his magick in check as his anger rose.

He walked out the door, down the steps, and over to where Jack was looming over the boy. Jack was still laughing when Gart's rough hands suddenly shoved him hard enough to make him stumble sideways. Jack staggered a couple of steps, righted himself, then turned to gawk at Gart, outraged that a stranger would have the gall to touch him. Will was still on the ground. His hat had fallen off, revealing quite a lot of bushy red hair that framed a pair of big, terrified brown eyes.

"Hey, what's your problem, old man? This kid's pretty small for you to be slapping around like that!" Gart's voice was low, but fierce.

Old Jack turned his red-rimmed eyes on Gart, and yelled his reply. "What's it to you, stranger? Nothing, that's what! This here's got nothing to do with you, so bugger off, before I make you even uglier than you already are!" Young Will scrambled backwards, but fetched up against the wheel of the wagon, and had nowhere to go. He cowered there with his arms crossed over his face, shaking in fear.

Gart felt his anger flare within him; no child should have to feel that way. He glanced at the lad to be sure he was out of harm's way, then turned his attention to the sputtering fool in front of him.

As Gart's intense, icy stare focused in full on the older man, Jack's blood suddenly ran cold. There was power in that gaze, and Jack could feel it. For just a moment, Jack was visited by doubt. Then his anger returned in full force, clouding his mind even more than the wine he had drank that morning. With a snort, he brushed his doubts aside and puffed up his chest.

Before Jack could speak, Gart said, "You know, if you really need to hit someone, I'll volunteer. Let the kid go. You want to beat someone up, then I'll stand in for him."

Jack's mouth fell open. Then his eyes fell on Gart's sword and a sly smile crossed his grizzled face. "Oh, easy for you to say, stranger, wearing that fancy sword and dagger! I'm unarmed!"

Slowly and deliberately, Gart removed his sword and dagger from his belt and gently laid them aside, his cold, blue eyes never leaving Jack's. Taking a slow step forward, Gart stuck out his chin and tapped it with one finger. "Now that we're both unarmed, go ahead. Give me your best shot."

Jack needed no further goading. He hauled off and swung for Gart's exposed face as hard as he could, already planning to kick him afterwards until his ribs broke. Just as he was expecting to make contact with Gart's chin, pain blossomed in Jack's own head and he reeled from a powerful blow to the face. Rocked back on his heels, it took Jack a moment to recover from the punch, and he looked up at Gart to see that he had not moved in the slightest. Moreover, his own fist was stinging.

Gart's voice was steely, but calm, and the icy blaze of his eyes stayed locked onto Jack. "No, I said you could hit ME...not yourself, you jackass. Care to try again?"

"You...you son of a..." Jack launched himself at Gart, flailing punches, only to somehow strike his own face with each one. After one particularly nasty blow, Jack fell dazed to the ground, his lips split and bleeding. The world spun crazily and then went dark for Jack.

Gart shook his head as he looked at the man in the dirt before him. It had been an easy thing for Gart to intercept Jack's punches with his magick and redirect them back into his own face with a little added power. Jack would not be out long, but for now, he was unconscious in the dirt. Turning to the boy, Gart saw that he was staring at his downed employer with wide eyes and a look of shock plain on his face. Blood oozed down his chin from the split lip that Jack had given him, but apparently, Will had forgotten all about it for the moment. Bending down, Gart snagged the boy's floppy hat from where it had fallen under the wagon and stepped closer to the lad. He turned the hat over in his hands and examined it. It was dusty and worn, but still had some use left in it.

"This here is a nice hat. Is it for sale?" Gart knelt by the boy, who finally managed to tear his eyes from Jack's supine, unmoving form and focus on him instead. It took a moment for the lad to find his voice.

"Um...well...it was my father's hat, but I'd be willing to part with it if the price was good, sir."

For all the residual anger Gart felt at Jack's behavior, Will's careful, businesslike reply almost made him laugh, but he managed to remain serious and keep the unaccustomed smile from creeping onto his face.

"You father's hat, eh? Well, then, I'd expect that the price for an heirloom like this would be somewhat high." Gart pulled open his pouch and fished around in it. He was suddenly glad that he had taken the money from the cavern. Now, it would do some good. He pulled out three gold coins, more money than Will and his mother would see in months of working whatever odd jobs they could find, and held them out to the boy. "Would that about cover it?"

Will stared at the gold in the scarred man's hand in front of him. He looked from the coins to Gart's shattered face and back again.

"Sir, I believe that it would."

Gart smiled, and noticed how odd it felt to do so after avoiding it for so long. He doubted that it made his face any more attractive, but he couldn't help grinning at the boy. He twirled the hat with a flourish and placed it on his head, where it fit surprisingly well.

"Then it's a deal. I've been walking for far too long without a hat, and I'm pretty sure that the sun has baked my brain something awful. Thank you, lad, I appreciate it." He reached over to give the money to Will, who held his hand out to take the coins. As Gart placed them in his palm he suddenly clasped Will's hand in both of his, not unkindly.

"Listen, this money won't last forever, though you might think it would. Take it straight to your mother. After that, I want you to do two things, boy. First, find another job." Gart tilted his head toward the store, knowing that the owner was watching through the window. "I'm pretty sure that Geordie can help you. Second, stay away from Jack. I'll talk with him and see that he leaves you alone from now on, but he's far more trouble than you need. Can you do those things for me?"

"Yes, milord! I will, I promise!" Will's eyes were wide and his head nodded as though it might fall off.

Gart snorted. "Boy, do I look anything like a lord to you? I'm...was...just a farmer. Where I'm going, I don't need a lot of money, I don't think, but you do. So take it and get out of here before he wakes up. And remember what you promised!"

Will nodded frantically, his reddish mop of hair flopping as he did so, and then he scampered away to disappear around a corner. Gart watched him go, and a warm spot blossomed deep within him, a sense of satisfaction that he hadn't expected. Just then, Jack groaned and started to push himself unsteadily to his feet, muttering curses as he came back to himself.

Before Jack could recover his bearings, Gart grabbed him by one arm and forcefully escorted him, stumbling, around to the side of the store where they were out of plain view of the street. Quickly, he slammed Jack against the wall, gripping his tunic in two unyielding fists. Jack struggled for a moment, enraged, but then fear replaced anger in his eyes when Gart easily slid him up the side of the wall, holding him there with little visible effort.

"Who...who are you?" Jack's eyes were wide with fright and his gravelly voice was little more than a choked whisper. He was a big, sturdy man, and though the man holding him up was much smaller, he was handling Jack's weight as easily as he would a child's. His arms weren't even shaking under the strain. Eyes of frigid, icy blue bored into his own, searing his withered soul with the intensity of their gaze. There was no give there whatsoever, and Jack knew it.

"I'm a man who thinks it's wrong for you to beat up children, Jack. I think you should mind your own business from now on, and leave good people alone. I'd hate to have to come back here and...discuss...this with you again." Gart let one hand fall to his side, slowly so that Jack could see it, and he easily held Jack on the wall with only one hand. Jack's face went even paler than it had been. "My name is Gart. Not that it matters. Are you hearing me, Jack? You touch that boy again, and I'll break you. I don't need a sword for the likes of you. Understand?"

Jack nodded frantically, not trusting his voice.

Gart continued, "I have some business to finish up with Geordie, then you can tend to yours. Young Will may end up working here soon...don't give Geordie a hard time about it either."

In a voice thick with fear, Jack croaked, "I...I understand. Leave Will and Geordie alone...yes, sir."

Gart allowed Jack to slowly slide down the wall until his feet were solidly on the ground. He released his grip on Jack's tunic, straightened his new hat while still glaring right into Jack's frightened eyes, then dismissed him from his attention. Gart walked back out into the open and retrieved his sword and dagger. Sliding them back into his belt, he headed back up the steps to reenter the store. Geordie was holding the door open for him, craning his neck to see what had happened around the corner. He had most certainly heard the whole exchange.

"Sorry about that, Geordie. I...um...couldn't help myself. I don't like men like Jack being mean to kids that way."

Geordie's eyes were wide, but he nodded quickly. "Oh, no sir, I understand! I'm actually glad you did something! I always wanted to, but..." and he looked away for a moment before bringing his gaze back to Gart. "I'm not much of a fighter, sir. Thanks for helping the boy. I heard what you told him, and I'll give him a job here the next time he comes in."

"Thank you, Geordie. I'm sure he'll work hard for you." Gart nodded at the goods he had chosen, now all bundled up in an efficient package. "Let's settle up here, how much do I owe you for all this? And the stew?"

Gart paid Geordie what he owed, and although Geordie tried to give him the stew for free, Gart paid for that too. Geordie helped him load up his pack and settle it on his shoulders once more. Gart picked up his wooden Jidaan and shook Geordie's hand in thanks with the other.

"Thank you, sir. I truly appreciate your hospitality...and the stew was pretty tasty."

Geordie smiled, "Oh, thank you, sir! It's my wife's recipe," Geordie leaned in close to almost whisper, "But I put more spices in mine." Geordie winked slyly at Gart. "By the way, I do think the hat suits you."

Gart had almost forgotten he was still wearing the floppy old thing, it fit so comfortably on his head. He reached up and felt the brim of the hat with one hand, and was pleased at how it felt. Although old, it was still sturdy enough to keep the rain off, and somehow just felt *right*. "You know, I think so too, Geordie. I think so too."

With that, Gart turned and walked out of the store. Old Jack had been sitting on the steps, and rose to allow him to pass. Gart was ready in case Jack tried something, but the older man kept his eyes cast down towards his own boots. The fight was gone from him. Without a word, Gart found the center of the road and started making his way through town. He still wanted to find a decent horse before leaving the town behind. The sun shone down steadily, warming Gart's shoulders. In the shadow of his new hat, Gart almost smiled.

Chapter 11

"How long do you think it will take us to get to Laro?" Bekah was eager as always, and kept busy hustling from one camp chore to the next, chattering all the while. The other nuns of Rowann smiled to themselves as they, too, busied themselves at their evening tasks as they settled in for the night. They were camped in the forest, just away from the path that led to the distant city, and the evening was rapidly approaching. There were seven women, all dressed in traveling cloaks and leggings, and although unaccustomed to life on the road, they were firm in their resolve to make the best of it. Their mission was an urgent one, and perilous, but that did not mean they had to be glum about it.

"I reckon we can be there within the fortnight if this weather holds clear," Eli replied, running a hand through his scruffy salt-and-pepper beard. Nearing fifty summers, Eli was still hale and fit enough to escort the nuns across the plains and through the forests to Laro, as he had made the trek many times in his youth and was no stranger to life on the road. His eye was yet keen, his arrows remained true in flight, and the scars on his forearms were not from kitchen work. "Though I've heard tell of foul things happening east of here. I'm hoping we can stay clear of that kind of thing. At least, that is, until we ride right into the lion's den at Laro. I still don't understand why ye ladies insist on going there if'n you KNOW there will be trouble!"

"Because that is where the goddess Rowann needs us the most," Fiona's voice drifted over the campsite. She was the eldest of them, her hair showing far more silver than black, and though her face was lined with years, she still possessed a stern beauty. Her deep blue eyes yet twinkled with unvoiced laughter and her hands were still quick and sure.

Weeks earlier, Fiona had wakened from a vivid dream in which she had seen shocking, horrible things. War was coming, of that she had no doubt. The moment her feet had hit the floor, she knew what she must do. She gathered six of the strongest Sisters, women adept in healing and other useful skills, and set out on a mission most dire.

Fiona finished rubbing down the horses, and walked closer to her old friend as she spoke. "The 'trouble' of which you speak will most certainly require healers, Eli. And mayhap some of our other talents as well. It is our responsibility to go where we are needed, no matter the danger. Lives depend on it."

A grimace crossed over Eli's weatherworn face and he wrinkled his bushy, graying eyebrows as he grunted his response. He rubbed his chin again, then cracked a toothy grin. "Well, be that as it may, milady, it be a perilous thing you walk into if what you say you saw in that dream is even half-right. Bein' in your debt as I am, know that ye can count on me. I'll get ye ladies there, no matter what, and I'll stay as long as I'm needed. There's still a little fight left in this old man, and if I can use it to help ye at all, Milady Fiona, then I'm glad of it." Fiona smiled and placed a hand on Eli's arm in thanks before moving back to her tasks.

The trees thinned on the western side of the road as the forest gave way to the plains beyond. The sun was drawing near the distant horizon, and the clouds were swirling pink and orange in anticipation, as if playing as much as possible before the coming of night. A breeze rustled the leaves in the trees and brought the clean smells of earth, stone, and flower, causing everyone to pause briefly in their duties as they unconsciously savored the peace of the moment. Perhaps they knew in their hearts that soon enough, such moments would be few and far between.

The horses suddenly started nickering softly, stamping their feet and snorting. As Fiona moved to calm them, Eli felt a tautness in the air that had not been there before. An intense, opalescent light suddenly shone from somewhere past the trees, its brightness filtering through the great trunks without betraying its origins. As quickly as it had come, it winked out. As Eli stood listening, the gentle sounds of horses and soft conversation in a handful of voices drifted through the forest to his ears, travelers upon the road where there had been none only moments before.

"Ladies, 'ware the camp! Someone comes; hide yourselves!" Eli warned them in as quiet a voice as he could, even as he nocked arrow to string and squinted in the direction from which the light had shone. He heard frantic shuffling behind him as the Sisters moved about, followed by a sudden silence. The old veteran turned to glance over his shoulder, and was astonished to find himself completely alone in the clearing. The horses and gear were still in plain view, but of the Sisters, there was no sign at all.

"Hello, the camp!" a stately voice carried through the forest, strong, but without a hint of menace. "If you are headed to Laro, we would warn you to turn back. Ill times approach that city, friend."

Eli stood with nocked arrow pointing to the ground, grizzled chin thrust out defiantly. "And how would ye know that, *friend?*" He scanned the forest before him until he saw the shapes of horses and ponies being led through the trees by their riders, becoming clearer as they approached the light of the campfire. There were nine that he could see. All carried weapons and had the bearing of warriors, though only two wore armor. The others were clad in cloaks and leathers. There were four men (one of them a GIANT!), two women, and three children riding upon their ponies. And then one of the children let his hood fall back upon his shoulders, and Eli gasped to see that they were not children at all, but Weya. Eli's eyes widened at the sight of the small ones as they rode calmly into the light and then dropped lightly to the ground from their mounts.

"Eli! It's so good to see you! You can put the bow away, these are my companions," a sweet, musical voice reached Eli's ears. His expression of surprise turned to a huge grin as he saw Alyssa step forward near the fellow who had spoken. That one was black-haired and bearded, lean of limb and graceful as he moved. The staff he carried looked sturdy enough. Intricate carvings could be seen near each end of the smooth wood. Eli turned his attention back to Alyssa.

"Lady Alyssa? What the Hels are ye doin' out here? I heard ye went off with some wizard or...um..." Eli's eyes darted from Alyssa to Brunar and back again. "That be him, I suppose?" He gestured to Brunar, who stood smiling at Alyssa's side. Alyssa's laughter drifted across the clearing.

"Why, yes, Eli...this be him," Alyssa's sly smile put Eli at ease at last. "And these are my fellow Guardians. We are bound for Laro, to help fight against the forces of Mordak, which are apparently headed that way. Now, why are *you* out here?"

"I can answer that," a feminine voice answered from somewhere behind Eli. All eyes turned toward the sound, and where there had been no one before, suddenly six cloaked women appeared seemingly from nowhere. One simply stepped from behind a tree, while two dropped nimbly down from unseen hiding places within the lowest branches of the same. Bjarke gasped in startlement as a pile of dirt on the ground right behind Eli suddenly stood up, becoming a Sister in a dusty brown cloak, a shy smile upon her pretty, smudged face as she shook dirt from her clothes.

"I'll be damned," Nessar muttered in admiration before Kiran elbowed him for his crudity. Even without the power of his Jidaan, he was as skilled at concealment in city and forest as any alive, save the Weya, and he would not have seen anything amiss in the clearing. He would never have seen the women, so well-hidden were they.

The voice answered Nessar's quip, "Well, sir, I certainly hope not." Suddenly a seventh woman simply appeared next to Eli. There had been no transition whatsoever. She had simply appeared, standing quietly, as though she had been there all along, unseen.

"Fiona!" Alyssa gave her reins over to Brunar and then raced over to the newcomer and embraced her warmly. The two started talking over each other in their excitement, and then laughed.

"I take it you know each other?" Brunar asked with a raised eyebrow.

"Yes, Brunar, Fiona and I have known each other for years. She's a healer such as I, from the Alder Branch Home. It's a mission, um, similar to the one where you found me. She's an old friend, to say the least." Alyssa smiled hugely at Fiona, who smiled just as hugely back.

"While I am a healer, Alyssa, I'm certainly not one such as you. Were I half the healer you are, I'd be thrilled!" Fiona's praise made Alyssa blush only a little. It was widely known that Alyssa's skills in healing surpassed any of the Nuns of Rowann, although none but she now knew that it was her own innate magick that set her apart. "I'm so glad to see you, I can't begin to tell you!"

Alyssa beamed and embraced her friend again. "I am too, my dear! Let us get settled, and I want to hear what has brought you out this way. It's dangerous out here, and by all indications, will only become more so the closer we get to Laro."

The Sisters waded right into the Guardians and Weya, introducing themselves at every turn, leading the horses to their picket line behind the trees, and chattering softly at their new friends as they helped them to settle in for the night. Their mounts tended and their packs stowed away, Alyssa and Brunar sat with Fiona and Eli while the others got to know each other and busied themselves preparing the evening meal.

The next morning dawned bright and clear, and found the group already packed up and moving along the trail. Layton and Eli rode in front, wary eyes scanning the road ahead, while the rest chatted quietly as they rode. The Sisters mingled freely with the Guardians, asking seemingly endless questions of them, their training, and their families, to which they got modest answers for the most part as well as an occasional grunting acknowledgement from a surly Nessar. The Weya rode in gentle silence, but now and then, one or another of them would sing softly for a while, passing the time, their quiet music lifting the hearts of the group. The sun rode higher in the sky with each passing mile, and although the weather was beautiful and the birds were singing, the cold knowledge that every step brought them closer to war was always with them.

When the sun fell close to the tops of the trees in the west, Brunar called a halt to set up camp for the night. The party found a suitable spot just off the road, and there they settled in. The horses were picketed under the sheltering branches of nearby trees and soon everyone was busy preparing their bedrolls and tending the animals, each grateful for the chance to be out of the saddle for the day. Bjarke immediately set up a cooking station and began to dole out a meal that he seemingly whipped up out of nowhere. The smell of rabbit stew wafted over the campsite and made mouths water in anticipation.

Fiona came and sat next to Brunar on the large rock he had appropriated as a seat. "I see you're enjoying your food, sir Mage."

Brunar chuckled as he finished sopping up his stew with a bit of hard bread. "In my days of travel, I've had far worse than this, and Bjarke is a surprisingly good cook."

"Thank you, sir!" Bjarke waved a spoon from across the clearing, having somehow overheard the compliment.

Brunar waved back and continued more quietly, "These may be the last days of peace before a long and difficult time. We had best enjoy them while they last."

Fiona nodded slightly. "Yes, I feel that too. My dreams showed me some awful things that may come to pass," a chill ran up her spine as she spoke. She shook it off and continued, "Even so, we are prepared to help in any way we can."

Brunar looked up at her and was about to speak when he froze. He sat motionless for a heartbeat...then two. Fiona said, "Sir Mage?"

Brunar quickly held up a hand to still her, placed his bowl down on the stone and began to scan the surrounding trees intently. His fingers closed about the weathered staff, and a slender ribbon of violet power pulsed along its length, as if readying itself for battle.

"Something is coming. From the east. I'm not quite sure what, but I have a very bad feeling about it." *Bad* did not quite convey the oily, crawly, dark sensation that had begun to creep into Brunar's awareness, but the word would have to suffice. Brunar reached out with his mind and touched the Guardians, beckoning them to his side. As one, they tossed aside whatever they were doing and made their way to where Brunar stood. Brunar noted that Kiran had unconsciously drawn her sword. The Weya quickly followed suit. Valelder Moihra, Cohl, and Ginn had felt Brunar's sudden tension as though someone had loudly plucked a guitar string off-key, and Brunar was glad they were so perceptive.

To Fiona, he said, "You need to ready the Sisters, have them prepare the horses in case we must flee. Eli," he nodded to the rugged guide as he walked up to see what was amiss. "Scout to the east, bring word if you see anything at all. I fear that it won't be long before it overtakes us. Be careful, I know not how close or far, or how many they may be." Eli nodded, picked up his bow and strode into the eastern forest with a grim, determined look on his craggy face. Cohl and Ginn looked at each other for a beat, then at a nod from Moihra, they wordlessly picked up their own bows and quivers before following Eli into the woods. Not a leaf moved out of place to mark their passing.

Fiona nodded her assent to Brunar, and then turned to her Sisters. She quietly whistled once to get their attention, and then switched to handsignals thereafter, her hands shifting through a short series of quick movements. Two of the women produced short bows and disappeared soundlessly into the surrounding forest after Eli and the Weya, while the others broke down the newly-made camp, moving with an efficient speed that made Brunar raise an eyebrow. He turned to Alyssa.

"What exactly do they teach nuns of your order, Alyssa? They behave like soldiers, not like...well...not like nuns."

Alyssa smiled as she replied. "They're from a...how do I say this...a 'special' order of Rowann. They are extremely proficient at a broad range of tasks."

Brunar watched the nuns bustle about for a moment longer. One had produced a dagger and a hand axe from somewhere and was sharpening the axe, while another pulled a slender yet wicked-looking sword from somewhere in her baggage. A dark-haired lass with a long braid nimbly climbed into a nearby tree only to disappear in the uppermost branches, a bow and a full quiver of arrows hanging from her back. "Broad range of...yes...those should come in handy." He then turned his attention back to his pupils, tension plain on their faces.

"Guardians, something is drawing near, and I fear that it is of a fell nature. We need to prepare ourselves..."

Without warning, an ear-splitting roar rolled out of the forest, the sound of it rattling their very bones. Trees at the edge of the clearing exploded as the massive, horrifying head of the Killith burst into view, followed instantly by its scaly front claws and thickly-muscled body. It roared again, enjoying the release of its anger and hatred towards the humans it had smelled from afar. Its baleful eyes raked over the puny figures in the clearing. Shock had frozen them for an instant in fear, which was pleasing to the Killith. Had it the ability to do so, it might have laughed.

The horses were still tied up, whinnying frantically at the presence of the Killith, and they kicked and strained to escape their tethers. Giant yellow eyes turned in their direction, and suddenly, the Killith's tail whipped overhead, spearing its deadly spike into the nearest horse, cracking its spine and splitting it nearly in two with the blow. The Killith roared with pleasure at the sensation of killing the large animal, the smell of the blood and the sounds of the remaining horses going berserk in their traces. The Killith turned its attention back to the humans.

Ssssthok! Sssssthwack! Arrows began to appear in the creature's head and neck as if by magick, loosed by the nuns and Moihra, though they seemed to bother the Killith not at all. Some bounced harmlessly off of its scaly hide to no effect, while others only penetrated a short distance through muscle and skin. It growled deep in its throat as it swished its scorpion-like tail overhead and glared down at the little humans in the clearing below, as if choosing which to kill first.

Brunar raised his staff and barked a word of power, and great, roaring flames burst into being in front of the Killith. With a roar of fury, the monster reared away from the curtain of fire, for it knew the perils of such a flame. Were it real, the fire would have incinerated the beast instantly, but Brunar's power was illusory.

"Get to the trees!" Brunar yelled as he struggled to maintain the illusion. "We can shelter among them!" The Mage expanded the flames until the Killith was completely obscured by the fiery illusion, raging and tearing at the earth in frustration. From the corner of his eyes, Brunar saw his charges turn to rush to the safety of the trees. As the Mage fed power into the phantom fire, a chilling sound reached his ears...the yowling and hissing of Gholans. Before Brunar had time to adjust to the new threat, a horde of bloodthirsty creatures boiled out of the forest behind them, biting and slashing mercilessly at the Guardians and Sisters. The sounds of hacking and slashing of sword, axe, and Jidaan into Gholan flesh accompanied the war cries of both nuns and Guardians as they turned to face the swarm.

Layton was in his element. He danced and twirled and with every slice and stab and strike of his Jidaan, a Gholan fell dead. Their slavering jaws snapped shut on nothing but air as he moved among them, dealing death with a faint smile on his face. He had never been able to move so well as now; Brunar's training had further awakened his ki and every movement was fluid, fast, and perfectly balanced. The Gholans may as well have been standing still as Layton wove among them, killing with every stroke.

Off to the side of the clearing, Bjarke stared through the curtain of Magefire at the enraged Killith and felt terror crawling up his spine. He knew that the monster would quickly discover that Brunar's flame was an illusion, and then it would run amok and cut them all down in moments. His gaze darted around to see his friends fighting for their lives, Kiran and Nessar back-to-back, staving off the yowling little creatures. Alyssa was defending Brunar's exposed back, jabbing her spear at anything that came near the Mage, a panicked expression on her face but sureness in her movements. The nuns and Moihra were fighting frantically in an attempt to stay on their feet as the horrid Gholans snapped and bit and slashed at them, trying to drag them down to the ground. The big forester looked back at the Killith behind the tall sheet of illusory flame only to find its serpentine gaze locked on him. It snorted, taunting him, and that's when Bjarke felt rage for the first time.

"No...no, you're not going to hurt my friends, you hateful beast!" Bjarke had been mostly alone for many years, and he was not about to allow his companions to get hurt, not without a fight. His Jidaan suddenly glowed scarlet, its power awakening as Bjarke hummed angrily, calling to it. Raising his right hand, Bjarke channeled a bolt of force directly at the monster's head, and the crimson blast hammered into the Killith's face. Roaring in pain, the beast rocked back into the trees, staggering at the power of the blow. Its glaring eyes found Bjarke again, and it righted itself, its deadly tail swinging over its head like a cobra.

"Come for me, you pile of filth! Take me if you can!" Bjarke blasted it again, and once more, each time enraging the Killith further, then he sprinted through an opening in the trees, goading the Killith to follow. It immediately turned to pursue him, smashing trees out of the way as it thundered after the fleeing Guardian.

Brunar watched the creature go, marveling at Bjarke's bravery and quick thinking, and he let fall the fiery illusion so that he could turn his attention to the battle raging around him. Purple fire blazed at the top of his staff and he whirled to slam it into the nearest Gholan, cracking its already misshapen skull in a burst of violet power. The dead beast had hardly fallen before Brunar had downed two more. Alyssa continued slashing and cutting, her resolve strengthened by Brunar's example.

"Kiran! Ward us!" Brunar's strident voice cut through the din of battle, striking like lightning.

Kiran had her sword in hand, and was smoothly cutting apart the small, snarling Gholans that came howling and thirsting for her blood. Small rips and tears had appeared in her light chainmail as if by magick, and thin trickles of scarlet oozed from within. Without turning from her defense, she barked back at the Mage, a frightened edge in her voice. "HOW?! What can I do against this many? I haven't done anything like this!"

In a heartbeat, Brunar and Alyssa were fighting at her and Nessar's side, Brunar's staff blazing violet in the darkness, flashing and sparking with power as he smote the attacking Gholans. Kiran could hear bones crunching with every strike, and the crackle of power in the air made her hair stand on end. In a moment, his flaring might had cleared a small area of calm around them as the remaining Gholans regrouped for another attack.

Keeping his eyes on the snarling throng of creatures that was preparing to swarm them both, Brunar spoke directly to Kiran's mind, and her eyes widened as she heard the calm, deep voice of the Mage thundering gently in her head. *Invoke the gift. Call to it. Beckon it with your spirit, and it will come. Once you have it, I will guide you. Do it now!*

Kiran took a single deep breath and let it out, fighting to remain calm. She could hear the others fighting all around her, and she heard one of the Sisters scream as she was brought down. Layton was a blur of motion off to her left, and she could feel the thrum of Bjarke's power as he loosed it at the beast somewhere behind her in the trees, flashes of scarlet leaking through the closely-packed leaves of the forest. By will alone, she tuned out those sounds as she dropped her sword and drew her Jidaan smoothly from the scabbard at her back.

Silently, Kiran looked inward, searching for the magick that she knew was there. *I call upon you.* Her simple plea was instantaneously answered, and she felt her power swelling within, filling her with calm and strength. That power was echoed by her Jidaan, and its sapphire pommel-gem blazed in cobalt fury as it awakened, ready to give its Chosen the gift she had been born to wield. The connection between Kiran and her weapon flared to life within her, and she gasped at the intensity of it. When she felt she would surely burst, Brunar's calm voice rumbled again.

Look, the Mage's voice said. Kiran closed her eyes, and an image abruptly formed in her mind that clearly illustrated Brunar's plan to gain them a few moments to regroup behind her shield. It would work, of course, but Kiran's mind turned over another idea. Warding wasn't just a shield; it could be a weapon as well. She opened her eyes and took in the battleground around her, sapphirine light from her Jidaan shining into the night. She now had a good idea of just what this Jidaan could do, and she was aching to use its power.

To me! To me! On my signal, turn and run to me! Kiran's silent voice echoed in the minds of the other Guardians, and they fought on. They didn't know exactly what was to happen, but in that brief burst of mindspeech they had caught the raw emotion of Kiran's command. It was not to be denied. Brunar relayed her command to the Sisters of Rowann, who grimly fought on with bows, short swords, and one with only a hand axe and a knife.

A heartbeat passed, then two...and then Kiran's voice thundered aloud, stronger this time. "NOW!"

With a final slash or thrust at their vile attackers, the entire group turned and rushed to the middle of the clearing, then stopped and turned to defend against any foe that followed. Two of the Sisters dragged an injured third, still fighting all the while. In their center, her Jidaan held in both hands over her head, stood Kiran. Cobalt fire burst from the blazing pommel-gem, boiled along the length of the weapon, and engulfed Kiran's arms to the elbow. That fire also shone in her wide eyes. They heard her grunt suddenly, and then a great wave of magick erupted from her, spreading outward in a growing dome of power that rolled over them all, stunning them with its potency. They found themselves thrown to the ground and the air pushed out of their lungs as the blue force rolled over them. It continued outwards for a few feet more, then stopped a few yards away from the group, where it grew brighter.

Kiran stood her ground, the Sisters of Rowann now encircling her, bows held ready and arrows nocked, and her fellow Guardians in their midst, their spears dripping with brownish Gholan blood. Their eyes darted in all directions, shocked to see the wonder she had wrought to save them. They stood at the center of her creation, a glowing dome of power, an impassable barrier that protected them all. The dirt and grass churned where the writhing magick came into contact with the earth. The vicious Gholans could still be seen hurling themselves at the impenetrable shield. But they could not get through. The Warding was working, just as Brunar had suggested to Kiran that it would.

Before anyone could move, another grunt of effort escaped from Kiran. Everyone turned to see sweat pouring down her face, and the blue fire of her Jidaan intensifying. Another wave, less substantial than the first, burst from her to flow outward just as the first had done. Brunar watched the new glowing dome with wide eyes. He had not expected a second Ward! It reached the point of the first shield and pushed silently through it, and also through the screaming, slashing Gholans beyond it. The pale ward moved another few yards past the vile creatures, and then it stopped.

Kiran began to shake with the effort and her companions watched in awed silence as the outer Ward deepened in hue and become as solid as the first. One last, heaving breath hissed between Kiran's clenched teeth, and then with a final expulsion of breath, she convulsed. The outer ward instantly slammed back into the first, mercilessly crushing every Gholan within its confines.

Like a candle being snuffed by giant fingers, the Wards disappeared, allowing the pulped bodies of the Gholans to fall into brownish-black piles of vileness. As their crushed bodies fell, so too did Kiran's.

"Catch her!" The Sisters of Rowann were already heeding Brunar's call, and they eased her inert body to the ground. Alyssa was beside her in a flash, placing her hands quickly on Kiran's forehead and heart. Brunar turned to Layton and ordered, "Search for the others, and be careful! Find Eli and the two Sisters who followed him into the forest. Report back here if you see anything at all."

"Yes sir!" Layton's fist to heart salute was instantaneous, as was his subsequent departure. With his speed and his Gift, he could scout the entire area in a matter of minutes, and Brunar knew it. As he neared the treeline, Layton stopped. "What about the Weya?"

Brunar smiled. He doubted that a gang of Gholans could lay a finger on the Weya in the middle of the forest if they did not wish it.

"I'm fairly certain that they will be along soon. Find Eli and the ladies first." Layton saluted once more and disappeared into the trees.

"Will she be all right?" Nessar's worried voice came from behind the Mage. Brunar turned and put a hand on Nessar's arm. He could feel the worried tension in the old man's body. After a quick, reassuring glance at the old thief, the Mage turned his eyes back to the fallen girl.

"She seems fine, Ness," Alyssa called. "It seems to me like she's . . .well . . .she's asleep."

"Asleep?" Nessar sounded surprised.

"Yes, Alyssa's right. You've used your Gift a few times, Ness. You know how it makes you feel," A nod came from the slightly suspicious oldster. "Well, she just used about three times the power I would ever have expected of her, and it took its toll. She'll be fine in a few hours. We'll move our camp a bit and rest for the night, and she should be ready to travel again tomorrow. Find a spot nearby for us to camp, please Ness."

Reluctant to leave her side, but satisfied that Kiran would be well-tended by Alyssa and the Sisters, Nessar wandered towards the ring of brownish ichor that surrounded them, evidence of Kiran's power.

"Thanks for letting us find a less messy place to sleep. This stuff smells horrible already." He paused momentarily to kick dirt towards the gory pulp before walking over to retrieve Kiran's pack as well as his own. He then walked from the group, looking for another campsite. "Hey, where's our giant? He was fighting a damned Killith last I saw him, but it's quiet out there now."

Brunar looked around them, watching for any further sign of attack. A brief touch of mindspeech from Layton confirmed his suspicions that they were alone in the forest; the Gholans and Killith were all dead. Relieved, he sighed. The Mage reached out with his mind and felt Bjarke's distinctive presence nearby, slowly moving back towards them.

"He's all right, Nessar, though how he managed to slay that beast on his own will be a tale, I'm sure."

The old thief let out a low whistle. "The big one's tough, I'll hand him that. I thought we were all going to be served up for dinner when that thing poked its head through the trees." Shaking his head, Nessar slipped into the forest and disappeared.

Bright flashes from Alyssa's Jidaan lit up the clearing as she healed the cuts and gashes suffered by the wounded, but there were few. Alyssa carried her weapon over to Brunar and asked, "Brunar, can I help Kiran with this? The others are completely healed, feeling better than ever, they say, but what about her?"

"Nay, little one. This stupor is one of the few things that your Gift cannot heal. She can only recover at her own pace, though I'm sure you'll see that it won't be long before she's up and around. We can only make her comfortable in the meantime."

"All right then," Alyssa nodded her understanding. "We can do that. And by the way, I know I'm a bit on the short side, Brunar, but if you call me 'little one' one more time, I'm going to shave off both of your eyebrows while you sleep." She raised an eyebrow at the surprised Mage. "I mean no disrespect, but I swear, you make me feel like your granddaughter or something. I'm a perfectly competent member of this group, and I have been a full-grown woman for quite a while now. Just plain 'Alyssa' will be fine." Without further ado, she returned her attention to the Sisters of Rowann, some of whom were nervously giggling. All of them had known Alyssa for years, and they knew better than to judge her by her size.

Brunar frowned for a moment, but then a rueful smile creased his face. With a slight bow, he spoke.

"I am happy to oblige, Lady Alyssa. Please forgive my presumption. I meant no disrespect or offense."

In the process of directing the transport of Kiran's slumbering form by the Sisters, she nevertheless heard Brunar's apology. She acknowledged him with a satisfied nod and then moved to check on the one Sister who still had an injury. Fortunately, Sister Katalia had only twisted her ankle rather than suffering a gash or bite from the nasty beasts. She was far more embarrassed than hurt.

Brunar's smile widened as he watched Alyssa massage the woman's ankle. He had been pleased to see Alyssa stand up for herself. He knew in his heart that she was rightly Chosen, just as he knew it about all of the Guardians, but it always raised his spirits to see that fact reinforced by actions and words. Alyssa's Jidaan flashed again and Katalia gasped as the pain in her ankle vanished as though it had never been there at all.

Minutes later, Nessar appeared at one edge of the clearing and called for everyone to follow him to a new camp site, where Eli, the Weya, and the other two Sisters awaited. A tired cheer met Nessar's announcement that they were battered, but alive. Without delay, the Sisters carefully carried Kiran's slumbering form towards the thief, who led the way. He carefully pulled aside tree branches and shrubbery that barred their path to a thickly sheltered grove far enough from the main path to hide them all.

Turning to seek his pack--hastily discarded when the attack had begun--Brunar heard a rustling in the brush to his left. Taking a firm grip on his staff, he tensed for a moment, but then relaxed as Bjarke walked into the trampled clearing. His face, hands, and forearms were covered in gore, as was the blade of his Jidaan. His great brown eyes were wide and staring, and his massive hands were shaking.

"Bjarke? Are you injured?" Brunar quickly intercepted him and placed a hand on his arm to steady him. For a moment, Bjarke simply did not notice him, but then his gaze shifted to take in the smaller man.

Silence was the only reply for several seconds.

"The beast . . . it was . . . formidable." Bjarke's eyes were flat and cold. "I killed it. It's dead. It won't hurt anyone now."

Brunar said nothing for a while, just letting the bigger man stand quietly by. To say that a Killith was formidable was a gross understatement. The Mage was proud that Bjarke had taken the fight with the beast away from the group so that no one else would risk injury from it. It had been a brilliant move, however spontaneous. Brunar put a steadying hand on Bjarke's shoulder, reaching up to do so.

Looking into Bjarke's haunted eyes reminded him of the fact that just a few short months ago, Bjarke was a quiet, happy forester, living peacefully in a sheltered valley. Now he was a powerful warrior, expected to fight to the death against all manner of foul creatures, and win. The transition was not without cost.

"You've done well, Bjarke. The man who carried the Jidaan of Power before you could have done no better. Rhu would have been proud. Rest, now, and have Alyssa look after you."

Without reply, Bjarke slowly shuffled in the direction the others had gone, his head slightly bowed, his gaze fixed on nothing. He had barely taken two steps when Alyssa attacked him with a ferocious hug, then instantly released him to scold him mightily for being so foolish as to pit himself, alone, against such a massive and deadly beast. He finally sat down on a nearby rock so that she could reach his face, and she cleared off the worst of the blood with a rag, chattering angrily at him all the while. A ghost of a smile touched Bjarke's lips as she continued, and his hands finally stopped shaking.

Brunar picked up his own saddlebags and pack from the ground, dusted them off, and threw them over one shoulder. After a few steps, he stopped and looked over at the oozing circle of gore and grime that had once been a pack of Gholans. Though much of his power had been spent in battling the ferocious creatures, Brunar's eyes narrowed as he called forth his magick again. Within seconds, the noisome, pulpy mass burst into flame, real this time. It burned quickly, and Brunar watched the conflagration for a few moments. He carefully directed his power to stir the air currents and disperse the foul-smelling smoke that arose from the burning carcasses. Moments later, only a great, charred ring remained on the earth.

Satisfied, Brunar headed into the woods after his comrades. The sun was nearly gone, and the time for slumber would soon be upon them. He hoped that the night would be uneventful and offer them a chance to regain their strength.

The gentle purple twilight slowly gave way to a clear and starry evening, and the stirring of the night insects reassured the party that all was finally quiet in the forest as they settled into their new campsite. After a time, the Sisters followed Kiran into slumber, while the Guardians, Eli, and Brunar stood watch or busied themselves with other tasks. Cohl and Ginn meditated near the edge of the camp, facing the forest to keep their night vision intact, while Moihra and Fiona chatted quietly by the fire.

When night had fallen completely, and the fire had settled into a low flame, Brunar called for those still awake to talk together.

"We were fortunate today," he began as everyone got comfortable nearby. "No one was killed, or even hurt badly. Alyssa can heal much, but even she has limits."

Alyssa agreed. "Yes, even the little bit of healing I did today was tiring, Brunar. But I'll do whatever I can whenever it's needed."

Brunar continued, "We must make for Laro with all speed. We've been using Layton's Gift to help us along, but it's obvious that Mordak's beasts are on the move. The longer we are on the road, the greater is the chance that we will run into more of the same. I had hoped that we could avoid them for longer than this, but Mordak is calling his vile creatures from every dank cave and hole across the land. Separately, they avoid humans and Weya, but when led by the likes of Mordak, they'll come together in untold numbers. If he is, indeed, headed for Laro, the army he could amass would be enormous. Thousands upon thousands of Gholans, not to mention the riding dead that he has apparently reanimated."

Nessar spoke up. "Laro has a great wall surrounding the castle. That should keep out most of the little beasties and men, but if he's got more things like that Killith, it's going to be a mess. At least those things don't fly!"

"Well..." Brunar's grimace drew an open-mouthed stare from the old thief.

"Don't tell me, he's got things that fly. That's wonderful." Nessar sat heavily on a rock next to Brunar and put his face in his hands. "That's absolutely...wonderful."

The Mage sighed and put a hand on Nessar's shoulder. "There are a handful of flying creatures that may answer Mordak's call, but most have not been seen in centuries. Those that remain are difficult to control. Even so, if he brings rocs, Harpies, wyverns, or other such, we'll deal with them one way or another. I have a few tricks up my sleeves, so to speak. And the Laroan army will fight bravely to keep those creatures out of their city." Brunar turned back to the other faces looking expectantly at him from around the fire. "We are doing that which can be done. We just need to do it a bit faster."

"I'll do my best to move us farther each time, Brunar. I'm getting better at using the Gates over longer distances," Layton's voice was hopeful.

Brunar nodded. "Yes, you'll definitely be getting lots of practice, lad. We'll move as quickly as we're able without you exhausting yourself. It'll do us no good to get there in a hurry if you're passed out for a day as a result."

Turning back to the others, he continued. "I have never met Duke Gensen, the ruler of Laro, but I have heard that he is a reasonable man and a sturdy warrior."

"I knew his father," ValElder Moihra spoke up. "He was a good leader of men, though not as well-loved as I hear the younger Duke has become."

"Then let us hope that this younger Duke is up to the task of defending his city against Mordak's foul army long enough for us to find a way to defeat the sorcerer. If we can get to him, his army will fall apart. Murderous and cunning as Mordak's creatures are, without him to lead them, they will scatter and go back to their holes and swamps."

Moihra responded, "And the dead that he has awoken, those who ride with him against their will...they will finally be at peace." Sadness and determination mingled in her voice. Stern nods met her words, for all knew that the abomination Mordak had perpetrated upon those poor souls desperately needed to be put right.

Little else was said that night, for the path ahead was clear. The morning would see them all hastening along the road to Laro, desperate to reach it ahead of Mordak's horde in the hopes they could find a way to protect as many of the city's inhabitants as possible, while somehow striking a blow at Mordak's evil heart.

Chapter 12

Twilight had come, darkening the sky into a deep purple as night sought to cover the forest. Gart had finally found a horse in the last town, and had tried to make as much progress on the road as possible, but the approach of night had forced him to settle in under the sheltering boughs of a massive tree. The horse had been hobbled and stood not far from the tree, quietly cropping grass, and Gart found the sound somewhat comforting. From what Gart could tell, the Gholans had yet to disturb this part of the Realm, so he felt safe to start a fire and cook the meat he had bought from Geordie the grocer. The beef smelled delicious as he roasted it, the fire beneath hissing as grease dropped from the cooking meat. Gart pulled the spit carefully off of the fire and settled back against the huge trunk of the tree to eat.

As he brought the meat to his lips, Gart suddenly tensed. His new horse, Bessie, was snorting and shuffling. She had caught wind of something. Before Gart could move, he saw the newcomer and froze. Just beyond the light of his meager campfire, in the darkening shadows of the forest, two unblinking eyes shone back at him. His sword was leaning against the nearest tree, but Gart's free hand drifted toward the dagger at his belt, moving slowly so he wouldn't provoke an attack. For a moment, he thought he had been wrong about how far the Gholans had ranged, and that they had stumbled onto him. Strangely, no attack came. It occurred to Gart that the pair of glowing eyes was much lower to the ground, at about the level of his waist. Not only that, he heard none of the other sounds that he associated with the little monsters. Only the crackle and pop of the fire could be heard, along with the gentle rustling of the leaves in the trees overhead, moved by the night breeze. Gart held himself still, willing himself to relax, and watched the eyes watching him. After a few moments, a decisive, loud 'whuff!' came from the shadows, and the owner of the eyes slowly eased into the camp. Gart's own eyes widened in surprise.

Walking slowly towards Gart's fire, head down and tail lowered, was the enormous mastiff from the village. He had only seen it from a distance once, when two villagers had pelted it with rocks and chased it as it made off with a turkey. Gart had later heard more tales of the vicious beast, each worse than the last. Up close, the dog was even more startling than he had expected. There was a thick patchwork of old scars on the animal's face and side, lending a monstrous aspect to what might have once been a handsome animal. Its left eye drooped due to the thick, pale scars that crisscrossed its short snout, and that side of its mouth was left in a permanent snarl. Its coat was almost black, mixed with a dark brown, and more old scars raked across its flank. Although its ribs were clearly showing through its skin and it obviously had not been eating well or often, it was still a formidable looking creature.

The animal crept forward, keeping its eyes on Gart. It stopped just out of Gart's reach, then settled down on the ground and lay its massive head on its front paws. It licked its lips once, then stayed totally motionless.

Keeping still, Gart looked the beast over. Although malnourished, it was still so big that it could easily kill him if it had a mind to do so, and the old wounds that covered its face and sides spoke of many battles fought and survived. Gart's fingers touched the hilt of the big knife strapped to his leg for a moment, then gently settled back to the ground. A few heartbeats passed, and the dog simply lay there, watching. Hoping? Gart's gaze wandered over the animal's ravaged face and flanks, silently taking in the depth of pain and suffering the dog must have endured during its life. It didn't seem to be more than a few years old, at most. Gart gently shook his head as he looked back to the animal's damaged face. He knew that kind of pain.

"Well, finally, I meet someone uglier than me. I'm sure you'll want some food; it looks like that's been hard to come by for you, and that turkey couldn't have lasted very long." Gart looked at the meat he held in his hand, most certainly the source of the dog's interest. As if in answer, the dog licked its damaged lips again, and gently wagged its tail a few times. "Go on, then. Enjoy it. I have more."

Gart tossed the scrap of beef to the beast. Without warning, it lashed out and snatched the food from the air with unexpected speed. It was swallowed just as quickly, and the dog settled back into its original position as though it had never moved.

Unable to help himself, Gart laughed for what seemed the first time in years. The huge dog flinched, but then settled his massive head back down on his front paws. Gart looked into the beast's brown eyes and, oddly, felt no malice there. The men from the village had been quick to tell of the dog's viciousness, but looking at it up close, all Gart saw was a hungry and tired animal, huge but calm. Although he knew he shouldn't look a strange dog straight in the eyes for too long, there was something about this beast's gaze that drew his own. Their eyes met for a handful of heartbeats, and something passed between them. The dog huffed once, then wagged his tail back and forth a few times before becoming still once more. It wanted to be here.

Keeping his voice low, Gart spoke. "You know, I'm told that my face looks like this because of a dog like you. I was just a baby, barely walking, when a dog attacked me while we were at market. I don't remember any of it, which is probably just as well. I remember what it was like growing up with these, though, I'll tell you." Gart slowly raised a hand to his face to trace the scars that he knew so well, running his fingertips over them.

"You'd think I'd be angry at you for what your kind did to me." Gart watched the dog closely, but got naught but an eyebrow raise and a tail wag in response. "Funny, though, seeing you like that. It sure looks like you ended up far worse off than I did. No, I've got bigger fish to fry now. I had a wife, and a daughter..." Gart's voice trailed off as his throat closed up with grief and anger, and he looked away.

The dog whined softly--a soft and almost sympathetic sound—then it wagged its ragged tail again as Gart searched for his voice. Gart met the dog's eyes and continued, "Well anyway, from what I saw in the village, you get hassled enough. You don't need any more harrassment from me, so you won't get any. Even so, I don't have much use for you. I'd just have to keep feeding you, and by the size of you, I'd guess that you could eat an awful lot. That's just more work for me, so you may as well just move along." The dog chuffed again, then whined; its tail wagged tentatively.

Raising his voice and leaning forward, Gart tried to shoo the dog away. "Go on, get! Get away!" The dog recoiled and jerked away as if struck, but didn't immediately leave. It whined again, louder this time, as if entreating Gart to let him stay. Gart hopped to his feet and yelled, "GO! Go away, dog!"

The moment Gart moved, the dog bounded into the bushes and disappeared. Gart found himself yelling at nothing, the dog having vanished as though it had never been. He watched intently for any sign of its return, but saw none. "And stay away, dog! I don't want you!" His voice rang bitterly in his own ears. Softer, he added, "I don't need you..."

Reclining against the tree, Gart tried to feel satisfied that he had done the right thing. The taste of anger at the thought of what he had lost was still in his mouth, and he breathed deeply to calm himself. He reasoned that the dog would be naught but a nuisance, and possibly even a liability if it started barking when quiet was necessary. Gart pushed the rage away as RaeLynn had taught him, but even so, Gart had a faint, nagging feeling of unease, as though a part of him wished the dog had stayed. Snorting at himself, he ignored that feeling. He didn't need or want a companion on this voyage. Gart finished his meal in silence, and settled in for the night. His last thoughts before dozing off were of how much trouble a dog would be. Caring for a horse would be difficult enough, but at least he could ride Bessie and make better time.

The next morning dawned warm and bright, and Gart was up and saddling Bessie well before the sun had cleared the eastern horizon, his new hat firmly perched on his head. From what the merchant in the last town had told him, Gart knew that he had less than a day's travel on Bessie to make it to the next settlement. He could get better directions to the mountains from there, and he could easily replenish what little food he had eaten before the next, longer leg of his journey. Mounting Bessie, he carefully gathered the reins and gently urged her back towards the road. Gart's walking stick was tucked behind him in his bedroll, and he reached a hand back to check that it was secured well. Each night, he whittled and carved away at it, and it was slowly becoming more and more like the weapon he had seen and held in his dreams. He had already stripped the bark from it and flattened one end, but it was yet a far cry from the balanced, graceful weapon he remembered. At times, Gart would sit in the shade to sip water and rest, and he would shape the weapon to further match the one in his mind's eye. It still looked more like an odd walking stick than anything else, but he figured he could make a reasonable copy of the spear, given enough time.

Time, he had in plenty. After being immersed in the Lake of Whispered Sorrows and subsequently healed by the Lady RaeLynn, the ancient spirit of the Lake, the burning pressure to drive himself forward to collapse with exhaustion at the end of each day had eased somewhat. It had been replaced with a deeper, more enduring strength that he knew would carry him through to the mountains and beyond. He had only to keep moving one foot in front of the other, eat when necessary, rest when needed, and all else would eventually come.

He realized that had he actually found Jor Dayne before meeting the Lady, he would have been overwhelmed by the combined forces of Gholans and undead riders that accompanied the yellow-eyed villain. No, Gart now knew that his path was north and west into the mountains, where his Jidaan awaited. Once the weapon was in his hands, then he would finally be able to destroy Jor Dayne. A grim smile crept across Gart's face at the thought, and then drifted away again.

Miles fell away under Bessie's steady stride, and he moved through the forested lands that lay between himself and the mountains. He stopped into any settlements he ran across and filled his pack with provisions each time. It was always better to have more than he needed than starve along the trail if he couldn't find game to hunt. News of the vicious conflict that Gart had left behind apparently had not reached these towns, as their people seemed to have no knowledge of such things. As always, Gart's face brought a handful of gasps and stares, but he had no time to worry about that. Gart's mind was on the road ahead and the tasks that lay before him: reach the mountains, locate the Mage's keep, and find a way in. Only then would Gart have the weapon he sought.

Onward Gart rode, whittling his stick when he rested and practicing the use of his power whenever he could. He could feel the energy flowing within himself, eager to respond to his mental summons. Rocks floated up from their places in the dirt as Gart rode by, only to settle back to earth as he passed. At night he dreamed, almost always of the girl with the long, raven hair who wielded the weapon, *his* weapon, with such practiced ease. Upon waking, Gart spent much of his time thinking about what he had seen and felt within the dreams. As Bessie moved steadily down the trail, he let his mind drift to the dream he had experienced the previous night...

"LILLIA! 'Ware the bugs on your right!" The shout came from a massively muscled and hugely bearded man, his bald head gleaming with sweat. He was riding on Gart's left on the biggest horse Gart had ever seen, a Jidaan strapped to his back. The man and Gart's dream self were galloping across a rocky plain, driving the horses hard. Gart looked down and saw that one slender hand was strongly clutching the reins and the other held his fabled weapon, the Jidaan. The emerald in its pommel sparkled in the dying light. The sun was low in the sky behind them, and rapidly approaching from the southeast was a small group of things Gart could not readily identify. He stopped counting the shapes at twenty; they were moving fast. Light glinted off parts of the creatures, hinting at razor sharp claws or tusks, and he caught glimpses of shiny green and brown in the dying light. Whatever they were, they were the size of ponies and heading straight for the pair of riders.

Lillia replied in a strong, clear voice, "I see them, Rhu! There are too many of them to fight with just the two of us, but I think I can slow them enough for us to make that pass ahead if you can shut the gate behind us when I get there!"

"What gate?" Rhu yelled over the stamp of hooves. "There's nothing at the mouth of the pass but those big boulders...ah, I see, now! You want me to use those big rocks to shut them out! I can do that! Do what you can, milady, I'll have the 'gate' ready to close when you get there!" His beard split around a giant, toothy grin and Gart felt a burst of annoyance wound tightly around a deep sense of affection that must have come from his dream self.

"I've told you before, stop calling me that! I am NOT your lady, you swine! Ugh!" She turned her horse away from Rhu, toward the approaching creatures. His booming laughter carried on the wind to her ears. If she weren't insulting him every other sentence, he'd think she had stopped caring for him, she was certain of it, and she couldn't have that.

Lillia angled her horse so that she would cut across the path of the swarming, enormous 'bugs'. She just needed to buy Rhu enough time to get into position so he could bring his own power to bear. As she got closer to the creatures, their outlines became frighteningly clear, and she got a good look at the massive insectile beasts. Mutated by Mordak's dark magick, they might have once been ordinary, tiny insects, but now they stood taller than a man, with mantis-like claws and faces. They also possessed fangs and a cunning intelligence that was nothing like their tiny predecessors. They could run all day without tiring, and could burst into the air on huge wings for short distances to fall on their prey from above. And they could tear a grown man to pieces in the blink of an eye.

A herd of these was now close enough that Lillia/Gart could hear the clicking of their claws. The odd hissing sound they made as they saw their prey approaching sent a chill down Lillia's spine before she could remind herself that she had dealt with beasts like these before. Lillia drove her horse across their path and then looked over her shoulder to see if they had adjusted to follow her...they had. Looking ahead once more, she calculated the gentle curve that she would have to ride to take her back to the valley's entrance--to Rhu, to safety--and saw that she could make it.

And then her horse stumbled and fell.

Lillia landed hard, but managed to roll somewhat as she hit the rocky soil. Even so, the breath was still knocked out of her, and it took her precious seconds to get to one knee, gasping for air. Her horse was already up and running. It had left her behind without a second thought, and Rhu was much too far away to be able to reach her in time.

"Blast you, Daisy! Get back here!" The horse galloped onward, heedless of Lillia's commands. It knew the bugs were coming, and was obviously thinking that its time would be better spent elsewhere. Lillia had only moments before the bugs reached her. Frantically, she cast about herself for her Jidaan, and found it a few feet away. With a thought, she beckoned it to her hand and it leapt the distance as though it had been waiting to do so. The emerald pommel flared to life, and Lillia turned angry eyes towards the murderous insects, only a few heartbeats away from her now. Standing to her full height, she raised one hand before her and channeled the Jidaan's power.

The wind picked up instantly, answering her call. The bugs raced forward, fiercely clicking their slavering mandibles, reaching for Lillia with their razor-sharp mantis claws. Lillia watched them come as she increased the strength of the gale, used her Gift, and exulted in the power it gave her. In seconds, the wind had turned into a howling vortex, with dust, rocks, shrubs, everything spinning in the sudden storm. Lillia stood safely in the eye, while everything else churned ferociously around her. The walls of the storm rose high overhead, twisting, turning, looking for all the world like a dirty, swaying rope reaching for the clouds above.

The vicious mantids tried to escape the storm's wrath, but found themselves caught in the terrible wind. Some tried to fly, but their fragile wings tore to pieces in the howling gale, and then the airborne creatures bodies were ripped apart before hitting the ground. Others tried to reach the center, but they, too, were carried aloft and destroyed.

Too soon, Lillia's strength began to wane. They had been fighting a running battle for days, and the strain had finally caught up with her. Gritting her teeth, she tried to hold the storm long enough for the mantids to all be destroyed, but exhaustion rolled over her and forced her back down to one knee. The winds started dying.

"No! Not yet! Not...yet..." Lillia could already hear the insectile clicking over the dying winds, mantids that had not perished in the gale, but she had reached the end of her strength. With a gasp, she released the storm completely and tried to rise to her feet, desperately clutching the Jidaan in a fighting grip, wondering how long she would last against the bloodthirsty bugs.

The dust settled slowly, and three mantids emerged, one dangling a broken foreclaw, the others merely disoriented. Almost as one, they sensed her and turned to attack.

As Lillia tried to gather her strength to take as many of the vile bugs with her to the death as she could, a streak of scarlet light bolted from somewhere to her left, striking the head of the bug nearest her. The bulbous-eyed monstrosity exploded, and the carcass twitched and jittered for a moment before collapsing in a heap of legs and claws.

"What in the name of the Goddess...?" Lillia shook her head to clear it, and two more reddish bolts came flying over the plain to strike the remaining two bugs, cutting one in half, and taking the head off the other. They fell, and all was silent except for a gentle breeze that brushed Lillia's long, dark hair away from her face and cooled her neck. Without another word, she sat heavily on the ground and then lay flat on her back, staring up at the blue sky above. Her breathing slowed, and she watched the clouds roll by.

Several minutes passed before she finally heard the clopping of hooves and a familiar voice. "You know, lass, you shouldn't be laying about like that. It makes you look laaaaazy." Rhu's voice was laced with laughter and Lillia opened the eyes she hadn't realized she had closed. Rhu was there, sitting on his horse with Daisy's reins tied to his saddle horn, tossing a grapefruit-sized rock from hand to hand. "Fetching...but lazy."

"Lazy my arse, I gave that storm all I had, Rhu," Lillia replied, completely ignoring the compliment, as always.

"Well, apparently, you didn't have that much to give," and he smoothly ducked the rock Lillia tossed at his head. "You only got, what, twenty-five of them?"

"Twenty-seven, I think, but I wasn't counting. How did you get the last three? You were much too far away to use your power, I thought."

Rhu tossed the stone in the air and caught it again. "Here, watch this!" He dismounted his horse and pointed at the canyon's mouth far behind them. "See that big rock, there? The one that looks like a duck?"

"Yes, Rhu, I see it." Lillia slowly got up from the ground and began dusting herself off.

Rhu smiled and invoked the power of the Jidaan at his back. The ruby flared, and its power rolled along the weapon, into Rhu, down his arm and into the stone. Rhu drew his arm back and threw, and the stone launched itself in a scarlet burst of energy to fly unerringly towards the head of the stone formation he had indicated. The resulting explosion was quite impressive. They watched the debris settle from the impact and Rhu turned a great, toothy grin at her. "You like?"

Lillia smiled in spite of herself. "That," she inclined her head towards the valley. "That is a mighty impressive trick. My hero...now help me up on my horse so we can get to a safe spot before something else comes this way." Rhu's laugh had followed Gart out of the dream as he had drifted towards consciousness.

Gart had long since stopped fighting the dreams, or even being upset by them. Each dream showed him more and more ways to use the weapon, and indeed, how to use his own magick as well. He had decided that the best way to get justice for his family was to glean every single bit of information that he could find regarding the use of his power and that of the magickal spear. Thinking about his latest dream, Gart thought about the Gift that lay within the weapon, the Jidaan, as Lillia and Brunar had called it. He was starting to get a feel for the fabled spear through the dreams. Though he had never held it, he knew that it would fit him perfectly, and thought he had a good idea of how to invoke its Gift.

Bessie's hooves continued their monotonous stamping in the dirt of the seemingly endless road, and Gart let his eyes drift ahead to the miles before him. The instrument of his vengeance lay somewhere ahead, and if the dreams kept coming, he'd be more than ready to make use of it when he finally arrived.

A grim half-smile crossed Gart's face as he imagined how he could use that power on Jor Dayne.

"One day soon, Slayer," Gart whispered. "One day..."

Chapter 13

Duke Gensen slammed his fist down on his massive desk in frustration, and his aide, Rorian, winced at the sound. "Hells below, we needed the supplies in that caravan, and two others are still unaccounted for!" The Duke's face was twisted into a mask of anger and frustration. He placed both hands on his desk and leaned heavily forward, staring down at the map that Rorian had placed there. Red crosses marked the last known locations of the two missing caravans and more red marks on the outskirts of Laro noted a score of disappearances that had occurred over the last few weeks. The Duke reached over and angrily marked a third red cross on the map, then jammed the quill back into its inkwell.

"First, it was just a missing cow or a farmer's dog, then the farmers themselves started vanishing! Farms destroyed, livestock slaughtered and left to just lie there in the sun. I'd think it was a team of bandits, but I've never known bandits to just lay waste to everything and everyone on the outskirts of our lands, leaving valuables in plain sight. Not only that, but bandits MUST know that we'll be coming out in force to investigate at this point. Why would they do this?" The Duke sat down heavily in his chair with a sigh and ran a hand through his close-cropped hair, a sure sign of his distress. The Duke had been a fighting man, an oddity among the nobles of the Realm, but he had always figured that his pastimes were no one's business but his own. While other nobles chose to lead lives of leisure, he had instead chosen to lead the armies of his father into the field of battle as a young man, and had only assumed the role of Duke upon the elder's death. Since then, he had watched over the people of Laro with a stern but fair hand, as his father had done before him, but still made time to train with his officers. At the moment, he was wishing he were leading an army against a foe he could see. The absence of a tangible enemy was wearing his patience thin.

"Your Grace, we've already increased patrols in those areas, and they have found nothing. I'm as perplexed as you." Rorian was the opposite of the Duke in many ways. Where the younger Duke Gensen was dark haired, burned brown by the sun, and sported a pointed goatee, Rorian was clean-shaven, light-skinned, and had blonde hair flowing past his shoulders. His bright blue eyes missed nothing, and he forgot nothing. He had long been a valuable resource for the Duke's father and now for the Duke, and was proud to be considered as such. "I'm concerned, however, that this problem is far worse than a handful of bandits. I cannot yet say why. It's just a feeling, but this bodes ill for Laro, I'm sure of it."

At that moment, a solid knock came at the giant door in the corner of the Duke's chamber. Both men turned towards the sound and the Duke responded. "Enter."

The door opened and the captain of the city watch entered, adjusting his tunic as he walked. Captain Drattus was a solid man in his middle fifties, somewhat unimaginative, but a dependable, by-the-book soldier who had worked his way up the ranks to earn his command.

"My apologies, your Grace, but there is a group here to see you." A look of uncertainty washed across Drattus' worn face as he gathered his thoughts. "Their leader says his name is Brunar. He leads several nuns of Rowann, three Weya, and a handful of others that he called 'Guardians.' It just seemed like an odd bunch, and I thought you'd like to know of their presence right away."

The Duke raised one scarred eyebrow as he cast a quick glance at Rorian. He was surprised to see the older man's eyes widen as he sat heavily in his accustomed chair.

"You know of this man, Brunar? The name sounds familiar." The Duke's voice was a quiet rumble.

Not one to lose his composure for long, Rorian quickly found his voice.

"Yes, your Grace, if only by reputation. I had wondered if the tales were true, and I'm suddenly dying to find out. He is a Mage, reputed to be centuries old, and responsible for doing Laro, and indeed, the Realm, some great service in the distant past. By all accounts, he is a very powerful and honorable man. He led the Guardians long past in defense of our very own city. Surely, they cannot be the same ones, that was millennia ago."

The Duke's expression shifted as he settled back into his own chair. He steepled his fingers before him and considered for a few moments before responding.

"Hmmmm. Well, in that case, we should probably find out what brings him and his unlikely band of travelers to Laro. Captain Drattus, please escort Brunar to me."

"Yes, your Grace!" Drattus slapped his fist to his heart and turned to leave.

"On second thought, hold a moment." Suddenly, the Duke stood up at his desk and rose to his full height. "Where are they now?" he asked.

Drattus turned smartly back to his Duke and resumed his place at attention. "They were in the city market, last I saw. The leader said that he'd await word of your wishes at the Monument Arch. His people were hungry, so I allowed them to feed themselves in the market while I came to alert you. I left one of the guards there to keep an eye on the one called Brunar. Shall I bring him to you, my Lord?"

Duke Gensen could see that Drattus was hoping fervently that he'd done the right thing. "No, that won't be necessary. I've had about all I can stand of this dusty room, and the walk will do me good. I'd just as soon stretch my legs. Thank you, Drattus, please follow us to the Arch and bring an honor guard. A few men will suffice." To Rorian, he said, "If he is who you say, then this visit of his will likely be of some great import. Let us go and meet this Mage; I am quite intrigued." The Duke leaned over to grab his sword from a hook on the wall. He buckled it on with practiced movements as he strode purposefully out of his chambers. Rorian and Drattus followed close behind, both worry and curiousity etched on their faces.

Bjarke's eyes were wide as he goggled at the colorful, noisy bustle within the city of Laro. From outside the gate, the city had seemed peaceful and quiet. A massive castle of grey stone was surrounded by smaller buildings that peeked over its great encircling wall. The towering wall protected the city as it had for over a thousand years, and looked ready to stand for a thousand more. Once they had passed over the drawbridge, through the main gate, and into the city itself, the noise and activity washed over him in waves. After living such a secluded life in the forest, so many new smells and sights were overwhelming. Even so, that did not prevent him from wandering over to a meat pie vendor and buying an armful while the others spread through the market to find their own meals.

Nessar called out, "Hey, Bjarke! What have you got there?"

"Mmhmmpf hmpff!" the big man tried to reply around a mouthful of meat pie. He chewed for a moment, wiped his arm on his sleeve, and continued. "These meat pies are amazing after all the travel rations we've endured! Here, have one."

Nessar accepted a pie and took a bite. "Mmmmm," A crooked grin slid across Nessar's grizzled face. "Yes, the things they do with rat nowadays are pretty impressive. It's in the spices, you know." His eyes twinkled as he enjoyed another bite.

Bjarke's chewing slowed and then stopped. He stood very still for a moment, then swallowed loudly before speaking.
"Did you say...rat?"

Before Nessar could reply, Kiran's elbow sank into his belly, almost causing him to spit out his mouthful. He tried to look indignant but failed miserably. He was trying not to spit out his pastry and hold in his laughter at the same time. Neither effort was terribly successful.

Kiran rolled her eyes at the old man as she turned to Bjarke. "That's not a rat meat pie, Bjarke. It's plain old beef. Those over there..." she pointed across the busy market to a vendor cart whose pennant had a cartoonish emblem of a rat popping out of a pie and a long line of impatient customers, "those are rat pies. Nessar was just being funny." She elbowed him again for good measure.

Bjarke looked at Kiran, then at Nessar, who was turning red with suppressed laughter as he fended off Kiran's elbows. Bjarke gazed down at the meat pies still in his hands, then back at the old thief once more. After a moment of silence, Bjarke burst into great, booming laughter. It echoed back and forth all over the market square. He laughed until tears streamed down his cheeks and he was doubled over with glee, carefully clutching his remaining meat pies. Soon, even total strangers nearby were laughing with him without even knowing why. It was the first time he'd laughed since dealing with the Killith, and it was most welcome.

All this Brunar watched from his place in the shade underneath the Monument Arch, an ancient stone structure the size of a modest family dwelling. It occupied a place of honor at the center of the market square, a half-circle of stone rising from opposing corners of a rectangular base. The Arch was twice the height of a man at the center, and carvings decorated every inch of exposed stone. At each corner of the raised platform rose a short pillar, each one deeply chiseled with battle scenes from a long-ago conflict. The centuries had tried to wear away the intricate carvings, but they were deep and well-made, almost as clear as the day they were struck. Brunar walked from beneath the shelter of the Arch to view one of the pillars and was mildly surprised to see his own image staring back at him from the stone, looking very dignified and stern. The Mage had forgotten that the artisans of old had inscribed him there, and seeing himself pictured thus embarrassed him. In the carving, he battled a horde of monsters single-handedly, cutting them down in a great swathe with a bolt of magick from one outstretched hand. Although he was centuries old and had used his skills to save the lives of so many in the past, Brunar still felt himself to be no more than a simple servant of the land, not a hero deserving of such monuments. If only the carvers had known how terrified he had been during those battles, maybe they would not have drawn him in such heroic fashion. A half-smile played across his lips as his eyes wandered over the carving.

"Well, it looks like they captured your best side in that one, Brunar. We've never met, but my advisor tells me that your powers are, indeed, formidable." The voice carried strongly across the square, and Brunar turned from the carving to see a small group of men and city guards walking up to the steps of the Monument Arch, led by a man who wore his authority as easily as others might wear a cloak. Brunar stepped down to meet them and bowed politely as he addressed the Duke.

"Your Grace, I simply do my best and hope that it's enough for the task at hand. I'm glad we are remembered here in Laro. I wish that we were here under better circumstances, but I'm afraid that I bring ill tidings."

The Duke nodded as he looked into Brunar's grey eyes. "With all that's happened around here recently, I doubt that your tidings will be any great surprise. My advisor suggests that it would be wise of us to accept your counsel, whatever comes. I'm told you have a group of warriors, nuns, and Weya with you?" Brunar nodded.

"That is so, your Grace. They are here somewhere, famished after our long trek. I can have them here in moments, though. Shall I fetch them?"

"Indeed, we'll escort you to our council chamber where we can speak freely. We'll have a decent meal prepared for your people, as well."

"You are most gracious, my lord Duke. If you could stand back a bit, I'll bring the Guardians."

Duke Gensen raised an eyebrow at Rorian, who merely shrugged in return. With a curt nod, the Duke had his guards clear a space before the Mage. Brunar nodded, "That is fine, your Grace. A moment please."

Brunar silently called to Layton, sending a mental image of his location, and within moments, a Gate opened up nearby and the young man stepped into their midst, seemingly from nowhere. The Duke's guards gasped and the Duke quietly commanded them to leave their swords sheathed, as many had nearly drawn them in surprise. Layton was nibbling on a massive turkey leg and acting as though appearing in such a manner was perfectly normal. For him, of course, it was.

Upon seeing the Duke, Layton hastily switched the turkey leg to his other hand and saluted with his fist over his heart as he bowed in greeting.

"Your Grace! I apologize; I meant no disrespect."

The Duke had almost instantly regained his composure.

"None taken, young sir."

Layton bowed again, then turned to Brunar, who quickly asked him to round up the Weya and the nuns of Rowann and escort them back to the Monument Arch so they could proceed to the Council Chambers.

"Yes sir, I'll have them here as quickly as I can." Without another word, he opened a Gate and vanished into it.

In the meantime, the Duke had been quietly conversing with Rorian. He turned back to Brunar. "That would be the Guardian who has the power of Gates, I presume?"

Brunar replied, "Yes, your Grace, his name is Layton. The others are here too, all but one."

The Duke nodded again. "I see. I confess to not being as well-versed on the abilities of your colleagues as I would like, but Rorian has been enlightening me as best he could. I don't know what brings you to us, but it appears that it will prove most interesting, to say the least."

Brunar's eyes had been scanning the crowd and lighted on Bjarke, Nessar, Kiran, and Alyssa, who were all striding purposefully towards him from various corners of the market, answering Brunar's mental summons. Another Gate opened nearby, and the nuns of Rowann began filing through it, looking somewhat startled. "Yes, your Grace. You could certainly say that."

Chapter 14

The clip-clop of Bessie's hooves soothed Gart somewhat as he rode along. Since the last town, he had made good time towards what he now knew were the Heartstrong Mountains. He had been angling west towards the largest of them, and any time he had changed direction, he always felt pulled back to one enormous peak jutting above the others. Gart saw no reason to shy away from the feeling. He would bet his last coin that the huge mountain was the correct one. He reasoned that a Mage of Brunar's caliber would certainly make his home in the largest peak, rather than in one less impressive.

Every step brought him closer to finding the weapon; at least, he hoped that was the case. The rolling hills that surrounded him were lush and green, with tall, swaying grasses. To the east, Gart could see the edge of the Iron Highlands Forest, where the trees seemed to hold the shadows close within their sweeping branches, and travelers were often known to disappear. To the west, another ancient forest stretched across the horizon from north to south, but Gart didn't know its name. Although the countryside was quite pretty, it held nothing that truly interested Gart. He needed that spear--that Jidaan--and that was that. That was his Destiny: to find the thing and use it to bring justice to those who had killed his family. He knew it would take a long while--months, most likely—and Gart had nothing but time. He would see it through to the end, even if it took years.

Adjusting the brim of his floppy hat, Gart looked up at the peak that seemed to be calling him. Where snow didn't cover it, the stone of the mountain was an iron gray. It loomed ahead like a massive sentinel, watching over the lands that lay beneath as it had for thousands of years. From this distance, he could not see anything resembling a dwelling on the mountain, whether cottage or castle, but Gart still felt it had to be there somewhere. He hoped that a few days of travel would take him to the peak he sought.

Something in the distance drew Gart's gaze. He squinted into the brightness of the afternoon to see a trio on horseback on the road ahead of him. They were riding slowly in his direction, and Gart grimaced. He hoped to simply pass them by without interaction, as he needed no undue delays. Truth be told, he really didn't want to talk to anyone unless he had to, and he had neither the patience nor inclination to be polite to a bunch of louts on the road. He set his mouth in a grim line and took a firmer hold on the reins. Gart clicked his tongue at Bessie, urging her to move a bit faster, desperately hoping they wouldn't see the need to talk. Slowly, they moved closer, and Gart could see that there were two riders leading a third. The two in front were rough looking, and had not seen the wet side of a bathtub in quite a while. Gart eased Bessie to the right side of the road so they would have ample room to pass.

The man closest to Gart had dirty brown hair cropped at the shoulder. His ragged cloak was of a similar brown, and his leather armor and trousers looked as though they had seen better days. His beard was short, yet still gave the impression that something might live in it. He had a stern squint that missed nothing, though he worked hard at appearing nonchalant. An unadorned sword hung from one hip, a dagger from the other. The man rested one hand easily on the pommel of his sword as though he knew full well how to use it. His companion had the same hawk-eyed look, though he was clean-shaven and bald, and clothed all in black. He had no sword, but he wore two daggers at his belt and the head of a warrior's axe bounced over one shoulder. A scar slithered down the left side of his face from his ear, which was missing a piece.

Tied to the bald one's saddle was a rope leading a third horse. Its rider was cloaked and hooded, gloved hands tied at the wrists and lashed to the saddle horn. Gart couldn't see anything else about her.

Her? Gart caught himself. The cloaked figure was not particularly slight in build, and he had yet to see any movement that might reveal one sex or another. Why had he instantly thought of the hooded one as a female? Gart tilted his head a bit to keep his face in shadow while sneaking a closer look at the captive. She—if it was a she--slumped slightly, as though staying upright was an effort. As Gart watched, the figure swayed in the saddle, then righted herself. *She's either injured, exhausted, or drugged.* Then he shook his head as if to clear it. None of this was his affair and he had more important things to do. There was no sense in digging into whatever was going on with these three. Gart put his head back down and hoped that there would be no trouble. The trio drew closer.

"Ho there, stranger!"

Gart stifled a snort of frustration. Without looking up, Gart mumbled a greeting as the riders pulled on their reins and slowed their horses to a stop. He reluctantly pulled Bessie to a halt. "What do you want?" His voice betrayed his impatience.

The man in brown made a face. "Well now, we is only being polite, here, sir. There's no cause to be rude."

Gart sighed. As much as he'd rather just be on his way, he knew that these bravos would either attack him or leave him alone, depending on their mood. There was no sense in provoking them if he could avoid it. Calming his voice, he replied, "My apologies. I meant no offense."

Brownie smiled and lightly punched his bald comrade in the arm. "There, see? He's a nice fellow after all." Baldy grinned, showing cracked, yellow teeth.

"Yeah, he is at that! I bet he'd be happy to help us out." Baldy's voice was high-pitched and grated on Gart's nerves immediately. Gart turned his head slightly to get a better look at the men and saw that Baldy had a loaded one-handed crossbow on his lap, one dirty hand holding it steady. It wasn't yet pointed at Gart, but he could hear the eagerness in his screechy voice.

I really don't have time for this nonsense, Gart thought. Even so, the cloaked figure intrigued him. She had been silent so far, and had given no indication that she even knew they had stopped. Who was she and why was she being held captive? What had she done? *Blast...well, I'm already here, may as well jump into this and see what happens. They were going to attack me anyway.*

"Depends on what kind of help you need. Who's the girl?" Gart nodded towards the figure, and saw the two men glance at each other before Brownie replied.

"Well, you don't need to worry about her none. Just a criminal we're taking to Larkspur."

"For trial!" Baldy interjected, showing broken, yellow teeth.

"Yeah, for trial," Brownie agreed. "She started a ruckus back in Green Meadows, nearly killed a man over a horse. Gotta take her in."

It was ME OWN horse, ye ass! The girl's voice echoed in Gart's head as though she'd spoken directly into his ear, but it was obvious that the two men had not heard her comment. *And ye just want to collect the price on me heid!* Gart looked over at her, but she had not moved at all and it dawned on him that he was hearing her thoughts. He had the sense that she didn't know he could hear her, and he had no idea why he could.

On a hunch, he awakened his magick. He felt the energy swirl within him, and it occurred to him that he'd never done anything like what he was about to do. As gently as he could, he reached out and tried to touch the girl's mind with his own. He instantly felt her anger, raging hotly just under the surface, so similar to his own that it nearly made him smile in recognition. He also felt her pain and exhaustion. She had been beaten repeatedly by the men who held her, and could barely keep herself in the saddle. Gart's brow furrowed and he clenched his jaw in shared anger. No one should be treated that way, criminal or not.

Beneath that pain and anger, there was a strong sense of outrage appropriate to one wrongly imprisoned. Carefully, he probed deeper, not wanting to intrude upon her thoughts, but still trying to deduce from her emotions whether she were innocent or guilty. Finally, he found what he had unknowingly been looking for--fear. Deep down, what she feared was her fate at the hands of the Constable. She was afraid that she would never see her home again, her people. She had already been badly beaten, but she was a warrior and no stranger to such things. No, there would be far worse for her when they delivered her to the Constable in Larkspur. Some things are worse than death.

Satisfied, Gart used his magick to loosen her bonds. He could feel her surprise and a rush of excitement as she carefully worked her wrists loose. Gart broke the link between them, and took a deep breath to steady himself.

"She must be pretty dangerous for you two to have her trussed up like that. Did she give you any trouble?" Gart fought to keep his voice level.

Again, the pair of bravos looked at each other before the brown one answered. "Well now, she was pretty feisty at first, but we knew how to take the fight out of her, right, Joyel?" Brownie leered at his partner, who flashed his ugly smile again as he bobbed his bald head in agreement.

"Yeah, Roland, we sure did." Joyel chuckled nastily. "It's a shame the Constable wants her intact, but a good thrashing softened her up just fine." Roland laughed as well, a smirking, self-satisfied laugh.

That did it. Gart turned his face just enough that he could stare squarely at both men; their laughter died. Fierce eyes of icy blue glared unblinking from under the brim of his floppy hat. Though Joyel and Roland were hard men, the power they saw in Gart's eyes gave them pause.

A shuffling sound to Joyel's right made him turn his head. The world shifted as he was suddenly grabbed by the arm and yanked downwards. The girl had quietly dismounted, found the nearest stone, and crept close enough to strike. Joyel never saw the rock that slammed into his temple. Knocked out cold, he slid off his horse like a rag doll and landed in a dusty heap in the road, his crossbow falling to the ground beside him.

"You blasted wench!" Roland drew his sword and tried to wheel his horse around, but Gart had already pulled his wooden Jidaan. Holding it near the end, he reached out and smashed Roland in the side of the head with the flat of the wooden blade, swatting him right out of his saddle. All three horses skipped and shied around the bodies of the two men before trotting off a little way down the road and settling down.

Gart looked down at the girl he had just aided. Her hood had fallen away, exposing a head of frizzy red hair, badly cut just above the shoulder and held more or less in check by a leather headband. Her defiant eyes shone light green above her pale cheeks, which were scarred with intricate tribal tattoos. There were bruises on her face, and one eye was ringed in purple, showing where she had taken a heavy blow at some point. There was a harsh beauty to her, though the cloak hid the rest of her shape from view. Her movements were quick and efficient in spite of her exhaustion. She stripped Joyel of his axe, daggers, and crossbow, and tossed them all to the side of the road. The longknife, she stuffed in her belt as though it belonged there. Rolling the man on his side, she began tying his hands behind him with the rope that had previously bound her own wrists.

She glanced up at Gart, her tired eyes looking like chips of jade in shadowed hollows. "Thenk ye fer 'at. I cood hae taken him meself, but I appreciate yer help." The burr and lilt of her accent was thick, but Gart managed to follow her words in spite of it.

She looped one end of the rope around the bald man's ankles and hogtied him. She flipped her cloak off of her arms so she could work better, and Gart could see that she was strongly built. She was wearing a dirty long-sleeved shirt under a battered leather vest with steel rings sewn in, a knee-length skirt with a distinctive green and red pattern, and old calf-high boots. It took her only moments to bind the man and drag his unconscious body to the side of the road, where she leaned him up against a tree and tied him to the trunk. Swaying only a little from fatigue, she stood and headed for the other man.

"You're welcome. What's that about a price on your head?" Gart made no move to get down from Bessie's back.

The girl stopped suddenly and cast Gart a wary look as one hand drifted to the dagger at her waist. "How dae ye ken aboot 'at? Who are ye?"

Laying his wooden Jidaan across his lap, Gart raised his hands. "I don't mean you any harm, and I'm just passing through here. I just assumed that these fellows were bounty hunters or something."

She relaxed a bit and went back to searching Roland and relieving him of his weapons. "No, they be 'dep-u-ties'. Which is pretty much the same thing as bounty hunters in Blue Ridge, I ken. About a year ago, someone tried tae steal me horse there in 'at little toon. I knocked him senseless and left him in the street whilst I went aboot me business. Later 'at night, he attacked me as I was leaving toon and I defended meself."

"I take it that you killed him?" Gart would have done the same in her place. He couldn't abide thieves, and if the man had attacked her again out of spite, he had certainly deserved whatever he had gotten as far as Gart was concerned.

The girl shrugged as she removed a coin pouch from Roland's unconscious body and tucked it away in her belt. "I did nae have a choice in the matter. He came at me wi' a sword and wouldn't stop hacking at me until I ran him through." Roland groaned once and started to move, but the girl simply punched him in the face, sending him back to whatever dreams awaited him. "I had nae idea that he was a noble's son. He sure didna act like one. Anyway, I thought it was all over and done with until I rode through Blue Ridge again a few days ago and *these* scumsuckers," she kicked Roland soundly in the ribs, "clouted me in the heid from behind and knocked me oot. When I woke, they had me tied up and boasted that they were takin' me to the Constable in Larkspur for the bounty. He has a reputation for cruelty, the Constable does, and I have nae desire to get to know him at all." The girl bound the man in a similar fashion as his comrade, and then dragged him to the same tree as Joyel. After wrestling his limp body into position, she bound him firmly to the opposite side of the tree. She checked the knots to be sure they'd hold, then started kicking each of the men again. Gart winced as she landed a few particularly well-aimed blows. He knew the men would be in pain for a good long while after they woke.

"Why not kill them too? They've been rough with you, haven't they?"

The girl raised an eyebrow at him and paused before answering. His curiosity seemed genuine, and he had helped her without hesitation. She considered the man in the floppy hat for a moment as he sat atop his horse, his face in shadow, quietly watching her in return.

Shifting her focus, she engaged her ability to See. Opening her mind as her tribal elders had taught her when she had been but a girl, she gradually became aware of the living auras surrounding everything around her. Now, she could See that the horse glowed with a gentle light, a nimbus of energy that extended a few inches from its body. The trees, the grass, the bound and unconscious men nearby--all had their own energy that was visible to her Sight, each differing in color and intensity.

Although she seldom used it, the quiet man intrigued her, and she wanted to See him.

She stifled a gasp as she looked fully upon him. To her Sight, he shone more brightly than anything or anyone she had ever seen, far brighter than the most powerful shaman from her tribe. His aura was golden and bright green, colors she knew bespoke kindness and good. Although they ran deeper and more intense in him than she had ever seen, there was no evil in him. Other colors displayed a deeply ingrained pain. A quick glance at the bound ruffians showed her what she expected: auras with shades of brown, black, red, and a phlegmy yellow. She closed her eyes and let her Sight fall away. She had seen enough. The man had a story, for certain, but he would not hurt her.

"What's the matter? Are you hurt?" A touch of concern was in the man's voice, and she opened her eyes to look at him with her normal vision. His horse snorted, and he absently reached a hand down and patted the animal's neck to reassure it. The unconscious gesture spoke volumes about him as had his aura. He was simply concerned for her and nothing more.

"No, I'm nae really hurt. I've been beaten before. I've already paid these fools back in kind, and they're nae worth the killing. I kill only when I must, and I'd wager that their karma will come back on 'em soon enough. Someone less forgiving than I will come along at some point and they'll suffer for it."

The man grimaced under his hat and glanced at the two unconscious men at the side of the road. Their faces had already started to puff up where they had been struck, and they had drawn their legs up protectively over the other places the girl had kicked. He stared at them for a moment or two before turning back to her.

"Seems like your right foot must be named 'karma.' I suppose someone will come along and set them free before too long. If they don't, then it's probably no great loss to the world." He reached up and took off his floppy hat, exposing a head of blonde hair. One sleeve wiped sweat from his forehead, but he didn't put the hat back on immediately. He turned his gaze fully on her, and her breath caught in her throat as the power of his icy blue eyes washed over her. "I'm Gart. What's your name?"

She recovered quickly and answered, "I be Ishabel of the Iron Hills Clan. It's a pleasure to meet ye, sir." She caught sight of the scars on the right side of his face and thought for a moment that they were tribal like hers. She shrugged that thought off immediately, quickly seeing that Gart's scars were far more extensive and appeared to be animal in origin. Her own had been carefully applied upon her cheeks by her mother after Ishabel had passed all of their tribe's tests of combat and woodcraft, and so named a warrior.

Spooked momentarily by the ruckus, the other horses had moved away to eat grass at the side of the road. Ishabel walked slowly over to them and called one to her. She calmed it with quiet words and gentle hands and then set about searching it thoroughly. There was a bundle tied just behind the saddle, and from it, she pulled a scabbarded sword and another dagger, which she buckled around her waist. Satisfied, she moved to the other horse and searched it as well, transferring food and supplies into the saddlebags on the first horse. Once the first horse was loaded properly, she unsaddled the other two horses, removed and cut up their bridles, and then cut the billet straps on both saddles. Even if the two bravos did get free anytime soon, they'd not have an easy time chasing her.

"Where are ye headed, Gart? Ye don't look like a rich merchant, nor a soldier," Ishabel said as she smoothly mounted the horse and gathered up the reins. Gart put his hat back on and shifted in his saddle, still cradling his wooden Jidaan on his knees as she rode up next to him. "And what's wi' the stick?"

Chapter 15

"I think that's all of them." The Duke's voice rumbled in satisfaction as he leaned on the battlements and watched the last of the wagons roll past the outer gates of Laroan Castle. The previous few days had seen the entire population of Laro either stuffed into the keep, bearing as many supplies as they could carry, or headed west towards Rualtha with all of their possessions crammed into whatever modes of transport they could find. The Duke had sent a company of guards to escort the fleeing commoners as far as Broken Boulder Valley before coming back to add their swords to the defense of the city.

"Blast, I wish those stubborn fools would listen to us! I swear, some of them haven't the sense of a ball of twine!" The Duke clenched his fists in frustration at the thought of the farmers who either hadn't believed the magnitude of the threat that approached, or simply felt they could lock themselves in and weather the storm. They had stayed put, and nothing any of the guard captains had said could convince them to leave.

Brunar sighed. "In spite of our best efforts, there are those who will be lost. Dying in battle is one thing, but I agree with you, Your Grace. Those who choose to stay behind in their homes will face certain death at the hands of Mordak's vile horde." The Mage stood on the wall next to the Duke and watched the fleeing townspeople without further comment for a moment. Looking left and right, he saw the outermost wall of the Laroan Keep stretching away to either side. A modest barbican warded the wide drawbridge that spanned the moat. The canal of muddy water was deeper than it looked, and it surrounded the outer wall, protecting the keep and outer bailey within. Many of Laro's citizens had set up temporary residence in the open courtyard as best they could. Brunar nodded towards the obviously worried crowd below. "Should we lose this wall,Your Grace, then many of those people will die as well unless we get them into the keep proper."

The Duke grunted his agreement. "Yes, we've already issued orders for all of the townspeople to be ushered through the inner gate when the battle starts, while any able-bodies fighters stay to aid us out here. If the wall is breached by the enemy, then we'll retreat into the keep as well and make them pay dearly for it." The stern glint in Duke Gensen's eye promised that he'd face any threat to his beloved city with ferocious determination.

Brunar could feel strength emanating from the Duke, and fear as well. Brunar closed his eyes and opened himself to those feelings, quietly testing the Duke to see what kind of man would be defending the walls alongside his soldiers. The Mage was pleased to find that the strength ran deeply in Duke Gensen, so deep it seemed as firm as the stone upon which they both stood. This Duke wouldn't break under pressure; he would fight until his last breath was wrested from him. The fear was there, yes, but it was not at all for himself. Duke Gensen cared deeply for his people, even the stubborn ones, and wanted no harm to come to any of them. His birthright may have made him a Duke, but his spirit made him something more. He had a responsibility to his people, and he took that responsibility quite seriously. Brunar opened his eyes and smiled slightly. In the Duke, Brunar had found a rare combination of strength, humility, and honor, nothing like some of the nobility with whom the Mage had dealt in the past. Many of them had only been concerned with their own power and wealth. Brunar clapped a hand on the Duke's shoulder, a familiar gesture that would have startled any who had seen it.

"Your Grace, I'm glad that we're on your side. The wall is strong, and so are the Laroan soldiers. Hopefully, we've overestimated the threat, and it won't come to battle at all." Even as he said it, Brunar knew that nothing could be further from the truth. The band of creatures that had attacked them weeks earlier had included a Killith, and if Mordak had called more than that single beast, then the wall would most certainly fall at some point.

Brunar leaned over the battlements and looked at the dusty ground below, his gaze wandering along the outer wall and back towards the main keep, further assessing the defenses of Laro. The walls were yards thick and nearly thirty feet high. Ballistae were evenly spaced along the wall, capable of loosing giant bolts up to 500 yards away, as well as bundles of smaller arrows or stones that would spread out and rain down on the enemy. Archers headed the defense, followed by pikemen and footmen upon the walls. Although there had been no signs of imminent attack, the gates had been fortified, routines behind the walls established, and soldiers were at the ready. Thousands were safe within the courtyard and keep for the time being. Brunar hoped that he could keep them that way.

Behind them, the inner wall was twice as tall as the one on which they stood, with turrets at each corner that looked out over the land. Equally spaced around the wall and towers were statues of gargoyles in various poses of watchfulness. The great stone beasts looked ferocious with their sharp fangs and claws at the ready, sloping brows and vaguely canine faces framed by curving ram's horns lending them a sinister aspect. It had been centuries since Brunar had actually seen a living Gargoyle. The ancient sculptor must also have seen them in person; he had captured their likeness so closely.

The Duke turned and looked back at the castle. "Where have your Weya gotten off to, Mage?"

Brunar blinked a couple of times as he realized that he had not seen the three Weya since the meeting in the council chamber days ago. He took a few moments to search for them, sending his feelings gently over the city. He felt the strong energy of his Guardians at various places throughout the keep, but of the Weya, he felt nothing. This was not a true cause for alarm, as they were hard to sense on a good day, but Brunar could usually find some hint of their presence. Today, there was none.

"My lord Duke, I haven't the slightest idea. Moihra did mention to me that she wanted to explore the older parts of the keep, but she didn't explain further. I assume she's looking for weaknesses that Mordak could exploit. If she has found any, I don't know about them. I'm sure she'll turn up."

The Duke shrugged. "Well, if anything I've ever heard about the Weya is true, then I'm more than happy to let them have the run of the castle. If anyone can find such things, they can, and I'd be wise to heed their instructions."

Brunar smiled. He had known the Weya for centuries, and was glad the Duke trusted them already. Many humans were intimidated by the elusive Weya's various abilities, not quite grasping that they had millennia to learn whatever crafts they chose. Humans were often afraid of them. Small in stature, Weya were ferocious fighters, incomparable artisans, and possessed of a deep wisdom that often sounded like arrogance to the short-lived. Even so, Duke Gensen had not found them arrogant in the least, and had warmed to them immediately.

The Duke's steely eyes scanned the eastern horizon, carefully watching the distant line of trees that marked the beginning of the forest and the end of the gently rolling farmlands under his care. It all looked so peaceful, the land covered in green and brown, lush and thriving as it had been for centuries. The Duke's deep and sentimental love for his land and his people swelled within him, and a lump formed in his throat at the thought of all manner of foulness despoiling his beloved domain.

His voice hard, he spoke, almost to himself. "Whatever comes...we'll fight it with everything we have."

Brunar nodded in agreement; he knew the Duke spoke truly. The Mage turned his eyes back to the horizon, wondering at which point the forces of Mordak would emerge, and when.

Chapter 16

Gart and Ishabel rode in silence through the forest, listening to the quiet sounds of birdsong and breeze. There was no path, yet Ishabel knew these woods almost as well as her own forests in the Iron Highlands. She had travelled widely during her younger years, and she knew of the high peak that Gart sought. She had heard the tales of the wise one who dwelled there, though she knew of no one who had actually seen him. It had been said that he was a man of magick, not to be trifled with, but also a man of great kindness and wisdom. Gart had told her only that he had been searching for the man's abode, for he had something that Gart needed very badly. Whether annoying a Mage was the smart thing to do was definitely in question, but Ishabel felt that she owed Gart for his help with the two ruffians. She had agreed to guide him as best she could, at least to the foot of the largest mountain.

"Do ye have any family, man?" Ishabel asked, trying to be companionable. Only stony silence was the reply for several hoofbeats.

"I did, yes," Gart's voice was cold and matter-of-fact. "I had a wife and a...a daughter. They're gone now."

Ishabel felt his pain through the few syllables he had managed to utter. She felt sorry she had chosen that particular question.

"I'm sorry, I didnae mean to upset ye. I was just askin'," Ishabel replied softly. She knew that kind of pain all too well. Warriors were not supposed to show it, but they felt it just as deeply. Some ignored it, while others absorbed it and then let it go, and eventually became stronger because of it. Others let it turn them into something darker, more sinister. Pain and grief were powerful things, and capable of pushing a person to either greatness or ruin. Ishabel wondered which of these Gart was pursuing with such determination.

Gart spoke again, his voice quiet but calm. "It's all right, you had no way of knowing. They are dead and gone; it's just me now."

"I'm sorry," Ishabel said again. She decided to change the subject. "Ye've told me that yer looking for the Mage, but ye havenae told me what he's holding for ye."

More silence was her only answer for a while, and then he turned one blue eye her way. "You ask a lot of questions, did you know that?" His voice was flat, and Ishabel was unable to tell if he was poking fun at her or actually upset. There wasn't a hint of a smile on his scarred face, but then, she had not seen him smile at all yet, so that was no surprise. She decided to plunge ahead and hope for the best.

"So I've been told. Without asking, there be no answers, then, so I ask!" She nodded to herself, satisfied. "How the devil is a person supposed to find out things if they don't ask?"

Gart's cold stare held for a short time, and then the ghost of a smile crept up the corner of his mouth.

"Yes, well, it does seem that you've probably had a lot of practice at that. You've been trying to talk me to death ever since we met."

Ishabel turned and dropped her mouth open in mock outrage. "Are ye saying that I be a'talkin' too much, is that it?"

"Maybe," Gart managed to keep the smile from spreading, but only just. It had been a long time since he'd been able to talk to anyone in anything resembling a normal manner. Purchasing supplies for the road didn't count. Although he hated to admit it, he was enjoying himself. Ishabel was decidedly incensed, however.

"Why, the nerve of you! How dare ye suggest that I be some kind o' blabbermouth? I'll have ye know that I can be silent for hours at a time, ye ken? Huntin' and stalkin' takes smarts AND quiet, and I've been doing both since I was a wee bairn at me mother's knee, huntin' deer in the Iron Hills! Quiet, that's right, I can be silent as a rock when need be. I can sneak up on a deer close enough to touch it before it even senses me presence, how's that fer quiet, Mr. Gart? Yes, sir, silence is me middle name and...are you laughing at me?"

Gart's smile finally broke free of his control and it felt foreign on his face. He let it sit there, getting the feel of it, and decided that he would let it stay there for now. He rode that way for a bit before he turned back to Ishabel. "I'm sorry, did you say something?"

"WHAT? Oooh, yer sich an eejit!"

Ishabel leaned over in the saddle and swatted him hard on the arm. Gart accepted it in smiling silence until her swat actually connected.

"Ow!" Gart made a face and looked down at his arm. Although it had not detached itself from his shoulder, he knew he'd feel the sting of that playful blow for quite a while. Had she wanted to, she probably could have knocked him right off of Bessie. He looked back at her, a questioning look on his face.

"Och, quit yer whining, it was jist a tap!" She arched one eyebrow at him, almost daring him to complain. Gart finally allowed a chuckle to escape. Ishabel reminded him of his Gennie in some ways. Although Gennie had always been the kindest, sweetest, most compassionate person he had ever known, she had also had a tongue like a razor when she needed it. She wouldn't back down from anyone if she honestly felt she was in the right. Even as he laughed, the thought sent a pang of grief through him. He missed Gennie with every fiber of his being, and thinking of her loss filled his heart with ice. The rage was still there, the black despair that had threatened to claim him more than once, but he could control it better now. Thanks to the Lady RaeLynn, he had managed to focus on the job at hand rather than dwell heavily on that loss. He carried that pain close and always would, but Gennie wouldn't mind if he laughed a bit now. She'd have hit him in the arm, too.

Making a big show of rubbing his arm, Gart grimaced. "Indeed, it was just a tap. Hardly felt a thing. It was like the touch of a feather."

A smile brightened Ishabel's face immediately. "Ha! A feather, he says! If I'da wanted to knock ye offen your mount, I'd have done so, so count yerself lucky!" She nodded smugly to herself and then turned back to guiding her horse through the forest, watching for low hanging tree branches.

Gart shifted in his saddle and returned his eyes to the way ahead, trusting in Ishabel to lead him to the foot of the great mountain. After a time, he said, "It'll be dark soon. How much farther?"

With a shrug, Ishabel replied, "We'll have to camp tonight, but we'll be findin' our way out of the forest midmorn tomorrow, and the road leading up the mountain should be close by. It'll still take a few days to reach the big one ye've spoken of, ye ken, but we're nearly there." She glanced up through the trees, trying to gauge the time until sundown. "We should stop soon. There are wolves and sich in this forest that care nae a bit for people trampin' aboot in their domain.

"If we're just a few hours from the edge, we should keep moving. We could be out in the open by midnight and camp outside the forest." Gart turned his icy glare in Ishabel's direction. He had come a long way, and this close to his goal, his desire to find the Jidaan burned hot within him.

Ishabel was unmoved by his sudden intensity. "It's more like five or six hours. We canna move fast through the forest, and we'd be even slower in the dark. And did ye nae hear me mention the wolves? Ye know, big, hairy beasties that can rend ye to pieces with their sharp teeth and all? They hunt in packs, and if we find ourselves crosswise wi' one o' them packs, it'll go badly for us, I dare say. The noise that we, especially you, would make traveling at night would be like a dinner bell for them."

Gart wasn't willing to give up so easily. "Don't wolves generally stay away from people? And I thought that noise would scare them away?"

"Most wolves do avoid folks, but out here, it pays to be careful, eh? I've been around here me whole life, and I've known too many who came through these woods with fewer folks than they'd started with, and blaming wolves fer the loss. The wolves out here are nae afraid of us, and that makes them dangerous. I've stayed clear of them so far, but if we keep moving at night, they'll hear us and come for sure...especially the way ye blunder around." She arched her eyebrow again, looking sideways at Gart to see if he would rise to the bait. All she got was a stony silence.

Finally, Gart spoke. "All right then, I've no desire to fight off a pack of wolves. Let's find a spot to camp." In spite of the encounter that had left his face a mass of scars on one side, he had no particular aversion to dogs or wolves. No, wolves were just another danger to be respected, like snakes, bears, or thieves who would waylay a man for whatever coin he might have. Gart grudgingly agreed that they would be safer camped than tromping through the forest at night, and he started looking for an appropriate campsite.

An hour later, twilight had gently fallen. Fireflies were shining their lights here and there, their tiny, luminescent bodies glowing in the deepening dark. Gart sat with his back against a tree, eating cold rations from his pack, watching the insects flying lazily about him. They reminded him of the emerald glow he had seen in his dreams, the powerful emerald stone of his Jidaan come to life. *Storms,* the Mage had said. *I'll have the power of Storms.* In his dreams, Gart had seen Lillia call down lightning and create winds out of clear skies. He wondered what else he would be able to do with the weapon. If the Jidaan could control the weather, Gart reasoned, it would be the most powerful thing imaginable...as long as he could control it. Lost in his thoughts, he paid no attention to Ishabel as she laid out her bedroll nearby. A small fire blazed in a circle of stones they had laid, and the horses were hobbled in a clearing nearby where they could crop grass.

"Will ye be takin' the first watch, or shall I?" Ishabel said as she lay back on the ground, motionless for the first time since they had stopped. She looked at Gart, the light from the fire illuminating his face under the floppy hat and showing the full extent of his scars. She had seen worse, but not on anyone living. *Even so, he's still a handsome man. That is, when he's nae scowling like he's tasted something sour,* she thought to herself.

Gart stayed silent a moment longer, then turned to look at her, the piercing blue of his eyes shining in the dim light. "I'll take it; I'm not tired yet. Go ahead and get some rest." He took off his hat and ran his fingers through his unruly blonde hair, thinking absently that he could do with a haircut. He had never let his hair get this long, but then, Gennie had always cut it for him. A low rumble of anger coursed through him at the thought. He missed her unbearably, and the thought of her loss always brought the rage along with it--rage at what had unjustly been taken. He took a deep breath and let it out as he attempted to let the fury roll away. It served no purpose at this moment, so he managed to let it go. For now.

Ishabel had seen the anger flick across his face, and just as quickly vanish. She took a breath to ask him about it, but then decided to leave it alone. Whatever was bothering him, he'd talk of it when he chose, and not before. She settled into her bedroll and closed her eyes. Sleeping in the forest always calmed her, and the sounds of the wind in the trees lulled her to sleep in moments.

Gart watched her drift off and then finished eating the dried meat he had pulled from his pack. He sat for a time, letting his gaze rove over the forest that surrounded them, keeping his eyes away from the fire to preserve his night vision. Satisfied that nothing was about to jump out at them, Gart pulled out his carved Jidaan and began to whittle on it, carefully shaping and carving the wood. It was looking and feeling much more like the one in his dreams, and he worked on it whenever the opportunity arose. Running one hand across the flattened wooden blade, he estimated that another night of work would leave him with a reasonable facsimile of the weapon. It already felt properly balanced; he simply needed to smooth out a few places and maybe add a couple of decorative touches.

The stars slowly rotated in the heavens above and Gart scraped away at the weapon as the night passed. Ishabel slept soundly nearby, and Gart stole a look at her now and then. His gaze lingered over her strong features and the curves mostly hidden by the cloak she had curled up in. *She's kind of pretty,* he found himself thinking. *Not nearly so pretty as Gennie, of course, but pretty, nonetheless. And with a mean punch, too.* Staring at her, he felt his pulse quicken. A feeling of wrongness washed over him then, and he looked away. She wasn't Gennie, and never would be. He took a deep breath and let it out. He knew that being attracted to her would be natural, but the idea of holding anyone but his Gennie filled him with nothing but frustration and pain. He sighed again and looked back at his sleeping companion. No, he would not, could not, see her as anything but a comrade. Gart snorted and reminded himself that Ishabel had never once hinted that she intended to be anything more. Gart shook his head at his own presumption. *As if she'd have anything to do with an ugly lout like me.* As he calmed, he was able to admit that he was simply glad to have her companionship, even if only for the handful of days it had taken to get this close to the mountain.

Suddenly, Gart froze. Something was tickling at the edge of his consciousness, a presence he couldn't identify. Something was near--something dangerous. He scanned the clearing and saw nothing, but the feeling would not go away. Climbing to his feet and holding his wooden Jidaan at the ready, he tried to identify the source of his unease. With one hand, he released his hold on the stick and reached for his sword.

Without warning, a wolf leapt from the bushes, its fanged mouth reaching for Gart's throat. Gart struck out with his Jidaan on instinct, hitting the wolf on the side of its head and sending it to the ground on his left. The wolf landed heavily, but shook off the blow and immediately got to its feet, growling low in its throat and staring fiercely at the man who had just struck it. Gart drew his sword and started gathering his magick as he stepped back to prepare for the next lunge. Before he could unleash his power, he stepped squarely on a round stone and his foot shot out from under him. He fell faster than he thought possible, and the ground raced up to meet him. *No! Ishabel!* was all he had time to think before the back of his head cracked into the trunk of the closest tree with a loud thump. He fell hard, dropping his weapons from nerveless fingers.

Ishabel was already up, sword in one hand, dagger in the other. She saw Gart go down and yelled his name, but saw his head loll to one side as he passed out in the dirt. The wolf snapped at her, and she stabbed it in the throat before it could snap again. Another jumped out of the bushes to take its place, and then another joined in the attack. Ishabel slashed at them as they came close. Three more gray, fanged wolves stepped into the firelight, their amber and gold eyes burning into Ishabel. A pack had found them, and she knew that this would not end well. She tossed her knife near Gart's unconscious form, picked up a burning branch from the fire, and quickly moved to stand protectively over his body. She waved the flaming brand at the wolves as they warily approached, but they were not frightened overmuch by her torch. Ishabel was not happy to see that, at best, the fire was only keeping them at bay momentarily. Soon, they would circle around and attack from both sides and that would be the end of it. For now, the wolves moved restlessly back and forth just out of her reach, growling all the while.

Gart groaned underneath her feet, struggling to regain consciousness, and she kicked him lightly in the ribs with her heel. "Get up, ye lazy goodfernuthin; I be needin' a hand up here! They'll be tearing us to ribbons!" His eyes fluttered open. Still dazed, he tried to roll over so that he could get to his feet, but only succeeded in putting his face in the dirt. The world was a painful kaleidoscope of firelight, Ishabel's boots, and snarling wolves. Somewhere in his clouded mind, Gart knew that if he could just wake up enough to use his magick, they would be safe, but that was as far as he could get.

Ishabel moved the fire back and forth, yelling, "Hai! Hai!" but it dissuaded the wolves not at all. Suddenly a huge wolf slunk out of the bushes, bigger than the others, and Ishabel's jaw dropped. The smaller wolves made way for the newcomer-- obviously the leader of the pack--and its low growl was loud and strong enough to run chills up Ishabel's spine. Its golden eyes shone brightly in the firelight, and thick muscles played under its grayish fur as it moved. It was completely unafraid, and Ishabel knew that they had only moments to live. She could not defend against them all at once, and with their leader present, the other wolves made ready to attack.

Just as Ishabel began offering her silent prayer to the Goddess Rowann to accept their souls, something big burst out of the nearby forest and slammed into the lead wolf, snarling and barking. Instantly, the wolf turned to fight, and the campsite exploded into a flurry of fang and claw and movement almost too fast to see. Ishabel's eyes widened as she watched the whirling animals finally separate, and saw that the big wolf faced an enormous mastiff, battle-scarred and ferocious. It was a mottled brown and black, heavily scarred and just a hair bigger than the wolf it faced. Blood ran thickly from claw marks on both animals, but neither was backing down. They slowly circled each other, growling constantly. Keeping her torch in front of her,

Ishabel slowly knelt to check on Gart, who had finally opened his eyes, though they were unfocused and vague. For the moment, the other wolves only had eyes for the fight in front of them.

Suddenly, the mastiff lunged, and the wolf fought back, its wild instincts driving it to bite and tear and claw. It knew that its life was on the line, and it would either kill or be killed. As strong and fierce as the wolf was, it was no match for the huge mastiff. The dog was a veteran of hundreds of vicious battles with bigger animals, and sometimes more than one at a time. In just a few seconds, the big dog had the wolf's throat in its great jaws. With a vicious shake, the mastiff ripped out the wolf's windpipe, and let its body fall to the ground, its life bleeding out onto the dirt and grass. Blood dripped from its muzzle as it stood, one big paw on the body of its slain opponent. Its teeth were bared in challenge as it moved its great head side to side, daring the other wolves to attack. One gray wolf made a move and the mastiff snapped at it, taking an ear and leaving the wounded wolf yelping in pain. The other wolves milled around uncertainly under the mastiff's unforgiving gaze. Then, as if at some unseen signal, the wolves turned and vanished into the forest, leaving the mastiff standing victorious in the firelight.

Ishabel stared in surprise. The big dog looked around alertly for a few moments as if seeking signs that the wolves were returning, and then apparently decided that all was well. Its ragged ears relaxed, and it looked over its shoulder at Ishabel. The dog turned and left the body of the wolf and walked cautiously over to her. Still wary, Ishabel waved the torch in its direction and the dog backed off immediately with a 'whuff.' Unconcerned, it sat down just out of her reach and yawned. As Ishabel pondered her options, the dog sniffed the air and then wandered over to Gart's pack, still lying on the ground where he had left it. The beast pawed at it until one of the flaps came undone, then it nosed inside until it found the packet of dried meat that Gart had been carrying. It carried the packet back towards the fire and sat down, obviously intending to enjoy the snack.

"Dog...ow...Goddess, that hurts..." Gart's groggy voice called her attention back to the prone form beneath her feet. His eyes were open and he was starting to move around at last.

"Yes, yer quite correct. It's a dog, though it's in a wee bit of rough shape." Ishabel kept the torch between herself and the dog, though it largely ignored her in favor of the meat it had dug out of Gart's pack. "Even so," she continued as she knelt near him, "it saved our bacon."

Gart struggled to a sitting position, wincing as every move sent a bolt of pain through his swollen head. He reached back and explored his injury and his fingers came back with a bit of blood on them. The goose egg that had formed back there was already quite impressive. He groaned as he tried to get his eyes to focus on Ishabel's face, and then looked around the campsite to take stock of the situation. He had been partially aware of events, but was still unsure of what had happened.

"The dog saved us? That one?"

Ishabel raised her eyebrow at him. "Well, yes, that's the only dog I'm seein' 'round here at the moment, and yes, it flung itself at the pack leader. That would be the big dead one on the ground there." Ishabel gestured towards the body of the big wolf. "Ripped its throat out, it did. And scared the others away."

Gart looked at the big animal, which was calmly finishing off Gart's dried meat. It ignored him, concentrating on the food.

"I know this dog," he said. "It was run out of a town a ways back. I fed it once in the forest. Hard to believe it followed me this far."

"Well, it must've taken a powerful liking to whatever ye fed it, then," Ishabel quipped, "because here it is. And I'm pretty happy about it, let me tell ye. I thought we were dead!"

Gart managed to get to his feet and dust himself off. He looked at the dog, recognizing its brown and black coat, torn ear, drooping left eye and the permanent snarl. New wounds had opened up on the dog's flanks, but it paid them no attention, focused as it was on its meal. Gart crouched a bit, averted his eyes to avoid challenging the dog, and slowly moved closer to it.

"Gart, be careful, that thing's nearly as big as yer horse," Ishabel kept her sword and torch at the ready and Gart waved her off.

The dog stopped eating and froze, a quiet, low growl rumbling out of its throat. Gart immediately stopped moving.

"It's ok, boy...not going to hurt you. I just want to take a look at you, that's all." Gart's tone was soothing and quiet. The dog stopped growling and suddenly let out a loud, staccato bark. It lurched to its feet, promptly startling Gart. Still woozy, Gart fell on his rump and tried to crawl away from the dog. Before Ishabel could move, the dog bounded left, then right, then stopped right in front of Gart, who had thrown up an arm to protect his face from the giant animal's teeth. To their surprise, the dog didn't attack. Instead, it splayed its front legs out and stuck its wagging tail in the air, its huge tongue dangling out of its mouth as it panted happily. It barked again, and then bolted off into the bushes, out of sight.

Ishabel and Gart watched the spot where the dog had vanished, then looked at each other as they tried to get their bearings. Without warning, the dog burst back into their campsite, dropped a stick as long as Gart's forearm at his feet, stepped back and resumed its tail-wagging stance.

"Ye've got to be pulling me leg," Ishabel muttered.

Gart didn't move for a few seconds and the dog barked. Slowly, he reached out and picked up the stick. The dog's eyes followed it and it barked again. Gart tossed the stick into the bushes and the dog leaped after it, only to return moments later to drop the stick at his feet once more. Gart was speechless. He threw it again and got the same result.

"Well now," Ishabel said, lowering the torch. "It sure seems that the beastie has ta'en a liking to ye. And lucky for us, too; it's big enough to swallow us whole." She kept a close eye on the dog, who seemed to be having a grand time fetching the thrown stick while Gart recovered his composure.

When the dog returned and dropped the stick again, Gart gently reached out a hand to it, keeping his eyes averted and moving slowly. It stood up from its playful crouch and leaned forward to sniff the offered hand. Whatever it found there seemed acceptable to the giant mastiff, and it snuffled and licked Gart's hand. Carefully, Gart scratched the dog under its chin and behind its ears. It responded with a throaty moan of pleasure before rolling its massive body on the ground, playfully exposing its belly. Seeing the ferocious animal acting like a happy puppy almost made Gart laugh in spite of the pain in his head. He crouched down next to the dog and obliged it with a good belly rub. He saw that it was a female, and it wiggled around, obviously enjoying Gart's attention.

"Well now, I think you're right, Ishabel. It seems that we've just gained a new friend."

After checking on the horses and tending to Gart's head as best they could, Gart and Ishabel settled down to rest until dawn arrived. They were both far too alert to sleep, and Ishabel wanted to be sure that Gart was coherent for a while before letting him drift off again. The dog had curled up near the fire and fallen promptly asleep, though it pricked its ears up and opened its eyes often at sounds they could not hear. Ishabel had dragged the corpses of the wolves a fair distance from their campsite and left them for the scavengers.

"We could eat those, you know," Gart had said, his head pounding as he spoke.

"Wolves stink," Ishabel had quickly countered. "And they often hae worms. I can do without those, thank ye verra much."

Gart had shrugged his shoulders at that. He had to agree that, although they were handsome animals, most wolves did have a fair stench about them. They had enough food to last, so he didn't press the point.

As the sky started to brighten, they loaded up their horses and started on their way again, the dog quietly loping through the forest alongside them. Gart couldn't for the life of him figure why the dog had followed him for so long without revealing itself, nor why it had saved them. After pondering it for a long while and finding no answers, he decided to simply be thankful that it had shown up as it had. They wound their way through the trees, across streams and creek beds, and around any sections of forest that were too thick and tangled for the horses to get through.

Just after midday, as Ishabel had estimated, they broke free of the trees into a meadow that stretched east and west to both horizons. Looming ahead were the Heartstrong Mountains, stabbing into the heavens, an enormous, jagged wall of grey stone that stretched as far as the eye could see. Leagues away, across the swaying grasses of the foothills, the riders could see the pale line of a road that traveled along the base of the mountains. Ahead and a little to the east of the two riders, another road branched off and led up into the craggy rocks above. Snow covered the lofty peaks, though it was warm and sunny down below. Gart let his gaze wander along the range until he fixed on one peak that towered over the others. Its massive size inspired a feeling of awe and wonder in Gart for what felt like the first time in his life.

"Ye should shut yer gob, yer drawin' flies, man," Ishabel said with a smirk. Gart immediately scowled in her direction, but his gaze was soon drawn back to the majesty of the mountains before him. Ishabel smiled and continued, "The Mage's road is there," and she pointed to the branch in the road up ahead. "At least, that's what I've heard. Whatever yer searchin' for, it'll be at the end of that road. Though it seems close, it'll still take ye days to get through there and up. It's farther than it looks. As for me, I've got to head west to

Tamaransett. That's where I was headed afore those bruisers caught me, ye ken?"

Gart looked at her for a few long moments, then turned his searching gaze back to the mountains ahead. "All right, then. Thank you for guiding me here, I am most grateful."

Ishabel chuckled. "Sir, I be the one who's grateful! Ye helped me escape those de-pu-ties on the rood. Should ye ever have need of me or mine, you have but to ask. Here..." shifting the reins to her teeth so that she had both hands free, Ishabel rolled up her left sleeve, exposing a leather wrist brace. She deftly unbuckled the straps and handed it across to Gart, who ran his thumb over the intricate design and the few precious stones embedded in the leather. The swirling, circular knot depicted on the brace seemed to have no beginning and no end, an impressive display of artistic skill. "Should ye ever be anywhere near the Iron Hills, show that to someone and they'll know how to find me or me clan."

Gart strapped the brace to his left wrist and then rebuttoned his sleeve over it. He was touched by the gift, an object that appeared to be of some emotional value to Ishabel, yet she had handed it over without hesitation. His eyes threatened to mist in spite of himself.

"Ah, uh...thank you, Ishabel. I hope the rest of your journey is uneventful."

She laughed, a sound that Gart had come to enjoy. "After thugs and wolves and gigantic dogs and such, I'm pretty sure the rest of me trip will kill me from boredom!" Her face softened then, and she paused before she found her next words. "Gart, I dinna know ye all that well, but I've Seen ye, and yer heart is good. I know ye've got pain in there, too. Whatever yer quest, know that my heart is wi' ye. Farewell, my friend."

A lump found its way into Gart's throat, but he swallowed it down.

"You too. Farewell, Ishabel. Be safe."

Ishabel turned her horse abruptly and spurred it into motion, heading west across the great meadow. She didn't want Gart to make fun of the tears that slid down her face.

Gart watched her ride away, the dog loping along beside her horse for a short while before turning back to rejoin him. It walked close, its great head near Gart's feet in the stirrups. He didn't have to lean down too far to scratch the dog's ears, so he obliged, knowing how much the dog enjoyed it. Wiping his arm across his face, he sniffled once, then again, cursing the meadow and its grasses for aggravating his sinuses and making his eyes tear up.

Chapter 17

Owen Hawser stood at his post on the outer wall for the third night in a row. He looked out over the darkened fields, enjoying the cool air that brushed gently across his face. The stars were twinkling merrily in the night sky above, and he could see great, gray clouds rolling silently over the lands of Laro. He had always enjoyed guard duty at night because of the quiet time it afforded him, but for once, it was much harder to find the peace that he usually did. The keep would be attacked soon, and everyone knew it. What they did not know was when, and by what. Tensions ran high within the walls of the keep, and Owen did his best to allow the calm darkness to soothe him as it always had.

Owen leaned on one of the battlements and let his gaze wander to the edge of the cleared lands where the forest began. Something had caught his eye out there earlier, some kind of movement, but he had not been able to see the cause of it. Curiosity had drawn his gaze back to that same area more than once this night, but each time he had seen nothing.

This time was different.

In the distance, a tiny blot broke free of the trees and started moving towards the castle. Owen squinted into the dark and saw the figure racing headlong, though in retreat or pursuit, male or female, he could not say. As it drew closer, Owen realized that it was a horse and rider at full gallop, the rider nothing more than a dark, hunched bundle. There was no sound, as it was still too distant to be heard.

"Rider approaching!" Owen yelled, keeping a steady watch on the oncoming horse. Immediately, arrows were nocked, and all eyes fastened on the dark figure heading straight for the road that led to the outer gate. Finally, the horse was near enough that Owen could make out the iron helmet of a sergeant of the city guard, its wearer slumped over in the saddle and desperately trying to stay upright. His cloak was wrapped tightly around his body, making him look oddly like a caterpillar.

"It's one of ours; open the gate!" Owen yelled to the guards below, and immediately, the clanking of chains and rumble of winches echoed through the courtyard as the massive gates slowly opened. Other guards ran from their posts to intercept the rider. The terrified horse sped through the gate and shot past the waving hands of the guards, its eyes rolling frantically. Sturdy hands finally grabbed the reins and others helped steady the horse as the injured man rolled out of the saddle into the waiting arms of his fellows.

Carefully, they laid him down on the ground, still wrapped tightly in his cloak. One soldier said, "It's Sergeant Lonias! He was out with a squad trying to convince the holdouts to come here." Lonias held fast to his cloak, keeping it wrapped closely about himself. His face was white with pain, his eyes wide and staring, and he was shaking uncontrollably. Scarlet trails of blood leaked from his nostrils and the corners of his eyes, and stained his cloak in many places. His chest heaved rapidly, and he wheezed with each struggling breath. The soldiers tried to comfort him, and the call for a healer raced through the men.

"Back away, you louts! Give him room to breathe!" At the sound of his voice, the soldiers quickly stepped aside to let Captain Drattus pass. He knelt by the injured soldier, who reached up to clutch at the front of Drattus' tunic, staining it with blood. Lonias' eyes finally focused on the captain, and his words came out in a strained whisper.

"Captain! Oh, gods, Captain, they're out there! They came from the shadows...we didn't have a chance! I'm so sorry, sir!"

Drattus' face was stony, though inwardly, he was furious. He had known Sergeant Lonias since he first enlisted as a gawky youth and had watched him grow into a strong and dependable soldier. Now, he lay bleeding and terrified in the dirt.

"What was it, man? Tell us! What's out there?"

Lonias laughed hysterically, and a chill rippled through the surrounding soldiers at the sound. Fear and madness were in that laugh. The man they had once known had been brave and solid. This was no longer that Lonias. Just as suddenly, his laughter ceased and a grating, giggling whisper emerged.

"Demons, sir! M-monsters! Everywhere...they pulled us off our horses...we tried to fight, but there were so many! So...many..." Lonias' eyes lost focus again and his head started to droop. Drattus shook him insistently, trying to be gentle but failing.

"Lonias! How many are there? Where are they coming from? Lonias!"

The sergeant's eyes opened wide once more and fixed on Drattus. "Mordak sends his regards...and a gift. I'm sorry, sir. I tried to stop him, I did." Lonias unclenched his bloody hands from Drattus' stained tunic and let them drift towards his own chest. "I really tried, sir...I'm so sorry."

Shakily, Lonias grasped the tightly wrapped edges of his cloak and pulled them apart, exposing his chest. A gasp went up from the surrounding soldiers as they saw that he had been stripped of his armor. The pale skin of his torso, heavily muscled from years of training, now featured a long, ragged gash held together by bloody black stitches. As they watched, the skin of Lonias' belly started to move, as if pushed from the inside. The sergeant screamed hoarsely, just once, then the light went out of his eyes and his head lolled to one side.

With a wet ripping noise, the skin of the sergeant's belly burst open, and a nightmare emerged with a triumphant screech. It was impossibly long and spindly to have ridden inside the man's body, but it unfolded itself, dripping gore and blood as it stood on two slender legs. Skeletal arms shot out, disemboweling the nearest guard with sharp, gleaming claws before anyone could move. Another screech erupted from its catlike, fanged muzzle. It was covered in grey, warty skin. Deceptively strong and wiry muscles could be seen as it moved. A bony tail whipped out, lashing into one soldier, slicing cleanly through his neck even as the cat-thing slashed another man with its vicious claws. Blood flew on the air and suddenly, every soldier had his sword out, hacking at the hideous beast.

Swords rose and fell, and the men screamed their frustration and fear into the night. The hideous cat-thing roared defiance and slashed with claws and fangs, killing every man who came within its reach. Archers from the walls began loosing arrows into the creature as fast as they could bring them to string, and soon, the beast was bristling with shafts. Black blood flowed, and the creature yowled in agony and rage as it finally dropped to one knee, weakened by the arrows and a score of cuts and slashes. Seeing the creature's weakness, the hardened soldiers sprang forward, hacking and slashing at the beast until it was unrecognizable. At last, the men stopped their attack and stepped away from the scene. A ring of dead bodies surrounded the ghastly corpse of the cat-thing and its host, the poor sergeant who had carried it into the keep. A stunned silence fell over the men, broken only by their harsh breathing.

Duke Gensen made his way to the center of the crowd, his face a mask of anger. He glared at the bloody mess for a few moments, then turned his gaze to his men.

"Captain Drattus? Where was Sergeant Lonias patrolling?" A low anger burned in his voice as he gestured to the fallen sergeant.

"Your Grace, he led the squad that headed east. There were a few farmers out there who refused to come in with the others; he was trying to get them to change their minds and join us here."

The Duke nodded slowly.

"East, then. That's where they'll be hitting us. Get back to your posts and keep your eyes open. This was meant to scare us, but all it did was assure that we will kill every last creature they send against us. Demons or no demons, we will not fall. These creatures deserve no mercy, and they will receive none from us." As one, every soldier slapped a fist to his heart, then turned to move back to their defensive positions. Duke Gensen watched as a few men started to attend to the corpses. His eyes fell on the body of a man he recognized, but couldn't name. No more would Owen walk the night watch, and enjoy the cool breeze on his face.

Brunar watched from the tower balcony, where he had seen the carnage in the courtyard below. There had been no time for him to descend from the tower to help, but at least the creature had been dispatched quickly. More importantly, from up high, Brunar could see the forest from which the sergeant had come. To his unaided eye, there was nothing to see save the darkened fields and roads leading to the edge of the trees. This rankled the Mage. It was not at all like Mordak to send such a greeting and then wait. He liked to strike while fear was still coursing through the veins of his adversaries. As Brunar's grey eyes surveyed the landscape, he still saw nothing, but the back of his neck prickled in apprehension. Brunar squinted harder into the distance, trying to pinpoint the cause of his uneasiness. Minutes passed before he noticed a faint sense of motion that teased at the corners of his eyes. When he looked directly, he saw nothing but the moonlit fields and roads, but still...there was something.

Slowly, the Mage raised both hands and called on his power. A faint violet glow surrounded his hands, then flowed to cover his whole body. He closed his eyes, quietly chanting in an ancient language and concentrating on his magick. He would have to gamble this time. If what he thought was incorrect, then all he would do was alert Mordak to his presence. But if he was right, it would be well worth the effort.

Brunar molded the spell with his will, forming it to take the shape he wished. His energy swirled within him, growing stronger moment by moment until it was ready to be released. His hands clenched into fists as he prepared to cast the spell. He glowed atop the tower like a bright purple lighthouse searching the night.

With a sound like a thunderclap, Brunar threw all of the energy he had conjured in a bolt of violet lightning towards the east, from whence the rider had come. The power streaked out from the tower and over the lands of Laro, where it exploded as though it had struck a massive, unseen wall, outlined in a sickly scarlet radiance. Shocks of crimson battled with Brunar's violet energy, sparking across the sky, but Brunar's power held firm, and the vague form of the wall disappeared. It had been a powerful cloaking illusion, but it was no match for Brunar's expertly wrought spell.

Where before there had been naught but the quiet roads and fields of Laro, the foul might of Mordak's horde was now revealed in the pale moonlight. Brunar's eyes widened as he saw the staggering size of the army. Thousands upon thousands of writhing figures in ragged columns swarmed over the land, now only half a league from the moat and castle gates. Gholans, humans, and--Brunar squinted into the dark--Krell! Brunar gasped as he recognized the humanoid cannibals from the far East. Somehow, Mordak had tricked them into becoming allies, though they had been his sworn enemies for two millennia. Other larger shapes milled about in the darkness, shapes that Brunar had trouble identifying. Worse, there were some that he recognized, and wished he had not.

"Not good. Definitely not good." Brunar called the Guardians and Weya with his mind--waking most, finding others already awake in their rooms--and told them to meet in the courtyard below. The time for battle had come.

Chapter 18

Moving constantly uphill was starting to annoy Gart. The road he now followed had led up into the foothills at the base of the tallest peak, and was now zigzagging through the rocky land as it wound its way towards the mountain itself. He had tried taking Bessie directly overland to avoid the twisting, turning road, but he found that to be much more difficult than staying on the cleared pathway. Step by step, he rode Bessie towards his destination, the dog trotting along next to them. She would often bolt to chase something that she spied nearby, and occasionally she would flush a few birds from a bush. She never came back with anything to show for her efforts other than a somewhat satisfied look on her scarred face.

"If I was a bird, I'd fly away too, the likes of you coming after me like that," Gart said irritably to the dog, who pointedly ignored him in favor of keeping a watchful eye out for more birds. Gart shook his head. "You're either a lousy hunter, or you're just playing with them."

The dog finally turned to look at him and whuffed.

"That's right; I said it. You're a lousy hunter. It's a wonder you survived until I found you."

Still trotting alongside Gart and Bessie, the dog whuffed again, then sneezed.

"Oh, begging your pardon. Yes, I forgot that *you* were the one who found *me*. I apologize." Gart offered a mock bow from his saddle and the dog whuffed one last time before bolting off the road once again. Gart scoffed at himself. "Talking to a dog. I've been hit in the head too often lately, I think." He took off his floppy hat and rubbed his scalp with one hand, feeling the tenderness at the back of his head where he'd hit the rock. It seemed to be healing well, but the dull ache that remained did not help his disposition at all. He rode on, letting his anger warm him as the air slowly started to chill in the higher altitude.

The road snaked its way upwards, and soon Gart could see the path ahead rising sharply to follow the mountain itself. Looking up, Gart was awed by the sheer presence of it. Its base was lost in the rising land along with the neighboring mountains, but there was no mistaking the peak that rose above all the others. Looking at the snow that frosted the top of the mountain, Gart slowed Bessie to a stop and dismounted. Glancing often at the road ahead, Gart pulled a fleece-lined jacket from his pack, a pair of gloves, and a dark red scarf. Taking time to stretch his legs, relieve himself, and don the cold weather apparel, he allowed himself to believe that he was nearing his destination. This was the mountain. He felt it. All he had to do was follow the road, find the Mage's home, and take the Jidaan that was meant for him. Whatever powers it had would aid him in finding and killing Jor Dayne and his master Mordak. And then, at last, justice would prevail. Gart scowled as he buckled his weapons back on his belt and wound the scarf around his neck. "We're almost there, dog, so let's move." The dog came trotting back from her latest mission, this time with her head held high and carrying a small pheasant in her mouth. She walked up, turned in a circle and sat down, looking expectantly at Gart.

"Well, look at you. Finally made yourself useful, I see," Gart grudgingly allowed himself to be amused. "Here, I'll take that and put it on the horse. Give it." He held out a hand and the dog let the bird's carcass drop into his outstretched palm. It took only a moment for Gart to tie the bird onto the back of the saddle. He saw that the dog continued to sit, panting slightly and wagging her sturdy, scarred tail. Kneeling, Gart brought himself face to face with the dog and scratched her neck and behind her ears. The dog closed her eyes and let out several little grunts of pleasure.

"You've had a rough time of it, haven't you dog?" The dog did not reply, but merely leaned into the scratching. Gart had gotten used to the dogs scarred face quickly. None of the old injuries seemed to hamper her when she moved, save an occasional hitch in one of her rear legs. Gart began to pet her back, making note of all the scars there as well. She was thin, but still a big beast. Properly fed, she would be a monster. Against his better judgement, he decided that he liked having the dog around. She had brought food for him, saved him and Ishabel from the wolves, and was generally very little trouble. Something about having someone to talk to without worrying what would be said in return was deeply appealing to Gart, and it just wasn't the same with Bessie. "Well, I guess you're not that bad to have around. Just don't give me any trouble, and we'll get along." Suddenly, the dog started licking his face with her giant, wet tongue. Gart grimaced, but didn't immediately pull away. Then he chuckled and ruffled the dog's fur as she rolled over on its back, exposing her belly.

"All right, all right, no need to get all mushy about it," he said, gently rubbing the dog's belly. Absently, he thought that he should figure out what to call her. "Come on, you, let's get moving. We're close, I think, and I'd just as soon not get caught out here on the mountain at night." The dog eagerly rolled over and stood up, sniffing the air.

Moving quickly, Gart remounted Bessie and clicked his heels against her sides to goad her into action. "Get up there, Bessie girl. You come along too, dog." Bessie eased herself into motion again, and the dog trotted happily along beside them.

The road worked its way upwards, and Gart kept his eyes on the path ahead. It was wide enough for at least three horses to walk abreast, and fairly even. Gart tried to settle in for the ride, leaning forward a little to compensate for the gentle uphill rise that would surely get steeper.

The dog was the first to know that trouble had found them. She growled deep in her throat, looking out into the rocks, but did not bark. The road was passing through a series of small canyons and bluffs on the way to the main peak, and Gart had already been feeling somewhat hemmed in by the lack of visibility. The sound of rocks falling caused the hair on the back of his neck to stand on end. Gart reined Bessie to a halt and sat listening for a few moments. For a while, all he heard was the wind blowing softly through the rocks, and the gentle song of birds here and there.

"I don't like it," Gart spoke quietly to the dog. "This has the feel of something that won't end well. Such a shame, too, it's been a lovely ride so far." The dog whuffed in reply. Gart leaned down and scratched behind her ears again. In a louder voice, he said, "Well, girl, if there's anyone out here, we'll just have to hope they're friendly. We don't want any trouble, now do we?"

"I'm glad to hear that, friend! We don't either. Now, if you'll just pay the toll, we can keep any trouble from coming about." The voice was thickly accented and had an amused tone.

Gart tilted his head in the direction of the voice, and saw a man standing on a boulder on the left side of the road a few yards away. He was shabbily dressed, wearing mismatched armor, and a big furry hat on his head. One of his legs appeared to be shorter than the other, and he stood with his body angled to the left. He had a big, curved saber, and he carried it nonchalantly on his shoulder, angled so that Gart could see it. His grin was missing several teeth, and Gart could count the remaining ones in single digits. He was a comical figure, though Gart sensed his intentions were anything but humorous.

Anger rose in him, and Gart felt his magick waking. He remembered a time when he had fought his magick at every turn, and even denied its very existence. Now, it was as much a part of him as his arms or legs, and it was far stronger than it had ever

been. As his rage built, his magick swirled within him, aching for
release.

"Toll?" Gart said, trying to keep his voice neutral. "I
thought this was the road to the Mage's keep. Somehow, I doubt
that he'd send anyone to collect a toll."

"Are you saying I'm a liar?" the odd little man replied,
anger rising in his voice. He whistled through his few teeth, a
short, sharp sound that hurt Gart's ears. Within moments, a
dozen armed men appeared in the surrounding rocks, some with
bows already drawn. The dog started barking immediately, and
Gart reached down and attempted to calm her. She stopped
barking, but kept growling, low and menacing. The scruffy
fellow shook his head and continued. "Oh, that's not nice of you,
sir. Not nice at all. We were going to allow you through after
taking only a token payment, but now I'm afraid that we'll have
to take all that you have. For being insulting, you understand."
Laughter echoed among the rocks from the other ragged men.

Gart slowly looked around and took stock of the
situation. Some had swords or axes and a few had spears. He
noted the position of each man, especially the bowmen. They
would most assuredly send arrows flying at his first hint of
resistance, and they would need to be dealt with. Beneath the
shadow of his floppy hat, his mouth tightened into a grim line.
Moving slowly so that they could see that he was not going for his
weapons, he dismounted and kept his hands in view.

"My apologies, I meant no offense. Though I still don't
think that you've been commissioned by the Mage, I'm willing to
pay a small toll. However, I'd like to make you a bet."

The leader laughed. "A bet? Well, I'm a bit of a gambler,
you might say. What is it?"

Gart slowly opened his money pouch and pulled out a
single gold coin. He held it up so that the sunlight gleamed from
it, noticing that the bandit leader's attention was suddenly very
focused. "It's a simple one. If you can catch this, then I'll give
you everything in my money pouch."

The bandit barked a short laugh.

"You'll give us everything in your money pouch whether
you win or not, but I'll play along. What if you win?"

"Then you leave me alone, as well as any others who
travel on this road. Find another line of work. There's no toll
needed here, and I'm pretty sure that you're trespassing."

A toothless smile crossed the bandit's face. "Well,
fortunately for me, I'm pretty good with my hands. And unless
you happen to be the Mage, then you're the one who's

trespassing." A harder look settled in then, exposing the murderous thief that resided underneath the harmless looking exterior. "Toss it up here. Now!"

Gart held up the gold piece again, showing it to the bandit leader, and tossed it in a high, easy arc towards him. The leader's beady eyes flashed with greed as he tracked the coin through the air and reached out one dirty hand to catch it. The sun glinted and sparked off the coin as it turned, and all eyes followed it. The leader's hand lashed out and closed. He laughed. "Ha! Easy!" He opened his hand to view the coin and a perplexed look crossed his face.

His hand was empty. For a moment, he stayed silent as he tried to figure out where the coin had gone.

"Looking for this?" Gart's voice made the bandit lift his head to see the coin floating down from the sky to hover a few feet in front of him, slowly rotating in the sunshine.

Grabbing the gold piece with his magick had been easy. At the last instant, Gart had sent the coin moving skyward so quickly that none of the bandits had seen it, leaving their chief to catch only empty air. "It seems you're not so good with your hands after all." Gart reached out with his magick towards the surrounding rocks, finding each man and gaining an instant, almost physical sense of their positions.

"KILL HIM!" The leader yelled, pointing his sword at Gart, bringing a ferocious round of barking from the dog.

The twang of bowstrings was immediate, but Gart did not cower or try to dodge. He simply stood there in the middle of the road and raised one hand. Time slowed for Gart as he concentrated on the tendrils of magick he had extended between himself and each of the bandits. Six of them had loosed arrows at him, two of those at the dog. Curling his magick around the speeding shafts, he grasped them all tightly and simultaneously stopped their flight, leaving them to hover in the air. Through his magick, Gart could feel the astonishment of the bandits, and not long after, their fear.

"It's bad enough that you're trying to hurt me, but trying to kill my dog is downright mean. I don't like mean people. They make me angry." Settling his feet into the road beneath him, Gart reached out with his magick, grabbed every bandit, and *squeezed*. He was immediately rewarded with gasps and howls of fear. Gart took a deep breath and focused his mind. He had lifted many things since embracing his power, but this was the biggest test thus far--so many targets, each man-sized. Slowly, the bandits were drawn from their hiding places, Gart's invisible power hauling them into the air, arms pinned to their sides and feet kicking ineffectually. Those who had loosed arrows found their missiles slowly moving back towards them to stop an arm's length from their faces, their gleaming, sharp heads now pointed right back at the frightened ruffians. Once Gart was sure he could hold the men in place without undue strain, he ignored their cries for help and turned his attention to the bandit leader, who was trying to escape. His loud scuffling revealed his position, and Gart found him easily. Reaching out with his power, Gart snatched him up as well, kicking and screaming.

Gart moved him through the air at frightening speed, and brought him out from behind the rocks to hover close by so he could see him face to face. The little man continued to struggle and wail until he was just a few feet away. His eyes were wide with terror as he drifted in the air, his booted feet dangling as they reached for the ground but did not find it. Sweat beaded on Gart's forehead and rolled down his cheek, but the strain was manageable. He held the arrows, all the bandits, and the leader in the air in an inescapable grip. His heart thumped faster, but not unduly so, and Gart guessed he could hold them this way for several minutes before he started to tire. Staring into the face of the leader, Gart decided to scare him a bit more. He slowly rotated the little man until he was floating upside down, his frightened brown eyes on a level with Gart's piercing blue ones. Slowly and deliberately, he removed his hat so that the leader could better see his face, and his scars.

"I believe I won the bet. Wouldn't you agree?"

Upside down and near tears, the bandit leader whined pitifully. "I'm so sorry, sir Mage! We didn't know it was you, honest! We'll be on our way, yes sir. You'll never even know we was here! Just..." he started to cry. "Just let us go."

Gart's angry blue gaze bored into the bandit leader. There was no softness to be seen at all, and the bandit sensed it. Cobalt fire seemed to flash behind Gart's eyes and the dirty little man began to whimper. At Gart's side, the dog continued a low, rumbling growl.

"What is your name?" Gart's voice was quiet and cold.

"B-b-bojun, sir Mage. Please, I'm begging you!" His face was turning purple as the blood flowed into it.

Gart remained silent for a moment. Bojun was obviously mistaking him for Brunar. He saw no reason to correct him and decided to use the assumption to his advantage.

"I'm sure that others have begged for mercy as you took their money on their way through here, yes?" Gart rotated the man so that he was right-side up again; he was still shaking with fear. Gart continued, "I'm not inclined to be forgiving. Had I wanted a toll imposed on my road, I'd have done so. I have no need of that, and I'm offended that you are showing such disrespect." Leaning forward until he was only inches away from the bandit leader's nose, Gart continued, "*Deeply* offended."

"We didn't mean no harm, I swear! We're sorry; we'll leave here and never bother you or anyone on this road again." Several of the men hanging in the air nearby chimed in, echoing the leader's sentiments enthusiastically. Gart silenced them all with a sharp squeeze of his magick.

Slowly he turned to examine them all, giving each a long, penetrating look. In every face, he saw fear. Through the magick that held them, he also gained a strong impression of their emotions. All were strongly committed to escaping and running as far from the Mage's cursed road as possible--all save one.

He was a huge, burly man with a forked beard. Gart turned to fully face the man, staring into his eyes, and found only defiance and rage there. Cocking his head, Gart concentrated on the sensations that flowed back along his magick from the man. Flashes of barely suppressed rage, murderous hatred, and violence startled him with their ferocity. The others, though rough, hard men who would murder and steal, were not truly, deeply evil. This one, though...Gart knew to the bottom of his soul that the man was profoundly wicked, depraved, and dangerous. Black hatred poured from him in a steady wave, so much that Gart felt sickened by it. A name came to him, and he spoke it aloud. "Raben. That's your name. Raben." The man kept his mouth clamped shut, but Gart felt his sudden surprise, which was quickly overwhelmed by Raben's brutal anger. Raben was insane, and Gart knew it. Suddenly, Gart was unsure of what to do. He could kill the man now as he hung there, helpless. However, all of the other men were just as guilty of trying to kill Gart as he was. If he were going to kill any of them, then he should kill them all. Gart grunted to himself, frustrated, and then turned back to the leader.

"You lead these men?" he asked Bojun.

"Yes, sir Mage. They follow me," Bojun shakily replied, daring to let hope sneak into his voice. The Mage before him was powerful, but he had let them live so far. Bojun desperately hoped the Mage would be merciful and that he would escape alive. He watched the Mage think for a moment, his scowl puckering the vicious scars on the right side of his face. The eyes scared Bojun more than the scars, though...such power in those sapphire eyes.

"You tried to kill me. For that, you should pay with your life. However, what I face is far worse than your pitiful bunch. Take them far away from here, and find a way to atone for the wrongs you've done. If you do not," Gart's eyes flashed with the intensity of his command, "I will know. And you'll all pay."

Bojun nodded frantically. "Yes, my Lord, we'll do as you say. Yes, we will!" Eager cries of agreement came from most of Gart's captives.

Gart slowly lowered each man to the ground, feeling their relief as their boots made contact with the road. Gart released his hold on them, trying not to sigh as the stress of holding the men suddenly disappeared as he did so. The arrows clattered to the road as well. He kept his eyes on Bojun, who seemed about to pass out. Suddenly, a roar of anger echoed in the clearing, and Gart spun to meet it.

Raben had pulled a throwing axe from his belt the moment Gart's hold on him was gone. With a shout of rage, he hurled it at Gart's unprotected back. Without thinking, Gart snatched the weapon from the air and redirected it right back towards the man, burying the blade in his forehead with a meaty thump. Raben's angry yell was suddenly silenced. The dark-bearded thug stood still for a moment, a shocked look frozen on his face. Raben's body collapsed to the ground, raising dust as it settled there. A thin trickle of blood found its way down his forehead to drip on the road.

Gart sighed. He had not wanted to kill anyone, but if someone had to die, he supposed Raben was the best choice. He had killed scores of Gholans, but never a human. Although completely justified by the fact that Raben had just attacked Gart from behind in an attempt to murder him, Gart found himself wishing that he hadn't had to kill the man. Turning back to Bojun, he found the little fellow staring at Raben's corpse, shaking his head.

"Sir Mage, I'm so sorry. Raben was always a problem. He wasn't right in the head; it's good that you killed him." Gart raised an eyebrow at Bojun, who immediately tried to reassure him. "We'll move right along and not trouble you any longer!"

Gart stayed silent for a moment, then turned his attention back to the road ahead. "Go. Take your men and get out of here before I change my mind and decide to deal with you all more harshly." Removing his attention from them, Gart replaced his hat on his head and knelt down to calm the dog, scratching her ears and speaking softly to her as the men scrambled back over the rocks and disappeared. Moments later, the sound of hooves striking the stone of the road echoed throughout the small valley. Bojun appeared from behind a massive boulder, riding a stout little pony. The others rode behind him, the last towing a riderless horse in his wake. They left the body of Raben where it had fallen.

The men rode by, casting wary glances Gart's way as they did so. He watched them go, his cobalt blue eyes boring into the eyes each bandit as they passed. Before long, the sounds of hoofbeats faded away as they headed down from the mountain. Gart ruffled the dog's fur again before standing. He took a drink from his waterskin and gathered his thoughts before remounting Bessie.

The vile creatures he had faced on his journey seemed intent upon killing every human in sight. Good humans or bad, the Gholans did not care one bit. Raben, although dangerous, was ultimately nothing more than a distraction from Gart's real goal. Besides, the creatures under Jor Dayne's command were far more deadly.

"Still," Gart said aloud to the dog, who had remained sitting obediently. "Death by Gholan claw or by a madman's hatchet, they're the same amount of dead. I had to kill Raben or he'd have kept trying to kill me. I just…" He looked down at the dog, who looked back up at him with her permanent snarl. Her warm brown eyes were a soft counterpoint to her visible fangs, and Gart felt himself oddly comforted. "I just didn't want to."

The dog did not answer, but then, Gart had not expected her to. Gart looked ahead at the road and back to the dog, who had kept her calm, easy gaze on him. She whuffed at him, and Gart felt his spirits lift.

"Beauty," he said to her. She cocked her head to one side, making her torn ear flop. "I think I'll call you 'Beauty.' I may be the only one who thinks that about you," he shook his head slightly, "but I think it fits." The dog righted her head and whuffed back at him, then sneezed. Her scarred jaw dropped open and she began to pant easily as her tail started to wag. Gart looked back at the road and continued talking, more to himself than to the dog. "Yes…that sounds right."

The path rose sharply and angled to the left as it hugged the side of the mountain. Urging Bessie forward, he sighed and pulled his hat down harder on his head. He was ready to push forward and see what new challenges awaited. He put Raben and the bandits out of his mind, and focused on moving forward.

Suddenly, he thought about the fact that Bojun had mistaken him for Brunar and snorted at the irony. For the longest time, Gart had hated Brunar for intruding into his life and bringing such turmoil.

"I'm no Mage," he said aloud, musing. "Not even close." Beauty heard him and whuffed once, though whether in agreement or dissent, Gart could not say.

Chapter 19

"What are they waiting for, do you think?" The Duke's voice was curious, but held no fear. He and Brunar stood on the ramparts of the outer wall, surveying the sea of enemies camped on the castle's very doorstep, just out of bowshot. Brunar's grey eyes slowly crawled over the evil horde. It seethed and moved as various beings shifted position, occasionally fighting each other, like a vast colony of ants. Bestial howls and screams from within the enemy army kept all of the Laroan soldiers on edge. Sleep had been hard to come by, for those screams followed them into their dreams. The enemy had surrounded the castle on three sides, then simply sat there. They had not advanced for two days and still showed no signs of attacking. On this, the third day, the sun eased over the horizon to show a cloudless blue sky. Unfortunately, the clear weather gave everyone on the walls an unobstructed view of the horror below. The short, grey-skinned Gholans shied from the light, but held their ground. Morcats moved among them--taller than a man, and bulky with hard muscles that rippled under a short coat of coarse fur. Their fearsome claws and sharp teeth gleamed in the morning light, and the hatred in their cat-like yet reptilian faces was plain to see as they stalked among the snarling Gholans. No one had seen a Morcat for centuries, and most thought them to be wholly mythical. Yet hundreds of them now walked the grounds outside the castle, waiting to feast on the humans within.

"I know not, Your Grace, but they can afford to wait. They know we're not going anywhere," Brunar sighed. "That being said, I've never known the creatures of Mordak to be patient like this; it's not in their nature. Ordinarily, they'd have attacked us the moment they reached the castle. He is using some extraordinary power to keep them all held in check this way. It concerns me."

The Duke laughed without humor. "Well, I'd have to say that it concerns me as well, sir Mage. Our people are scared and restless. The soldiers are itching for a fight to break the tension, and that's certainly not good. Men in that state make mistakes. Mistakes here can be bloody costly." Duke Gensen ran his gloved hand over his close-cropped hair, as close to a nervous gesture as he would allow. "Is he out there, do you think? This...Mordak?"

At the sound of the Vile One's name, Brunar had to repress the urge to spit. "Unfortunately, his wards are too strong. I've tried to locate him and he strikes back before I can find him." He felt faint echoes of the tremendous pain that had been sent back along his search spell. "When he chooses to reveal himself, you'll know it. I would wager that he's out there somewhere, enjoying the spectacle he's created."

Without turning his eyes away from the horde of foul creatures that swarmed outside the castle, Brunar sent a mental call to all of the Guardians, beckoning them to come to the first wall. Within moments, an opalescent Gate opened up next to the Mage and Layton stepped through it, Alyssa and Kiran following immediately after.

Layton saluted, as always, and Brunar nodded to him. He had tried to get the lad to stop doing that, but he insisted it was a habit, long-ingrained from his time with the Eastern masters. It made him itch if he didn't do so. Brunar turned to them and spoke.

"I know the others will be along soon. I'd rather wait until they are all here before we talk."

"Well, I'm here." Brunar actually jumped at the sound of Nessar's voice right next to his ear, and the old man grinned slyly to see his reaction.

Brunar recovered instantly, and the ghost of a smile flitted across his face as the others laughed out loud. "Nessar, I see your skills are improving."

Nessar shrugged innocently. "Maybe a little, Mage. Just a bit," but the grin remained on the thief's grizzled face. He had indeed improved, he was forced to admit, and without the use of his Jidaan. Physically, Nessar was fitter than he had been in years. His senses had been enhanced dramatically, and his stealth was now of a level that astounded even him.

Brunar looked over Nessar's shoulder and saw Bjarke's shaggy head towering over the soldiers on the wall as he rapidly approached them. His face was stern, which was a look that did not sit well on his kind features. Before him marched the Weya, ValElder Moihra in the lead and Col and Ginn on either side. In moments, they reached the group, and Brunar greeted them all.

"Guardians, you've all seen the enemy as they surround us. As yet, there has been no move to attack, but I have the feeling it will be soon. We've discussed as many possibilities as we could, and there is little left to do but wait."

Duke Gensen gestured at the massive stone walls upon which they stood. "Fortunately, the walls are high and thick, and the moat is wide. There are caltrops on the ground between the moat and the walls, as well as pit traps. My soldiers are prepared to send boiling oil over the walls to dissuade them, and of course, we have our archers and the ballistae."

Layton's voice piped up, "I haven't seen any siege towers or scaling ladders on their side. How are they going to get in?"

"Gholans can climb like lizards," Brunar could not keep the disgust from his tone. "There are thousands of them, and it's likely they will swarm the wall to kill as many of us as they can before opening the gates to allow the rest of the horde to come in. They are vicious, and quite cunning. The larger beasts are called Morcats; they are even more deadly than the Gholans. They will slash and tear with claws and teeth, just as the Gholans do, but they are far bigger and stronger. In the last war, Mordak had only a handful of them, but I see hundreds of them out there. We must keep them out as long as possible."

Kiran spoke up, frustrated. "There are thousands and thousands of creatures out there! What are we supposed to do, just kill them all as they come at us until there are none left? That doesn't sound like a good way to win a battle, Brunar. They'll just flat wear us out. They've got enough numbers to keep throwing themselves at us until we break!"

Nessar said, "And I don't know that we could do enough damage to make them want to retreat. Those things out there are...are...they're *monsters*! I doubt they think like us. We can demoralize humans, but we can't scare those creatures away." He pointed one gnarled hand out at the evil horde outside the gates. "Call me crazy, but I think they scare us a lot more than we scare them!"

Brunar brightened. "Ah, that's where you're wrong, Nessar! Gholans will fight as long as they think they are winning. They are cunning, but not all that smart. They are driven by others among them, captains, if you will. Those captains will bully and harass the masses into attacking on Mordak's orders. If we take out enough of them, especially the captains, they will lose what courage they have." His voice hardened once more, "However, make no mistake. They are still capable of doing a lot of damage, so we must kill every single one that gets close enough for us to do so. And those Morcats? Well, they're not so easily frightened, but there aren't nearly as many of them to deal with, thank the Goddess."

The Duke peered out over the horde, still assessing their strength. "It looks like he's got humans out there too, sir Mage. They look somewhat odd from here, but I see a great many of them behind the creatures."

"Most of those are not humans, Your Grace. They are Krell." Brunar's words elicited a burst of babble from the group, and he gestured for quiet so that he could continue. "Yes, they are very real. They are from the far East, past the Gorran Plain, and they are vicious, bloodthirsty flesh-eaters. Their teeth are filed to sharp points and they are effective fighters based on their ferocity alone. How he managed to get so many of them to follow him again is completely beyond me, but nevertheless, there they are."

Bjarke's voice surprised them all. "The Krell followed Mordak centuries ago, but when they found out that he wasn't as powerful as he had claimed, many of them were so furious that they flung themselves on the spears and swords of their enemies. Thousands died with Mordak's name on their lips as a curse, and those few that remained swore eternal hatred. It's hard to believe they are following him again."

Brunar nodded, impressed. "That's exactly right, Bjarke. How did you know that?"

Bjarke shrugged. "I read your book, Brunar. The history you wrote of the last war with Mordak. It has been most illuminating." Turning to look out at the hateful creatures that covered the land outside the castle walls, he continued. "He must have somehow used his power to influence them. However he managed it, they are out there, and eager to tear our throats out. I can blast a lot of them with my Gift, at least. That should help. And of course, I will do what I can to keep them from breaching the wall." Bjarke's suggestion was met with general approval.

"Indeed, Bjarke. However, there are limits to your strength, however prodigious. We must find opportunities to use your power to best effect so that you're not exhausted too quickly. The foe is relentless and their numbers will allow them to push us hard."

Layton reached up and tapped Bjarke on the shoulder, and beckoned for him to lean close so that he could hear. Bjarke bent down and listened to Layton's idea and a huge grin split his bearish face. He nodded at the smaller man and slapped him on the back before turning his attention back to the Mage. Layton kept his feet, but only just barely.

Brunar continued, "Kiran, I need you to protect the main gate. If it looks like it's going to fall, use your power to hold it until we can get as many of our fighters back to the keep as possible. The same goes for any sizeable breach in the outer wall. Hold it until it's repaired or we must retreat."

Kiran nodded. "Yes, sir, I'll hold the wall for as long as I can. Making and holding a Ward that big for longer than a few minutes...I'm liable to pass out again. I may need one of you drag me out of there afterwards."

"Not if you're still wearing that blasted heavy chainmail under there...ow, hey!" Nessar always knew how to get a rise out of Kiran, and she rewarded him with a sharp kick to his shin.

Layton stepped forward to speak. "Kiran, don't worry about that. I'll come and get you. I can be there in an instant and Gate us both to safety, so you just do what you need to do. I'll get you out of there; you can count on it."

Kiran was touched. Through the heightened senses they all possessed, she immediately felt his sincerity and knew the younger man would die before he'd let anything stop him from coming to get her. Such was the strength of his simple pledge. After all the times she had picked on him during their travels, he didn't bat an eye. He would be there for her. Embarrassed, she coughed before replying.

"Yes, well, see that you do. You leave me hanging out there, and there will be Hel to pay, Laytie dear." Kiran popped a quick punch to his shoulder, hard enough to sting, which brought a smile from the lad. He saluted and bowed, which he knew would annoy her. "Ugh! With the bowing!" Kiran rolled her eyes in mock disgust as she turned back to face the evil horde outside.

Brunar cleared his throat and all eyes turned back to him. Addressing Alyssa, the Mage continued, "Alyssa, you will be sorely tested almost immediately. The temptation will be to heal everyone that comes before you because you can. However, you can't do that for very long before you become exhausted and at that point, you won't be able to heal so much as a scratch until you recover. You must be wise in your choices. Use conventional measures where you can and heal only those who need it most. There will be suffering and death that you cannot prevent. You must be strong and simply do what you can."

Alyssa nodded. "Yes, I've got the other Sisters working with Laro's physicians right now, preparing for the wounded. I'll do my part, Brunar."

Valelder Moihra's voice arose on the breeze like gentle music. "Though we are only three, we will remind the Gholans why they shy away from our fair folk. Also, there are defenses remaining in the old keep from Elder times. They have been long forgotten, but we have sensed them. We are not yet sure what they will do or how to enable them, but we are working on that. We are not Lormages, but we are not entirely unskilled." Her tilted jewel-like eyes glittered and the ghost of a smile touched her sculpted lips.

Duke Gensen was astonished. "Other defenses? What other defenses? My family has ruled here for generations and I've never heard of anything of the sort. Please elaborate."

Moihra bowed slightly in apology. "At this point, we know not," she turned her head and nodded towards the castle, which was far older than the outer wall. "There is a slumbering enchantment on the stones of the old keep. We feel it. We will continue to investigate as best we can. It is very, very old, but still potent. Cohl also said that he felt something in the Royal Crypt, but did not have time to delve further."

"The Royal Crypt?" Duke Gensen's astonishment reached new heights. "How in the world did you get in there? Those doors are formidably locked and foolproof!"

Cohl simply shrugged. "We are Weya," he said, as if that explained everything.

The Duke looked at Brunar for answers, and the Mage shrugged as well.

"What he means, Your Grace, is that most locks, including those on the Crypt, are somewhat...um...simple. To a Weya, I mean." Brunar inclined his head towards Cohl, and he nodded.

The Duke shook his head and smiled.

"I'm glad you're on our side, then. By all means, if it will help us in the coming battle, continue to investigate whatever you wish. If Rorian or I can help you in any way, please don't hesitate to call on us."

The three Weya bowed slightly to the Duke and turned to make their way back down to the castle. The sun continued to shine as the morning passed. Birds flew overhead and sang their usual songs, thoroughly unconcerned about the battle brewing below. The Duke watched the Weya leave, noting that ValElder Moihra walked over to face one corner of the keep--a tower. She sat down a few yards away from one wall of the tower and assumed a position of meditation. There she stayed, unmoving. Cohl and Ginn disappeared into the castle, presumably to further investigate the Royal Crypt.

The Duke turned back to Brunar and spoke again. "Well, we're as ready as we're going to be, I believe. Now, we wait."

A distant rumble caught their attention, and everyone turned towards the evil horde. The noise had come from within the forest behind the massed army; scarlet bursts of radiance showed through the tangled branches and sturdy trunks. Flashes of crimson continued for a few moments more, then vanished, though the deep rumbling could still be heard and felt for long minutes after the lights had gone. Finally, the sounds disappeared as well, leaving an ill feeling in the hearts of those who had heard it.

"Well, that can't be good," Duke Gensen spoke first.

"It's not," Brunar replied. "That's got to be Mordak, along with whatever kind of monstrosities he may have brought along with him." Brunar stared at the forest, searching it with his grey eyes.

As if that were a signal, a mob of man-sized figures began pouring through the trees, adding to the already teeming masses of foul creatures that lay before the castle. Some appeared to be riding while others walked. But all had glowing scarlet eyes, visible to the castle defenders even from that distance.

Brunar stared at them as they came. He had known they might have to fight Mordak's reanimated dead, and now, the reality was staring him in the face. He was not happy about it. Not happy at all. Hundreds, maybe thousands of them, had just been added to the force arrayed against the good people of Laro. The gentle breeze that had been carrying the vaguely swampish, sickly smell of Mordak's horde suddenly brought worse odors into the castle as the shambling merged with the larger force. Death was in the air, and hearts sank as the numbers of Mordak's foul army continued to grow.

At the far edge of the teeming horde, a monstrous figure on horseback began slowly riding towards the castle. The crawling, hissing creatures of the throng fell away before it, then closed ranks in its wake. Closer and closer it came, nearing the front lines. Finally, the horse broke free of the immense crowd of teeming horrors, and leisurely walked towards the outer gate of the castle.

Duke Gensen watched the rider approach, noting the sheer size and bulk of the man as he guided his horse along. The newcomer had long, flowing black hair and a short beard. His massive chest was covered in a patchwork of various types of armor, though his muscled arms were bare. His eyes were those of a serpent, glowing yellow in the clear morning light. The cruel smile on the man's face was chilling to those with vision sharp enough to see it. Even at this distance, they could sense an aura of death about him.

"Well, they've finally sent someone to talk with us. Is that Mordak?" the Duke said.

Brunar shook his head. "No, Your Grace, it is not. I have never seen that man before, though it is obvious he is one of Mordak's creations. Assume that nothing he says is the truth, for Mordak knows nothing of honor. He will only use the truth if it can possibly hurt us."

Their eyes followed the huge man as he approached the outer gate, stopping just shy of arrow range. His gigantic horse snorted and tossed its head as though it would rather be elsewhere, but the man paid no attention. His sly smile never wavered.

"Hallo the castle! I am Jor Dayne, and I lead this army for Mordak. I bid you to open the doors to us, or else there will be needless suffering." There was a taunt woven into his words, an unmistakable hint of sarcastic laughter.

The Duke bristled at Jor Dayne's tone, but kept his composure. He would not be goaded into looking like a fool. "If you wish to avoid needless suffering, then by all means pass us by. Whatever you want from us, we'll not willingly provide. You may as well get your...troops...out of here, and leave us be. We have no quarrel with you."

Jor Dayne laughed, and the sick sound of it made many of the soldiers at the wall somewhat ill. "Oh, no, we won't be doing that. I have orders to get inside and then recruit all of you. We need more soldiers, and you'll do nicely. So much the better if you're all dead."

Drattus turned to the Duke, anger flaring in his voice. "He's mocking us, Your Grace! The filth! I'd go down there and fight him one on one if I thought it would end this."

Duke Gensen shook his head. "I know you would, Drattus, but I have the feeling that even your strong sword arm would count as nothing against the likes of that. He's got the stink of evil magick about him, and it will take more than one of us to put him down." Turning his attention back to Jor Dayne, the Duke raised his voice again. "Begone, lackey! We care nothing for you or your words, you scum-sucking degenerate! You go back and tell that son of a whore, Mordak, that he'll not have Laro, no matter what he sends against us, so he should take his flea-bitten, mangy pets elsewhere!"

More hideous laughter rang out, echoing from the massive grey stones of the outer wall. The awful sound of it made the soldiers' skin crawl. "Thank you, my Lord Duke! I had hoped to have to wrest your people from you in battle, and you have not disappointed me! I do so love to hear the screaming..."

Jor Dayne drew his massive sword and held it aloft as his horse reared. The foul yellow gleam from his eyes shone as he looked over the defenders atop the wall, then he spun his horse in a circle before allowing it to put its front hooves down again.

"Soon now...very soon, you will all be nothing more than meat for our army. You'll either be joining it, or feeding it. You think you're safe in there, behind that wall? Bah! We'll have those doors open by nightfall." His voice somehow carried to every defender on and behind the wall, and the cold breath of fear touched the backs of their necks.

"Like Hel, you will!" Duke Gensen spat over the wall and looked over his shoulder towards one of the parapets, where a pair of soldiers stood ready next to something covered by a huge canvas. At the Duke's quick nod, the soldiers grinned and yanked off the cover to reveal one of the huge ballistae, already loaded and armed. In quick, efficient motions, they turned their weapon towards Jor Dayne. At the Duke's command, they took aim, and immediately let fly. A full load of fist-sized stones screamed through the air, aimed directly at the huge, taunting rider. Jor Dayne's laughter stopped as he realized the danger and frantically struggled to turn his horse, but it was too late.

The heavy stones pelted Jor Dayne and his warhorse,which went down, whinnying in pain as the stones impacted its body. Struck from the saddle, the yellow-eyed monster dove, rolled, and came up bellowing in pain with his left arm cradled in his right. His deep-throated roar sounded far more like that of an animal than a man. As he turned, his left forearm came into view, bent at an awful, awkward angle. Blood streamed from the new wound where the broken bone had stuck through the skin. The huge man roared his pain with each breath for nearly a minute. Then he started laughing.

The defenders' blood went cold as they heard the low, maddened laughter of the giant man outside the gates. He stood there with one arm broken nearly in half, just grinning and laughing at them all.

Still laughing, the big man gripped the wrist of his injured arm and, with a sickening wrench, yanked his left arm straight again. It took a few moments for Jor Dayne to settle the bones properly. Satisfied at last, he flexed his fingers a few times, then turned his gaze back to the Duke atop the wall.

"If that's the best you can do, this will be even easier than I thought. Ah, well...I was asked to try to do this as peacefully as possible to minimize damage to our new soldiers, but this way will be much more fun for me!" Jor Dayne picked up his sword and slammed it into its scabbard. "Since this is to be the case, my Lord Duke, please allow me to present you with a little gift before we start."

The Slayer put his fingers to his lips and let out a piercing whistle.

"What's he doing?" The Duke strained his eyes to see, but Jor Dayne simply stood where he was, smiling that horrid smile.

"I don't know, Your Grace. Whatever it is, we must be ready." Brunar's fingers tightened around his fighting staff and a pulse of violet power sparked through the wood. All the fighting men of Laro peered out over the horde of foul creatures arrayed against them, wondering what was about to happen.

"Your Grace, look there, to the west!" Drattus pointed and all heads turned in that direction. There was movement among Mordak's creatures on that side as something emerged from the nearby forest. It took several moments for the objects to become clear.

"Hels below, those are the wagons we sent to Rualtha," Duke Gensen growled. "They left days before this filth arrived. We thought they were safe."

"Nothing is safe where Mordak and his ilk are concerned, Your Grace. It looks like they didn't make it." Brunar's voice was cold and tired. He knew what was to come.

The soldiers on the wall could do naught but watch as twenty wagons were hauled closer to the castle by crews of Gholans and Morcats, who hissed and yowled curses at those within the city. Rents in the wagons' fabric became visible, as did great reddish-brown stains where blood had sprayed. Slowly, the wagons were pulled into a line just beyond arrowshot, and the creatures released the yokes they had been pulling. Unnaturally quick, the Gholans and Morcats jumped inside the rickety wagons as the defenders watched from atop the battlements. When the beasts emerged, each one carried a bundle which was dumped limply on the ground. Every man and woman on the walls could see the presents Mordak had brought for them. As each dropped its grisly burden, it turned and hopped back into the nearest wagon to drag another into the light.

"Those are...those are bodies. Our people..." Rorian was shocked, his voice a fearful whisper. His eyes went wide as he saw the monsters pile body after body on the dusty ground, tossing in the occasional arm, leg, or head that had fallen from the hideously mangled corpses. Flies started gathering immediately on the dead.

"Such is Mordak's way. He knows nothing of mercy, or honor. He is completely insane, and knows only death." Turning to the Duke, Brunar continued, "I'm sorry, Your Grace. I'm afraid this will get far worse before it gets better." Brunar's voice was low and calm. He had seen all of this before and survived, and he had no intentions of allowing a different outcome this time around. He planned to do everything in his power to spare the people of Laro the worst of Mordak's ill will.

"Those...those *monsters!*" The Duke spat at the Gholans beyond the wall. His fist was clenched tightly around the hilt of the sword he didn't even remember drawing from its scabbard. He ached to be able to strike a blow at the despoilers of his beloved land, murderers of his people. And yet, he could do nothing but wait.

Suddenly, Brunar stiffened. He gripped the edge of the battlements with one hand and leaned heavily on the wall with a pained grunt. Kiran grabbed his arm in an attempt to support him.

"Brunar! What is it? Are you hurt?" she said, concern in her voice.

"No, I'll be all right, Kiran. He's here—Mordak--he's coming now."

Kiran helped to steady Brunar as he regained his composure, casting worried glances out at the milling horde. "He's here now? Where?"

Brunar took a deep breath and pointed with one shaky hand. Everyone on the wall who had heard the Mage speak followed his pointing finger and looked to the East. The army was parting again, but this time, the figure for whom they made way was walking rather than riding. Creatures cleared the way for him as he passed, as though not wanting to get too close. As the figure walked regally into view, the air seemed to become thicker as though in response to the foulness that approached.

He was over six feet tall, and moved with a smooth grace that spoke of physical strength and control. Wearing a simple black robe trimmed in red, Mordak glided across the dusty earth as though he owned it. Glowing scarlet eyes revealed madness and horror, belying an otherwise noble and handsome face with an aquiline nose and a strong, cleft chin. A mane of silvery hair fell to his shoulders, blowing gently in the breeze. A cruel smile lingered on the sorcerer's face as he stopped and surveyed the castle. He turned his gaze on the larger man-demon, Jor Dayne, and was pleased to see him drop quickly to a knee in complete obeisance. He motioned for the massive fighter to rise, then

Mordak strolled a few steps closer to the castle to get a better view. His eyes flashed red as he continued to direct his power at Brunar.

Brunar spoke a few words in an ancient language and gathered his magick to fight off the influence of the evil sorcerer. After Brunar's dispelling of the cloaking illusion, Mordak certainly knew of his presence within the castle. Now, he had managed to send a wave of nausea, fear, and despair directly at the Mage, just out of spite. It was an old trick, and Brunar was surprised that it had affected him so strongly. His stomach clenched violently and threatened to send his last meal to the stones before him, and an overwhelming wave of hopelessness washed over him like a tepid, oily flood. For just a moment, he felt that all was lost before it had even begun. Clenching his fists, Brunar made himself stand taller as he took in a deep, cleansing breath, then let it out in one explosive exhale. Digging into his magick and asserting centuries of discipline, he finally managed to shut out the Vile One's power completely by creating an invisible shell around himself. As long as he could maintain it, he would be safe from both magickal and physical harm. Brunar sighed with relief as his body recovered. Brunar gestured for Kiran to move back to her place on the battlements, farther down the wall, before turning his attention back to his foe.

Using a touch of magick to augment his words, Brunar spoke, his voice reverberating so that all could hear. Some of the Gholans and Morcats on the front line flinched and moved away from the Mage's powerful voice.

"Mordak! We have done all this before. It ended badly for you back then, and this will end no differently. This time, you will most certainly be destroyed!"

Snide laughter from the black-clad sorcerer was the only reply. There was a moment of silence from the grounds outside the wall, the gently blowing wind the only other sound. The laughter finally stopped, and all was quiet.

Suddenly, Mordak spoke, and his thundering words were loud enough to make the stones of the wall shudder under his power.

"*Fools!*" Men covered their ears and cried out in pain as Mordak's foul voice slammed into them, dropping many of them to their knees. "Pitiful creatures, all of you! Every man, woman, and child behind those walls will die by nightfall. My creatures will flay the skin from your bones while you lie there screaming, and you will be helpless to stop them. Those that are not fit to join my riders will be devoured by my followers; most of you will still be alive when they tear into you. Do you think your puny magick can stop me, Brunar? I now wield more power than you could ever dream! Nothing you, or your 'Guardians'," Mordak sneered the word, "can possibly do will stop me this time."

As Brunar and the others watched, Mordak lifted an elegant hand and gestured towards the grisly pile of human remains that his creatures had brought from the wagons. A young girl's bloodied head slowly floated up from the dusty ground, its blank eyes staring at the men and women on the wall. Its long blonde hair was matted with filth, and hung limply beneath it. Two mismatched arms rose up as well, floating on either side of the disembodied head, and then a man's gashed torso rose on two unsteady legs. The parts all fused together to form a clumsy, ghastly body, and as the Duke and his followers watched in horror, Mordak made the lich dance and twirl among the other corpses. A mad, gleeful giggle escaped the sorcerer as he sensed the revulsion and fear from those who opposed him.

At his command, the dancing marionette fell back into its separate pieces, rejoining all of the other body parts lying in the huge, gory pile. Mordak raised both arms and engaged his power once more. Every bloody limb, torso, and head rose smoothly into the air, higher and higher, until the whole dripping mass floated above the level of the outer wall. Sneering, the Foul One flicked his hands towards the castle, and every bloody bit of flesh hurtled over the walls, flying over the defenders and spattering them with gore.

Brave soldiers cursed and yelled in anger and revulsion as they tried to shield themselves from the spray of blood. They turned to see the remains land wetly on the ground beyond the wall, leaving a huge, bloody mess of arms, legs, and hardly identifiable pieces that were once innocent men, women, and children. Flies immediately descended on the bodies, buzzing hungrily. Men and women from within the castle came running to see what horror had been done only to gasp in shock as they surveyed the macabre scene that greeted them.

Mordak's low, mocking laugh drifted on the ill wind. Enhanced by his evil magick, his vile chuckling found its way to every person within the castle walls. Pure hearts shuddered at the sheer malevolence of that laugh, and an unreasoning terror began to brew within the keep.

A low, animal sound came from deep within the Duke, and Brunar turned to see him staring at the bloody remains. Those were his people. They depended on him for their safety, and now they lay in the castle courtyard like so much rubbish.

Rage burned in Duke Gensen's eyes, so hot that it edged towards madness. Brunar grabbed the Duke's arm to steady him. The Duke's unfathomable rage was only barely held in check, and he could hardly speak.

"That bastard!" The fire in Duke Gensen's eyes was plain for all to see. Had he been able, he would have attacked the sorcerer and his entire monstrous army singlehandedly. His sword was in his hand, though he did not remember drawing it from the scabbard, and his fist ached from clutching it in an iron grip. "He can't DO this!! I'll kill him with my own two hands!"

Brunar's grip tightened, and he gave the Duke a shake to jolt him and draw his attention away from the sorcerer below. "Patience, Your Grace. This is what he does. If he goads you into attacking in fury, then he'll have already won." Brunar spoke quietly, very close to the Duke's ear, and used a touch of his magick to ease his rage. "Calm yourself, and lead your people. They watch you, and they need you to be rational and not dancing to the tune of a madman."

The Duke's wide, frantic eyes turned to the Mage and held for a heartbeat, then two. Brunar watched as reason slowly returned to Duke Gensen and he visibly relaxed. The bigger man took a deep breath, let it out, then gently gripped Brunar's shoulders for a moment as he spoke.

"Thank you, Mage; you're right. We'll not fall into his trap, not like that. If he wants Laro, he'll have to take it." The Duke turned to the soldiers on the wall and raised his voice. "Be strong, men and women of Laro. Do not believe his words, for he is vile and evil! We will defend our home, and emerge victorious!" The Duke raised his sword high for all to see, and a ragged cheer started. It gained strength as the Duke passed his gaze over them, showing that he was not beaten, nor afraid of the powerful sorcerer below.

"Is there any way we can strike at him, Brunar? Any way at all?"

Brunar sighed. "His power has grown immeasurably. However, I wonder..." Brunar called Layton to him, and the lad quickly saluted. The Mage outlined a strategy--a long shot-- and Layton grinned from ear to ear as he agreed.

The lad pulled his Jidaan from its sheath on his back and held it upside down in front of him, its razor-sharp tip pointing at the stones beneath his feet. He peered over the battlements at the evil sorcerer, who appeared to be awaiting a response. Layton estimated the distance and then waited for Brunar's signal.

Brunar stood where Mordak could see him and amplified his voice again. "Nice try, you fiend! Is that all you've got? Tossing corpses at us? Surely, you've lost much of your power over the centuries." Brunar added a taunting tone to his words, knowing that Mordak did not take well to such things. He saw the sorcerer clench his fists in anger, then start to speak. In that instant, Brunar raised his hands to attack, sending violent bolts of indigo energy to sizzle through the air towards the evil man below. Even as Mordak shielded himself from the blazing energy, Brunar threw another spell--not at the sorcerer, but instead at the ground beneath his feet. In an instant, Brunar's power turned the solid earth to wet, clutching quicksand. Mordak immediately sank to his knees in the muck as he struggled to fight Brunar's purple lightning. With a Word, Brunar solidified the ground again, sealing Mordak to the knees in unyielding rock. Keeping up the magickal assault, Brunar signaled Layton, "Now!"

Layton ignited his power, and a Gate the size of a dinner plate burst into being before him, a horizontal portal at the level of his knees. Brunar's sharp eyes saw its twin appear inches from Mordak's chest even as Layton thrust his Jidaan downward, into the Gate, with all his might.

Mordak screamed.

The sorcerer's black-robed body jerked as the Jidaan traveled through the Gate and slammed into his chest, the ancient blade passing completely through him and bursting his heart. Layton quickly withdrew his weapon and both Gates vanished, leaving Mordak stricken and unable to move. Brunar doubled his assault, flinging bolt after furious bolt of energy at the injured sorcerer below, obscuring his hunched form under a storm of destructive power.

"I got him, Brunar! That was a killing blow; I'm sure of it!" Layton's voice brimmed with excitement as he looked over the wall at the wounded sorcerer.

Brunar did not reply. He kept up the attack for a moment longer, scorching the earth surrounding the sorcerer for several yards in all directions. He finally ceased the flow of magick as exhaustion seeped around the edges of his awareness. Mordak had stopped guarding himself as the Jidaan went through him, and Brunar had felt his attacks strike true, mercilessly pummeling Mordak's trapped body. Dust floated in the air, obscuring the still form of the Foul One. As it cleared, the outline of the sorcerer slowly became apparent. He was silent, leaning lamely to one side, both hands clutching the wound in his chest. His legs were still frozen in stone up to his knees. His black robe was burned and torn, and smoke curled up and away from his body. The soldiers on the wall stared in tense silence at the still form of their enemy, waiting to see the results of the attack.

Long moments passed in watchful silence and then...Mordak laughed. It was a quiet laugh, low and raspy, yet it carried perfectly to the keep. Standing back up to his full height, Mordak spoke.

"That was almost amusing, Brunar. Almost." At Mordak's gesture, the stone that held his legs exploded, sending shards in all directions. Slowly, he rose into the air, smoke still trailing from his burning robe.

Layton whispered, "No, that's not possible. I felt it go through him!"

The Duke leaned close. "I'd have agreed with you, lad, but there he is, whole and unharmed...and now he's floating."

Brunar remained silent. His attack had been strong, and it had taken a toll on his reserves. He had feared Mordak would survive, but desperately hoped otherwise. In the past, that level of power would have certainly felled the sorcerer, especially with a burst heart. Somehow, his evil strength had increased twenty-fold, and Brunar's mind raced to come up with a way to deal with the necromancer's power.

Mordak opened his arms wide and majestically drifted back down to the ground, landing gently near the crater he had just created.

"As you said earlier, Brunar...'nice try.' I look forward to spending some very meaningful time with you, Mage. Oh yes, when every one of Laro's citizens is either dead or walking undead in my army, you and I will have a wonderful little chat. I look forward to destroying you one...inch...at a time. I'll see you soon."

His evil smile never wavered as he turned away to walk through his legion of creatures. As soon as his face was averted, a ripple passed over him, altering his appearance. His silver hair and weathered features transformed into a long, blonde braid and the fresh-faced countenance of a much younger man. It took only a moment for him to assume the illusion of Balroth, the wicked Daemon-God. All of the beasts shied away from him as he walked, obviously terrified of their master. As Mordak approached the area occupied by the Krell, the fearsome warriors dropped to their knees and cast their faces downward, lest they offend the one whom they thought to be their god. Mordak, they would tear limb from limb, but they would follow Balroth unto death and beyond. Unhurriedly, Mordak disappeared into the sea of horrifying faces, leaving an eager Jor Dayne staring up at the castle with an evil grin on his devilish face.

Brunar gripped the stone of the wall before him, a sinking feeling in the pit of his stomach. He had heard Mordak's threats before, many centuries ago. Back then, the Mage had the King's army and six fully trained Guardians to wield in defense of the Realm. The slaughter that followed washed the land in blood and fire, and left scars that had taken hundreds of years to heal. Mordak had lost, but he had taken thousands of lives, including those of Guardians, before he had finally been stopped.

"This time, your power is far greater than it was, you fiend. And ours is diminished. How can we even hope to fight you like this?" Brunar thought aloud. He clenched one fist, but stopped short of hammering it down onto the battlements in frustration. He must not lose hope, must not show such weakness. Those who had chosen to fight with him deserved that much. Brunar took a deep breath, held it, and let it out. Resolute once more, he turned and stepped to the Duke's side.

The Duke's eyes were scanning the milling horde that lay before them, his sword in hand and ready. Without turning, he said, "Well Brunar, I'm sorry we had to meet under such dire circumstances. That being said, I'm glad you're here. We'll meet this evil host with cold steel and bravery, but you'll have to deal with whatever sorcery he throws at us."

Brunar nodded. "Indeed, Your Grace. I know how he thinks, and we'll do what we can. His power is great, and he has thousands of vile creatures at his disposal. Even so, he's still just one man. We've beaten him before, and we will find a way to do it again. We will fight until he's captured or destroyed."

"I vote for the second option. Scumsucker!" Kiran voiced the thought they all shared. "There's no way we can let him live. He won't stop until he's dead or we are. We'll see if he can heal himself if we lop his smirking head off!" Her face was dark and grim, her warrior nature on full display.

Duke Gensen suddenly pointed to the sky over the horde. "Brunar, look. I'm guessing this is the start of it."

Brunar's keen eyes saw what the Duke had indicated. Silently, he sent a mental call to the Guardians and felt their response as they steeled themselves for combat. Likewise, the Duke commanded his soldiers to readiness, and the rattle of weapons and yells of men and women in preparation drifted across the morning air. Down below, Jor Dayne rode back and forth, holding his great sword aloft, bellowing orders to the creatures that surrounded him.

Out of the clear dawn sky, a tiny black cloud appeared in the distance. That one cloud began to churn and grow, seething and roiling as though it had a life of its own. In moments it expanded to twice its original size, then twice that again. The lone thunderhead stopped and hung motionless for several heartbeats. Even from a distance, the tingle of ill magick could be felt. Suddenly, the dark cloud exploded outward, spreading across the distant sky like water poured onto a stone floor. A distant rumbling reached those standing in the tower and on the wall. It was more felt than heard, and the earth, itself, seemed to protest the foulness now spreading mere yards above its surface.

As the fearsome mass grew, a gentle breeze picked up, cooling the backs of the watching soldiers. Gradually, the blow rose in intensity as air from miles around was pulled into the rising storm--feeding it, building it. The churning thunderheads had become gigantic, and their hearts of deepest black swirled with crimson power.

When it seemed the mass of seething evil had consumed the eastern sky from horizon to horizon, the wind at Brunar's back suddenly ceased. The entire city fell into a deadly silence.

Moments passed in that tense quiet, while all eyes stared out at the hellish stormbank on the plain. A few sharp thunderclaps punctuated the stony silence, and hints of scarlet lightning flickered in the clouds. The storm convulsed violently and surged forward, rolling quickly across the plain. As it advanced, the very stone beneath their booted feet began to shudder.

"Such *power*!" Brunar's voice was but a shadow of its usual self. He watched the monstrosity forming on the plain and tried desperately to think of a way to counteract it, but without the Jidaan of Storms, they were nearly helpless. Nothing in his two thousand years had prepared him for this. This was no old spell from a moldering book. No, this was the nightmare of a madman, gleefully brought to life. Nevertheless, Brunar began to call his magick, preparing to lay as much of a defense on the outer wall as he could.

The tempest rolled in like a malevolent living thing, a great, inexorable mass sweeping towards the city, towering for what seemed like miles into the unbroken blue of the sky above.

Crashing bolts of thunder threatened to split the world apart, and onward the roiling storm moved, swirling with murderous power, rushing to embrace the city and the stone castle. The border between darkness and light advanced, accelerating across the open plain towards the city walls, moving faster than the fastest horse could dream. A faint howling could be heard from the plains, growing louder with each passing second. It soon became apparent that a fell wind rushed before the storm, pushed forward by the incalculable force of the seething cloudbank.

As if in answer, Duke Gensen's voice rang out across the city.

"Stand fast, warriors of Laro! Yon comes the Evil One, and we will meet him with steel in our hearts and in our hands! We will kill every monster that shows its ugly face above this wall! We will destroy them all, and show that foul, sorcerous idiot that he chose the wrong city to plunder! Ready your weapons! Fight for Laro!" His clear, strong voice galvanized the soldiers that stood facing the oncoming storm. As one, the fighting men and women of Laro raised their weapons and shouted defiantly at the boiling, churning mass that hurtled towards them, taking heart from their Duke and from the knowledge that the Guardians would use their magick to defend them all.

The wind reached the walls of the city long before the storm. As the gale attacked the ramparts, it became painfully clear that the fierce wind was ice cold. Plumes of breath were torn from the mouths of the determined soldiers, and thin sheens of ice formed instantly on their sweaty faces. Hearts pounded as fear tried to work its way into the soldiers, but they would not be moved. As the gale threatened to steal the very warmth of their souls, they stood firm and resolute. These were the soldiers of Laro, proud of their city and their Duke. They shied not, and instead turned their faces outward, towards the seething bank of approaching clouds. Gritting their teeth against the sudden chill, they held their weapons at the ready and bravely stood their ground.

As one, they roared their defiance as the power of the Vile One slammed into the city, covering them all in ghastly, red-limned darkness. A few hapless warriors fell screaming from the walls as the intense winds blasted them into empty space. Others held grimly to the battlements as best they could, trying desperately to see through the swirling murk of the conjured storm.

Brunar slapped his hands against the wall and spoke a few Words in an ancient language, his voice lost in the gale. A faint, purplish glow arose around the Mage's hands as his magick began to flow, illuminating his stern face. Brunar channeled his power into the unyielding stone, reaching into it with his senses. He felt a solid sense of immovability and strength throughout the entire structure of the wall. The wind pounded against it, but the ancient stone barrier was far stronger than even this powerful gale. It would have laughed at the wind, had it been able. A slight grin crossed Brunar's face and he thanked the Goddess for the enduring strength of the stones of Laro. Bearing down, he forced more of his power through his glowing hands, sending his energy all through the East Wall. Gradually, the stones began to glow a pale shade of purple, fighting back the swirling, maddening dark of the storm. Warriors were soon cheering as the wall shone brighter and brighter, blunting the force of the storm and allowing the warriors to see again.

One of the captains atop the wall pointed with his sword and bellowed, "Here they come! 'Ware the Gholans, they attack from below!" Swarming like ants, a huge wave of the hideous little creatures climbed dripping from the moat and rushed the bottom of the wall. Handfuls of them screeched as they fell into pit traps or were stung by the caltrops that lay scattered along the ground. The injured were simply trampled as others took their places. They hesitated as the violet light blazed from the stones, burning their eyes, but leaders among them yowled and spurred them to attack. As Brunar had predicted, they latched onto the stone of the wall as though born to do so and climbed with frightening speed, snapping their fanged jaws in anticipation of the slaughter to come.

"Pour the oil! Now, before they reach the top!" Duke Gensen's commanding voice galvanized the soldiers. Several huge cauldrons of boiling oil were hoisted into place by teams of soldiers, and carefully tipped outward until their scalding contents began to rain down on the hapless monsters. Inhuman screams of agony immediately drifted over the wall as scores of Gholans died and fell, taking many of their brethren with them. Rather than coating the walls as was expected, the blasting wind sprayed much of the oil away, leaving great clear patches and allowing the next wave of Gholans to cling easily to the stone and climb unhindered.

"Archers! Keep them from reaching the top! Refill the oil cauldrons!" The Duke yelled orders to his nearest captains, who quickly relayed them up and down the walls. In moments, archers were loosing arrows as quickly as they could nock them to string. The driving wind made aiming difficult, but even so, Gholans were sent screaming to their deaths. More oil was brought, but the blowing wind made the process difficult. Keeping the fires lit under the cauldrons was nearly impossible in the storm. Brunar's power kept the entire wall glowing brightly, lending strength to the defenders and repelling the foul little creatures below.

The Mage pulled away from the wall, satisfied that it would continue to shine and allow the defenders to see their attackers for the next few hours. That accomplished, he searched for a safe spot where he could focus. Striding across the battlements, he made his way around the archers and other screaming warriors until he reached the relative shelter of the barbican. Kiran and Nessar were there, squinting into the wind, loosing arrow after arrow into the crowd of Gholans that continued to assault the wall and the front gate. As he drew closer he could hear Kiran muttering to herself.

"Try and get through MY gate, will you? Not today, you nasty little buggers. Nope. Eat this!" An arrow twanged from her bow, lodging in the eye socket of one snarling Gholan and knocking it off the wall. "And THIS!" Another arrow found its mark, taking another monster in the forehead. She took a moment to nod at Brunar, then went back to work, eyeing a new target as she took an arrow from the massive pile of shafts next to her. So many of the beasts were assailing the walls that there was no shortage of choices. It was a testament to the fortitude of the defenders that the creatures had yet to reach the top. Nessar had never been very good with a bow, but had found a crossbow instead and was methodically picking off Gholans while humming a quiet tune to himself.

Brunar sat down, out of the worst of the howling wind, and closed his eyes. He needed to do something about the storm. For now, they were keeping the Gholans at bay, but Brunar knew Mordak. The Gholans were only the first move in a much bigger game. The storm had to be masking something. The longer it went unchecked, the more time Mordak had to prepare his next attack. Brunar took a deep breath and gathered his power, preparing to search the storm for weaknesses.

Elsewhere on the wall, several of the Gholans had managed to reach the top. The warriors had dropped their bows in favor of swords and began hacking away at them. Snarling and yowling, the monsters climbed over the battlements and flung themselves onto the defenders, slashing with their wicked claws. Blood flew--human crimson and Gholan brownish-black-- to be borne away on the howling winds. The soldiers held for a moment, but a flood of the creatures poured over the wall and spread out across the battlements, rending and slaying as they went.

The Duke yelled, "Fill the breach! They're coming over the wall; someone stop them!!" Swinging his great sword in short, vicious arcs, he chopped and slashed at the Gholans that reached him as well as the ones trying to climb over the wall nearest him. He could not move to help plug the hole in the defense without leaving his own spot on the wall undefended. His curses flowed freely as he brutally killed everything that wasn't human. His loyal soldiers surged forward, driving themselves into the horde of Gholans that befouled the stone of Laro with their oily touch.

Just then, one of the Morcats topped the wall. Nearly seven feet tall, over three hundred pounds of bulky muscle and coarse fur, the beast howled. It was wearing crude plate armor strapped to its body, but carried no weapon. Morcats needed only fangs, wicked claws, and their incredible speed. With a ferocious roar, it slashed through a soldier's face and neck, sending gouts of blood into the air. It didn't even take time to watch the body fall to the cobbles below before grabbing another soldier and ripping him apart. More soldiers died screaming as the Morcat cleared the way for Gholans to pour over the wall.

Suddenly, a bright light blinded the Morcat and nearby Gholans, making them shield their eyes. A roughly circular Gate opened near the Morcat and Layton stepped through it onto the wall. Before the creatures could recover, Layton lashed out with his Jidaan and felled the four nearest him. Another slash dispatched the few Gholans that had just popped their heads over the wall, sending them crashing down into their fellows below. Now, there was nothing between the enormous Morcat and Layton. In the violet gleam of the wall, Layton stared into the beast's golden, slitted eyes, and saw only an alien emptiness. There was no mercy there, and no fear.; there was only an inhuman hatred. Muscles bunched under the Morcat's thick skin as it tensed to attack the small man, and its razor sharp claws slid from its fingertips as it readied itself for the kill.

Layton saw all this in an instant and knew the beast could easily kill him. It was twice his size and blindingly fast. He also knew he had to close the gap on the wall to keep any more Gholans from getting inside. Warriors were dying all around him, and time was running short.

A happy little half-smile appeared on Layton's face and his mind cleared of all thought. Nothing existed for him save the sensations of movement, both his own and that of his attackers. And it was beautiful.

The Morcat launched itself at Layton, swiping one massive paw at his chest, intending to rake it completely open, but Layton was no longer there. He had dropped to a knee and slashed upward with his Jidaan, catching the creature at the wrist as its attack whooshed over his head. The paw went flying off into the darkness, and the maimed Morcat howled in pain. Its remaining paw immediately whipped downwards, its talons already bloody. Layton rolled out of the way and the vicious claws gouged deep furrows into the stone instead.

Furious, the Morcat lashed out again and managed to slash Layton's left arm. The young man gritted his teeth in agony, but maintained his clear mind. It was a wound, nothing more; he could work around the pain. With a daring leap, he placed one foot on the wall and launched himself up and over the Morcat, twisting in mid-air to avoid its razor-sharp claws. He cleared the beast by an arm's length and landed deftly behind it, bringing the Jidaan down hard and chopping the Morcat's monstrous head in half even as it turned to attack him again. The beast froze for an instant, then fell lazily over the side of the wall, adding to a growing pile of dead Gholans and Laroan soldiers at the edge of the courtyard. Layton turned and immediately cut down three more Gholans as they tried to climb over the battlements, and then four more soldiers came to help him seal the breach in the wall.

Layton, you're hurt! Alyssa's voice echoed in Layton's mind.

'Tis naught but a scratch, Layton Spoke back to her. *I'm fine!* He felt a note of worry from the healer, but then the contact was broken as she apparently decided to take him at his word. Without pausing, he turned his attention to the attacking horde of hideous creatures. Like lightning, he continued to slash and stab, block and kick and punch, moving to a kind of music that only he could hear, and the smile never left his face.

Elsewhere on the wall, Bjarke was grimly manning an entire section of the wall almost by himself. He had asked that a pile of massive logs be placed near his station, and told others to stay clear. In the lull before the battle, he had affixed thick rope handles around the middle of each timber and then placed them where he could reach them easily. Duke Gensen asked what he was planning, and upon hearing immediately set a small team to preparing more logs and hoisting them up to Bjarke's place on the wall. The Duke suggested that he soak them with oil and set the timbers on fire, and Bjarke had readily agreed. Since the attack had begun, Bjarke had dropped three of them, and was looking over the wall to guage how close the next round of climbing Gholans had come. When they were just a few feet below the battlements, Bjarke squatted down and wrapped his hands around the rope handles of the nearest timber. With a sharp jerk, he stood and heaved the giant log up to his chest. He held it balanced, then carefully took the couple of steps to place it atop the wall. Once there, another soldier set it afire, then Bjarke pushed it so that it fell on the outside of the wall, taking scores of monsters with it. The huge, fiery timber cleared the stones completely of Gholans and Morcats, crushing and burning those below. By the glow of Brunar's power, he would watch them swarm around the growing bonfire at the base of the wall and then start to climb again. Before long, the new bunch of creatures would be close enough for him to repeat the process.

"We're going to run out of timbers soon, Master Guardian." one of the soldiers tasked with supplying Bjarke with logs yelled into the wind. Bjarke didn't turn around, so he moved closer and yelled again. The big man heard that time and turned with a startled look on his face.

"I'm not a 'master' of anything, sir, and you can just call me Bjarke. But thank you, I'll just use what we have and we'll move on from there." Bjarke turned back to watch the climbing monsters below, still too far away.

The soldier shook his head grimly as three of his fellows helped to move another massive log in place. As far as he was concerned, any man who could lift what amounted to an entire tree and make it look like he was lifting nothing more than a single piece of firewood, just HAD to be a master of something.

Bjarke carefully leaned out to check the progress of the Gholans below, his stern face illuminated by the violet glow of the wall. He looked into the upturned faces of the hideous creatures climbing towards him, snarling and spitting hatred with every putrid breath. *Each and every one of them would like nothing better than to rip my heart out and watch my life's blood flow into the stones.* Bjarke looked over his shoulder at the inner wall and the stone castle behind him, remembering the terrified faces of the people who had rushed inside when the evil horde had come. They were not fighters, yet the creatures below would kill them all with the same ferocious glee as they would any warrior on the wall. The big man sighed and squatted down to pick up another log. Hatred did not come easily to him, but he knew what needed to be done. He knew his duty to the land, knew deep in his heart that he was doing the right thing. And he would do it with all his might. Without so much as a grunt of effort, Bjarke yanked the massive timber up to his chest and gently placed it atop the wall. He nodded at the soldier nearby, who set it ablaze by touching a torch to it. Flames raced along the length of the oil-soaked wood, and Bjarke sent it rolling down the other side of the wall, again clearing it of crawling Gholans.

Just inside the Keep, Alyssa walked from patient to patient. They had started coming in immediately, and she had each of them taken to cots where the Sisters of Rowann worked with Laro's own healers to stitch them up as best they could. Some of the wounds were ghastly, and yet the power of her Jidaan had healed them completely. Others were too far gone even for her power to save. Desperate warriors clutched at her as she walked by, begging her to ease their pain, and although she was fighting exhaustion, she always complied.

And we've only just begun, she thought to herself as she leaned against a wall for support. Brunar had warned her that she would want to heal them all and he had been right. She couldn't bear to see such suffering when she had the power to take it away. Alyssa had trained hard, but she was rapidly approaching her limit. *These people need me, though, no matter how tired I get.* Breathing deeply, she focused her attention inward, finding the center of her energy as Brunar had taught her. She found it, and tried to rebuild it as best she could. She closed her eyes for a moment and stilled her mind. She only needed to catch her breath; surely, it would only take a second or two...

"Lady Alyssa, we need you here. Are you all right? You've been standing there for ages," one of the Sisters was gently shaking her and she came back to herself suddenly, startled.

"I'm fine, Bekah. I'm sorry. Where do you need me?" Alyssa had no idea how long she'd been standing against the wall, but she did feel a bit better. Bekah took her by the arm and pointed her towards the infirmary, where it seemed that the number of wounded had suddenly tripled. *Goddess give me strength,* she prayed silently, *I'm going to need it.* Alyssa reached one hand over her shoulder to touch the pommel of her sheathed Jidaan. It was just as she had left it--hanging at her back, awaiting her call. Reassured, she stepped forward to see which warriors' lives were hanging by a thread and which ones just needed a quick stitching.

Hours passed, and the battle raged on. The brave defenders of Laro kept most of the evil horde from getting over the walls, but many fell wounded, Alyssa healed a good number of them, sending them back to fight once more.

Brunar sat, unmoving, locked in a silent battle with the storm that Mordak had sent. He could almost feel the foul sorcerer's laughter from somewhere out in the whirling dark, belittling him as he strove to deconstruct Mordak's monstrous creation. Just when he thought he had found a way to pull the storm apart, something would shift, and Brunar would have to start over again. Though there was chaos all around him, he did not move. He was fighting on another plane, entirely.

"I don't know how long we can keep going like this," Rorian had made his way to Duke Gensen's side on the battlements and yelled so that he could be heard, "but we're holding up well thus far. Our own soldiers are fighting effectively, and the Guardians have been most impressive." There had been a slight lull in the fighting on the Duke's side of the wall, though combat raged elsewhere. "There seems to be no end to these monsters, Your Grace."

"There's an end, Rorian," the Duke countered. "Even if that evil bastard brought every last one of those disgusting creatures from across Talwynn to throw at us, there's only a finite number of them. And if we must, we'll kill them all. We've only just begun, and we're fortunate enough to have the Guardian Alyssa healing many of our wounded. Those nuns of Rowann have been a big help as well. The beasts out there, on the other hand, have no such assistance. They have numbers, but once they're stabbed or hacked apart, they're done." The Duke looked around at the warriors who manned the wall. Many of them sported gashes and cuts wherever their armor failed to protect them as they fought the bloodthirsty Gholans and vicious Morcats who had managed to break through. Taking stock of the situation at a glance, the Duke said, "Keep the men rotating in shifts as much as possible. I want fresh sword arms replacing tired ones."

"Yes, Your Grace. I'll see to it right away." Rorian bowed slightly and moved towards the stone steps that led to the courtyard below. He was already planning the distribution of fresh warriors who would relieve those ready to drop from exhaustion.

"I knew I could count on you, Rorian," the Duke said to himself. His words were carried off by the wind as he watched his trusted advisor carefully feeling his way along the wall in the uncertain light on his way to the courtyard below. The man had been his family's faithful servant and counselor for decades, and Duke Gensen had thanked the Goddess for Rorian's effectiveness more than once during the battle.

Just then a voice carried over the blowing of the wind. "They're pulling back! They're pulling back!" A ragged cheer went up around the wall and the Duke rushed to the battlements to peer guardedly over the edge. Sure enough, the Gholans and Morcats were moving away from the glowing wall, backing into the shadows of the storm, snarling at the cheering soldiers as they went. The frustrated shouts of Jor Dayne were mostly carried away by the howl of the wind, but still occasionally drifted up to the defenders as he whipped the creatures into formation down below.

The Duke wasted no time in replacing tired soldiers with fresh ones, knowing that this was only the first wave in the assault. For all of the hundreds of horrid creatures that now lay in gory piles at the base of the walls, there were thousands more out there, hiding under the shelter of the storm. Other, more massive creatures had yet to show themselves, and the Duke knew that it was only a matter of time before they were finally deployed. Duke Gensen looked for Brunar, but the howling winds and flying dust obscured anything more than a few yards away. After a short search, the Duke finally located him above the Gatehouse. Brunar was still seated with his legs folded under him, unmoving, his eyes closed in deep concentration. Nessar and Kiran sat nearby with their backs against the battlements. They had fought tirelessly since the storm hit and were finally eating rations that had been brought to them hours ago.

"How long has he been like this?" Duke Gensen asked Kiran, keeping his eyes on the still form of the Mage.

"A couple of hours, I think. Hard to tell time in all this nonsense, Your Grace," Kiran waved a hand at the storm.

The Duke raised an eyebrow. "A couple of hours? What's he doing?"

Nessar rubbed his grizzled chin with one hand before replying, "I believe he's fighting Mordak somehow. He didn't tell us anything, he just came out here and sat down like that." The old thief took a bit of dried meat and chewed thoughtfully. "I can feel that he's doing something, but I'll be a Gholan's uncle if I know what it is."

At that moment, Brunar stood and thrust both hands overhead, an intensely bright purple radiance bursting from his fists and forearms. Gooseflesh broke out on those nearest the

Mage as they felt the power that emanated from him. Several soldiers dropped to their knees as the pressure mounted. Suddenly, a massive bolt of brilliant purple lightning exploded from Brunar's hands and crawled across the clouded sky, heedless of the howling winds. The power sought a point within the storm, a nexus of forces bound together by Mordak's will. The bolt found that point and latched on, pouring Brunar's enormous cache of energy into it. There was a single earsplitting thunderclap, the force of which knocked many surprised warriors off their feet and burst several eardrums. And then there was quiet. Slowly, the heavy black and scarlet clouds that had obscured the sky began to fade. Within moments, the enormous storm had entirely disappeared to reveal the bright pinpoints of stars overhead, like diamonds on black velvet. A thick crescent moon shone down, bathing the city in silvery light, and cool, clean air breezed gently through the city of Laro.

Brunar dropped to his hands and knees, then rolled over on his back in utter exhaustion. Sweat had soaked through his shirt, and he was breathing heavily. Duke Gensen and Kiran rushed to his side. Brunar saw them coming and weakly raised a hand to reassure them both.

"I'm fine, Your Grace, just weak from casting. If you would please help me to my feet? It's unseemly for me to be lying here like this." The Duke and Kiran helped Brunar until he was standing unsteadily on his own again. He carefully walked over to where Nessar sat, still eating, and slid down the wall to take a seat next to him. Assured that the Mage was in no danger, the Duke walked over to the battlements to assess the enemy, glad that he could finally see them without the concealment of the storm.

Nessar continued chewing for a moment, then offered some of his rations to the Mage. "Beef? You look like you could use it," the thief said quietly. Brunar took the dried meat and ripped off a piece with his teeth.

"Thank you, Ness, you're right. Food will help me recover more quickly," Brunar said around the mouthful. "That took a lot out of me, but that storm had us at far too much of a disadvantage. It had to go."

Kiran grinned. "I agree. It sure did take you long enough, though."

Brunar stopped chewing and raised an eyebrow at her before replying. "Well, Kiran, I just figured you needed more time to thin out the numbers of Gholans for us," he leaned slightly towards Nessar and mock whispered, "Her archery still needs some work."

The gruff old man nodded and kept chewing. "Yep. That it does."

Kiran snorted at them both and walked back to the wall to join the Duke, who had been standing silently during the exchange, gazing at the enemy. "Well, Your Grace, what do you think their next move will be?" Kiran finally looked out and saw what the Duke had been staring at. "Oh...oh, that's bad."

All of the houses nearest the castle had been demolished, their timbers used to construct a dozen or so makeshift bridges across the moat. On the other side, thousands of silent creatures awaited their master's command—Gholans, Morcats, and other nightmarish forms that twitched and jerked unnaturally as they moved. Among the hideous creatures were hundreds of humans. These stood silently, shoulder to shoulder with the monsters, their eyes glowing with a bloody, hideous light in the cool darkness. Scores of them were wearing the distinctive crest of Laro over bloodied and dented armor; many were missing limbs. They swayed side to side in unison as though listening to the same slow, eerie music that only they could hear.

"Sweet Goddess above..." the Duke said, unaware that he had spoken aloud. He shook his head, then continued in a louder voice so that the others could hear. "Some of those are our soldiers, only killed this very day. He's already taken them."

Brunar stepped up to the wall next to the Duke and responded, "Yes, that is Mordak's way. He'll use them against us, not only for their numbers, but also to demoralize our warriors. The undead won't fall to ordinary wounds, Your Grace. They must be hacked to pieces; else they'll just keep coming. Beheading works best."

Horrified, the Duke turned to the Mage and grabbed the front of his robe with one steel-gauntleted hand. "Those are my PEOPLE, Mage!" He turned back to the silent mob outside the walls and pointed at one of the undead humans on the front line. "That one there...his name is Kalin, nephew to Rorian. I watched that boy grow up. We must find a way to free them somehow!"

Brunar put a hand on the Duke's shoulder to calm him and quietly replied, "The only way to free them is to release their souls from their flesh, Your Grace. They're dead. There is no bringing them back. Their souls are trapped under Mordak's foul control, and must watch their bodies perform whatever heinous acts Mordak wishes." Brunar turned to look out at the lad the Duke had indicated. "Rorian's nephew is in there, yes, but his soul is screaming to be released. Only we can do that. We must render them unable to fight us, and then behead them. Only then can their tortured souls to find peace." Brunar watched the pain in the Duke's eyes slowly shift and resolve itself into steely determination. The Mage continued, "Tell your men, Your Grace. We must be strong enough to do the right thing."

The Duke turned his eyes back to the merciless enemy massed outside the castle. He sighed heavily before speaking. "Aye. I trust your counsel, Mage. It shall be as you say. If you have any other suggestions that will help us against these...creatures, then send for me."

Turning towards the nearest soldiers, he bellowed, "Captain!" A warrior wearing a captain's scarlet cloak stepped forward and saluted. The Duke took his arm and escorted him along the wall, explaining Brunar's strategy as they walked. Kiran watched him go, then heard the distinctive twang of a crossbow behind her. Whirling, she saw Nessar just lowering his weapon with a satisfied look on his face.

"What..." she started to speak, then looked out at the front lines of the enemy just in time to see one of their number slump to the ground, a bolt jutting from its forehead. She watched the hideous red glow fade and disappear from its eyes as Mordak's hold on its spirit was broken by a true death.

"Kalin?" she said quietly to Nessar, who had already leaned the bow against the wall and sat down again with his back to the battlements.

"Yep," her old friend replied. "Figured it had to be done, might as well save the Duke the trouble of doing it himself or seeing it done right in front of him. He's a hard man, that one, but that would have hurt him. To me, it was just one less body to wield a sword against us." The old man drank from a waterskin, then placed it on the stones next to him before wiping his sleeve across his mouth.

Kiran grinned, "You're such a softy, Ness."

He shrugged. "The Thieves Guild in Rualtha would agree with you, I'm pretty sure." He looked out over the courtyard, watching the soldiers and civilians of Laro bustling about. He hadn't thought of the Guild for weeks, not since the *Damsel* had foundered on the rocks evading the Shipsbane. Many of the Guild's members had been only too happy to hear that he was abdicating Mastership of the Guild to his trusted lieutenant, Boyd. One contingent of thieves, led by the outspoken Jared, had not attempted to hide their opinion that Nessar had outlived his usefulness as Guildmaster. Every time he let some minor transgression go without an instantaneous death penalty, they started squawking like crows. They said he wasn't hard enough to do what needed to be done, never realizing that those who Nessar let live were so grateful they ended up bringing in more profit to the Guild. No, they only saw weakness in Nessar, rather than good planning with a dose of compassion. Those short-sighted fools had made Nessar's life a living Hel.

Of course, there were others who were fiercely loyal, but every day had been a struggle. Before Brunar had come bearing the news that both he and Kiran had been Chosen to wield the fabled Jidaan, he had caught himself thinking of how pointless his life had become. Sure, he was the leader of the Guild, respected by most, and far more wealthy than he could ever have expected given his tragic beginnings. Even so, he had just felt empty. He kept order within the Guild as best he could, and during his term had furthered business to levels of prosperity previously unheard of. But, it had still felt pointless.

Then, everything had changed. He had been given a real responsibility, and great powers had been awakened within him so that he might be able to meet it. He was needed. His age simply didn't matter in this war. No matter what was required of him, no matter what danger he might face, Nessar would die before he let the people of Laro down.

Kiran snorted. "Who gives a horse's fart what they think? This here is a bit more important than whatever they've got going on, eh? And if we don't stop it here, how long before Rualtha falls? The Thieves Guild will be up to their armpits in it then." She arched an eyebrow as she smacked him on the shoulder.

"A horse's fart? Really? That's not proper talk for a lady, Kiran," Nessar's good humor had returned.

"Well, when a lady shows up, I'll be sure to tell her not to talk about such things. Get up, Grampy, I don't know why they haven't attacked us yet, but this respite can't last much longer." She held out a hand to help him to his feet, and he made a show of favoring his back. Fresh soldiers came walking along the wall and offered to spell them at their posts, and Kiran opted to find a privy while Nessar waited with them. Minutes later, she returned, and Nessar hustled off to take his turn.

Time passed with agonizing slowness, and the soldiers patrolling the wall became more and more uneasy. The sight of the malevolent horde only yards away was unsettling, and the courage of those who protected the keep was beginning to unravel.

The Morcats pushed their way to the front lines, their bulky, muscular forms towering above the smaller Gholans and the crimson-eyed, undead humans. Their bestial growls and snarls drifted on the gentle breeze, as well as the rank smell of decaying flesh. For a few moments, they surrounded Jor Dayne to receive orders before they spread out among the horde. Still, no attack came.

"They do like to make us wait, don't they?" asked Layton. He had come to check on Bjarke on the northern wall, bringing him water and food.

"It certainly seems that way," the big forester responded. "It doesn't bother you?" To say that Bjarke had been on edge throughout the entire conflict was an understatement. He had seen and caused so much death; he simply couldn't fathom it. For all his enormous size and strength, Bjarke was a kind and loving man. Even when he killed animals, it was only for meat or in the rare event that he was in danger, such as the time a wounded mountain lion had attacked him. He felt a measure of sadness each time he took the life of any animal, and now, he had been thrust into the forefront of a war where it was kill or be killed. The wounds to his soul were already deep. The only thing that kept him sane was knowing that every creature he felled would have happily murdered every person within the castle walls if given the chance. It felt as though it had been years since he had laughed, and worried that he had forgotten how.

"Oh, not at all. I know it's just their strategy," Layton answered almost cheerfully as he bit into an apple. "They'll attack when they're told to, and not before. Whatever Mordak is cooking up will likely arrive soon, and then we'll find out what's going on. What will be will be."

Bjarke shook his head, "I don't know how you do it; I'm trying not to lose my mind with all this. There are so many creatures out there, all wanting to kill us. The Laroan people are depending on us, and we barely know what we're doing." He rubbed a hand across his face before speaking again. "I'm supposed to be the strongest of us, but I'm barely holding myself together. You seem as though you're just out for a walk."

Layton chewed thoughtfully for a moment, then swallowed and wiped his face with a sleeve. "Well, one of my masters once told me 'A thing is neither bad nor good, it simply *is*.' We attach meaning to everything that happens based on our own beliefs and experiences. But it doesn't matter what we think; things happen anyway. Emotions don't influence events, but actions do. Remembering that helps me stay outside of it so that I can do what I need to do."

Bjarke scratched his massive head. "That doesn't make sense. You mean that innocent people dying is neither bad nor good? I think it's abominable, Layton. It's evil! How can you be so uncaring?"

"I didn't say I didn't care, my friend. Far from it. I care very deeply, and I'm honored to be here fighting for the lives of all of these people. I'll lay down my life to protect them. Not one of them will die if I can prevent it. I think Mordak is of the very worst kind of evil, and I'd kill him in a heartbeat if I knew how." Layton recalled how he had plunged his Jidaan into the sorcerer's heart, and how the fiend had just shaken off the wound. "No, it's just a matter of perspective that allows me to clear my mind when I fight. That way, I can do what needs to be done without worrying about how important the outcome might be. Here...catch." Layton tossed the half-eaten apple at Bjarke, who caught it easily in a massive fist. "That was easy, yes?"

Bjarke nodded, listening intently. Layton reached out his hand and Bjarke returned the apple to him. Layton stepped closer and a dreadful coldness swept across his face. His eyes narrowed and his voice lowered menacingly.

"Now, I'm going to toss it again, but if you miss, everyone in the castle will be ripped apart by those beasts out there. All of them--men, women, children and babes--all slashed to pieces to die screaming in pools of their own blood. And it will all be your fault."

Horror and anger started to register on Bjarke's face, but before he could speak, the apple was arcing through the cool night air towards him. He gasped as he made a grab for it, and it bounced off his palm at first. A moment of frantic juggling later, Bjarke had the apple cradled close against his chest with both hands. Angry now, Bjarke growled down at his young comrade, "That wasn't funny, Layton."

Layton smiled, returning to his usual, amiable demeanor. "I didn't mean for it to be, my friend, and I mean you no disrespect. I'm just making a point. Let me ask you this, was it harder the second time?"

Still incensed, Bjarke nevertheless answered calmly, "Yes, much harder. I knew it was silly, but I was thinking about what you said, and I was suddenly terrified I'd miss."

"What was different? I tossed it to you at exactly the same speed and angle. It was exactly the same. So what was it that made the second time more difficult?"

Realization dawned on the big man. "Nothing. Nothing at all had changed except the fact that I was so concerned with 'what ifs' that it made my heart pound and I got nervous."

Layton smiled. "Correct. Now, when you remove all of that, remove the emotions surrounding the consequences you imagined, did you save all of those people from certain death? No. What did you really and truly do?"

Bjarke stood quietly, thinking. Slowly, understanding dawned on him and he realized what Layton was trying to show him. He smiled then, and took a big bite of the fruit before handing it back to the young warrior.

"I caught an apple in the air. Nothing more and nothing less."

Layton clapped him on the shoulder, reaching up to do so. "Exactly, my large friend. When you strip it all down, every task is just a set of physical actions, whether it's catching an apple or beheading a Gholan to save a child. Focus everything solely on the action itself, with every fiber of your noble being, and not on the possible consequences. Doing so doesn't mean that you don't care about what happens, it just makes it easier to perform that task better. You are a good man, Bjarke; I know that you will make the best choices you can. Trust in that, and let the worry go."

Bjarke was surprised to find that Layton's words made sense. From the look of it, there was a long and dangerous road ahead. Bjarke needed to find a way to navigate it without being destroyed by it. Layton had long since found a way to do so, and Bjarke knew it. Standing taller, he replied. "I hear the truth in your words, my friend. I shall strive to do as you say. Defending these people is the right thing to do, and I think I can let that be enough for now."

Layton saluted, fist over heart. He bowed low to the big forester before turning toward the stairs that led to the courtyard below. He wanted to take advantage of the lull in the battle to visit Alyssa and get the worst of his wounds healed. Bjarke stepped up to the battlements to peer over the wall, feeling somewhat renewed in his heart.

"Oh, Bjarke!" Layton's voice called from below. The forester turned just in time to see something small come hurtling up from the courtyard. Quick as a striking snake, Bjarke's massive hand lashed out and snatched the object from the air. A grin shone through his bushy beard as he opened his hand to find a shiny new apple. "Nice catch, big man!" Bjarke smiled as he took a big bite and turned back to the wall.

Inside the keep, Alyssa lay facedown on one of the pallets that had just been vacated. Earlier, a young soldier had nearly lost an arm from a vicious swipe of a Morcat's claws, but the healing power of the Jidaan had reattached the limb with only the thinnest of scars to show where the wound had been. Alyssa had learned how to adjust the amount of healing she performed to conserve her energy. A complete healing that left the patient whole and sound took far more out of her than a healing that left ordinary scars. The power of the Jidaan was inexhaustible, but hers was not. The strain of healing so many had taken its toll, as she had known it would, and she had finally pushed long past the point of exhaustion. As a result, she slept more deeply than she ever had in her life. Her snores buzzed loudly in the stone chamber, making the Sisters smile as they bustled nearby, tending the wounded.

Fiona walked by and took a moment to draw a thin sheet over Alyssa's sleeping form, brushing a stray lock of hair from the tiny healer's sweaty face. There were still more wounded coming in, and many were calling for Alyssa after hearing from their fellows how she had healed them. Unfortunately, the little Guardian had already done as much as her body could handle for the time being. The Sisters of Rowann hustled as fast as they could, using their own skills to good effect, but nothing compared to the complete healing that Alyssa's Jidaan accomplished. Trying to keep the pained soldiers calm when they were told Alyssa wasn't available seemed to be the biggest problem they had. For the most part, though, the soldiers did their best to stoically endure the ministrations of the healers as they worked to save lives and limbs. Fiona had masterfully directed the Sisters as the wounded came and went. She dealt with those who didn't survive their injuries so that Alyssa could focus on her own work.

Another group of soldiers came in, Layton among them, and Fiona sent Bekah to deal with them. Still energetic, the young Bekah raced over and got them sorted by severity of injury and dispatched other Sisters to tend them before swarming Layton.

"What is it? Are you hurt? What happened?" Her hands were all over him, probing, poking, and expertly searching for wounds underneath all the blood on his clothing and armor. She found the slashes on his left arm before he could speak, and sucked in her breath at the sight of them. "Ah, those are from Morcat claws; we've got to clean those immediately, or else they'll fester. Those things have rotting meat in them, worse than poison. Get that mail off, I'll take care of it." Bekah led Layton to a stool and gathered the things she needed to clean his wounds.

Layton removed his bloodied clothes and shrugged out of his armor so that Bekah could tend him. "Can't Alyssa just heal it?"

"She could, but," Bekah pointed a thumb over her shoulder towards Alyssa, who still lay sleeping, "she'd have to be awake to do it. She pushed herself hard, nearly passed out while she was finishing up one lad. A head wound, I think it was, or maybe an arm...anyway, she finished with him, staggered to that corner and has been out cold ever since."

The young nun efficiently cleaned Layton's arm and began expertly stitching the vivid gashes closed. She leaned close and her eyes went wide as she spoke, "It was amazing, Layton! There were men in here who had moments to live, and she healed them! They were good as new when they walked out of here." She took a moment to snip through a bit of thread before starting on the next set of stitches. "I've never seen anything like it. No one died in here for the first three hours, and most walked out to fight again right away. She's truly amazing!"

Layton's eyes drifted around the room, seeing how many men wouldn't survive the night. It was nothing new for him. He had seen his way through scores of battles in his young life, but it never became any easier. He knew how to set his feelings aside when he was fighting, but seeing the gruesome results of such battles affected him far more than he would ever admit. He sighed, looked down to see Bekah tie off another stitch. Moments later, she was finished and the arm was tightly bandaged.

Flexing the arm a few times, Layton said, "Perfect! You're a wonder, Bekah. This feels fine."

Blushing slightly from the praise, Bekah responded by lightly swatting the young warrior in the back of the head. "Yes, well, maybe cover your head next time so I won't have to stitch that too."

Layton flashed his boyish grin, his good humor returning. "Yes, mother, I promise." Bekah laughed and hustled off to see to the other soldiers as Layton put his armor on and prepared to go back outside. As he stepped towards the door, he saw Alyssa dozing in the corner. Walking as quietly as he could, he moved to her and knelt by her side.

She was exhausted, that much Layton could easily see, but her sleep was sound. She'd likely rouse soon, and immediately fling herself back into her work. Careful not to disturb her slumber, Layton reached out and placed his hand on her shoulder. Using an ancient technique he had learned from one of his Eastern masters, Layton shut down his senses, leaving his mind in a place of complete silence. Once there, he looked inward and began to gather his energy, his ki. He was pleased to find that he was far stronger now than he had ever been, thanks to the Jidaan and his own newly-awakened magick. Layton guided his power within himself, making sure that he would use enough to be helpful, but not so much that he rendered himself incapable of fighting. Soon, he found the balance point and opened his senses once more so that he could again see and feel Alyssa before him. Focusing carefully, Layton allowed his ki to flow from himself along his arm and into his sleeping comrade, hopefully speeding her recovery. He knew that his form of battle-healing could only aid in increasing a person's energy level, and was nothing compared to the incredible power of her Jidaan, but it seemed like the right thing to do.

"Your work is far more important than mine, Alyssa," he whispered. "Any fool can kill the enemy, but what you do is truly noble. What strength I have is yours."

He stayed like that for a few quiet minutes, channeling his ki into her tiny body. Finally, he started to feel drowsy, so he cut off the flow and stood. Alyssa immediately stirred and opened her bright blue eyes to look uncomprehendingly at him. She stretched and sat up, rubbing her eyes.

"Oh, hello Layton. I'm sorry, I just needed to rest a bit. Are you all right? Wait, you were hurt, I remember..." She picked up her Jidaan from where it had lain beside her. She was still groggy but was already reaching for him, about to ignite the power to heal him.

"Don't worry, I'm fine," Layton gently closed his hands on hers to stop her. "Bekah already tended my wounds, I'm all right. You save your strength for those who need it. Why don't you get something to eat? They've stopped attacking the walls for the moment, so we're all resting as best we can. You need food!"

Just then, another of the Sisters walked up, carrying a small tray of food, and Layton stepped away to make room for her. "Here, Alyssa, I was saving this until you woke," Emmi said, placing the tray on Ayssa's lap. A small bowl of stew, a hunk of buttered bread, and a jug of water made Alyssa's mouth water and stomach gurgle. She had been healing patients for hours without a break, and had only just realized how famished she was.

Smiling, Alyssa said, "Thank you both, I feel..." she paused, assessing. "I feel better! Let me eat this, and I'll get back to work. I want to see if we can clear this room before things get ugly again." Without another word, she started slurping up soup and ripping into the bread with her teeth.

"Wow, watch your fingers, Layton. You're likely to lose one if you get too close," Emmi smiled crookedly at the young warrior as she turned to leave. Layton stifled a laugh.

"You sure you're all right, Alyssa?"

"Yes, Layton. I'm feeling much better, thank you. What's going on out there is horrible, judging by what makes its way in here, but we're fighting back as best we can. We'll not let Laro down." Alyssa burped somewhat less than daintily and kept eating.

Layton looked around the infirmary, noting the large doors that led into the main part of the keep.

"I don't know what's coming, but there's a good chance that we'll lose that wall. They're holding back now, and I have a bad feeling that whatever's in store for us is going to be more than we can handle. Be ready to move everything farther inside the keep if they breach the wall." Layton stood, absently checking his Jidaan in its sheath along his back. "I'd better get back out there and see what's happening."

Alyssa wiped the soup bowl clean with the last of the bread and popped it into her mouth as she stood. Still holding the soup bowl in one hand, she reached up and wrapped her arms briefly around Layton's neck to give him a quick hug before moving away. They had been Chosen together, trained together, traveled together, and fought together. Layton, and all the other Guardians for that matter, felt like family to her. Her heart swelled with concern for him, but she steadied herself and focused on the job at hand.

"Ok, we'll be ready if that happens. Call for me if I'm needed out there."

Layton grinned. "If we need you that badly, I'll just come and get you." An opalescent portal burst into life next to him, startling the nearby nuns and soldiers with its sudden brightness. Layton stepped into it and vanished, leaving the room dimmer by comparison.

Alyssa had gotten used to his abrupt comings and goings, and was amused at the surprised looks on everyone else's faces as they turned back to their tasks. She turned around and saw Bekah staring at the spot where Layton had been standing. The young nun was smiling and idly playing with a lock of her own hair, obviously lost in her thoughts. Just then, Fiona called for Bekah to help her move a larger soldier, and she snapped out of her daydreams. Alyssa smiled. She knew that Bekah had been smitten by the young warrior. So did everyone else, with the notable exception of Layton himself. With a sigh, Alyssa reached for her Jidaan and strapped it to her back so that she could move freely with it. In her heart, she dared hope that both Bekah and Layton would survive to see what might arise between them.

As the night wore on, the evil minions of Mordak held their ground and continued to wait, though for what, no one could guess. Nevertheless, the defenders of Laro used that time to rest, eat, redistribute arrows and oil for the cauldrons, and generally compose themselves. They knew that the attack could come at any moment.

"Your Grace, I think something is coming," Captain Drattus pointed into the darkness. "There's something moving out there in the distance. Something big." The pale light of the moon above filtered down through the drifting clouds, sporadically illuminating the milling horde outside the wall. Duke Gensen strained to see in the direction that Drattus had pointed, but saw nothing more than the thousands of Gholans, Krell, and Morcats that made up the bulk of Mordak's foul army.

A tremor vibrated through the wall, very faint, but unmistakeable. More followed, an odd, disjointed rumbling in the earth that crept up into the soldiers through their boots, unnerving them. All eyes strained into the darkness, searching for the next monstrous attack. Within moments, several massive shapes came close enough to be seen in the pale moonlight, and Gholans and Morcats skittered out of the way, frantically scrambling over each other in the process. Those who were too slow were slapped aside or crushed under the massive, three-toed feet of the oncoming beasts.

They were easily twenty feet tall, their grayish-green skin covered in old scars and warts. Their faces were brutish, with tiny eyes and sloping foreheads. Short tusks jutted up from their lower jaws and their thick, matted hair hung down over their shoulders, rattling from the bones braided into their greasy tresses. Filthy furs were wrapped around their hips, and more bones decorated them. Hugely muscled, each carried a fearsome club consisting of a tree trunk with jagged sword blades jammed through one end. As the earth shook with their heavy footsteps, the largest of them raised his club and let out an angry, ear-splitting roar, and the others followed suit.

"Sweet Rowann above, those are Forest Ogres! Arm the ballistae! Get those bolts loaded right now!" Duke Gensen's powerful voice echoed in the still night air, and the cry was picked up by the captains scattered along the wall. Soldiers rushed to turn the winches to arm the huge, mounted crossbows. There were four of them, two on the barbican and one on each tower, and in moments, all would be armed and ready to loose their deadly bolts.

It would not be soon enough.

With a mighty roar, one of the enormous creatures picked up a huge boulder from the opposite side of the moat and heaved it through the air towards the northeast tower. Soldiers rushed to get out of the way, all save the one man aiming the ballista, his face white with fear. Even as the giant rock hurtled towards him, the young soldier carefully lined up the tip of the bolt with the Ogre's chest, adjusted for the distance, and pulled the lever to loose the shaft. The enormous bowstrings thrummed mightily and the heavy bolt shot through the air, barely clearing the incoming rock as it flew towards its target. Ballista and soldier were smashed to pieces by the boulder, but the young man's bravery was rewarded by a loud, agonized howl. The bolt had struck true, spearing the great beast through the heart. It gripped the wooden shaft as though it meant to pull it out, even as it died on its feet. As it fell, it crushed a handful of hapless Gholans that were too slow to escape.

"By the Goddess, he got one!" The Duke raised his sword in triumph. "Feather those brutes! Loose the shafts as fast as you can, lads! Ready the oil!"

Earth-shaking roars erupted from the six remaining Ogres as they approached the moat, and the night air was suddenly filled with a great swarm of razor-tipped, deadly arrows. For the most part, they bounced off the Ogres' thick hides or else missed them completely, mowing down scores of Gholans and Morcats instead. One huge Ogre bellowed furiously in pain as one of its eyes was put out, but it yanked the offending arrow loose and kept coming at the wall. Massive bowstrings twanged and two more of the creatures fell, with bolts as thick as a man's arm driven deep into their bodies. Other missiles flew astray, but by then, the remaining Ogres were past the moat, almost too close for the ballistae to reach.

"Ready the pikes!" The Duke yelled, and warriors quickly sheathed their swords and picked up the long, sturdy pikes that had been laid aside ahead of time. Even as the brave soldiers steadied the weapons atop the battlements, turning the wall into a bristling porcupine of steel, they knew that it would avail them not against the enormous monsters that bore down on them.

The first Ogre came within striking distance of the wall and lashed out with its massive war club, shattering the battlements and killing several soldiers. Their broken bodies fell along with jagged shards of stone to the base of the wall. The beast roared as it swung again, clearing away several defenders even as more rushed to fill the gap.

Farther down the wall, the one-eyed Ogre reached up and swatted at the men above it, but they managed to stay well clear while sending arrow after arrow to sting the beast. It brushed at the arrows that stuck out of its skin, and yelled in frustration. Suddenly, it lowered one shoulder and ran straight at the wall, slamming into it.

The wall was hugely thick and strong, but the impact had thrown several warriors to their knees, and one had fallen backwards to the cobbles below. The Ogre shook its head and backed up again, more out of anger than any real plan, and charged again, hitting the wall in the same place.

Something moved.

It was small, only the slightest shifting sensation within the ancient stones, but every soldier felt it. The Ogre felt it too, for it backed up and snorted with satisfaction. It squinted its one eye and watched the puny humans evacuate the battlements above. The huge creature dimly realized it could probably break through the wall with a few more blows, and then dine on as many of the crunchy little humans as it could catch. Arrows continued to rain down and the Ogre ignored them, though it kept its head moving from side to side to make it more difficult for the archers to hit. As it prepared to lower its shoulder and charge once more, a lone figure appeared atop the wall. In the moonlight, he glowed a pure, clean red, and the bushy-haired, bearded man drew the monster's attention.

Bjarke had felt the wall shift and seen the warriors scrambling to safety, and knew that it was up to him to stop the Ogre. Pulling his Jidaan from its sheath along his back, he hummed quietly to call its Gift. Instantly, the ruby flared and

Bjarke felt its potency flow through him, filling him with an incredible sense of power as he walked out to stand atop the wall across from the massive beast. He let the power build for a moment, then raised his left hand and released an intense burst of energy. The scarlet beam struck the Ogre full in the chest, knocking it flat on its back. It scrambled up immediately, its chest still smoldering from Bjarke's power, and roared its defiance. With frightening speed, it reached out and snatched a chunk of wreckage from the moat and threw it directly at Bjarke. Another bolt of magick shattered the wooden mass, sending dangerous shards in all directions. Bjarke glowed fiercely as he maintained his control of the Gift of his Jidaan.

Without another thought, Bjarke stepped from the battlements and dropped the thirty feet to the earth below, landing solidly on his feet among scores of Gholan corpses. He broke into a run directly towards the enraged Ogre. He knew he had to take the fight away from those on the wall.

"I think Bjarke has lost his mind!" Nessar said as he and Kiran peppered another Ogre with arrows and crossbow bolts. Though they had little effect, they seemed to sting the beast enough to keep it away from the main gate long enough for the ballista to be loaded. Aiming the huge weapon at a target this close to the wall was tricky, but possible.

Kiran loosed another arrow at the creature and spoke without turning, "Just keep an eye on him, old man. If we can help him somehow we will, but we've got our hands full with this one and I dare say that Bjarke can handle himself." She focused her arrows on the Ogre's face, making it flinch and cover itself with its arms each time she hit it. The beast roared in frustration and got a crossbow bolt in its mouth as a result. "Hurry up with those things!" Kiran bellowed at the nearby soldiers as they struggled to winch back the massive bowstrings. Bright blasts of scarlet lit up the night as Bjarke did battle with the Ogre, but Kiran had no more time to watch.

Suddenly, a dark shape swooped down and snatched up one of the soldiers. Another followed right after, leaving Ness and Kiran alone on the barbican, the ballista useless without a crew to work it. There were terrified screams before a pair of sickening cracks silenced the abducted soldiers. A heartbeat later, their still forms plummeted out of the dark sky to slam into the cobbles below, spraying blood from shattered skulls.

"What in the name of Rowann was that?" Nessar turned and peered into the darkened sky, glad the moon gave at least some light for him to see by. A shape darted across his field of vision, then swerved in the air to head towards one of the other ballista crews. "Oh, Hels, I can't believe this." Quickly cocking his crossbow, Nessar let out a string of curses that made even Kiran's ears burn.

"What? Speak up, Ness, what is it?" Kiran continued loosing arrows at the Ogre, which backed away and started searching the ground for something. As it moved just out of range Kiran lowered her bow and turned to see Nessar aiming his crossbow into the air as he tracked something in flight.

"Harpies," he said without looking away. "They're throwing Hels-damned Harpies at us now. I KNEW they'd have something that flies!" Nessar pointed his crossbow nearly straight up and pulled the trigger, sending a bolt hissing through the dark. He was rewarded by an unearthly shriek. "Gotcha, you hag!" Then he jumped back as the body of the harpy slammed into the spot where he had been standing. It had been returning for one of them.

Kiran jumped back in surprise as the reptilian body shuddered and convulsed on the stones in front of her. It was bigger than a man, but thinner, and more spindly. Its skin glistened wetly in the moonshine, and she could see scales all over its wiry body. Hands and feet ended in long, skeletal claws, and great bat wings flapped crazily as the creature died. Its face was that of an ancient crone, gnarled and hideous, its eyes blazing with hate and insanity. Long, stringy hair splayed out on the stones beneath their feet, and its body curled around the quarrel that Nessar had lodged deep in its black heart. Nessar reached down and pulled the small arrow out of the Harpy's body with a sickening, wet sound, wiped it off in its hair, then quickly reloaded his crossbow. "I really hate Harpies, Kiran. Just hate 'em."

"Well that's just wonderful. Juuust wonderful." Kiran turned back to the Ogre she had been harassing and her blood ran cold. The enormous creature had picked up a section of wall from the ruins of a nearby house and was using it as a shield. "And that's even better." Leaving Nessar to deal with the Harpies, Kiran nocked another arrow and watched the Ogre, waiting for it to lower its guard, even for a moment. Holding the shield up to protect its face, it advanced step by step towards the main gate. Her arm tiring from hours of loosing arrows, Kiran knew that if the brute made it to the gate, nothing could stop it from getting in. Looking past the oncoming Ogre, she saw that the Gholans and Morcats had crossed the moat again, joined by the undead walkers and the ferocious Krell. They were following close behind it, betting on the chance it would breach the gate, allowing them to swarm through. Furiously, she tried to figure out a way to stop the big monster from getting any farther.

Brunar, too, had seen the horde amassing behind the battling Ogres, and was dismayed to see they brought Laro's dead with them. Shambling forms missing limbs walked shoulder to shoulder with monsters, moving with silent purpose towards the walls they had once protected. Brunar knew Laro's army could not defend against both the mob and the Ogres, but suddenly he knew how he could even the odds a bit.

Walking over to one of the boiling cauldrons of oil, Brunar gestured at the massive iron kettle, quietly speaking a few words in an ancient language to focus his mind. The kettle obediently rose, bubbling and steaming, out of its cradle. Looking over his right shoulder, Brunar saw one of the Ogres attacking a nearby section of the wall, smashing soldiers with every swipe of its wicked club. With a sudden heave, Brunar threw both arms towards the beast, directing the cauldron to shoot through the air and slam into the monster's great, misshapen head. At the moment of impact, the creature simply grunted, but then the boiling oil poured out and slithered down the Ogre's body, scalding and burning everything it touched, and the grunts became agonized howls of pain. Brunar gestured at a nearby torch, and it flew out of its bracket to strike the Ogre directly in the chest, setting the beast aflame. Its howls became frantic as it tried vainly to beat the fire out with its massive hands, spinning in a violent dance of death. Burning furiously, it stumbled back into range of one of the ballista.

"Now!" Duke Gensen yelled at the nearest crew. It took only seconds for them to aim and loose the razor-tipped harpoon with a mighty twang of bowstrings. The bolt took the screaming creature in the side, bursting its gigantic heart. The Ogre stopped fighting and dropped to its knees, then toppled onto its side, finally dead.

A ragged cheer went up, but was soon silenced when a horde of screeching Gholans boiled over the walls. Distracted by the battle with the Ogres, many of the defenders were startled by their sudden appearance and they paid dearly. Blood flew, monsters were killed, and men and women died as they were bitten and slashed by gleeful, evil creatures. Morcats, too, reached the battlements and began clawing their way through the warriors there. More defenders rushed to fill the gaps, but the losses were staggering.

Just outside the wall, Bjarke had blasted the Ogre off its feet thrice, but each time it got up and fought back, slamming gigantic fists into the ground, shaking the earth with its power. Thankful for Brunar's training, Bjarke managed to evade the Ogre's clumsy attacks, but hours of defending the wall and repeated uses of the Jidaan's Gift were tiring him. He dodged another crashing blow from the Ogre that almost landed and tried to keep his footing. Fortunately, the other fell creatures nearby gave him and the Ogre a wide berth, as they had no wish to be crushed to death beneath the giant's fists or feet. Steeling himself for what he knew had to happen, Bjarke tried to clear his mind and ready himself.

The Ogre roared at Bjarke, its foetid breath washing over him, but he ignored it. He was watching the monster's hips to see where it would move next. Sure enough, the great beast shifted to its right and brought up its giant fists in an attempt to squash the puny human. As it did, Bjarke hummed his gravelly song and unleashed a much smaller blast of crimson power from his Jidaan, striking the Ogre full in the face. It flinched, and that was all the opening Bjarke needed. Bursting into action, Bjarke sprinted towards the Ogre and dove between its thickly muscled legs. Bjarke hit the ground and rolled. Coming up fast and turning as Brunar had taught him, Bjarke ignited the power of his Jidaan with a ferocious yell and swung the weapon with all his might at the Ogre's exposed hamstrings. Realizing too late where the little human had gone, the Ogre tried to turn, but it was far too late. Bjarke's Jidaan flared bright crimson and sheared cleanly through both legs, severing them completely. Caught in mid-turn, the Ogre twisted and collapsed to the ground. Its legs fell to the dusty earth, useless. As it struck the ground, it began to howl in agony. Bjarke jumped up and plunged his weapon into the Ogre's massive heart in one powerful strike. Its eyes locked with Bjarke's for a moment, then its enormous head lolled back into the dirt as it died. Bjarke pulled his Jidaan from the Ogre's chest and jumped down, running even as his boots hit the earth.

Layton! I need you! Bjarke ran as fast as he could towards the wall, noting the massive cracks the Ogre had put in its center. Without warning, a Gate burst into being in front of him. Bjarke ran into it and instantly found himself racing across the courtyard behind the wall. He slowed and stopped, breathing heavily from the fighting and the run, and looked for Layton to thank him.

I'm up here, Bjarke. Thanks for handling the Ogre!
Bjarke looked up and saw Layton atop the wall where the fighting
was thickest, whirling, slashing, and stabbing in a graceful dance
that left nothing but corpses in its wake.

Bjarke was tired, exhausted all the way down to his
bones. More than that, he was heartsick. A minor entrance to
the keep was nearby, and Bjarke walked over to it. It was no
more than a doorway covered by a stone overhang, but Bjarke
saw it as a haven. He stepped out of the open courtyard, away
from the fighting, away from the wounded being carried into the
infirmary and the soldiers battling desperately to regain control,
away from everything. The torches weren't lit in the alcove, and
Bjarke was glad of it as propped his Jidaan against the wall and
sank down onto a small bench. He leaned back against the cold
stone and sighed, letting the dark calm him. His hands were
shaking, so he clasped them together and slowed his breathing in
an attempt to still them.

Tears flowed down his cheeks and he wept harder than
he ever had in his life. Sorrow engulfed him, and great wracking
sobs shook his powerful frame. In the instant he had stabbed the
Ogre, its eyes had found his. Their spirits had connected for the
briefest of moments, and Bjarke had *seen* inside the creature's
mind. It knew itself as Nom.

When at first the connection occurred, there was a
profound malevolence there, a presence that reeked of evil and
insanity. Suddenly, as though it had realized the Ogre was dying
and of no further use, the presence dissipated, leaving behind
nothing more than Nom's own dim intelligence. The creature
had no idea what it had been doing. It had not known where it
was, only that it was suddenly in greater pain than it had ever
experienced in its long, solitary life. It didn't even realize that its
legs were gone, only that they hurt. As Bjarke ended its life, Nom
knew only confusion and pain, and a longing to return to its cozy
cave in the forest. Now, the big man mourned for the Ogre he
had slain, and for the others he knew would also die far from
home, unwitting pawns of a great evil.

It was long before the tears finally stopped and Bjarke
could take a breath without hitching. He stared into the silent
dark, turning events over in his mind until he had completely
regained his composure. Killing the Ogre had broken his heart,
but because it had assailed the castle, it had to be stopped. The
huge Guardian hated killing, but knew that he would have to step
up again and protect the people of Laro. At least he knew the
Morcats, Gholans and Krell were vile creatures, known for their

hatred of humans. Those, he could kill without a second thought.

Searching the dark for Brunar's telltale purplish outbursts of power, he quickly found the Mage fighting atop the western wall. Focusing his will, Bjarke called to him with his mind. Instantly, the Mage answered, and Bjarke told him as briefly as possible what had happened. The forester felt Brunar's anguish at the plight of the Ogres, and the Mage thanked him for the information before severing their mental connection. Bjarke hoped knowing the Ogres were naught but puppets might help Brunar find a way to free them without taking their lives.

Bjarke stood and stepped back out into the moonlight. He looked up at the fighting atop the battlements, and found one area that looked as though the defenders could use him. As he watched, three Morcats made it to the top of the wall and began pushing the defenders back. Bjarke took a deep breath, then took a few running steps towards the wall before channeling his energy into his jump as he had been taught. His Jidaan blazed crimson as he landed in their midst, scything through the vicious beasts as though they were no more than wheat at harvest. Still more clambered over the wall to assail him, and Bjarke grimly settled into the rhythm of combat.

The Harpies were causing more trouble by the minute, swooping in to snatch fighters right off the battlements. Some soldiers managed to stab their abductors as they were lifted into the air, but often did not survive the resulting fall. One man got snatched not an arm's reach from Layton, who finally saw the danger. Scanning the walls and keep behind him, Layton quickly opened a gate and stepped into it, arriving atop the tallest tower of Laro. A flag arose from the center of the conical slate roof, and Layton grasped it firmly to steady himself. From his vantage point so high above the fighting, things did not look good for the citizens of Laro. Beyond the outer wall, Layton could see the vast horde of Mordak's creatures, swarming like ants over the land, surrounding the castle on three sides. Fortunately, the keep backed up to the River Corris, and was protected by the powerful flow of the water on that side. Searching the night sky Layton detected several flitting shapes, but the deepening dark made them very difficult to track. Using the Mindspeech that Brunar had taught them, Layton reached out to the Mage.

Brunar, I need to be able to see up here. Can you do something?

From one corner of the wall, a bolt of purple energy shot skyward, flying up past Layton until it was far overhead.

Suddenly it exploded, turning into a brightly glowing ball of violet fire hanging in the air, casting light in all directions.

Layton was at once grateful and dismayed. Brunar's flare showed twenty or more of the wicked, reptilian shapes in the skies over the castle-- darting, diving, and killing everyone they touched. Engaging the power of his Jidaan, Layton tracked one of the creatures as it flew nearby, screeching defiantly. He timed his casting carefully, and a Gate burst into existence directly in front of the flying Harpy. It flew into it before it could veer away. The Gate's twin appeared mere inches from the inside wall down below, and Layton was pleased to see the beast slam into the unyielding stone at full speed, smashing its skull with a sickening thump. The dead Harpy collapsed on the ground at the base of the wall and a group of passing soldiers immediately began to hack at it, making sure it was dead. Layton spied another Harpy and sent it, too, into the wall below. It did not take long for the soldiers to realize what was happening, and they began to anticipate the appearance of each shrieking monster, eager to help it along the road to death.

Unfortunately, the use of his Gift gave away his position to the harpies as his Jidaan flared brightly with its opalescent fire. He was also tiring quickly with each Gate he created. The Harpies' awful squawking increased as they figured out what was being done to them, and the next Gate Layton created was deftly avoided. A Harpy screeched in triumph, and pointed one long, bony talon at the shining man atop the tower. As one, the beasts flapped their leathery wings and flew to the attack.

Layton hated to admit it, but he was exhausted. He started to create a Gate to take himself to safety, but was struck a stunning blow from behind as a Harpy took him unawares. He lashed out with his Jidaan, but the creature was already long gone, and just then another one flew in from his left, shrieking loudly. He pivoted and lopped off its head in midair, only to be struck again by another of the vicious creatures. Pain erupted along his ribs from the long talons that slashed through his chain mail. Suddenly, stars whirled in front of Layton's eyes as he was struck again, this time in the head. He was glad he had heeded Bekah's advice and worn a helmet. He dimly realized he was falling. Some part of him knew that he had a long way to go, though the fall would seem short. He tried to create a Gate, but everything whirled and danced in the dark, and he couldn't remember how.

Without warning, Layton landed in two immensely strong arms and was carried aloft. Rock dust exploded into his face, making him cough. As the young warrior tried to focus his eyes, he was startled to find himself staring into a gray, pugnosed face, with short tusks poking up from a strong lower jaw.

"What the...?" Layton exclaimed in surprise. The creature that had caught him merely grunted in response. It flapped its massive leathery wings and descended to the rooftop of the main keep, where the Weya leader, Moihra, stood waiting. It landed lightly and made sure that Layton could keep his feet before it turned and launched itself back into the night sky. Layton marveled at the obvious strength of the creature, its enormous muscles bulging as it moved. It was manlike, but flew on huge bat wings. It possessed a long, snakelike tail that ended in a sharp spade. Its powerful back legs were more like a dog's, as was its thick brow and short snout.

Another of the creatures flew close and hovered, holding Layton's Jidaan out to him with its nimble tail. Layton reached out and took it. The beast flew skyward, joining two others, both newly arrived. Within moments, a horrendous screeching was heard as the airborne battle was joined, the four new creatures attacking the Harpies with brutal efficiency. One by one, the Harpies fell, mangled, from the sky.

Layton looked at Moihra, his questions plain on his face. She laughed, a lovely sound to his ears after hours of the noise of battle.

"They are gargoyles, Layton. Or at least, stone likenesses of them. They've been sitting atop the castle for centuries, placed there in the event they were needed. That was the enchantment I felt in the stones; it just took me a while to find a way to call to it and awaken them. They will defend the city ferociously until the enchantment runs its course. They'll turn back to stone at that point, but will kill many of Mordak's foul creatures before that happens."

Layton watched the battle in the skies under Brunar's slowly dimming flare, noting that the gargoyles were quietly and efficiently dispatching the howling, reptilian Harpies. Wherever the Harpies managed to strike a blow, he could see puffs of rock dust in the air as their wicked talons gouged into the stone skin of the gargoyles.

"It appears they don't like Harpies," he said, with a fair amount of wonder in his voice. He had never dreamed he'd see a gargoyle in flight, much less in battle, and it awed him more than a little.

Moihra laughed, "No, they absolutely do not. They have been mortal enemies since the dawn of time. Although those are only statues, they have been imbued with a spark of true spirit, donated by a living gargoyle. The statues live and think as true gargoyles, but only for a while." Layton swayed on his feet and Moihra steadied him with a small hand on his arm. "Come, we need to get you to Alyssa. Can you Gate us there?"

In answer, a Gate appeared in the air next to them. Layton gestured for her to step in ahead of him and she did so, disappearing as she crossed the plane of the portal. With one last glance at the powerful gargoyles overhead, Layton stepped through as well.

At the front gate, Kiran watched one of the last Ogres as it inched its way towards her position. A new crew had manned the ballista, and were firing stones and quarrels at the enormous beast as fast as they could load the weapon. It was still shielding itself with a chunk of debris, and the crew had already loosed the last of their large bolts. More and more, it was looking as though the Ogre would make it to the gate.

"Staring at it won't make it any prettier, Kiran," Nessar quipped, sending another crossbow bolt out into the dark.

"Indeed, the more I look at it, the more it looks like you, Grampy," Kiran replied without turning.

"Lucky fellow, then," Nessar replied, recocking his crossbow and laying another bolt in position.

Kiran was wracking her brain to think of a way to deal with the enormous beast, and they were running out of time. If it made it to the gate it would surely try to break it down. Then it would only be a matter of minutes before her strength ran out and her Ward crumbled. Before she could think any further, Nessar burst into a coughing fit beside her. Without thinking, she turned to him and pounded on his back. After a moment, he stopped and sighed heavily.

"Thanks, Kir. For a second there, I couldn't breathe. Spit went down the wrong way."

Kiran's eyes widened and she exclaimed, "That's it! Thanks, Ness, you're a genius!" She jumped up and kissed Nessar's scruffy cheek, leaving him bewildered.

Kiran moved quickly back to her place at the wall and laid down the bow she still carried in her left hand. She reached up to touch the haft of the Jidaan, safely scabbarded along her back, and focused her attention on the oncoming Ogre. Sweat broke out on her brow as the sapphire in her Jidaan came to life, answering her silent call. Its deep blue glow crawled over the surface of her body, enveloping her as she prepared to focus the Gift. Extending one hand, Kiran gestured at the oncoming Ogre.

A faint blue radiance appeared in front of the beast--a huge, square-shaped wall. The Ogre bumped into it with its makeshift shield and stopped. It nudged the wall a few times more, then slowly lowered its shield to see what it had encountered. That was all the opening Kiran needed.

With a sharp gesture and a grunt of effort, Kiran lifted the Ward she had created, flinging it at the Ogre's brutish head, where it wrapped around its face like a wet towel. The Ogre's roar was muffled by the Ward. It instantly dropped its shield and started clawing at its face, desperately trying to remove the strange glowing thing that had attached itself to its head.

Kiran tried to control her breathing, and prepared to completely solidify the Ward and connect its edges. Doing so would decapitate the Ogre instantly, and then the gate would be safe.

Kiran, NO! Don't kill it! Brunar's voice boomed in her head, and she almost lost control of the Ward. In spite of her surprise, she managed to keep it intact.

Mage, have you lost your MIND? Why in the Hels not? For the life of her, she could not understand why Brunar would want her to stay her hand. Straining to hold the Ward while the Ogre struggled to rip it off its head, she turned to see Brunar making his way to her along the top of the wall.

Reaching her side, he immediately pointed his staff at the Ogre and ignited his own power. Cold, violet lightning poured out of the end of his staff, lancing out and merging with the blue Ward of Kiran's.

"Hold it steady, Kiran. That's it," the Mage's focus was intense. Kiran was fuming, still waiting for an explanation. After a few moments of watching the Ogre struggle against both magicks, Brunar sent one last surge of power from his staff and said firmly, "Now, release him! Quickly!"

Kiran released her Ward and sagged heavily onto the battlements, exhausted. "What did you do, Mage? Why didn't you want me to kill him? I had finally figured it out, and was just about to..."

"Yes, you did, and I'm proud of you for that. However, these Ogres have been enspelled by Mordak. They don't want to be here. They don't even know that they *are* here. Look, there," he pointed at the Ogre who had gone down to one knee and was shaking its head in confusion. Arrows still rained down upon it, and it flinched as though it had not been already experiencing those small pains for hours. It lurched to its feet and looked frantically around, trying to figure out where it was. With a pained howl of anguish, it turned and ran straight for the forest, crushing any hapless creature that could not get out of the way fast enough.

"Are you kidding me? Those things have been killing the people of Laro all night!" Kiran was furious, and shocked as well. "You should have let me kill it, Brunar! What if it comes back?"

Brunar's voice radiated calm authority. "It won't be back. Through the combination of your powers and mine, I was able to break the spell on that Ogre. It was difficult, but I think I can do it again if you're willing to help me with the remaining beast," Brunar's voice lowered and he leaned in so she could hear him, "As ferocious as they are, Kiran, the Ogres are innocent. Mordak forced them to do this. Left alone, Ogres only attack when threatened. I should have known that so many of them together like that was because Mordak was controlling them; they'd never do it on their own. Had I known sooner, we could have spared more of them. I, myself, am responsible for the death of one, and I wish it were not so."

Kiran scowled at Brunar. In her mind, the only good Ogre was a dead Ogre, but if what Brunar said was true, even they did not deserve to be used that way.

"What about the rest of them? The Gholans, the Morcats, and all those Krell? Are they enspelled, too?"

Brunar shook his head. "No, those races have always harbored a deep hatred for pretty much every other race on our world except for themselves. I think Mordak did somehow trick the Krell into being here, but they need little in the way of encouragement when it comes to making war on humans." Brunar pointed at the remaining Ogre, battling a host of archers and pikemen while trying to stay inside the firing arc of the ballista. "We can save that one, though. Cast your Ward about his head, Kiran, the same as you did with your Ogre."

Kiran snorted, "*My* Ogre? It's not like he was my sweetheart or anything, but I hear you, Mage. Give me a moment and I'll snare him for you." Kiran took a deep breath and called to her Jidaan. It answered instantly, the sapphire clutched in the weapon's pommel flaring brightly. Kiran focused intently on the Ogre and reached out with one hand, guiding her magick. She grunted, and a blue sheet of energy wrapped itself around the Ogre's face just as before. Brunar aimed his staff and spoke a Word of power, sending his magick arcing through the air to meld with Kiran's Ward.

This time, it took only moments for Brunar to sever the connection with Mordak, and when it happened, Brunar heard the furious scream of the necromancer in his mind. Brunar smiled as he cut off the flow of his power.

"There's one less creature you'll use against us, you fiend," Brunar muttered. "Kiran, please Ward that Ogre for a few moments until he's out of range of the ballistae. I'd hate to have freed him from Mordak only to have him impaled moments later."

Kiran grimaced, but ignited her power anyway and created a dim Ward between the Ogre and the defenders on the wall. Arrows bounced off the blue shield for a few more moments, then stopped as the defenders realized that they weren't getting through. The Ogre had fallen to his knees as Mordak's influence was broken. It shook its great head and rubbed its huge hands over its face as it looked around, trying to understand what was going on. It grunted in fear and confusion as it rose to its feet, then it turned away from the castle. It stepped over the wreckage of the moat, and Jor Dayne rode up, yelling furiously at the beast. The Ogre stared down at Mordak's Champion for a few seconds and then simply swatted him and his horse out of the way. Within moments, the Ogre was racing to the east, crushing Gholans, Morcats, and Krell alike and leaving Jor Dayne in a heap on the ground. Kiran sighed and let the Ward fall.

A ragged cheer went up as the Ogre ran away, even as combat continued. Gholans continued to swarm the walls, Morcats among them. The Krell stayed back for some reason, still not attacking. The wicked cannibals stalked back and forth on the far side of the moat, as if waiting for a signal, and with them, the pirated dead of Laro. As defenders fell on the outside of the wall, Mordak's bloody glow slowly appeared in their eyes and they dragged themselves to their feet, shambling over to join ranks with the other undead.

The night wore on, and although the warriors of Laro were strong and determined, their numbers were slowly dwindling. Wave after wave of evil creatures fought their way up from the ground, only to be repulsed by the stalwart defenders. Each time, though, the cost was high. The oil had run out long ago, and archers were running through their supplies of arrows at an alarming pace.

Atop the wall, Layton had just cleared one area of enemy creatures, giving the soldiers there a momentary respite from the constant fighting. He called to Bjarke with his mind, eager to finally implement his strategy.

Bjarke, are you ready? I think now is a good time.

Bjarke answered quickly, *Yes, though I'm nearing exhaustion. Let's do this before I'm completely spent.*

Layton looked over and spied Bjarke waving at him from the north wall, and instantly created a Gate near the big man. Bjarke stepped into it and vanished. Layton followed with a Gate of his own and found himself standing next to Bjarke on a balcony, high up in one of the keep's towers. It overlooked the battlefield, and Bjarke leaned heavily on the railing as he surveyed the tremendous horde still arrayed against them.

"Where do you think we should hit them?" Bjarke's gravelly voice was tired, but resolute.

Layton scanned the scene, noting the concentration of creatures spread out on the far side of the moat. Picking a suitable location, Layton pointed, "There. You see that statue on the corner of the road?"

Bjarke's eyes searched and found the statue indicated by the young Weaponsmaster. He recalled riding past it on their way into the castle. It was a lifesized sculpture of a warrior, fully armored and holding a sword at the ready. "Yes, I see it."

"Right, then. At this distance, I can only hold the Gate for a few moments, so blast away as hard as you can. With any luck, they'll think the statue did it, and it'll confuse them."

Bjarke grinned, the pale moonlight glinting off his teeth in the dark, and held his Jidaan at the ready. The big forester started a deep, rumbling hum as he willed his power to life.

Layton sheathed his own Jidaan in the scabbard at his back and turned to look out at the milling horde of creatures once more. He gauged the distance carefully, then raised both hands as though he were about to conduct a group of musicians. He took a deep breath, let it out, and smiled. Opalescent Gates burst into being, mirroring the bright opal that shone in Layton's Jidaan. One gate held steady right in front of Bjarke, and another opened far below, just in front of the statue's sword.

Bjarke gripped his Jidaan tightly and unleashed a massive beam of intense energy through his Gate. He was rewarded by the sight of that beam lancing through the night below, looking for all the world as though it had originated in the blade of the faraway statue. The bolt of magick was as thick as a man's arm and burned through anything it touched, killing scores of evil beings in the middle of the vile sorcerer's army. Sweat broke out on Bjarke's brow as he widened the beam, cleaving through more of the foul creatures as they scrambled in an attempt to escape its burning touch. Careful to keep his energy inside the Gate on his side, Bjarke moved his weapon from left to right and back again, sweeping the intense blaze in a wide arc down below and killing everything in its path. Hundreds of creatures succumbed to the focused power of Bjarke's crimson ray.

"Can't...hold it...much longer. Please...hurry." The tremor in Layton's otherwise calm voice was the only indication of the strain of holding Gates open so far apart. Bjarke instantly shut off the flow of his power and collapsed to the stones, exhausted. Layton allowed the gates to disappear and dropped to one knee beside the panting Bjarke. Suddenly, lying down seemed like the better option, and Layton found himself staring up at the stars overhead as he recovered. He noted that he did not see any more Harpies flying overhead, and he silently thanked Moihra for waking the gargoyles to defend the city. As his breathing slowed, he wondered where the stone creatures had gone.

Bjarke moved first, though slowly. He groaned and managed to sit up. "That seemed to thin them out a bit," he said tiredly, "though there are still thousands of them out there. It may take a while before I can do that again, though. I feel as if I could sleep for a week." Silence was his only response. Bjarke leaned over to check on Layton, concerned that he had hurt himself, but relaxed when he heard a light snore from his fellow Guardian. A wry chuckle escaped the big man. "Well, I see that you, too, have reached your limit. I guess we'll be taking the long way down."

Moving slowly, Bjarke got to his feet, then carefully hoisted the sleeping young man up and over his shoulder. Layton did not even stir. Bjarke managed to settle his own Jidaan in its scabbard as Layton had. Up close, he noticed that Layton's weapon was smaller by far than his own, and he wondered at the difference. Back at the Hall of Jidaana, they had all appeared exactly the same when they saw them on the wall. Shrugging to himself, Bjarke walked over to the door that led to the interior of the keep. Layton let out a particularly loud snore that made Bjarke chuckle again in spite of his exhaustion. It had been too long since he had laughed, and it felt good. The big man kept a smile on his face as he wearily headed inside to find the stairs, Layton dozing peacefully on his shoulder.

Chapter 20

Gart's feet crunched in the snow and his breath steamed on the air as he trudged upwards on the mountain path. He had been climbing for what seemed like ages. Though it was only midday, he was weary beyond belief. The icy air hurt Gart's face each time his scarf fell away, and his lungs burned with the cold as he tried to keep his breathing steady. Thankful for the gloves and jacket he had bought at the last town, he steadied himself by keeping his left hand in contact with the nearly vertical face of the mountain, while holding the reins of his horse with his right. Bessie was far from her prime, but she had borne Gart all through the foothills and into the mountains without complaint. Even now, as they worked their way up the sloped path that skirted the edge of the largest mountain Gart could see, the old horse showed no signs of slowing. Of course, Gart was moving at little better than a walk at the moment, so that may have had more to do with the horse's stamina than anything. The dog padded along quietly next to them, its breath clearly visible as well. The path was easily wide enough for three people to ride abreast, but Gart gave more than a healthy respect to the drop on the far side of the path, and he kept himself and the horse close to the mountainside. Bessie plodded steadily along next to him, snorting occasionally in the cold.

Finally, the road leveled out into a large, circular, flat space, ringed with a low wall. Near the edge of the plateau, a massive pile of both large and small stones rested. Gart wondered if the huge snow-covered mound was an ancient rockfall. A squat building, also made of gray stone, was set into the side of the mountain, and Gart made straight for the entrance. It was easily large enough to host both Gart and Bessie, plus a dozen others. He eagerly led the horse inside the empty building, and the dog quickly followed, glad to be out of the wind and cold. There was a fireplace in a corner of the one-room building with a large, neat stack of dry wood nearby. Gart wasted no time in getting a fire burning. He carefully groomed the horse, watered her, and set a feedbag in place. That accomplished, Gart rested for a moment and took time to pull rations from his pack, feed himself, and spare a few mouthfuls of meat for the dog. He still had enough food for a few days, but after that, it would be rough going for the three of them. Gart nodded to himself and put back half the food he had taken out.

He knew they'd likely need it, since he still was unsure how far they had to go.

Fed and satisfied, Gart bundled up again and went back out into the cold, taking his wooden Jidaan with him. It had taken quite a lot of work, but he had finally managed to achieve the proper balance of the weapon. He felt better with it in his hands even though it was only a replica, and he still wore his short sword on his hip. The dog left the warmth of the cabin to keep an eye on Gart, snuffling about here and there as he surveyed their surroundings.

The stark beauty of the mountains was new and somewhat alien to Gart, and he carefully walked over to the low wall near the stone pile to look out across the range. Gazing at the neighboring mountains, Gart's eyes scanned the snow-covered trees and vast expanses of space that separated the enormous peaks from each other. He knew they were actually very far away, yet they seemed so close. That sense of vastness, the height, and the rawness of the mountains awed Gart. Not for the first time, he wished Gennie could see it as well, and the thought of her brought his pain and anger to the surface as it always did. Goddess, but he missed her. He tried not to think of her bloodied corpse, looking so small in his arms back at Tiller's Grove. To dwell on that would ignite the deeper wells of rage and hatred that the Lady RaeLynn had only just managed to calm, and he couldn't afford that at this point. He had to keep his mind clear for whatever lay ahead. Gart wiped ice from his face where tears had briefly flowed as he thought of his love, and he took deep breaths of the cold air to regain control of his ragged emotions.

Turning from the stunning mountain vista, Gart looked for the path upwards. Although the view was beautiful, he could not imagine that the spot was built as nothing more than a scenic overlook. It was far too long and arduous a climb for something so trivial as an afternoon picnic in the summer, or a place for young lovers to enjoy on a lark. No, this had to be a way station for travelers on a much longer journey. Besides that, this *felt* right. The closer he had come to this particular peak, the stronger that feeling had become. Without knowing how, he *knew* he was in the right place.

He turned and looked back down the path on which he had arrived. The road hugged the mountain, and the stone rose almost straight up to form a massive wall on that side. On the other side there was nothing but a four thousand foot drop. The road led right up to the small plateau upon which he stood, which held only the circular courtyard and the stone cabin that backed right up to the mountainside. There was no outlet in sight.

Gart adjusted his scarf to cover his head and face better, then walked back down the road a bit, following his own footprints. When he was far enough away, he turned and retraced his steps, sliding his hand along the mountainside to his left as he had before. He felt nothing unusual in the stone, and saw nothing new. The road seemed to lead only to the cabin, a dead end. Gart scowled in frustration. This simply couldn't be the end of the trail. He knew the way was before him if he could only find it.

Removing one glove, Gart walked back along the wall for several steps and stared up at the towering mountain above him. Much more slowly this time, he started moving towards the cabin--sliding his bare hand along the icy stone. He was soon rewarded. Two deep, thin cracks ran vertically along the wall, as wide apart as the road upon which he stood. Snow had hidden them before, but now his bare fingers found them. Stepping back to widen his view, Gart could see that the cracks ran straight up the mountain wall for at least ten feet, where they were connected to each other by another crack, this one a gentle curve, and the stone within the outline was recessed slightly. It was a door; it had to be. But how was he to open it?

The wind plucked at Gart's headscarf as he stood in the trail, and he shivered as his eyes slowly searched every inch of the massive wall of stone. Snow obscured much of it, and Gart reached out with his magick. He had been using his power to move stones, branches, and other things for weeks. As his control improved during the trek, Gart found other uses for it besides simple lifting. This time, Gart let his magick sweep across the stone in a wide arc, scraping the crusted snow from its icy surface, leaving the full outline of the doorway exposed to the frigid air. More and more, Gart was feeling his magick as an extension of himself. He was becoming increasingly adept at interpreting the sensations that came back to him when he reached out with it.

Gart scanned the newly-clean surface of the stone and saw the outline of the door much more clearly. Oddly, he also noticed hundreds of shallow holes scattered across the vast side of the mountain that had previously been hidden by the snow. Some were only fist-sized, while others were huge. Carefully, he caressed the face of the wall with his magick, probing the seams and hollows as deeply as he could. The stone was ancient and unyielding. Gart could sense nothing beyond the pitted surface of the mountain, nor very deeply into the seams.

Gart stopped the flow of magick with a frustrated snort. He had found nothing that could tell him how to open the way, if in fact, this even *was* the gate he sought. It certainly looked like one, and there were no other paths he could see. Gart scowled as he turned the problem over in his mind.

Just then, Gart felt a tremor in the earth beneath his feet, and he heard a deep growl and a *whuff* from Beauty. The dog wasn't given to barking for no reason, and Gart was instantly concerned. A loud grinding, crunching, rumbling came from his right, and he swiveled his head around to see that the great pile of stones was no longer sitting quietly as it had been--it was moving. Gart staggered back a few steps in surprise as he watched.

The stones grated loudly against each other as they slowly rose from the earth, and puffs of snow fell away to reveal the rough surfaces of the individual rocks. The pile had seemed enormous before, and now it rose high over Gart's head and slowly began to swirl and rotate before his eyes. Beauty quickly placed herself between Gart and the stones and stood her ground, growling ferociously. The mass gained speed as it spun, a giant globe of spinning granite chunks. A powerful humming sound vibrated Gart's bones, and he felt the immense power of an ancient elemental magick coming to life. The sphere hovered several feet above the snow-covered ground, rotating steadily. Incredibly, a deep and cavernous voice issued from within the sphere of moving stones.

"Who are you?" The voice held no anger or malice, only a faint curiosity.

Gart realized he was holding his wooden Jidaan in a fighting posture before him, and at the same time he saw how futile it would be against such a creature. If it chose, it could crush him under a pile of rubble in an instant, and even his black-bladed sword would be no help. As foolish as he felt, he quickly recovered his composure and replied.

"I am Gart. A farmer. That Mage, Brunar, said I was supposed to come here, so I have. I wasn't certain this was the right way, but after seeing you, I suppose that I'm on the right track." Gart lowered his wooden weapon and stuck the butt end in the snow so he would not appear quite so defensive. "And what, exactly, are you?"

The stones continued their steady rotation, and the sphere drifted slowly towards Gart. "I have been asked to guard the path. None shall pass this way without permission from the Mage. You say you are such a one, but that has yet to be determined."

"Well then, oh pile of stones, how do we determine that? Brunar said there's a weapon in there that only I can wield. I'm here to claim it, and it's important that I do so."

The sphere tightened in on itself and its rotation intensified. Gart tensed and hoped he had not said the wrong thing. After a few moments, the stones replied, "No Chosen has ever walked this path without their Jidaan in hand. The one you hold is wooden. What is the Word of Passage? All Guardians know it."

Gart scowled as he strained to remember if the Mage had mentioned a password of any kind, though he knew Brunar had not. "Brunar didn't say anything about a 'Word of Passage' when he tried to get me to come here. I have no idea what it might be."

The rumbled reply came quickly. "That is unfortunate. If you do not know the Word of Passage, then I cannot allow you to continue to the Keep. Please depart in peace, lest I be forced to deal with you."

Gart grimaced. He had an idea what that meant, and it meant nothing good. Frustration rose in him, but he took a few deep breaths to steady himself and managed to dispel it. His whole life, Gart had responded to every challenge with anger. It had always worked before, but things were different now. This was no village bully picking on him, easily cowed by his quick temper and willingness to back that temper with his fists. Even with his magick, this creature could easily crush him, and although Beauty was formidable, she'd end up crushed as well. Getting angry would be no help against this creature. The rock thing was apparently just fulfilling its purpose as a sentry; it was even civil about it. Gart sighed and decided on a different approach.

"Have you a name? If we're going to talk, I'd like to call you something, and I, uh, don't want to be impolite."

The creature was silent for a moment, its stones slowed in their swirling. "No one has ever asked for my name before. You may call me Orith, thank you."

"All right, then...Orith it is. I'd say it's a pleasure to meet you. I've never thought something like you existed, but then, I've run across many things lately that fit that description. The Lady RaeLynn said that there would be those who would help me on my way, but I don't know that she meant you in particular."

The stones began to spin faster again, and a tone of excitement crept into the rumbling voice. "The Lady of the Lake sent you?"

Gart felt hope flicker within him. This was a good sign. Beauty's tail started to wag at the change in tone.

"In a manner of speaking, yes. I was attacked by a group of Gholans while I was tracking their leader. Someone...a Weya, I think...tossed me into her lake. She healed me and somehow moved me much closer to this mountain than I had been when I was when I spoke to her. She told me that if I wanted to have any chance at beating Jor Dayne and Mordak," the stone sphere instantly tightened in upon itself and spun even faster at the mention of Mordak's name. Gart continued, "She said that I would need the Jidaan. I got here as fast as I could."

The gravelly voice of Orith deepened with anger. "The one you call Jor Dayne is unknown to me, but Mordak is vile and evil. This, I know." More calmly, the stone creature continued. "The Lady RaeLynn is very well known to us. She would not send you here unless you were, indeed, Chosen. Did Brunar give you a token?"

"A token? No, I don't think..." Gart suddenly remembered the emerald he wore. He had long since forgotten it underneath his coat and cloak. Quickly, he pulled it out and was astonished to see it glowing brightly, its deep green light shining against the white snow. He removed the necklace and held it before him, letting the emerald dangle freely so that Orith could see its gleam.

The sentinel drifted closer, close enough that the emerald glow reflected off the nearest of Orith's stones as they swirled past. Gart's breath caught in his chest as he felt the power that radiated from the elemental being, immense and deeply strong. Silently, he waited as the creature seemed to observe the glowing pendant.

"Chosen, you shall pass. Follow the road upwards, and you will find the Keep. Your Destiny lies within."

The stones of Orith immediately broke away from the whirling sphere and sailed towards the face of the mountain above the outline of the door. It took only a moment for Gart to see that each stone was seeking its own particular hollow. One by one, they sank into their individual divots with apparent eagerness. As the final, largest stone drifted into place, there was a thump deep within the rock, and a grinding sound could be heard above the wind.

The stone within the outline of the door Gart had discovered was rotating, slowly turning clockwise, gradually exposing an opening that grew larger as it turned into place. Moments later, the turning stopped with another loud thump in the earth, and there before him lay a wide tunnel leading to the other side of the mountain.

Gart stared into the passageway, noticing its gentle upwards slope. It was long enough that he could not see the end, but light was filtering in from the other side. He was almost there. Without another word, he whistled for Beauty to follow him as he hustled to the cabin to prepare Bessie for the next leg of his journey. The Jidaan was within his grasp, and Gart wanted to waste no time getting his hands on it.

Chapter 21

There seemed no end to the hideous army Mordak had created. Wave after wave of viciously howling Gholans and Morcats swarmed up the wall to be cut to pieces by the determined defenders. Alyssa and the Sisters of Rowann did the best they could, but hundreds had died. Those still fighting were covered with stitches and bandages aplenty. The Duke was exhausted, yet he continued to fight. His sword rose and fell constantly, hewing down anything that climbed his wall.

The dead had been coming more often, and soldiers had to cut down friends with whom they had fought side-by-side only moments before. They kept fighting, even with severed limbs, pulling themselves towards the surviving soldiers with whatever arms or legs they still possessed. Tears covered many faces as the defenders furiously did battle with their former comrades, and morale was low. Still, they fought on.

The afternoon sun shone off of the Laroan swords and axes where they weren't covered with blood, and glinted off the wickedly sharp talons and teeth of Mordak's hideous creatures. Every so often, the monsters would pull back, giving the soldiers a brief respite before the Morcats howled and drove the smaller Gholans back up the wall.

During one of these pauses, Brunar found his way to the Duke, who shook his head as the Mage came near. "We can't last much longer. We'll have to retreat to the keep soon, and I don't know how long we'll hold out after that. We have supplies for weeks in there, but we may not be able to keep them out for that long once they breach the wall."

"Indeed," Brunar was grim but resolute. "We've got to find a way to get as many people out of here as we can, but I don't yet see how it can be done."

"Can't your Guardian use his Gates to get my people out?"

Brunar shook his head. "His range is far too limited. Mordak has us surrounded, and the very farthest he could reach is still well within the midst of Mordak's army. At that distance, he could only make a Gate big enough for one person at a time. It would be like sending lambs to the slaughter. If I could lure Mordak close enough, I might be able to do something, but even then..." Brunar's voice trailed off as both he and Duke Gensen remembered how Mordak had shrugged off a mortal wound.

Just then, the Morcats signaled another attack, their ferocious yowls cutting through the relative silence. The Duke took a deep breath and let it out. He clapped Brunar on the back and said, "We'll discuss this further, Mage. Sorry for the interruption." Turning to the soldiers nearest him, he bellowed, "All right, lads, a bonus to the soldier who kills the most Gholans this round!" A weak cheer answered him, and Duke Gensen strode away, standing tall with his shining sword held aloft. His presence gave strength to the weary fighters, and they gathered what energy they still had as the wave of bloodthirsty fiends made its way across the moat on its way to the wall.

Brunar walked to the barbican, where Kiran and Nessar had already gone through vast piles of arrows, and had just dumped another armload on the ground between them. Nessar still had a small bundle of bolts remaining for his crossbow, but had also found a longbow and had it close at hand. Kiran was rolling her head from side to side, eliciting soft pops as she did so. Nessar was sitting on a stone, his chin on one hand, his eyes closed. "How are you two holding up here?" the Mage asked.

Kiran nocked an arrow to string, and replied, "Just peachy, Brunar. They haven't come close to breaching my gate, but I'm almost out of arrows. Usually, I'd at least be able to gather up whatever they sent my way and shoot them right back, but these little creeps don't use bows. It's frustrating!" She drew her bow and let fly an arrow that took a Gholan in the head just as it reached the wall below. Kiran looked over her shoulder to see her old friend still sitting with his chin on one hand, unmoving, as if in deep thought—or sound asleep. "Nessar. Ness. Nessar, wake up!" When he didn't answer, Kiran reached out and lightly kicked at his leg.

Without opening his eyes, he deftly caught her foot with his free hand and let it drop. "I'm awake, baby girl. I was just resting my eyes." He stood and stretched. Kiran rolled her eyes at him as she picked off another Gholan below. Nessar leaned over her shoulder with his crossbow and took out a Morcat that was just reaching the bottom of the wall.

Brunar walked over to the edge of the battlements and watched the Gholans and Morcats climb towards them. As they neared the top, Brunar held up both hands and began whispering words of Power. His quiet voice chanted melodically and his outstretched hands took on a violet glow that intensified as he spoke. His voice rose and his hands started to shake as the brightness slowly became too much to bear. With a final syllable, Brunar clapped his hands. The light around his hands vanished, leaving the others blinking and shaking their heads. For a moment, nothing happened.

Nessar spoke first. "Well, what was that all about? I saw no explosions, fire, or Gholans dropping dead out there." He squinted out over the battlefield, watchful for signs of magick.

Brunar leaned heavily on the battlements, his breath ragged. "Just watch the wall, Ness. Watch the wall," and he pointed across to where the defenders awaited the uppermost of the climbing monsters.

All eyes followed Brunar's gesture. The first wave of Morcats and Gholans was almost within reach of the soldiers who bravely awaited them, weapons ready. Yowling and screeching with a mad glee, the brutes climbed quickly up the rough stone. Suddenly, the topmost started frantically flailing about. They were sliding back down the wall, unable to catch a clawhold on the stone. Faster they slid, taking those below with them and ending up in a massive jumble of angry arms and legs down below. Furious, the creatures screamed harshly, and some even turned on each other in their frustration. Again and again, they attacked the wall only to find they could get no grip on it. Bewildered defenders cheered and slapped each other on the back. They had no idea why the monsters had slipped, but they were thrilled about it. Many took the opportunity to rain down arrows, rocks, and other debris, crushing backs and cracking skulls below.

Kiran turned to Brunar with an eyebrow raised. "Well that's a neat trick. Took you long enough to throw it. We've been fighting forever out here. Where was that two days ago?"

Alarmed, Nessar grabbed her arm. "Kiran!"

Brunar laughed sadly and put up a placating hand. "It's fine, Nessar; she's right. I could have cast this particular spell at any time, but it takes a lot out of me and I wanted to wait until it would give our people a bit more rest. The walls will be too slippery for the creatures to climb for an hour or so, but I can do nothing more while the spell is in effect."

Kiran snorted, but said no more. Brunar was looking away from her, and she took the opportunity to really, truly look at him. The man was wrung out, as were they all. Dark circles had appeared in the hollows of his eyes and he moved slowly, almost painfully. Although she doubted he was at the edge of his power, he was getting close. She knew from the limited use of her own magick that it drained a person in ways that transcended the physical. Her weapon bore the brunt of the power that she was able to use but it still took a heavy toll on her to engage her Gift, even for a few moments. Brunar had been wielding his magick for days in defense of the entire city, using astounding amounts of power. She realized that his exhaustion was very likely deeper than she could ever imagine. She let out a sigh and put her hand on the Mage's arm.

"Sorry if I was prickly, Brunar. All that wailing down there is just making me irritable," she said, her voice low and apologetic. His hand, long fingers shaking slightly, covered hers.

"It's all right, Kiran." He looked and sounded like a much older man than the Brunar that had trained her back in the mountains. With an effort, Brunar straightened up and took a deep breath. He wasn't finished yet. Kiran smiled as she saw him gathering strength, and was pleased to hear the steel in his voice when he spoke again. "Let's get back to it. We've got to figure out a way to either stop this attack or get everyone out of here. If not, then this is nothing more than a prelude to a massacre. I had no idea he'd bring a force of such vast numbers."

Suddenly, an opalescent Gate appeared next to them and Layton stepped halfway through it, leaving the rest of his body elsewhere. It shimmered around him, sparkling, even in the sunshine. The young warrior looked around, as if to be sure he'd arrived where he had intended.

"Hello, Kiran...Nessar," They nodded in greeting and Layton continued. "Brunar, I've spotted something, and I think you need to see it. Come with me, if you please." With that, he disappeared into the glittering doorway.

Brunar quickly moved to follow him. "I'll return soon. Tell the Duke about the spell on the wall," he said as he disappeared into the portal. It winked out of existence as soon as he was through.

Kiran looked at Ness for a moment and then shrugged. "I'll do it. It'll do me good to stretch my legs," she said. Jabbing a finger at Nessar, she admonished, "Don't let any of those little maggots through here...this is *my* gate!" Before Nessar could reply, she strode off to find the Duke.

On the high tower Layton and Bjarke had used earlier, Layton pointed into the distance as Brunar squinted in an attempt to see what the young man had spotted.

"There was a flare of red out there. It looked like your magick, Brunar, but had that sickly red color." Layton grimaced as he remembered the flare of scarlet radiance that had animated the dismembered corpses.

Brunar's gaze reached out over the devastated town of Laro in search of Mordak's crimson glow. He found it in the hills to the far north of the castle. "Yes, I know it well. He's throwing his power around, but to what end?" Turning back to the young warrior, Brunar said, "Layton, make a gate up there, please." He pointed to a spot high in the air out over the town, far from the safety of the castle.

Layton was puzzled for a moment, then realization dawned on his face, bringing a grin with it. "Ah, you want to lean out and look from there! For a moment, I thought you were going to fly!"

Brunar chuckled briefly, "Well, there's a certain amount of floating I can accomplish, but that height would be far beyond my limits."

Layton ignited his power again and created a Gate high in the air where the Mage had indicated, twin to the one that sprang into being right next to them on the balcony. The strain of holding the Gates open at that distance caused sweat to drip down Layton's smiling face, but they held steady. Brunar leaned into the nearest Gate and his head and torso appeared on the other side. The wind at that height was stronger, and it ruffled his hair and beard. The air was clearer away from the castle, lacking the smells of blood, fire, and death that had been so pervasive there. Brunar took a deep, welcome breath before scanning the grounds below. It took only moments for him to find Mordak's foul magick.

To the north, the forest crawled into rocky hills, the dark green of the trees leading into a gray stone labyrinth of valleys and hollows. In one particular canyon, bursts of sickly crimson light were visible, exploding from within the folds of the land. They continued for a few heartbeats more, then stopped. Brunar leaned out a little farther and shielded his eyes from the sun with one hand, straining to see the results of Mordak's work. Although he could not determine what Mordak was doing, he could clearly see the Krell hard at work below, building some kind of structures at frightening speed.

Suddenly, a bloody red flash appeared at the entrance to one arroyo, and the radiance immediately started growing in size. Brunar's eyes widened as he realized it wasn't growing, but was instead speeding directly for him. He pulled back through the Gate and fell to the stones on the balcony, yelling, "Close it! Close it!"

Layton allowed the Gate to vanish, but too late. A burst of scarlet power came through the closing Gate at an upwards angle, pulverizing the balcony roof. Bits of rock and dust fell down on Brunar and Layton, but they had escaped the worst of the blast. Layton helped Brunar to his feet.

"Well, Brunar?" Layton asked as the Mage dusted off his robe. "What did you see? Could you tell what he's doing out there?"

The expression on Brunar's face was grim. "Nay, Layton, it was still too far away." Shaking his head, Brunar continued, "Get me back to the Duke, right away. Whatever Mordak is doing out there cannot be good for us."

Layton's mouth tightened, and he nodded. Quickly, he looked over the balcony at the battlements below. It took only a moment to find the Duke, seeing to the repositioning of soldiers, shuffling rested warriors in to take the place of those who were already spent. Layton took a deep breath, smiled, and another Gate appeared. He gestured to the Mage to step through.

Brunar noted that the lad's skills were improving remarkably quickly. He was obviously exhausted, as were they all. In spite of that, the young man was using his Gift more than all of the other Guardians combined. A rueful smile appeared briefly on the Mage's lips as he amended his thought. *By now, though, Alyssa's likely the most practiced of them. I hope she's well.*

On the battlements, Duke Gensen was startled to see Brunar and Layton step out of one of the lad's bright circles of opalescent light. He'd almost gotten used to Layton's mode of travel, but not quite. He recovered his composure quickly, and addressed Brunar. "What news, sir Mage?"

Brunar's voice was grim. "The sorcerer is up to something, but I cannot see exactly what. Even so, I have the feeling that the assault will intensify soon, and they will eventually breach the wall. We need to do two things..."

Duke Gensen cut him off, "Fight them off and prepare the retreat to the keep at the same time."

"Exactly. We've done well to keep them out for this long, but that may change soon. He's got the Krell building structures out there, some kind of siege towers, I'm thinking. That's why they haven't been part of the main assaults here. When the attack comes, I think we may have no choice but to retreat."

The Duke looked out over the field, trying to see the structures Brunar had mentioned. Finally he spotted them—they were hastily built wooden platforms, but sturdy enough. Fitted atop each other with ladders inside, they would make a tower that could be pushed up against the outer wall. The uppermost wall of the top chamber would then fall onto the battlements, making a ramp for the Krell to traverse.

"It looks like it will take them some time to fit those chambers on top of each other, Brunar, and then they'll have to navigate the moat. Even though they've clogged it and bridged it in places, they should have a rough time getting those things close enough to be a danger." The Duke's gray eyes scoured the distant construction sites.

"Unfortunately, they'll have Mordak's magick behind them," Brunar countered. "I believe that they'll come sooner than you think. And I saw bursts of Mordak's power back in the hills," he pointed and Duke Gensen followed with his eyes. "He's busy out there, but doing what, I simply can't guess." The two men stared off into the distance, but the sparks of ill magick had vanished. Even so, Brunar knew what he had seen. Something was coming.

Although battered from the escaping Ogre's blow, massive rider Jor Dayne rode back and forth near the castle moat. He had found another war horse and now delighted in taunting the defenders on the wall. Every arrow they winged at him went astray or bounced off the small shield he had strapped to his broken left arm. Any other man would have been felled by the pain of an arrow hitting a shield positioned thus, secured directly to a broken limb, but the pain was nothing to Jor Dayne. Indeed, it was a welcome sensation after the Void from whence he had come. He intended to use his stolen body to the full and experience every nuance of human feeling.

As he rode, he suddenly jerked in the saddle as if struck. Mordak had summoned him with a mental call that had hit him with such force he had nearly been unhorsed. He shook his head to clear it and wiped a forearm across his face to catch the blood that had momentarily gushed from his nose. Enjoying the pounding headache that had suddenly erupted in his temples, Jor Dayne regained control of his horse and angled it away from the castle, towards the heart of the horde. His master had beckoned.

Within the keep, a flurry of activity had begun. The wounded had been carried away from the original infirmary and taken to an inner chamber, more easily protected. Supplies had been moved, barricades had been readied, and the citizens inside the massive castle were preparing for the worst.

From deep within the lowest reaches of the castle, Cohl and Ginn sprinted up the stairs towards the main floor. They had been in meditation in the Royal Crypt ever since the battle had begun, and had walked the entire castle in spirit many times over. It had taken days, but they had found something at last. Dodging the people of Laro with the natural agility of the Weya, they wove through the crowd like ghosts, leaving stunned faces in their wake.

Cohl spoke, mind-to-mind, with ValElder Moihra as he ran. *We found a way out, ValElder. I doubt the Duke will like it, though.* He sent her a brief explanation of their discovery and felt her flinch through their mental connection.

Go and tell him. It will be the difference between life and death for these people.

Cohl ran on, his soft boots making almost no sound on the stone floor, Ginn running smoothly alongside. They found the massive front door heavily barred and reinforced, but a smaller door was nearby. They slowed long enough to nod at the startled guard before bursting through it and into the courtyard, squinting their jewel-like eyes in the brightness of the sun. It took only moments for them to find the Mage. His power tingled on the air and in their bones, and they felt him strongly enough that they could have found him anywhere in the castle. Barely touching the stone steps, they found their way to the top of the wall and easily wove through the milling warriors until they had reached the Mage's side.

"What have you found?" Brunar's voice was hopeful.

The two Weya glanced at each other before replying. Cohl spoke first. "We think we have found a way out, a huge passage leading away from the Royal Crypt. It leads to the west, and is big enough that everyone here could likely make it out." Their expressions were stern, and Brunar felt their tenseness.

"I would think that would be good news, but I sense that there's a catch. What is it?"

There was a moment of silence before Ginn replied. "There's an intricate spell cast upon the entrance, which is currently nothing more than a blank wall of stone. To open it, the stones must reorganize themselves in such a way that the castle will implode. Everyone will have to be ready to move, for the castle will fall only minutes after the way is opened."

"What do you mean, 'the castle will implode?' Can't we just break through the stone? Or have your man, Layton, Gate us there?" Duke Gensen had walked up just as the Weya started talking to Brunar. He had heard the tentative escape plan, and was aghast at the thought of the castle's destruction.

Brunar turned to the Duke to explain, "Layton can only Gate to places he can see or has already seen," he looked at Ginn again. "Could we simply break through the stones, leaving the surrounding structure intact?"

Ginn shook his head, "No, Sir Mage, not only is the wall there incredibly thick, but the builders somehow tied the entire support system into that particular wall with a powerful enchantment. Once it goes, the castle will begin to crumble in upon itself with great force, killing anyone who remains within. It will take but a few minutes, then the castle will be nothing more than a massive pile of rubble."

The Duke grunted in frustration and turned to look at the fortress he had protected ever since he had come of age. It had been the refuge and pride of the Laroan people for centuries, and was filled with memories, relics, and priceless artifacts. Thousands had called it home over the years, and many traveled far simply to view it from outside. His father and his father before him had walked its many halls, as had many fathers before that. It was a piece of living history. Duke Gensen let his eyes rove over its walls and towers for a moment longer before bringing his gaze back to the Weya, who had waited quietly for his response. The Duke drew himself to his full height and took a deep breath.

"The castle, though much loved, is just a castle. Naught but stone and wood. Make ready to get our people out if it comes to that. Find Rorian and enlist his aid, you will need him. Drattus!" Duke Gensen bellowed over his shoulder and the captain immediately made his way over to them.

"Yes, Your Grace?" Drattus was worn and dirty, and new gashes in his mail showed that he had been in the thick of the fighting.

"Go with them and see that what needs to be done is done, and quickly." Duke Gensen clapped the man on his shoulder, lending his own strength to the tired Captain. Drattus nodded, slammed his fist over his heart as he bowed slightly, and then looked to the Weya.

Both of the Weya bowed respectfully to the Duke as well and then glided away with Drattus close behind. They could feel the hurt emanating from the Duke at the thought of what might come--the destruction of his beloved castle. They also felt his love for his people, which eclipsed everything else. They knew he'd trade cold stone for flesh and blood any day. Although the Weya tended to stay aloof from humans, they liked this one. They had found most humans to be selfish and petty, but Duke Gensen was neither. Though passionate and volatile, he ruled his emotions with discipline, and had dedicated himself to the protection of the Laroan people. Moving easily through the gathered warriors, they went off to coordinate the evacuation, determined to help the Duke's people as best they could.

Just then, Nessar said, "The creepies are pulling back. However, those, what do you call them...Krell? It looks like they're bringing us a gift."

Everyone moved quickly to the wall and peered out at the enemy. Sure enough, the Gholans, Morcats, and undead humans were making their way back across the rubble that had been piled across the moat. The Krell were massed around the platforms they had built. Their harsh, guttural language carried across the distance and grated on the nerves of all who heard it. There were several platforms, each resembling a three-walled cabin with no roof. Logs were run underneath each structure, providing the Krell with a way to lift the finished chambers. Jor Dayne rode among the beasts, directing their movements with loud commands and gestures from the point of his blade. As one, the Krell bent down, grabbed the wooden supports, and stood again, lifting the structures off the ground. One started chanting, and hundreds of bare feet began moving in unison, carrying the platforms towards the castle. There were no less than twenty of the wooden chambers being carried by the vicious humanoids.

"I've never seen the Krell before," the Duke declared, his eyes on the oncoming force.

Brunar's voice was grim. "Most who have are now dead, Your Grace."

Slowly, they came into view, and a murmur rolled through the warriors atop the wall. The Krell were a dark red-brown in color, with hair that ranged from black to brown. Many had their heads shaved but for a long ponytail behind, and some wore a strip down the center, spiked tall with dried mud. They were all heavily muscled, sinews bulging as they carried the weight of the platforms, and yet they moved with the athletic grace of the great hunting cats of the southern jungle. Their eyes were completely black, and their teeth were filed to sharp points. Tribal scars, intricate and deep, covered many of the warriors, telling tales of enemies conquered and slain. Armbands and bracelets of bone rattled and clinked together as they moved, making a macabre kind of music for them to march by. Those who did not carry the platforms strode alongside them, bearing the weapons of their burdened comrades. The sun glittered from the razor-sharp edges of brutal axes and short, hacking swords. Jor Dayne now rode ahead of the central structure, and behind him walked a handful of the largest, strongest Krell, each nearly the size of Jor Dayne, himself. Thousands of them marched relelentlessly towards the castle, bringing death closer with every bare-footed step.

"Archers!" the Duke yelled. Tired though they were, the army of Laro moved with impressive precision as the command was relayed down the wall, foot soldiers moving aside to allow the archers to take their place at the battlements. "Let's see if we can slow them down when they come in range. Make those arrows count. And give that gods-blasted Jor Dayne a few feathers in his hat as well!" The archers waited for the Krell to make their move.

Nessar moved closer to the Mage, keeping his squinted eyes on the oncoming force. "Brunar, what are they playing at? I've seen siege towers before, and those aren't even close to being tall enough to reach up here."

"I'm not quite sure, Ness, but Mordak has a plan. We'll have to see what it is before we can counter it, I'm afraid."

As if the mention of his name had conjured his presence, Mordak glided through the horde, coming to rest alongside Jor Dayne. The army stopped short of the moat, and the Krell moved to surround the castle on all three exposed sides, taking the structures with them. At a command from the huge Slayer, the Krell set the platforms down on the dusty ground. The bearers retrieved their weapons and then streamed into the open-roofed chambers until each was full of heavily armed warriors. There they waited.

"LOOSE!" The Duke's command was instantly echoed by his captains, and bowstrings twanged as a storm of arrows were sent on their way. They arced up, over, and then fell like rain on the exposed Krell.

Just before the arrows could find their marks, a shield of dull crimson light burst into being over the enemy army. The missiles struck the barrier, splintering or bouncing astray as they encountered its unexpected solidity. As quickly as it had appeared, the barrier vanished, leaving Mordak, Jor Dayne, and the Krell unharmed.

The Duke cursed colorfully and slammed his fist down on the wall. His frustration was felt by all, and no more arrows were loosed. Brunar laid his hand on the stone and whispered a few words of Power, sagging in relief as he finished.

"Brunar?" Kiran said, worried that he might fall.

"I'm fine, Kiran," he replied. "I doubt that the spell I cast on the wall will help us now, so I removed it. I'll need as much energy as I can muster, and soon, I fear." Gathering strength, he continued, "Let us see what the Evil One has in store for us."

The answer was not long in coming. Mordak turned to face the platforms and raised his hands. A nimbus of light the color of blood appeared around him, and the air became charged with foul magick. The defenders clutched their weapons apprehensively, watching to see what the vile sorcerer would do.

On the east and west sides of the castle, two platforms suddenly lifted off the dusty ground, leaving a few feet of empty space underneath. On the north, two more platforms floated up as well, awaiting Mordak's command. The brightness that surrounded him intensified, and with a gesture, he sent all of the Krell-filled structures across the moat, bringing them right up to the base of the wall on each side where he set them down gently. The same hazy reddish light covered the open tops of the wooden chambers, deflecting the few arrows that were sent down at the Krell.

Beyond the moat, Mordak gestured again, and more platforms lifted off the ground. They floated across the moat to settle atop the first structures, doubling their height and bringing the feral warriors closer to the top of the wall. Their sharpened teeth gnashed with manic glee as they glared up at their enemy, their black eyes shining like pools of ink.

"He's building his damned siege towers right in front of us!" shouted the Duke. "Ready the pikes! Push those demons over as soon as they are within reach!"

Mordak's laughter rang out over the battlefield, echoing between the curtain wall and inner wall of the castle. It seemed to be everywhere at once, and his scorn and triumph squeezed the hearts of all who heard it.

From atop one of the towers, a low, rumbling hum suddenly vibrated through the stones. Magick flared, and a massive bolt of energy leapt from Bjarke's Jidaan to strike one of the platforms that remained on the ground. It shattered into a thousand pieces, and Krell warriors screamed defiance even as they died in the blast. In answer, Mordak brought his own power to bear. A bolt of sickly crimson lightning, laced with darkest black, lanced from his outstretched fingers. Soldiers dove for cover as the lightning scrawled across the stone of the wall and Bjarke's tower, incinerating any flesh it found there. Men died screaming as their bodies melted under Mordak's evil energy.

"BigBear!" Kiran yelled. Instinctively, she threw a Ward up around the tower, a glowing sphere of energy as blue as the sky above. She convulsed as Mordak's power raked over it and she felt the acid touch of his magick as though it had actually reached her. She gasped in agony as she fell to the stones, eyes clenched shut as she battled the pain. Others rushed to help her, but she had succeeded in protecting those on the tower, including Bjarke.

More platforms raised off the ground as the Krell swarmed over the shattered chamber, rebuilding it with frightening speed. Soon, it would be repaired enough to support another troop of Krell warriors, and would be added to the towers that would assault the walls. The other platforms glided easily over the moat, settling on top of the first and second chambers. Only one level remained before the towers would be tall enough to assault the battlements directly.

Brunar raised his hands and threw bolt after bolt of his own magick at the oncoming platforms, intent on slowing Mordak's progress. At every turn, he was blocked by the sorcerous madman whose power seemed inexhaustible. The Mage was, indeed, nearing his limit, and was more weary than he had ever been in his long life.

Suddenly, the Krell surged across the debris-filled moat, howling fierce war cries. Many had small, vicious bows that curved back on themselves, and they used them the moment they got close enough. Black-shafted arrows slammed into the defenders above, bringing cries of pain as they drove deep. Arrows sped back in return, striking down many of the enemy. Those were soon trampled into the bloody ground by others intent on taking the wall for their unholy god. Mordak's illusion had worked well, and the Krell were in a frenzy to please him.

Mordak lifted the final chambers into the air, each filled with eager Krell warriors, and sent them drifting towards the nearly-completed towers. As they approached, the defenders of Laro frantically pushed at them with their pikes and threw everything they had at the floating structures, but it was no use. Mordak settled the chambers in place, and for a moment, all was still.

At some unheard signal, the closest walls on the uppermost chambers of each tower dropped onto the battlements, each forming a ramp from the towers to the wall. Wicked hooks anchored the ramps, and Krell warriors poured out of the openings, hacking, stabbing, and clawing as the battle was joined.

The fighting was fierce, the people of Laro defending not only their own lives, but the lives of every living thing in the castle. The thought of their loved ones dying at the hands of such vicious creatures lent strength to their arms, but even so, the Krell were fresh and ferocious. Men and women fell from the walls, bleeding, broken, dying from gaping wounds left by Krell axe, sword, and spear. The Duke cursed aloud as he fought with all his might. Slashing left and right, he prepared to order the retreat.

Just then a loud, low hooting sound reached the Duke's ears. He had never heard the like of it, and the deep, animal grunting soon overwhelmed the war cries of the Krell. He saw the vicious humanoids look around in fear as though they had never heard it either.

It had come from the south, where the rear of the castle butted up against the River Corris. Mordak's horde had not massed there because the river was far too wide and swift to deal with. The sounds of combat rang up from the base of the walls at the southeastern and southwestern corners of the castle, though the Duke was mystified as to who was attacking.

"Drattus!" he yelled, cutting down another Krell warrior with a sweep of his sword. "What the devil is going on back there? We've got all we can handle here!"

As the captain dodged a spear thrust and stabbed the Krell in the face with his dagger, he panted in reply, "I know not! They're not ours; all of our fighters are in here with us!"

From around the back of the castle, still dripping wet from the River Corris, the Fist of the Augenan had come. The giant red gorilla-people plowed into the Krell with warhammer, club, massive fists, and sharp teeth, overwhelming them with sheer bestial strength and ferocity. The Krell feared nothing, and flung themselves at their new enemies only to be broken and bashed without mercy. Long, furry arms lashed out in every direction and the gorilla-folk used their immense strength to shatter every Krell they touched. A thousand strong, the Augenan fought their way from the back around to the front of the castle, pulling down the Krell towers on the east and west sides of the curtain wall as they went, killing every Krell inside. They had apparently come from across the river to the south, and Brunar shook his head in amazement as he realized that each and every one of them must have swum across the swift current of the river to reach the castle.

The moment Brunar caught a glimpse of the huge gorilla people, hope rose anew within him. The Augenan were a noble race of fierce warriors. That they were attacking the Krell was a very good sign. Although he had no idea how they had come to be near the city of Laro, Brunar was not one to question such gifts.

Across the field of battle, Mordak screamed in fury. He reached a hand towards Jor Dayne, who was mounted on his warhorse nearby, and with a clench of his fist, yanked the Slayer through the air to grovel on his knees at Mordak's feet. Looking into Jor Dayne's serpent-yellow eyes, Mordak saw no fear there, only an insane glee as the daemon within the man enjoyed the sensations that coursed through his human body.

"Send the Gholans, the Morcats, and the rest of the Krell, every single one of them! Destroy those damnable apes and take that castle!" he ordered. Grabbing Jor Dayne's muscular throat with one hand, Mordak augmented his strength with magick and squeezed tightly.

"As...as you wish...Lord!" Jor Dayne barely managed the words through the strangling hand of his master. The sorcerer released him, and the Slayer clutched his throat as he struggled to breathe. Gasping, taking in the smell of fire, blood, and death, Jor Dayne recovered and got back to his feet, towering over Mordak. A huge smile crossed his face and stayed there as he remounted his horse. It reared and whinnied in anger as he sat atop it, but he pulled on the reins and quickly regained control. Using the words he had been taught, he called to the creatures that had stepped back to allow the Krell to lead the assault. A sea of hideous faces turned towards him, then looked eagerly back at the castle, hungry to be on the attack once more. Mordak's Champion drew his sword and yelled for the charge as he kicked his horse into action, racing for the moat and the castle beyond it. Thousands of evil creatures followed him, lusting for the reward of human flesh.

On the wall, Brunar watched the Augenan lay into the Krell, killing them at every turn. The gorilla folk possessed awesome strength, and were far faster than their great size might suggest. They crushed the enemy, smiting them with their clubs and war hammers, and even used their bare hands to good effect. Soon, the Krell began to know fear.

Although his dealings with the Augenan had been few and very far between, Brunar knew that they would never travel this far from the jungles of Triagga without their leader. He scanned the frenzied battle below and found him almost immediately. Towering over the others, he swung a massive double-bitted axe, and wove a tapestry of death through the screaming Krell.

Layton! Brunar called with his mind. *I need to speak to their leader, the one with the axe, right now! Gate him to me, quickly!* He sensed that Layton was fighting on the western wall, cutting his way through the Krell as though they were standing still. A mental grunt of acknowledgement came back, and the Mage knew that he had been heard.

A few moments passed and one of Layton's opalescent Gates appeared right behind the massive warrior down below. Even as the mighty creature clove an attacking Krell nearly in half, the Gate swiftly moved forward to engulf him, moving him and placing him a few paces away from Brunar atop the gatehouse. The great warrior was startled, but quickly focused on the human before him. The man was down on one knee with his head bowed, and held his hands high to show that he carried no weapons. The Augenan's eyes narrowed as he assessed the Mage. Blood from the recently departed Krell dripped from the huge blades of his axe and pattered on the stones beneath their feet.

"We mean you no harm, mighty one! We thank you for attacking those who beseige us." Brunar kept his eyes downcast until he was sure the huge gorilla understood that he was not a threat.

The beast snorted through his cavernous nostrils, looking quickly around at the humans that surrounded him. Although obviously startled, none had moved to attack him, busy as they were fighting off the monsters that climbed the wall. He decided that the man nearest him meant no harm. Holding the axe between its razor-edged blades, he let the butt-end rest on the stones at his feet. Although his legs were short in relation to the rest of his body, he was still a formidable figure, towering head and shoulders over Brunar. Enormous muscles played beneath the reddish fur of his arms and legs, and he radiated a raw, inhuman power. Beneath his massive eyebrow ridges were a pair of surprisingly humanlike eyes that shone with intelligence. Copper ornaments glittered on his biceps, wrists, and his iron helmet. Copper also accented his burnished iron breastplate, and a brief kilt of leather protected his lower body.

"I am Ch'shok," his voice came out as a deep, bass rumble that Brunar felt as well as heard. The sheer strength of presence that Ch'shok possessed was staggering. Struggling to find the words in the common tongue, he continued, "I have brought the Fist to aid your people. This battle is good! Very good to fight those..." Ch'shok sneered and nodded towards the Krell below, "...things. More creatures come, though. The Fist is strong, but we will not beat them all."

"That may be, mighty Ch'shok, but you have given us valuable time to regroup. We can get all of your warriors behind this wall so that we can decide what to do next, and you've certainly stopped the Krell from getting in here for now. Please allow us to bring your people inside. We can do it quickly."

"The same way you brought me up here? That is powerful <magick>."

Brunar nodded. "Yes, mighty one, just the same. But we'll put your people on the ground below," he said, pointing to the area between the curtain wall and the main keep.

Ch'shok tugged at the copper baubles that were braided into his short beard as he turned things over in his mind. He grunted sharply and nodded once. "Put me back there," he pointed to the battlefield below. "I will rally the Fist. You make the door, we will enter." He picked up his great battle-axe and readied himself.

Brunar called Layton through the Guardians' mindlink, and Ch'shok instantly found himself back on the ground at the base of the wall. His Augenan warriors had destroyed all of the siege towers and were handily mopping up the few Krell that remained. "<To me! To me! Rally to me, my brave Augenan warriors!>" With amazing precision and speed, the gorilla people began shifting their positions, even as they continued to battle the last of the bloodthirsty Krell. Although many of the red-furred warriors now bore wounds, they had not lost a single fighter, having won through with surprise and ferocity. Seeing them all moving towards him with such confidence and strength made Ch'shok's heart swell with pride.

The roar of oncoming Gholans, Morcats, and the remainder of the Krell grew louder as the evil horde rapidly approached the moat, preparing to swarm over the newcomers. Although hundreds of Krell now lay dead or dying nearby, thousands remained. On they ran, brandishing their weapons of blackened steel, bloodlust singing in their dark hearts.

Without warning, a huge, writhing wall of flame appeared on the far side of the moat, and Mordak's fell creatures frantically skidded to a stop to avoid being incinerated. The towering flames were twenty feet high, and so thick that nothing could be seen through them. Gnashing their teeth, the creatures yowled and screeched in frustration. Behind them, Mordak shook his fist in rage as he tried to find a way to extinguish the barrier.

Brunar's hands were glowing as he fueled the spell that had raised the fiery wall. It was nothing more than an illusion, given a touch of heat to scare the enemy, but neither Mordak nor his army knew that just yet.

Layton, bring the Augenan into the courtyard inside the wall, right now! Put a Gate near Ch'shok, the big one, and he'll guide them in. I'll get down there to help put them at ease. Brunar knew that often, relations between Augenan and humans were strained. Old feelings died hard in the jungle, and humans had a history of being less than kind to the gorilla folk.

If the huge, reddish warriors were surprised by the glowing opalescent Gate that appeared next to their revered leader, they did not show it. Ch'shok started herding the first of his warriors into the huge circular portal, which looked like a massive, glowing coin stood on end, its surface a pool of shimmering colors. In rapid and orderly fashion, they filed into the Gate and appeared on the other side of the great wall, where they were quickly met with words of welcome from three captains of Laro. Soon, a thousand and one Augenan warriors were safe behind the wall, their eyes wary as they surveyed their new surroundings. Relieved, Brunar allowed the illusory wall of flames to disappear.

Mordak's horde surged forward when the flames vanished, making their way quickly across the debris-filled moat. This time, the Krell sent a hail of black-shafted arrows hurtling up at the defenders, protecting those who assaulted the wall from below. Men screamed as the deadly quarrels slammed into them, killing some, wounding others badly. One hit Brunar, but glanced from the skin-shield of magick he had enabled when the battle had started. The force of it rocked him, but the arrow bounced harmlessly away. He dropped down behind the merlons to gather his strength. Atop the wall, the defenders loosed their own deadly hail of arrows, killing many of the horrendous attackers below.

Nessar knelt at Brunar's side, checking on the Mage, while Kiran continued to use her bow to good effect.

"Are you all right, Mage?" Nessar's sure hands moved over Brunar's shoulder and upper body, but found no wounds. Brunar did not answer right away and Nessar continued, "I've got to learn that shield trick from you, old man. You showed us that back at the Hall of Jidaana, but never showed us how to do it."

Brunar turned his tired gaze on the former thief. He had come to like the crusty oldster in spite of his general surliness. Time and again, Nessar had displayed a deep respect for his fellow Guardians and helped in many ways, though complaining loudly even as he did so.

"Indeed, Nessar, I've seen more than enough years to be called 'old man' by you," a tired grin crossed his face as he elbowed Nessar gently, "but at least I still have my looks."

Kiran overheard and started snickering, even as she sent another arrow into the mass below. Nessar waggled a finger at her. "You hush! That laughing is disrespectful!" Thoroughly ignored by Kiran, Ness turned back to the Mage and helped him stand up, wary of more incoming quarrels from below. "Well, I'm glad to see that you're fit enough to joke, Mage. Who are they? That big one turning up like that just about scared the life out of me!"

"They are the Augenan, Nessar. They are a tribal people from the jungles of Triagga. I have no idea why they are here, but I'm glad to have them. They are mighty warriors, and for whatever reason, they are on our side." He looked at the milling crowd of Augenan and humans below and saw that the Duke was heading towards Ch'shok. "I'd better get down there," He turned back to Nessar. "Just keep picking them off, you two, and protect the gate as best you can. We will most likely have to retreat to the keep soon." With that, he set off toward the stairs that led to the courtyard.

"You heard the man, Grampy. Get over here and help me with these scumsuckers." Kiran feathered a Morcat that had nearly reached the top of the wall opposite her. Nessar walked over and crouched between the merlons, rearming his crossbow as he did so.

Down below, the Duke, Captain Drattus, and advisor Rorian were standing across from Ch'shok, his face a stern mask. He had seen the brutal efficiency with which the gorilla folk had dispatched the Krell. Although he was grateful, he was leery of having such powerful creatures within his walls without knowing who and what they were. A thousand huge Augenan warriors stood in ranks, swaying nervously back and forth as they awaited orders, their eyes darting in every direction. They looked more than a little concerned that they were hemmed in behind Laro's massive outer wall. The human warriors that surrounded them looked equally ill-at-ease. The shortest of the gorilla folk were taller than the humans and easily weighed several hundred pounds more. Even so, every man and woman on the walls had seen the Augenan fling themselves at the Krell, killing the entire breaching party. That gained the Augenan instantaneous respect and gratitude, and none of the Laroans would attack without the Duke's express orders. Indeed, seeing them up close, none of them *wanted* to start any trouble with the gorilla people.

"Are you ruler here?" Ch'shok's gravelly voice rumbled down at Duke Gensen.

"Yes, I am, sir. I am Duke Gensen, ruler of Laro. We are grateful for your intervention. Our warriors are near exhaustion, and those siege towers would surely have brought the Krell inside. Many of us would have died. I thank you." He sketched a short but respectful bow to the huge creature before him, gesturing for Drattus and Rorian to do the same.

Ch'shok was taken aback. No human had ever addressed him with such respect, even though he was the acknowledged High Chief of the Augenan. Moving slowly so that he would not startle the little human, Ch'shok carefully affixed the Tugan, his massive battle-axe, to its strap on his back. The High Chief nodded his head with exaggerated slowness towards the Duke in his best imitation of a bow, leaning heavily on the knuckles of both hands as he did so. Astonishment showed in the Duke's face, mingled with relief. He had only heard stories of the gorilla folk, and had never in his wildest dreams thought to meet one.

"I...am Ch'shok. High Chief. These," he swept one massive hand around to indicate the surrounding warriors, "are the Fist of the Augenan. They are clan Na'tam. Brave warriors. I also am clan Na'tam." A round of heavy grunts rolled through the Augenan, accompanied by the scattered pounding of chests as they voiced support for their Chief. He continued, "Our seer said we need be here to help you. What she saw, very bad. We come."

Duke Gensen nodded as he replied, "Yes, I think this counts as very bad. Thank you for coming to our aid...Ch'shok."

"Your warriors...tired. I send mine. My Augs all strong, ready to fight! Yours go rest. No enemy will get inside, I promise that."

The Duke's relief was visible. "I will leave some of my captains atop the wall in case you need them. Thank you, sir." Turning quickly to Drattus, he said, "Have our warriors leave the wall in shifts to recover. See to it, Captain, and quickly!"

Drattus saluted and sprinted towards the nearest set of stairs to relay the commands to the other captains. The brief rest they had gotten when the Augenan had attacked had ended as the remainder of Mordak's evil creatures crossed the moat and assailed the wall once more. The sounds of battle were thick as the defenders desperately hacked and slashed at anything and everything that poked its ugly head into view. Word of the Augenan relief was eagerly welcomed, and soon, Drattus waved that all was ready.

Ch'shok turned and loudly grunted a few short, harsh commands, accompanied with a few quick gestures of his massive hands. Immediately, the Augenan began hooting and bellowing war-cries as they burst into action, heading for the walls. Laroan soldiers were streaming down some stairs while others had been left empty for the Augenan to use, but they need not have bothered. Most of the gorilla folk simply climbed whatever structures they could find and swung their way to the wall walk with enthusiastic efficiency. At once, they began clearing the top of the wall of the enemy, swinging clubs, warbars, and hammers to good effect. Gholans, Krell, and Morcats fell in broken heaps on both sides of the wall, their heads and limbs shattered.

Ch'shok looked down at the Duke once again, pride showing in his bright eyes.

"They will fight good fight. I go help. You rest too...seem very tired." He carefully reached out one gigantic hand and completely covered the Duke's armored shoulder with it.

Duke Gensen was startled by the sheer weight and power of Ch'shok's hand, but tried not to show it. The thought of leaving the protection of the castle to someone else, anyone else, was alien to him. Even so, he felt the strength in that enormous hand and looked up into eyes that managed to convey not only intelligence and determination, but also a deep understanding of the feeling the Duke held for his people and his city. Ch'shok was a leader as well. The Augenan High Chief knew that sense of love and responsibility, and would defend the walls of Laro as though they had been built by his own massive hands. Leader to leader, the Duke bowed once more.

"Thank you, Ch'shok. I will rest for a short time, then fight again."

Ch'shok snorted, satisfied. In a flash, the big Aug reached up and freed his battle-axe from its harness. With a loud whoop and a grunt, he made for the top of the wall with amazing speed. The Duke and Rorian watched him go, then looked at each other. Duke Gensen spoke first.

"Glad they're on our side, Rorian?"

"Your Grace, I'm beyond glad," Rorian replied. "Ecstatic is more like it. Come, let's find a spot for you to rest."

Brunar fell in beside them as they walked toward the Keep. "You handled that brilliantly, Your Grace. Augenan are not known for dealing well with humans, but that is only because humans are always so disrespectful to them. Their command of our language is not good, but that does not mean they are not as intelligent as we are; they are quite astute. By showing respect to their leader, you will receive the same in return from each and every one of them."

The Duke shook his head. "It wasn't a plan, Mage, it just seemed the right thing to do. They saved us just then, no doubt about that, and I'm grateful. Now I'm going to spend an hour or so facedown on a bed somewhere. Please wake me if anything gets interesting." He clapped Brunar on the back before turning to head towards the infirmary. It was far closer than his own quarters and he knew that he could find a pallet there. Rorian followed along, intent on seeing his Duke settled in before finding a corner of his own where he could doze until needed again.

Brunar watched the battle from below, admiring the power and ferocity of the Augenan. Although he had seen them before, it had been centuries past, and to see them at war was an awesome thing. Using the mindlink that he shared with the Guardians, he told them he was going to retreat into meditation for a short time to gather his strength. Replies of varying intensity reached him, though Nessar remained quiet for several seconds until he suddenly burst into the conversation, sounding startled. Apparently, he had already been dozing, for real this time, until Kiran kicked him awake.

He has the right idea, Guardians, the Mage replied with his mind. *Take this chance to rest, for we will be needed again very soon. For now, allow the Augenan to shield us.*

The battle continued for the remainder of the afternoon. Hundreds of Gholans and Morcats climbed the walls, and the Krell started using tall ladders to make their way to the top, but the ferocious Augenan and newly rested Laroans held them at bay. The ranks of the undead swelled as brave warriors fell from the wall only to have their sightless eyes filled with a bloody, shining gleam that brought them to their feet once more. The Augenan lay where they fell, apparently immune to Mordak's magick.

The Duke stalked the wall after his brief rest, defending his city with brutal efficiency. After snatching a few moments of meditation, Brunar used his arts to harry the oncoming creatures mercilessly: sweeping them off the walls, turning the ground below into a sucking bog, and causing thorny vines to grow and entangle the legs of the hideous enemy. Seemingly numberless, they came on, callously stepping over their own dead as they did so.

Humans, Augenan, and Weya fought side by side, repulsing each wave of evil as the sun rode lower in the western sky. Resting in shifts and aided by Alyssa and the other healers, the defenders lost far fewer than they expected. Even so, the numbers of warriors on the wall dwindled. The Duke began to calculate how long they could remain before they would be forced to retreat to the Keep.

Outside the walls, Mordak watched the conflict with narrowed eyes. He had taken over a vacant dwelling and used his magick to blow out an entire wall facing the castle so that he could sit in comfort and watch his creatures attack. He had enjoyed watching the conflict over the last few days, savored the screams of the dying and felt the horror of the good people of Laro as their dead rose again to fight them. He sipped at a mug filled with wine as he went over the events of the last few days in his mind. The strong drink brought no relief as his anger rose.

The Harpies had done well at first, but then Brunar had somehow loosed those damnable gargoyles. The living statues had killed every last one of Mordak's flying creatures before suddenly falling out of the sky, their bodies again immobile as their enchantment had run out. The Ogres were making good progress until they had either been impaled or somehow freed from Mordak's compulsion. Even so, the sheer numbers of Mordak's horde would have eventually prevailed, but then the blasted Augenan had emerged from the river behind the castle, destroyed the Krell siege towers and decimated their ranks. Now that the gorilla-folk walked the walls, his army had made little progress. They had managed to pile their own dead at the base of the walls on all sides, making a grisly ramp to help them get to the top faster, but the ferocious might of the Augenans saw them all die as they strove to clamber onto the battlements.

Fast as a striking snake, Mordak flung the mug at the wall, shattering it and splashing wine in all directions. The Gholans who lurked nearby to satisfy Mordak's needs cowered in fear as he furiously stood and paced the room, keeping his eyes locked on the fortress, its walls yet standing in defiance of him. Filled with rage, he slammed his fists down on a nearby tabletop, breaking it to shards in his fury.

"Enough of this!" he growled. "It's time for me to show them that their puny wall is no match for my power!" Engaging his unholy magick, Mordak lifted himself until the soles of his boots hovered a few inches off the floor. Propelled by his will, the sorcerer glided out of the dwelling, leaving his confused Gholan servants behind. He moved off to the north, where he had prepared a little surprise for the good people of Laro.

Atop the wall, the defenders were weary beyond measure but still holding, bolstered by the unflagging strength of the Augenan. They fought with enthusiasm and gusto, only stopping when the combined attacks of tooth and claw and arrow and thrown axe finally dealt a death blow to one of the huge gorilla warriors.

Those that fell behind the wall had almost all been brought back from the dark halls of death by the curative Gift of Alyssa, who had ventured out of the infirmary to help. The Augenan were too heavy to be moved into the keep, and many died before Alyssa could reach them. The tiny healer now stalked the base of the walls with some of the Sisters, bringing her powerful Gift to bear where it was needed most. She helped many brave warriors rise again to defend Laro and its people. When the hideous creatures of Mordak fell, they received a different kind of assistance as Alyssa and the versatile nuns dispatched them with axe, dagger, and the flashing blade of the Jidaan.

"By the Goddess, we're holding, Brunar!" Duke Gensen had rested and eaten, and the fire had come back into his eyes. Atop the northwest tower of the curtain wall's battlements, the Duke saw a lull in the fighting around him as his warriors fought alongside the Augenan to clear the space. Brunar nodded in response as he used his staff to focus his power, blasting a Morcat off the wall nearby.

"Indeed, the Augenan may have helped us turn the tide; the numbers of the enemy are far less. Although thousands remain, many more lie slain outside." Brunar leaned on the edge of the wall, looking out at the masses of fell creatures that swarmed over the land, waiting for their opportunity to attack. The horde had noticeably diminished. "If we can keep them out of here, there's a slight chance he will call off the remainder and regroup. If he keeps this up, his numbers may dwindle so low they will become vulnerable."

"When this is over, I'm having a statue erected of these Augenan; they are mighty fighters!" The Duke turned, a sly smile forming on his tired face. "You've already got a monument, Mage."

Exhausted though he was, Brunar laughed with the Duke, relishing the brief pause in the fighting. Just then, his mind echoed with Kiran's voice, sounding more than a little concerned.

Mage, something is heading this way, and I don't like it one bit. Look to the north.

Brunar's expression hardened as his hawk-like eyes scanned that direction. He had seen flares of Mordak's power from within a valley out there earlier, but naught had come to pass. As he looked, he again saw bursts of the sickly scarlet radiance that he associated with the vile necromancer. Something huge moved in the distance, surrounded by the tell-tale signs of Mordak's power, but the Mage could not yet make it out.

Suddenly, silence fell outside Laro's wall. Looking down, Brunar saw the Gholans, Krell, and Morcats pulling back, deftly crossing the debris-laden moat to mass on the far side, followed soon after by the slower-moving undead. Rank after rank of the creatures stood patiently, waiting, as something evil drew near.

Bjarke strode along the wall walk towards the Duke and Brunar, sheathing his massive Jidaan as he came. "What do you make of it, sir Mage?" He squinted into the distance, but although his vision had improved mightily since the Choosing, he could not tell what approached.

All eyes faced the north as soldiers and Augenan peered into the distance, trying to decipher the new threat they would soon face. Before long, it became clear, and dread fell upon the defenders of Laro.

Pushed along by bursts of oily, crimson magick, a colossal boulder rolled and thumped towards the outer wall of Laro. More than twenty feet high, it crushed anything and everything in its path as its massive bulk moved jerkily toward the ruined town. Mordak's creatures were not immune to its enormous power, and many who were too slow to move aside were smashed into a grisly pulp as the huge mass rolled by. The shape of the immense whitish stone seemed familiar to the defenders, and terror began to work its way into their souls. As it drew closer, two vast hollows, two smaller slits for a nose, and an array of tombstone-like teeth came clearly into view, covered in spots with gore and blood from those it had already crushed. Its death's head grin and vacant eye sockets glared out at them, promising death and destruction as it drew closer to the wall.

"Is that...is that a...?" A soldier near the Duke forgot himself, he was so shocked at what seemed to be approaching.

"It looks like a skull," the Duke agreed as he watched the gigantic thing come closer with each passing moment.

Surely enough, a skull larger than any ever seen upon Talwynn was rapidly approaching the castle. It smiled grimly at the defenders as it finally rolled to a stop across the moat near the northernmost wall. Its huge, empty eye sockets seemed to be mocking the living as it gently rocked back and forth, settling into place. A soft, reddish light surrounded it. Glowing even more brightly than the skull, Mordak emerged from behind it. He strode confidently forward, a sneer on his face as he surveyed the terrified army that opposed him. He laid one hand on the side of the skull and poured magick into it, making it shine more intensely, its crimson glare glowing evilly as twilight fell. Jor Dayne rode up to stand on the opposite side of the skull, grinning in anticipation of the slaughter to come.

The bizarre relic sent horror sweeping through the men, women, and even the Augenan on the wall. Ferocious men and women began to tremble as they stared at the massive skull. Icy fingers of soul-withering fear traced their way into quickly-beating hearts.

As he battled his own feelings of dread, Brunar realized what was happening. The skull was not a skull at all, but simply a boulder carved to appear as one. Regardless, the bloody glow was Mordak's insidious attack on the morale of the defenders. Its size and shape were meant to inspire fear, which was augmented by the sorcerer's power. While terror froze their hearts and minds, Mordak would surely attack. Brunar squinted his eyes shut for a moment and called his power to purge the effects of Mordak's spell from his own body before doing what he could to shield the others. This casting was far more powerful than the one Mordak had used before, and Brunar strained to break its hold on the defenders.

His amplified voice echoing in the unnatural stillness, Mordak spoke, "I have tired of watching you defend what is already mine! You should have known that you could not stop me; now you will all pay for your insolence!" He raised his hands, and channelled more magick into the grisly mass. Slowly, ponderously, the huge skull lifted off the ground, still dripping gore in several places. It hovered there, held aloft by the will and power of a madman.

Brunar recognized the danger and yelled to Kiran. "Kiran! Ward the wall!"

Before she could respond, Mordak launched the grinning skull at the wall with frightening speed, directly at the same spot the Ogre had weakened with his ferocious attack. Warriors atop the wall scrambled frantically to escape, even as the evil missile bore down on them.

Suddenly a huge, glowing barrier of sapphirine blue burst into life in front of the cracked section of the wall. Kiran grunted with the effort, her Jidaan held tightly in both hands as she concentrated every fiber of her being on the Ward, strengthening it and making it as solid as stone. She hoped it would be sound enough to keep the giant boulder from striking the weakened wall. Doubts plagued her as she stole a glance at the giant crack left by the Ogre, but she gritted her teeth and poured everything she had into the shimmering shield. It darkened and thickened, turning a strong cobalt blue as it gained solidity.

From farther down the wall, a blazing bolt of clear ruby power slammed into the skull, blasting a huge chunk out of it and spinning it on its axis as it flew. Bjarke threw another massive burst of power, hoping to at least push the thing over enough to miss the weakest part of the wall, but the heavy, battered skull continued on. It slammed into Kiran's sapphire Ward at sickening speed. Mordak's vile crimson power met Kiran's in a tremendous explosion that shook the ground and knocked dozens of defenders off their feet. Kiran screamed in agony as her Ward disintegrated under the vicious attack, and she fell into Nessar's arms even as the giant skull-stone crashed into the wall, bursting through and sending screaming warriors and chunks of stone in all directions.

It took a few moments for the debris to settle, and then all was quiet. The outer wall of Laro had stood for over a thousand years, unbroken and unchallenged. Now it had been shattered, and a gaping, jagged-edged hole beckoned the vile horde of Mordak. Clouds of rock dust obscured everything and made breathing nearly impossible.

Behind the wall, Duke Gensen found himself facedown on the hard cobblestones, and he shook his head to clear it. Agony shot through his left arm as he doggedly rose to his feet. It was most certainly broken, victim of a hard fall off the stairs. Steeling himself against the pain, Duke Gensen shouted orders, striving to bring order to his troops as quickly as possible. Moans of the injured and dying reached his ears as those crushed under huge chunks of debris breathed their last or cried for help. As uninjured soldiers rushed to aid their fellows, the Duke was pleased to note that not one warrior had fled into the keep during the massive assault, but all had immediately shifted to the defense. The Augenan smoothly moved into action, moving the larger pieces of stone to help those trapped beneath. Raising his voice again, he called the nearest warriors to him and headed for the breach, blinking furiously through the pain of his arm and the gritty dust that dug into his eyes.

Suddenly, a wind rose within the courtyard, and the dust cloud began moving towards the massive hole, flowing outwards as if seeking the open land beyond. As the air cleared, Brunar emerged, his hands glowing gently as he chanted minor words of power.

"We must defend the breach until our people get into the keep!" Urgency suffused the Duke's gravelly voice. His throat burned as he spoke, adding to the mass of pains that plagued him. He squinted through the huge hole in the wall, seeking the evil army that waited just beyond the moat. As the dust dissipated, he could see them eagerly awaiting the command to attack.

"We are with you, Your Grace," Brunar replied. "We will hold as long as we can."

Bjarke suddenly landed near them, the power of his landing cracking the stones beneath his booted feet. His Jidaan was held at the ready and though weariness showed in his eyes, his demeanor was all business. He greeted the Duke with a brief nod, but that nod spoke volumes.

A loud grunt from the gigantic Augenan High Chief let them know that Ch'shok was at their side as well. Leaning forward on the knuckles of one hand, he held his massive axe in the other as though it weighed nothing. He snorted as he surveyed the enemy.

The Duke spat to one side, then drew his sword with his good arm. "Come on then. Let us show them we are unafraid!" With that, he stepped up on a block of stone and bellowed commands at the surrounding soldiers. Those who were not actively aiding the injured flowed into the courtyard just behind the breach, with hundreds of hooting Augenan in their midst. Within moments, a small army of defenders had gathered to repulse the evil tide of creatures that was sure to come.

They did not have long to wait.

Jor Dayne rode into view on the far side, his sword held high. Nearby, the black-robed figure of Mordak gloated. Scarlet light bled through his eyes as he surveyed the results of his monstrous attack. With a curt word to his Champion, Mordak ordered the final assault.

Jor Dayne yelled gutteral words in an ancient tongue as his horse reared high. He kicked the beast into a ferocious gallop, and it exploded into motion, leading Mordak's bloodthirsty, fanatical army towards the wall. He watched them step up to the breach and laughed as the battered Duke and his puny allies stood in defiance of Mordak's mighty host. They would be swept away by the monstrous tide that followed in Jor Dayne's wake.

His great war horse picked its way across the debris-laden moat, and quickly found purchase on the solid ground beyond. The daemon-bred man raised his massive sword and headed straight for the Duke, preparing to strike off the insolent man's head as he rode past. Hoofbeats pounded in his ears as he drew closer, laughing to himself as his target stood unmoving, awaiting his doom. Jor Dayne began his swing as his horse jumped...and slammed face first into a shimmering wall of sapphire energy that had not been there an instant before. Jor Dayne did not hear the sickening crack that accompanied the breaking of his horse's neck as he fell, senseless, to the ground, his face broken and bloodied. The first rows of the advancing horde tried desperately to stop, but the momentum of those behind smashed them into the glowing Ward, leaving scores of creatures hideously broken before they were able to cease their headlong advance.

"Take that, you bastard!" Kiran screamed in fury at the unconscious Jor Dayne, even as her entire body shook with the strain of holding the Ward. She glowed like a sapphire in the sun, flooded with power from her Jidaan. Kneeling on the wall walk at the edge of the gaping hole, she held her hands before her as she summoned the last of her strength and poured it into the Ward. "I may not have been able to stop that blasted rock from getting in here, but I sure as Hel can stop YOU, you piece of filth!" Nessar knelt between Kiran and the outside, holding a shield he had taken from a fallen soldier to protect her from any arrows the Krell might send her way.

You'd better hurry, Mage, Nessar sent along their mindlink. *You know she can't keep this up for very long...that's a big wall she's holding up out there.* Brunar's mind raced as he planned his next move.

A ragged cheer went up from the astonished soldiers behind Kiran's Ward, and they brandished their weapons at the furious creatures on the other side of the translucent blue wall that protected them. Brunar quickly spelled out the situation for the Duke, who then turned to address his troops. He stopped their cheering with an upraised hand.

"Warriors of Laro! The Guardian, Kiran, cannot hold this breach for very long. We must get our wounded into the Keep. Those of you who are not helping with that task, get as much of this rubble to the wall as possible to make it higher. The harder it is for those brutes to get in before we all retreat to the keep, the better! Now MOVE!" He cast a glance at Kiran and saw that her face was a mask of pain and determination. "Hurry!"

A flurry of activity resulted. Soldiers uncovered the wounded and helped them move while others continued to fight the creatures that were trying to overrun the other three walls. Alyssa and Fiona ran over to check on them, redirecting the more badly injured to a different area within the keep. Brunar hastened up the stairs to take a position near Kiran so that he could see the entire courtyard. Using his magick, he then began lifting hefty pieces of the shattered skull-stone and floating them into the gaping hole in the wall. Swords were scabbarded as many hands, both human and those of the gorilla-folk, started hauling debris into the breach as well. Here, the incredible strength of the Augenan was invaluable, and the makeshift repair grew higher by the moment.

Outside the moat, Mordak had seen Jor Dayne slam into Kiran's Ward and then watched helplessly as his beasts died against the shimmering wall of power. "Gaaaahhhhh!" He clenched his fists in rage. Suddenly, he stood still as inspiration struck him, and a mad glee soon followed. Yes, he knew what to do! In a swirl of black robes, Mordak quickly strode towards the main gate that the Guardian of Warding had been defending for days. He knew she was doing all she could to keep the huge hole in the wall defended, which meant the gate would finally be unprotected. A maniacal gleam appeared in Mordak's eyes as he hurried towards the moat, angling towards the raised drawbridge at the castle's entrance.

Pulled shut by massive chains that disappeared into small portals in the stone of the gatehouse, the drawbridge covered the portal itself, providing yet another layer of protection for the castle entrance. Beyond it, the massive oaken doors, banded with iron and seasoned to incredible hardness, stood barred and locked, and even those were protected by an iron porticulis.

Gathering his rage and using it to bolster his unholy power, Mordak chanted the words he needed to bring his anger to life. Harsh, grating syllables echoed in the air, causing even his own creatures to shy away from him as he made his way through. The sickly crimson glow around his body increased as he moved, and his words grew louder.

Just as he reached the road where the near end of the drawbridge would ordinarily rest, his chanting ceased. His hands began to glow with a nauseating reddish light that became brighter by the moment. Mordak gestured sharply towards the closed entrance, and a wicked gout of liquid Helfire instantly burst from his hands. It leapt across the moat to cover the shuttered portal, completely engulfing the closed drawbridge. Flames hotter than those of any forge flowed hungrily over the wood and metal barrier, eating through it in seconds, the iron bands, rivets, and even the porticulis melting like ice in the fire. Those atop the gatehouse flung themselves away from the conflagration, desperate to avoid the searing heat. In seconds, both the shuttered drawbridge and the gates themselves were simply gone, incinerated by the intense inferno. The short, wide tunnel leading into the keep lay open and completely unobstructed. Nearby, the blue barrier of magick that shielded the huge breach in the wall flickered as the Guardian's power waned.

Mordak raised his fists in triumph, but before he could give voice to his exultation, blinding agony exploded behind his eyes. He pressed his palms to his forehead, trying to relieve the pain and failing. A sickening wave of dizziness took him as darkness crept into the edges of his vision. He staggered a couple of wobbly steps and dropped to his knees. Through the flickering blue curtain of Kiran's Ward, Brunar saw Mordak stumble and a burst of hope flowed through the Mage at the sight. *Aha! You DO have limits, you fiend!* The sorcerer struggled to regain his composure as his head threatened to split in half. Finally, the pain eased, leaving him on his hands and knees in the dirt with a dull ache still throbbing in his skull.

Relieved that the pain was mostly gone, Mordak sat back on his heels and wiped a hand across his face. It came away bloody. He wiped again and discovered streams of thick blood still oozing from his nose. Angrily, he scraped his face across his sleeve until he was sure the flow had stopped, and then he slowly got back to his feet.

Having regained his senses, he scanned the scene before him. There were now two breaches in the wall, one wide open and the other nearly so. Mordak amplified his voice until it thundered across the battlefield, commanding his savage creatures to focus on the main gate until the Ward had fallen. "Swarm the keep, my children! Kill anything that breathes!"

Even as the flood of hideous beasts surged toward the opening, Bjarke stepped into the gatehouse tunnel with half a dozen mighty Augenan and a handful of human soldiers at his back.

"We will hold them here; get the others out!" Grunts of assent came from the burly gorilla-folk, and the rearmost man of Laro turned and sprinted away to convey word of Bjarke's plan to the Duke. After seeing Bjarke defeat an Ogre in single combat, the entire Laroan army considered his orders worth following.

The burly forester strode to the halfway point of the tunnel and pulled his massive Jidaan from its scabbard. Turning the point downwards, he thrust it into one of the wide flagstones at his feet. The bright blade slid into the stone as though it were soft soil. The weapon stood there, its ruby pommel gem already glowing a bright, clear scarlet. Bjarke hummed quietly as he brought the Jidaan's Gift to life. He stood just behind the weapon, one hand on the shaft, the other raised before him as though he could simply push the army of Mordak away with it. In truth, that's exactly what he planned to do, though it would not be nearly so gentle. His deep bass hum gained strength as his mind cleared, and the inside of the tunnel became bright with the Jidaan's shining vermilion light. Behind him, the powerful warriors of the Augenan shifted and grunted, their weapons at the ready.

Just then, the horde of Mordak burst into the tunnel on the far side, Gholans in the lead, howling Morcats and Krell alongside. Their thirst for blood and fanatical loyalty to their god drove them forward, their weapons gleaming red in the Jidaan's light. They surged towards Bjarke, shrieking as they came.

Bjarke waited until the vicious creatures were within arm's reach before he unleashed his Gift. A burst of intense scarlet power exploded from him, slamming into the oncoming mob and shattering those in the front, smashing their bones to pulp. The power spread out until it filled the tunnel completely, demolishing everything in its path. Broken bodies with tangled limbs exploded out of the end of the tunnel as though thrown from a catapult. A few Morcats and Gholans on the far sides had escaped Bjarke's power, but the Augenan smashed them mercilessly to the stones in moments. The huge, furry warriors looked on Bjarke with awe and respect even as they waited for more of Mordak's army to charge.

Two more waves of Mordak's filth rushed to the attack, only to meet the same fate at the hands of Bjarke and the mighty Augenan. Bjarke was already exhausted, but he knew he had to make a stand, to keep Mordak's forces outside the walls until the last moment so as many as possible could seek shelter within the Keep. He repelled a third rush with another blast of power and then a fourth. Even as he loosed the last explosive burst to clear the tunnel, bright sparkles began to dance before his eyes and dizziness overtook him. Clutching his Jidaan with one hand, Bjarke dropped heavily to a knee as he struggled to remain conscious. Outside the gatehouse, he could hear Mordak's creatures massing for yet another charge. Steadying himself with his Jidaan, he pushed himself to his feet, using every ounce of strength he still possessed. Bjarke took a cleansing breath and began the deep bass rumble in his chest that he used to ignite his Jidaan. *I can do this,* he absently thought to himself as he watched more vermin pour into the tunnel. *If I just hold them a while longer, more will be safe.* He unleashed another bolt of power, momentarily scouring the tunnel of Mordak's filth. It was too much, and he nearly passed out. Bjarke clutched his Jidaan tightly, and the giant, furry hands of the Augenan steadied him before he fell. *Just a little longer...*

In the courtyard, the repair to the breach had reached only fifteen feet, but would get no higher without a supporting structure. There was fighting on every wall but that one, shielded as it was by Kiran's Ward. The sparkling blue barrier fueled by her anger was flickering more each second as her deepest reserves were emptied. Nessar sat with her, his shield abandoned as he knelt at her side, holding her by the shoulders and keeping her steady.

"Hold on, baby girl. You've got this, just hold on a bit longer, the rest of them are almost safe in the Keep."

She drew strength from his closeness, as she always had. Kiran's breathing was heavily labored, but she stayed focused on keeping her Ward intact even as her whole body shook. Blood had started flowing from both nostrils, but she did not spare the effort to wipe it away.

Duke Gensen bellowed, "Mage, we can't wait any more! We've got to get everyone inside!" He looked to the walls, his eyes taking in the brave, exhausted soldiers who were still repelling the creatures that climbed up to assail them. He knew the rearmost would suffer heavy losses as they tried to reach the Keep before Mordak's hideous beasts overran them from behind. Once Bjarke and the Augenan left the gatehouse tunnel, the remainder of the horde would get inside. "Damn that Mordak! We're going to lose many as we pull back!"

Brunar turned on him, his storm-grey eyes determined. "Not if we can help it! Order the retreat, Your Grace, we'll do what we can!"

Duke Gensen caught the look in the Mage's eyes and nodded. Something told Duke Gensen that, whatever his plan, the Mage would make it work. Taking stock of the situation, he sheathed his sword and used his right arm to pull a small hunting horn from his belt on the left side. He raised it to his lips and blew a call he never thought he'd have to use. *Tan-tan-tarooooo! Tan-tan-tarooooo!* Instantly, each soldier responded by throwing a few last strikes at the nearest enemy to gain some room, then they all turned and sprinted away from the fighting. The Augenan stayed longer, using their great strength and size to give their smaller comrades more time to make it down the stone steps to the courtyard below before easily jumping or climbing down themselves. The moment the great gorilla-warriors left, Gholans, Morcats, and Krell clambered over the battlements, howling in triumph.

Brunar planted the end of his staff firmly on the stones at his feet and held one hand before him. Questing with his senses, he reached out and quickly gained a sense of the battlefield, assessing the position of every living and non-living being within range of the spell that grew within him. Brunar knew his internal store of magick was only a shadow of what it should be, but it would have to be enough. He knew he had to get the spell correct or he'd not have another chance. He saw one of the Augenan carrying the unconscious form of Bjarke out of the gatehouse tunnel, still clutching his Jidaan, while the other gorilla-folk fought ferociously as they backed into the courtyard, step by step. One of them went down as a Morcat ripped out his throat, and then another fell as a Krell warbar cracked into her knee. The others fanned out in an attempt to contain the vicious creatures, but it was obvious that the brave Augenan had only moments to live.

The blue Ward in front of the north wall winked out of existence with a soft popping sound as Kiran finally succumbed to exhaustion. Instantly, the sounds of Mordak's beasts intensified as they attacked the makeshift repair. Rocks started to fall into the courtyard, and Brunar knew it would not hold. Soldiers were streaming into the Keep entrances as fast as they could, but there was no way they would all get inside before Mordak's horde swamped them.

Brunar focused his power and chose his targets, being careful to differentiate between the Laroan forces and the evil creatures that harried them. Using the iron discipline he had learned over centuries of intense training and study, Brunar crafted the spell. He spoke the Ancient Words of power that formed the base for the enchantment, and his resonant voice echoed from the walls of Laro. The Mage raised his staff in the air a few inches and held it there as he finished the chant. The staff suddenly glowed with a painfully bright indigo brilliance as Brunar charged the ancient wood with magick. He held it for a moment more, then slammed it to the flagstones with a deafening thunderclap that cracked the stones beneath his feet.

A bright purple wave of light exploded out from the Mage in an ever-widening circle, rolling effortlessly over everything in its path. Every dark-hearted being that strode into the courtyard froze in its tracks, suddenly turned into living statues as the spell hit them--every Gholan, every Morcat, each and every raving Krell--all stood perfectly still as Brunar's spell stole their ability to move. The shambling dead froze as well. Although they were once human, the unholy force that now drove them was vulnerable to Brunar's enchantment. The Laroan soldiers flinched but did not slow as it passed over them, and they continued their rush to get into the keep. The Augenan saw the hateful creatures freeze and instantly capitalized on the opportunity, bashing and crushing as many as they could lay their hands on. Although it went against their grain to smite helpless opponents, the noble gorilla-folk knew that each monster they downed was one less that could attack them later. They took no relish in the slaughter, but set to the task of eliminating as many of their enemies as possible as the humans finished dragging the wounded into the entrances to the Keep.

Duke Gensen only took a moment to marvel at the spell Brunar had wrought, then turned to bellow, "We've only moments; get everyone inside! NOW!" The sounds of booted feet slapping against the stone of the inner courtyard merged with the panting of the soldiers as they complied. Soon, the walls were emptied, and only the Augenan remained, still slamming their way through Mordak's creatures. The Duke sheathed his sword and reached out to help a soldier who had taken a slash to his thigh. Using his good arm, he supported him until others took him inside one of the entrances, then the Duke looked for another. There was no shortage of wounded who needed help.

Brunar was severely depleted, and sagged heavily on his staff. Any further casting from the Mage this day, and maybe the next, would be dangerous for him. His store of magick was nearly spent. He scanned the battlements, searching for Kiran, Nessar, and Layton. He had already seen Bjarke dragged into the Keep by a handful of Augenan, so he knew the big man was safe for now. Brunar was just about to send a mental call after them when Layton came jogging out of the gatehouse, his Jidaan strapped safely to his back. He deftly dodged through the frozen Gholans, Morcats, and Krell, and stepped over the fallen undead until he was even with Brunar. He saluted, as always, before speaking.

"I figured there was no sense in making it easy for them, sir," Layton's face was coated with blood, grime, and rock dust, yet a bit of a smile shone through anyway.

Before Brunar could ask what Layton meant, the outer entrance to the gatehouse collapsed, crushing every evil creature inside and sealing the passageway thoroughly under tons of fallen stone.

A ghost of a smile flitted across Brunar's exhausted face. "How...?"

"Oh, I just relocated a few rather important stones in the foundation. As it turns out, a structure really needs those to be in place or else it'll...well...collapse."

Brunar slapped him on the back. "Obviously, you are quite correct, Layton. Kiran and Nessar were up there, were they not?"

"They were, sir, but I've deposited them in the Keep. Kiran is unconscious, but otherwise all right. Nessar is cranky, so he's also fine."

Brunar managed a faint chuckle at that. "See that everyone is inside at once, my spell will only last a few moments more, and I'm sure that those beyond the reach of the casting will be here soon."

"Yes, sir Mage," The young warrior slapped his fist to his heart and trotted off. Brunar turned to find the mighty Ch'shok approaching.

"Humans...all inside, I think," the massive warrior snorted. "We go inside, too?" His distaste was obvious. The Augenan spent their lives in the jungle, able to move about at will and see the sky. Going into a dark, enclosed castle was not something they had considered.

"Yes, High Chief," Brunar replied. "There is a way out through tunnels that lead away from here. We will have to use them, or we will die here."

Ch'shok snorted again and looked out at his warriors. All of them sported wounds, and he could see more than a handful of dead Augs littering the courtyard. Many of Mordak's frozen creatures were starting to move again, albeit slowly, and it was only a matter of time before the full might of the remaining horde was brought to bear inside the walls. Reluctantly, the furred warrior nodded.

"I will call them. We no like inside, but we will go." Without further comment, Ch'shok turned and barked a series of commands. Instantly, his warriors turned away from their grisly task and converged on the entrances to the Keep. Although the looks on their faces betrayed their uneasiness, they shuffled inside along with their human allies. In moments, Brunar, the Duke, and a few guards were the only allies remaining in the courtyard, along with hundreds of dead, dying, and mostly immobile creatures of Mordak.

The Duke bumped unsteadily into the Mage before righting himself to stand as regally as possible. He scanned the great wall that had stood for centuries, now blasted into rubble in one section, and eyed the remains of the gatehouse Layton had collapsed. Dead bodies--human, Augenan, and those of the sorcerer's fell folk--lay scattered all about the grounds. Such a sight tore at the Duke's heart.

"Mordak has much to answer for, Mage," he said, his voice shaking with emotion.

Brunar leaned heavily on his staff, at the end of his physical and magickal stamina.

"Indeed he does, Your Grace," the storm-grey eyes of the Mage had seen it all before. "Indeed he does." Brunar turned and shuffled as quickly as he could towards the Keep's main entrance, a huge pair of double doors he knew would never be opened in welcome again. He and the Duke crossed the threshold from light into shadow, and the Duke ordered the doors closed.

It took several guards on each door to get them to swing shut. The resulting thunderous boom as they fell into place sounded dreadfully final. The Duke ordered all entrances to be completely barred and every piece of available furniture pushed up against them to afford the people of Laro as much time as possible to retreat.

Even as he ordered it, he knew he was saying goodbye to his beloved castle. Once the ancient passageway in the crypt was opened, the Keep would fall in upon itself, destroying centuries of accumulated artifacts, memories, and history. The kitchens where the Duke had played as a child, the great hall, even the Laroan Library famous for its holdings, all would disintegrate under the force of tons upon tons of falling stone.

Suddenly, the Duke stopped in mid-stride. For a moment, the pain of losing his home, his land, and everything else he held dear was shoved aside. A sly grin played on his blood-streaked face and he picked up his pace, hurrying to find the Weya, who were somewhere in the Royal Crypt preparing the way for the townspeople and soldiers to escape.

Outside, the evil soldiers of Mordak's horde who had been beyond Brunar's magickal influence were clambering over their frozen brethren, even as those struggled to break free of the spell. Slow minutes passed, and at last the enchantment fell away completely, allowing creatures that yet lived to move freely once more. They swarmed over the castle, searching out every possible entrance. Windows in the highest towers were shuttered, and balcony doors were barred from the ground floor all the way up to the highest, but they would not hold against the single-minded ferocity of the Gholans and Morcats.

Floating a few feet over the rubble of the makeshift barrier in the shattered wall, Mordak led the Krell into the courtyard that had been denied him for so long. After expending so much energy hurling the boulder and the Helfire so soon after, the sorcerer was having trouble maintaining the effortless control he had shown before now. He floated into the middle of the courtyard and caught himself before he stumbled upon landing.

Mordak thought it such a beautiful sight--the gargantuan castle of Laro, covered with Gholans as they searched for a way in. The pure white stone of the towers looked befouled by the creatures as they crawled across its surface like lizards, and that made Mordak smile. He muttered to a nearby Morcat, ordering it to send its comrades climbing to hunt for additional entrances. It growled in response, then loped away to spread the word among the vicious catfolk. Mordak watched it go, then focused his attention on the last obstacle that stood in his way.

The main entrance was sealed even more solidly than the gatehouse had been. Its massive double doors were triple-banded in thick iron and covered with another portcullis, even more densely woven than the one at the front gate. If Mordak had not been so woozy, he'd have simply blasted it with Helfire and been done with it, but that spell had nearly knocked him senseless. It seemed that the power he had stolen from Balroth was not unlimited after all. Instead, he ordered the Krell to attack the door, knowing they would eventually get through it.

Jor Dayne staggered alongside him, having finally dug and clawed his way out from under a huge pile of dead creatures. After slamming into Kiran's Ward he had lost consciousness. The remainder of the horde had washed over him, crushing the first several ranks to death against the shimmering blue shield and covering him with their bodies. He had awakened under that charnel house of filth and found his way to his master.

"Be ready, my Champion," Mordak hissed. "Once those vermin get the doors open, the castle will be mine! You will lead the others inside to be sure that all are dead. Find the Duke, so that I may sit upon a new throne made of his bones!"

"Yes, my Master," he said with a grin. Spears of pain, deep and delicious, were shooting through Jor Dayne's fleshly body, and he relished them. Bones were broken and muscles torn, but all was naught but sensation to him, a massive contrast to the nothing of the Void. And it felt wonderful. "What about that Mage? And the others, the ones with the spears of power?"

Fast as a striking snake, Mordak lashed out and back-handed the huge daemon-bred Champion. Wounded and surprised, Jor Dayne dropped to one knee before recovering his composure.

"You will kill them! Those puny Guardians are nothing! NOTHING! Bring them to me and I will flay the skin from their bones!"

Relishing the new pains that jangled across his nerves, Jor Dayne smiled as he rose to his feet. He ran a massive hand across his face where Mordak had struck him, wiping a smear of blood from a split lip. The sorcerer was his master, and he must follow his orders...for now.

"I hear, my Master, and I will obey." He smiled, and his serpent's eyes gleamed an ill yellow as he thought about the joys of torture he could extract from the spear-wielders. They would be good practice, he was sure.

Mordak turned his attention back to the Krell at the doors. They were already chipping away at the exposed wood with relentless fervor, desperate to please the one they thought was their god. Their blood already stained the door in places as they worked with feverish intensity. The sorcerer's eyes gleamed scarlet in the deepening dark as he scanned the face of the castle. It was crawling with his creatures, and they would find a way in before long. Then, the castle would become a massive slaughterhouse.

Inside the Keep, confusion reigned. Thousands of people were crammed together in the first two floors of the castle, trying to figure out what was going on. The sounds of Mordak's horde outside banging, clawing, and shrieking, had set everyone on edge. The remaining guard captains moved through the throng, doing their best to keep everyone calm. Panic threatened to break out at any moment as everyone was herded towards the lower levels of the castle, below ground. The Sisters of Rowann--some still bloodied from fighting on the walls alongside the other warriors--also moved through the crowd. Ripples of serenity followed them as they took the time to lay a comforting hand on someone's shoulder, or pause for a brief embrace to bolster a battered soldier's spirits. Their magick was of a very subtle kind, borne of their love of the land and their connection with the Goddess Rowann. They, more than any, kept the survivors of Laro from unraveling. Soon, everyone had been guided away from the main floors of the castle and down to the basement levels below. Sturdy doors were slammed shut and barred, leaving the rest of the fortress empty of life.

The Royal Crypt was a vast, high-ceilinged chamber, set deep into the bedrock under the castle. It had always been considered an oddity, being far too large for its stated purpose. An array of stone sarcophagi clustered at the far corner of the room, leaving an enormous amount of empty space, and statues of generations of rulers surrounded the entire hall. A wide corridor gently sloped from the level above, rather than a set of stairs. Over the centuries, there had been quite a bit of discussion and complaining about the odd ramp that led into the tombs of past nobility, but no one was complaining any more. Wagons and carts had been rolled into the Keep from the outside and loaded with as many supplies and wounded warriors as could be safely transported, then eased down the ramp into the crypt. The usually empty chamber was filled near to bursting with yelling, shoving, pushing townsfolk, guardsmen, and agitated Augenan, all trying to talk at once.

ValElder Moihra deftly climbed on top of one of the larger statues where she could be seen and heard. Settling her feet firmly on the shoulders of the likeness of a man long-dead, she clapped her hands five times, each clap louder than the last. The final clap was deafening, so loud that it echoed in the cavernous space and dust fell from the lofty ceiling onto the startled crowd. The ValElder raised her hands, palms out, and a beautiful golden light emanated from them, illuminating the entire cavern. All eyes turned towards her, and talk in the Crypt drifted into silence as she gained the attention of every soul in the room, calming their minds with the beauty and warmth of the light that flowed from her hands.

"Good people, the time has come for us to escape the violence above," she said, her lilting voice so sweet it actually brought smiles from many in the room. "You have been told of the passage that we will open here. We sense that it leads away to the west, towards Rualtha, though I doubt it goes that far. Once the way is open, you must move quickly through it, for the creation of the portal also dooms the castle above. It will fall in upon itself, and I'm sure you'd prefer to be elsewhere when that happens." The ghost of a smile played on her lips as she spoke, reassuring the frightened folk of Laro that she was in complete control. She brought her glowing hands together and they shone more brightly. She twisted them, somehow creating a ball of light that sat on her palms. She gave the sphere a gentle push, and it drifted toward the high ceiling above. As it moved, it suddenly multiplied into several identical glowing orbs that drifted to all corners of the room, providing a serene, comforting light for all to see by.

As the room brightened, the Duke and his advisor, Rorian, made their way to the base of the statue on which she stood. Cradling his broken arm, the Duke stepped up onto the base of the same statue, doing his best not to grimace in pain.

"My people, I trust Moihra and her companions completely." Though strained from the pain of his injury, the Duke's familiar, resonant voice further served to calm the assembly, and many visibly relaxed. "We will be leaving through the passage in moments. Please help each other, and we will escape with our lives. In time, we will return to rebuild Laro, but for now..." he was silent for a moment before continuing. "My only concern is for the safety of our people, and that of the brave souls who have come to help us in our time of need." Many nods greeted his comment. The Duke was known as a pragmatic man who cared deeply for those under his rule. "Brunar and the Guardians have done all within their power to protect us. The Augenan, though fearsome, are noble and wise. They traveled far from their own homes and many gave their lives to help us. Let us all work together once more as we move to a place of safety."

From the crowd of onlookers, a middle-aged merchant tentatively moved towards one of the massive Augenan, who turned a wary eye on the little human. The man was obviously fearful but determined, even though others tried quietly to stop him. Ignoring the hushed voices of those around him, the merchant walked up to the furry warrior, squared his shoulders, and nervously reached out a hand in welcome. The Augenan looked at him for a moment, then engulfed him in a massive hug, eliciting gasps from the crowd. The young Aug grunted with laughter and quickly set the surprised man back down. The merchant straightened his tunic, then sketched a careful bow. Relieved, more Laroans came forward and introduced themselves to the Augenan warriors, who hooted and laughed as they spoke in their halting humanspeak, and a certain amount of tension lifted from the room.

Brunar made his way to the Duke, leading the exhausted Guardians. Each had used their Gifts repeatedly over the last few days, and were nearly asleep on their feet, leaning heavily on each other for support. The Augenan High Chief shuffled over, carrying the unmoving form of Bjarke, who remained unconscious. The townsfolk, though calmed by Moihra's light, still looked askance at the huge gorilla leader. However, he paid no attention other than to politely snort now and again. Kiran leaned hard against Nessar, but was managing to stay awake only through sheer stubbornness. The oldster looked much the same as always, though dirt and blood now soiled him thoroughly. He supported Kiran with his usual sour expression.

Alyssa stumbled as she approached, and Brunar gasped at the sight of her as she caught her balance and came closer. Where her auburn hair used to shine a deep brownish-red in the light, it now looked listless and dull. Grey streaks shot through it, and it seemed to have thinned as well. Her face was sunken and pale, and she looked far older than her twenty-five years. She was focused on the Duke, whose broken arm was obviously paining him.

"Excuse me, Brunar, I need to heal the Duke." Keeping her eyes on the Duke, Alyssa tried to move past the Mage to reach him, but he blocked her with upraised hands.

"Alyssa, you must rest. I don't even know how you are on your feet!" His concern was evident. Centuries past, Willen had used his Gift repeatedly, but never to the level that Alyssa apparently had. She seemed to have aged greatly since he had last seen her.

She stopped moving and tilted her face back to look at the Mage. Brunar was both surprised and pleased to see that, although her face had aged, her eyes were yet bright and clear.

Alyssa looked at him, then back at the Duke, then shrugged. "As you wish, Brunar." Without warning, the pommel of the Jidaan she had strapped to her back ignited in a short burst of sparkling, multicolored radiance before dimming once more. A knowing smile appeared on her lips as she turned away from the Mage and sat down on the wheel of a nearby wagon.

Brunar looked at her, then looked behind him to see the Duke flexing his left arm in amazement. She had healed it from several feet away, something Willen had never been able to do. Turning back to Alyssa, he raised a questioning eyebrow.

She shrugged again, a faint smile on her worn but pretty face. "Had to be done. These people are all looking to him for leadership, and he'll do a better job of that if he's not in agony. Now, if you'll excuse me, I think I need some rest." Exhausted but triumphant, Alyssa clambered up into a wagon with a group of oldsters, women, and children, who welcomed her with open arms. Her healing powers were widely known by now, and they happily moved over to make space for her to lie down on the floor of the wagon. She was asleep in moments. Brunar shook his head and turned to find the Duke standing next to him, Rorian close behind.

"It's time, Brunar," the Duke said. "I don't know how Alyssa did it, by the way, but my arm is as good as new. I feel ten years younger!"

"That woman is stronger by far than I ever dreamed possible," Brunar shook his head in amazement, then turned his full attention to the Duke and ValElder Moihra, who had climbed down from the top of the statue to join them. "And yes, we must get everyone out of here." Turning to Moihra, he said, "How long will the way stay open before the castle falls in on us?"

The ValElder's face took on a hint of frustration as she spoke. "We are uncertain. Minutes only, perhaps as much as a quarter of an hour, but I'd not hope for more than that." She looked around at the tightly-packed throng of desperate citizens, wagons, carts, soldiers, and huge Augenan. "We will have to hurry through the moment the opening is large enough to enter, and we may still lose the hindmost in the destruction."

"Not if we can help it," Brunar replied. "We will do what we can to allow everyone out. Do we know what's on the other side?"

Cohl spoke up from behind Moihra. He had been with Ginn in discovering the passageway, and had the best impressions of what lay beyond the stone of the Crypt wall. "From what I can tell, sir Mage, it is a wide tunnel with a relatively flat floor. It feels as though it was carved that way. Farther down, it connects to a natural set of caverns, and the footing may be more difficult there."

The Duke nodded tersely. "We will deal with that when we come to it. Drattus!"

The weary Guard Captain appeared, shouldering his way through the crowd. "Yes, Your Grace?"

"We will open the passageway in a few moments. Spread the word to the other Captains to listen for my command, and get everyone through as quickly as possible. Leave behind anything that will hamper our movements. Rualtha is not that far, and should we survive the journey, we can resupply there. The people are more important than any odd item they might think they need. Pile everything you can find against the doors leading from the floor above to here."

"Yes, Your Grace!" Drattus saluted and immediately turned to convey the Duke's orders to the other captains. A group of soldiers broke away and started carrying whatever they could lay hands on to throw against the doors in the hall outside. A handful of Augenan grabbed some of the heavier items and shuffled along to help.

Duke Gensen turned back to the Mage with a conspiratorial gleam in his eye. "With your permission, I'd like to have Layton perform a task for me. I think he'd be the one with the best chance of doing it safely."

Brunar mentally beckoned Layton to approach, and felt his acknowledgement. A moment later, a Gate opened nearby and Layton stepped out of it, looking somewhat haggard. He saluted the Mage and bowed to the Duke. "You have need of me?"

"Yes, Guardian. I need you to go and unbar and unblock the doors to the main entrance to the Keep. I want the castle to be full of Mordak's creatures when it collapses. I don't even want them to know that we've escaped from under their noses...let them search the entire castle for us as we head into the tunnels. We can't afford to open the doors to this level to let someone else out. Will you do it?"

A big smile crossed Layton's tired face as he saluted and bowed to the Duke. "Oh, it'll be my pleasure, Your Grace. Just tell me when."

The Duke paused for a moment, then spoke. "Now is good."

Layton grinned. In the space of two heartbeats, he was gone.

The Duke stood quietly for a moment, staring at the floor where the young Guardian had been. Sighing, he turned to Moihra. "Open the passageway. Let us get these people to safety."

Moihra inclined her head to the Duke, then turned to Cohl and Ginn. A wordless communication passed between them and they walked in unison towards the blank face of the western wall. The wall was bare of adornment, save for a single carving in its center. It was an ancient sigil, a triquetra, intricately carved so that a single line wound around itself to form a flowing three-lobed figure. The Weya raised their hands and focused their attention on the symbol, reaching out with their spirits to awaken the ancient enchantment that had been imbued into the stones. A hush fell over the crowded chamber as their magick began to awaken the spell, and the air became thick with power.

A low rumble started somewhere beneath the stones, increasing in volume and intensity until the entire floor was vibrating. Cries of alarm echoed from the walls as the people of Laro held each other in fear. The Weya began to chant, their voices merging in a haunting harmony as they asked the stone to perform the task it had been given so long ago. The symbol on the wall began to glow a fiery gold, and a great grinding, scraping sound assaulted the ears of all present as a crack appeared in the wall. From floor to high ceiling, the crack widened an inch, then two, ever widening as the ancient enchantment took effect.

In the courtyard above, Mordak ran a hand through his hair as he watched and waited. The outer portcullis had been removed, and it was only a matter of time before the Krell managed to hack their way through the big double doors. Even with the iron reinforcements, they could not hope to stand up to the intense assault.

A faint tremor in the earth reached Mordak through the soles of his boots, but it soon faded, and he dismissed it. Suddenly, Mordak thought he saw one of the doors shift as the Krell worked on it. He peered more closely, trying to decide if what he had seen had been a trick of the fading light. Without warning, the rightmost door swung completely inwards, and the Krell immediately whooped in victory, their piercing shrieks echoing in the courtyard. They picked up their weapons and rushed inside, eager to spill the blood of those within.

Mordak was elated. "Jor Dayne! Lead our forces inside, and have them open every door and window you can find to let more in. This will be easier than I thought!"

The big man-daemon drew his massive sword and immediately moved forward, calling the Gholans and Morcats to attend him. The undead of Laro had been standing immobile until Mordak needed them, and he silently ordered them to follow Jor Dayne as well. Within moments, a steady stream of vicious killers entered the castle of Laro. Only when well over a thousand of his bloodthirsty creatures had entered the building did Mordak stride regally across the courtyard and cross the threshold himself. An evil grin played across his face as he envisioned the bloody rituals he could enact with the bodies of the Laroan captives. Balroth was not the only dark power to which he had access, though none were nearly as powerful as the evil Daemon-God. Even so, the lesser beings had their uses, and required quite a lot of blood. Imagining the fear of the captives that surely awaited, cowering and hiding in the upper levels of the castle, Mordak chuckled with mad glee. Another rumble from deep within the stone floor passed unnoticed by the sorcerer in his excitement.

In the Crypt, the two halves of the western wall were still ponderously moving apart to expose a huge, empty passageway beyond. The tunnel was squarely cut and large enough to drive two wagons through abreast. It led into darkness at first, then two wall sconces nearest the Crypt flared brightly with ancient magick which settled into a warm glow that brightened the tunnel. Farther down, another pair of sconces ignited, and then another, illuminating the pathway to safety.

The doors locked themselves into place with a deep thump that they all felt within their bones. Captain Drattus and Ch'shok led the first desperate Laroans into the tunnel, hastening them as quickly as they could.

"Hurry!" the Duke bellowed over the heads of the crowd. "We may have a candlemark, at best. Help anyone around you who might need it, and abandon anything that slows you down. GO!"

Brunar stood on one of the nearby sarcophagi, watching hundreds of people moving through the opening, crushed together so tightly that it was a wonder any could even draw breath. The floor had started to vibrate and a huge crack suddenly crawled across the length of the ceiling, sending dust and debris down onto the fleeing townspeople. He felt the tension rising, the fear of each person multiplied as it seemed to move around the room. Delving deeply within himself, he called forth enough magick for a very minor spell and chanted the few necessary words to invoke it before raising his shaky hands to direct the power. A gentle calm fell over the frightened crowd, easing their worries and slowing the frantic beating of their hearts. The pace remained the same, but the frenzied feeling was gone, and Brunar relaxed. Had panic erupted, many would have been trampled beneath the feet of the others in their rush to escape.

As he clambered down off the ancient sarcophagi and its silent cargo of moldering bones, Brunar looked at the stone lid of the tomb and noticed it was carved in the likeness of Duke Reinhold, a noble who had ruled Laro over a thousand years ago. He had known the man, an obstinate fool far more concerned with his own comforts than those of his people. If this horrific war had to happen, Brunar was glad that Duke Gensen was the living ruler of Laro, rather than someone like the swine that lay in that particular tomb.

There seemed to be no end to the people who rushed into the gaping tunnel. Hundreds had gone through already, but many still remained inside the Crypt, edging forward in tiny steps as the crowd ahead moved with agonizing slowness. The rumbling increased and dust filled the air as larger chunks of stone started falling from the walls and ceiling. In spite of Brunar's calming spell, screams of fright echoed in the vast chamber. Overwhelmed with fatigue and fighting a blinding headache from using so much magick, Brunar staggered to one side of the huge opening and leaned his back up against the stone. It vibrated constantly now as the structure of the entire castle began to fail. Soon, the highest towers would topple, and the uppermost rooms would begin to crumble in upon themselves. The rumbling below grew steadily louder and the floor vibrated more with each passing moment.

A huge chunk of jagged stone broke off the ceiling and plummeted towards the unknowing crowd below. Brunar's hands flashed up and he cast a spell without even thinking, catching the stone in its fall and guiding it off to one side. A blinding pain struck behind his left eye, but the Mage ignored it as best he could and struggled to move the chunk of debris to an unoccupied corner. It shattered on the stone floor, sending a spray of sharp chips and rubble at everyone nearby. Screams and startled yelps resulted, but no one appeared to be badly hurt, and they kept moving towards the exit. Another chunk fell, and he guided it aside as well, in spite of the increasing pain in his head. Then a third, much more massive piece suddenly detached itself from the ceiling and began its deadly descent.

No! He didn't have time to voice the thought as he threw the previous piece of rock aside and reached out for the huge chunk of falling stone. The instant he touched it, he knew he was not strong enough to move it.

In that moment, a cobalt blue Ward appeared underneath the mass of rubble. It neatly caught the ragged piece of stone and stopped its fall several feet above the heads of the townspeople, who cowered in fear. The Ward carried the stone to the empty side of the room and abruptly disappeared, leaving the rock to fall heavily onto the cracked floor. Stunned, Brunar turned and searched the room with his eyes until he found Kiran, sitting on the base of one of the statues on the opposite side of the room. The steadily moving river of Laroans lay between them, but even from that far away Brunar could see she was dangerously exhausted.

I know that you're spent, Mage, Kiran's voice echoed in Brunar's head, making it throb with pain. He wiped his nose and found a spot of blood on his hand. 'Spent' did not begin to cover the depth of his fatigue, but he dared not let her know that. Her voice continued, *Busy yourself with something else; I'll keep the ceiling from killing anyone. For Goddess' sake, though, get them to hurry!* The floor rumbled again beneath their feet, and another chunk of ceiling fell, only to bounce off another of Kiran's Wards, followed quickly by another. Once more, her voice rang in his mind. *HURRY!*

Above, Mordak walked into the main audience chamber on the second floor. Its wide open space was usually filled with people waiting to speak to the Duke on some issue or other, but only Mordak's creatures filled it now. They had found a handful of townspeople, mostly well-to-do merchants who had tried to hide in the various closets and smaller rooms. Although those had provided a bit of bloody entertainment, Mordak was getting aggravated. He had driven thousands of people into this very castle. Where were they? The stones rumbled beneath his feet, and he stumbled on his way up to the simple throne at the end of the hall. Frustrated, he kicked the nearest Gholan, who snarled and scuttled away from him as he put a hand on the arm of the throne to right himself.

"Jor Dayne!" Mordak bellowed for his Champion, who quickly entered through a nearby doorway.

"Yes, my Master?" There was blood on Jor Dayne's hands and on the sword he carried.

"Where are they? The castle was full of people only minutes ago! There's no way that Guardian could have transported so many out of our hands. We've got the castle surrounded and it's too far for that pathetic fool anyway!"

The huge man shrugged, his serpent-yellow eyes never leaving those of his master. "They are probably hiding in the upper levels. Doors leading to the higher floors are locked and barricaded. I have the Krell working on them, and we'll be able to swarm the area any moment now."

Mordak climbed the steps of the dais upon which the throne of Laro sat. It was a solid, blocky seat, carved entirely of a beautiful dark wood. It was inlaid with gold filigree and gemstones, not nearly as ornate as the King's throne in Bos Aldas, but befitting a Duke of the Realm. Mordak slid into it with a triumphant grin upon his face.

"First Laro, then Rualtha, then the royal city of Bos Aldas...and everything in between. This time, it will all be MINE!" He slammed a fist down, hard, on the armrest of the throne.

In that moment, a massive piece of the ceiling came crashing to the stone floor at the far end of the hall, crushing a dozen Gholans and a Morcat to death in an instant. The rumbling Mordak had felt increased beyond anything he had felt so far and huge cracks formed in the walls nearest him.

Chaos erupted around Mordak and Jor Dayne as Mordak's army panicked. They howled and screeched as they clawed at each other in their haste to escape, and blood flew on the air. Another chunk of stone hit the floor, then another, and suddenly the air was full of falling debris as the castle finally succumbed to the enchantment down below.

Jor Dayne lashed out with one big hand and grasped the front of Mordak's robe before the sorcerer could even speak, and yanked him off the throne. Without pausing to hear Mordak's screams of outrage, Jor Dayne tucked the smaller man under one massive arm and burst into a sprint towards a nearby stairwell, batting aside anything that got in his way. He bounded down the stairs three at a time, carrying Mordak as though he were naught but a child. There was a sense of power building around the sorcerer, but Jor Dayne had no time for whatever Mordak was trying to do. It was obvious the castle was coming down, and the only sensible thing was to get as far away from it as possible.

It took only moments for Jor Dayne to reach the ground floor, and he kicked open the door to the enormous entrance hall, then headed towards the main doors that led outside. The huge chamber was filled wall-to-wall with Gholans, Morcats, and Krell as they fought each other to be the first ones out. Huge chunks of stone fell, crushing them to pulp. Jor Dayne drew his sword and began cutting his way through them, scything them down like wheat at harvest. The noise had become unbearable-- the rumbling from deep in the earth, the crashing of massive blocks of stone-- the ancient castle of Laro was not dying easily. Jor Dayne dimly realized that Mordak was screaming something. A scarlet light flared from the sorcerer's hands, but Jor Dayne kept moving, kept cutting his way to the doors.

Frantically, he continued driving forward, dragging Mordak as he went. More rubble fell from the ceiling, striking him hard in the back and shoulders. Jor Dayne went down to a knee, covering his master's body with his own. He staggered and rose to his feet once more, then a massive slab came loose directly above him. He looked up, saw the huge face of rock falling down on top of him, and knew there was no time to dodge it. Covering the chanting sorcerer with his body, he tensed for the impact. He did not have long to wait.

"Come on, come on!" Brunar herded the last of the townspeople into the tunnel, but before they could make it through, the huge doors began to shut on either side. Brunar could see that they were moving too fast. "You won't make it unless you run! HURRY!" Battered and exhausted, the people of Laro tried to run, but many fell as they tried to sprint across the threshold. Brunar stumbled over and attempted to help some of those who had tripped, but there were too many. More and more debris had fallen, and Kiran was struggling to keep the biggest pieces from hitting the townspeople. Blood ran down her face and she swayed on her feet as she pushed her body beyond its limit, her Jidaan flaring bright blue in her hands.

Just as Brunar helped two more people onto their feet and into the passageway, a half a dozen Augenan burst through the diminishing opening. Without a word, they scooped up every slowpoke they could and bore them through the closing gap. More Augenan came right after and did the same, and suddenly the Royal Crypt was empty except for Brunar and Kiran.

Brunar raced to her side as the doors drew shut behind him. Kiran collapsed in his arms, nearly sending them both to the floor. The entire chamber was shaking and debris from the structure above was making its way into the crypt; it would be filled with rubble in moments.

LAYTON! The Mage yelled in his mind, knowing that the young Guardian could get them out even if the doors shut. *Layton, we need you!!!* There was no answer. Indeed, Brunar felt no acknowledgement of any kind. A shadow settled on his soul. He had last seen Layton dispatched to make the castle doors easier to open so that more of Mordak's ilk would be inside when it collapsed. Had he made it back?

Shutting out the darker possibilities, Brunar heaved himself to his feet and shifted his grip on Kiran so he could move faster. Rock was falling on all sides, and dust clouded his vision. He could hear the massive stone doors grinding as they moved to close off the passageway from the destruction of the castle, and then he caught sight of them just a few yards away. They were nearly shut, but he could make it.

In that instant, something struck him solidly in the head and everything shifted. Time suddenly had no meaning, and everything went black. Even as he lost consciousness, he could hear the resounding, final thump of the doors closing for good. And then, he knew no more.

Chapter 22

The road on the far side of the tunnel was much easier to walk, even in the deepening dark, and Gart was relieved to be back in the open. His horse, too, seemed pleased, and she snorted and tossed her head as they walked. Gart caught himself talking to her, and to Beauty, far more often than he had expected. He had grown up with farm animals, and though he had seen his father talk to them constantly, he had never done so himself. They were just dumb animals, after all, and unworthy of his attention. He had always been too angry, too inwardly-focused to ever entertain such a notion. But as unlikely as it was, after weeks of following a path of cold vengeance and nearing a token of unknowable power, Gart somehow felt more relaxed when he spoke to them.

"Yes, yes, we're almost there, I think. You can make it, Bessie. Let's just keep moving." A snort and an eye roll was his only answer. Gart shook his head in mock dismay. "I know, we've been doing a lot of that since I bought you. At least this road is wider and easier to travel, and I think we're...almost..."

They rounded a bend where the road widened out ahead of them, and entered what appeared to be a courtyard. Gart's breath caught in his throat as he walked the horse closer. Ancient, weathered stones made up a low wall that surrounded the area in a great circle. At the western side, where the small plateau butted up against the mountain, a massive pair of wooden doors stood, closed and solid as the mountainside itself. Shuttered windows were visible in the cliff wall. A balcony, its own small wooden doors tightly closed, was situated directly above the huge entrance. Gart realized that the keep was built right into the side of the mountain, rather than being a castle sitting atop the peak as he had imagined.

Gart led Bessie into the courtyard with Beauty quietly sticking close by. His eyes were drawn to the northern side of the walled space. Three stone benches surrounded a stunning statue of a woman, her arms outstretched as though to embrace someone. Gart was drawn to it. Indeed, he could not have bypassed it had he tried. He slowly approached, taking in the amazing beauty of the statue. The sculptor must have used magick, for the woman was captured perfectly in a moment of flowing movement, her hair blowing in the wind, a vision frozen in time and yet somehow alive.

Beauty trotted ahead of him, and turned rapidly around in circles before the statue. She then sat, gazing upwards into the stone figure's face. Gart stopped a few feet away from the statue and looked upon it. Snow had covered the pedestal, obscuring it completely, so he used a touch of his magick to sweep it clean. In simple script, the name became clear: Rowann. The Goddess of Life, Mother of All.

Gart had seen many representations of the Mother Goddess, and none had ever moved him in the least. They were all just stone, or paint on canvas, nothing more. This one, though...this one was different. It appeared to be made of pure marble, yet its lines and curves spoke of a living being, a beautiful woman full of life and love. It almost made him believe she was truly there, within the stone, just awaiting the right moment to move freely. Gart thought if he moved closer he might see her chest rise and fall as she breathed in the cold mountain air. The statue had a presence; he could feel it. Somehow, he just knew she would step off her pedestal to dance and twirl the instant he took his eyes off of her.

He stood there for several minutes, simply looking at her. Finally, the horse snorted and brought Gart back to the present. He shook his head to clear it, and wondered how long he had been standing in the lightly falling snow staring at the statue. Oddly, he felt lighter, more relaxed than he had in weeks. Turning, he saw a small stable off to one side of the courtyard, and he walked the horse into it. He wasn't sure how long he would be inside the main keep, but he definitely felt that a decent rest was in order for both himself and his four-legged companions. He unsaddled, groomed, and cared for Bessie, making sure there was ample food and water for her. He gave Beauty some water and a bit of food as well before unstrapping his wooden Jidaan. Although he still had the black-bladed sword, he had never warmed to its use, so he left it with the saddle. He shouldered his backpack and walked back outside where the main doors awaited, Beauty at his heels.

Looming twenty feet high, the massive wooden doors looked strong enough to withstand any assault from either man or the elements. They were elegantly carved, yet gave the impression of great, enduring strength. Gart walked slowly up to them, his carved Jidaan in his hand. As he came closer, he noticed a faint greenish tint reflecting back at him from the wood. With each step it became brighter, and his hand suddenly went to his throat where the emerald pendant rested. He held it up in front of his eyes and was not surprised to see that it was glowing brightly in his fingers. He let it drop against his chest once more and reached a hand out to the doors.

At his touch, Gart heard heavy locks disengage somewhere within, and then the massive slabs of wood slowly swung inwards on silent hinges. Gart stepped inside, letting his eyes adjust to the shadows within the massive hall that lay before him. Supported by huge stone pillars, the room was vast, and his footsteps echoed in the cavernous space. Beauty walked along beside him, her nails clicking against the stone floor. As soon as the pair had walked far enough away, the doors swung shut and locked themselves again, a huge wooden beam falling into place from alongside the doorframe. Instinctively, Gart knew the doors would open at his touch as before, and was unconcerned. At the far end of the hall against the back wall stood a raised marble platform. Somehow, light was reflected from an unseen source up high in the vast ceiling to illuminate the dais, and Gart saw the glint of steel and a flash of emerald among five other sparkling points of color.

The back wall was divided into six equal sections, each carved with runes of archaic aspect. Gart approached until he was close enough to clearly make out the shapes of the characters. The dreams Brunar had left for him to view each night had given him a vague understanding of what was before him, and what some of it meant. Even so, he could not read the ancient runes.

Each section had a great gemstone embedded above the text and hanging brackets that were now empty of the weapons they once held--all save one. Gart scanned each panel and thought about what he had learned so far. The leftmost was the ruby that represented Power. Gart recalled the big man named Rhu had carried that one. He had seen some of what it could do in his dreams. The next bracket hung below a glistening opal, but Gart could not remember what that stone represented. Its rainbow of fiery colors impressed Gart. He had never seen anything remotely like it, and he wondered what powers it afforded its Chosen. An ebony jewel, onyx, marked the resting place of the next weapon. Gart had trouble looking at that one straight on; each time he tried to fix his gaze on it, he found himself looking elsewhere. *Stealth,* he thought to himself, recalling one of his many dreams from the last few weeks. He could not remember exactly what he had seen in that dream, or what the weapon could do, but that word rang in his mind.

On the far end of the dais, a cobalt crystal blazed out of the wall, catching Gart's eye. The sapphire, and the sparkling diamond in the section nearest it, twinkled at him, sending beautiful glints of color into the darkness of the hall. Again, he could not quite remember their powers, or Gifts, as Brunar had referred to them in their first meeting. His eyes wandered over the ancient runes that covered those sections of wall until he was satisfied that there was nothing further he could learn from them.

Finally, he turned his full attention to the one bracket that still held a weapon. His weapon. The Jidaan of Storms awaited him. The emerald pommel gleamed and sparkled at him, as though it were alive and greeting him warmly. Gart looked down at Beauty, who sat on the floor next to him. Her brown eyes looked back, but she remained silent, giving no advice whatsoever. He gave her a good scratch behind her ears, more to reassure himself than her, and she grunted quietly in response. Turning away from her, Gart took a deep breath and mounted the first step to the dais.

The instant his foot hit the stair, the necklace at his throat exploded in fiery green brilliance, its light beaming at a space on the dais right in front of the emerald Jidaan. A shape formed there, tall and slender, gradually becoming more solid. Gart held himself very still, waiting to see what would come of this new magick. Slowly, the light gathered enough substance to resolve itself into a form that Gart knew well, though he had only seen it once. Remembered anger flowed through his heart at the sight of the man who had accosted him on the road so long ago.

"Brunar," the single word came out more as a growl. The image of Brunar stood on the dais looking not at Gart, but straight ahead. He was dressed differently from when Gart had first seen him. Gone was the simple robe the spectre of Brunar had worn on the road. Instead, the Mage was wearing a light cloak over boots, dark trousers, and a shirt, all cast in shades of emerald green as the image projected from Gart's gemstone. When the likeness of Brunar was complete, it spoke.

"Gart," the familiar voice of the Mage grated on Gart's nerves. The young man still remembered the anger and resentment he carried for the Mage. On some level, he blamed Brunar for everything that had happened, though somewhere deep down, he knew none of it was Brunar's fault.

"If you are seeing this, then you have somehow found your way to your Destiny. The weapon on the wall, the Jidaan of Lillia, is to be yours. It has Chosen you. To claim it, all you must do is come up here and lay a hand on the weapon, and it will do the rest." The Mage paused then, and appeared to take a deep breath before continuing. "I can only surmise that something terrible has happened to bring you here, judging by your reluctance at our first meeting. I am truly sorry for that. The evil of Mordak is beyond imagining, and if left unchecked, will touch everyone in the Realm. If you have experienced it already, then you understand what a horror he is. I, and your fellow Guardians, have gone to the city of Laro to fight him. We have information that he and his vile army are headed in that direction, and we plan to arrive there and prepare that city's defenses. This is the fourth day of the third month, and we will be leaving momentarily."

Gart counted quickly. They had left more than two months ago, and that was weeks after he had first seen the Mage on the road. It would take nearly that long just for him to reach Laro himself, and that was if he could find a ship. He cursed silently. There was no way to know if Jor Dayne was there. Although, if he was, in fact a minion of Mordak, it would stand to reason that he would probably be part of whatever army Mordak had amassed. Although furious at the delays revealed by Brunar's message, Gart kept silent, not wanting to miss any important information. The Mage continued.

"Gart, I saw tremendous power in you. The Jidaan always Choose wisely...you were meant to wield it. No one but you can do this. Take the Jidaan, be Chosen, and then follow your heart. It will lead you where you need to go. Since I was unable to instruct you personally, I took the liberty of leaving you with certain memory-shadows from Lillia, provided by the Jidaan. They are harmless, and will dissipate in time. While you experience Lillia's memories as dreams, take care to observe her use of the Jidaan. She was an adept, highly skilled in using her weapon's Gift of Storms, and also in using it in hand-to-hand combat. Although learning from her in this way is far from being the most effective method of training, it was the best I could do. I'm sure it felt like an intrusion, a violation of sorts, and I apologize for not having a better way. I have left a scabbard, maps, and a few other supplies for you here. I think you'll find them most useful." The image of the Mage gestured towards a neat stack of gear off to one side of the dais, previously unnoticed.

"May the Goddess keep you safe, Gart."

The image of the Mage grew silent, and then simply vanished. Gart kept his customary frown as he thought about all that he had heard. He didn't want to admit that Brunar was right about anything, but he had seen the evil of which the Mage spoke. Jor Dayne fairly reeked of vile magick and violence. The murderer had even named his master, Mordak. Even though Jor Dayne commanded the undead, as well as hundreds of the vicious Gholans, he was apparently still just an underling. The true leadership of the evil that had taken Tiller's Grove, and Gennie and Rheann, was Mordak.

Gart's icy blue eyes narrowed. *That's it then,* he thought. *They both have to die. Simple enough. Let's get on with this Choosing thing so I can get to work.*

Slowly, deliberately, the man who had once been a farmer climbed the few steps to mount the dais. He walked towards the one remaining weapon on the wall. With each step, the emerald in the pommel of the Jidaan shone more brightly, welcoming him. His eyes roamed over every inch of the steel and oak of the spear, taking in its exquisite workmanship, its polished shine, the grain of the wood in the handle. He looked at the wooden replica he had created, a substitute for him to familiarize himself with the balance of the weapon while on the road. It had come a long way with him, but its time had passed. Compared to the real thing, it was nothing but a toy. Carefully, Gart leaned it on the wall next to the mounted Jidaan, and then stood tall before the spear.

Gart's right hand rose slowly. He reached for the Jidaan, but hesitated. Two heartbeats went by, then three. Then Gart grasped the handle, and his world exploded.

A MAGE AWAKENS

Book 3 of the Fire of the Jidaan Trilogy

Rolling Scroll
Publishing

Whit McClendon

A Mage Awakens

Book Three of the Fire of the Jidaan Trilogy

By Whit McClendon

Prologue

Wendall's head was hurting abominably, and it took a few moments for him to realize exactly where he was. Squinting his eyes, he struggled to get them to focus, finally making out the stones in the ceiling above. The slats of the chair he had been using dug uncomfortably into his back and he realized he was lying flat on the floor in his laboratory. An acrid smell stung the wizard's nostrils and bright spots still danced before his eyes as everything started coming back to him. A dull ache began in the back of his head. Wendall let out a low groan as he pushed himself up from the floor, untangling his legs from the chair so he could get to his feet. Had the procedure worked? He was dying to know.

As wizards went, Wendall was still young at not quite a hundred years of age, though he appeared to be a man in his late thirties. His dark hair was shorn close to his head so it would stay out of his face. Wendall was a man who disliked distractions. His cheeks showed several days' worth of salt and pepper stubble, lending him a somewhat ragged appearance. His face was lean and worn from days of intensive experimenting and lack of sleep, but his dark eyes were afire with intensity. Placing both hands on the edge of his massive worktable, Wendall leaned forward to see if his latest project had survived the final step.

The table was bare of the papers and materials Wendall had placed there earlier, and winding curls of smoke drifted up from its scorched surface. Blast lines radiated outward from the table's center, where a small block of wood supported the source of the explosion, a palm-sized golden medallion. It was inscribed with ancient runes and designs that seemed to writhe and squirm if gazed upon for too long. The firelight glinted from its golden surface, yet it held a look of shadows about it, as though it would prefer the darkness to the bright lights that bathed it now. At its heart was a huge blue diamond, exceedingly rare and cut so that its many facets danced and sparkled with color. It had a peculiar presence, and the air surrounding the amulet was thick with power for a few moments before the energy dissipated, leaving the area around the piece empty and cold.

A few silent seconds passed, and nothing further happened. Slowly and carefully, Wendall eased closer to the artifact he had created. He cast his senses into it, desperately hoping that all of his painstaking work had paid off. Reaching out with his magick, the wizard sensed...nothing. Where the amulet should have been there was nothing but a void, a distinct lack of presence that was stunning for its absence.

Wendall's eyebrows went up and he grunted with excitement. The lack of any discernable aura around the object was a good sign that his creation was working. Tearing his eyes away from the amulet, the sorcerer turned and shuffled to another nearby table.

"Yes, yes, so far so good. But we must test it before giving it to the King, yes, we must." Wendall chattered absently to himself as he shuffled objects around on the table until he found the item he needed, a box he had laid there earlier for this very purpose. He opened the lid and carefully retrieved a simple wand of wood from within. It was slightly crooked, less than the length of his forearm, and had leather wrapped around one end for use as a handle. The tool looked fragile, but was in truth a powerful weapon in the proper hands. Wendall picked it up and turned back to the amulet he had assembled.

The sorcerer pointed the wand at the amulet and spoke the proper Word. Instantly, a ray of intense fire as thick as his own wrist flew across the laboratory at the amulet, only to disappear just before striking it, leaving the gold completely undamaged. Moving a step closer, Wendall called forth the wand's power again, but with a different Word. Greenish lightning burst from the end of the slender wand only to be absorbed just as easily as the fire had been.

Moving even closer, Wendall stood quietly for a moment before completing the final test. The wand's third Power was extremely volatile, and if the amulet did not function properly, he would be hard pressed to contain the magick he was about to release. Unchecked, the Black Portantis Mist would devour everything with which it came into contact. Wood, stone, flesh and blood - the deadly mist would dissolve it all with equal eagerness and ease.

Wendall took a deep breath to calm himself, and let it out. He raised the Wards he hoped would contain the mist, and enabled the additional safeguards and enchantments he had laid within the room for this very experiment. When all was ready, he aimed the wand at the amulet. In a shaky voice, he spoke the final Word.

An oily black tendril oozed from the end of the wand, snaking its way through the air towards the amulet. It spread as it extended, additional strands reaching hungrily in all directions as the Power moved forward, getting closer to its destination. One questing finger of inky darkness touched the table, and the wood instantly dissolved under the intense power of the Portantis Mist. More tendrils found their way to the wood of the table, hungrily devouring it, cutting through the hardened surface like a scalding knife through fresh butter.

The lead tentacle kept moving forward, eager to reach the amulet. As the table disintegrated behind it, the black finger of death approached the gold and diamond amulet until it was only a few hand spans away. There was a soft popping sound, and Wendall's eyes widened as he saw the result.

The mist had instantly and entirely vanished. It had disappeared into the amulet, completely absorbed at its first touch. It took a few moments for Wendall to fully grasp the impact of what he had seen. The most powerful destructive force he had ever known had been totally nullified. Absorbed completely into the artifact he had created with his will and his own two hands, the Mist had been utterly destroyed.

"I've done it." Wendall whispered the words at first, then yelled at the top of his lungs, "I'VE DONE IT!" He thrust his fists skyward and started to dance, then he remembered that he still carried the wand. Quickly but carefully, he settled it back into its usual resting place in the box before continuing his jig, howling and laughing to himself in glee.

As he settled down, he set about preparing the ornate little chest he had built for the occasion. He polished the outer surface once, though it already gleamed, then carefully placed the amulet, his greatest creation, on the folds of velvet inside. Locking the chest firmly, he stood silently for a time, enjoying the feeling of accomplishment he had justly earned.

The King had given him a commission to complete an extraordinary task: create an artifact that would defend against all magickal attacks. Although peace had reigned in the kingdom of Samidia for years, the King had become increasingly wary of spies and traitors of late. For reasons all his own, he felt particularly vulnerable to magickal attack. He wanted to be sure that no one could use any mystical means to harm him, and so had set Wendall to the task.

It had sounded simple enough at the time, but as Wendall had dug into his research, he had discovered that the issue was far more complicated than he had thought. There were thousands of ways to harm someone with magick, only limited to the power, will, and creativity of the attacker, and so there were just as many defenses to be found. Fire was easy to defend against, but there was also ice. There were tales of magickal weapons that could cut through anything, and those, too, had to be considered. He discovered ways to throw lightning, cover a target with a sticky goo that would suffocate in moments, and send acid attacks that would eat the flesh from an opponent's bones. All of those spells could easily kill a man, and no single defense mechanism could deal with them all. It had been quite perplexing. Wendall had thrown himself into the task with enthusiasm, learning the ways of magickal destruction in leaps and bounds as he tried to find ways to counter it all.

As the months rolled by, Wendall spent less time at court as he spent more and more of his waking hours working on the problem. He had tried every kind of magickal ward and shield. Many of the different types of wards would cancel each other out, sometimes with explosive, disastrous results. Nevertheless, Wendall pushed forward, learning from each failed experiment and delving into ancient spells that should likely have been left undisturbed. Dark magick mixed with light as he quested for answers. He became obsessed with the challenge, and only slept for a few hours at a time as his mind turned the problem over and over, seeking a solution.

One day, he turned too quickly and bumped three small containers of arcane liquid to the floor with his elbow. Fortunately, none were volatile, and he quickly grabbed a towel and knelt to clean up the mess. As he watched the different colored liquids all soak into the folds of the single cloth in his hand, he had an epiphany: he was going about his task the wrong way.

With a gasp, he realized there was no way he could form a shield that would work against all of the myriad forms of attacking magick, but if he could find a way to *absorb* them instead, it would have the same effect. Leaving the damp towel on the floor, he hurriedly got to his feet and rushed over to his overflowing bookshelves. Standing on a rickety stool, he reached one of the larger volumes on a dusty, high shelf and brought it to his worktable. Excited, he began an entirely new course of research - that of absorption, rather than shielding.

Now, after over five years of intense study, analysis, and painstaking experimentation, Wendall had finally achieved his goal. The solution had been simple enough in theory, yet amazingly difficult to accomplish. Magick, at its most basic level, was nothing more than energy. It was either shaped by the direct applied will of a conjurer, or wrought into a predetermined form by an enchanted object. Whatever form the spell might take, whether it be a blast of fire, a disintegration ray, or even something as benign as an illusion spell, it all began with the same kind of power.

Wendall had found a way to attack any incoming spell and touch it on that fundamental level. Any spell that came within reach of the amulet's power was instantly turned back into its original form of pure energy and then safely absorbed into the shining metal, leaving the wearer unharmed. It was a masterpiece of magickal engineering, and Wendall was flush with pride at his achievement.

After taking the time to bathe and change into clean robes for the first time in weeks, Wendall carefully lifted the chest and held it close. He took a deep breath to calm his excitement, then left his chambers to present the potent magickal device to the man who had put so much trust in him, the wise and benevolent King Lareno.

Secluded as he had been for many months, Wendall had no way of knowing that the King had gone completely, irrevocably, insane.

Chapter 1

The pounding, scratching, and clawing at the castle's massive double doors was persistent and ferocious. It was accompanied by inhuman shrieks and howls of frustration as the evil creatures of Mordak's army struggled to gain access to the ancient castle of Laro. Fortunately, the doors and windows were all shuttered tightly, and protected by the stone in such a way that it would take ages for anyone to get through them. Even so, the sharp talons of the vicious little Gholans slashed and cut away at the seasoned wood, while the savage, humanoid Krell used more conventional tools to try to create a way into the keep.

Suddenly, the shadows in the huge, empty entrance chamber were chased away by a glowing, circular portal that burst to life a few feet away from the massive doors. Layton, the youngest Guardian, stepped through the shining surface of the Gate as easily as if he were walking through an open doorway. Once he was through, it winked out of existence, leaving him alone in the room. He was already weary beyond measure, but he yet had a job to do. Tired though he was, he was looking forward to his task.

Upon his left shoulder rested his Jidaan, the powerful magickal spear that allowed him to open and use the Gates. Looking carefully, he examined the doors before him. Laying a hand on the rightmost door, he reached out with his senses to the other side and recoiled at the horror he found there. Thousands of creatures had stormed the courtyard when the outer wall fell, and now they were all trying to find a way into the castle so that they could feast on the sweet flesh of everyone inside.

A weary smile crossed Layton's face. The townspeople had all retreated to the Royal Crypt, and would soon be making their way out through an ancient and secret passageway that had been discovered by the Weya. The huge stone doors would close behind them, sealing them off from the rest of the castle, and keeping them safe from the resulting collapse of the great stone structure. Layton had been asked to make it easier for Mordak's creatures to enter the castle so that many of them might be killed within as it fell. It was an assignment that Layton was honored to fulfill.

The young warrior had noted that the doors were tightly latched and locked, and a massive iron-capped beam had been laid in place as a locking bar. With a smooth, practiced motion, he slid his Jidaan over his shoulder and into its sheath. The short spear's long blade slipped into the leather holder easily, leaving the sparkling opal in its pommel to sparkle just over Layton's right shoulder. Moving quickly, Layton stepped over to the locking bar.

The huge timber likely weighed more than a handful of men, but Layton had already decided not to try to lift it. His newfound power as a Guardian might well have allowed him to pick it up, but the effort would cost him dearly, and he did not need to work that hard. Instead, he went over to one side and pushed one end of the bar until it slid out of its bracket and fell with a ponderous thump onto the flagstones of the floor. He repeated the maneuver on the other side, and the bar slammed down to the flagstones. The timber still held the door shut, but out of its brackets, even its great weight would eventually be shoved aside by the hideous creatures who were determinedly working on the other side.

Layton stepped away from the doors, bringing his short spear into a fighting position again, holding its long blade in front of him. Like all of the Jidaan, Layton's weapon was not quite as long as he was tall. It had a wickedly sharp blade on one end, almost a short sword, and an ornate steel diamond shape on the other. Within the clutches of the pommel glimmered a large opal, its rainbow fire shining in the dim light of the chamber. His was the Jidaan of Gates, carried centuries ago by his ancestor, Dani. She had been a warrior priestess, according to Brunar, and she had been highly skilled in the use of both the Jidaan itself and its Gift.

Although Layton was known throughout the Realm as the Weaponsmaster and could fight with any weapon, learning to use the Jidaan's ability to create magickal portals had taken far more time to understand. After days of almost constant combat in defense of the castle of Laro and using both muscle and magick to the full, the young warrior was very nearly spent. Even so, he had happily accepted the task of luring the evil creatures of Mordak to an almost certain doom. The doors rocked and shuddered as the Gholans and Krell worked at them. Cracks started to appear in the hard wood and Layton knew that Mordak's horde would soon swarm into the castle in an angry flood.

Satisfied, Layton turned away, preparing to open another Gate that would take him back down to the Royal Crypt where his fellow Guardians awaited. Before he could invoke his Gift, something huge, furry, and powerful slammed into him from the shadows of a nearby stairwell, driving him to the floor. The

Morcat was a head taller and thickly muscled, and only Layton's heightened reflexes kept him from being killed outright. The part of his mind that wasn't immediately concerned with saving his own life dimly realized that the Morcat must have gained entry through an upper window or balcony and crept back down to the first level.

Dropping his Jidaan to the floor, Layton grappled with the beast, straining to keep hold of its thick wrists so it could not use its fearsome claws. He levered a knee up in between their bodies and only barely avoided the Morcat's snapping fangs. Exhausted as he was, he knew he had only moments before the creature would overpower him.

Shifting one hip towards the ground until he was lying on his side, Layton scissored his legs sharply while rotating the beast's arms at the same time, flipping its back to the stones. Rolling with the movement, Layton ended up sitting on the surprised Morcat's chest, still grimly hanging on. He slid his right knee up to pin the creature's left arm to the floor. Moving with ruthless efficiency, Layton released the beast's wrist, pulled a dagger from his belt, and drew it across the struggling monster's throat. A scarlet spray of hot, coppery blood fountained up at him as the Morcat continued to struggle. It took only a few tense moments for the light to leave the creature's eyes and its body to sag limply to the floor. Layton wiped his bloody dagger on the Morcat's matted fur and then stuck it back in its sheath as he slowly got to his feet. He walked over and picked up his Jidaan, glad to have it back in his hands again. He gathered his will to invoke its Gift, eager to join his comrades in their escape below.

Suddenly, the massive double doors cracked. Shards of jagged wood flew inwards, showering Layton as he covered his face with one arm, and the howls of the creatures on the other side intensified as they felt the barrier begin to fail. One of the doors was pushed inwards a few inches, the massive locking bar on the floor slowly scraping along the stones. Another shove gained more ground, and a final, tremendous heave pushed the rightmost door open enough for the first of Mordak's creatures to burst through. Layton turned to face them, his Jidaan vibrating in his hands.

The Krell that had first breached the door was strongly built, his skin the color of dark red clay. He wore a leather cloth around his hips, and little else. Trinkets and designs covered much of his muscular body. His partially shaven head showed intricate tattoos intermingling with battle scars, and the remaining shock of raven hair was bound up in a knot held with tiny bones and rawhide cord. One hand gripped a wicked looking axe; the other held a long dagger at the ready. Obsidian eyes gleamed in the dying light like inky pools of hate as they fastened on the bloody figure of Layton. The Krell warrior opened its mouth wide as it screamed a chilling battle cry, showing off its sharpened teeth. It hurled itself at Layton in a killing frenzy even as others of its kind began to push their way through behind it.

Fortunately, Layton had been through this scenario before - hundreds, if not thousands, of times in the last few days alone. He was well-acquainted with the fighting style of the Krell, having spent hours defending the outer wall of Laro and sending many of them to their deaths. Although fatigue was burning in his muscles, a lifetime of fierce training combined with his own newly-awakened magick gave him strength. Layton moved gracefully and quickly, almost without conscious thought. The Krell may as well have been moving in slow-motion. Layton glided forward, a distracted half-smile on his face, and dispatched the attacking figure before it even had time to be startled. The follow-through from the killing blow swept into the next Krell, and with a whirling step that any dancer would have envied, the young warrior mortally stabbed a third.

Those that clawed their way through the widening opening clambered over their fallen comrades, attacking the lone warrior without hesitation. For every Krell he left bleeding on the floor, three more scrambled for a chance to remove Layton's head from his shoulders. Wounds started to appear on the young man's body as if by magick. Layton's skill and strength were legendary, but even he had limits, and he had come upon them at last. One knobby war club hurtled towards him, and though he shifted properly, he was a bit too slow. It glanced from the side of his head even as he killed the snarling Krell in mid-swing. The blow left Layton stunned and dizzy.

Still more Krell, and now the hideous little Gholans as well, poured into the entrance chamber. Layton knew that he had to escape. He swung his Jidaan around him in a flash that cleared a space. The creatures nearest him already knew how deadly his shining weapon could be, and they stepped back a pace to regroup. A low rumble rolled through the stone of the castle, causing dust and tiny bits of debris to fall from the ceiling. Layton knew that the doors below were open, and the castle would begin to collapse at any moment. He glanced over his shoulder and saw a group of Krell already attacking the doors to the lower level, where the townspeople had gathered. He knew they could not have all escaped through the secret doors down below. If the Krell broke through and found them now, the slaughter would be devastating.

No! He thought. *I must give them more time!*

He gathered what strength he had remaining and burst into a run that surprised the Krell, leaving them behind as though they were standing still. As he sprinted past the creatures at the door to the Crypt, Layton reached out with one hand and slapped several of them on the backs of their heads, all in a row, *pop- pop-pop-pop-pop!* This immediately drew a round of infuriated howls and murderous glares. Layton stopped at an archway, an entrance to the wider corridor that led to the upper levels. As the Krell frantically tried to catch up to him, he had just enough time to look over his shoulder, bend over, and smack his own backside a few times, taunting the fierce warriors before running away. Layton couldn't stop himself from grinning as the Krell howled in outrage and furiously raced to follow him. It had been childish, he knew, but effective. All of the Krell that had been working on the door to the Royal Crypt were now in hot pursuit, howling for his blood.

He waited until they were within reach, then turned and efficiently killed the foremost so they would fall and impede those behind. Layton retreated a few steps and repeated the process, drawing the frenzied cannibals towards him and away from the Crypt with each step. Fatigue burned all through him now, and the dizziness had become a problem. As he moved backwards, he found the steps leading to the next level and carefully moved upwards, his Jidaan flashing out and killing more of the ferocious Krell and smaller, but no less vicious, Gholans. As he mounted the steps, the entrance chamber beyond became visible over the heads of his attackers. Layton grunted in satisfaction as he saw the main doors burst fully open, admitting a bristling, howling flood of Mordak's creatures. Layton felt another, stronger rumble that shook the stone beneath his boots. He knew that he should hold the attention of Mordak's forces for just a little while longer, drawing as many of them after him as he could. Then he could Gate himself back to the Crypt and escape with the others, leaving the evil invaders to die under tons of falling stone.

Giving ground only grudgingly, Layton continued fighting as he backed up the stairs. His head still ached and spun, and his arms were starting to shake. His time was running out, and he knew it. If he could just hold on for a while longer.

As he moved to attack a Krell warrior on his left, something slammed into him from the right, sending him stumbling back into the stone wall behind him as pain exploded from the impact. The wall knocked the wind out of him, and Layton glanced down to see that a small hand axe had sheared through his mail and was still embedded in the thick muscle of his right shoulder. A dagger clanged loudly from the stone near his head, and another axe, the handle this time, clipped his left knee. The Krell had learned that they could deal death from a distance while staying out of reach of Layton's deadly spear blade.

Wincing in pain, Layton tore the small axe from his shoulder and promptly buried it in the nearest Krell's forehead before lunging into an awkward sprint around the next corner. His head was spinning and the pain was making it difficult to think. He knew he needed to Gate himself out, but he suddenly realized he couldn't picture a safe spot in the Crypt below. Hundreds of townspeople would be crowding through the passageway; there was no way to know where he could safely appear. Layton turned and slashed at a Gholan that had gotten too close, and then at a Krell that had climbed over the corpse. He had to get out, but to where? The pain and exhaustion threatened to overcome him, but he stumbled onward, up the stairs, drawing still more of the evil creatures in his wake.

He came to a wooden door at a landing and yanked it open to find what appeared to be a storage chamber. Without hesitation, he flung himself inside and slammed the door closed, only to hear the frustrated howls of the foul monsters outside as they attacked it. They would be inside in moments, but a moment was all Layton needed.

Taking a deep breath and finding the core of stillness that he drew upon, that peaceful place within himself that nothing could touch, he found the strength to invoke the Gift of his Jidaan. A shimmering, opalescent portal opened in the air before him, brightening the small room with its radiance. Clutching his bleeding shoulder with one hand, and holding his flaring Jidaan in the other, Layton fell into it and was gone.

The wooden door splintered and crashed open barely an instant later, but the ravening Krell and bloodthirsty Gholans found nothing. Nothing at all.

Chapter 2

Slowly, deliberately, the man who had once been a farmer climbed the few steps to mount the dais. He walked towards the remaining weapon on the wall. With each step, the emerald in the pommel of the Jidaan shone more brightly, welcoming him. His eyes roamed over every inch of the steel and oak of the spear, taking in its exquisite workmanship, its polished shine, the grain of the wood in the handle. He looked at the wooden replica he had created, a substitute for him to familiarize himself with the balance of the weapon while on the road. It had come a long way with him, but its time had passed. Compared to the real thing, it was nothing but a toy. Carefully, Gart leaned it on the wall next to the mounted Jidaan, and then stood tall before the spear.

Gart's right hand rose slowly. He reached for the Jidaan, but hesitated. Two heartbeats went by, then three. Then Gart grasped the handle, and his world exploded.

A burst of emerald green radiance overwhelmed his senses, along with the scent of rain, of earth and growing things. The hair on the back of his neck and his arms stood in response to the energy that crackled around and through him, and Gart's vision blurred and dimmed until he saw nothing but the darkness of a moonless night. He looked down, but could see nothing of his own body or the Jidaan he held. Indeed, he could feel nothing from any part of his body save a vague feeling of weightlessness. Recognition dawned for a brief moment as he realized he had experienced a similar feeling while in the Lake of Whispered Sorrows under the care of the Lady RaeLynn. Her magick had felt something akin to this, though this felt stronger, more intense.

The dark deepened, then there was a sensation of rapid movement that left Gart disoriented. He tried to squeeze his eyes tightly against it, but it did not help. Long heartbeats passed as he fought a rising sense of nausea and dizziness. Eventually it cleared, and Gart found a certain sense of balance again.

Far in the distant dark, his sight was drawn to a cluster of flickering lights ahead and below him. They were indistinct at first, but resolved into tiny dancing pinpoints of light. Torches, he realized, and a few larger fires, blazed in the distance against the dark of night. He sensed that he was high in the air. Gart cast his eyes downward and saw a leafy canopy far below him, a forest that stretched for miles in all directions. Of his own body, he saw no sign, but everything else came into sharp focus. Sensations assaulted him: the smells of the woodland below, the scattered songs of the night birds, and the wind as it rushed by. There was something vaguely familiar about his surroundings, and soon enough, he discovered why.

His awareness swept towards the distant fires, and dread blossomed in his heart. "No. Oh, no..." On some level, he felt and heard the words leave his lips back in the Hall where his body yet stood. He knew this was just a vison, a shadow of what had been, like the dreams Brunar had given him. But this was not something he wanted to see. "Goddess, please. Not this."

The vision continued unabated. His shade hurtled towards the fires until he could see his worst fears realized. At the edge of the forest was a small town. Some of the fires were torches, while others were buildings that had been set ablaze. Figures were running everywhere, some hastening into the shelter of the buildings, others coming together in combat. As he approached, he could finally hear the screams of the townspeople, yells of ferocity, agony, and fear. The smells of burning timber, blood, and other unsavory things reached him, and he found himself fighting the urge to retch.

It was Tiller's Grove, his village, the night of the Festival. The night that Jor Dayne and a small army of Gholans and undead riders killed everyone in sight. The night that Jor Daye had killed his Gennie and Rheann. Although Gart knew it had occurred months ago, in this place of spirit, it was happening again right before his eyes. Rage and despair boiled up within him, yet he was helpless to do anything but watch the scene as it played out before him.

He saw the hideous little Gholans darting everywhere, slashing and biting anything that came within reach of their razor sharp claws and slavering jaws. Ragged, foul-smelling humans with glowing red eyes wandered through the town, hacking and stabbing as they went. People Gart had known his whole life ran by, bleeding, screaming, dying right in front of him. Gart's anger was equaled only by his desperation as he realized that somewhere in this melee were his wife and daughter. He tried to move and found that he could not; he could only observe. Cursing silently in frustration, he scanned the chaotic scene, searching for Gennie and Rheann. From somewhere, he heard the laugh that had haunted his dreams, the evil, beautiful laugh of the Slayer, Jor Dayne.

Just then Gart saw a figure burst from the forest, a longbow in his hands. Blood from a slain buck was still on his shoulders, and his blue eyes blazed with an icy ferocity as he started loosing arrows into the murderous Gholans. The man's blond hair and the scars on his face left no doubt as to his identity. Gart was startled to see himself this way, dealing death to every snarling creature that crossed his path, desperate to save his family.

Just as Gart watched himself draw the final arrow from his quiver, every living thing within his sight suddenly froze. Nothing moved. Gart looked around in disbelief and saw men fighting with broken bagatt sticks frozen in mid-swing as they tried to defend themselves. The flames of torches and bonfires were completely still in their mindless dance. All was still.

Without warning, Gart was whisked to another part of the village, away from where his other self battled Jor Dayne's creatures. Before he could protest, he found himself looking right at the town baker. The man had tormented Gart many times over the years, even splitting his lip once when he thought Gart had been stealing from him. Now, he was just another old man. His once strong body was now bent and stooped, a victim of some kind of illness that had robbed him of his vitality these last few years. His wrinkled face was contorted with terror and one spindly arm was raised as if it could ward off the sword blow that was about to end his life. The scarlet-eyed dead man before him was already in mid-swing, the already bloodied sword frozen in a downward sweeping arc that would kill the baker.

Gart looked at the baker and realized that the old man was not alone. Behind him cowered three children, their tears making shiny tracks along their dirty faces. The surly oldster was protecting them, even though it was obvious that he was no match for the undead Rider. Without warning, everything burst back into motion and the sword came down.

"NO!" Gart screamed, and tried to surge forward to save the baker and the children, but it was no use. The old man continued to fight after the killing blow had landed, but he finally fell, bloody, to the earth at the Rider's feet. Even then, the old man reached up with one liver-spotted hand to clutch at the Rider's boot. With a series of brutal chops, the Rider finished the baker, and then the children, before moving on. Gart's heart ached with rage and sorrow.

Before he could begin to collect himself, all movement ceased once more and his spirit was instantly somewhere else. This time, three men, farmers all, were defending a small tavern against a band of vicious Gholans. The men had swords, and although obviously clumsy with the unfamiliar weapons, they were determined.

"No, Goddess, there are too many of them..."

Gart's observations proved correct as the vision snapped into motion once more. Suddenly, the Gholans were everywhere, and they swarmed the three men. They went down screaming in a flurry of slashing claws and rending teeth. Blood flew on the evening breeze. It was only then that Gart saw the faces in the windows of the tavern – women, children - all doomed, and they knew it.

In the next instant, Gart was inside the tavern. He had seldom been inside, but knew the place well enough. There were two women and a lad of thirteen summers trying to barricade the door with one of the big wooden tables, while one of the older children tried to calm the younger ones in the corner farthest from the entrance. Just as they managed to get the table levered against the door, the Gholans chose the windows instead.

Gart tried to scream, but no one could hear him. He watched, helpless, while the women and the oldest boy fought valiantly against their monstrous attackers, armed with nothing more than knives and a skillet from the kitchen. It was hopeless, and they had no chance of winning, but still they fought. They fought not for themselves, but for those who could not fight. And they gave everything they had.

Again, Gart was taken somewhere else. Again he witnessed a snippet of the battle that he had experienced only in terms of what it had cost himself. He saw ordinary people rising up to fight against fearsome creatures and overwhelming odds to protect others. Again and again, he saw them die.

But still they fought.

Emotions that felt far too large for him to hold inside all warred within his soul - anger, despair, rage, frustration – if only he had been there when the attack began...

"I'd have died with the rest of them."

If only he'd been able to use his power...

"I had been taught that it was evil, and I held it back. But it's not." He had just seen, up close, the nature of true evil. For as long as he could remember, Gart had been unloved, ridiculed, and feared because of his power and his unfortunate scars. He now knew, without a doubt, that he was nothing like the creatures he had seen. Neither he, nor his power, were evil.

"My parents and the townspeople...they were just afraid of me. They knew no better."

He remembered the baker. Though always rude and testy, he nevertheless had been willing to give his life for the children. He could have escaped into the trees, but he had not. In every instance he had seen, these simple people had given their lives while attempting to save those who couldn't fight.

All movement ceased again, and Gart was moving through the frozen figures, locked in combat. Dread blossomed in his heart as he saw that his shade was heading for the barn. He had last seen Gennie dragged from the structure by her hair, a captive of the monstrous being that called itself Jor Dayne. The doors were firmly closed now, but they were no deterrent to Gart in his spirit form, and he moved through them without slowing.

He saw her immediately. Gennie was in one corner of the barn, surrounded by a dozen terrified children. She knelt among them, and although Gart could not make out her words at first, he could hear her calming tone. His heart nearly broke at the sight of her. She tossed her long black hair over one shoulder and mustered a smile for the children.

"Logan, you're the oldest," she was saying to one little boy, a little taller than the rest. "You have to lead the others now." The boy had obviously been crying, but sniffed once and tried to be strong for her. Gennie continued, "Everyone hold hands until you reach the forest." The children reached for each other and clasped tightly. To Logan, she said, "Once I kick out this board, all of you run for the trees. Make no sounds, and run as fast as your little legs can carry you!" Logan nodded, determination battling with fear on his dirty face. "Someone will find you soon." As she added this last, tears spilled down her pretty face. She hoped and prayed that her words were true. She reached down to the last child in line and hugged her fiercely. Her hair was dark, just as Gennie's was, and when she turned, Gart found himself looking at eyes as blue as his own. Gart's whole world came to a stop as he recognized his daughter, Rheann.

Gennie kissed Rheann once more, then stifled a cry as she stood and turned towards the wall of the barn where she kicked repeatedly at one board in the corner. It had already been loose, and it came out quickly, leaving an opening just large enough for Logan and the others. "Hurry! Go now!" Logan ducked out of the hole and began helping the others through.

Just then, something slammed against the barn doors. They held, but the noise came again. Frantic, Gennie raced to one side of the barn and began pulling bales of hay towards the corner, piling them up to hide the children as they escaped. She managed to get four bales in place before the wooden beam shattered at the barn doors. Leaving the corner, she moved as far from the children as she could, intending to draw attention away from their escape, hoping that all, including Rheann, would make it out in time. Although she was filled with terror, she managed to hold herself together as the children escaped.

Gart watched her display of composure and bravery in silence, his heart aching to be able to help her. For the first time since that night, Gart allowed hope to blossom in his heart. Rheann was escaping! She might, even now, be safe!

The doors finally crashed open and a score of hissing, snarling Gholans burst into the barn, followed immediately by the hulking figure of Jor Dayne atop his horse, his great blade held high. Gennie screamed, her fear finally winning through. The huge figure reached for her with one hand and she screamed again as she dodged away. She caught sight of the Gholans crawling like evil spiders all over the inside of the barn, and a new fear gripped her. They might find the children! She had to do something. Looking around her, she spied the nearest possible weapon and snatched it up.

The Slayer took one look at the young woman, alone in the barn, awkwardly holding a pitchfork in front of her, and burst out laughing. Before he could move, Gennie had lunged towards him and stabbed him in the belly with the pitchfork. She yanked it out again and backed away.

He stopped laughing.

"I don't know who you are or what you want, but you'll not take me without a fight, you murdering bastard. Want some more? Come and get it!" Gennie spat at him, her fury plain to see. Tears ran freely down her face, but she did not cower. She knew she had to draw the attention of as many of the evil creatures as she could.

An impossibly wide grin appeared on Jor Dayne's face as he looked down at the determined young woman who opposed him.

"Well, well. You're a spirited one, aren't you?" he purred. The huge figure lifted one leg over the saddlehorn and lazily slid down to stand in front of Gennie. He slid his sword into its scabbard and raised both arms in a gesture of surrender as he slowly walked towards her. Gart raged inside. He knew what would eventually happen.

Before Jor Dayne could speak again, Gennie darted forward and slammed the pitchfork into his body again as hard as she could. Its tines went all the way through his torso, yet he did not flinch in the least. Instead, he dealt Gennie a vicious backhanded blow that sent her sprawling senseless to the dirt. The swarming Gholans nearby hissed with glee at the sight.

Gart's fury was indescribable. He would have given anything in that moment to be physically present, to be able to do anything that would change the outcome of that awful night. At least he knew Rheann might be safe, hiding in the woods somewhere nearby.

Gart watched as Jor Dayne extracted the pitchfork from his body and tossed it contemptuously away. He reached down and grabbed Gennie by her hair, her beautiful hair, and dragged her back towards his horse. The huge figure mounted up, then spurred the horse out of the barn, dragging Gart's love as he went. Moments later, one of the undead Riders walked by and almost casually tossed in a flaming torch. The hay caught fire immediately, spreading hungrily to the old walls of the barn.

Gart was reeling from all he had seen, and his focus began to blur. He was moving again, slowly this time, his awareness leaving the barn as the flames grew. Just then he heard a familiar cry and looked back at the barn to see that Rheann was still in the corner, cowering behind the hay bales as the barn burned.

Despair claimed Gart. He had found her bloody shoe back then, and had thought her dead. Seeing her like this, alive again but soon to die, was nearly more than he could take. He lost sight of her tiny figure as his spirit floated upwards, out of the barn, away from the slaughter and smoke and blood. Soon, he was high enough that he could no longer make out individual faces, only the dancing of the flames as the town burned and his people died. As his spirit left the barn, he knew now that it was as he had first believed. Both Gennie and Rheann were dead, along with everyone he had ever known.

But they had fought. They had not given in, even though they were outnumbered and overwhelmed, they had fought. Seeing Gennie like that, determined to protect the children, had marked Gart, had changed him.

As he floated higher, and the fires of his village merged into a single flickering light in the vast forest below, Gart saw something to the north. Another flicker. In an instant he was there, and was shocked to see that it was another village much like his own, only smaller. It, too, was under attack. Gholans, undead Riders, and strange cat-like creatures he had never seen before were raging through the humble town, slaying everyone they met.

Before Gart could respond, his spirit moved away again, higher, and he saw another glimmering light to the south. Again, his spirit was abruptly there, and he discovered a much bigger town with cobblestone roads and stone buildings. Its fate was much the same. The dead lined the streets and their blood mingled in sticky pools on all sides. Gart was shocked at the display of bloodshed.

Gart drifted higher once more, and finally he caught sight of more lights in the distance, more dancing flames at more villages and towns. Just a few at first, then a score, then hundreds. Somewhere out in the dark, Gart heard harsh evil laughter. Some part of him knew it was the man behind it all - Mordak. The many fires below merged until he saw nothing beneath him but flame and blood and death.

Gart squeezed his eyes shut and was surprised to find that they worked again. For a moment, he saw nothing. When he opened them, he was standing back in the Hall of Jidaana, his feet firmly upon the dais. In his right hand, finally free of its brackets on the wall, was the Jidaan of Storms, its emerald fire still shining in the dimly lit hall. Gart's body vibrated with its power and he felt its awakening deep within his soul. It was his.

Concerned, Beauty whined. Gart turned to look at her and discovered that tears had been streaming down his cheeks. The huge dog leaped forward to nuzzle at Gart's legs, nearly knocking him down in the process, and Gart steadied himself before he could fall. He wiped a sleeve across his face, which did nothing but smear the tears around. Exhausted in both body and spirit, Gart knelt beside the huge dog, carefully laying the powerful and ancient Jidaan on the floor within easy reach. Beauty tried to lick his face and he barely managed to avoid the huge tongue as he ruffled her fur in return. Her concern touched him, and he welcomed it.

He spent a few moments in silence with the dog, letting it all sink in. What had seemed to be an eternity to him had likely only been a couple of heartbeats, though he had experienced much. Quelling his turbulent emotions, he turned everything over in his mind as he decided what to take from it. Then he turned it all over again.

He wanted to wallow in his rage, in his lust for vengeance against those who had taken his life away from him. Gennie and Rheann had been the only things that mattered to him, and they had been savagely killed. He ached for justice. His anger was almost a living thing, screaming for release.

Then he sighed. He had seen that it was no longer just about Gennie and Rheann. As much as he loved them, as much as he was outraged at their deaths, there were hundreds, no, thousands of others dying. All were falling prey to the very same horror that had taken his family from him.

Everywhere he had looked, he had seen people rise to fight that horror, even those who had no power against it, no chance whatsoever of winning or even emerging alive afterwards. Overwhelmed by evil and faced with certain doom, the powerless fought back. They fought with everything they had to protect themselves and the strangers that stood beside them.

Having settled Beauty down, Gart reached over and picked up his weapon. As his hand touched the smooth wooden handle, the emerald nestled in the Jidaan's pommel flashed brightly in welcome, and its power rumbled through his body again. He looked at the shining steel of the blade, untarnished and gleaming after untold centuries, razor-sharp and beautiful. Its magick called to him, awakening his own, joining with it as it was meant to do. He smiled.

He was not powerless. He could stop them.

"Jor Dayne. Murderer," Gart spoke quietly into the emptiness of the Hall. "Mordak. Whatever you are. I'm coming for you both. May the Goddess have mercy on you, because I surely as Hel will not."

Chapter 3

The castle of Laro had always been there, it seemed. It had watched over its citizens for centuries, its tall spires and thick walls lending the people a sense of steadfastness and security as they lived their lives within its benevolent shadow. It had towered over the city, a prime example of ancient architecture that blended defensibility with beauty.

Now, only the broken outer wall and an immense pile of rubble remained.

Within that rubble, thousands of evil creatures had died, crushed to death as the castle collapsed. They had stormed the towers, filled the castle from top to bottom. They were caught unawares, just as the Duke had intended. Thousands more milled around outside the broken wall and within the rubble-filled courtyard, deciding what to do next. Without orders, they were directionless. Mordak and his Champion, Jor Dayne, had been inside the castle when it had fallen, and had not been seen since. Some of the Gholans had fled, their cowardly nature asserting itself, but the compulsion laid upon them by the evil Mordak was yet strong in the rest of the horde. At a loss for anything better to do, they waited.

The night sky was just beginning to show signs of the coming dawn, and the creatures relished the remaining darkness as best they could. Many, especially the Gholans, would find nooks and crannies to hide in during the day unless otherwise ordered by Mordak himself. The day held no true harm for them, but their black hearts yearned for the cover of night, where evil deeds could more easily go unseen. A few of them carefully picked through the huge jumble of broken stones, finding an arm here, a leg there, something to nibble on until new directives were given. The Krell had lost many warriors, but the survivors felt no remorse or sadness for them. They quested through the remains of the shattered castle in search of anything interesting, valuable, or of use. If they found a piece of an old comrade, so much the better. Food had been scarce of late.

One of the Morcats ventured near the area that had once been the main entrance. A familiar smell was there, but deep down, beneath the jumble of stones and shattered wood. The Morcat sniffed a few times, then started to move away, not wanting to get any closer to the owner of that particular aroma.

Without warning, an area several yards across violently exploded in a burst of sickly scarlet magick, sending a deadly hail of stones in all directions. Those nearest the blast died instantly as their bodies were shattered by the flying debris, and others scrambled away from the site. From a safe distance, the survivors gathered to see what would arise from the devastation.

It had been hours since the walls had fallen in upon Mordak and Jor Dayne. Shielded as he was by Jor Dayne's massive body and his own magick, the evil sorcerer had escaped certain death. He had not, however, been completely unaffected. Although he had rested for a time beneath the heavy pile of rock and regained much of his strength, he was far from wholly recovered. As he strode purposefully from the jagged crater he had just made, he cloaked himself in the image of Balroth that the Krell needed to see. Had the fierce cannibals from the eastern desert thought for a moment that he was actually Mordak the Betrayer, they would have torn him limb from limb. Instead, he appeared to them as their wicked Daemon-God, thus ensuring their undying loyalty. Masked by the illusion, Mordak's cracked and bleeding lips widened into a ghastly grin unseen by the nearest Krell warriors, who hurried to bend a knee in obeisance.

Suddenly, the sorcerer was pulled to an abrupt stop, and he looked over his shoulder to see what was impeding his progress. He had grasped his Champion by one ankle and had begun dragging him out of the crater when Jor Dayne's limp and broken body had snagged on a jutting piece of stone. Mordak snorted in contempt and gave a sharp yank, freeing Jor Dayne and leaving a smear of blood on the stone behind him. The daemon-bred warrior had certainly done his job. He had protected Mordak's body with his own, allowing the sorcerer to erect a shield to keep from being crushed under the weight of the falling stone. Of course, Mordak had not included Jor Dayne in the shield, and his unprotected body had been completely shattered.

Mordak stepped carefully through the debris until he finally set foot on the flat stones of the courtyard. Morcats, Krell, and Gholans crowded around their master, eager to hear his bidding but also reluctant to get too close lest he decide to make an example of one of them. They surrounded him on all sides, instinctively keeping a respectful distance, firelight reflected in their wicked gazes.

The sorcerer kept walking until he found a stone large enough to serve as a chair. With a disgusted smirk, Mordak released Jor Dayne's misshapen leg, letting it fall heavily to the ground as he seated himself. Once he was finally comfortable, he surveyed his Champion.

Jor Dayne had been completely pulverized. He had left a long, bloody smear behind him, and Mordak doubted that a single bone had been left unbroken. His face was mashed and nearly unrecognizable. Reaching out with his senses, Mordak found the slender thread of life that glowed within the broken form. Jor Dayne was still in there. Mordak was somewhat surprised to discover that the consciousness of the man he once had been, the simple mercenary named Lucanos, was there also. The daemon that had assumed control of the mercenary's body had mutated its flesh to suit itself, making it bigger and stronger, better to serve Mordak's needs. Lucanos could no longer do so much as lift a finger of the body that was once his. Even so, his awareness was still there, watching, listening, experiencing every brutal, vicious act of barbarism that Jor Dayne enjoyed, feeling every burst of pain from his abused body. Most men would have been driven insane long ago. Mordak did not know whether Lucanos' spirit had been driven mad, and he did not care in the least. In fact, knowing that he was still in there at all only enhanced Mordak's enjoyment of the task to come.

"Well, my brave Champion," Mordak's silken voice purred, "you're of no use to me like this. I'll have to rebuild your body. I can reknit your bones, fix your organs, and make you whole again so that you can serve me."

Behind the illusion of the blonde, boyish Daemon-God Balroth, Mordak's weathered face broke into a huge, elated grin.

"But it's going to hurt."

He could not contain his evil laughter any longer. It echoed among the ruins of the castle of Laro as he called upon his malevolent power. His long-fingered hands glowed a bloody red as he used his power to lift the shattered body of Jor Dayne/Lucanos off the ground to float in the air. A pained sound emerged from somewhere deep inside Jor Dayne and his one undamaged eye rolled frantically in its socket. He had awakened at last, and was in absolute agony. Mordak's power enveloped Jor Dayne as the sorcerer went to work.

Jor Dayne's guttural, agonized screams were a symphony to Mordak, a special kind of delicious music that made his malicious heart sing. He did so love a good performance.

Chapter 4

The massive stone doors slammed shut with a ponderous thump, narrowly missing the last Augenan, burdened as he was with a struggling human in each arm. The huge slabs of stone locked together at an impossibly narrow seam. It had been chiseled millennia ago to seal off the way from the Royal Crypt of Laro to the underground escape tunnel that ran westerly towards Rualtha. There, in the bright glow of magickal lanterns, the survivors of Laro stared at the empty wall of stone that shielded them all from the destruction of the castle above.

"No!" Nessar yelled. "Kiran! Kiran!" He struck the wall with his fists, far more strongly than one of his advanced age might be expected to do. His magick and rage gave him strength; even so, the closed doors were unaffected. The old thief continued hammering at the doors for a moment longer, then rested his forehead on the unyielding stone in despair, his breathing ragged and heavy.

Kiran had been much more than a friend and fellow Guardian; she had been the only daughter he had ever known. The thought of her being crushed under tons of stone as the castle of Laro destroyed itself emptied his heart in a rush, leaving nothing but anguish and pain. After surviving days of steady combat with the evil forces of Mordak, all slashing teeth and razor-tipped talons, to have her fall this way with escape so near was unthinkable. She was only a few feet away, just on the other side of those damnable doors. She had stayed with Brunar, the Mage, to protect the townspeople from falling debris so that they might escape the Royal Crypt. And now, both she and the Mage were gone.

The Laroans were quickly moving down the ancient passage, away from the destruction of their beloved castle. However, a small group of Augenan and humans remained to witness Nessar's pain. Ch'shok rumbled forward and stood silently observing. Although his face remained stoic, the huge leader of the gorilla-folk could feel the older man's pain keenly. He, too, had lost loved ones in the past.

ValElder Moihra, tribal elder of the mystical Weya people, slowly came forward to put a hand on Nessar's arm. She saw the tracks of tears winding their way through the dusty wrinkles on Nessar's craggy face, and could feel his agony as though it were her own. Her ancient and beautiful countenance was caught in an unaccustomed frown as she leaned close to comfort the old thief.

"Nessar, hold a moment. There is a chance we may save them!" Her melodious voice was filled with urgency. "I have yet to feel their spirits depart; they may be merely unconscious and trapped in the chamber beyond." The old thief turned tired, yet suddenly hopeful eyes towards the lovely Weya. Although her pointed ears and tilted, jewel-bright eyes were still startling to a city dweller like Nessar, they now gave him hope. He knew her to be capable and wise. She had opened the ancient doors in the first place; surely she would know how to open them again.

"How?" he rasped. "Just tell me how, lady, and I'll do it!"

Moihra gave the old man's arm a gentle squeeze. "I don't know if I can, but I will try. I will require your strength, yours and that of the others as well."

Somewhat confused, yet willing to do anything to save Kiran, Nessar gave her a sharp nod and turned reluctantly away from the closed doors.

Moihra nodded in return, then turned away to call out, "Bjarke! Duke Gensen! Alyssa! I need you all here with me if this is to work."

Moments later, the Duke stepped out of the shadows behind the Augenan. He had been overseeing the escape of his people, setting the remaining captains to the task of guiding them safely along the ancient passageway. He had returned to check on the Guardians. He was battered, bloody, and covered in rock dust, as were they all. His stern face showed neither the bone-deep sadness at the loss of his beloved castle, nor the cautious optimism he felt at seeing so many of his people still alive. His face revealed only a tired determination that was reflected in his gravelly voice. "I am here, my lady. You have need of me?"

A weary Bjarke ambled along behind the Duke, his great Jidaan sheathed at his back, a sleeping Alyssa in his arms. She looked very much like a child next to Bjarke's hulking figure, and he carried her as such. Her reddish hair hung limply over her shoulders, still damp with sweat. The past several days had taxed her healing ability to its limit and beyond. Once the massive doors had locked behind them, Alyssa had finally allowed herself to rest. Bjarke glanced down at her often, lines of concern clear on his face. Suddenly, she opened her eyes to smile up at him, and relief flowed through the big man.

The ValElder nodded in answer to the Duke and beckoned them all closer. Her Weya companions, Cohl and Ginn, said nothing as they made room for Ch'shok. The leader of the gorilla-folk shook himself and patted some of the dust out of his reddish fur before settling onto the floor. Sitting put him more or less at eye-level with the others, and his wide feet with their prehensile toes were aching furiously from days of standing combat. He turned one ear slightly towards the diminutive Weya woman so that he might hear better.

"These walls and doors were made to be impregnable once closed. However, I spent hours examining the enchantment that was laid on them eons ago, and I think I can *ask* them to open again for a short time."

"*Ask* them?" Nessar hissed. "Just like that? Are they alive?"

The ValElder gently shook her head. "Not in the way you think. These stones are ancient beyond our imagining, and have lain silent for millennia. Even the violence of the castle's demise is naught but a whisper to them. But although its purpose has already been fulfilled, the enchantment laid upon the foundations here is still present enough that I may be able to use it to open the way once more. Not for long," she cautioned, "and it will be difficult. I will need you all to invoke the power of your Jidaan and lend me what strength you have left."

"How can I help? I have no Jidaan, my lady." The Duke was perplexed, but willing.

Moihra's lovely face brightened. "You are of Royal blood, Your Grace. The doors would never have even opened had you not been present. You must add your strength to ours to let the enchantment know that you wish this to happen."

Turning to Ch'shok, she continued. "If my attempt to open the doors succeeds, I will need you and yours to get inside and retrieve the Mage and Kiran as quickly as possible. They will not stay open long. And watch for falling stone before going in; I'm sure it's piled up against the doors just waiting to fall on us when they're opened. I'll do what I can to steady it."

The massive Ch'shok nimbly got to his feet again as he replied, "If they can be rescued, we will do it." He turned and grunted sharply at some of his warriors and they snapped to attention. At his gesture, they followed him to stand near the doors, and waited.

Moihra turned to Nessar, Duke Gensen, Bjarke, and Alyssa, who was now standing with Bjarke's help, leaning on her Jidaan to steady herself. "When I turn to face the doors, all of you put your hands on my shoulders." To the Guardians, she added, "Call to your Jidaan. Awaken your Gifts. I will do the rest."

"And me?" The Duke asked quietly.

A smile lit up the ValElder's face, and she almost laughed. "Just be the Duke. I'm pretty sure you can do that, Your Grace."

"I have had a bit of practice, yes," he replied with a slight grin as he placed his hand on her shoulder.

"Can we hurry this up? They could be dying in there!" Nessar's hand was shaking as he placed it on top of the Duke's. He was trying to stay calm, and failing.

The others placed their hands on Moihra's small shoulders, Bjarke's giant mitt being the last. There was a moment of stillness, and all was quiet. Slowly, the ValElder raised her hands until both palms faced the stone door. She began to chant softly in a language that none of them knew, and her hands began to glow with a warm and comforting light.

Bjarke's deep, rumbling hum broke the stillness and his ruby Jidaan flashed into wakefulness. The ValElder gasped quietly as his immense power flowed into her, and she barely managed to keep her incantation steady. Bright multicolored sparkles suddenly danced across the blank stone as Alyssa, drained as she was, added her own energy to the spell. Nessar's inky black stone seemed to vanish within the clutches of his Jidaan's ornately wrought pommel, leaving an oily dark blot that seemed to draw light into itself. Detected only by the Weya ValElder, Nessar's silent, unseen power joined with that of the others and flowed into her small body. Her chant continued, and the glow around her hands brightened as she channeled the combined powers from those behind her. She narrowed her sparkling, tilted eyes as she focused on the doors. Gently, she made contact with the lingering enchantment embedded in the stones. Her voice rose and fell, shifting into a soft melody as she rode the magick of the enchantment, imploring the massive doors to open. For a few moments, nothing happened.

Then a loud scraping sound echoed in the cavern as the doors answered the ValElder's call. Inch by torturous inch, they began to slide apart.

Rocks began to fall out of the opening, small ones first, then larger stones followed. As Moihra had predicted, the rubble from the collapsing castle above had completely filled the subterranean chamber. Behind her, Nessar grimaced at the sight. Kiran and Brunar were somewhere under that rubble. Tons of it.

Nevertheless, he kept a firm grip on the small Weya leader's shoulder and continued sending his power to her.

Moihra changed the tone of her song, increasing its tempo and intensity. The stones stopped tumbling out into the passage, held in place by her will. Slowly, ponderously, the doors continued grinding open, but the rubble stopped falling. The opening revealed a great, jumbled wall of rock, the debris held tightly together by the pressure from above and the magick spell woven by the ValElder. It was a precarious balance. The doors continued moving until they were halfway open, and then stopped.

Still chanting, Moihra inclined her head slightly at Ginn, who instantly turned to the Augenan High Chief. "Now! We must be careful not to upset the balance of the rocks too much, for Moihra cannot hold it immobile for much longer." He pointed to the debris at the rightmost edge of the opening. "They were on that side when we lost sight of them. If you can open a way, we can probably crawl in and pull them out."

Ch'shok grunted his assent. With a quick nod to his warriors, he led them to the rocks and began carefully clearing a path into the Royal Crypt, keeping close to the door. Behind them, Moihra sang, and the Duke and Guardians held firm, lending her the strength she needed. Bright colors danced in the dimness of the underground passageway and the magick of the Jidaan shone forth in the enclosed space.

Although the strength of the gorilla warriors was immense, the going was slow. The rocks were packed together so tightly that it was difficult to move them without causing a collapse. Ch'shok was in the lead on his hands and knees, and he gradually disappeared into the Crypt. He carefully dislodged the rocks before him and handed them to the warriors who followed behind, who passed them back until they could be discarded. Inch by inch, stone by rough-edged stone, a small tunnel through the debris began to form.

Moihra's song wavered for a moment as she tired, and the entire wall of precariously balanced stones shifted with an ominous rumble. The effort of holding the massive pile of debris in stasis was a tremendous strain, but she was equal to the task. The ancient Weya leader steeled herself with a deep breath and steadied her song, concentrating on the flow of energy from those behind her. The Augenan had not even broken stride in their work, trusting the tiny woman and the power of the Guardians completely. They continued to push their way into the tunnel as they searched for Kiran and Brunar.

Suddenly, Ch'shok grunted something in Aug and his warriors paused, waiting. There was the sound of shuffling and more grunting from within the tunnel. Moments later, two limp, gray bodies were passed along the chain of sturdy gorilla warriors, from one huge pair of hands to the next. Nessar could not stifle a cry of despair as he saw Kiran's lifeless body gently laid to rest in a safe spot well away from the doors. Brunar's limp form was laid right next to hers and the Augenan began to extract themselves from the hastily made tunnel.

"Move aside, quickly! Once she allows the doors to close, they cannot be stopped!" Ginn's voice echoed from the walls of the cavern. The Augenan had all come out of the tunnel; only Ch'shok remained inside as he carefully made his way back out.

Suddenly, Moihra's song faltered and died as she collapsed. Duke Gensen clumsily caught her before she struck her head on the stone floor. Blood stained the front of her tunic and trickled from both ears, signs of the immense strain she had undergone as she channeled the intense power of the Jidaan. The instant her song had ceased, the multicolored sparkle of power winked out, leaving the cavern almost dark in comparison. Stones immediately began to fall out of the huge jumble revealed by the doors, which had already begun to scrape towards each other once again. Ch'shok had yet to emerge from the tunnel, which would soon disappear forever.

Bjarke immediately saw the danger and staggered forward. He laid his ruby-pommeled Jidaan on the floor at his feet, steeling himself for what he knew he must do. Heedless of the stones that crashed to the floor around him, he pressed both hands on the rightmost door and firmly placed one boot on the other. Applying pressure against the closing doors, he was able pick up his other foot and jam it against the opposing door as well, leaving his body suspended between the huge stone slabs as they slowly, relentlessly inched towards each other, the opening to the tunnel just beneath the big forester's suspended form. Bjarke hummed his song of power and his Jidaan answered by flaring to life once more. Its inexhaustible power flowed through Bjarke's tired body, flooding it with strength. He pushed with everything he had in him, calling forth as much of the Jidaan's magick as he dared.

The doors did not stop in their inexorable, unstoppable progression...but they slowed.

The Augenan warriors frantically dove back into the narrowing tunnel, in a frenzy to get their leader out, moving stones out of the way at a rapid pace. Boulders continued falling around them, clipping one on the shoulder and breaking his massive arm. He merely grunted and continued heaving rubble away with his good arm. Smaller stones struck the others, but they ignored the pain.

Suddenly, one of them yelled something in Aug, and the others grabbed him around his thick waist and pulled for all they were worth. At last, the bruised and bloodied form of Ch'shok flew out of the tunnel and into the arms of his warriors, knocking them all down in a heap on the floor.

"He's out! Bjarke, for Rowann's sake, get out of there!" Nessar yelled from his place at Kiran's side, having hastened to check on her the moment he was free.

Bjarke's body still glowed with the power from his Jidaan, his bass hum rumbling in his chest. He dislodged one foot and carefully placed it on the ground. The moment he had firm footing, he pushed as hard as he could, flinging himself away from the doors to land awkwardly on the stone floor. The entire cavern rocked with the impact of the huge slabs slamming shut, pulverizing the debris that stood in their path. A cloud of rock dust blew out over the exhausted figures that had stayed behind to rescue Kiran and Brunar. As the echoes slowly died away and the dust settled, silence finally fell in the cavern.

Here and there, scattered coughs could be heard as the Augenan, Guardians, and Weya slowly recovered from the ordeal. Cohl cradled ValElder Moihra's head in his lap and carefully cleaned the blood from her face and neck. In spite of the bleeding, she seemed to be breathing normally, and he was much relieved.

Suddenly, Kiran gasped loudly, the sound echoing in the stone passageway. She sat up with a startled yelp, her arms flailing over her head as if to protect herself. Nessar tried to calm her as best he could, and finally, his voice seemed to reach her. Kiran's wild eyes focused on his craggy, dusty features, and she stopped thrashing. Confusion was plain on her face for a few moments more before she seemed to find her wits. She took stock of her surroundings, noticing the pile of Augenan slowly rising, the battered Ch'shok among them. Bjarke lay facedown on the cold floor near the Duke and Cohl, who tended the still form of Moihra. Alyssa was curled in a ball on the floor, facing away from her. Finally, her eyes settled on the motionless form of Brunar lying next to her, unconscious. She raised an eyebrow and shook her head as she spoke in an exhausted, ragged voice.

"Well, this doesn't look good. Nope. Not good at all."

Chapter 5

Guided by the sure hands of Cohl at the reins, the wagon rolled steadily onward, shuddering here and there as it passed over uneven spots in the cavern. The stone floor of the passageway had been surprisingly flat for nearly a mile beyond the doors of the Royal Crypt, offering no hindrance to those who walked along the ancient way. The walls, too, had been as smooth as the surface of a calm lake, unusually uniform in their perfection. The wagon wheels creaked amiably as they turned, the monotonous sound echoing gently in the tunnel. The glowing sconces in the wall cast their warm and comforting light at regular intervals. After the harsh flames and the horrid sights and sounds of days of intense violence, Kiran had finally allowed herself to relax. Comforted by the presence of Nessar and Brunar in the wagon next to her, Kiran lay her head down on her arm and drifted into a contented doze.

That's when the easy, gentle ride suddenly ended. The wheels of the wagon abruptly left the carved portion of the tunnel and the passage roughened substantially, causing the last two wagons in the long chain of fleeing people, horses, and carts, to jostle in what seemed every direction at once.

Kiran was not happy.

"Oh, for the love of...gaaah!" She sat up and looked around, taking in the natural stone walls and occasional pointed stalactites that hung from the coarse ceiling above. In spite of the fact that a few thousand people had just passed through that section of the tunnel, the wide cavern still had an air of archaic majesty. From what little they knew, the cavern had not seen the presence of a single living thing for several centuries. Looking at the primeval stone, Kiran had the distinct feeling that the unyielding rock cared not one bit for the humans who trespassed in its domain. It would silently, grudgingly tolerate their presence until they had passed by, and then resume ignoring them and their kind for another handful of centuries. A chill ran down Kiran's spine as she wondered what else might be down there, lurking in the everlasting darkness of millennia, only catching its first sight of humans as they passed by in the light of the magickal sconces.

She dropped one hand to her Jidaan. It lay next to her in the bed of the wagon, and its realness and solidity comforted her. She closed her fingers around the oaken shaft and pulled the weapon closer until it lay across her lap, then she scooted rearwards until her back fetched up against the inside of the wagon. Nessar lay snoring next to her, while Brunar lay completely still on the other side of the old thief. Concern crawled across Kiran's face as she looked at the Mage. He had yet to regain consciousness, and Alyssa had been far too exhausted to even attempt to heal him. He had a large swelling on the back of his head. Kiran had seen worse, by far, in the training halls when someone had taken a good thump like that and happily survived to tell of it. However, those kinds of head injuries were nothing to toy with. Kiran wished again that Alyssa would recover soon enough to heal whatever was keeping Brunar unconscious.

The Mage had saved her in the Crypt, protecting her from the worst of the falling debris with his own body. Not for the first time, Kiran saw the irony of the fact that her singular Gift was that of Warding.

"Leave it to you, Mage, to shield the shield bearer." She reached a gentle hand down to touch his brow and was comforted to find no fever there. He seemed to be breathing well enough, and she hoped that Alyssa's diamond-pommeled Jidaan would be able to bring him back to wakefulness.

In the wagon immediately behind Kiran's, Duke Gensen held the reins and carefully guided the old cart horse around some of the bigger rough spots in the cavern floor. Ahead, he could make out hundreds of shuffling forms, the last of the few thousand survivors, all steadily moving away from the destruction of their beloved city. They were all covered in dust and many bore wounds and bandages. The strong helped the old and infirm over the more uneven areas, and the Duke saw several children being carried on the shoulders of members of his City Guard. A few of the Augenan had taken some of the more adventurous children and let them clamber up on their immensely broad shoulders, which were easily wide enough to hold three or four of the youngsters. They rode along, hanging on tightly as the huge gorilla-folk made their way along the tunnel.

Rather than curse the fact that there were so few survivors, the Duke chose to celebrate those that had made it out alive. It could have been far, far worse, and he knew it. He felt the anger rising in him, rage at Mordak for bringing death and destruction on his fair city, but he quelled it. One way or another, he'd make the sorcerer pay in full for what he had done. In the meantime, though, the safety of his people was his first and only priority.

Ordinarily, he preferred to lead from the front, but for now, he wished to be nearest the end instead; if any of Mordak's vicious creatures somehow discovered their escape route, he wanted to be there to meet them. His trusted advisor, Rorian, and the sturdy Captain Drattus were leading the exodus, and runners were moving back and forth, relaying messages as necessary.

Duke Gensen looked over his shoulder and saw the Guardians and Weya ValElder resting more or less peacefully. Bjarke had been first to recover from the ordeal, while Alyssa still slept. The big forester was furiously attacking a piece of dried meat, attempting to regain some of his prodigious strength. Ginn continued tending to Moihra, who had yet to regain consciousness, but at least seemed to be in no immediate danger. The wheels of the wagon continued to turn and creak and thump, the old horse snorted lazily as it walked, and for the first time in many days, there was no immediate threat. The Duke turned his gaze back to the tunnel ahead and allowed himself a relieved sigh.

Near the middle of the long stream of evacuees, the mighty Ch'shok walked warily, his eyes constantly scanning the sides and roof of the natural cavern. Often, he would reach over his shoulder to touch the blades of his double-bladed battle-axe, the Tugan, to reassure himself. As always, it was there in its harness, and its cool solidity calmed him. After spending a lifetime in the humid jungles of Triagga, where the sky was always visible through the towering trees and life pulsed around him, Ch'shok was ill at ease surrounded by the lifeless stone. He prayed to the Lady Donda, his goddess, that he would see the sky again.

Just then, another Aug warrior, Ba'hak, approached, and the Augenan High Chief stepped away from the constant flow of refugees to greet him. Ba'hak approached his leader with head bowed and one palm held out. Ch'shok grunted in acknowledgement and accepted the gesture of obeisance with a gentle scrape of his own palm on Ba'hak's, and the smaller gorilla warrior lifted his eyes to his leader's.

"My Chief," Ba'hak said quietly in their own language. "All is well with our people. We have lost few, and the others are strong."

"How many have we lost?" Ch'shok's voice was a low rumble.

Hurt flashed across Ba'hak's face as he answered. The Fist of the Augenan was tightly knit. Every Aug knew the others, and losses were keenly felt. "Not quite a hundred, my Chief."

A pang struck Ch'shok's mighty heart. Nearly a tenth of his warriors would never see the trees again. He sighed, too pained to speak.

"If I may ask," Ba'hak chose his words carefully, "has the Fist fulfilled its purpose here, my Chief?"

Ch'shok snorted and turned sharply back to Ba'hak, who immediately bowed his head and raised his hands.

"I meant no disrespect! I only know that some of the warriors were asking...we will all follow you unto death, my Chief!"

Ch'shok glared at Ba'hak for only a moment before snorting again. After gathering his thoughts, he put one massive hand on the young Aug's shoulder in reassurance.

"I wish I could say, Ba'hak. Renelda the Seer warned of a human who cloaked himself in the power of Baulotha." At the mention of the Augenan's evil god of the underworld, Ba'hak shuddered. "Her vision certainly appears to have been accurate. There is still the Prophecy to consider."

Back in the Augenan's tree-city of Neronda, their Seer had received a vision of such horror and power that it had killed her. Before her death, she had implored Ch'shok to take the Fist, a thousand Augenan warriors, to the human-city of Laro. She had said that in doing so, the ancient Augenan prophecy would be fulfilled. The battle-axe carried by Ch'shok, made eons ago of an unknown metal, was destined to strike a blow directly at the evil god, though no one knew when or how.

Although Mordak did indeed appear to have been invested with the evil god's power, no opportunity had arisen for Ch'shok to strike directly at him. Moreover, Ch'shok had a distinct sense that cleaving Mordak, although ridding the world of an obvious and deadly evil, would not fulfil the prophecy. The High Chief was puzzled.

Ch'shok shook the young Aug's shoulder roughly in reassurance. Ba'hak looked up at his leader, doubt obvious in his eyes.

"I think our path lies with these humans a while longer. Spread the word among the warriors to stay strong. Baulotha will reveal himself to us at some point, and then..." In a motion so smooth and quick it was almost magickal, Ch'shok whipped the Tugan from its harness on his back and held it up to gleam in the dim light. "The Tugan will fulfill its destiny."

Doubt vanished to be replaced by a broad grin on Ba'hak's face and he hooted loudly, startling many of the exhausted Laroans as they walked by. Sparing a brief glance at them, Ch'shok swiftly put the battle-axe away and slapped the young warrior on his back, sending him off to convey his words to the Fist.

Watching the enthusiastic Aug disappear among the milling figures up ahead, Ch'shok searched his feelings. Had he spoken truly? Would he really have a chance to strike that fabled blow? Somewhere, deep within his heart of hearts, he felt a tiny spark of...something. And it was enough.

Chapter 6

Gart sat on the stone steps of the dais, holding the Jidaan across his knees. He gently examined it, letting his callused hands explore the weapon. His rough fingers traveled over the wooden shaft, carefully touching the shining steel of the rune-etched blade before inspecting the diamond-shaped pommel and the radiant emerald gem it clutched. Although the dreams had been vivid and clear, they had not truly prepared him for the beauty of the weapon. The craftsmanship was so exquisite that it took Gart's breath away.

Beauty pushed in close to him, burrowing her head under his right arm as he sat there, almost knocking him over. She was panting and wagging her tail, still eager to have reassurance from Gart after the display of power she had just witnessed. It had only taken moments, but she had deeply felt the intense magick in the air and was still anxious.

"Hey, hey, take it easy! I'm fine, you big furball, just fine." Gart petted her roughly only to have her huge tongue flop out and hit him in the face several times. For once, he didn't shy away from it, but laughed instead. "Yes, yes, I know. Everything's all right. Come on, let's look around."

Gart nudged Beauty away and gently laid his Jidaan down. He stood and removed his backpack, which he dropped on the floor next to the shining weapon. The scabbard that Brunar had left for him was on top of a bundle of parcels, and Gart picked it up. After studying it for a few moments, he worked out the right way to wear it and slipped his arms into the straps. He cinched the few buckles that held it in place, making sure it didn't pinch anywhere.

Gart retrieved the Jidaan, marveling again at how wonderfully balanced it was. It took him a few moments to get the blade into position and then slip it into its sheath. As soon as it settled into place, Gart was astonished to find that he felt completely free to move as he wished. He walked around, swinging his arms and twisting. The weapon rode in its place along his back with perfect balance, and did not impede his movements in the least. *Must be more of Brunar's magick,* he thought. He rolled that idea around in his mind a bit, then shrugged to himself. Until now, he had only used his magick to move things. He hadn't thought of its other uses, while Brunar was obviously a master of it. Gart wondered what else he could do with his own power.

As he contemplated, Gart walked slowly around the Hall of Jidaana, his soft footsteps and the clicking of Beauty's nails echoing in the vast and empty space. The chamber was enormous, its lofty ceiling supported by eight wide stone pillars. Gart's eyes were drawn up to the glowing globes high up in the room's corners. They had no visible means of support, yet hung there, suspended, providing ample light to see by. Gart shook his head at the sight. Again he thought how Brunar's understanding of magick was far beyond his own comprehension.

Beauty snuffled at the floor and ambled towards an open doorway on the south wall. There were several closed doors along both the south and north walls. Set in the walls above six of them was a sparkling gemstone, each a twin of the stones on the dais where he had found his Jidaan. He assumed they were the living quarters of the other spear-bearers like himself. He saw a ruby, a diamond, a bright blue sapphire, a stone of deepest black, and another that seemed to combine all the colors of the rainbow in a single, fiery gem.

"Guardians," he said out loud, remembering what Brunar had called them. He tried to laugh at the name, thinking it sounded pretentious, but something deep in his soul responded with a feeling of rightness he could not ignore. The Jidaan held power - immense power. It was meant to be wielded in defense of the land, to protect it, and Gart had been Chosen to use it for that very purpose. He had tried to stubbornly rebel against the thought of being some kind of high and mighty paladin, but he now knew that where others had no power to fight against the demons that were out there, he did. He sighed. "So be it, then. 'Guardian' it is."

Beauty barked from an open doorway and he walked up to it, not surprised to see a gleaming emerald embedded above the lintel.

"Yes, of course you managed to find my room. All right, let's take a quick look and then be gone. We need to be on our way." As Gart stepped into the open doorway, he wondered exactly where he was supposed to go. "Follow your heart," the Mage had said. He had also said they were heading south to Laro to meet Mordak in battle, but that was months ago. Still, it was a place to start. South it would be.

Gart looked around the room, taking in the simple furnishings - bed, desk, privy, and simple shelves cut into the walls. It was austere, but comfortable. On a hunch, he turned and walked over to the room nearest his own and opened the door. A vaguely floral smell reached his nose and Gart could immediately see the room had been lived in. Extra blankets and pillows lay on the carefully made bed. The arrangement of furniture was different from that of Gart's room, and a vase of dried flowers sat next to a neat pile of books upon the desk. Other small decorative touches had been added, and Gart guessed the room's former occupant had been female. He wondered what she would be like, the bearer of the diamond-pommeled weapon. His own predecessor, Lillia, had also been a woman, and a potent warrior.

Beauty whined good-naturedly and brushed up against Gart's legs, nearly knocking him down. He chuckled as he reached down to scratch her ears. "All right, you, I'm sure you're hungry again. Let's go see what that Mage left for us; there might be some food in those bundles." Gart ushered the huge mastiff out of the room and looked around one last time before closing the door behind him.

Chapter 7

Mordak stood on top of the gatehouse where the Guardian had used her powers of Warding against him. The memory made him snort in disgust, thinking of how the girl had kept his forces outside the damaged wall of Laro for as long as she had. She had failed at the last, though. Brunar and his cursed Guardians had failed!

A wide grin crawled across Mordak's face and he relished the moment. His spirit had languished, awake but imprisoned, in the cold depths of a great chunk of stone for over two millennia because of that meddling Mage and his pet warriors. They had dogged his every step centuries ago, and now he, Mordak, had finally made them pay! He laughed, loud and long, and hoped that Brunar and his new lackeys had died screaming in the rubble. For all their vaunted power, they had been helpless before his own unstoppable might. "You thought you could stand against me...ME!" he shouted in triumph at the spirits of his old adversaries, "and look at what your feeble attempt to stop me has wrought!"

Corpses were everywhere. Humans lay among the bodies of Gholan, Krell, and Morcat alike, their blood mixing in viscous pools. The evil sorcerer smiled to see so many soon-to-be soldiers. Thanks to the powers he had received from the Daemon-God Balroth, whom he now impersonated, he was able to animate and control entire legions of undead bodies. They were his favorite kind of soldier; although slow, they were completely relentless. They never tired, never gave up, never fell to small wounds. They continued to strike at Mordak's enemies until they were cut to pieces. Now, thousands of them were just waiting for him to use his dark magick and bring them to unlife to do his bidding.

Mordak looked over his shoulder at the shattered remains of the Castle of Laro in irritable disappointment. He had wanted the rest of the Laroan population to add to his army, but now the great majority of cityfolk lay crushed and unusable under tons of stone. No matter. He had more than enough to assault Rualtha to the west and the forest city of Alverton Falls to the north as he pressed on towards the Royal City of Bos Aldas. By the time he reached the Heartstrong Mountains, his army would be unstoppable. This victory was but the first of many.

"Master," Mordak turned at the sound of Jor Dayne's ragged voice from the courtyard below. The fool had screamed himself hoarse while Mordak had repaired his broken body earlier. He smiled at the memory.

"What is it?" the sorcerer replied as he leaned on the broken railing, looking down at the daemon-bred being who was his eyes and ears on the field.

Jor Dayne's baleful yellow eyes burned dimly, even in the afternoon sun, giving off their own sickly glow. He looked up at the man who had brought him to this world, seeing through the glamour Mordak used to dupe the Krell into following him. The half-breed noted the prominent nose and scarlet-tinged eyes, the silvery mane of hair that fell to just above the sorcerer's shoulders. A smile crept across Jor Dayne's face before he could stop it. If the Krell could see Mordak as he could, they'd tear him apart.

Two thousand years in the past, Mordak had led thousands of Krell warriors into battle against the Realm. Using lies and false promises, he had convinced them that they would win, gaining control over the lush forests and farmland the Krell coveted. When defeat at the hands of Brunar and the Guardians was imminent, they turned on Mordak and Realmsman alike, furious that they had been misled. Over the centuries that had followed, the name of Mordak had been a curse on the lips of every Krell, an eternal hatred that burned in each of the cannibalistic, tribal warriors of the Gorran Plain. Only Mordak's appearance in the guise of their god, Balroth, had swayed them. That, and the displays of unholy power Mordak had received directly from the god himself, had won their loyalty. Mordak had to maintain a cloak of illusion about himself at all times, portraying the likeness of the wicked god, lest the Krell realize his deception.

Jor Dayne's smile widened at the thought. Although he was bound to Mordak body and soul, and compelled to do the sorcerer's bidding, there were ways around such compulsions. Jor Dayne would enjoy turning the tables on Mordak, oh yes he would. Until then, he would play the dutiful second-in-command. His throat still stinging, Jor Dayne answered his master.

"The townspeople have perished in the castle, my lord. We lost nearly two thousand of our own, but..." he turned and made a sweeping gesture to indicate the vast horde of creatures that seemed to stretch to the horizon, "we have thousands remaining. Your army is assembled and awaiting your orders."

Mordak stared down at him for a few moments and then looked away. For an instant, he had seen something in his

Champion's eyes that he did not like, but then it had disappeared so quickly he couldn't be sure it had been there at all. *No matter,* he thought to himself, confident of his control over the half-daemon. He returned his gaze to Jor Dayne and spoke.

"Gather the host and divide them into two armies, the smaller consisting of two thousand of our creatures. You will come with me and the larger group to assail Alverton Falls to the north, while the smaller group will head for Rualtha to cut off any aid they might supply. Once we have accepted the dead of Alverton Falls into our forces, the city of Rualtha won't be able to stand against us, and then we can take the rest of the Realm." His scarlet eyes gleamed brightly as he clenched his fists in his excitement. Recovering his composure, he continued, "Go and see to it!" He dismissed Jor Dayne with a curt wave. He did not see the sly grin that reappeared on the bigger man's face before he turned to organize the horde. Mordak's mind was already on other things.

"I must have a way to see what occurs at Rualtha...hmmm." Mordak scanned the battleground, his scarlet gaze roving over the bodies and blood of the dead, human and otherwise. Bent and damaged weapons were scattered everywhere like broken toys. He spied a large helmet, little more than a pot with a T-shaped opening in the front. It sported a large dent in one side and blood within. With a gesture and a flick of dark magick, Mordak called the helmet to his hand, and it floated through the air towards him. As it hovered there, the sorcerer turned it this way and that, examining it.

"Yes...yes, this will do nicely." Again using his magick, Mordak pushed out the dent even as he fished around in one of his pockets. His fingers closed on a ruby the size of his thumbnail, and he pulled it out to rest on his palm. Taking the helmet in his other hand, he gathered his will and chanted a few sentences in an ugly language that grated on the ears. Squinting, he pushed the spell into the small gemstone, bringing it to a sickly scarlet glow. Once it was afire with unholy power, he placed it on the front of the helmet, where it instantly fused itself to the metal. Mordak shook the helmet sharply to be sure the ruby was secure, and was satisfied with his handiwork.

Looking up from the helmet, he saw a pair of burly Morcats walking among the rubble in the courtyard below. Igniting his magick once more, Mordak stepped from the roof of the gatehouse to float gently to the flagstones below.

"You two! Come here!" The creatures' heads turned in the sorcerer's direction, and they approached immediately. Each of them was a full head taller than Mordak, and far wider through the shoulders. Their rank odor assailed him long before they stopped moving, and Mordak's nose wrinkled at the noisome beasts. He held out the helmet to one of them. The Morcats looked at the helmet, its ruby glowing scarlet, and then back at the sorcerer, but neither immediately moved to take it.

Without warning, Mordak unleashed a bolt of crimson power at the leftmost Morcat, blasting its body across the courtyard until its corpse slammed against one of the ruined castle walls. It slumped there, charred and lifeless. Its comrade stared at it for a moment, then turned back to Mordak, its feline face showing no emotion whatsoever, though its golden eyes narrowed slightly. It growled softly, almost to itself, as it took the helmet from the sorcerer. Its eyes glittered as it stared down at Mordak, its expression betraying nothing.

"Well, put it on, you dolt!"

Moving slowly, the Morcat reached up and began to stuff its head into the helmet. Oversized for a human and made so that a padded arming cap could be worn beneath it, the helmet was still a tight fit for the larger creature. Its growl continued, one long, low growl that voiced its displeasure without being overtly disobedient. It had seen how Mordak dealt with those who did not immediately follow orders. Once it was finally on, the Morcat shook its head several times, disoriented by the magick that the sorcerer had imbued into the helmet.

"There! Now I'll be able to see what you see at Rualtha. Go and tell that big lunk, Jor Dayne, that you are to lead two thousand of these vermin towards Rualtha. I want you to cut off any aid they might send to the north. I will give you orders as necessary through the helmet. Do you understand me, swamp cat?" Mordak's disgust was clear in his tone, and not lost on the Morcat. Even so, the Morcat obeyed completely for reasons not even Mordak fully understood.

In a rumbling voice, the Morcat spoke, carefully enunciating the words so that Mordak could understand them. "Yes, Lord. I...command...the troops...stop help...from Rualtha."

Mordak snorted, "Yes, good. You understand. Very well then, go and tell him!" He made shooing gestures at the large creature. It stared at him with its golden, inscrutable eyes for only a moment longer before leaving to find Jor Dayne. It flexed its claws absently as it walked away.

The sorcerer surveyed the carnage around him once more. Most of the human corpses that lay scattered about were far too damaged to be reused as undead soldiers. Even so, there were thousands of them both inside the shattered castle wall and out in the community, if the Gholans and Krell had not eaten them all. Mordak shouted to a nearby Gholan in its own foul language and ordered it to gather more of its kind and then scour the battlefield for relatively fit corpses.

"And don't eat them, you filth!" Mordak yelled after them as they scuttled away. "Bring them to me!" He rubbed his long-fingered hands together with undisguised glee. "We'll just wake them up and take them with us. No sense in letting perfectly good bodies go to waste!"

His laugh was harsh, raw, and thoroughly insane. An icy chill crawled up the spine of every living thing that heard that sound of madness.

Chapter 8

Captain Drattus trudged along the passageway as he had for the last few days, more tired than he had ever been in his life. That included his induction into the City Guard when he was but a lad. The drill sergeants had run him completely ragged, day after day, running, fighting, loading rocks into wagons and then unloading them, then running again. He had fallen asleep on the privy that first evening, much to the delight of his squadmates. He had never lived that down, save for the simple fact that he had outworked every single one of them that day. And the day after. And the day after that, as well. Drattus was no bigger, or stronger than any of them, but he simply would not quit.

That said, the last several days of constant fighting, no rest, and now endless travel underground had almost broken his spirit. Every stone he saw looked like a wonderful place to sit down, but he did not. He plodded on. Almost broken was not the same thing as broken. He would make it. He was leading the column of Laroan survivors, and they were depending on him to see them safely to Rualtha. He'd die before he let them and his Duke down.

Wearily, he turned and looked at the sea of faces behind him, all shuffling along the same as he. Behind the first few rows composed of the strongest soldiers, he could see the frightened and exhausted townspeople. All were dusty, and several that Drattus could see were wounded. Many helped support others or carried children; others were empty handed. Having become too tired to carry their bundles with them any longer, they had laid them alongside the walls of the ancient tunnel and continued on. They were only things, and could be replaced when they were safe and sound somewhere else.

Drattus turned his eyes forward once more, towards the darkened end of the tunnel in the distance. The magickal lights along the passageway flared into life whenever they drew near and went dark shortly after the trailing warriors and Augenan passed by. *A handy device*, Drattus absently thought as he watched another pair of lights brighten in the tunnel ahead, illuminating another section identical to the one through which they now traveled. He looked ahead, but saw no sign of the scouts they had sent earlier. Surely the lights would signal their approach if they came back with news.

Rorian shuffled up beside him, drawing him out of his contemplation. "Captain, the Duke sends word." Drattus arched an eyebrow and looked at the Duke's advisor expectantly. "He says that...hey, how are you faring, Drattus? Are you holding up well enough?" Rorian's voice held a quiet note of concern.

Drattus blinked at Rorian for a few seconds before replying with a sigh. "Sir Rorian, I regret to inform you that it appears I will survive. And thank you for asking."

Laugh lines suddenly creased Rorian's face, and his blue eyes managed the barest of twinkles as he slapped the captain on his back, sending a cloud of dust into the air.

"Well, Captain, I've seen walking dead before, and I'm just making sure you aren't one of them."

A grin finally made its way across Drattus' face. "Not just yet, Sir...not just yet."

The two men laughed together for a moment, finding a warrior's joy in a stolen moment of camaraderie, and Rorian relayed the Duke's message that all was well thus far. They were to continue until nightfall, and then the train would stop for a rest.

Drattus laughed again. "Did he say exactly how we are to know when nightfall might be? It's hard to read my sundial down here."

Rorian tried to look shocked at Drattus' impertinence, but the advisor couldn't manage it. He knew that the captain would have said the same thing straight to the Duke's face. With respect, of course. Before he could answer, a lovely feminine voice startled him nearly out of his skin.

"It is currently an hour or so before midday."

Rorian and Drattus turned to find one of the priestesses walking next to them. Neither had seen or heard her approach, and they were both somewhat discomfited by the fact. Her chestnut hair fell down her back in a single braided plait, bound at the end in a shining steel sphere. She wore a brown traveling cloak over a once-white shirt, a brown skirt, and sturdy black traveling boots. A gracefully curved longbow was slung over one shoulder, a full quiver of arrows rode at her hip, and a canvas bag was settled on her other shoulder. Above one of her pale blue eyes, Drattus noticed she had a thin scar that cut through one eyebrow. Rather than detracting from her beauty, he thought it was rather enhanced by the mark. She caught the captain staring at her and threw him a wink, causing him to jerk his eyes forward again. Her delighted chuckle did not amuse him in the slightest. It did, however, amuse a nearby Aug, who huffed deep in her chest in unsurprised mirth. Drattus glared up at her, and the huge gorilla warrior promptly puckered up and made kissing noises at him before laughing again, then turned to chat in Augenan with one of her fellows. Drattus fumed quietly to himself and proceeded to ignore everyone around him.

"Gentlemen, I'm Muriel," the priestess introduced herself. "Fiona sent me up here to aid you."

Understanding dawned in Rorian's eyes while Drattus stared straight ahead. "Ah, you're with the priestesses of Rowann! Yes, you have all been of great assistance, my lady. The Weya say there is an exit up ahead, and we should reach it eventually. I'm not sure what you can do for us up here at the moment; we are simply putting one foot in front of the other until we get there."

Muriel smiled, examining the captain's angry profile over Rorian's shoulder. *Oh, he's just darling,* she thought. She had seen him during the fighting and been impressed by his straightforward, working-man approach. Nothing fancy there, but his men certainly held him in high esteem. For that alone he'd be worth talking to, if he could lighten up the least bit. And he wasn't bad looking.

"To be honest, I'm not sure either. However, when Fiona says for me to do something, I do it." Muriel thought she saw Drattus' eyebrow raise for an instant. She could practically hear him approving of her almost military obedience to what he considered a superior officer. *Ah well, let him think what he likes; it does no harm.* She continued, "Fiona occasionally has visions of things that come to pass." Both Rorian and Drattus turned alarmed expressions her way. "She hasn't had any yet," she quickly reassured the two men, "but she had a strong feeling that she should send me up here. So..." she spread her hands wide, presenting herself. "Here I am!"

Chuckling, Rorian replied, "Well, no matter why you have been sent, we're pleased to have you with us. How did you know what time of day it is? That's got me curious."

Muriel could see that Drattus was listening in spite of himself, and she smiled broadly as she spoke. "It's something we are taught in our first year of training. It's about connecting with the magick of the world around us, getting in touch with it all. It's a very powerful lesson, and least of all it gives us the ability to tell where the sun and stars are in the sky above us at all times."

"What else does it allow you to do?" Drattus asked the question before he could restrain himself. Her voice was just so gentle and sweet, yet possessing a wiry kind of strength. It had pulled him away from his anger and embarrassment before he even realized it.

Muriel beamed at him, a big smile lighting up her face as she spoke. "It's different for each of us after that. Some are healers, some are seers, and some of us..." she paused, deciding how to phrase her words. "Some of us are, um...our gifts end up being more physical in nature."

Both men looked puzzled for a moment.

"We're good fighters and scouts," she added.

"Oh, of course!" Rorian exclaimed with a chuckle. "Well, that doesn't surprise me at all. I've heard tales of your prowess from both Eli and Brunar."

Just then, a cool breeze washed over their faces, and they all gasped quietly at the unexpected pleasure. It was a welcome feeling after so long in the dead air of the tunnel. Drattus was instantly on alert.

All business, the captain turned to point out the first two rows of guards, ten hardened soldiers. "You men, come with me. If there's an opening up ahead, we need to check it out before the entire train gets there."

Muriel frowned. "Hey! I just said that some of us are scouts. Did you not hear me?"

He blinked at her for an instant, then waved her on. "Fair enough, then. If you're any good with that bow, then maybe we can use you."

Muriel rolled her eyes and tilted her head towards Rorian. "Well, I'm glad he thinks I'll be able to lend a hand."

"Don't let him bother you. It's been, shall we say, a rough week."

She flashed a smile as she moved forward with the others. "Yes, that is quite true. I'll just try to keep him from hurting himself." Her grin was infectious, and Rorian grinned back. He liked these priestesses; they were capable and intelligent, and likely to give Drattus fits.

Three Augenan also moved forward with the advance party, eager to see the sky again. They moved their enormous bulk with surprising speed on their hard knuckles and broad feet, and Drattus was pleased to have them.

They moved quickly along the corridor. The lights burst to life ahead of them, showing yet more of the tunnel until they abruptly stopped. As the party drew closer, it became clear that a cave-in had occurred at some point, almost completely filling the passageway with broken stones big and small. An opening, hardly larger than a man, was still passable next to the leftmost wall. Through that narrow space, a golden spear of sunlight was visible in the near distance. A refreshing breeze issued from the opening, cooling the rank sweat on their faces and necks and bringing a collective sigh of relief.

Drattus narrowed his eyes as he examined the rockfall and the cramped passage that seemed to lead to the outside. He held up a hand for those around him to stop, and they did, falling silent as they surveyed the area. The captain stayed quiet for a few moments, then voiced his concern.

"Where are the scouts? At least one of them should have come back to let us know about this, even if the others moved on ahead."

Muriel's voice seemed to startle Drattus, coming as it did from right next to his shoulder.

"I agree completely. Someone should have been left behind."

Drattus eyed her warily for a moment, receiving only a pretty smile in return, before turning back to the scene in front of him. He edged closer to the gap and examined the surrounding debris. After a time, he decided that both scouts must have gone to survey the exit. That wasn't much of a problem, but the fact that they had yet to return did not sit well with Drattus. Procedures were in place for a reason, and the scouts had not followed them.

Drawing his sword, he pointed out five of the nearest guards. "You all come with me. We'll see if we can figure out what happened to those scouts. The rest of you, start moving debris away from this opening, but be careful. If it starts to become unstable, stop immediately!" The remaining soldiers saluted and moved to place their weapons aside, but within easy reach, before starting the work. Drattus turned to the Augenan and bowed politely as he continued. "And we thank you also for your help. Your great strength will certainly be of use here if you don't mind helping to widen the tunnel." The Augenan that had made kissyfaces at him earlier grinned and huffed loudly at the smaller officer before clapping him on the back hard enough to make him stagger. She chuckled as Drattus regained his balance and then turned to speak a few words to her fellows. Moving lightly for such huge creatures, they immediately moved to the rocks, picking up the biggest ones and hefting them onto their shoulders to be carried out of the way. Drattus, the guards, and Muriel headed for the gap.

When he saw that Muriel was coming, he tried to protest and warn her away. But she was having none of it.

"I'm not a kitchen maid, Captain, though some of them are awfully tough. You may need me out there. I'm going."

Muriel's mouth was set in a stern line and she radiated confidence.

He stared at her for a beat, outraged at her refusal to follow his orders. Then he closed his mouth with a snap and raised an eyebrow at her.

"All right then. Try to keep up. If you slow us down, I'll send you back to your Fiona." As he turned away from the young woman, he found himself admiring her attitude. He needed all the help he could get, and if she thought she could hold her own, then so be it.

Muriel rolled her eyes, but said nothing. She was used to having men underestimate her, but it was still frustrating. Pulling an arrow from her quiver, she notched it to her bowstring and kept it pointed at the floor as she lined up with the others behind the captain.

Drattus kept his sword ready as he edged towards the opening. Although the disappearance of the scouts had him on edge, the lure of fresh air was a Siren song he could not resist. Stepping carefully, he entered the cramped tunnel, his eyes squinting at the bright daylight up ahead.

They moved slowly, ears pricked for any sign of trouble. At first, only the sounds of the Augenan and remaining soldiers clearing rubble behind them were audible, but gradually, the murmur of wind rustling through leaves and the distant rushing of a river reached them. Step by step, they approached the opening. Drattus shielded his eyes with his left hand as he halted close to the exit, his sword at the ready. He squinted into the glare as best he could, tears forming at the corners of his eyes from the contrast of long hours in the dimness of the tunnel.

The tunnel had emerged on the side of a towering cliff that rose into the sky alongside the River Corris. The passage had originally run its course completely enclosed within the stone, but at some point, an enormous landslide had occurred, causing a great portion of the upper cliff to break away and fall to the river valley far below. The slide had exposed the tunnel to the sky for over a hundred yards, though much of its floor was covered with debris. Presently, there was only a narrow ledge upon which they could walk. At the far end of the slide, Drattus could make out a larger opening where the passageway dove back into the solid stone of the cliff to continue on its way towards Rualtha to the west.

Drattus took a few careful steps out into the sunlight to allow the others to join him. Awed, he looked out over the land to his left. Their high vantage point afforded a spectacular view of the southern lowlands and the lush forest that swept across the rolling hills from horizon to horizon. It was beautiful, and Drattus felt his heart leap at the sight.

"Beautiful." As if echoing his thoughts, Muriel's voice startled Drattus enough that he couldn't stifle a gasp. She had somehow moved up beside him so quietly that he had no idea she was there. It was maddening. Quelling his embarrassment, he turned to voice a sharp retort and was shocked to silence at the sight of her face, her profile clearly visible as she swept her gaze over the land.

The sunlight played across her features, caressing every curve and hollow. There was experience there, and laugh lines in the corners of her sparkling eyes. She was older than he had first thought. The scar above her eye was much deeper than it had appeared in the dim light of the cavern. Drattus knew scars like that; the wounds that left them hurt like Hel and were never accidental. She continued to stare out over the land, drinking in the sight and breathing in the fresh air. Drattus felt his heart thump harder in his chest. Suddenly, he felt foolish and looked away.

"It is, yes," he confirmed. He turned to scan the cliffs above, noting that they were far too high for most of Laro's survivors to climb. He could see huge tree limbs peeking over the edge of the escarpment overhead. The branches swayed in the breeze, shining green and white in the sun. Something about them struck Drattus as odd, but he could not easily define why. He watched them for a few moments more before turning his gaze back to the rocky path that lay ahead.

"We'll have to clear as much of this debris as we can to make it easier for everyone to make it across. Fortunately, we can just pitch the rocks over the edge, and we certainly don't have a shortage of labor."

"Indeed, that's the truth," Muriel agreed. Suddenly, something caught her eye. "Look there!" Without waiting for Drattus to comment, she swiftly strode farther down the path and knelt to examine something. Drattus sighed in exasperation as he motioned for the other guards to follow and hurried to join her. He peered over her shoulder and was instantly perplexed.

Muriel had pulled a dagger from somewhere and was gently prodding a whitish-gray, stringy mass about the size of a soldier's bedroll. It appeared to be stuck to the surrounding stones with tiny white fibers.

"And just what is that?" Drattus asked.

Muriel continued to poke gently at the bundle with her dagger. "I'm not sure. If it weren't so big, I'd think it was a..." abruptly, she stopped talking and bent forward to saw at the bundle with her dagger blade. She worked at it until she had managed to cut halfway down the length of the mass, then she gently pried open the edges. Inside was the desiccated body of a mountain lion, its dry lips pulled back from pointed fangs. Muriel stared at the creature's empty eye sockets without speaking for a moment.

"It's a mountain cat," Drattus commented. "But why is it all dried out like that? And what is that stuff?"

Muriel stood hurriedly and turned to face the captain, her eyes wide. "If that's what I think it is, we need to get back into the tunnel as fast as...hey, weren't there five guards with us?"

Drattus turned to see the four remaining guards looking at each other in surprise.

Before anyone could speak, a rock tumbled down from the sharply sloping cliff overhead, drawing their eyes upwards. There they saw a horror that turned the blood in their veins to ice.

A spider the size of a horse clung to the stone just a few yards away, black-furred with long spindly legs and fangs as long as daggers. Its body was divided into two parts: a bulbous, furry abdomen, and the cephalothorax, its head and torso combined. The front of its head was flat, dominated by two huge black, unblinking orbs surrounded by six smaller eyes. Two curved fangs dripped venom behind its pedipalps, tiny limbs alongside its mouth used to steady its prey. Using quick, darting movements, the spider pulled flat sheets of silk from its spinnerets and wound them tightly around the struggling form of the hapless guard, mummifying him in moments, leaving only his terrified eyes showing above the grey-white strands that held him prisoner.

Suddenly, a bowstring thrummed and an arrow sank deeply into the spider's abdomen. Without a sound, the beast flinched away from the pain. Drattus turned to see Muriel already loosing another arrow to fly unerringly into the spider's body. Far too quickly for something so big, the spider whirled and skittered up the steep slope, leaving a smear of black blood on the stone. Its claws made sharp clicking sounds as they carried the wounded creature up the nearly-vertical rock face. It disappeared over the top of the cliff, leaving its wriggling bundle to fall to the narrow path with a heavy thump. A muffled groan issued from within, and the feebly struggling form started to roll over the ledge.

"He's falling! Grab him!" Sammis, the nearest guard, was already moving even as he yelled at the others. The four of them dove for the bundle, burying their gauntleted hands deep in the encasing silk and hauling at it with all their strength. Together, they managed to keep it from falling to the rocks hundreds of feet below. When the guard, Ranier, was settled away from the ledge, the others began sawing away at the silken cocoon with their daggers as fast as they could without endangering the wild-eyed man within. As his limbs came free, it became apparent that he could barely move, his limp, nearly lifeless body a stark contrast to his frantic, darting eyes and agonized groans.

Muriel quickly approached and examined Ranier, finding a pair of thumb-sized holes in his right shoulder. They still oozed blood and a pus-like substance that had a faint metallic odor to it. She carefully touched the gunk with her pinky and the tip of her finger promptly went numb.

"The venom in that first bite was only enough to paralyze him. Any more would liquefy his insides so that the spider could slurp them out through the holes." Muriel laid her hand on the frightened man's cheek. "Don't worry, we'll take care of you." Though obviously terrified, relief passed through the man's eyes at her gentle touch. Muriel looked up to address the others. "One of you run back in there and tell the others right away. Get the Sisters, and whatever soldiers are handy, out here as quickly as possible."

The confused guard looked from her to Drattus, who had the good sense to offer a terse nod in confirmation. That was good enough for Sammis, who turned and sprinted back into the tunnel through which they had come.

To Drattus, Muriel said, "Come on, let's get him back into the tunnel as well before the spider comes back."

"It's got two of your arrows lodged deep in its belly. Do you really think it'll be eager to accost us again?" He tried to sound hopeful, but he urgently scanned the overhang above them as he spoke. He helped get Ranier settled on another guard's shoulders in a soldier's carry and sent them towards the tunnel. "Hurry, Charel; get him safely in there."

Before Muriel could answer him, a sound carried to them on the wind - a sound that chilled them to their bones. The wounded spider's claws had clicked sharply against the stone as it had climbed up the cliff, its eight spindly legs pulling it quickly along. Now, the sound reached them again, but it was gradually getting louder. And the clicking was increased a thousand fold.

Drattus saw something moving at the top of the cliff, and for a moment, could not make it out. Then his face went pale as he saw the entire overhang go dark with huge, bulbous bodies, their long, slender legs carrying them down the side of the cliff with frightening speed.

"Sweet Goddess above..." Drattus whispered as he watched scores of enormous spiders as big as horses, and easily as fast, bearing down on them from above. It was a staggering sight. They came on, waving their forelegs and gnashing their curved fangs in anticipation of the meal that lay ahead. Drattus knew he was done for, but he drew his sword anyway and shifted his stance in preparation. If he was going to die, he was going to take quite a few of the giant spiders to the grave with him.

Muriel's bowstring hummed in rapid succession, and no less than four of the huge creatures lost their grip on the stone and plummeted past the ledge, bristling with her arrows. Encouraged, the guards brandished their swords and yelled war cries at the eerily silent beasts as they closed in.

Her quiver empty, Muriel shouldered her bow and pulled a slender sword from underneath her cloak in the same motion, whirling to the attack even as Drattus flung himself at the spider nearest him. He hacked a pair of legs away from one beast then smashed his sword into the creature's head as it reeled back in pain. The guards grunted and howled as they fought, and the spiders hesitated as they discovered that their prey had fangs of their own.

Muriel was a blur, slashing and stabbing as she took the fight away from the guards, into the heart of the swarm of giant arachnids. They were fast, but the priestess was in her element, leaping deftly from rock to rock on the debris-laden precipice as she fought. She wove through them as though they were standing still, almost dancing, dispatching every spider that came close with surgical precision. For all their size, speed, and numbers, they could not touch her.

One guard screamed as a spider pounced on him and plunged its fangs deep into his back, only to be killed by an enraged Drattus an instant later. Another guard became hopelessly ensnared in his attacker's web. As it came in for the kill, he managed to pull a dagger and stab it repeatedly in its underside, causing it to spasm and fall. They plummeted to the valley floor together, joining each other in death. Another guard went down and Drattus howled in fury as he tried to aid the fallen man. They were losing - losing and dying. They would not last long like this.

Just then, the stamp of booted feet echoed among the rocks as twenty guards boiled out of the tunnel, adding their swords to the fight. Drattus screamed in triumph and skewered another spider that had come too close.

"They're circling below us! Watch your backs!" Muriel warned, her voice clear and loud. Drattus risked a glance over his shoulder and, sure enough, almost half of the crawling monstrosities had broken away from the group and scuttled down the cliff face on either side of them, obviously planning to come at them from below.

"Half of you, keep those buggers from getting too close! Use the stones!" Drattus kept hacking at anything that crawled too close and edged nearer to one of his soldiers, protecting him. A veteran, he had figured out Drattus' plan already. He sheathed his sword, quickly picked up a hefty stone in both hands, and threw it in the same motion. It slammed into one of the spiders that had already crawled into position below them, just as it was about to spring up at their unprotected backs. The stone smashed into the beast's face with a sickening crunch, hurling the spider's body down and into its fellows that followed too closely behind. All three fell into the depths below only to be replaced by more of the skittering arachnids. The guards were already hurling stone after stone, and more spiders fell.

Though they held for a few long moments, there were too many swarming creatures to fight. They were too fast. Drattus bellowed in frustration as he saw another pair of men go down, impaled by the spiders' murderous fangs. Almost instantly, the men were cocooned in grey silk and borne away from the battle. Another man went down, and another, and Drattus knew that soon, they would all suffer the same fate.

"Hold!" A feminine voice rang like a struck bell, echoing from the rocky cliff face, its power freezing every living thing in its tracks in an instant. A bright light shone forth, a great, glowing sphere of rainbow colors that swirled and danced, drawing every eye into its mesmerizing depths. The spiders stood immobile, completely entranced by the sphere. It floated upon the air, gently turning, spinning lazily, and every creature that gazed upon it grew calm. The sphere moved away from the cliff and upwards, drawing the gaze of hundreds of unblinking black eyes as the spiders followed its slow movement.

Drattus managed to tear his eyes from the lovely sight and shook his head to clear it. He quietly reached over to the soldier nearest him and shook him until he, too, came out of the light trance he had been in. The captain looked around in awe at the sea of spiders that surrounded them, each one now swaying gently in time with the movements of the sphere. He could scarcely believe what he was seeing.

Surefooted as a mountain goat, Muriel threaded her way over the rocks to stand next to Drattus, still holding her sword in one hand, a dagger in the other, both arms covered to the elbow in black gore. Her hair was a mess, she had a new cut on her forehead, and Drattus thought that he'd never seen anyone so beautiful in his life. She blew a stray lock of hair out of her face and grinned as she leaned in to speak.

"That would be Fiona. I'm glad she showed up, it was getting dicey out here." She nodded her head to indicate the woman who now stood just outside the tunnel entrance, her hands raised and glowing with the same colors as the sphere, a look of concentration on her face. Behind her stood several of the other Sisters, some with weapons drawn and others already digging in bags and pouches for bandages and other supplies.

Drattus turned back to Muriel, and before he could say a word she grabbed his face between her hands and kissed him soundly before releasing him. He gaped at her in utter astonishment, completely oblivious to the sticky handprints she had left on either side of his face.

"Sorry," she grinned at him sheepishly. "I love a good fight! Gets me all excited." She wiggled her eyebrows at him briefly before moving past him towards one of the downed soldiers. Drattus, to his credit, said not a single word.

Her blue eyes shining in the sunlight, Fiona walked along the ledge, treading carefully as she stepped past the injured, making room for the Sisters to attend them. A few were beyond help, but most would survive, and for that, Fiona was thankful. She wished she could have arrived sooner, but the visions that guided her came when they would and not before. She was pleased that, at least, she had sent Muriel ahead, as she had obviously been needed. Fiona shook her head, enjoying the feel of the breeze flowing through her silver and black hair.

She approached Muriel and Drattus and was about to speak when a new voice echoed among the rocks. It was silky and sibilant, very nearly a purr, but loud enough to be easily heard over the wind.

"What is thisss? Who art thou, to impose your will upon my children?"

Their eyes were drawn toward the top of the cliff, and their blood froze in their veins as the biggest spider they would ever see crawled over the ledge and slowly moved towards them. It was enormous, far bigger than the horse-sized spiders they had been fighting, and yet it crawled over the stone just as lightly as the others had. Its long legs moved almost elegantly as it approached, obviously in no hurry. Its huge black eyes focused directly on the trio, who were captivated by the sight of her. Although it was nearly as big as a full-grown dragon, there was something about the way it moved that almost suggested daintiness, femininity, as well as incredible deadliness.

As it approached, Muriel spoke aloud before she could stop herself. "She's beautiful..."

Stepping carefully through the other spiders, the massive creature stopped mere yards from them and jerked once, its inhuman features somehow giving an impression of surprise.

"Beautiful, you call me?" The creature's pedipalps tested the air, constantly moving in front of its huge fangs. "None of your kind has ever called me that. Many things, I have been called, but never that." It paused for a moment before continuing. "I am, of course, quite beautiful. It is, however, kind of you to say so."

Fiona spoke, her voice strong and sure. "Indeed, my lady, we have never seen anything such as you. And we apologize for causing you or your..." Fiona looked around at the horde of spiders, "children...any harm. We are only passing through."

The massive spider lowered itself into the midst of the others. It idly moved its two front legs, gently caressing the backs of other spiders who still gazed longingly at Fiona's swirling ball of light. "My children are many. They often die. I will have more; it is of no consequence. That said, the colony needs food. Why should you not be it? Your kind are very tasty, I must admit. Now that I am here, we could easily overwhelm you all, in spite of your magick."

"My lady, we agree that you most certainly could do that very thing. We humbly ask that you do not."

Drattus slowly turned wide, astonished eyes toward Fiona. His expression fairly screamed, *Is that the best you can do?* She narrowed her eyes at him before turning her full attention back to the spider queen. Sweat began to trickle down her face as the strain of holding the mesmerizing spell began to take its toll. She would not be able to hold it in place for much longer.

The purring voice replied, "You are very polite, for a human. Most are much more indelicate with ussss. What would you offer usss instead?"

Drattus could not believe their good fortune. "Ahem...um...my lady, we would be quite happy to present you with a number of cattle sufficient to suit your needs, provided we have enough." The spider queen regarded him without speaking for several long moments. Drattus used that time to send a frantic, silent prayer to the Goddess Rowann, asking that they not end up as food for a massive spider colony.

"Thisss is unexpected. As tasty as humans are, they are small and not terribly filling. Cattle, however..." its forelegs flicked at the air in anticipation, "are both tasty and substantial. We accept your offer."

Before they could voice their enthusiastic response, the queen spoke again, her voice rolling easily over the rocks. "I do have an additional boon to ask of thee, however."

Fiona's voice, though strong, had begun to shake slightly. "If it is within our power to grant, my lady, we will be pleased to do so."

The spider queen slowly raised herself up to her full height, towering over the humans as she spoke. "I would ask that one of you come back and visit with me every so often. You interest and intrigue me. I would know more of you. Do you agree to thisss?"

Fiona glanced at Muriel and then quickly at the other Sisters, seeking their assent before answering. As she knew they would, they all nodded in agreement. "My lady, it would be our pleasure to send one of our number back to visit you once the people in our care are safe. We flee the violence of Mordak, and this tunnel is our only way to safety. You have my word on it."

At the mention of Mordak, the spider twitched sharply several times. "Mordak...yessss, we know that one. He called to usss some time ago. He asked usss to join him." Fiona and the others held their breath as they waited to hear more. "We do not follow him or his ilk. He is..." Agitated, her fangs gnashed for a moment before stilling again as the spider queen regained her composure. "He is...not polite."

Chapter 9

The trip down from the high mountain Keep was uneventful, thanks in part to the map that Brunar had left for Gart among the ample supplies. Bessie seemed pleased to be on flat ground again and Beauty was back to chasing birds and rabbits alongside the road. There were still hours of daylight left, and they were making good time. Gart tilted his hat so that the brim shaded the back of his neck from the afternoon sun as they traveled towards Green Meadows. The town was still at least three more days' ride, but the terrain appeared to be gentle and the weather clear.

Gart had thought long and hard about which direction he should take upon leaving with his Jidaan. The Mage had said they had gone to the city of Laro, far to the south, to prepare for battle. Gart had looked at the map for several minutes and thought that they most likely went west and boarded a ship, sailed down the coast to Rualtha, and then traveled overland to Laro from there. That would have been the most logical way to go. So why was he feeling drawn to go east?

Tracing his finger along the map back at the Keep, he had seen the road to Green Meadows and noted that the Blackthorne River cut right through the town. It ran directly south, passed through the city of Alverton Falls, and then angled westward slightly until it joined with the Corris River, not far from the very walls of Laro.

That way felt right, down deep in his bones.

"The Mage said to follow my heart. I suppose that starts now," he had said aloud to Beauty, who had only wagged her tail in response. That had been days ago, and they had been met with naught but clear skies and easy traveling ever since.

Gart often reached down to check on his Jidaan. Wanting to be inconspicuous, he had strapped it alongside Bessie's saddle rather than carry it openly in its scabbard across his back. He could feel its potent magick, a quiet hum that played just on the edge of his senses. It felt as though the Jidaan lay sleeping, only awaiting his call to come awake. He knew he should practice with it, but had so far only swung it around in imitations of the patterns he had seen Lillia use in his dreams. The weight and balance of the thing was uncanny, but he had yet to unleash any of its magick. Even after seeing what Lillia had been able to do with it in so many dreams over so many nights, he could not seem to bring himself to try anything. After a while, his own reluctance began to irritate him.

As the sun neared the horizon behind him, bringing gentle breezes and the soft songs of night birds, Gart found a comfortable spot to camp for the night. He settled under a massive oak tree that was far enough from the road that he wasn't worried about being seen. He saw to Bessie and Beauty before pulling out rations for himself. He sat with his back up against the ancient tree, grumbling at himself as he ate.

He had been using his magick for weeks now, and his strength and control had both grown considerably. The weapon had Chosen him after all, and was now his to wield as he saw fit. How could he bring justice to Mordak and Jor Dayne if he could not use the power of his own weapon? The thought was absurd! As he scowled his way through a ration of dried meat, he decided that the time had come for him to better acquaint himself with the weapon's uses.

Gart abruptly stood and brushed his hands on his trousers before removing his hat. He laid it on the ground where he had been sitting and picked up his Jidaan from where he had rested it against the tree close by. He looked around and found a clear spot not far away, a small meadow empty of trees, and he headed towards it. Beauty instantly got up to tag along with him.

"No, girl; you need to stay here. Stay. I don't know what might happen when I use this thing." He gestured for her to stay put and she sat obediently, whining quietly as she did so. Gart left her there and strode to the center of the clearing, where he planted his feet and held his Jidaan in both hands.

Gart took a few deep breaths to calm himself, incensed that he would be nervous in the first place, and then breathed more slowly until his irritation was under control. He thought back to the dreams in which Lillia had called down lightning to obliterate her attackers. Gart carefully examined the memory, turning it over and over in his mind as he relived the sensations she had experienced as she had ignited the power of the Jidaan.

Often she had used no words, no gestures, nothing more than the flexing of her own will. Gart looked inside himself and found his own magick instantly ready, almost eager to answer his call. He reached out with his power and picked up a fallen tree branch, large enough that he had to focus on the task. As he did so, he examined what he was doing, observed his own actions as though he were separate from them. He held the branch in the air for a few moments, and then allowed it to settle to the ground once more, satisfied with his discovery.

It was the same. His own use of magick to move things required the same kind of flexing, the same kind of focus, as Lillia had used to engage the power of the Jidaan. He could do this.

Without a word, he held the Jidaan out in front of himself with both hands and sent his energy into the weapon. The emerald clutched in its pommel flared instantly to brilliant life, casting its green light in all directions, brighter than a bonfire. Gart angled his face away to lessen the glare, but kept a firm hold on the weapon, which vibrated and hummed with power. Gart created an image of lightning in his mind, something he could definitely use against Jor Dayne and his master, Mordak. Before he could even complete the mental picture, the Jidaan bucked in his hands, sending a dazzling bolt of green fire into the sky to manifest Gart's wish.

Gart stumbled in shock, astonished at how easily the weapon had channeled his will. Before he could catch his balance, there was a blinding flash. Gart felt as though he had been struck in the chest with a huge hammer, swung by the immense fist of a giant. The ground rose up and slammed into him, or so it seemed to Gart. The world spun wildly for a few moments; then he found himself staring into the cloudless sky above, just purpling with the first signs of twilight.

He blinked several times and tried to catch his breath. There was a powerful ringing in his ears at first, and as it diminished, Gart made out the distinct rumble of thunder as it receded in the distance. He waited until it was completely gone before he tried to sit up. Groaning loudly, he managed to push himself to a sitting position and sat there, breathing heavily.

Everything hurt. There was a loud buzzing in his head and he struggled to focus. He stayed still, giving his body time to recover, and his vision gradually cleared. Steam arose from a few places on his body, but he did not feel burned. What he did feel was thoroughly beaten and bruised all over. Back in Tiller's Grove, he had once slipped down a steep hillside and fallen head over heels to the valley below, seemingly hitting every single rock and branch in the process. That was an afternoon picnic compared to this.

His bewildered gaze fell on his boots. They were more or less where he expected them to be, on his feet in front of him. His right boot was fine. His left, however, had a charred hole through which he could see all of his toes. Gart managed to wiggle them and confirm that they were unharmed, though like the rest of his body, intensely sore. He was still disoriented, but after sitting quietly for a minute, he started to feel more like himself - just a very beaten up version of himself. Frustration and embarrassment rose in him, familiar shades of anger coloring his mind red as they always had, and his hands clenched into fists.

Just then, Gart heard a soft whine and turned to see Beauty sitting a few yards away from him, eyeing him warily. Her tail was wagging uncertainly as the residual energy from the Jidaan's lightning strike dissipated. She was obviously anxious. Seeing her so agitated at his plight, worried about her friend and chosen master, burst the bubble of his rage as easily as if it were made of soap. The old anger vanished, leaving a feeling of gratitude behind.

"I'm all right, girl; come here." He beckoned her closer.

Beauty whuffed and stayed right where she was.

Gart raised an eyebrow at her, surprised at her disobedience. "Oh, c'mon Beauty. I'm fine...I think." He snapped his fingers and tried to whistle to her, but had to stop as the pain in his head flared anew. He groaned and clutched his head in his hands.

Beauty whined again and sniffed the air for a few long moments before she padded over and tentatively licked Gart's hand. As his pain slowly eased, he reached up and scratched between her ears and felt her finally relax. She sat next to him and licked his face happily.

Looking up at the massive canine and feeling her hot breath and slobbery wet tongue on his face, he managed a weak smile for her.

"Well, that could have gone better, I suppose."

Beauty whuffed in agreement.

Chapter 10

Magick raced through Brunar's arm and exploded into his torso, setting every fiber of his being afire. Blinding pains erupted all over his body, dominated by a spear of agony in the back of his head as the magick filled him completely, scouring every inch. His spine arched, lifting him off of the wooden surface on which he found himself. His eyes flew wide and he sucked in a great, gasping breath.

As his vision focused, he became aware of the stone ceiling above him, dancing with bright sparkles of color. The power that coursed through his body seemed to burn him from the inside out, and it rushed to every angry flare of pain as if eager to reach them all. Like ice melting in the noonday sun, Brunar's hurts vanished under the flow of healing magick. The internal fire raged for a moment more, but then it diminished in intensity, and the Mage gradually eased his body back down to the boards.

As the magick dissipated, it left him feeling warm and strong in a way that he'd almost forgotten he could feel. The bright lights danced overhead for a few heartbeats more, then vanished, leaving the cavern dark in contrast. Brunar lay still and inhaled deeply, enjoying the feel of the muscles in his torso working as they expanded his lungs to the full. Everything had hurt for so long, it was a shock to feel sound again. He pushed himself to a sitting position, then looked at his hands. They had been battered and torn, like the rest of him; now, they were whole. He flexed his fists, testing his strength, and the ghost of a smile found its way onto his face. He looked around to see several people hovering nearby.

Alyssa was seated next to him in the bed of a wagon, one small hand on his arm, the other holding her Jidaan. She looked healthy and well-rested, her auburn hair pulled back and bound into a ponytail. Her soft brown eyes twinkled above a broad smile.

"How are you feeling, Brunar? Can you walk?"

A huge grin played across Brunar's bearded face, displaying white, even teeth.

"Alyssa, if there were music, I'd be dancing to it! It's been centuries since I last felt the magick of your Jidaan; I'd forgotten how incredibly powerful it is. I feel fifty years younger!"

A snort drew Brunar's gaze toward one of the wagon wheels. Kiran leaned against it with a lopsided smirk on her face, oozing nonchalance. "In your case, Mage, that's not really saying much."

Relieved laughter greeted the jibe, and Brunar joined in as he got his feet under him and nimbly leapt down out of the wagon. He was pleased to see Nessar nearby and Bjarke looking like a huge grinning bear. The Duke stood off to one side with Ginn, the Weya. Everyone looked healthy and strong, though their clothes and armor were filthy and battered. "How long have I been unconscious? What has happened?"

The Duke stepped forward and grabbed the Mage in a mighty bear hug, surprising him. He held Brunar tightly for a moment, then stepped back to speak. "Brunar, thanks to you and those you brought with you, thousands of my people have survived. Once we managed to pull you and Kiran out of the Crypt, we continued down the tunnel. You remained unconscious, but Fiona and the other priestesses examined you. Although many of your bones were broken, they said that you'd survive. We made you comfortable until Alyssa awoke and could aid you. She had also collapsed from the efforts of the battle and from your rescue. As you can see, she has fully recovered."

Smiling, Alyssa twirled and performed a curtsy which brought a round of light laughter from the group. Brunar laughed with them, then turned to Kiran.

"You are unhurt, then? I don't remember very much after the ceiling started to fall in at the Crypt."

Kiran waved a hand in dismissal. "You shielded me with your own body, you old fool. You got those broken bones in my place. I must have passed out because the first thing I remember after that is waking up in this goddess-forsaken tunnel. I'm fine, though; Alyssa healed me too." She turned her attention to her sword, which she had been sharpening before Brunar woke, but her mindvoice was suddenly loud and clear in the Mage's head. *Thanks for helping me out in there. I owe you one.*

He smiled and turned away to talk with the others, but his reply was heard nonetheless. *You owe me nothing, Kiran. You are a Guardian. We are family.* Kiran cast a sideways glance over her shoulder at the Mage but said nothing more, though an answering smile did turn up one corner of her mouth.

The Duke was grinning hugely. "We think we have nearly reached the end of the tunnel. The ValElder says that we approach the ruined city of Caffian, which is nearly a third of the way to Rualtha, and that is likely where the exit is located."

"How long have we been traveling? Have I missed much?" Brunar hated the idea that he had been unable to aid the caravan as it had traveled beneath the ground. After such hardship at Laro, he hoped the voyage had been relatively easy.

The Duke laughed and shook his head. "Well, not much, really. Oh, there was that issue with the spider queen a while back, but Fiona settled that for us."

Brunar's eyes widened. "Spider queen? You mean Kulcania? She attacked us? But she's enormous! She could never fit in this tunnel."

"Oh, you know her!" The Duke was not terribly surprised. He knew that the Mage was over two thousand years old and had probably run across her at some point.

"Of her, only. I never had the chance to actually meet her. Fiona dealt with her, you said?"

"Indeed she did. The tunnel is exposed to the outside at one point due to erosion on the cliffs above, and that spot happened to be just beneath the queen's lair. We lost a few good soldiers before Fiona stopped the queen's children from attacking and somehow engineered a truce. You'll have to ask her about it when we reach the front of the caravan. She's up there now."

Brunar shook his head slowly in appreciation. "Fiona has always impressed me with her ingenuity. It doesn't surprise me a bit that she devised a way to keep us all safe."

"That she did," replied the Duke. "We left the queen behind us two days ago." Gesturing with one hand, he continued, "Come. Now that everyone is functional again, let us move forward and discuss our options. We have stopped for the night, so it won't take too long to reach the front."

Brunar nodded his head towards the Guardians, indicating that they should follow as well, and then he stepped forward to join the Duke. They strode towards the distant head of the caravan, slowly passing the still forms of the Laroan people. They were bundled up on the stone floor in whatever they had managed to bring with them, most sleeping heavily. Horses stood quietly among them, and other livestock could be found amidst the sleepers' bodies.

Walking alongside them, Ginn spoke at last in his quiet, melodic voice. "The ValElder has news, Sir Mage. She asked to speak with you."

"Yes, of course. I want to speak with her as well. I feel as though I've been gone for an eternity; I want to get caught up." Suddenly, Brunar stopped in his tracks, causing the others to stop as well. He turned to find Alyssa closest behind him. With concern in his voice, he asked, "Where is Layton? Has he returned?"

Alyssa sighed, her beautiful face creased with an unaccustomed frown as she spoke. "No, Brunar. He did not come back from the castle." Her voice brightened then, "We don't know for certain that anything has happened to him, but…" Her voice trailed off, unwilling to continue the thought.

Brunar put a comforting hand on her shoulder. "Layton is very resourceful. It's not only possible that he survived, I think it's highly likely that he did so."

Nessar's gravelly voice rasped from somewhere in the back. "Yes, he's a sneaky pup, that one. I'd bet a gold crown that he's out there somewhere, causing trouble."

Brunar gave Alyssa's shoulder a gentle squeeze of reassurance before turning away. "I'm sure he is, Nessar." More quietly, he continued, "Yes. I'm sure he is." Raising his voice slightly, he addressed the others again. "All right then, let's see what's going on in the front; we've ridden in the back for too long." As he started walking again, he hoped his concern had not been too obvious, even though he knew that it had been.

Chapter 11

Rain fell in sheets and thunder rumbled through the night sky, rolling across the forested hills, though the army who slogged through the mud below paid it no attention. Swarming almost silently over the countryside, thousands of fell creatures headed northward, leaving the ruins of Laro behind them. Woodland beasts both large and small fled before the teeming horde, sensing its malevolent nature from afar. Any living being that could not escape quickly enough soon fell to the slashing talons and sharp teeth of Mordak's inhuman soldiers. Gholans and Morcats led the way, followed soon after by the humanoid Krell and a legion of scarlet-eyed, undead Riders, animated by Mordak's stolen magick. Those animals that could hid safely until the evil multitude had passed them by, its foul wake scarring with each step. Occasionally, fights would break out among the undisciplined mob of Gholans, and only the yowls and cracking whips of the Morcats would subdue the unruly brutes into forward motion once more. The dead were simply swallowed up by the mob, eaten on the run. The hideous creatures corrupted everything they touched, and the land would have cried out in agony had it the power to do so.

Mordak rode above it all, floating high in the air upon the magick he had stolen from the evil Daemon-God, Balroth. The unholy power filled him near to bursting, but he had learned to control it. He smiled often as he recalled how he had offered the world of Talwynn to the evil, yet naïve, being. All he had asked for in return was a sliver of the Daemon-God's own sorcerous might so that he could prepare the way for Balroth's coming. He had no intention of enabling Balroth to do any such thing, but the Daemon-God did not know that. Mordak laughed aloud at the very thought of it. Now that the power was his, he would use it to fulfill his own destiny, crush the rulers of the Realm under his heels, and become Emperor of the known world. His authority would reign supreme, and every living thing would either bow down to him or die horribly.

Touching his temple with long, artistic fingers, Mordak sent a mental command to Jor Dayne far below. He knew it would be loud enough to give the half-daemon a splitting headache, but he cared not. He only needed Jor Dayne's obedience, not his affection. Doubling his effort, Mordak again sent the command to turn east and was rewarded with an agonized reply. Applying his magick to allow him to see through the dark and weather, the sorcerer peered at the vast army that moved across the hills below. From that height, it looked like an enormous flood of ants, tiny pinpricks sliding over the muddy terrain. He saw an individual spot out ahead of the main mass. Through his augmented sight, he could see Jor Dayne's yellow eyes glowing in the darkness as his warhorse reared and bolted towards the east. The swarm of creatures and undead soldiers immediately shifted to follow him.

Mordak smirked to himself, pleased to see his Champion following orders so efficiently. He turned his gaze back to the darkened horizon, seeking what had caught his attention earlier. Far in the distance, visible through the storm only due to the sorcerer's use of magick, was a small town. It slumbered quietly, shuttered against the driving rains of the storm. Its people slept in peace.

In an hour or so hence, that peace would be shattered by the sounds of screaming, fighting, and dying as Mordak's army unleashed itself onto the unsuspecting townspeople. Some would end up as food, while most of the others would die only to rise again and ride for Mordak. The sorcerer mused to himself, thinking that he might reanimate some of the children this time. They were small and might be useful...if he could just keep the Gholans from eating them all.

Chapter 12

Standing barefoot, Gart thumped a new pair of boots on the counter and waited. Upon hearing the sound, the kilted bootmaker walked through a doorway from his workshop in the back. He was intently running a cloth over a newly-made boot, making his way to the counter from sheer force of habit without ever bothering to look up. Gart watched him approach and angled his head to the right slightly, presenting his unscarred profile to the man. Folks had a tendency to be startled if he looked them straight on at first.

"Yes sir, what can I do for ye?" The man set the single boot and polishing cloth aside and stepped up to the counter, finally setting eyes on Gart.

Still looking away, Gart kept his tone light. He waffled between being angry that he had managed to strike himself with lightning and being amused at the fact, and he figured there was no sense in letting his own anger cause him trouble.

"I'm in need of a good pair of boots, and these fit me well enough. How much do you want for them?" Steeling himself for the shopkeeper's gasp, he finally turned to face the man.

"Och, let's see. This particular pair be...sweet baby monkeys!" He stammered for a moment as he collected himself. Suddenly amused rather than offended, Gart said nothing and kept a straight face. "I'm terribly sorry, sir, but I was startled by yer scars. Please dinnae take offense, I beg ye!" The bootmaker started wringing his thick-fingered hands together, obviously distressed.

Gart was surprised at the man's reaction. Rarely had anyone ever apologized for commenting on his scars. Back home, they had usually assumed he was somehow evil, or that his scars were sinister in origin, rather than merely the result of a chance encounter with a strange dog. His entire life, he had been a pariah because of his damaged features, but as he traveled far from home, he found that more people were willing to overlook them.

Smiling slightly, Gart reassured the man. "It's all right; no offense taken, friend. I just need the boots and I'll be on my way. How much?"

The bootmaker's relief was evident as he sighed and produced a clean handkerchief from one pocket and wiped his fleshy face with it. "Thank ye for yer understanding, kind sir! I surely meant ye no disrespect." Pocketing the kerchief again, he steadied himself by reaching for the boots. "As I was saying, this particular pair of boots ordinarily be four silvers, but eh..." he sheepishly looked around to see that the shop was empty before continuing, "seeing as how I acted like a horse's arse, I'll give them to ye for three."

Gart's grin widened at the little man's words. Three silvers was a handsome sum for a pair of boots, but the stitching was tight and the leather in excellent condition. And he liked the fellow. He dug around in his money pouch, sifted three silver pieces out of it and placed them on the counter.

"Sold. I need to head downriver today. Are there boats available?"

The bootmaker quickly tucked the silver pieces away in his sporran, the pouch he wore in front of his kilt. "I'd say so. Just head down to the docks and ye should find something to suit ye, depending on how far ye be headed."

Gart thanked him and took the new boots off the counter, tossing his old ones onto a pile of worn out footwear in a corner. Then he sat on a nearby bench and eagerly began putting the new ones on his feet. As Gart slid his feet into the firm leather, the cobbler picked up Gart's old boot, the one with the charred hole in it. He looked at it quizzically.

"Beggin' yer pardon, kind sir, but," he frowned in confusion, "how did ye manage to do this?" He stuck his arm inside the boot so that his fingers poked out through the hole and wiggled them for emphasis.

Gart stood up and sighed happily, relishing the feel of the new footwear for a moment before responding. He turned a stern eye towards the puzzled bootmaker and replied without a trace of humor. "Lightning. Gotta watch out for that stuff. It's tricky."

Gart tipped his hat politely to the befuddled shopkeeper and then stepped outside where Beauty and Bessie had been patiently waiting. Beauty whuffed at him and wagged her tail ferociously as he approached. He scratched her ears before untying Bessie's reins from the shop's hitching post. For the hundredth time, he pondered his course, letting his thoughts wander. *South,* came the answer, strong and clear in his mind. The Blackthorne River was the fastest way to travel in that direction, so there it was.

"Come on then, you lot. We have a boat to catch."

Chapter 13

Moihra's melodic voice echoed quietly in the tunnel, "I've been thinking about Mordak. The power he is manifesting is most unusual." She, Brunar, Fiona, and the Duke walked together several yards behind a rank of guards and Augenan at the front of the caravan. Behind them, the river of Laroan refugees continued its steady flow towards the safety of Rualtha, far to the west. Brunar nodded, one hand rubbing his bearded chin as he contemplated the ValElder's words.

"I agree. Not only its magnitude - which surpasses any of his previous capabilities - but its very *feel* is different." Brunar winced as he recalled the oily scarlet force that emanated from the evil sorcerer. "It's ancient. And far more powerful than anything I can face directly. If it came down to a duel, there is a good chance he'd simply overwhelm me. We're fortunate that controlling his army keeps him somewhat distracted for now."

The Weya woman continued musing, "The Jidaan are likewise powerful, but each in its own way. If there were another magickal artifact that could amplify your own power or have enough power in its own right, having such a weapon might tip the scales in our favor."

Brunar rubbed his bearded chin as he searched his memory for anything suitable. A handful of magickal artifacts existed on Talwynn, but he was aware of only a few. As far as he could recall, even the most potent of those would not aid them against the power that Mordak brought to bear. Still, something tugged at the back of his mind, but he could not yet put a finger on it. Suddenly, he remembered that Bjarke had brought along one of the histories that Brunar had written to chronicle the first war with Mordak. "Excuse me, milady, but I need to go check something with Bjarke." She inclined her head politely, and Brunar left her to walk back towards the middle of the caravan.

Many faces stared at him as he walked by, the tired and dusty survivors of Laro. Some brightened visibly as he approached, while others turned their eyes away in awe and not a little fear. Brunar's magickal ability was well-known to them all. He nodded and smiled to each as he passed, trying to reassure those who would otherwise be frightened. Soon, he spotted Bjarke walking with Alyssa and Fiona, looking much brighter and happier than the last time the Mage had seen him.

"Bjarke, do you still have that book with you? The one I wrote?"

Surprised, Bjarke nevertheless nodded that he had, and produced it from a pouch on his belt. It looked positively tiny in his huge hands, and he carefully passed it to the Mage. "Yes, I've kept it on my person ever since we set out on our journey. It seemed only right, and I've read from it often."

"Thank you, Bjarke, I'll return it to you presently. I just need to verify something."

"As you wish, Brunar."

The Mage exchanged a few words with Alyssa and Fiona before stepping aside to allow the caravan to pass him by. He seated himself on a nearby rock near one of the magickal lights and cracked open the ancient tome, its leather binding still stiff and strong. Although he recalled writing it, so many years had passed that it felt as though someone else had set quill to parchment to record the history. The smell of the old pages brought back many memories of a time long past.

As he carefully paged through the book, he noted the swirling script he had used, the maps drawn by the light of multiple candles back in his room in the mountain Keep. Nothing new jumped out at him. On a hunch, he flipped to the last page of the history and saw that a few blank pages remained after he had finished. He flipped through those as well, and there, pressed tightly between the final two pages, he found two pieces of paper. They were sharply folded and flattened from centuries of being compressed in the back of the book. Brunar carefully extracted them and laid the book on his lap so that he could focus on the loose pages.

He slowly pried the first one open so that he could examine it and saw that the handwriting was not his own. It was in an obscure Eastern language; the script was very stylized, but he could read it. Focusing his mind to the task, he pored over the contents, making sense of all the swirls and lines that made up the words and phrases.

My Dear Ranaud,

The amulet is almost ready, I think. Only a few tests remain, but all of my previous experiments have led me to believe that the final infusions will have the desired effect. Some of the things I've had to do, some of the paths I've trod, have been dark. So very dark, my friend. I'm not quite sure I'm the same man I was when we studied together. Had I known that accepting the King's commission would have forced me to learn such things, I don't know that I would have so blithely agreed to make the thing for him.

However, I'm on the verge of doing something that no one else has ever done! Me! I, Wendall the Wise, have created a device capable of nullifying any spell cast upon it! It absorbs the fundamental energy that makes up a spell, Ranaud! It's difficult to explain, but I found a way to break down ANY magickal attack into its base particles and then absorb that energy. Just a few more tests, and I'll know for certain if it works. Even now, the lion's share of work has been completed, and I'm positive that it will function impressively well. I know not why the King has requested such a thing, although it is certainly his right to do so. However, he is King, and so I strive to obey.

I should not even commit this to the page, but I feel I can trust you, Ranaud, my boyhood friend. I wonder if the King might have some treachery planned for me. He has nothing to fear from me, of course, for I have always been loyal. He must know that it would be foolish of him to accost me in any way. The things I have learned have given me power beyond anything I had ever known before, and he would pay dearly for such a betrayal, one way or another, even if he was wearing the token I've made for him.

Ah, but I am rambling, my friend, and surely allowing my fears to run away with me. In thinking of it more, I am sure that the king will elevate me to a much higher status for achieving the impossible.

I will complete the final procedures over the next two days. I look forward to writing you soon with news of my success and promotion.

Warmest Regards,

Wendall

The letter was signed with even more ornate swirls and symbols, and Brunar could feel the tiniest bit of magick still clinging to the parchment. He carefully placed it aside and examined the other page. Rather than a letter, it appeared to be a short journal entry, carefully torn from a book and dated over a thousand years past.

The sorcerer Wendall has yet to answer my repeated attempts at communication. Indeed, a peculiar silence has fallen over the entire kingdom of Linbourne, and I fear the worst. I will be leaving on the morrow for Linbourne to try to make contact with Wendall and to ascertain the situation within the city itself. I am concerned that King Lareno might have taken Wendall's device and then tried to betray him. Wendall was already a powerful sorcerer, but his recent studies appear to have taken a darker turn, so I cannot venture to guess how he might have responded to such an attack. I fear that he might do something violent and drastic in response to an attempt on his life, and it could endanger all of Linbourne. Goddess willing, I will find him alive and well and the city in good standing when I arrive.

Ranaud Silverlark

Brunar read and reread both pages before carefully slipping them back into the book. He recalled very little about the tiny kingdom of Linbourne, as it had been a small, far eastern city and he had never been there. He stood and strode quickly to catch up with Bjarke, holding the book in one hand.

"Bjarke, why exactly did you bring *this* book with you? There were hundreds of others."

Bjarke looked startled at the question. "I was looking for something to help me learn more about our adversary, Sir Mage. I saw that one and that you had written it, and it seemed the logical choice."

Brunar nodded and was about to turn away when Bjarke continued.

"Of all the books I looked at, that one felt the most right."

Brunar's eyebrows raised. "It *felt* right?"

Bjarke nodded. "Yes, sir. It just felt right to bring it along."

"Hand of the Goddess..." Brunar's words were barely above a whisper as he examined the book's cover with new eyes. He did not remember tucking those papers between the last few pages, but he had a habit of absently keeping such things in books to keep them safe. That it was these particular pages and this particular book...Brunar shook his head in amazement.

"Thank you Bjarke. You may have just given us what we need to fight Mordak."

Chapter 14

"How far 'r ye headed?" The lanky, kilted sailor eyed Gart up and down as he stood on the docks with Bessie and Beauty. The man's gaze lingered for only a moment on Gart's scarred features, but then ignored them and turned back to the business at hand.

"As far south as you're going, sir. I'm trying to get to Laro. How much will that set me back?" Gart was not used to having so much money at hand, but he was smart enough to know he should hide the fact that he had gold in plenty.

The sailor shook his head. "Nae, we're only goin' as far as Alverton Falls. That'll get ye aboot half the way to Laro. And it'll cost ye a gold, what with yer horse and…" he eyed Beauty dubiously, "yer dog, there. Does he be the bitin' kind?"

"Well, yes *she* does," Gart smiled as he said it. "But only if you get on her bad side. Her name is Beauty." At the sound of her name, she wagged her battered tail happily, belying the fierceness of her permanent snarl. "Alverton Falls will be just fine."

The sailor looked at the huge, scarred animal and back at the scarred face of the young man on the dock. A slow smile spread across his face. "Beauty, eh? I like that. I'll do me best to stay on her good side, then. Come aboard sir!"

Gart thanked the man and began walking Bessie and Beauty along the gangplank to board the ship. As they passed, the sailor casually glanced at Bessie and noticed the sheathed Jidaan riding alongside the saddle. His eyes widened as he saw the bright emerald clutched in the ornate pommel of the weapon. Without thinking, he reached one hand towards it.

"Don't touch that," Gart's voice was sharp. The sailor yanked his hand away and turned to glare at Gart. Before he could speak, Gart continued, his voice much more polite. "Please. It is very old. Been in my family for generations. Sentimental value, you understand." Gart's blue eyes were icy beneath the brim of his floppy hat. The sailor looked into them and saw the hardness there. As much as he might be intrigued by the shining emerald, one look at Gart's eyes made it clear that it was none of his business.

"I hear ye, then. No problem, I was just lookin' at the pretty thing, eh?" He held up both hands to show he meant no harm.

Gart's intense gaze burned into the man for only a moment longer before he turned to dig in his money pouch. "No harm done, friend. Here's payment for us three." He stepped closer and put two gold coins into the man's callused palm. The sailor's confusion quickly gave way to excitement. Gart leaned close so that only the sailor could hear. "That second coin is for you. Please see that we have an easy ride. Does that suit you?"

The sailor grinned widely. Easy money was his favorite kind of money. "Friend, it most certainly does. All me lads, they be good lads, and we'll get ye to Alverton Falls as safe as can be. I be Darryn, and this is me own ship. It's a decent little ship, the *Goshawk* is, and with a little luck, it'll be smooth sailing for ye, Mr... er...what was your name?"

"Gart," the man who had once been a farmer replied. "Just call me Gart."

Chapter 15

As Brunar made his way to the head of the caravan, he heard a commotion. He picked up his pace and saw that the flow of traffic had stopped completely up ahead, and weary travelers had all set down their packs to rest until whatever had caused the slowdown could be resolved. It took several long minutes for Brunar to reach the front of the column, and there he found the Duke, the Weya, Muriel and Fiona, and a crowd of soldiers staring at a blank wall. The tunnel had finally ended, but there was no doorway in sight. The Duke already had soldiers moving through the crowd, calming those who were distraught after so many painful days of travel only to find their way completely blocked. Brunar saw that the Weya and priestesses were already examining the walls, searching for anything that might lead to a way out. The Duke turned at Brunar's approach.

"Well, we've made it this far. I'm hoping there's a way out here. I don't relish going back and asking the spiders to help us reach the top of the cliffs. That just sounds like trouble to me." Tired, but healed and strong, the Duke sounded almost jovial.

Brunar grinned. "If anyone can find it, they can," the Mage tipped his chin to indicate the priestesses and elf-like Weya. He stepped forward to assist.

ValElder Moihra brushed a lock of her dark hair over one pointed ear and looked intently at something on the leftmost tunnel wall. Brunar approached her, and she rewarded him with a dazzling smile.

"You seem pleased, milady," Brunar was encouraged by her expression.

Her smile only widened. "The builders of this passage made it easy for us. Look." She stepped away and gestured towards a golden plaque set directly into the stone of the wall. It was slightly larger than a serving platter, its script boldly embossed and easily read. "It's written in Common."

Brunar leaned forward to read the script aloud.

"What has fallen shall rise again. Laro only sleeps. The ring, forged of metals three, shall awaken the dragons and serve as the key. Say the words by which you live, and the world above will be yours again."

The Duke and Rorian made their way over as the Weya leader and the Mage pondered the phrases in silence. Duke Gensen read the words softly to himself and realization hit him.

"Goddess above, look here!" he said, his voice tinged with excitement. He held out his left hand, upon which rested a large signet ring. A pair of curling dragons, cunningly engraved, made up the official Seal of Laro, their tails twining around the gold band on each side. Moihra leaned in to examine it.

"One dragon is platinum, and the other is silver." Rorian observed.

"And the band is gold." Brunar said. "That fits the requirements of the plaque."

Moihra looked up at the Duke, cultured eagerness in her lovely face. "The passageway in the Royal Crypt could not have been opened without you present. You're of the royal bloodline. It stands to reason that the makers of this tunnel expected you or someone of your line to reach this point if the passageway were ever opened."

Duke Gensen looked at his ring with new eyes. It had been given to him during an elaborate ceremony upon the death of his father, many years ago. He had initially thought it a gaudy thing, slightly too big for his hand. He had grown into it quickly enough and had come to see it as a symbol of everything he held dear. He had been given a great trust: to keep the people of Laro safe and guide them to the best of his ability. His father had done so while wearing that same ring, as his father before him had also done. Duke Gensen had vowed to do likewise. He had kept that vow with every breath and every action, and always wore the ring as a reminder of his oath.

"What do I do? How do I use it to open the way?"

The answer came from Brunar, who had been examining the smooth face of stone that barred the way. Still gazing at the blank stone face, the Mage indicated a spot on the ground a few feet away from the center of the wall.

"You'll need to stand here, Your Grace. But we must still figure out the words you will use."

The Duke stood quietly for a moment, then turned and firmly ordered the nearest of the townspeople to move back, allowing room for more of his soldiers to settle into position. Ch'shok had come forward with a few of his warriors, and Fiona and several priestesses quickly found places among the men of Laro. The Guardians had all walked forward and stood nearby as well. Bjarke pulled his Jidaan from its sheath, a dim sparkle shining from the ruby pommel. Instantly, the other Guardians followed suit.

The Duke smiled and turned back to Brunar and Moihra. "We know not what awaits on the other side, so I'd just as soon be prepared for anything."

Brunar raised an eyebrow. "The words...?"

The Duke smiled wider. "In my heart, I know them, Mage. I've known them since I was a boy, and lived by them every single day." He uttered a short command and his men instantly came to battle readiness. Several had bows drawn, as did the priestesses. Swords were raised, and Kiran shouldered her way forward to see better, knowing that if anything threatened to overwhelm them, she could best shield them all. The Duke stepped to the spot Brunar had indicated.

Moihra's words were heard by all, though they were quiet. "It is late afternoon, and by our reckoning, we are a third of the way to Rualtha. We may find ourselves in a ruined town or in the middle of a dense forest, we know not for sure."

The Duke drew his own sword and readied himself. He nodded to the Mage, and saw Brunar shift his staff into a fighting hold. Duke Gensen took a deep breath, let it out, and faced the barren stone wall.

His family had always been noble of birthright, but not always of spirit. For centuries, the rulers of Laro had been mostly decent men, occasionally petty ones. Only a few had been mean-spirited, and those had been quietly endured by the people until their deaths, which were just as quietly celebrated. Somewhere along the way, a code of behavior and responsibility blossomed within the ruling family of Laro, and it had changed everything. Under the guidance of a succession of honorable, passionate Dukes, Laro grew from a tiny backwater into a thriving city over the course of a century, and prosperity reigned.

Duke Gensen had been raised with this code in his heart. He believed that his family existed for Laro, not the other way around. The first part of the code was simple, but it had forged a driving passion in him to better himself for the sake of his people, to never give up. It encapsulated such a spirit of optimism and determination that it had burned itself into the young Duke as a child. Those words burned there still.

"While I breathe, I hope."

The Duke's ring suddenly burst into silent flames, two silvery and one golden. The flames twirled around each other as they rose from his hand, forming a blazing pillar of light. It rose to the level of the Duke's eyes, then shot forward to strike the wall directly in its center. The magickal flames spread over the entire surface of the wall, eliciting gasps of amazement and fear from those nearby. Soldiers shifted in their stances, but swords and nocked arrows remained steady. The warriors watched and waited in tense silence.

The flames crawled over the solid rock face for a few heartbeats, then swirled together to form the great seal of Laro, two dragons entwined, right in the middle of the wall. Then, as suddenly as it had appeared, the blaze vanished, leaving everyone blinking in surprise.

A low grating sound filled the tunnel, the ponderous noise of stone against stone, and a horizontal crack of daylight appeared at the top of the wall as it began to sink into the floor. It widened as the wall descended. The light from the afternoon sun blinded them all at first, and their eyes streamed tears from the glare. A cool breeze wafted over the assembled people of Laro, but still, no one moved or spoke.

The wall finally vanished flush into the floor with a loud thump, and all was quiet. Beyond the threshold lay a forest, though not a dense one. The songs of birds reached them, such beautiful music to their ears. The ground sloped gently away from the opening, and the distant sound of a river could also be heard.

Soldiers and Augenan alike were still rubbing their eyes as they carefully peered out into the forest, wary of any threat. Brunar was about to step forward when a familiar voice reached them from outside.

"Hey there! Glad you could make it! If you could, um, point those bows elsewhere, we'll be happy to help everyone out. From the looks of it - and, whew! The smell of it - you're all very ready to get some fresh air."

Kiran stepped forward, disbelieving her ears, both thrilled and somehow annoyed at the same time.

"Layton? Is that you?"

Walking slowly with his hands held high, a figure stepped out from behind one of the trees. His clothes were soiled and bloodied, and his armor beaten and pierced. His Jidaan was clearly visible over one shoulder, its opal pommelgem quiescent. He moved with a slight hitch on one side, but the smile on his boyish face was wide and his eyes were bright with amusement.

"Yes, it's me!"

Without another word, Kiran raced past Brunar, handing her Jidaan to him on the way. She flung herself at the young warrior, embracing him fiercely. Before he could speak, she released him, took one step back, and then planted a ferocious kick squarely in his chest, knocking him to the forest floor.

"That's for making us all think you'd been eaten by Gholans or something! What is wrong with you? Ugh!" Without another word she whirled and stomped back into what she could now see was a cave at the base of a rocky cliff. She grabbed her Jidaan from an amused Brunar and walked back in among the others, grumbling quietly to herself.

Brunar and the Duke tried not to laugh and failed. They led the first of the survivors out of the cave and walked over to Layton, who still lay on the ground, his hands crossed over his chest.

Brunar knelt by the lad.

"Are you all right, my boy?"

"Ow. I was until just now."

Brunar chuckled. "I believe Kiran was concerned for your welfare."

Layton pushed himself up on his elbows and grinned. "Right. I'd hate to see what she'd do if I had actually upset her." He winced as he got to his feet.

The Duke approached. "I thought I heard you say 'we' a moment ago, Guardian. Who's 'we'?"

Before Layton could respond, a platoon of green-clad soldiers virtually appeared out of nowhere, their weapons still sheathed. Their armor was all of a kind, leather and plate, dulled and darkened for better camouflage. As one, they saluted the Duke and then stood at parade rest. A tall woman, similarly garbed but wearing a dark maroon beret, stepped forward to meet them. She stopped before the Duke and bowed in greeting.

"Your Grace, I am Jayden Luca, Captain of Rualtha's Shadow Troop. Your man here," she gestured at Layton, who shyly nodded, "he showed up at our gates a fortnight ago, asking to speak to Duke Fergus. He was sorely wounded, and we aided him as best we could. Upon seeing Layton's power and hearing his story, Duke Fergus acknowledged that he is whom he says he is - a Guardian, as of old. Duke Fergus has pledged his support. As we speak, our army is mobilizing to defend against Mordak's forces, should they be foolish enough to attack Rualtha. This young man used his extraordinary powers to transport us here."

Layton spoke up. "I managed to escape the castle before it went down. Just so you know, it was loaded with Gholans and Morcats when it collapsed!" A wide grin appeared on his face as he continued. "I knew that Rualtha was downriver, so I just followed it, using my Gates to speed me along. Once I had recovered sufficiently, it was fairly simple to transport groups of soldiers a good distance each time. I had already traveled the way there, so I knew where to 'hop', as it were, on the way back. I knew the tunnel followed the river on this side, so I brought everyone this way until..." A puzzled look crossed his face for a moment. "I don't know, it *felt* right to me. I kind of followed my nose to this cliff and we waited. I'm glad it worked out!"

Duke Gensen stood silently for a moment in disbelief. He had always been on decent terms with Duke Fergus, but this show of support was more than he had expected from the crusty old leader, especially so quickly. And the young Guardian's capabilities astonished him. Not only had he survived the fall of the castle, but he had alerted Rualtha and brought a small army to the rescue! Turning to the captain, he bowed elaborately.

"Captain Luca, I am very pleased to make your acquaintance. I have what remains of my people, only a few thousand, in that tunnel. How long will it take to get them to the safety of Rualtha?"

The captain smiled and turned to Layton, who responded with a grin of his own.

"Your Grace, if we can get everyone organized, I can get us all there in a day, maybe two. Ordinary travel would take another three weeks at top speed. I've been there and back already, and I know the best places to put my Gates. We can get everyone to safety."

Captain Luca spoke up. "We've brought medical supplies and food. We weren't sure what your situation would be or how many had made it out, so we came as prepared as possible."

Relieved, Duke Gensen sighed. "Although tired, I believe that no one carries any wounds. By now, Alyssa has reached those who needed her talents. Everyone is ready for food and rest, I'd wager. We'll start bringing them out." He paused for a moment before continuing. "Captain, I thank you, your soldiers, and your Duke. After all that's happened, you are a very welcome sight."

Captain Luca smiled a lopsided smile as she saluted. "It's my pleasure, Your Grace." She turned away then and began ordering her soldiers to spread out and prepare for the multitude that would come streaming out of the tunnel. Some of them moved towards the many tents that had been set up in preparation for the refugees' arrival.

The Duke stood quietly for a moment, facing the setting sun as he finally allowed a sense of relief to flood through him. Although he could not save them all, thousands of his people would survive. Their children would live to grow strong. Eventually, he would take them home and begin to rebuild. It would take time, but Laro would rise again. Duke Gensen's breath hitched in his chest at the thought, and he did not even try to stop the tears that flowed down his face.

Chapter 16

The rain continued to fall, drenching everything under the silvery light of the half moon. Mordak's undead simply stood in the deluge, unperturbed, as they awaited further orders, while the rest of his horde tried to huddle under hide tarps and tents. The sorcerer himself was untouched by the torrential downpour, shielded as he was by his magick. Droplets bounced off of a hazy scarlet nimbus that surrounded him, and the rain bothered him not at all.

The horde had grown far too large for him to transport with the dimensional portals he had used to get his creatures to Laro. He had already spent more energy than he cared to admit, and now, he paced angrily as he chafed at the delay. He had no problem running the Gholans to death, but it would not serve him to reach Alverton Falls with an exhausted army. He grudgingly allowed a few hours of sleep each night as they swept across the land during the day, slaying and ravaging with every step.

They had made camp alongside the edges of the Poravian Mire, an ancient swamp most often avoided by men and Weya. Dire things were said to live within, and many who braved the Mire never returned to tell of it.

But Mordak had no fear of the Mire. Indeed, he had once lived there for nearly a century as he experimented and delved into the lore of certain dark magicks. It was another home to him.

"Jor Dayne!" He ordered his Champion to attend him.

"Yes, my Master?" The big half-daemon lumbered into view almost instantly.

"See to our forces. I must enter the Mire for a time. I plan to...visit some old friends."

Jor Dayne's eyes gleamed yellow in the dark. He had no idea what Mordak might have meant, but knew better than to ask.

"Yes, my Master. You wish us to wait for your return before we move forward?"

Mordak snapped his head towards Jor Dayne.

"Yes, you fool! I shan't be long. Just keep an eye on things until I return. You can do that, can't you?" Contempt dripped from the sorcerer's words.

Jor Dayne kept silent for a heartbeat before replying. "Yes, my Master. I can, and will." A slow smile spread across his face, unseen in the dark. *One day soon, sorcerer...*

Mordak turned away, oblivious. "Good! See that you do!"

Without another word, Mordak levitated a few inches above the muddy ground, just high enough to keep his feet out of the mud, and glided into the dark embrace of the Mire.

Jor Dayne watched the sorcerer disappear into the swamp, already planning various delightful activities for the future. The time was coming when Mordak's hold on him would weaken just enough, and then things would become very interesting. He turned away and hummed a little tune to himself as he went to harass the unruly Gholans and remind the Morcats that he was their superior officer. The Krell, he left to themselves.

The rain continued to fall, as if trying to wash away the stain on the surface of the land. Try as it might, it failed.

Chapter 17

The wind on the river nearly took Gart's hat off, but he clamped one hand on it in time to keep it from flying out into the water. He settled it more firmly on his head and returned to his task. The leather bag he had fashioned slid over the end of his Jidaan, completely covering the diamond-shaped pommel and the glittering emerald it clutched within. Using a slender lace of leather, he bound it tightly to the weapon's shaft. He shook the weapon to see if the cover would stay in place and was pleased with the result. Satisfied, he slid the Jidaan's blade into its sheath and then slipped his arms into the straps so that it would hang properly at his back. Its size and shining, unblemished blade made it noticeable enough. At least now, the sun would not make the emerald sparkle and draw more stares from the riverboat crew.

He stepped up to the railing and looked out over the Blackthorne River, watching the tall trees on the eastern riverbank move slowly past and enjoying the clean smell of the piny woods. The ship had its sail unfurled, and they were making good time on their way south. The sailors moved about their tasks with smooth efficiency, proving Darryn's earlier words. The *Goshawk* was moving mostly cargo on this trip, so Gart was able to avoid most of the other passengers without being rude. Beauty's size and fearsome appearance also gave him a bit of privacy, since the others were reluctant to engage her.

At the moment, Beauty had her front feet on the railing next to Gart, her head on a level with his. Her eyes were nearly closed and she seemed to be enjoying the sensation of the wind blowing in her face. Gart smiled and ruffled the fur on her neck before moving away to take a seat nearby, leaving her to enjoy the breeze.

He leaned back against the main cabin and looked up at the sail. It was decently filled, but fell slack now and again as the breeze wavered. He wondered idly how steady the wind would be throughout the southerly journey, and realized suddenly that another opportunity to practice was right in front of him. However, he would have to be far more careful than the first time; he couldn't have anything happen to the ship.

He needed to learn better control. He would have to start smaller - much smaller - than a bolt of lightning. He looked over at Beauty, her face still turned into the wind, enjoying herself.

Yes, that would work. If he could touch the wind, just a little, maybe he could speed up their travel.

A wry grin crawled across his face. *Or I could end up smashing this boat against the rocks on the opposite bank,* he thought. He had seen Lillia perform wonders with her Jidaan, commanding the elements of wind, rain, and lightning as adeptly as any famed bard might have plucked the strings on a lute. He, on the other hand, felt like a bull trying to learn to dance. His skills with his own magick had grown immensely, especially since taking up the Jidaan, but he was still a complete novice where its power was concerned.

Gart let his eyes rove over the sail and mast above him, getting a feel for its structure and function. He let a trickle of his magick out to caress the canvas, feeling its rough texture and its tautness as it caught the breeze. He felt the solid yet flexible strength of the mast, and through it, the rest of the ship. Then he closed his eyes and expanded the range of his senses. For long, silent minutes, his awareness floated high above and around the boat, gaining a sense of the sweeping air currents that surrounded the world. He was awed by the vastness of it all. He had always taken for granted the air that he breathed, but riding the wind like that, he could sense its incredible, limitless power. It could caress a feather so that it drifted gently to rest in a child's upturned palm, or it could literally wipe an entire city from the face of the world.

Slowly, Gart brought his awareness back to his body and opened his eyes. He began to form a vivid picture in his mind, a detailed image of exactly what he wanted to happen. He spent several minutes imagining the sail filling out completely, hearing the sounds of the mast as it held the strain, and replayed the scene over again several times. He would not rush this as he had the lightning.

Once he felt confident in his visualization, he awakened his magick and sent it towards the Jidaan. It answered his call immediately. He could feel its intense thrum at his back, but this time, he held his command. It awaited his will. Cautiously, Gart held back, working to control his use of the Jidaan's power.

Gart waited a few seconds before he sent the picture in his mind towards the Jidaan, and it vibrated sharply as its power was enabled. He felt the magick leave the weapon, seeking the very air that surrounded him.

In moments, the wind picked up, and the sail snapped forward, its ropes straining to contain the blow. Gart used his senses to feel everything that was happening, carefully gauging the amount of stress on the ship. He felt the ropes tighten further and heard the mast groan under the increasing gale.

The sailors began shouting to each other as they increased the pace of their tasks to keep up with the gusts, tying some lines while loosening others, and generally swarming over the deck to see that all was well as the *Goshawk* sped faster and faster down the river.

At the railing, Beauty whuffed and barked, wagging her tail in glee at the increasing wind.

Sweat trickled down Gart's face as he felt the tempest continue to rise. The sailors' shouts became louder and concern crept into their tone as they hurried to keep the ship under control. A rope snapped and the mast groaned loudly. Beauty barked in alarm, the sound carrying over the wind. Old, familiar anger and frustration rose in Gart. This was exactly what he had feared would happen.

Shoving those emotions away, Gart took a deep breath and let it out. Delving deeply into his magick, he reached out to the winds as he held the scene he had visualized in his mind more firmly, sending it out in an attempt to impose it upon the situation he had created. Heartbeats flew by, and at first, nothing changed.

Just when Gart's concern threatened to edge into panic, the wind finally began to slow. Gart kept his eyes closed, sweat soaking his shirt as he struggled to control his power and that of the Jidaan of Storms. As the wind subsided into the speed he had originally envisioned - a strong breeze just enough to speed the *Goshawk* along without undue stress - his taut muscles finally relaxed and he let out a sigh of relief.

He opened his eyes and felt a wave of weariness wash over him, exhaustion of a kind he had never felt before. Gart leaned back against the firm wood of the cabin, relieved to hear the sailors' shouts fade back to their usual timbre as they expertly piloted the ship to ride the wind he had created. He was weary right down to his bones, and felt as though he could sleep for a week. Beauty padded over to him and licked his face amiably, and he didn't bother to defend himself.

"All right, girl, all right. Settle down; everything is fine." She obediently turned in a circle and curled up next to Gart with her massive head on his lap. He absently stroked her tattered ears with one hand, trying to calm himself as much as her.

It had almost gotten away from him, but he had managed to rein in the power of Storms. No one had died; he had not been lightning-struck, and all was well.

Gart wearily tipped his floppy hat down over his eyes and leaned his head back. Although he had succeeded, he was frustrated. He had only managed to summon a tiny fraction of the abilities he had seen Lillia wield in his dreams, yet he was completely spent. He knew that he had to find a way to get stronger and more skilled with the weapon's Gift, or else he would never stand a chance against the likes of Mordak and Jor Dayne. He tried to curse in anger, but found he just did not have the strength. Before he could dwell on his frustrations any further, sleep took him by the ankles and dragged him under. Beauty sensed her master's unease, but as she felt his body relax in sleep, her own tension lessened. Moments later, she dozed off herself. And she snored just as loudly as he.

Chapter 18

The pennants atop the great pavilion snapped in the breeze, the colors of Rualtha on the western side and the Laroan flag on the east. The leaders, both human and otherwise, had been in battle council since dawn. Several ideas had been born, modified, discarded, and the whole process started over again many times. Mordak would be on the move, most likely had been since the fall of Laro, and it would only be a matter of time before his murderous forces would attack another settlement.

"If Mordak has sent his army this way, toward Rualtha," the Duke was saying, "we'd have seen them by now. They travel overland much faster than we were able to cross through that tunnel. Why are they not here?"

"We know not, Your Grace," Captain Luca replied earnestly. "We have a wide line of scouts on both sides of the river to alert us of their approach, but all are accounted for and have seen nothing yet."

Brunar leaned back from the table. "They will surely be heading this way soon enough. Whether they come in full force or split their army to move to the north as well, that is also a question."

The table's surface was covered with one of Brunar's illusory maps, a spell that created a three dimensional representation of the terrain for miles in all directions. Their own location glowed purple to one side of its center. An ornate compass shone in one corner, establishing the cardinal directions. The Corris River ran along the length of the table, labeled in a flowing script. Spots of gold and green showed the cities of Laro and Rualtha, and a spot of blue far north of the Corris denoted the city of Alverton Falls. The terrain rolled gently across the tabletop; Captain Luca reached out a hand to touch it, so real did it seem.

Brunar's brow was furrowed as he contemplated. "If he were bringing his whole army this way, he would have already come this far. No, something else has happened. I am sure of it."

Moihra's voice entered the conversation, its melodic tone like music on the air. "Brunar, can you use a spell to spy on him? I thought that was something you had done in the past."

Brunar grimaced. "Indeed, honored ValElder. Only, each time I have done so, Mordak has struck me down ere I saw anything of value." He paused for a moment, remembering the blinding pain that the evil sorcerer had visited upon him back at the Keep in the Heartstrong Mountains, and again at the site of the *Damsel's* shipwreck. He took a deep breath and shrugged off the memory. "Even so, it is vital that we gain some intelligence regarding his position. I must risk it." Rising smoothly from his chair, he stepped towards the opening in the tent that served as a door. "This should not take very long. I shall return." With that, he strode out the door as conversation resumed around the table. Fiona watched him go, a calculating look on her stern yet beautiful face.

Outside, the Mage looked around, happy to see the people of Laro being tended, fed, and finally resting comfortably. They would be moved to Rualtha the next morning, with Layton speeding their transport. Brunar smiled at the thought of the young warrior. *That boy has come a long way,* he thought. *When newly Chosen, he could barely move the six of us across a room through a single Gate. But then, he takes to such challenges quite well, it seems.*

After a few moments of aimless walking, Brunar found a secluded spot with a stone big enough for him to sit upon. He settled himself and cleared his mind, deciding on his course of action. The last time he had tried a Search spell, he had been immediately stricken by the Evil One. This time, he would approach it differently. He took a deep breath to focus his will, and then mouthed the ancient Words that helped him engage his magick. There was a feeling of separation within him, and then Brunar floated upwards from his place on the stone. His body remained seated with legs crossed and eyes closed. The Mage's spirit rose higher and then higher still, until he could see the surrounding terrain for miles around. He figured as long as he did not specifically Search for the evil sorcerer, then his presence might not be detected right away. This time, he was simply an unknown phantom, a wisp within the ether, and as long as Mordak was not also Searching for him, Brunar felt he should be safe.

He drifted high above the land, relishing the view of the rolling grasslands and forests below. Far to the east, he could already see columns of smoke in the distance, revealing the location of the shattered remains of Laro. He willed his spirit in that direction. Not far from the bluff through which they had exited the tunnel, Brunar saw the side of the cliff where they had met the Spider Queen, Kulcania. None of the huge spiders were in sight, though Brunar could feel their peculiar energy in the forest that spread across the land away from the cliffs. They were there, for certain, and Brunar was shocked at how vast their numbers seemed to be, hidden as they were in the trees below. His spirit flew on towards Laro.

It was not long before he caught the oily, rank sensation that accompanied those of Mordak's ilk. As he soared overhead, he saw them as dark spots on the grass, a horde of ants that swept over the countryside. There were a few thousand of them, but not nearly so many as Brunar had expected. They were indeed headed to Rualtha, but at a pace no faster than that of a running Gholan. There were nearly enough of them to take the heavily defended city on their own. They must not have started out their journey as early as Brunar had feared they might. *Interesting,* Brunar thought. He turned that fact over in his mind as he continued onward.

The remains of Laro devastated Brunar. The once proud city was completely destroyed, fires still burning in many places. Its castle had collapsed into a shattered ruin, and the smell of death was thick in the air, so strong that even Brunar's shade perceived it. After a quick look around to ascertain that none of Mordak's troops had been left behind, Brunar left the dead city, moving northward.

A few days ride from the city, Brunar beheld a sight that hurt his heart. A small village, its name unknown to him, had been razed to the ground. No complete corpses remained, only a few grisly bits and pieces lay strewn about. Not for the first time, Brunar cursed Mordak's black heart. He flew on.

Soon, a strong sense of dread started to eat at him, and an icy chill shot through his spirit. Hoping to avoid detection, Brunar moved higher into the clouds. He scanned the land ahead of him, hunting for the source of his unease. It came soon enough.

Near the edge of the Poravian Mire, legions of dark creatures waited. Seen from afar, the army resembled an enormous black lake, but as he drew closer, he could see the individual figures scurrying about. Gholans made up the bulk of the force, but there were Morcats aplenty as well. The Krell had a sizeable island of space to themselves, having already established that they did not care to rub elbows with the lesser creatures they considered little better than vermin. Scarlet-eyed Riders in the thousands, Mordak's undead, were scattered among the army, unmoving until called upon.

Brunar skirted the throng, trying to gauge its size, but it was so vast that it confounded his efforts to quantify it. His heart sank as he circled the colossal force. Of Mordak, there was no immediate sign, but he had to be nearby. The Mage marveled at the sheer size of the horde. He had no idea that so many fell creatures even existed on the face of Talwynn. Nevertheless, they apparently did, and Mordak had managed to enslave them all. Disheartened, Brunar had seen enough. He turned to leave.

That's when he found that he could not. His shade hung in the air, motionless. Alarmed, Brunar willed himself to move-down, up, anywhere-but he was frozen in place. Fear blossomed in his heart.

A dark swirling cloud appeared before him in the air, no bigger than a handprint. It churned and grew until it was twice the size of a man, its interior as black as midnight. From within its inky darkness came a laugh that Brunar knew well. It was tinged with madness.

"Brunar, how good of you to come. That your body is not here is disappointing, but your spirit...ah, that's even better! I'm going to enjoy shredding your soul, Mage!"

Brunar tried to cast a spell and found that he could not. His spirit was bound in rings of magick stronger than any steel. He had been caught completely unawares, and now he would pay the price.

"Brunar, fly!" Fiona's voice echoed like a thunderclap, and a blinding flash exploded between Mordak's cloud and Brunar's shade. Mordak howled in anger, and a bolt of sickly scarlet power shot out of the darkness to strike the spot where Brunar had been. The Mage was not there.

Rather than try to break through his bonds, he simply compressed himself. He focused his will until his shade was naught but a slender thread that shot out from Mordak's shackles before they could tighten on him again. The Mage's spirit flew faster than it had ever flown, the land racing past beneath him. It took only moments for him to return and plunge back into his body in the secluded glade. He gasped and his eyes flew wide only to see Fiona, who had apparently been standing next to him, just starting to fall unconscious to the ground. He staggered forward and caught her in his arms, then carefully lowered her to the grass below.

"Fiona! Fiona!" He urgently tried to wake her. As he watched, a shining silver streak began at her right temple and worked its way through her dark hair all the way to the ends, and her face took on a worn, tired look. Before Brunar could move to get help, her eyes popped open, wild and darting, and she sucked in a great lungful of air as she struggled to sit up.

"Are you all right? Fiona! What did you do?"

After taking a few moments to calm herself, Fiona turned her deep blue eyes toward Brunar, and smiled a rueful smile.

"I can't let you have all the fun, now can I? Two heads are better than one where that evil sorcerer is concerned, so I figured I'd tag along. And I'm glad I did."

Brunar smiled. "I am also glad, my lady. He had me for a moment there. I might have been able to escape, but then again I might not. Thank you, Fiona." He helped her to her feet.

"You're most welcome, Mage. Besides, I wanted to see what you saw for myself." She took a couple of careful steps, making sure that her balance would not fail her. "Come, sir. Let us go tell the others."

"Indeed, they need to know what we saw." Brunar shook his head. "Though they're not going to like any of it."

Chapter 19

Once Brunar explained what he and Fiona had seen, it did not take long for everyone to agree on a plan of action. The refugees from Laro would be taken to safety in Rualtha, and that city would prepare for the oncoming assault. Although the force that was headed towards them was not nearly as large as the main army, it was uncertain what other threats might arrive with them. Mordak was wily, and everyone agreed that they should prepare for the worst.

The following dawn saw Layton begin to escort group after group of soldiers and survivors through a succession of his opalescent Gates until they ended up safely behind the walls of Rualtha. There, they entered several warehouses that had been emptied and prepared for them. Before entering Layton's portals, many of the Laroans stopped to speak to Brunar and the Guardians to thank them, tears in their eyes and gratitude in their hearts. Although their future was still uncertain, they had been saved from the clutches of nightmarish creatures by a Mage and warriors wielding the fabled, shining Jidaan. They would tell their children and grandchildren of their valiant rescuers.

There was still a sense of urgency; everyone knew that Mordak's assault force drew nearer with every passing moment. Although they were yet many days away, there was no use in taking chances. Layton strained his abilities to the full to get everyone evacuated. His skill and strength had improved greatly since Laro, where he had been forced to use his Gift repeatedly. Now, he created Gates large enough for huge groups to pass through, and far enough apart that the entire journey to Rualtha felt to them like less than a day's walk. It took a toll on the young man though, and by dusk, he was completely spent.

As the sun set beyond the hills to the west, only a handful of soldiers remained with Duke Gensen, the Guardians, and the Augenan, who had elected to stay behind. His work mostly finished, Layton sought out the command tent, weariness dogging his every step.

Inside the tent, Brunar sat across from Duke Gensen at the table, endlessly discussing possible scenarios, while Nessar sat chatting with Kiran and Alyssa in one corner. Bjarke stood with Ch'shok nearby, discussing the finer points of Augenan cuisine. Bjarke gnawed on a massive turkey leg while the Aug High Chieftain somewhat daintily worked his way through a huge bowl of fruit. Fiona and Muriel looked up from another table where they had been talking with Captain Luca and the Weya, sharing their mutual love of joint locks and throwing techniques.

Brunar watched Layton drag himself into a corner and fall facedown on a pile of hide tarps. The exhausted warrior was asleep and snoring in moments.

Duke Gensen spoke up. "That young lad astounds me. My people are safe in Rualtha tonight thanks to him, and to all of you here." He swept the room with his sincere gaze. "I cannot tell you enough what your presence has meant to me and to all Laroans. You have all risked your lives many times over for us. If any of you ever need anything from me or my people, please know that it is yours for the asking."

Without a word, Alyssa stood and walked over to the Duke. She opened up her arms to him and he bent forward to receive her hug. She kissed him on both cheeks, tears standing in her eyes. "The honor was ours, Your Grace." The Duke sniffed once, then stood tall, his own eyes shining.

"I wanted to be sure you all knew of my gratitude, for I will leave in the morning. Or sooner, if Layton is willing."

A loud snore came from the pile of hides and everyone laughed. "I think morning will be soon enough," the Duke chuckled.

Brunar stood. "Guardians, we must discuss our own travel plans. Mordak moves to the north. Based on what I saw, I fear that Alverton Falls will be the next target of his teeming horde."

Captain Luca announced, "Alverton Falls is larger than Laro, but not nearly so well defended. They've never had need of a large standing army, and they don't have a wall like Rualtha and Laro. They will be decimated by the creatures you described unless they prepare. We can send pigeons bearing messages this very night to alert them to the danger."

Brunar nodded his agreement. "Yes, the sooner the better. Add Duke Gensen's seal so they know the news is authentic." He sighed heavily. "They *must* prepare. If Mordak takes the city, you can bet he will make use of every human body he finds to build his army. If he does that, he could triple the size of his horde. He does not discriminate - the old, the infirm, the young, women, children - he can use them all as undead soldiers with the amount of power he's manifesting. With that many, he could easily overwhelm either Rualtha or the Royal City of Bos Aldas in the far north, not to mention any settlements in between. Any villages or towns would be easily overrun."

Nessar spoke up from his chair. "How in the name of the Goddess Rowann are we supposed to fight an army that size? They've already beaten us at Laro. We knew they were coming, and we had a giant wall to hide behind. Now their army is even bigger! I'm not one to give up; I'd just as soon spit in Mordak's eye if he comes close enough. But even with all of us together, it sounds like a losing battle!" Others murmured in agreement.

Brunar held up a hand and all fell silent.

"We need something to tip the balance. We can't take on the horde directly; we have to fight its leader. I have an idea." He took a deep breath before continuing. "There is an amulet that may help us. It was created in the kingdom of Linbourne a millennia ago."

"Linbourne? I've never heard of it. Where is it supposed to be?" Nessar scratched his white-haired scalp as he searched his memory for anything resembling the name.

"I have heard of it. And I've been there." Ginn's low, warm voice surprised them all. The Weya walked over to the table. "Brunar, the map, if you would be so kind."

With a wave of his hand, Brunar recreated the vivid map of the entire continent on the tabletop, complete with glowing representations of the cities and glowing north arrow in one corner. Ginn looked it over and pointed to a spot far to the east, almost to the barren reaches of the Gorran Plain. Brunar created a dot of red light to mark the location Ginn had indicated.

"I was there over a thousand years ago, just passing through on my way to one of our solstice celebrations. It was a small city, not nearly the size of Laro but very," he thought for a moment before continuing, "pleased with itself, if you catch my meaning. Somewhat pompous and gaudy, if I recall. In any event, I heard nearly a hundred years later that the city was gone. Just...gone. Not a stone remained from what I was told, though what became of it, I do not know. I never heard much beyond that and never went to investigate. Cities rise and fall for any number of reasons, I honestly never thought anything more of it."

Brunar nodded gravely. "That makes me think all the more that the artifact we seek may be there."

"*May* be there?" Nessar interjected. "Whatever this thing is, you don't really know if it's there?"

"A thousand years ago, a wizard named Wendall created an amulet that absorbs magickal energy. Such a device would nullify any sorcery, even Mordak's. If the city did indeed vanish as legend says, then some fantastic magickal calamity may have occurred. If that is what happened, then even now there will be traces that can be detected, especially by those who are sensitive to magick. The amulet was said to have incredible power, never seen before or since. Just imagine such a device! Mordak could throw whatever he likes at the amulet, but it would gain him nothing. Instead, it would drain him of his power!"

This was greeted with a moment of silence. If such a thing existed, then it would indeed turn the tide of battle. To render the foul sorcerer powerless would make him vulnerable, possibly weak enough that even ordinary weapons could kill him. The concept sunk in and slowly, heads began to nod.

Bjarke stepped into the conversation. "This amulet...how can we find it? Can we even get there before Mordak reaches Alverton Falls?"

Brunar looked over his shoulder at Layton, who snorted and rolled into a ball, still sleeping soundly. "If Layton is up to it, he should be able to get some of us close enough to Alverton Falls to help them mount a defense, then turn towards Linbourne with the others, find the amulet, return to us with it. It will be difficult, but necessary. Judging by his performance in the past week or so, he can do it. We can find a way to hold Mordak until the amulet is found."

Frowning, Kiran pulled a dagger from her belt and began to clean her nails with it. "All right, so you'll need two teams. Who goes to find the amulet?"

Brunar turned to face her. "I was thinking of sending you, Nessar, and Layton together. On horseback, with the use of his Gates, you will make good time. You'll need Nessar. Once you find the city, I think his particular set of skills may be necessary."

Nessar laughed at that. "You mean in case I have to steal it for you?" He tried to look insulted, but could not manage it. He wanted to act the part of the crusty old curmudgeon, but truth be told, the idea of a mission that suited his skills was intriguing to him.

Brunar raised an eyebrow in response. "I was thinking more along the lines of keeping everyone alive in case the amulet is warded somehow, but otherwise, yes!" Nessar chuckled, and Brunar continued. "Although, I have a feeling it is simply there, waiting to be found. Either way, you are needed, Ness."

The old man nodded his assent and leaned back in his chair. He'd go along, though he didn't see the need to let everyone know that he was even remotely happy about it. He cast a glance at Kiran and saw her frowning. He could practically hear her thinking she did not like to be running away from a fight, but knew that her skills would be necessary too.

Ginn's voice filled the room again. "I can guide them, at least to within sight of the city. Then I need to get word back to our people. I'm sure they've been fighting against Mordak's ilk wherever it has assailed them, but they need to know of his plans."

ValElder Moihra tucked her hair behind pointed ears as she spoke. "Brunar, if Cohl and I may accompany you at least as far as Alverton Falls, we shall rally the Weya in the area and aid you as best we can."

Brunar inclined his head at the Weya leader. "You have my thanks, my lady. The assistance of the Weya would be most helpful to the people of Alverton Falls."

Fiona immediately entered the conversation. "Some of us will go with you as well. Of the seven of us, three have gone on to Rualtha to assist them there. Bekah, Melina, Emmi, and I will go to Alverton Falls. The Goddess wishes it."

Brunar bowed deeply to the priestess. "We will be honored to have you and the other ladies with us, Fiona." When he stood tall once more, he could not hide the ghost of a smile that crept onto his face. Fiona intrigued him. She was a strong and intelligent woman, and her robe could not completely hide her feminine curves and natural grace. Suddenly scolding himself, he pushed aside those feelings and became the stern Mage once more. He didn't see that Fiona's eyes glittered brightly and her own smile echoed his.

Turning to the huge Augenan Chieftain, Brunar continued, "Mighty Ch'shok, you have our undying gratitude. You and your warriors saved us at Laro. What are your plans?"

Ch'shok pulled gently on the copper ornaments in his beard. Even seated on the ground as he was, the massive gorilla warrior was taller than Brunar. He wrinkled up his face for a moment, then spoke in his strong, gravelly voice. "Our Seer say we come, so we come. Fought good fight. Many want to go home now." Ch'shok picked up his chin as he thought further and made a decision. Slowly, an enormous grin brightened his dark face. "We attack the Erchalin, instead!" His voice dripped disdain as he referred to Mordak's creatures in his own language. "We will crush! Keep other human-city safe." In one smooth motion, he pulled the massive battle axe from his back and twirled it in one hand before replacing it. "We fight against Baulotha. Not go home until we win."

Brunar was pleased to hear that the hardy warriors would continue to fight. Indeed, at nearly a thousand strong, they might be able to completely decimate the oncoming enemy forces, though they were outnumbered more than three to one.

"Thank you, Ch'shok! I'm sure that they will fear the very sight of you!" Turning back to the others, he continued. "All right then, it's settled. Tonight, we rest and make ready for our journeys tomorrow. After Layton transports the Duke and the remaining Rualthan soldiers to their city, he will take us all north until our missions diverge. Agreed?"

As one, each in the tent voiced their assent. Brunar was glad to have a plan. In his heart, he prayed to the Goddess Rowann that it was the correct course of action, for many would die otherwise. He rose from his seat and walked out of the tent to meditate in the deepening dark of the forest. The night sounds had always calmed him, and he hoped they would again.

Chapter 20

The day had dawned gray and damp, the sun completely hidden behind a low blanket of heavy clouds. Moisture was thick in the cool breeze, hinting strongly of the rain to come. Gart's life as a farmer had left him sensitive to the turns of the seasons and the changes in the weather, but now that he had been Chosen, he felt that connection with the earth and sky far more acutely. He knew somehow that the rain would come at midday, but not before. It was a very tactile sense, similar to the way he could tell if a stone in his hand were heavy or light, and he was not at all used to it. He stood at the railing of the *Goshawk*, watching the scenery go by, idly reaching out to see what else he could divine with his heightened senses. He knew that, with the Jidaan or without, he had only recently begun to understand the power that he wielded, and he knew he needed to work at it. Letting go of his worries, he drifted, a part of him exploring far from the little ship.

Beside him, Beauty groaned good-naturedly, shook herself, and yawned loudly. Gart reached down with one hand to scratch her ears and she leaned into him, her bulk making him shift his weight lest he fall over.

"That's a good girl, Beauty," Gart murmured absently. Still riding the winds above on his questing senses, Gart could feel the heart of the oncoming storm approaching. Unsure of exactly how he managed to do so, he surged forward and joined with it. It was not a terribly strong storm, only a bit of lightning and rain in rumbly black clouds, but the power that Gart felt there awed him. This was nature's might, not his own, and even a brief thundershower contained far more energy than he had ever bothered to imagine.

As his essence drifted among the clouds, he began to understand how his Jidaan worked to control the weather. His power was funneled through the magnifying lens of the ancient weapon, which amplified it a thousandfold. The Jidaan then reached out to the atmosphere and manifested whatever picture Gart held strongly in his mind by adjusting the conditions of the wind, rain, even the temperature, to answer Gart's call. The entire operation completely amazed him, and he marveled that he had been given control of such staggering power. Suddenly, he realized just how dangerous, how devastating, such power could be.

A part of him wanted to celebrate his new understanding. He knew that with such power, he would make short work of Jor Dayne. But the thought also made him frown. At what price would come that victory? His gift came with great responsibility. He knew he could raise a storm of such fury that it would wipe out Jor Dayne, Mordak, and any creatures foolish enough to attack him. However, if they were in a village like Tiller's Grove had once been, that storm would destroy evil and innocent alike.

Gart reined in his spirit and opened his eyes. The trees along the far bank were starting to bend slightly in the wind. A fine drizzle was just beginning to fall, and Gart pulled his hat down farther on his head to keep the rain from hitting his neck. Beauty shook herself again, then padded to a sheltered spot near the main cabin and curled up there, out of the rain.

Gart chuckled at her, only to receive a *whuff* in return. Smiling, he turned away and moved towards the bow of the ship to see what lay ahead. The sailors waved in greeting as he passed, as did some of the passengers he had spoken with during the voyage. When he arrived, he found Darryn already there, leaning against the railing with his gaze fixed downriver, a worried look on his sunbrowned face.

"You don't seem happy, Darryn. Or should I call you Captain?"

Darryn kept his gaze focused on the river ahead. "Darryn be just fine, man. Me boys know I run the ship; I be Cap'n enough to them." He fell silent for a moment before continuing. "There's a bad feelin' in me bones." He ran one callused hand through his hair and then gripped the railing again. "We've made good time, that's certain, but there usually be more traffic headed upriver from here. For the last few days, there's none to speak of. For some reason, that bothers me."

"Sorry, I wish I knew what to say. This is my first time on a riverboat; I don't know the first thing about it." Gart would never have noticed the lack of other ships on the wide river until Darryn pointed it out.

The grizzled captain grunted in response and managed a grin. "Aye, ye be far more comfortable with mud on yer boots, I know. Nothin' to be ashamed of." But then his demeanor turned somber once more. "Not meaning to worry ye any. I just have the creepy crawly feelin' in me." Abruptly, he changed the subject. "We'll be going ashore soon. There's a little town ahead, Hollowthorne. We always dock there on our way south."

Gart grimaced. "With a name like that, it's no wonder you have a creepy crawly feeling."

Darryn laughed as he turned to attend to his other tasks. "The name be awful, yes, but it's a nice little place. Ye'll see! A handful of families live there and serve riverboaters like us, keep us from starving to death, ye ken? The mayor's a bit of a windbag, but otherwise, they're right friendly folk." Without waiting for a response, he swept up into the rigging to help another sailor tie off something that had come loose.

Gart looked downriver for a few long moments after the captain had gone and noticed that Darryn had been right. The river looked amazingly empty and lonely, as far as the eye could see. Try as he might, he could not sense anything amiss, but Darryn had passed on the feeling of foreboding. Gart hoped the captain had been wrong.

Chapter 21

It had taken most of the morning for Layton to transport the Duke, Captain Luca, and the few remaining soldiers back to the safety of Rualtha, then return. While they waited, they bid farewell to Ch'shok and the other Augenan, who had assembled in the shining light of the dawn. It was an impressive sight, so many of the enormous copper-furred gorilla people in one place, almost a thousand brave warriors. At a word from their High Chief, they turned and melted into the trees at a run, eager to lay hands on the approaching evil force. Ch'shok went last, waving at his new friends one last time before loping off into the trees as well, using his knuckles to propel himself at surprising speed.

Once they had gone, Brunar gathered his small force together. Horses were mounted and pack ponies tethered behind. Supplies had been well-packed beforehand. For the first leg of the journey, they would all travel north together, but once they neared Alverton Falls, Layton would take Ginn, Nessar, and Kiran to the East in search of the amulet at Linbourne. They gathered their horses on the spot that had previously been occupied by the command tent. Brunar led his horse up next to Layton.

"All right, Layton, it is time. If you would Gate us northward to get us started, we can ride a bit so you can save your strength before moving us all again."

Layton gave Brunar a tired smile. "It's all right, Brunar. I've had a lot of practice lately. I'm tired, yes, but I think you'll be pleasantly surprised. Hold on..." Without warning, a Gate appeared right near Layton's shoulder, an opalescent portal about the size of a small shield. The young warrior leaned into it, his head disappearing for only a moment, then he leaned back again and allowed the Gate to vanish. "Ok, sorry, I just needed to see where we're going. I'm ready."

Brunar smiled. Layton was growing into quite the adept with his Jidaan-bestowed Gift. "All right then, let's move!"

Layton created a Gate right in front of the little group, large enough for all of them to ride through at once. Moments later, the Guardians, Weya, and a handful of priestesses were gone from the clearing as though they had never been, and birds sang their sweet songs into the empty forest.

Chapter 22

The clouds had gotten darker as the day progressed. The sun had long since disappeared from view, leaving a rainy landscape that felt more like midnight than late afternoon. Lightning rumbled in the clouds at odd intervals as jagged flashes lit up the sky. The winds had died down a bit, and although Gart considered doing something about the storm, he had a strong feeling he should let nature take its course. He was reluctant to meddle with the delicate balance of energies in the skies unless it was necessary.

He checked over Bessie's tack and saddlebags, making sure that nothing had been damaged in the rain. The horses had been sheltered in a small pavilion at one end of the ship, and Gart was pleased to find her none the worse for wear. One shoe seemed to be working itself loose. It wasn't a problem yet, but it soon would be, and Gart made note of it.

Suddenly, he heard Darryn bellowing commands from somewhere on the deck, and the sailors burst into action. They had finally reached Hollowthorne. Gart made his way to the starboard railing and peered into the gloom. He was rewarded with the sight of a handful of buildings and several large docks that jutted out into the water up ahead. A couple of other riverboats were already anchored there, but something was off. He stared at the docks and buildings as they approached and noticed that there was no movement there. There should have been people moving about at this time of day even with the wet weather, but there were none to be found.

Darryn's crew expertly piloted the *Goshawk* into place at one of the docks and attached the mooring lines with the ease of long practice. A gangplank was lowered, and a handful of crewmen escorted the few passengers off of the boat. Gart pulled Bessie gently by the reins and found that she was eager to set foot on solid ground again, even if it meant stepping out into the heavy drizzle. He pulled his hat down, shifted his Jidaan in its harness at his back, and gave a short, soft whistle that called Beauty immediately to his side.

Gart walked them carefully over to the dock and up onto the shore, where there was a gravel trail leading between two of the large buildings. He figured there would be a blacksmith or a handyman who could take care of Bessie's shoe faster than he could do it himself. The drizzle started coming down harder, slowly turning into a pelting rain, and Gart was thankful for the old hat he'd bought from the boy some time ago. It had served him well.

He led Bessie around the nearest corner and found himself looking down a single road with wooden buildings on either side. At the far end of the road was a slightly larger two level structure. It looked more like a home than a business, though Gart could not imagine why someone would ever need a house that big. He began looking along the storefronts for the blacksmith's shop, Beauty at his side. Ahead, he could see the others entering a couple of the buildings, likely a grocery and a tavern. Other than the crew and passengers from the *Goshawk*, the street was deserted. In spite of the rain, there should have been signs of someone, somewhere. A crawling sensation crept up the back of his neck and a knot of dread began to form in the pit of his stomach. Something was wrong here.

Suddenly, Beauty growled deep in her throat, then whined softly. The hair on the back of Gart's neck stood up at the sound, and he stopped. He scanned the rainy street carefully, but saw nothing. No one came out of any of the buildings, but then, they were likely settling down to eat. He waited a few heartbeats, and seeing nothing else amiss, he started forward again.

Almost immediately, he found the blacksmith's shop, a three-sided building with a glowing forge in the back. It was still hot, but it seemed to be unattended.

"Hello?" he called. "I don't need much, just a repair on a horseshoe." Gart led his animals into the open shop and out of the rain. He wrapped Bessie's reins around a hitching post and stepped deeper into the darkness of the shop. "Is anyone here?"

Silence was his only answer. Gart stepped closer to the forge to ward off the chill left by the rain. Beauty shook herself, and drops of water hissed slightly as they hit the metal hood over the firepit. A pair of tongs lay with their ends in the fire and Gart carefully reached down and nudged the handles. Although the fire was burning down to coals, whatever had been held between the forceps had been there long enough to lose its shape. It was naught but a blob of molten metal, and the ends of the tongs were red with the heat. Gart moved the tongs out of the fire and carefully placed them near the edge of the pit where it was relatively cool.

"Hello?" he called out once more, and again, there was no answer. Gart knew something was very wrong. No smith would leave his forge untended like that, but there was naught to be done about it that Gart could see. He looked around and found what he needed to fix Bessie's shoe in one corner of the shop. He led Bessie to it, gathered the tools he needed and went to work. Beauty positioned herself just far enough inside that the rain did not touch her and stared down the street, eyeing the big house at the end of the lane. She whuffed several times and growled twice, but never moved from her lookout post.

It took Gart longer than he'd have liked to remove the old shoe, prepare her hoof, adjust a new shoe and nail it in place. However, when he was finished, even Bessie seemed pleased. He carefully put the tools away exactly where he had found them and pulled a few coppers from his money pouch. It more than covered the cost of a single shoe, and he placed them on a worktable in the back before untying Bessie's reins.

Just then, voices reached his ears and he tensed, one hand reaching towards his Jidaan. Gart stopped short of drawing it as the voices became clearer. It was only Darryn and the other sailors and passengers returning from the inn. Gart relaxed, but then noticed that their voices were taut and anxious. They passed by the smithy with hunched shoulders and darting eyes, obviously eager to return to the *Goshawk*. Darryn spied him and spoke a few words to his crew, sending them on with the passengers. Then he angled away from the small group to talk to Gart. The riverboat captain's face was a mask of concern.

"Find what ye need in there, eh?"

"Yes, she's all fixed up. Had to do it myself, though. There's no one here."

"Aye, it was the same at the inn. All the rooms, empty of people. Belongings, we saw in some, spare clothes and the like, but there be not a soul in that place. Those riverboats at the docks...where be their crews?" He looked around suspiciously, then shook his head. "I be thinking that something foul has happened here. I dinnae like it one bit. We gathered ourselves some food and drink and dug in. Left payment behind the bar, we did, I'll no hae anyone thinkin' we be thieves!"

Gart smiled briefly at Darryn's declaration. He liked the man, and his brogue reminded him strongly of Ishabel. "I did the same here. Whatever happened, it could not have been long ago. The forge was still warm when I got here."

Darryn rubbed his chin. "Aye, there was cooked food cooling in the inn, as well. Could nae have been more than an hour since it were set out. I've sent the lads back to the *Goshawk* to see to the passengers, but I've a mind to look about a bit and find the mayor. He needs to know about this, if'n he doesn't already."

Gart mulled that over. Whatever was going on in Hollowthorne, it was not his business. He was just passing through, heading towards much more important dealings with a sorcerer and untold numbers of violent creatures. His first thought was to tell Darryn to head back to the ship with him and shove off.

Just then he spied something across the road that he had missed before. It was lying in the doorway of a small basket shop, shielded from the rain by the porch awning. Leaving a bewildered Darryn with Bessie and Beauty, Gart stepped into the rain and crossed the street to retrieve the small item. He brought it back into the smithy, where he held it out for Darryn's inspection.

It was a child's doll, made of bits of leftover cloth. It was a simple thing, nearly faceless but for a pair of tiny blue buttons for eyes. It wore a shabby dress, but the stitches were tight. And the back of it was splotched brown with tacky bloodstains.

They both stared at the doll for a moment and then looked at each other, Gart's icy blue gaze boring into Darryn's brown eyes. Without another word, Gart tossed the toy into the fire. He doubted that the doll's previous owner would need it anymore. He led Bessie out of the corner to the hitching post near the outside of the shop and tethered her there. He finally reached over his shoulder and pulled the Jidaan out of its sheath, its blade shining even in the dim light of the rainy afternoon.

"All right then, let's go find the Mayor. Then we can get out of here." With a short whistle, he called Beauty to his side. She bolted to her feet, eager to be in motion alongside her master. Something definitely did not smell right to her, not right at all.

Chapter 23

Days of idleness had taken a toll on the forces of Mordak. Contentious by nature, the Gholans had often squabbled and even killed each other without compunction. The dead were quickly made use of; nothing went to waste. The rain had continued off and on, though it only seemed to bother the Morcats and the Krell. The light was slowly dying as the sun crawled unseen towards the horizon behind the thick blanket of thunderclouds. With the coming of night, Mordak's creatures became even more restless.

Jor Dayne stalked the fringes of the horde, allowing every creature in the army to see him. The ferocious yowling and screeching of the Gholans would quiet as he approached, then pick up again as he passed by. They all knew that he spoke with Mordak's voice, and obeyed him without question. They also knew he would not hesitate to kill any of them without a second thought. He had proven this multiple times when a surly Morcat or a belligerent Krell thought to test him. He left those lying in the dirt, broken and bleeding from the severe beating he had gleefully administered, not even deigning to use his jagged blade.

Even so, he knew he could only intimidate them all for so long. As he rode his enormous charger through the mud, he alternated between being frustrated that Mordak was still gone, yet happily imagining what he would do to the sorcerer at the first available opportunity.

Suddenly, Jor Dayne heard a swell of noise from the western edge of the throng, near the border of the Poravian Mire. The Gholans were agitated and had begun howling and chittering, even clicking their wicked talons in their anxious state. Jor Dayne turned his horse in that direction and spurred it into a gallop, peering through the rain to see what was causing the disturbance.

From the twisted trees that marked the very edge of the Mire, a dark, hunched figure was making its way towards the horde. Cloaked and hooded, it moved at a very deliberate pace, neither hurrying nor dawdling. Every so often, it paused as if to consider whether to continue before pushing onward once more.

Jor Dayne was puzzled. Mordak had floated majestically into the Mire on a swirling mist of scarlet magick. What was this shambling creature?

Jor Dayne positioned himself between the shadowy shape and the edge of Mordak's army. He drew his bloodstained sword from its sheath, and a flash of lightning glinted from the deadly blade. He pointed at the oncoming figure and bellowed, "You there! Name yourself, lest I release the Gholans to feast on your corpse!" Hearing his words, the nearest Gholans howled eagerly at the prospect of a fresh meal.

The figure did not slow or hurry. It simply continued walking directly towards Jor Dayne. Just as the massive half-daemon was about to order the attack, the figure raised one hand and blasted him with a bolt of blood-red magick. The energy bolt slammed into his chest, knocking the wind out of him and sending him tumbling off his horse to land heavily in the mud. He lay there, dazed, while the figure crossed the last few yards between them.

"You *fool!*" The voice was odd, strained, but unmistakably that of the evil necromancer. "Just whom did you think would be coming out of the Mire towards a horde of fell creatures? An old woman out for a walk? Bah! Imbecile!" His hood still cast over his face, he moved closer and laid hands on the reins of Jor Dayne's warhorse. It shied away for a moment, but then its training reasserted itself and the beast stood still. "Get out of the mud, you idiot, and help me up. I'm taking your horse for now; you can find another one."

Finally managing to suck in his first gasping breath, Jor Dayne croaked, "Yes, my master! I am sorry; I did not recognize you!" The agony in his chest had felt like fire, but it had dissipated quickly. The Champion struggled to his feet and moved to help his master mount the horse. As he made his way around the animal, he took a moment to scratch its neck and pat it on the nose so it would not buck or shy away again. As he neared Mordak, the sorcerer's hood fell away, tugged sharply by the wind. What lay beneath gave Jor Dayne a start, though he hid it well.

Behind Mordak's glamour, the illusion of the evil Daemon-God Balroth, Jor Dayne's half-daemon vision could plainly see that Mordak's patrician features were covered with fiery welts the size of peas. Although the darkness of the stormy afternoon made it all but impossible for anyone else to see, Jor Dayne could nevertheless make out Mordak's ravaged visage. Raised bumps also covered his prominent hook nose and even flowed down his neck into his dark robe.

Not wanting to be caught staring, Jor Dayne immediately looked down and formed a stirrup with his laced fingers for Mordak to step into. He allowed the evil necromancer to steady himself with a hand on his shoulder, and then he hoisted him up and into the saddle. Mordak expertly gathered the reins in one hand so that he could pull his hood back over his face. As his sleeve fell away, it exposed yet more welts on his hand, wrist, and forearm. Jor Dayne wondered if it was just the bright flicker of lightning in the clouds that made it appear as though the welts were moving.

Mordak's voice was little more than a croak, but still a recognizable one, and the sorcerer gave his orders without any further explanation about his appearance.

"Alert the horde. We begin moving to the north in half an hour." He gestured tiredly with one hand at the Mire from whence he had just emerged. "I have bolstered our strength somewhat. In addition to certain surprises that I will keep to myself for now, we will be adding a handful of shamblebeasts to our ranks. Be sure they are fed a Gholan or two when they look hungry!" he snapped this last, irritated.

As if to illustrate Mordak's words, a dozen or so massive shapes separated themselves from the stunted trees at the edge of the mire. They were nearly twice as tall as Jor Dayne, huge and bulky. As they approached, it became apparent that they were covered in huge roots and vines, making them difficult to spot among the thick foliage of the swamp. Their eyes, faintly glowing yellowish orbs, stared out of vine and leaf covered faces, constantly scanning and searching for prey. As they lumbered towards the horde, one of them lashed out with an impossibly long arm and snatched an enormous crocodile out of the water nearby. The huge croc thrashed its powerful tail and snapped with its dagger-like teeth. The shamblebeast grabbed it in both clawed, misshapen hands and broke its back in one sharp movement, killing it before it could get away. A wide, fanged mouth opened in its featureless face, and the creature began tearing into the dead reptile with obvious enthusiasm, never slowing its steady shuffle.

Jor Dayne answered quickly to avoid any further punishment. "Yes, my master. I'll see to it!" Spying one of the undead Riders nearby, he then walked up and yanked the silent corpse out of the stirrups and into the mud before swinging himself up into the saddle. He spurred the confused horse into a gallop and Gholans and Morcats alike scrambled to avoid its flashing hooves.

The Champion would do his job, and do it well; it was what he had been summoned to do. But, whatever Mordak had brought back from the Mire was obviously taxing him. Jor Dayne smiled at the thought. *My day will come, sorcerer. And sooner than you think.*

Chapter 24

The wind caught one of the shutters of an upper story window and slammed it closed. It drifted open and slammed shut again as the shifting winds toyed with it. The big house at the end of the lane was otherwise silent. No candles burned, no lanterns were lit, and its other windows gaped like vacant eyes staring into the gloom of the storm.

The knot of dread that had appeared in the pit of Gart's stomach made him feel hollow, but anger was working to fill the emptiness there. If the doll they had found was any indication, something was preying on children in Hollowthorne. Gart would simply not allow that to continue. His rage threatened to boil over for a moment as the image of his own murdered child appeared in his mind, but he managed to calm himself. *Think of the job at hand, man,* he told himself. *Rheann's murderers will pay, one way or another. But something here needs to be dealt with first.* He, Darryn, and Beauty carefully approached the mayor's big house, their eyes darting watchfully about and finding nothing.

"That be 'is 'ouse," Darryn volunteered. "Ne'er been in it meself, being just a sailor and all, but it seems the best place to look, ye ken? There's nae a soul in the whole town, but something's got to be here."

Gart shifted his grip on his Jidaan. He kept its razor-sharp blade in front of him as he crept towards the pavestones that led to the mayor's front door. "I agree. In any case, it's the only place in town we haven't searched."

As they moved closer, they could see that the door was open a few inches. It moved slightly in the wind, but would go no further, as though something on the other side impeded its movement. Darryn pulled a wicked looking knife from his belt and crept onto the stoop. He carefully pushed against the door and was rewarded with a scraping sound as a fallen chair rasped across the polished wooden floor inside. Darryn stepped across the threshold, followed instantly by Gart and Beauty.

Even in the darkness, they could see that the room was a shambles. The expensive furniture had been overturned, and broken bits of crockery and other decorations were scattered everywhere. A stairway led to the upper floor, but it was covered in debris. Darryn noticed a candle lantern that had escaped destruction and picked it up. Pulling a small tinderbox from one of his pockets, he managed to get the stub of a candle lit. Warm firelight bathed the room, much to the relief of both men.

Their relief was short-lived, however. Gart pointed at one wall. "Look there," he said in a quiet, stern voice.

A smear of blood arced across the wall, like a scarlet rainbow. As their eyes became accustomed to the gloom, they saw that more spatters and splashes covered the other walls as well, and a pool of blood had formed in one doorway that led deeper into the house. Beauty growled low in her throat and snorted twice, as if trying to clear her nostrils of the coppery smell.

Gart watched her and instinctively sniffed the air as well. He recognized the thick, cloying scent of blood, but there was also a dank, rotten smell of decay that seemed very out of place in such a richly furnished dwelling. He approached the pool of blood and carefully dipped a finger in it; then he scrubbed the crimson stain away on his trousers.

"It's still wet. And warm. This is fresh, Darryn." He stood up and gripped his Jidaan with both hands again. "Whatever happened in here *just* happened." Fighting to remain calm, Gart willed his magick to life. He had no idea what kind of creature they were dealing with, but he wanted to be ready for anything. He could not risk using the Gift of Storms inside the house for fear of bringing it down on top of them all, but he knew his own power well enough to use it.

The sailor snorted in frustration. "I should'a brought some o' the lads wi' us!"

"There wasn't time. Let's keep moving. If anyone is left alive, maybe we can help them." Gart motioned for Beauty to move into the next room and she obediently jumped over the puddle, her nails clicking quietly on the floor beyond. He and Darryn followed after, careful to avoid the blood.

They found themselves in a kitchen, and again, the room had been demolished. Remnants of a dining table and chairs lay in splinters and jagged boards all around the room. Many of the cupboards had been ripped from the wall, their dishes and pots broken and strewn about. More blood decorated the walls.

Two doors were closed on either side of the room. Beauty snuffled at one of them and quickly abandoned it in favor of the other. She sniffed along the bottom for just a moment before scratching softly at it and then stepping away. She looked over her shoulder at Gart, as if to be sure he had seen her actions.

Darryn walked carefully to the first door and opened it as quietly as he could.

"'Tis just a pantry," he said, and closed the door again before joining Gart at the second door.

Gart looked down at Beauty's scarred face. He took a moment to scratch her behind her ears - the gesture calmed him more than her - before reaching for the door handle. The rotten smell was stronger here. It reeked of dead things, decaying things, things that had long ago shied from the light of day. Gart readied himself and pulled open the door.

As it swung open, the light from the lantern fell on a portly little man huddled on the floor with his back against the wall. He held his arms tightly around his drawn up knees. His eyes were wide and staring. A greying fringe of hair stood out in messy tufts around his otherwise bald head, and his jowls shook as he trembled in obvious terror. He stared straight ahead, taking no notice of the blood that spattered him from head to foot. Beauty whuffed at him and growled once, quietly, but made no move towards him.

"'Tis the mayor!" Darryn whispered. He stepped over to the little man and knelt beside him. Setting the lantern down on the floor so that he could keep his knife ready, Darryn shook the mayor gently by the shoulder. "Sir! Do ye be all right? What in the name of Rowann and Theonas happened here?" The sailor shook him again, more urgently, and the mayor's eyes finally began to focus. He turned to Darryn, his pupils tiny dots of black in watery irises of pale blue.

A cold wind passed through the house just then, and Gart peered into the darkened room beyond the two men. The lantern's light was blocked by the mayor's body, and although Gart strained his eyes to see more, he could not make out anything but vague shapes.

"I...I called her," the mayor spoke at last, his voice quivering with fear. "I called her, and she came. But it wasn't supposed to be like this!"

"Like what?" Darryn urged. "Who came?"

"The river daemon," he answered, looking away from Darryn and back at the spot on the wall across from him. That spot was safe to look at. There was nothing but empty wall there - no blood, no death - just wall. "I used the book the tinker sold me; it's very old. He said she would make me the richest, most powerful man on the river. She was supposed to help me, but as soon as she saw my wife, she...she *took* her. Went inside her. She slashed her face open and...and then asked if I thought she was pretty." Gart and Darryn looked at each other, aghast at the older man's words. "She killed them all...everyone...but she said I'd be last." Tears slid down his fleshy face as he spoke, but he took no notice of them.

"Great goddess above, ye went and summoned a daemon, man?" Darryn's voice was incredulous. "What in the name of...ye be such a...I cannae believe ye'd be so stupid, man!"

Gart kept his focus on the darkened room beyond them. Something was in there. Something hungry. A low scraping sound came out of the darkness.

"Get him out of here, now. Beauty, go with them and keep them safe." Gart's sapphire eyes began to blaze as his magick roiled within him. He had no idea what was truly in that room, but there was no way that he could leave without doing something about it. It had killed children. Somehow, he would kill it, daemon or no.

Darryn looked up at him. "Are ye mad, man? Ye cannae fight a daemon!"

Gart looked down at the sailor and saw the man gasp at the sight of him. Gart's power was rising now, and the air was becoming thick with it. Something thumped in the darkened room, then another scrape. A high-pitched giggle reached them. It sounded like a girl, perhaps, or maybe a young woman.

"Out. Take Beauty. I'll be along."

The giggle had been enough for Darryn. He yanked the silent mayor to his feet and started manhandling him out of the doorway towards the front room and the exit beyond. Beauty looked up at Gart and whined once. Gart looked down at her.

"You heard me. Out. I'll be fine." Beauty wagged her tail uncertainly, looking into the shadows ahead and then back up at Gart before making up her mind to go. With a couple of running leaps, she vanished safely into the dark.

Gart reached down for the lantern and stepped into the doorway. He held it in his left hand and shortened his grip on his Jidaan so that it balanced better in his right. There was a short hallway that opened out into another room just a few feet away. He slowly eased himself forward towards whatever had been giggling at him. The warm circle of light preceded him and gradually illuminated the large chamber and all it contained. Gart tried not to gasp at the sight that met his eyes.

Seated four and five deep on the floor, all the way around the edges of the huge room, were the silent figures of the townspeople. There were scores of them, men, women, and children, and not one had been spared. Their heads lolled on their shoulders, their bodies only erect because they had been pressed so tightly together. Each one had been brutally slashed, especially at the throat, and the coppery smell of blood was thick. They all sat together with their vacant eyes staring out at nothing.

Gart leaned in and examined one of the corpses more closely, a young man. He was horrified to see that the man's face had been viciously sliced open, his mouth widened by a crooked cut that ran almost from ear to ear. Shifting his gaze to the next body, he saw that the same thing had been done to it as well. And the next. Every single one of them had been given a hideous death's grin.

Fueled by his anger, Gart's magick threatened to burst free, but he held it in check. He needed a target. Gart listened intently, but heard naught but the mournful wind and the banging of the loose shutter somewhere outside. Keeping a careful watch over the crowd of bodies, Gart eased over to one wall and placed the lantern on a shelf he found there. Its light brightened the macabre scene before him and he was relieved to have both hands back on his Jidaan. Using careful, deliberate steps, he moved to the center of the room where he had a better view. Seeing all the corpses from that angle made him feel as though he were on a stage, facing an entire audience of the dead. A chill crawled down his spine.

Gart was getting frustrated. Whatever had giggled and made the other noises was definitely still in the room. The only other doors were closed and barred from this side; the windows were firmly shut. And yet, all was still. He gripped the Jidaan more tightly and scanned the sea of dead faces before him, finding nothing but the evidence of insanity and violence.

Suddenly, Gart recalled riding the winds of the storm earlier. He had sent his senses out beyond himself, and felt everything in a way he never had before. He also remembered hearing Ishabel's thoughts once from several feet away, though he knew not how he had done so. He set his jaw and released a bit of his magick.

Like a living thing, Gart's power poured out of him and rolled across the empty space between him and the sea of dead bodies. All at once, he could feel their cold skin, the tackiness of the blood in their hair and on their clothes, and the ragged edges of their wounds. Repulsed, he steeled himself against the horrors he felt and pressed forward, reaching out farther with his senses.

There. Two rows back, right in the center of the crowd, something was different. Where all the corpses were cold, their spirits and warmth long departed, one body was as cold as ice. Gart turned his piercing blue gaze towards the wrongness and saw brackish water on the floor underneath some of the corpses in the front row. Something giggled again, and Gart saw one of them move, as if trying to hide behind another. It was playing a game.

Gart really did not feel like playing.

With a sharp gesture and a shout of anger that rocked the walls, Gart used his magick to clear an empty space around the icy being. Bodies flew away from it in gangly tangles of arms and legs, coming to rest in piles far on either side of the creature. His eyes blazed with cobalt fury as the lone figure, a woman, got to her feet almost shyly, a wicked, ghastly grin on her mutilated face.

Shredded though it was, her pink dress seemed of a finer cut and material than the others. *The mayor's wife*, Gart absently thought in some corner of his mind. But no longer was she the spouse of the town leader. Water dripped from her arms and stringy black hair, making a quiet pattering sound on the floor. Her eyes were impossibly wide and round, the irises white around tiny black pupils. She raised one hand to her lips in a coy, little girl gesture. Once slim and pretty, the woman's hands were now instruments of death, the fingertips completely worn away to reveal razor sharp claws of bone.

"Daemon! I don't know where you came from, but I'm sending you back there right now!"

Her response was immediate. She opened her slashed mouth impossibly wide and screamed her own rage into the night. The windows shattered and Gart covered one ear while turning the other away from the blast. Then she launched herself at him, reaching for his face with her deadly fingertips. Gart threw up one arm in defense and took a powerful clawing blow that raked bloody furrows across his shoulder. It sent him sprawling to his hands and knees, his Jidaan clattering to the floor a few feet away. The sheer power of the blow rocked him and he shook his head to clear it.

The daemon's screech turned into eerie, high pitched tittering that raised goosebumps on Gart's flesh. He rolled over on his back just as she flung herself towards him again, bloody fingers slicing through the air as she came. He managed to bring one booted foot up to intercept her as he caught hold of her bony wrists with both hands, holding her above him. Grunting, he held her there as she strained mightily to reach him. She was unnaturally strong, and Gart struggled to keep her from slashing him to death. Her maimed face was inches from his, and he could see that her skin was gray and slick with river slime. Her rank, rotten smell assaulted him and he gagged as her gaping mouth snapped at his throat. Her tongue snaked out and caressed his face, leaving a wet trail across his skin.

Gathering his strength, he kicked her off of him as hard as he could, sending her flailing through the air to land on her back. He desperately rolled towards his fallen Jidaan and scrambled to retrieve it. The daemon let out an unholy shriek and scuttled back to her feet with frightening speed just as Gart turned to face her. The emerald in his Jidaan burned through its makeshift leather cover, eager to unleash its power, and its light danced in the shadowy room. He pointed the blade at her chest. She smiled hideously at him.

For a moment she stood there, swaying gently as though in time with music only she could hear, moaning shrilly all the while. Gart took a step closer, preparing himself to attack. The daemon feinted to Gart's right, and he stepped that way to intercept her. Instantly, she shifted to his left and leapt to the wall, clinging there like a sinister insect. Before Gart could recover, she raced across the wall and flung herself at him again, her bloody jaws open wide and her bony talons questing for his throat.

This time, Gart lashed out at her with his magick. He swatted her out of the air and sent her crashing back to the floor. Reaching out with his power, he finally grabbed her, throwing unbreakable coils of magick around her slender, but supernaturally strong form. She screeched at him in fury, and Gart's eyes blazed right back at her with his own outrage. Flexing his will, he picked her up and slammed her into the far wall with devastating force. Bones shattered and water sprayed across the wall instead of blood. Her body slid to the floor in a jumbled, quivering heap.

Before Gart could even take a deep breath, he heard her giggle again. Slowly, with sharp, jerky movements, she began to pull herself to her feet. Parts of her were broken, and she stood awkwardly tilted to one side with one arm dangling crookedly. But her rictus of a smile never wavered.

It was obvious to Gart that the daemon had invaded the woman's body, and no matter what he did to its flesh, the daemon could still animate it. His mind racing, he wondered if it could take another body if the first became unusable. That would not do. He had to do something dire.

Rushing forward, he slammed his Jidaan into the daemon's chest, impaling her and pinning her to the wall. She wailed and reached out to slash at Gart, but he had already backed away, leaving the Jidaan in her struggling body. Desperation lent him focus. Forming a sharply detailed picture in his mind, he finally called to his Jidaan.

It answered.

A massive bolt of lightning slammed into the house from the outside, and the wall exploded in an earthshattering thunderclap. Gart shielded himself from the debris with his magick even as he threw an arm over his eyes. When he opened them again, an entire section of the wall was gone. Among the ruins, Gart spied parts of the daemon's stolen body, though no blood flowed from any of the severed limbs. A few bits of pink fabric swirled on the wind before being carried out into the storm. Inside the room, fires had started, spreading where the rain could not reach. Aside from the intruding elements, nothing else moved.

Recovering his composure, Gart reached out with his magick and found his Jidaan in the rubble. He levitated it back to his hands and was not surprised to see that it was completely unharmed, though the leather covering on the pommel had disintegrated. Moving quickly, he sheathed it and then ducked through the door back into the kitchen. It was the work of only moments for him to find spare lamp oil and use it to aid the blaze. Soon it was burning out of control, consuming the horrors that had occurred in the Mayor's home. Gart left through the front door as the house burned, his face set in a grim mask. He knew he had done the right thing; it was just an awful thing, no matter how right it had been.

Up ahead, Beauty had waited in the blacksmith's shop with Bessie, and she barked and jumped with joy at the sight of her master. Bessie neighed her welcome as well, and Gart leaned heavily against the hitching post as he gathered up her reins. The aftereffects of adrenaline and the use of his Jidaan had caught up with him, and weariness weighed heavily on him. After catching his breath, he gently guided Bessie away from the smithy and back towards the *Goshawk*, Beauty at his side. As he approached the corner that led to the docks, they met Darryn and six of his men, all heavily armed with swords and axes. They looked over his shoulder at the steadily burning house and then back at him, silently waiting for an explanation.

Gart looked at Darryn wearily and said, "It's done. As far as I can tell, the daemon isn't a threat anymore."

Darryn's face betrayed his awe. "What in the name of Rowann did ye do? That was the biggest lightning bolt I've e'er seen, and you're nae hurt at all? What are ye, man?"

Gart sighed before answering.

"I'm just me, Darryn. Just Gart. And I'll be damned if I let some daemon hurt children and get away with it."

Darryn stared into Gart's icy blue eyes and saw the power there. He also saw the deep, abiding sadness that exhaustion had brought to the surface.

He was quiet for a moment before he spoke again.

"Aye, I hear ye. We were comin' back to help ye, but it seems that ye didn't need the help at all."

Completely exhausted, Gart remained silent as they headed back to the *Goshawk*, but he turned Darryn's remark over in his mind again and again.

Yes, he decided. As powerful as he was, and as powerful as he seemed to be becoming, he was going to need help. A lot of it.

Chapter 25

The sun shone through the iron-gray clouds only when they allowed it, which was seldom. They rolled and churned slowly across the sky, a seemingly endless blanket of shifting darkness. The rain came down and then stopped, soaking the lush, grassy plains that led up to the squat mountains nearby. They were hard mountains with blocky, steep cliffs that rose towards the low clouds as though a giant fist had pressed them up from below.

The Blackthorne Range strode down from the north, overseeing the wide river that ran along the eastern side of the mountains. The range rose steadily as it marched southward, culminating in an enormous crater. Its ridged outline was worn and eroded from thousands of years of weather. In the center of the huge depression lay a sparkling, clear lake that fed the verdant foliage that filled the crater. Alverton Falls' namesake lay at the southern edge of the basin, and there a constant flow of crystalline water cascaded. Those who had climbed the mountains and braved the crater had found that its beauty was in direct opposition to its name: Balroth's Abyss.

According to legend, the massive crater had been the very spot where Balroth had been struck down. Born of Theonas and Rowann, gods of light and love, Balroth had nevertheless chosen to pursue only evil. The dark path he trod had corrupted his essence over the eons until he could no longer control his lust for power. He had become a Daemon-god, mighty and treacherous. Jealous of Theonas' influence and authority, Balroth rose up and murdered his father. Rowann had wept to discover that her only son had willfully shunned the light and come to despise all that was noble and good.

Enraged at her husband's murder, Rowann battled Balroth for forty-nine days, all across the world of Talwynn. At last, she struck a final, overwhelming blow that shook the earth and rendered Balroth senseless. Unwilling to kill her son, she banished him forever into a dark dimension from which escape was impossible. It was only then that she looked upon the world and saw the devastation they had wrought as they had clashed. Mountains were shattered and forests burned to ash; the land was a barren wasteland as far as the eye could see. She was ashamed. As she cried, her tears fell into the crater, forming a deep lake that never went dry. It filled the great bowl of earth and continually emptied over one side in a vast and majestic waterfall. In time, her tears brought life back to the world of Talwynn, and peace reigned. Although Balroth raged in his faraway prison, he could do no more harm on this world, save through those depraved enough to work in his name - those such as Mordak.

Brunar took a deep breath, letting the damp air fill his lungs. It was most welcome after so many days in the stuffiness of the tunnel. He drank in the sight of the green plains and stocky mountains, grateful to be out in the open again, even in the rainy weather.

His gaze lingered on the enormous cascade that shared its name with the city below. The Mage was pleased to see that Alverton Falls appeared to be safe for the moment; none of Mordak's vermin were nearby. Brunar and his small company were not close enough to see what preparations were being made, but the pigeons sent by Duke Fergus in Rualtha would have beaten even Layton's accelerated travel time by several days. Brunar hoped that Count DeRoberds had taken the warning seriously.

Nessar's gravelly voice echoed his thoughts.

"I hope they're getting ready over there or this could be a really short battle."

Brunar laughed. "I agree, Ness. We'll know soon enough." Turning his horse around so that he faced the group, the Mage raised his voice. "All right then, this is where we go our separate ways. Ginn, I know you'll guide them well."

Ginn inclined his head politely to the Mage. "I will, sir Mage. You have my word on it."

Brunar nodded, knowing that Ginn would honor his word unto his own death if need be. "According to Ginn, it should take you three or four days to make it to Linbourne, or where it is supposed to be, and the same to return here. How long it will take to find the amulet is unknown, but we can only hope you'll find it quickly."

Nessar replied before anyone else could speak. "Well, don't get your breeches in a twist, Mage. We'll be back before you can say 'Mordak sucks bilge water.' I'm good at finding things that people would prefer to keep hidden."

Brunar blinked at Nessar's banter and then laughed. "I expect no less from a master thief! And I will indeed keep my breeches from twisting; they are most uncomfortable that way." Addressing them all again, he continued. "May the Goddess go with you, for our hearts surely shall."

Layton slapped his fist over his heart as usual while Nessar just grunted and waved. Kiran reached over and smacked the old thief in the arm for being rude, and then offered a jaunty salute of her own before turning her horse in the direction they would be heading.

As they all prepared to leave the larger group, Bekah spurred her horse and pulled it up next to Layton's. She said nothing, but beckoned him closer. He leaned forward to hear her and she surprised him by wrapping her arms around his neck, hugging him tightly. He nearly fell out of the saddle but managed to right himself, then tentatively hugged her back. She held him for a long moment and then released him, embarrassment plain on her face. She reached into her cloak and pulled out what looked like a short, thin rope with tiny metal clasps on each end.

"Hold out your hand," she said, in a tone that brooked no argument. Layton held out his left hand and Bekah quickly fastened the token around his wrist. "This is so you'll know that I'll be waiting for you. You come back safely!" She embraced him once more and kissed him firmly before she could change her mind. Her mission complete, she guided her horse over to the other priestesses who were smiling broadly and talking quietly to each other. Bekah's face was bright red, but her expression was one of satisfaction. Layton was completely bewildered. He reached down and touched the bracelet she had given him, and was surprised to discover that it was made from a tightly braided lock of her own hair. It was soft and silky, and he decided he liked how it felt against his skin. He looked over at Bekah and watched her talking with Fiona. There in the dim light of the overcast, rainy day, he saw her as if for the first time. And he thought she was beautiful.

Ginn cleared his throat to catch Layton's attention. "We need to head east, Guardian. The land is fairly flat, as you can see, so we should make good time."

Layton responded, casting one more glance back at Bekah over his shoulder. "Um, yes...I'll need to rest tonight, but we can still cover a lot of ground before we camp." He looked at Kiran and Nessar to see if they were ready.

Nessar made a sweeping gesture in their general direction of travel. "If you're quite through with your canoodling, young sir?"

Layton blushed furiously and quickly willed a Gate into being, large enough that they could ride through two at a time. Far across the plain to the east, tiny in the distance, an identical burst of brightness revealed the Gate's twin. Without another word, he and Ginn rode through, followed by Kiran and Nessar. They had been gone but a heartbeat when the Gate vanished. Brunar's hawkish eyes spied Layton's next Gate, only ignited for a few seconds before it, too, disappeared.

Fiona commented, "I know we've been walking through his Gates for the last few days, but they never cease to amaze me. I can't even fathom the magick that his Jidaan employs."

"I've studied magick for over two millennia and it still awes me. The creators of the Jidaan imbued them with such potency that I sometimes think there's no end to it. It's the strength of the wielder that determines a Jidaan's efficacy." Brunar shook his head. "And that lad has taken to his powers better than almost anyone I've ever seen."

Bjarke rode his enormous horse nearer to Brunar and joined in the conversation.

"Indeed, Sir Mage, Layton sets a good example for us all. What do we do now?"

Brunar looked across the plain to the north, where the city of Alverton Falls awaited them.

"Bjarke, let's go see what awaits us in the city. I hope that Count DeRoberds is as accommodating as Duke Gensen was, for his own sake and that of Alverton Falls."

Led by Brunar, Fiona, and ValElder Moihra on her white pony, the company began the ride across the soggy terrain, heading for the nearest road that led into the city proper. They listened to the thunder rolling across the sky above them, each lost in their own thoughts. They could see another large patch of rain making its way towards them over the wide flatlands spread between them and the river. They all wrapped their cloaks more tightly and cast their hoods over their heads as the pelting rain approached them in an unwavering line. The storm moved rapidly, as though determined to soak them through and through, and all they could do was endure it.

Chapter 26

Mordak's brow furrowed in concentration as he rode. Controlling the legions of undead soldiers he had created, as well as keeping up the illusion of Balroth with which he cloaked himself, was beginning to tax him. Too, he needed to maintain control over the creatures he had carried out of the Mire. It took quite a bit of energy to keep them dormant.

The sliver of unholy power he had conned out of Balroth was far more than he had ever dreamed he could wield. At times, it felt inexhaustible, omnipotent. It seemed the only limiting factor was that of his own frail flesh and will. Centuries of disciplined training in the dark arts had prepared him, but his body required constant magickal upkeep, lest his stolen power incinerate him completely. Mordak carefully focused his mind through various cantrips and spells so that he could remain in control of everything that raged inside him.

The horde was sweeping over the rolling hills in the intermittent moonlight, slowly leaving the Poravian Mire behind. They moved no faster than the Gholans could run, and Mordak was secretly relieved he could ride at an easy trot rather than a gallop. Patience was difficult for Mordak to stomach, but he knew that the taking of Alverton Falls would be worth the time spent to get there. His army would swell with undead, and then no city in the Realm would be able to defeat him. That thought made him smile, a cruel grin that echoed the malice in his glowing scarlet eyes.

The sorcerer wondered how his creatures were faring in the south. He reasoned that they should be nearing Rualtha, though they were to remain far enough from the city to avoid detection. Their only function was to prevent aid from reaching Alverton Falls, and unless Rualtha had sent its entire army, it would be an easy task for the two thousand Gholans and Morcats that Mordak had sent.

Focusing his mind on the corrupt gemstone he had attached to the Morcat's helmet, he sent a slender tendril of energy far out into the night towards it. Once he felt it connect, he opened the link he had created so that he could see through the creature's eyes. Chaos met his gaze and Mordak concentrated as he tried to make sense of what he was seeing.

The moon's light was brighter there, and no rain fell where the Morcat could see. The drops that flew across the beast's field of vision were black in the silvery light, and they flew sideways, splattering across the face of a ferocious Augenan that let out a defiant yell of agony as the Morcat's claws raked across its massive arm.

The Morcat ducked the Aug's next swing of its war club and slashed deep into the gorilla warrior's thigh before darting away. The creature's lithe muscles sent it in a graceful leap through the air to land atop a jutting boulder, where it turned to survey the battlefield.

To the Morcat's left, the ground fell away as sharply as if it had been cut, and the sound of the Corris River flowing in a rush at the bottom of the cliffs could be heard far below. To its right, the swaying grasses of a wide meadow were being trampled beneath the feet and bodies of hundreds of Gholans and Morcats as they did battle with a large number of Augenan. In the center, where the fighting was thickest, one Augenan slightly larger than all the rest was laying waste to his attackers with a huge double-bladed battle-axe. The warrior bellowed in triumph as it cleared a space around it, daring more of its enemies to come close.

Mordak recognized him instantly as the Augenan leader he had seen at Laro. Somehow, the beast and his blasted gorillas had made it out alive! If they had escaped, Mordak wondered, could any of the others have also made it out? He had thought that everyone, including the Guardians, had perished in the castle's collapse. But had they?

Suddenly, Mordak heard through the Morcat's ears a dreadful yowling and screeching from the faraway battlefield. He turned his attention to it, and was astonished at what he saw. The Augenan, led by the large one, were sprinting towards the trees, leaving their adversaries in confusion in the center of the meadow. After a moment of indecision, Mordak's creatures began to race after them, screaming for blood.

The Augenan vanished smoothly into the thick foliage as Mordak's horde gave chase. What exploded back out of the forest made even Mordak shrink back in terror and surprise.

Spiders the size of horses burst out of the deeper shadows between the trees, their giant bodies skittering with incredible speed. Their fangs clicked in anticipation, but otherwise, they were oddly silent. They were hulking yet graceful creatures, and they swarmed over the oncoming rush of Mordak's forces in moments.

Spiders boiled out of the trees in untold numbers, an oncoming wave of death for the creatures of the dark. The spiders' huge fangs struck at every turn, leaving their victims lying paralyzed in the grass as the venom worked to dissolve their insides. Those at the outer edge thought to escape into the woods opposite, but the spiders reared up and slung their webs forward with blinding speed, capturing scores of fleeing Gholans and howling Morcats before they could reach the safety of the trees.

Soon, the far side of the meadow was covered with a thick white blanket of silk, moving here and there as the captive creatures tried to wriggle free of the clinging web. Their attempts amounted to nothing, and the spiders leisurely stalked over to begin their feeding. Not a single one of Mordak's wretched folk was spared, save the single Morcat atop the rock through which the sorcerer's eyes watched the scene unfold.

That creature growled quietly, deep in its throat, and crept backwards until it had crawled down from its perch and set its feet upon the ground below. It crouched there, peering around the sheltering rock, watching the immense spiders that crawled over the meadow as they patrolled their new webs. Each writhing bundle was pierced by the dagger-like fangs until its struggles died away, and the Morcat wanted no part of it. It turned stealthily, planning to melt into the forest and escape.

The Morcat had not taken a full step before coming face to face with its own death. Another huge spider had crawled over the lip of the cliff behind the Morcat, and now stood only a few feet away. The spider lunged, and Mordak felt its fangs pierce the beast's huge chest as though it were his own, the Morcat's pain stabbing into Mordak's breast as well. In agony, he severed the magickal connection with the Morcat and reeled with remembered pain. He clutched at the saddlehorn in front of him and fought to stay erect.

"Master, are you all right?" Mordak turned to see Jor Dayne riding next to him, his baleful yellow eyes shining in the dark.

"I'm fine, you dolt!" Mordak snapped. "Keep watch on the horde, lest I decide to make an example of you!"

"As you wish, my master." Jor Dayne turned away so that Mordak would not see his smile.

Chapter 27

Layton lay facedown on his bedroll, snoring loudly. After another day of travelling through his Gates and covering miles upon miles in mere steps, he had reached the end of his endurance. He had managed to eat his ration of dried beef, fruit, and water and had scarcely laid down before his world had gone dark.

Kiran poked at the fire with a stick, irritated and not trying to hide it. The source of her irritation was difficult to pinpoint, and that irritated her even more.

"Penny for your thoughts, baby girl." Nessar's gravelly voice was soft and relaxed. He had pulled a hammock from somewhere in his pack and secured it between two of the short, scrubby trees near their campsite. There he swung, seemingly without a care in the world. He knew Kiran was upset, and that talking to her was more likely to wind her up further than to calm her, but he felt the odds were in his favor this time. The wind was cool, they had left the rain far behind them, and all was quiet for the first time in weeks.

"I'm not a baby, old man," Kiran punctuated her comment with another stab into the fire. Sparks flew and the wood shifted, but it continued burning in spite of her interference. She stabbed it again, just because she could. "Haven't been for a long time, in case you hadn't noticed."

Nessar sighed quietly before responding. "No, you certainly have not. You're a grown woman now, who is acting like a baby. Would you care to tell me what's got you in a twist?"

Kiran nearly snapped back at him but stopped herself. She knew Nessar well enough to know that he wasn't trying to goad her. *It's my magick,* she thought. Concentrating on the odd sensations that flowed through her, she identified Nessar's predominant emotions: fatherly concern with the tiniest dash of annoyance. The annoyance was so typical of Nessar that it nearly made her laugh. It brought her back to herself enough that she realized she was being unnecessarily short with him. She sighed, and then walked over to him and sat on the sparse grass near his hammock.

"I don't know, Ness," she admitted. She pulled out a dagger and began to clean her nails with it. Although Kiran was no stranger to roughing it on the trail, she couldn't abide seeing her nails get filthy. She had to eat with those hands, and did not enjoy a side order of dirt with every meal. "I'm just annoyed. I guess I really want to be back where the action is, rather than out here on a wild goose chase. It's like they wanted to get rid of me."

Nessar pondered her words for a moment, but it was Ginn that answered. He had just finished tending his horse and was settling onto his own bedroll with an apple in one hand, his dagger in the other. His words drifted across the campsite almost as though he were singing, so musical was his Weya voice.

"My lady, they sacrificed much to send you on this mission. Alverton Falls has no wall such as Laro did. Your Gift of Warding would have been instrumental in defending the city, and yet they chose to send you anyway, thinking that your skills and experience gave the best possible chance of success." He paused for a moment, contemplating. "I would consider that an honor." He deftly cut a piece of apple and popped it into his mouth, his jewel-like eyes of jade green shining in the firelight at Kiran. There was no reproach there, just a quiet sureness.

Kiran glared at him for a moment, but then turned her eyes back on her hands and nails. His words made sense, and even that irked her, but she held her tongue.

Making a living with a sword was a tough business. Doing it as a woman had been doubly challenging, with every braggart and lout opposing her right to her chosen occupation. She was used to being thought of as "less than", and "not quite good enough", never mind how many times she had proven quite the opposite. If Ginn's words were true, then her abilities had finally been recognized for what they were: extraordinary. Brunar and the others expected her to succeed. Her skills were valued. So what reason did she have to be upset?

"None whatsoever. At least, that's my opinion. I'm glad you're here." Nessar answered her unspoken question, and Kiran turned sharply towards him. He held up both hands to forestall her. "Look, it was written all over your face, Kiran, I didn't need magick to tell me what you were thinking. I know why you've always had a chip on your shoulder, and I never blamed you for it. But let it fall. You're a Guardian, for what it's worth, and you don't need it anymore." Without another word, he squirmed onto his back in his hammock and closed his eyes. As she watched him, he started snoring, already blissfully asleep.

Shaking her head, she got up and wandered over to sit next to Ginn, who had finished his apple and was cleaning his dagger. Kiran noticed that it was a beautiful blade, and apparently razor sharp.

"Nice blade," she said, wanting to change the subject.

Ginn wiped it once more and then pulled the matching scabbard from his belt. He sheathed the weapon and held it out to her. "I'm glad you like it. It's yours."

Kiran's eyes widened. "What? No, I can't take that! It's yours! I have my own dagger, thank you."

Ginn smiled, his jeweled eyes shining. "Ah, but accepting a gift honors the giver. You don't want to slight my honor, do you?" He raised one eyebrow as he awaited her response.

Kiran sighed heavily and took the offering from Ginn's outstretched hand. "No, I certainly wouldn't want to do that. Thank you. I don't need a dagger, as I said, but this..." She pulled the blade free of its scabbard and it gleamed in the firelight. The balance of the weapon was perfect for Kiran's hand. "This is really beautiful. I wasn't asking you to give it to me."

Ginn's laughter sparkled on the air like tiny bells. Still smiling, he reached up and tucked his hair behind one pointed ear. "Of course not! You are far too polite to do that. Among my people, the giving of gifts is not reserved for special holidays. It brings us happiness to give something to someone who may delight in it. I can see that you appreciate good blades; this is a very fine one. Please enjoy it."

Kiran laughed and thanked Ginn again. Their talk flowed into the night, Kiran asking about blades and joint locks and Weya customs and Ginn happily explaining as much as he could. Eventually, the long day caught up with Kiran and she went to lie down on her bedroll, thankful that Ginn always took first watch. His need of sleep was far less than that of the humans with whom he traveled. He could drift into a light meditation that allowed him to be aware of everything around him and still be refreshed in the morning.

Hours later, Nessar snorted awake at Ginn's gentle prodding, and extracted himself from his hammock. He shuffled quietly around the fire for a few minutes as he came to full wakefulness. Ginn rolled over and promptly fell asleep. Nessar decided on a quick tour of the camp's perimeter to stretch his legs and also, just to see what he could see. The fire had long since been banked, and it shed little light, so Nessar's eyes were still adjusted to the darkness. He made sure his Jidaan was securely sheathed at his back and then moved away from the campsite, stepping carefully so he wouldn't rouse the others.

The half-moon was often hidden by clouds, its silvery light playing over the rocks and scrub brush that covered this part of the Realm. The soil was sandy, not worth farming, and the trees were thorny and shorter than those to the west.

Although not nearly as majestic as the elder forests that Nessar had seen, there was a stark beauty to the plains that touched him deeply. Somewhere in the distance, a nightbird screeched. Nessar found a large rock to lean on as he let his gaze travel the skies, lazily looking for the bird.

That's when he heard the deep, rattling growl nearby. Nessar froze in place, using only his eyes to search for the source of the sound. For a few moments, he saw nothing, but then he heard the growl again to his left. Whatever it was, it was moving, circling him. And it was big. Really big.

Alarmed, Nessar engaged his power and called to his Jidaan. It answered, like a burst of cool air at his back. The coolness flowed over him, covering him completely. When Nessar looked down at his boots, they were no longer there. He had vanished. There was silence for a moment, and then an enormous tiger pushed through the shrubbery and stalked closer to the boulder on which Nessar had been sitting. It seemed confused. It stood just a few feet away, sniffing the air carefully.

It can't see or smell me, he thought, deeply grateful for the power of his Jidaan. Moving carefully, he picked his way around the boulder and quickly headed for the camp. He had to rouse the others before the tiger stumbled across them.

It took only seconds for Nessar to reach his companions, and he released the power of his Jidaan so that he could be seen and heard again. He woke Kiran first, then Ginn. They rolled to their feet with blades drawn as soon as they heard Nessar's news. Layton was still exhausted and groggy, but he managed to stand up and drew his Jidaan as well.

"How big did you say it was?" Ginn's voice was barely a whisper. Nessar leaned down to answer.

"Not as big as an Augenan, but damned near! Maybe three hundred pounds, I'd say!"

"Shhh! It's here!" Kiran pointed a finger into the night.

Surely enough, the great beast nosed its way into the clearing, its tongue hanging out between long pointed fangs. Its head was low, and its eyes had already locked onto them. Its gaze was bright and keen as it stalked forward, and they could hear its breath wheezing in and out of its massive chest. Muscles bunched and moved under its sleek coat of stripes, and they knew they were in for a fight.

Suddenly Ginn cocked his head to one side and looked hard at the huge cat. He stayed that way for a few heartbeats, then he slowly sheathed his sword.

Kiran saw him and whispered fiercely, "Have you lost your *mind*? What are you doing?!"

Without answering, Ginn stepped away from them, moving in slow, deliberate steps. The tiger growled and turned its attention to the small figure of the Weya. It snarled loudly, baring its fangs once more.

Kiran caught a better grip on her Jidaan and tensed to spring at the tiger. If Ginn kept its attention long enough, it would expose its side to her and she could stab it through the heart.

As if sensing her intent, Ginn raised a hand to stop her. "Wait," he said, just loud enough for her to hear. Her eyes widened in astonishment, but she did as he said, staring at the massive cat that faced her friend.

Ginn stared into the cat's eyes for nearly a minute and then opened his arms wide. It pounced on him with shocking speed, bearing him to the ground in an instant.

"No!" Kiran said, leaping to the attack, but Nessar's strong hand pulled her back. She struggled to break free, but his hand was like iron.

"Wait, Kiran! Look!"

Ginn was not being mauled by the tiger. They were wrestling, and Ginn was winning. Moreover, he was laughing.

Kiran stopped fighting against Nessar's hand and stood there in shock. Relief and anger flooded her in equal measure as she tried to decide whether to be happy that Ginn was not hurt or upset that he had scared her nearly to death.

Ginn rolled with the great cat, who was now making decidedly playful growls and snarls. He threw his arms around the cat's neck in a headlock that the tiger easily escaped. The huge beast climbed on top of the laughing Weya and gently gnawed on his belly without doing any damage. Finally, Ginn grabbed it in a big hug and ruffled the fur under its chin, which it appeared to enjoy immensely. It made a low, rumbling sound that the Guardians were shocked to identify as purring.

To his companions, he said, "Let me introduce you; this is Brunella. She is far from where I last saw her, but these plains are her home. She is friendly with the Weya, and I know her. She won't harm us."

Nessar did not lower his Jidaan, and neither did Kiran.

"You're sure?" Kiran finally said, her voice tight. "It's not going to eat us?"

Ginn had already walked over to his pack to pick up a hunk of dried meat. He brought it back to the big cat and held it out to her. She almost daintily plucked it from his fingers with her enormous, raspy tongue, then settled down to chew it. Ginn petted her muscular neck and sat down beside her.

"Yes, I'm sure. The Weya are very friendly with many of the big cats, both here and in the deep forests. Some of our ValElders are even allowed to ride them into battle. I've met Brunella here before, but it was far to the south. She really should not even be here." Concern edged into his voice at the last.

Without explaining further, he shifted his position so that he could look into the cat's eyes. She continued to rumble loudly as she chewed, but when her gaze locked with Ginn's, she froze. They stayed like that, gazing into each other's eyes, Weya and tiger, for several heartbeats. Then, Ginn broke the connection by turning away even as he reached up and scratched her ears. Her contented growls and rumbles resumed. The Weya rose to his feet and walked back to his companions, a stern expression on his face.

"What in the name of big fanged kittens is going on?" Nessar still held his Jidaan in front of him, not quite willing to accept Ginn's word that he would not be eaten as a snack.

Ginn put a calming hand on the old thief's arm in reassurance. "I just spoke with her. Well, as much as any of us can, anyway. We Weya can communicate with the big cats by exchanging thoughts. To be more specific, I can see her thoughts if she lets me, and she can see mine."

"What did she say?" Kiran's eyes were wide, but she finally slid her Jidaan back into its sheath at her back.

Ginn grimaced. "Mordak's creatures are definitely headed towards Alverton Falls. She traveled long and hard to get away from them. They're south of us now, moving northwest. We'll miss them entirely on our way east to Linbourne, but judging from what she showed me, you'll return after they arrive."

Kiran's face settled into its battle mask. "So we'll have to cut our way through them to get the amulet to Brunar. I'm fine with that."

Nessar spoke up. "Well, if we can keep making good time, then maybe we can find the thing and still beat them back to Alverton Falls. It'll depend on Layton, and..." Nessar's voice trailed off and he began to chuckle.

Kiran and Ginn turned to see that Layton had apparently decided to take Ginn at his word regarding the tiger's eating plans for the evening. He had already curled up on his bedroll,

Jidaan in hand, and fallen back to sleep. He was still exhausted from the many uses of his Gift.

"Layton has the right idea. Morning is still hours away. I'll keep Brunella company and make sure that she moves on from here when she's ready. You'll be perfectly safe. Get some sleep, both of you."

Nessar needed no urging, though he left his hammock hanging empty and found a spot that kept the fire between himself and the big cat. He threw down a blanket and laid down with a grateful sigh.

"You're sure it's all right?" Kiran asked the Weya, wanting to be absolutely certain.

Ginn had leaned his back up against the huge cat's side, making himself extremely comfortable. "Oh yes, Kiran, Brunella likes me. I'll wake you in the morning and she'll be gone."

Kiran reluctantly wandered back over to her bedroll and sat down on it. She stared at Ginn and the tiger for a while; she had never seen one of the big cats up close. Now that she had, she could vouch for the fact that they were terrifying. And beautiful. With that thought in her mind, and listening to the quiet rumbles of the tiger nearby, she laid her head down on her arm and drifted off to sleep.

Chapter 28

"I still cannae believe that bugger...summonin' a daemon. Whisht! He already had more'n anyone else in town, and t'weren't enough!" Darryn shook his head in disbelief as he spoke. "The man's got the sense o' a bag o' rocks."

Gart leaned on the railing and felt the wind on his face. "Agreed. He was supposed to care for those people, and now they're dead." Gart's anger had been simmering ever since they had gotten the man off the *Goshawk* a few hours ago.

They had stopped at Riverlily, the next town downriver, and left the former mayor with the local authorities, who had promptly dispatched riders to Hollowthorne to assess the damage. The man had been mostly catatonic by the time they had left him, chained in the single cell in the constable's building.

Gart turned the situation over in his mind. In his greed, the mayor had called a malevolent being up from the depths of whatever Hel it had come from purely for his own gain. He had not meant to kill the townspeople; the daemon had done that on its own. Gart was furious at the loss of life, and aghast at the horror the mayor had caused, but the gibbering little man's wide-eyed stare had stuck with him. Most likely, his sanity had been forfeit, along with his own wife and children. Was that payment enough for his crimes?

Gart grimaced as he pondered further. "Regardless of what they decide to do to him, the daemon is gone. I'm glad of that much, at least. It killed those people, and now it's dead, too." He sighed and stared downriver, letting his eyes rove the trees and rocks along the riverbanks, finding that it soothed him. "I'm just glad no more were hurt. Any other sailors docking there or even travelers passing through on the road would have been lured in and slaughtered. Hel of a way to die."

Darryn nodded in agreement. "Aye, man. Ye've the right of it." The sailor turned and leaned his back against the railing so that he could face Gart. He paused for a moment before speaking again. "I know there's something about ye." Gart looked into Darryn's eyes and saw a calm resolve there. "That shiny spear ye carry has the look and feel o' magick about it, and it nae takes a scholar to see that ye be a dangerous man. Not tae mention that the company ye keep is, um...unusual." He nodded to the huge mastiff that sat curled up on the deck near Gart's feet. Beauty appeared to be resting, but had one eye fixed on the sailor as he spoke. Darryn squared his shoulders firmly, as though he had come to a decision. "That said, yer first inclination was to protect the townspeople and our crew. I'll no forget that, sir." Darryn reached out a callused hand and Gart gratefully clasped it.

Releasing Gart's hand, Darryn grinned and leaned closer before continuing. "So, do ye be a Mage, then?" Shocked, Gart's mouth fell open at the question. Darryn's voice was low and teasing, yet eager. "Go on, man! Ye can tell me! Calling down lightning like that, carrying a magickal weapon, surely ye must be one. I'll nae tell a soul if'n that's what worries ye; cross me heart." Darryn suddenly moved one dirty finger in an X pattern over his chest. "I promise!"

At one time, Gart would have been annoyed, even angered, at Darryn's questions, but the sailor's eagerness brought an unaccustomed smile to his face. Gart knew he was no Mage, though the power that lived within him was, indeed, extraordinary. No, Brunar had named him when they had first met on the road, seemingly ages ago. Gart had begun his quest as a single-minded pursuit of revenge, but he had been ill-equipped to face even a small company of Gholans led by the Slayer, Jor Dayne. He had nearly died back then, alone in the road.

A lot had happened since then. Things were different. *He* was different. He would have justice for those who had so needlessly died, his wife and child among them. His heart still ached painfully each time he thought of their smiling faces, and he knew that it always would. Gart shook his head once, sharply, to clear it. Mordak and Jor Dayne would pay, and dearly so, for what they had wrought. However, he was no longer the crazed avenger he had been when he had set his feet upon the road from Tiller's Grove. He had become something else.

Turning his icy blue eyes towards Darryn, he watched the young sailor's expression turn somewhat fearful. He stayed silent for a few long moments before allowing himself to speak the truth at last.

"I'm...I'm a Guardian, I think. Certainly not a Mage. I have some powers, yes, though I'm still figuring them out. I'm liable as not to kill myself trying to use them."

He looked down the river, not really seeing it, but instead imagining what lay far beyond it. Jor Dayne was out there with a horde of murderous creatures and undead men. Mordak was out there too, and likely ten times more dangerous.

"Be that as it may, I'm being drawn south. There is evil there that needs to be stamped out before it kills more innocent people. I'm only one man, but I plan to face it and do whatever I can to stop it."

Darryn cocked his head to one side. "Guardian, eh? That sounds suitably mysterious," he said with a grin. "Right, I knew ye were *something*, ye ken?" He scratched his head amiably. "Well, I know naught about stamping out evil, and all that; I be no more than a simple riverboat captain. But the *Goshawk* be at yer disposal. We'll get ye to Alverton Falls so ye can begin yer work, eh?" He clapped Gart firmly on the shoulder and made as if to move away, but then stopped. Quickly, he looked around to see if anyone was watching. Then he crossed his heart again, putting a shushing finger across his lips before throwing Gart a last wink and disappearing into the rigging.

Gart watched him go and heard Beauty give a good-natured yawn and a *whuff* from her resting place at his side. He knelt beside her and scratched her neck the way he knew she enjoyed. A feeling of warm contentment and approval washed over him, and he knew that it had come from the dog. His senses were becoming keener all the time.

"Yes, Beauty, I know. I like him, too." He looked down the river again and wondered, as he sailed closer to a war that promised to be filled with blood and death, why he could feel a faint trace of peace in his heart.

The next few days passed without incident, and the weather began to improve. Every so often, Darryn would catch Gart's eye and throw a wink his way as he climbed in the rigging or worked on deck. Gart would ignore the young sailor and continue about his business, grooming and regrooming Bessie. He tried to keep Beauty out of anyone's way, which was important simply because she was the size of a bull calf. She weighed nearly twice as much as Gart, and he did not want her to cause problems by wandering about. Fortunately, she obeyed his every command, and generally behaved herself.

Evening approached and Gart watched the bloody sun setting behind faraway mountains. Darryn had said they would dock in the next town and Gart was eager to set foot on land again. The wind from the south was warmer than it had been, and the evening was pleasant.

Suddenly, Gart's whole body tensed. The smell of smoke had reached him from somewhere nearby. He had smelled the smoke of many a campfire since he had left Tiller's Grove, but this was different, sharper. It wasn't just wood that was burning, and it brought back bloody memories. At his feet, Beauty growled low in her throat. She lifted her head, sniffing the air, her dark eyes peering into the deepening dark ahead.

Gart moved towards the bow of the *Goshawk*, his eyes focused downriver. At first, he could only see the water and the trees on either side. The Blackthorne River had been straight as an arrow for days, but up ahead he could see a sharp bend in its course where it angled to his right. As he carefully surveyed the approaching terrain, he began to see a glow on the underside of the low clouds, just on the western side of the river.

"How close are we to the next town?" Gart yelled over his shoulder. He knew that Darryn was somewhere nearby and was not disappointed. From up in the rigging, Darryn's voice drifted down.

"Just minutes away, really. We're almost there. Willowbranch should be just around that bend up there. Why?" With a thump, he landed right beside Gart, having jumped down from above. Beauty quickly got to her feet and stepped between Gart and Darryn, obviously protective of him, and Gart absently scratched her ears. Reassured, she wagged her tail and leaned hard against her master.

"I think there's trouble ahead. See that light?" Gart pointed at the flickering brightness that lit up the clouds ahead.

Darryn was a canny sailor, and he, too, knew a fire when he saw one. "I do. And it nae looks good to me, not one bit." Without hesitation, he turned and ordered his crewman to arm themselves, which they did in a clatter of swords and axes hastily drawn from their hiding places about the ship. "I've a mind to turn us around and row back to Riverlilly."

Without turning, Gart replied, his voice as cold as ice. "You'll need to let me off first." In his mind's eye, he saw again the destruction of Tiller's Grove. He had no idea if that was happening up ahead, an attack on a helpless town by evil, bloodthirsty creatures. It could have been naught but a communal bonfire. As quickly as the thought occurred to him, it was discarded. Something felt wrong, and Gart was learning to trust his senses. "Whatever is going on up there, I think I need to see it."

Darryn scratched his head and grimaced. "Well, we're almost there, so we'll be seein' what's goin' on soon enough. Make yerself ready to disembark; we'll get to the Willowbranch docks in a wee bit."

Gart nodded and walked over to Bessie, who had become restless. She smelled the burning in the air, too. Beauty was alert and stayed close to Gart as he prepared the horse to take to the land once more.

Tense moments passed as the *Goshawk* rounded the bend. They saw the docks, which were empty at the moment. The buildings alongside the river, both large and small, were deserted.

The riverboat eased into place, and nimble sailors jumped down to the docks and secured the lines. It took them only moments to get the gangplank down. The smell was getting stronger by the moment, and dark smoke had begun to find its way to the river.

"This has been a Heluva week for riverboatin', Mr. Gart! We may not stay long. If we can escape unharmed, we will, but I want to see for meself what's goin' on."

"Darryn, whatever happens, keep yourself and your crew safe. Hopefully, it's nothing more than a house or shop on fire, but if it's not, then get the Hels out of here," Gart said as he led Bessie towards the gangplank. Darryn threw a few final orders to the crew that remained on the *Goshawk,* while he gathered the roughest of his bunch, armed to the teeth, and led them onto the dock.

Gart got Bessie ashore and quickly mounted her. He left his Jidaan strapped to his back, knowing he could call on its power without taking his hands from the reins, and checked the black-bladed sword at his belt. Taken from an ancient, mummified guard in an isolated cave, the weapon was light and sharp, and although Gart was no swordsman, he knew enough to be dangerous. He could feel his magick roiling inside him, ready to be used, but he knew that he would not rely on that unless it was absolutely necessary to unleash the power of Storms. Gart settled his hat firmly on his head and urged Bessie forward.

Darryn let Gart take the lead, and they carefully moved down the path that led to the center of town, passing various buildings and shops along the way. The smoke was becoming thicker, and finally, they could hear the distant sounds of voices yelling and screams of anger, pain, and fear. They turned one corner and looked over the nearest rooftops, only to see flames blazing high into the sky from multiple sources somewhere near the town's small plaza.

Another sound brought Gart's rage back to the surface: the unmistakable sounds of Gholans yowling as they attacked. Human screams and shouts answered them.

"Gholans!" Gart shouted at Darryn, and then he spurred Bessie forward, furious that the creatures had attacked more innocent people. Beauty bellowed ferociously at his side as she loped ahead, her strong muscles propelling her as fast as Bessie in a sprint. Without waiting to see what Darryn chose to do, Gart drew his sword and followed the noise and flickering firelight. The last time he had faced the Gholans, he was easily overmatched. But not now.

Gart guided Bessie around the last corner and burst into the town square, a large plaza with a stone gazebo in the center. There, a ferocious battle raged. It was just as Gart had imagined. Scores of hideous little creatures were slashing and killing at every turn while the townspeople did what they could to defend themselves. In addition, there were larger beasts that Gart had never seen before. Huge, dark-furred cat-creatures that walked upright, some even wearing armor and wielding swords, howled war cries as they killed and maimed without mercy. Many people of Willowbranch were already dead, their bodies littering the ground, and Gart could see that three of the surrounding buildings were already blazing madly.

Without slowing, he leaned sideways in his saddle and lopped off the head of a snarling man-cat just as it was about to take a swipe at a terrified teenage boy defending two young girls. A few steps later, he hacked a Gholan to death and then another. Turning Bessie sharply, Gart galloped through the square again, venting his anger by killing every Gholan and huge cat-thing that came into range of his ebony blade. He knew that their numbers could pull him down if he was not careful. More of the horrid brutes turned to attack him, trampling those Gart had already felled, but Gart's blade sang a song of death, and none reached him.

As they gathered around Gart and prepared to overwhelm him, he whirled Bessie in a tight circle, slashing and cutting without pause. Beauty was a snarling, roaring blur as she grabbed the repulsive Gholans in her powerful jaws and shook them so hard that their spines and necks snapped under the strain. Blood covered her mouth and neck, none of it her own, and she was terrifying to see as she ripped and tore into every Gholan that came within reach. Gradually, the creatures started howling and pointing at the whirling, hacking, biting duo, and the foul beasts began to pull away from the townspeople in favor of concentrating their attack on the dangerous newcomers.

The moment the Gholans turned towards the new threat, the townspeople immediately fled towards the safety of the nearest buildings that weren't in danger from the fires. Men and women frantically worked to get everyone barricaded inside as quickly as possible, leaving a handful of determined folk outside armed with axes, pitchforks, and an occasional sword. Quick, tearful goodbyes were said before doors were slammed shut and furniture pushed against them. Those who turned away from their loved ones had fire and blood in their eyes as they prepared to defend their town, and they fell upon the marauding creatures from behind in a frenzy of rage.

Fatigue started to burn in Gart's arm and shoulder as he fought, and his frustration lent him strength. His power seethed within him, eager for release. Gart spurred Bessie with his heels and she leapt over a pile of dead Gholans, gaining a brief respite from their attacking claws and teeth. Taking a deep breath and letting it out, Gart finally released his power. It rolled out of him in a rush, flowing over the rapidly advancing creatures. He could feel them, each and every one, and the touch of their matted fur and leathery skin disgusted him. Even so, he reached for more, until he had nearly thirty of the howling beasts within the gentle touch of his magick.

With a flex of his will, the gentleness was replaced with a vicelike grip of iron that instantly halted the vicious creatures' advance as it seized them, holding them in place. Their howling increased in pitch and intensity, changing from bloodlust to fear as they found themselves clutched in invisible bands of power that they could not budge.

Gart cast his icy cobalt gaze over them all, sensing their spirits through the probing touch of his magick. He could see into their very souls, the twisted and hateful evil that drove them to follow the orders of the madman, Mordak. The sorcerer had bade them all to gather and make their way towards Alverton Falls, killing any humans they came across.

In turn, the Gholans got a look into Gart's mind as well, and what they saw terrified them all. As one, they yowled in defiance, fear, and desperation, knowing without doubt that they had met their doom.

Gart extended one hand towards the frozen figures, honing his focus, and then violently clenched his fist. The howling was abruptly cut off as Gart's power crushed the life out of the evil monsters, as quickly as if he were blowing out a candle. Exhausted, he allowed his magick to dissipate, and the creatures' broken bodies slumped to the ground in boneless heaps.

Suddenly, Gart heard an agonized shriek from the other side of the plaza. Beauty had attacked a hulking cat-thing as it had prepared to leap at Gart, and it had fought back with a powerful swipe of its dagger-like claws. Bleeding from long gashes on her side, Beauty landed and immediately sprang back to the attack, latching onto the snarling creature's throat and tearing it out in a vicious yank. Blood ran down her flank and legs, but she paid it no attention as she turned to take on a Gholan who got too close.

Although tiring from the strenuous use of his magick, Gart had decided that enough was enough. He stabbed his sword down into one of the Gholans and let go of the weapon, leaving it embedded in the dying brute's body. He then reached over his shoulder and drew his Jidaan from its scabbard, pointing the glimmering blade up to the roiling storm clouds that blanketed the city. The emerald in its pommel blazed brightly as if eager to be used in the battle; its power vibrated on the air.

Raising his voice so that it could be heard over the din, Gart shouted to the townspeople, who had finally begun to gain the upper hand against the marauding creatures. "Herd them towards the corner! Push them towards that wall!"

Gart's voice echoed across the plaza, and a burly shopkeeper with a huge club took up the call as well. He had seen Gart slay many of the repulsive beasts and had already decided that he was on the same side as the townspeople.

"Push them back! Do as he says!" The man yelled and pressed forward to fell another Gholan with a swing of his weapon, and the man next to him did the same. Suddenly their numbers were reinforced by Darryn and his sailors as they slammed into the mass of shrieking creatures, filling the gaps left by the townspeople. Together, they pushed forward and formed a rough skirmish line that began to shove and bully the mob towards the wall that Gart had indicated. The fighting was brutal, but the determined townspeople refused to retreat, stepping over beastly corpses as they advanced.

Gart moved Bessie to a better vantage point, then engaged his magick once again, snaring any cat-beasts or Gholans that seemed in danger of escaping. Straining, he threw them against the stone wall that made up one corner of the plaza. He caused many to trip and stumble on unseen tendrils of magick only to be trampled by their own brethren as they tried frantically to escape. Using his power to create an invisible wall around the creatures, he isolated them from the valiant townspeople. His strength diminishing, he knew that he could not hold them for much longer.

"Move away! Get as far away as you can, now!" Gart bellowed at the locals. To their credit, they immediately followed his order, stopping only to collect their wounded. Gart heard another gurgle of pain and anger and turned to see Beauty standing over a dying cat-creature that twitched its last as she crushed its throat. Gart had missed it; it would have either escaped or attacked him from behind, if not for Beauty's interference. "Beauty, run! Hide!"

The huge dog released its kill and threw a quick glance over her shoulder at Gart as if to confirm his order. He sharply motioned for her to retreat and she took off as fast as she could in an awkward, limping gait, her blood staining the ground behind her. Gart watched her until she found shelter behind a corner, and then he turned his full attention back to the furious herd of vile creatures he had captured.

"Evil scum like you destroyed everything at Tiller's Grove. You killed everyone there. But not here. Not today." His words were cold and fierce, and echoed so loudly that every fell beast within his magickal prison shied away for a moment before resuming their screams of rage. They felt his magick buzzing in the air, and suddenly they came to fear the man with the blazing blue eyes and the emerald-pommeled spear.

The powerful magick inside him leapt at his silent call, plunging into the Jidaan of Storms and bringing its emerald ferociously to life. Its viridescent glow shone brightly, forcing away the shadows and terrifying Mordak's creatures so that they cried out and shielded their eyes. A blast of green fire burst from the blade of the weapon, lancing into the low layer of clouds overhead.

No more than a few heartbeats passed before the first Gholan cried out in pain as his skull was cracked by a hailstone the size of an apple. Another yowled in agony and then fell to the bloody earth, dead. Another was struck and killed, then another.

Just then, the sky opened up and a thick, deadly rain of enormous hailstones pelted the defiant creatures. They screamed in agony and rage as their bones were broken by the huge, rock-hard chunks of ice that slammed into them from above. The storm was mostly confined to the roughly circular area in which Gart held the beasts captive, though a few hailstones crashed into the surrounding buildings with tremendous force. The sound of the deluge was deafening in the confined space of the plaza as thousands of stones rained from the sky upon the doomed creatures of Mordak.

After less than a minute, Gart reached the end of his strength. The Jidaan's blazing emerald fire winked out like a snuffed candleflame. The downpour of hailstones slowed and then stopped completely, leaving a huge pile of bloody ice that covered the broken bodies of the Gholans and cat-beasts. Gart sagged on Bessie's neck, barely holding his grip on his Jidaan. For a few moments, nothing moved in the plaza save the drizzling rain and the defiant fire that burned in three of the nearest buildings. Gart's vision began to darken. He felt hands on his body, supporting him, as he dimly realized that he was sliding out of the saddle. They bore him to the ground, and suddenly, Beauty was there among the dirty, curious faces of the townspeople. She licked his face and whined quietly at her master.

"I'm all right, Beauty...I'm...fine..."

The darkness claimed him completely, and he knew no more.

Chapter 29

The city of Alverton Falls was nestled between the southern border of the Shadowed Forest and the Alvion River, which flowed west from Balroth's Abyss. The enormous crater gave birth to the Falls that gave the town its name. The roaring of the waterfall was still audible in the city proper as the streets emptied after nightfall. The farmlands that stretched north along the Blackthorne Mountains had been prosperous for centuries, and the city knew peace.

No one had felt the need to construct a wall around the city. It had been founded long after the wars had ravaged the face of Talwynn, and Alverton Falls had started so small that the topic of a wall simply never came up. Even as the city grew and prospered, and the DeRoberds family came to power, naught but a small militia was ever created to police the populace. Although the militia had grown into a small army, it was nothing compared to the vile horde that approached.

Fortunately, Count Addama DeRoberds had taken the message he had received on the leg of a Rualthan pigeon seriously. Within three days, the army had swelled to nearly twice its size as able-bodied men and women answered the call to arms. Ramparts and pits were dug, supplies and weapons were gathered, and wagonloads of civilians had departed for the relative safety of the Shadowed Forest, on their way to remote villages where they would stay until summoned back to their city.

By the time Brunar and his small company of Guardians and priestesses had arrived, the soldiers had already erected several checkpoints on the road. They had to move spiky obstacles aside for them to pass. Rows of logs covered with sharp, pointed projections were alternated with deep trenches that were also spiked. Closer to the city, a series of earthen ramparts had been hastily constructed as the final defenses. All of the preparations had made the best use of the natural terrain, so that any force coming from the south would have to fight through the obstacles to get anywhere near the city. All the while, they would be under fire from the city's archers and trebuchets, which had been quickly fabricated by the Count's men.

Brunar had been impressed with the amount and efficacy of the hastily constructed fortifications, though he knew that they would only delay Mordak's forces for a short time. He hoped that time would be enough for Layton, Kiran, and Nessar to retrieve the amulet and return.

In the Count's chambers, Brunar took stock of the ruler of Alverton Falls. He was a tall thin man, with long dark hair that fell past his shoulders. He had a wispy mustache and goatee that he tended to toy with whenever he was thinking. He had been thinking often of late. In his late thirties, he had welcomed Brunar and his people with respect and a surprising willingness to cooperate. After seeing to their needs, he had quickly called a war council that evening.

"I know of Duke Gensen," the Count said to Brunar, looking at a parchment map of the city. Its new defensive additions were marked clearly in charcoal. "He is a warrior, through and through. I," he stated emphatically, "I am not." He ran a slender finger over the map. "In physical combat, I am all but useless." He shrugged his thin shoulders in resignation. "I have a weak constitution, you know. I'm a chess player, not a warrior." He straightened up and turned to Brunar and a stern glint appeared in his eye. "That said, I'll protect the people of Alverton Falls as best I can. I'm somewhat learned in tactics, at least. I'm glad you're here to help us."

"The defenses you've already built will help, but the horde is vast," Brunar explained. "I've been able to rest and recover, so my magick is stronger now than it was at Laro. That goes for all of us, and we will do our utmost to protect the city." Bjarke and Alyssa nodded their agreement from where they sat. Alyssa's healing had restored them all to glowing good health. "If Layton, Kiran, and Nessar are able to provide us with the amulet, then we may be able to stop Mordak here and now." *And this time, we will stop him permanently,* Brunar thought to himself.

Alyssa spoke up from her place at the table. "Is there nothing we can do but await their arrival? This sitting around leaves me feeling as though there is something we are leaving undone. I've checked and rechecked the infirmaries and spoken to the physicians a dozen times. They are as ready as they will ever be."

Brunar nodded. "I understand, Alyssa, and I agree. The Count has everything well in hand here for the moment, and I think that we, meaning Bjarke and I, should see if we can lay eyes on Mordak's army. There's a chance that we might bring Bjarke's power to bear and possibly thin out that herd somewhat."

At the mention of his name, Bjarke stood, his reddish curly hair nearly touching the low ceiling of the chamber. He clasped his hands together, wringing them nervously, but his face was set and resolute. "If you can get me close enough, I can do that. I understand my power better now." He paused and looked at the ground for a moment and left his eyes downcast. When he next spoke, his voice was quiet. "I hate all this killing. It's unnecessary and it tears away at my spirit each time I take the lives of even those foul creatures." His chin rose then, and everyone could see that although his words had been sad, nearly despondent, his eyes were filled with determination and strength. "But those monsters have already killed thousands of innocents, and will gleefully kill thousands upon thousands more! That is, unless we stop them. I will send as many of them as is necessary back to the pits from whence they came."

Brunar wanted to applaud, even though a part of him was deeply saddened. Bjarke had been a jolly man without a care in the world. Then Brunar had come to inform him that he had been Chosen to wield a Jidaan. He had once laughed as easily as breathing, but now, his laughter was seldom heard. Even then, it was but a faint echo of what it had been. He was a warrior now, for better or ill. The Mage walked over and clapped the huge forester on the back in encouragement.

"I know you shall, Bjarke. Hopefully, we can put an end to Mordak's threat once and for all." He left unvoiced the thought that, unless the quest for the amulet was successful, there was a good chance that they themselves would be the ones to fall. Nevertheless, they would stand and fight. It was within their power to do so, and it was their responsibility.

The Count pored over the map. "If they are heading north from Laro as you say, then they will have to make their way through here," he indicated a spot several miles to the south of the city. "Redleaf Valley. It is heavily forested and riddled with caves. You can use strike-and-run tactics effectively there. I can send a squad of archers with you, but not many. Too many would be easier for this Mordak to find. A handful, though, could melt into the forest and disappear. If we put a group on each side of the valley, they could alternate their attacks to keep the enemy off balance."

Brunar nodded and said, "Yes, I agree completely. Bjarke and I can unleash our magick on them, then fade away into the forest. Depending on how far it is, we can communicate with each other and relay information to the archers as well."

"Aye, you take one side and I'll take the other. We can catch them in a crossfire they'll not soon forget." Bjarke smacked one meaty fist into his palm in ire.

"Right. Count DeRoberds, if you could have your men ready, we'll set out just before dawn." Brunar turned to the nearby Weya advisor. "Cohl, how long will it take for the

ValElder to make contact with the Weya that live in the Shadowed Forest?"

Cohl stood and bowed. "It may be a few more days, I cannot say. I am yet somewhat unfamiliar with this area. Moihra has lived near here before, however. She'll know where to go, and if the Weya are willing, she'll bring reinforcements."

The Count looked up from the map. "How many troops do you think she will bring?"

Cohl shrugged, a very Weya gesture. "As I said, I am unfamiliar with this area. She could bring a hundred, or five hundred. I know not."

The Count grimaced as he pondered Cohl's answer. "Since we do not know how many will come, we must plan as though she will bring none at all. Then any help she brings will be a welcome blessing and can be used to best effect." He looked down at the map again. "Is there anything else you have not told me that might be helpful, Sir Mage?

Brunar had briefed him at length upon their first meeting on the nature of Mordak's strength, both in troops and magick. He shook his head. "No, but if anything comes to mind, I will surely provide you with that information."

The Count leaned away from the table at last, stretching his back with a groan before straightening up to his full height. "All right, then. We shall continue our preparations as best we can while you and Bjarke take the archers to Redleaf Valley. May the Goddess Rowann guide your steps."

Chapter 30

"There," Ginn said firmly as he pointed towards a curiously barren spot in the distance. The sun had already crawled high enough in the sky that it was no longer directly in their eyes, and the small party stared in the direction the Weya indicated. They were standing on what seemed to be an ancient road paved with wide, flat stones, now mostly covered over with sandy soil and shrubs that had found their way to the surface. The pathway led straight to a wide entrance of sorts, with two large stone pillars capped by a weathered arch of the same stone. Beyond the ancient gateway, there was nothing but empty land as far as they could see; no trees or bushes grew there. From their vantage point, it appeared to be a desolate waste that covered a huge, circular area. "I passed through that gateway nearly a thousand years ago and there was a thriving city beyond it. What happened here is unknown to us, though to my knowledge, no one has truly delved into that mystery."

The wind blew mournfully across the vast, empty space. Kiran shielded her eyes with her hand and peered out at the perimeter, noting that there were stones standing here and there. A few yards of a stone wall remained on the far side of the clearing. She shook her head. "There was definitely something there. I mean, it's obvious. But where would an entire city go, exactly? And how?"

Nessar glared out at what little remained of Linbourne. "I don't know, Kiran. I guess it's time we found out." He turned and extended a leathery hand to Ginn, who gripped it firmly. "Thank you for getting us here, Ginn. Easy trails to you."

Ginn smiled. "And to you as well. It was an honor to meet and battle side by side with the Guardians. May you find what you seek." The small figure bade farewell to Kiran and Layton before he turned his horse to southward. They watched him go until he disappeared behind some scrubby trees and could be seen no more.

"Well, let's get to it! If that thing is out there, we'll never find it sitting over here." Layton guided his horse forward until he was alongside Nessar and Kiran on the road, which was easily wide enough for the three to ride side by side. The young warrior's enthusiasm was in good supply since he had only used his Gift a few times before they had reached their current location, and he was still full of energy.

Nessar, on the other hand, had slept badly and awakened irritable. He was about to say something sarcastic when an odd sensation ran through him. They had just started their horses in the direction of the stone archway, and Nessar stopped them again.

"Did either of you feel that?" He looked at Layton, who quickly shook his head.

"What do you mean, Ness? I didn't feel anything." Kiran gave her old friend a puzzled look, then looked back out at the lonely stones at the end of the path.

Nessar stayed still, watching and listening. He realized that the disturbance he had detected was not out there; it was inside him. He had felt it deep in his core - a fluttering, a definite sense of unease. He reached inward in an attempt to find it, focusing his awareness as best he could. At first there was nothing.

"Honestly, I'm not sure. I know I felt something, though. Let's keep our guard up and head towards that entrance. Slowly." He gently nudged his horse and it started forward. They had not gone more than a few steps when Nessar felt it again.

"There! Did you feel that at all?"

Layton and Kiran sat quietly before finally admitting that they had not felt anything. "What is it that you're feeling?" Layton asked.

Nessar frowned for a moment before answering. "It's odd. It's deep inside me, but it's not like something I ate; it's the magick. It feels like a muscle twitch, but it's not physical at all. And it is definitely getting stronger the closer I get to that archway."

"It doesn't hurt?" Kiran asked, concerned.

Nessar shook his head. "No, Kiran, it's just an odd feeling. I've grown somewhat used to the magick that the Jidaan have awakened in us, but this is much stronger."

"Let's keep moving, but we'll take it slowly." Layton suggested. "We need to be careful, but time is not exactly on our side just now."

"I'm more than a little concerned there's something wrong with that arch. I don't know if it's a trap or something else. Let's just go around it." Nessar guided his horse off to the right, leaving the remains of the road, the others riding on either side of him. Whatever wall had once surrounded the kingdom of Linbourne was not there any longer, so they angled for an empty spot just to the right of the enigmatic archway.

The three riders drew even with the structure. Kiran was looking off to the east when she heard Nessar grunt, a short, strangled sound. She whipped her head back towards the old man but saw only Layton across from her. He had been carefully watching the archway for any signs of mischief when he heard the sound and turned to find only Kiran staring back at him. His mouth dropped opened in shock just as Kiran's had.

Nessar had been riding between them, and although the horse remained, there was no sign of the old man. He had completely vanished.

Chapter 31

The voices were muffled at first, but they became clearer as Gart fought his way back to consciousness.

"I've told ye, his name is Gart. He says he's nae a Mage, but some'at else instead." It was Darryn's voice, in a tone that made it clear that he was annoyed. "Whate'er he be, he saved yer bacon back there, so gi' the man some room to breathe!" A low growl came from somewhere very close by. Beauty was being protective of him; it made Gart smile. Finally, he opened his eyes.

He found himself lying on a wooden floor with a rolled up blanket under his head. His Jidaan and sword were within easy reach, and Beauty was seated right next to his feet, growling softly. Darryn was standing nearby, talking to a small group of people led by the burly townsman that had wielded a club against the Gholans. The club was no longer in his hands, and his bearded face was wrinkled in concern. When he saw Gart sit up, his face brightened.

"He's awake! Are you all right, sir? Can we do anything to help you?" The men and women with him murmured similar questions and their faces echoed the man's eager expression.

Before Gart could answer, he was assailed by Beauty, who nearly knocked him flat on his back again as her tongue slapped him in the face with great enthusiasm. He grabbed her around the neck to steady himself, only to have her whimper in pain and suddenly shy away. Gart let go quickly, and Beauty instantly came back and licked him again as if apologizing for moving away from her master. He carefully petted her and then got to his feet, bringing his weapons with him. He looked around and saw that he was inside a small inn, surrounded by people from the town. They seemed very pleased that he had awakened unharmed, so Gart slid his Jidaan into its scabbard at his back and reattached the sword to his belt.

"I'd..." his voice was rough from exhaustion. "I'd like some water, please." His stomach let out a loud gurgle. "And food, if you have any."

Half the group burst into action, apparently heading for the kitchen while the burly man with the beard hustled to the bar and grabbed a platter with a pitcher and mugs already on it. With awe written plainly on his face, he approached Gart with the platter held before him.

"Yes, sir! There's water here, and I've wine in the back if you want any. You just say the word, it's all on the house!"

"No, no, I can pay." Gart moved a hand towards his money pouch. Before he could open it, one of the women moved in close and put her hand on his.

"I'm Belinda," her voice was bubbly and girlish, although it sounded as though it had been a long while since it had come out that way. "Brynn and I own this inn, so if we say it's on the house, then your money's no good here, sir." When she was sure that Gart was not going to try to pay, she stepped over to the bar and accepted a trencher of steaming beef and hot buttered bread from one of the men who had just come from the kitchen. She walked over to a nearby table and set it down, motioning for him to come and sit.

Gart offered her a smile. "A moment, please." He knelt beside Beauty to examine her. The dog nuzzled him happily. "Could we get her something to eat as well? She fought hard out there, and I know she's hungry." He carefully ran his hands over her coat and was distressed to find several large gashes along her right side. She whimpered as he gently probed her wounds, and he frowned in anger. His piercing blue gaze immediately found Darryn.

The riverboat captain immediately held up his hands. "She wouldna let us do anything to help her, Gart. We tried to, but once we laid ye down in here, she curled up next to ye and wouldna let anyone get near either of ye again."

Gart's anger softened then. "Yes, that does sound like something she'd do." He looked at her scarred face with its permanent snarl. Her battered countenance sported a few new cuts here and there, and he felt a wave of affection for the huge animal. She licked his face again and wagged her tail. She was obviously in pain, but happy that her master was there.

Gart looked over her injuries again. In addition to the claw marks on her body, she was also favoring one of her rear legs. He gently ran his fingers over it, relieved to find that it did not seem broken. "I'll see what I can do for her...stitch her up if she'll let me." Then and there, he knew what he would have to do for Beauty. He owed her for saving him so many times. Even as he made the decision, he knew that neither he, nor she, would like it. He went back to examining her gashes and was pleased to see that although they were deep, they were far from life threatening.

Just then, one of the men brought a haunch of beef and set it before her. She looked down at it, licked her lips, and looked at Gart. "It's yours, girl. Eat up." She tore into the meat immediately and settled down to eat.

Gart moved to the table and began to eat also, using somewhat better manners than Beauty. He looked up and found that Belinda and Brynn had come out of the kitchen and stood beaming at him.

"Thank you very much for the food. I was really starved," Gart said between mouthfuls.

"Oh, you're very welcome, sir!" Brynn's smile shone from within his bushy beard. "And anything else you need, you just say the word. So many of us owe our lives to you; we'll help you however we can." His voice turned angry as he continued. "Those things just swarmed into town, killing everyone and everything they came across."

Gart nodded and returned to his meal. Brynn and Belinda finally turned away from him and began directing their workers to bring food and drink for the rest of the locals who had wandered into the inn while they were dealing with Gart. Darryn was handed a plate of food, and he sat opposite Gart, ready to eat.

"Darryn, I need a favor from you, my friend."

"Och, jest say what ye need, I'm good fer it," the sailor replied around an improbably huge mouthful.

Gart paused, trying not to let his welling emotions show on his face. A lump had appeared in his throat, both surprising and frustrating him, and he swallowed until he could speak freely again. "I need you to take Beauty back north with you. I've a friend there, her name is Ishabel; she's from the Iron Hills. Take her to Ishabel. Beauty's hurt, and she needs to heal. She can rest on the way back and then Ishabel will take care of her." A cobalt gleam appeared in Gart's eyes as he worked to contain a sudden rush of anger. "Where I'm going, there's a lot more to deal with than this. I don't know that I'll survive it, and I know she won't either if she goes on with wounds like that."

Darryn chewed a mouthful of beef, swallowed, and chased it with a long drink of ale before responding. "Gart, it would be my pleasure. After this, there's no way we're goin' any further south, not a single league. If ye can get the wee beastie to stay wi' me, then I'll be happy to take her. And if yer talkin' about Ishabel from the Iron Hills Clan, I ken that name. I'm nae from that clan meself, but some of me lads be from there, and they'll ken where she is. Ye have my word on it." The sailor wiped his hand on his shirt, which was no cleaner, and extended it across the table.

Gart looked at it for a moment before reaching over and shaking it firmly. "Thank you, Darryn. I owe you."

Darryn made a rude noise. "Ye certainly do *not*. Wi'out you along, me crew and I would either have been killed in Hollowthorne or most certainly would have met our bloody end right here. Gholans and Morcats...Goddess above, who would have thought! Nay, ye kept us alive, and the people here too. Dinnae give it a second thought. Just see that ye let Beauty know that she is to come wi' us, eh? We'll leave at first light."

Gart merely nodded and turned back to his food, which seemed to be the best tasting fare he'd ever encountered. He finished the platter and then excused himself. Beauty was nearly finished with her own food, gnawing determinedly on the bone, and Gart approached Brynn to ask for bandages and supplies to stitch her wounds. The innkeeper bustled away and returned with a small bundle moments later.

"These should do for her. There's a salve in there that should numb the cuts for the stitching. Will you be needing a room, then? Our beds are clean, no bedbugs at all!"

Although the food had helped restore much of Gart's strength, he was still weary. He laid the bundle of bandages and herbs on a nearby table as he considered Brynn's offer. A glance out of the nearest window showed that night had fallen. "Yes sir, that would be perfect. Some sleep would do me and Beauty some good."

Before Brynn could reply, Gart snatched a few gold pieces out of his pouch, slipped them into the innkeeper's hand, and folded the man's fingers over them. Brynn started to protest, but Gart's intense blue stare froze him in place before he could speak.

"You don't owe me, friend. Take this and use it where you need to. There was a lot of damage done out there tonight, and some of it was caused by me. Just take it."

Brynn closed his mouth with a snap and managed to nod his agreement, and Gart stepped away, satisfied. He picked up the bundle and walked over to Beauty. "Beauty, come." Without missing a beat, she picked up the bone and hobbled to Gart's side. Seeing her limp made Gart's heart ache.

Belinda appeared, drying her hands on a towel. "This way, sir. If you need anything at all, you just let us know." She gestured for Gart to follow her down a hallway. After bidding Darryn and the others a good night, he did, moving slowly so that Beauty could follow him.

The next morning dawned gray and dreary. The weather suited Gart's mood. Even though the townspeople had been very gracious, he knew that darker days lay ahead, and he did not relish what he was about to do. Darryn and his men had gathered in front of the B and B Inn, as it turned out to be called, and Gart walked Beauty out to them. The salve had worked well, and he had managed to stitch all of Beauty's wounds without hurting her. Gart had thanked Brynn and Belinda profusely before leaving. As they stepped outside the inn, Beauty bumped repeatedly against Gart. She wagged her tail constantly, happy as only a dog can be. She was eager to see what the day would bring, in spite of the lingering pain she was in.

Gart took off his hat and bent down so that he could see her eye to eye. She was tall enough that he did not have to bend far, and her deep brown eyes met Gart's startling blue ones.

"Beauty, I need you to go with Darryn. Find Ishabel. Understand?"

Beauty just continued to look at him, tail wagging. Gart snorted in frustration. He had to make her go. On impulse, he looked deeply into her eyes and awakened his magick. Ever so gently, he reached into her mind with it, and was completely shocked at what he found there.

Among the sensory inputs of smell and sound that were far stronger than his own, one emotion overrode everything else. It shone like the sun, bright and warm, and its light fell into every nook and cranny of the dog's mind, guiding her every move. It was more powerful than anything Gart had ever felt, more powerful than his own anger, stronger than the winds he had ridden, or anything he had ever seen.

It was love. It was pure, simple, and almost overwhelming in its intensity. Beauty loved him with all her heart. She would die without a second thought if it meant defending him. He was her entire world.

Oblivious to the tears that slid gently down his face, he sent an image of Ishabel to her. He felt the sense of recognition as she saw it, and he sent the simplest command he could think of. *Find her.* Again, a strong sense of recognition flowed back along the invisible link of magick Gart had forged between them, and he caught a flash of her intense desire to please him. Beauty would find Ishabel or die trying.

Gart reached over to his left wrist and unlaced the leather bracelet he wore there. It had been a gift from Ishabel, given when they had parted at the road to the Heartstrong Mountains, before Gart had claimed his Jidaan. He removed the ornately tooled leather wrap and let Beauty smell it. Through their connection, he felt her recognize the woman's scent very clearly. Beauty remembered her well. Keying on her memory, Gart sent the image of Ishabel once more and the command to find her. Beauty's love for him glowed strongly, and her devotion to the task was clear. From a small pouch he wore on his waist, he pulled a length of leather lacing. He attached the bracelet to it and tied it firmly into a makeshift collar around the dog's neck. Gart looked into her eyes again, but had to squeeze his own shut lest his heart break right in two. He pressed his forehead against hers and felt her wag her tail enthusiastically. Sensing his sadness, she whined sweetly, as if letting him know that everything was all right. She would do as he asked. She loved him.

Gart broke the contact and wiped his eyes as he stood. He took his time replacing his hat on his head and cleared his throat repeatedly so that his voice would not break when he spoke again. "Beauty, go with Darryn." Gart pointed to the riverboat captain, and Beauty obediently walked over to stand by him. Darryn's eyes widened, though he said nothing.

"She'll go with you. Just keep her fed and get her to Ishabel. She'll recognize her."

Darryn looked at the enormous dog and back at Gart with wonder in his eyes. Then he cracked a sideways grin.

"Aye, I'll do that. Though I'm thinkin' we'd better lay in some extra food. We wouldn't want her chewin' on me lads if she be peckish along the way."

Gart nodded his thanks, his jaw firmly set. He hauled himself up into the saddle and turned Bessie away from the group. Without another word, he gently kicked his faithful horse into a trot, wanting to put some distance between himself and his companion. *You know it was the right thing to do. She'll just die out there. Stop being silly*, he thought to himself.

He left Willowbranch and kept Bessie moving along the southern road. Although the sky was still iron-grey and filled with distant rumbles, the rain had yet to fall. Gart settled into the familiar rhythm of travel on horseback. He did not like feeling so deeply for Beauty. *She's just a dog, after all.*

He kept telling himself that as he rode. He never once managed to believe it.

Chapter 32

How much longer until they come? Bjarke's voice quietly echoed in Brunar's mind. It was only a few hours past midnight, and a warm wind was blowing through Redleaf Valley, named for the stunning shades of scarlet the leaves took on before they dropped in autumn. Fortunately, it was still summer and the leaves were thick, green, and plentiful. They provided ample cover for the two squads who lay in ambush on either side of the valley, awaiting the foul folk of Mordak's horde. The waning sliver of moon gave just enough light for them to see by without revealing their position. Bjarke's archers had spread out on the eastern side of the valley while Brunar's forces were settled in on the western slopes. They had each been given command of fifty veterans bearing three full quivers of arrows apiece. They were steely-eyed men and women, all awaiting the chance to rain death down on the invaders.

Soon, now. I can feel their presence growing stronger. We'll wait until the first ranks have filled the valley, and I'll send up a signal. Have your archers loose a volley in their midst, and keep sending arrows into those brutes until they all fall; we'll do the same. I will aid the attack with one of my own; that will be the signal for you to do your part. Brunar's grey eyes roved over the sloped forest across the valley where Bjarke and his forces were well-hidden. Brunar had cast a gentle cloaking enchantment to hide them all from Mordak's sorcerous eyes as best he could. Anything stronger than that would alert the heightened senses of the madman. If he truly *looked*, he would still likely see them, but only if he focused his will on the task. Otherwise, they were invisible, concealed as they were in the trees and rocks.

With any luck, Brunar thought to himself, *Mordak thinks we died in the fall of Laro. If he thinks himself superior, he'll likely not give the valley a second thought.*

Just then, Brunar felt rather than heard the approach of the horde. It was a subtle vibration that drove through the earth and up into Brunar's boots. The first distant sounds reached his ears, thousands of feet striking the ground in anything but unison. Gholan howls and mutters dirtied the air with their foul tongue, and every so often a Morcat would roar at some infraction. The rumble drew steadily closer, as did the sounds of the hideous creatures as they began to swarm into the southern end of the valley.

They were led by a single armored man on an enormous horse. Brunar spied the tell-tale glow of the man's serpent-yellow eyes gleaming in the dark. He recognized Mordak's right hand, Jor Dayne. He was the leader in the trenches, relaying Mordak's orders. Surely at least part daemon, he would be formidable, to say the least. At Laro, Brunar had seen the man reset his own broken forearm, laughing all the while. The Mage made a mental note to hit the big brute hard when he unleashed his attack on the horde.

Brunar focused his breathing to calm himself. He quickly found the stillness within the motion, that place of calm from which he could fight or cast spells in a fury of manifested will and power, riding in the eye of the hurricane while the maelstrom raged around him. Alyssa's healing had unexpectedly brought him almost back to his full strength, and he planned to use his increased power effectively and in impressive fashion.

Moments crawled by and the horde made its way up the center of the valley. Legions of dark, scuttling Gholans defiled the grassy land upon which they walked, while the haughty Morcats strode among them, aloof and deadly. A pang struck Brunar's heart as he noted the presence of hundreds of scarlet-eyed Riders, those who had once been living, breathing humans now perverted in death into soldiers for Mordak. They made no sound, for they had no need to breathe. They shuffled or rode with their glowing, blood-red eyes fixed straight ahead. They endured any discomfort, caring for nothing as they followed the relentless compulsion under which they lived. Such was Mordak's way.

Brunar remained calm as he observed the movements of the deadly creatures. For now, they just kept moving, paying no attention to the slopes on either side. Enemy soldiers continued their march into the valley from the south, filling the relatively flat space between the two tree-laden slopes. The Mage stoically watched them go by, concentrating on keeping the cloaking spell engaged while gathering the energy necessary for his attack. He allowed a few hundred more to make their way into the valley, and then he sent a tiny burst of indigo light lancing into the night sky to signal the attack.

The response was immediate, but almost silent. Brunar heard the muted twangs of the bowstrings on his side of the valley and watched a massive flight of arrows leave the forest and begin their slow arc down to the valley. His sharp eyes picked out a similar sized cloud of deadly shafts from Bjarke's side, winging quietly through the air towards the unknowing horde.

Moments later, enraged howls and screams of pain echoed up from the valley floor, and the archers were already loosing another volley. The front rank moved quickly downslope until they were close enough to pick off individual targets without being easily seen, and began their deadly assault. Gholans died by the hundreds, as did the ferocious Morcats. The animated Riders continued marching, not noticing that they bristled with arrows. Only those whose heads had been pierced by the wooden shafts or whose hearts had been burst by the flying arrows had fallen to the bloody earth, while the others continued to plod forward until they received further orders from Mordak. For now, it appeared that the sorcerer was far enough in the rear that he did not yet know what had befallen the first third of his army.

Brunar smiled. *He'll know soon enough. Bjarke, when I hit Jor Dayne, you do the same with your target!* The huge warrior responded silently and Brunar gathered his power, his eyes locked on the hulking figure of Jor Dayne down below.

The massive warrior's horse had been downed by several arrows but he jumped free of the saddle as it fell. Bellowing in anger, Jor Dayne broke off the shafts that had penetrated his armor, leaving the heads embedded in his body. The pain was exquisite. A few had gone all the way through his muscular arms, and those he removed after breaking away the barbed arrowheads. Bright sparks of pain burned in his back and he knew that a couple had lodged there as well, but he could not reach them. They would have to stay. Paying no attention to the dying horse at his feet, the half-daemon brutally hacked through the leather straps of his saddle and pulled it free to use as a makeshift shield. He covered his upper body with it as best he could and started to make his way towards the western slope, intent on dealing as much death as he possibly could.

Brunar gathered his power and unleashed a violent indigo bolt of force at the huge figure. At that same instant, a clear ruby beam of energy burst free of the forest on the opposite side of the valley, aimed at the western slope near the southern end, just where Mordak's army was pouring in. The two blasts exploded almost simultaneously, and the earth shook with the power unleashed by the two men.

Bjarke's power blasted an enormous chunk of the bluff away from the valley slope, causing a devastating rock slide. Boulders great and small slid downwards in a deadly river of earth and stone, engulfing the forces of Mordak, crushing them, and cutting the bulk of the evil army off from the killing ground within the valley.

Brunar's blazing purple blast slammed into Jor Dayne and hurled his battered body high into the air. His scream of rage echoed over the sound of the explosion, only to be clipped short when his body smashed into the unyielding earth below. It came down awkwardly, breaking one of his great thigh bones on impact, as well as several ribs. The yellow light in his eyes dimmed and went out as the huge half-daemon lay still, his scarlet blood mingling with the brown and black ichor left by Mordak's other fell creatures.

Seeing the imposing warrior finally down sent a thrill through Brunar, but he had no time to celebrate. Quickly, he turned his attention to the remainder of the group that had fallen into their ambush. The archers on his side had all taken advantage of the confusion below to move forward with their comrades at the tree line where they could better see their targets, and creature after howling creature fell to their deadly arrows. Bjarke unleashed another blast of pure scarlet power, causing an even bigger wave of rock and earth to pour into the far end of the valley. Soon, the way was completely blocked. No one was getting in or out of the southern pass.

Brunar scanned the valley floor and was both pleased and sickened at what he saw there. The dead and dying were piled everywhere, and faint yowls of pain drifted up to his ears. A few human undead remained standing amidst the carnage, awaiting orders from Mordak. These, Brunar killed with quick bursts of energy, a rapid-fire attack that left him feeling soiled inside. They had been ordinary humans once, innocent of the crimes and abominations they would commit under Mordak's compulsion. Whatever good they might have done in their lives before then had been washed away in rivers of blood. Mordak's evil had corrupted them as he used their bodies as his servants and soldiers. Now, at least, they were truly dead, and would hopefully find peace.

When nothing moved in the valley, and the crows began to swoop down and look for food, Brunar finally called the retreat.

That worked better than we'd hoped! Bjarke's voice in Brunar's mind sounded relieved and hopeful.

Yes! Not only did we deprive him of a few thousand of his creatures, but we've cut off the horde from Alverton Falls for the time being. It will take them days to get through there, if they can even manage it. Otherwise, they'll have to go all the way around the Blackthorne Mountains to the east or fight their way through the Tanglewoods to the west. Either way, we've won some time. For the first time since he had awakened in the Heartstrong Mountains, Brunar felt the hope of victory blossom in his chest. *Have your squad retreat to the north, back to Alverton Falls. We have much to do!* Brunar smiled at Bjarke's enthusiastic whoop, heard all the way across the valley. He turned and signaled his own archers to start making their way north as well. *We may have hurt him, but he'll come back strong.*

As they began their trek, one warrior stopped and waited for Brunar to draw up alongside her. Meliantha was a slender woman of middling height, not imposing from a distance. Her long brown hair was tightly braided against her head, and she sported a thin scar that ran along her jawline on the left side of her face. Her eyes were keen even in the dim light, and the hands she held crossed atop her longbow were strong and sure. Meliantha stood before a small group of hard-looking warriors, both men and women. She signaled to Brunar to come closer, and the Mage complied.

"I'd like to stay behind," she said quietly, her voice soft yet firm with resolve. She nodded to the small group of steely-eyed soldiers behind her. "These here have volunteered to stay as well. We'll harass those nasty things a bit if they start to get through that mess. We'll use the caves to move about unseen. A few of them reach all the way to the southern side of the range here, so if we're careful, we can harry them on the other side of the barrier, too. We'll send word of their progress when we know more, and then fall back when the time comes."

Brunar's mind suddenly raced with possibilities. The city of Alverton Falls was vulnerable due to the lack of a surrounding wall, though the river protected it on the southern side. Furthermore, Count DeRoberds had initiated defensive measures in the open land south of the river that would hamper the enemy's approach. However, between that killing ground and the valley in which they stood lay many miles of hilly, lightly forested terrain. It was perfect for a guerrilla war.

The Mage smiled.

"Meliantha, that's a fine idea. Do what you can to slow them down; teach them to fear what they can't see. We'll reach Alverton Falls as quickly as we can and bring back more troops. I think we can bleed this beast before it gets close to town. Then we can really hit them hard!"

Meliantha grinned slyly at the Mage and clasped his hand briefly. The she melted into the foliage, leading her crew into one of the caves nearby. Brunar watched her go. He knew she had no intention of falling back at any point. She would fight until either she won or the enemy did. Brunar prayed to the Goddess Rowann that the brave archer would live to see Mordak fall.

The two squads silently picked their way through the sloping forest on either side of the valley, each warrior excited that they had dealt such a telling blow and received none in return. They failed to see the glimmer of sickly scarlet that perched atop the newly settled earth and rock of the slide. Mordak's gleaming crimson eyes missed nothing. He could see where his enemies were traveling as they thought themselves beyond his notice. A minor spell and shift in focus allowed him to see the entire valley in shades of red, based on heat. The soldiers appeared to him as a line of tiny red figures among the cooler trees, shrubs, and stone of the surrounding area.

"That's right...flee, puny creatures!" he snarled. "You think you've gotten the better of me, I'm sure. I look forward to proving you wrong, you feeble-minded idiots!" Cloaking himself in his magick and making himself as blurry and indistinct as possible, Mordak drifted through the air and down to the valley floor. He did not wish for Brunar to see him, not yet.

He had been impressed at the sight of Brunar's distinctive purple magick as he saw his Champion blasted into the air, broken and battered. Brunar seldom went in for brute force, but the bolt he had loosed at Jor Dayne had been potent, indeed. The ruby-hued power of the big man surprised him, though, for he had thought the red-bearded ruffian had perished at Laro. Even so, it would be of no consequence. Mordak was confident that he would triumph at Alverton Falls, no matter how many of those spear-bearing buffoons had survived.

Mordak's feet gently came to rest on the sodden ground of the valley floor, and the sorcerer frowned with disgust at the gore that fouled his boots. Stepping as carefully as he could, Mordak moved closer to the prone form of Jor Dayne. The huge, burly warrior lay face down. His right leg was twisted at an improbable angle, and the stubs of broken arrows protruded from his back. Mordak sent his awareness into the body of the half-daemon and was pleased to find that life still flickered there. The daemon had remained within the physical shell of the man, Lucanos, and that shell had not yet died completely.

He clucked his tongue at the fallen warrior. "Fool! Look at yourself. Always getting broken at the first sign of trouble." The necromancer started to roll up his sleeves, but then stopped as his hands found the hundreds of bumps that had covered his skin since his visit to the Poravian Mire. The bumps squirmed under his fingers, and he decided not to touch them again. "Pah! If I didn't need you on the field of battle, I'd send you back to the Hel from which I summoned you!"

After a quick check over his shoulder for signs of Brunar and the huge Guardian, Mordak raised his hands and set himself to the task of healing his Lieutenant again, starting with Jor Dayne's broken femur. As always, he elected not to ease the brute's pain in the process. Already, his mind was busily figuring out a way to get his army through the pass. If they could not move through Redleaf Valley, they would have to trek farther east, then north, and make their way through the Blackthorne Mountains. Going farther west was out of the question, as the Tanglewoods were there. That ancient, shadowed forest was dangerous even for the likes of Mordak. He would not brave them yet, not even with his army.

Amidst Jor Dayne's hoarse yells of anguish and pain, Mordak smiled as he finally decided on a plan. When he felt that he had healed the majority of his Champion's wounds and knitted his broken thigh bone, he turned away and looked at the mass of debris that now clogged the southern pass. Moving it with magick would be an enormous task, costing him far more energy than he could spare. Though he certainly would succeed, it would leave him vulnerable for far too long afterwards until he recovered.

"We'll just have to go over it." Mordak surveyed the barrier a few moments more, then glanced over his shoulder at Jor Dayne. The fallen warrior had finally risen to one knee, his massive chest heaving as he struggled to catch his breath. "Gather your wits, you lout. You'll oversee the work on this side, while I handle things on the other."

"Work?" Jor Dayne had only just regained consciousness, and had no idea what the sorcerer was talking about.

Mordak turned and backhanded him across the face, knocking the weakened warrior back to the ground.

"Yes, you fool! *Work!* I'll bring a few squads over to this side to begin clearing a path over all this! Use ropes, wood, whatever you need to do to make it stable enough for the army to traverse. I'll have them do the same on the other side and aid them with my magick. It should only delay us for a day, maybe two at most if we put those repulsive creatures to work." A malevolent grin appeared on his face. "I don't know how that Mage survived the fall of Laro, but I do know how he thinks. Right now, he thinks we will be on our way around the mountains or through the Tanglewoods, delaying us for weeks. He'll get a nasty surprise when we show up in Alverton Falls in mere days instead!"

Jor Dayne had recovered from the blow and was standing tall once again, enjoying the sensations of pain that still wracked his muscular body, but hating the man before him. He was a daemon, not a lackey! But that was the deal when he had been summoned. Even so, Jor Dayne did not have to like it...or follow the rules forever. For now, he still needed to obey orders. "Yes, Master. It shall be as you say."

"Of course it will!" Mordak snapped. "See to it!" Without another word, the sorcerer spread his arms and invoked his stolen power, lifting himself through the air on the arms of a misty scarlet magick that flowed from his body and carried him aloft.

Jor Dayne watched silently, his yellow eyes gleaming in the dark. And he smiled.

Chapter 33

Nessar's boots hit the dusty ground in a jarring thump, and he crumpled into a heap, breathing heavily. The pain had become unbearable, and Nessar felt like he was going to split in half. Just as quickly, his agony had vanished. He had felt an intense sensation of falling, and when it passed, he had found himself in a cold and alien landscape.

In time, he was able to raise his head and look around, but what he saw was not at all what he expected. The noonday sun had vanished, leaving behind not one, but two pale blue moons in the darkened indigo sky overhead. One closely resembled the moon Nessar had seen his whole life, while the other was smaller and misshapen. They glowed with a baleful light, illuminating a city that had not been there a moment before. Squat, rounded buildings covered the land before him, with taller towers poking up here and there.

Nessar managed to bring himself to his feet, shrugging off his disorientation as best he could. His insides roiled with a nauseating, crawling sensation, but he ignored it. He brushed dirt off of his trousers as he looked farther out into the city. Squinting into the darkness, he could see a cluster of larger, domed structures that arose near the center of the city dominated by one huge dome, almost certainly the palace. A cold wind howled across the land, and the old thief shivered as he wished he had brought warmer clothing.

He wanted to call out for Kiran and Layton, but instinct kept him quiet. He saw no movement in the city ahead, but that meant nothing. Turning, he saw that the wall that encircled the city was fragmented. Parts were missing as though sharply cut away by some maddened stonemason. A road of wide, flat stones led away from the city, right up to an empty space. Beyond that, in a ring that surrounded the entire city, there was nothing but an impenetrable darkness.

The arch was there; it was right there, Nessar thought, making a mental note of its location. He had no idea how he had arrived without his companions, but obviously, this was the place Brunar had mentioned. Linbourne. The Cursed City, gone from the world of Talwynn for over a thousand years.

The fact that neither Layton nor Kiran had arrived with him only made him roll his eyes in disgust. *Of course they didn't come along. Why in the world would we want to do things the easy way?* He shook his head and reached over his shoulder to check his Jidaan. He was relieved to find it still there, its wooden shaft solid and reassuring at his back. Nessar turned to survey the crescent of land between the darkened border and the first buildings and did not see anything that looked like a person, moving or otherwise. A rock here and there, but nothing else.

Moving silently, he approached the nearest buildings and slipped into an alley between them. The moment he stepped out of the odd moonlight, his nausea vanished as though it had never existed, and Nessar relaxed a little. He unshouldered his backpack and found the small waterskin that hung on one side. After taking a long drink, he restoppered it and laid it aside. Looking in all directions first to be sure he was unseen, Nessar opened the pack and began sifting through its contents. Several small items he removed and secreted about his person in hidden pockets designed to carry such things. Extra throwing knives found their way into concealed sheaths, and a small leather case filled with the highest quality lockpicks clipped onto his belt where he could easily reach it.

The darkness, although tinged with that peculiar blue-violet light, was far more comfortable to the old thief than the bright of day, although he did wonder what other things might be lurking unseen in the shadows alongside him. He tried to put that thought out of his mind so he could stay focused on his goal. If there was an amulet created and presented to the king, then it would most likely be in the palace. Nessar closed up his pack and then hid it in the shadows. Hugging the wall on his right, he eased himself forward until he could see the next street, and then pulled back quickly.

There, frozen in midstride across the way, was the first person Nessar had seen in the silent city. He appeared to be exiting a shop. He was completely still, his body like a statue carved in the act of taking a step through the doorway. Nessar's eyes narrowed as he tried to make out the man's face, and he thought he saw an expression of startlement on his static features. His clothing was odd to Nessar; the man was not wearing pants. He wore what appeared to be a single long piece of cloth wrapped around his body in a strategic fashion that left his arms and legs bare. He had a wide belt and sandals that laced up to the knee, and a satchel of some kind hung from his shoulder. Nessar studied the man for a few moments more and then looked up and down the street, noting other still forms near the entrances to other buildings.

It seems that the people here are...frozen? From the looks of it, they've been that way for a very long time. And why is no one in the street? Questions filled his mind as he surveyed the area.

In the next few moments he saw something that would have kept him out of the street forever. It started with a scraping sound just at the edge of his hearing. Nessar pressed himself against the side of the building, blending with the shadows. The sound grew louder as something approached. Peering carefully around the edge of the building, he saw it, and his blood ran cold.

It was taller than a man, and more slender. Its skin was leathery and mottled in the pale light of the moons. Its body was hairless, and draped in the tattered remnants of the kind of garment Nessar had just seen. Wide, pale eyes without pupils stared out of a nightmare face. It looked as though it had once been made of wax, then sat too close to a flame for too long. Its features seemed to be sliding down its skull. Its mouth was open and far too large, and even from far away, Nessar could see its pointed, jagged teeth. Long spindly arms ended in sharp, bony claws, its fingers far longer than normal. It was carrying something in one hand, something about as long as Nessar's arm, though he could not quite make out what it was. The thing shuffled forward on bony legs and bare feet that were gnarled and misshapen. Every so often, it raised the item it held to its mouth and tore a great chunk out of it with its teeth.

Cripes! That's not good. Nope. He watched the silent creature as it approached. It did not see him and the thief awakened the power of his Jidaan to be absolutely certain that he escaped its awareness. The magick within him rumbled and moved, calling to the Jidaan. It answered immediately and Nessar suddenly vanished. The creature approached, staying in the middle of the gravel street and passed by without even glancing at Nessar's hiding place in the alley. It kept walking, lumbering along as though it had no particular place to go.

Remaining hidden beneath the cloaking power of his Jidaan, Nessar kept a watchful eye on the creature as it moved away from him. He had finally seen that the creature was chewing on some poor soul's arm. *Something tells me I need to avoid those things. They don't exactly seem friendly.*

He wondered about the creatures. He had never seen anything like them, nor even heard of anything similar. And it was wearing a tattered toga, as though it had once been human. Nessar dwelled on that thought as he carefully peered around the corner, checking on the creature's progress. It had kept walking and was several buildings away, and Nessar judged it safe to cross the street. He stopped the flow of power to his Jidaan and it responded, allowing him to be seen and heard again.

The instant he stepped out of the shadows, the nausea and crawling sensation hit him hard again, nearly driving him to a knee. He stumbled, one foot catching in the loose gravel, but then quickly righted himself as he continued into the shadowy alley on the far side. As soon as he escaped the light of the moons above, the queasiness and disorientation passed, and Nessar paused to catch his breath.

Immediately, he heard an unearthly screech from the monster that had passed by. Hasty footsteps in the crushed stone of the road alerted Nessar. The thing had heard him and was coming back to investigate.

Again, Nessar invoked his Gift and vanished from sight. In that same moment, the beast stormed into the alley and passed Nessar without a single glance. It hurried a few more steps, then stopped, confused. It seemed to sniff the air for a few moments, making wet snuffling sounds. Another beast entered from the far side of the alley and the first creature hissed at it. It hissed back, though it did not come any closer. The creatures looked around the empty passageway and, finding nothing, each turned to leave. As they lumbered away, Nessar stayed cloaked, not willing to take chances. He waited for a full minute for them to move away before he allowed himself to relax his Gift once more.

Those things were real people once. What could have changed them?

His gaze was drawn upwards. He leaned out from under the overhang he had been hiding under and the light from the moons above hit him. Immediately, he felt sick. His skin started to crawl and itch everywhere the light fell upon it, and he quickly pulled himself back into the shadows.

Right. It's got to be the light of those Helsbegotten moons up there. Not that I know how they can do that, but playing it safe sounds like a good idea.

Nessar reached into one of his many pockets and found a small tin. He opened it, dipped a finger into its contents, and began to smear the black substance liberally over his fingers, hands and wrists, then on his forehead and around his eyes. Checking his face in a tiny mirror he pulled from another pocket, he nodded, satisfied, then stowed the tin and mirror away again. Moving as quietly as he could, Nessar drew his dagger and cut wide strips from the bottom of his cloak. He wrapped them carefully around his hands and wrists to shield as much of his body from the harmful light as possible, then wrapped a bigger piece of cloth around his face and neck before casting his hood over his head. He fished a piece of twine out of one pocket and used it to secure the hood more tightly so that it would not fall off during any of his more dynamic movements.

Satisfied that he had done all he could to protect himself, Nessar took a few more deep breaths, tried to clear his mind, and stepped out into the light once more. He was pleased to discover that he felt all right. He had relied on his own special blend of camouflage paint for decades, and it seemed to be thick enough to prevent the eerie light from harming him. *All right, then. Let's get on with this. It'll be easy-peasy,* he thought as he crossed the next street, moving deftly from shadow to shadow. He deduced that staring at the moons was not a good idea, and now that he was otherwise immune, his movements were strong and sure. *This is my kind of game. I've got this.*

The city was eerie in the pale moonlight, everything shaded in dark hues of deep purple and indigo from the orbs overhead. Nessar pressed himself against the wall of a small structure, pausing for a moment to look up at the two shining satellites again. He realized he was no longer in the Realm of his birth, not even on the world of Talwynn. The earth beneath his feet was much the same as he had trod his entire life, but the sky above was certainly not. Black clouds drifted among the stars, and Nessar watched some large ones heading towards the moons.

He thought back to a time before all this, before he had been Chosen. Nessar silently snorted as he remembered how hopeless, how pointless everything had seemed. He had been inducted into the Thieves Guild in Rualtha in his early teens. He had worked his way up through the ranks to become Guildmaster, only to find that the politics were just as cutthroat among the thieves as the nobles. Challenged repeatedly by subordinates who showed no respect for his authority, asserting that he was a washed up and useless old man, Nessar had slowly come to believe them.

The moment the clouds shaded the city from the glow of the moons, the old thief flexed his long legs and jumped lightly up to the nearest rooftop, using his magick just as Brunar and Layton had taught him, adding a flip just because he could. Carefully timing how long the deeper darkness would last, Nessar raced along what he had known as the Thieves Highway back in Rualtha, deftly moving from roof to roof, making almost no sound. After seeing the aggressive creatures that roamed the streets preying on the frozen citizens of Linbourne, he wanted to make the most of the shadows to remain undiscovered. His magick flowed through him as he leapt across wide gaps and danced along the tiles high above the ground. He felt like a lad of twenty again.

Washed up, indeed! he snickered to himself as he ran. *I can do this all day!* Nessar ran and jumped and twisted and flipped, all the while drawing nearer to the great domed palace up ahead. He caught sight of more creatures roaming the alleys and streets below. He saw one of them carry the frozen form of a man out into the street, only to tear into his helpless body a moment later. Other creatures howled and came running, swarming over the body until each of them had a hunk of meat to eat. Nessar grimaced at the grisly sight, but kept moving.

Soon, Nessar ran out of rooftops, and skidded to a stop before he fell out into empty space. Gripping the edge of the roof with both hands, he slowly flipped over and lowered his feet until they were close to the ground before letting go. He dropped quietly to the earth below and hugged the wall just as the misshapen moon burst free of the blanket of clouds above. Its odd light shone down on the wide open space between Nessar and the fifteen foot high wall that surrounded the palace. It was a clearly defined killing ground. Nothing could get across the expanse without being seen by sentries posted on the wall above. He doubted any of the beasts he had seen would have the forethought to patrol atop the walls, but he always felt it was better to be safe than dead.

Nessar eyed the wall and looked along its length to the left and right. The main gate was not in sight in either direction, but a guard tower was close by. He grinned. Fortunately, the clouds were plentiful. They moved fast, so the shadows they provided were fleeting, but he didn't need much time. Nessar waited until the glow of the moons was blocked once more, then he leaped nimbly back up onto the rooftop and ran across the neighboring roofs until he was directly across from the tower. From an inside pocket, he pulled a small coil of slender rope with a blackened metal grappling hook attached to one end. Both were Weya made, and had cost him dearly many years ago. They were lightweight, but nearly indestructible. Standing tall, he whirled the hook a few times around his head to gain momentum and flung it towards the guard tower. The moment he let go, he could tell that it was not going to fly far enough.

Concentrating, Nessar extended his right hand and reached out with his magick. It churned within him, answering his call instantly, flowing through his outstretched arm and extending away from him until it enveloped the grappling hook. Carefully, Nessar lifted the hook across the space until it reached the guard tower. He dropped the hook over the railing and pulled on the rope to make certain it was secure. Releasing his magick, Nessar hauled back on the rope to take up the slack. The line had a bit of stretch to it, and he pulled it to its limit before tying it to a small stone chimney that jutted out of the roof nearby. Nessar looked up at the moon and noticed that the clouds were about to thin out, allowing the moonlight to shine down once again.

No matter, the old thief thought with a grin. *If any of those things are in there, they'll never see me coming.*

Just as the city brightened under the moons' light, Nessar called to his Jidaan, awakening it so that he could use its Gift of Stealth. In that instant, the old man vanished completely. Cloaked by the Jidaan's power, he stepped on the slender line with first one booted foot, then the other, quickly finding his balance. He suddenly wished he had brought his catburglar boots with their soft soles and quiet tread, but he'd made do without them before. One foot after the other, almost at a fast walk, Nessar made his way across the line. *Glad I'm not afraid of heights,* he thought to himself as he glimpsed the cobblestones far below. At that height, an ordinary thief would be dead if he slipped. But Nessar was no longer an ordinary thief. He was a Guardian. *Albeit a slightly old and shady one,* he mused.

It took only a few seconds for him to reach the guard tower, and he dropped lightly behind the wall. He looked down at the courtyard and saw no one. Kneeling in the shadows again, he willed the Jidaan into quiescence once more. A crooked smile crossed his face as he remembered being in the woods with Kiran after the shipwreck of the *Damsel*. Back then, a single use of his Jidaan in order to sneak up on a small band of thugs had rendered him senseless with exhaustion. Had Kiran not been there, he would have been at their mercy, which would most certainly not have ended well.

Since then Nessar had practiced at every available opportunity, almost always when no one was looking. He had come to delight in disappearing and reappearing moments later before anyone even knew what he was doing. During their ride to Laro, he had spent many nights on watch engaging his Gift, practicing, slowly growing stronger and more adept in its use. He had begun to experiment as well, finding other uses for his Gift that had not initially occurred to him. He never saw the need to share this fact with the others; it was simply something he needed to do. He had improved vastly in his abilities, and as far as he knew, he was the only one aware of that fact. Which was exactly how he liked it.

As he rested, his eyes roved over the grounds, and he had to admit that the Linbourne Castle was impressive. The main tower was off to his left, topped in a massive dome that might have been beautiful in the sunlight. It was a wide, squat structure that dwarfed the buildings on either side. The keep was the tallest structure within the walls, and the smaller buildings spread outward from it in a diminishing crescent that partially encircled a huge courtyard in the center. Nessar could see the main gates far away to his right, massively ornate doors that seemed sturdy enough to keep out an elephant. *Or an Ogre,* Nessar thought.

There were windows aplenty that Nessar could see, though they were all shuttered, and several doors as well. He guessed he was looking at the utility entrances.

Perfect, he thought with a grin. He knew his way around the back rooms of a castle.

A set of stairs led down from the guard tower and into the courtyard below. It was mostly in shadow, so Nessar made his way down to the bottom and picked an entrance to try. It was a huge set of double doors with a small ramp leading up to them. Carefully and quietly, he slipped across the courtyard towards them. He watched for any signs of movement, but saw none. When he reached the doors, he put a hand on the lockpicks at his belt, then thought better of it. Avoiding the handles, he pushed gently on one door and was rewarded when it opened inwards with only a slight creak of hinges. Nessar slipped inside.

Once the door closed behind him, Nessar stood quietly in the dark, letting his eyes adjust to the deeper shadows inside the castle. Gradually, shapes started to resolve into recognizable objects. He could faintly see that he had stepped into a storage room with boxes, crates, and barrels lined up neatly in rows against one wall. A desk and chairs was pushed up against the wall to Nessar's left; a man was seated there.

The man sat as he had for centuries. A fork bearing a small piece of meat was lifted halfway to his open mouth in one hand while the other was still holding a small goblet. He wore the same kind of wrap that Nessar had seen in the town's other immobile denizens, and looked to be a young fellow in his twenties. A wide doorway stood opposite him, and Nessar crossed over to it. As he passed the dining man, Nessar felt his stomach growl.

A thousand years has passed since that meal was served; nothing on that plate could be good anymore. A slight chill passed along his spine as he idly thought of eating anything from the man's meal, but he shook it off and kept moving.

The doorway led to a wide hallway that branched off to his left, with other doorways leading to unseen rooms on either side. Some had doors that were closed, while others either stood open or had no doors at all. Here and there, Nessar saw more of the frozen citizens of Linbourne, everyone from servants in meager togas to guards in leather kilts and bronze breastplates with short stabbing swords at their waists. All of them seemed startled, their faces turned slightly to look down the hallway. Nessar guessed that the corridor most likely led towards the main building. *Whatever happened here probably originated there,* he thought. The floor was clean of dust and he saw no footprints. The air was still as a tomb, and just as silent. Nessar used all of his skills to keep it that way as he moved noiselessly down the hall, dodging the immobile figures wherever he found them.

An ancient city lifted to another place where the light of the moons (moons, I say!) turns normal people into hideous monsters, everyone else frozen for centuries...I don't like this. Nope, not at all. Nessar touched the long dagger at his belt and ran his fingers over the smaller throwing knives he had brought. They reassured him in a way the Jidaan could not. He knew how to use the long-bladed weapon well enough after weeks of training with Brunar and Layton, but he'd been throwing knives for decades, and he'd much rather neutralize an attacker with a dagger in the eye from a distance if at all possible. He thought about the huge, shambling creatures he had seen and hoped that one blade in their awful bulbous eyes would suffice.

Finally, he reached the end of the long hallway. It ended in a massive pair of double doors and branched off to either side, skirting the edges of the huge, round chamber. A great stairwell led upwards on Nessar's left, though he ignored it for the moment, choosing instead to concentrate on the double doors. Two armed guards stood there with spears in their hands and swords on their hips, but they were as frozen as everyone else. Both were caught in the act of turning towards the doors when time had stopped for them.

Nessar pressed his ear against a door and listened carefully for a few moments. He heard nothing, but there was a strong feeling of pressure that pricked Nessar's senses. It was very similar to the feeling he often got when Brunar had invoked his own magick during the battle of Laro. That piqued Nessar's curiousity.

If there is some kind of superpowered magickal amulet, I'd bet it could cause a disturbance like this, he thought to himself. *I can't detect any movement, but there's definitely something going on behind these doors.* He pushed gently on the wooden portals. They were solid and very heavy, and they were locked. Peering from side to side again and noting that the guards had not moved, Nessar knelt at the big keyhole and pulled out his set of lockpicks.

The ancient lock clicked open in half a minute, and Nessar grinned in the darkness. *Yep, I've still got it.* Guessing that this was an audience hall or other important chamber, he decided a little extra insurance was warranted. Just because most of the people he had seen had been frozen did not mean that they all were. For all he knew, the room beyond the doors had a giant hole in the roof that allowed the moonlight to corrupt and change everyone inside, leaving a score of vicious monsters to await him.

He carefully pulled a tiny vial of oil out of one pocket and affixed a slender, needlelike attachment on the opened end. He moved quickly to the edges of one door and was relieved to see that it was not flush with the stone walls alongside. He carefully reached the thin spout through the crack and applied oil liberally to the hinges on the far side. He repeated the process with all four hinges and then stowed the vial and spout away again.

Nessar moved back to the middle of the double doors and took a deep breath, then let it out. He engaged the magick in his Jidaan, rendering himself completely invisible and silent, then gently pressed on the leftmost door. Soundlessly, it swung inward just enough to admit him, and he slipped inside.

Beneath the cloak of Stealth that his Jidaan wove about his body, Nessar's mouth dropped open in surprise as he entered the huge circular chamber. The pressure he had felt from outside the doors was much stronger here, and the air felt thick with magick. A deep purple light blazed from the center of the room, illuminating scores of figures. There were nearly fifty people, all frozen in time as the others had been. Some were seated in pews that resembled those in a church while others had individual chairs. There was a circular dais off-center in the room, and there was an ornate throne upon it. Everyone was staring at the source of the light, their faces stretched in horror and many hands thrown up as if to defend against an attacker. On the throne, a wiry, crazed looking man sat, his crown sitting crookedly on his head. He was recoiling from the scene, shielding his snarling face with one arm.

Nessar peered into the violet glow. He could just make out the form of a man in sorcerer's robes reclining on the flagstones. He was pushing himself up off of the floor with one hand while the other stretched toward the dais in an angry claw. The man was seemingly oblivious to the half dozen arrows that protruded from his torso. Nessar looked around to see six guards with bows still in hand also shielding their eyes with upthrown arms.

It looks like you got doublecrossed, there, Wendall, Nessar thought as he stared at the sorcerer on the floor. *That's what you get when you deal with crazy kings. Tough break.*

Nessar turned his gaze towards the king, presumably King Lareno. He caught sight of something that twinkled in the King's right hand, something he was clutching quite tightly.

The old thief smiled broadly.

Taking care not to touch any of the frozen forms around him, Nessar made his way up to the dais. He mounted the steps slowly, keeping a careful eye out for any movement. He knew he could not be seen or heard as long as he used the power of his Jidaan, but he also knew that his ability to use it was limited. He would pass out soon if he stayed cloaked for too long.

A few more steps brought him face to face with the ancient king. Nessar looked into his wide staring eyes and saw naught but anger and madness frozen there. It sent another chill down his spine to look at the man, his teeth bared in an animal snarl, frozen forever in the moment of betrayal. The glint Nessar had seen in his hand was a fist-sized medallion with a huge gemstone in the center. Moving with extreme care and precision, Nessar reached one steady hand towards the amulet.

The instant his magickally cloaked fingers touched the cold metal, a thunderclap exploded, its power hurling Nessar's body across the room. With an impact that drove the air from his lungs, he slammed into the far wall and slid down to the floor, momentarily blinded and dazed. Pain shot through his battered body, and he gasped for breath as he struggled to his hands and knees. He shook his head to clear it.

Hel's bells...well, that didn't go quite as planned, Nessar thought, irritated. Movement in the room grabbed his attention and he turned to see what was going on. The eerie purple light had begun to ripple and pulse. As Nessar watched, the frozen figures all around the room started to move almost imperceptibly. The sorcerer on the floor slowly leaned forward, his mouth working as he strained one hand towards the figure on the throne, who recoiled even farther from the menacing gesture. All around him, men and women were reacting to the scene before them, but in extreme slow motion. As he watched, the figures began to gradually increase their speed. The pulsing light that came from the body of the dying sorcerer intensified, casting stark shadows on the walls of the circular chamber. A buzzing noise, at first low and menacing, became audible and the sense of magickal pressure increased exponentially. Whatever had been about to happen a thousand years ago was ramping up to finally come to its conclusion now, and the noise increased in pitch bit by bit as the pulsating light emanating from Wendall began to speed up.

Nessar's mind raced. What could have caused that powerful a reaction? Then he had it. *Whatever massive spell Wendall was throwing must have yanked the entire city out of space and time, until it hit the amulet. The spell has been continuously running all this time, held in stasis, while the amulet struggled to counteract it.* Keeping wide eyes on the slowly moving people of Linbourne, he struggled to his feet. *The power of the Jidaan must have shorted out that process somehow, and...great Goddess, Wendall's death curse is picking up right where it left off! I've got to get that thing and get out of here before that curse does whatever it was intended to do!*

Ignoring the sharp pains that shot through his body, Nessar dashed back to the dais. The movements of the people around him were slowly speeding up, and the thief guessed that they would likely be back to normal in moments. Nessar stopped before the king, this time avoiding the use of his Jidaan. He reached in and snatched the amulet away from the doomed ruler. It was cold and heavy in Nessar's hand, and he looked from it back to the king's crazed eyes. He saw them begin to widen in surprise as King Lareno perceived Nessar's presence, a man-sized blur in an already frenzied scene. Nessar held no pity for the man. From what he had discovered, the king had brought this on himself. It was a shame that his entire kingdom had suffered over a thousand years for his arrogance.

Nessar had no time to ruminate further on the fate of Linbourne. He knew he had to escape. Stuffing the amulet into one of his pockets, he ran for the double doors, hitting them with his shoulder and bursting into the hallway beyond. The guards ever so slowly turned in his direction, but he was already running back down the corridor. Somewhere up ahead, he heard the howls of the tall, misshapen creatures. He tried to engage his Gift as he ran, but found that the amulet completely absorbed any attempt to cloak himself. He would remain in full view of anyone or anything he encountered. A wave of magickal pressure rolled over his back as Wendall's spell gained momentum, nearly knocking him down. Struggling to stay on his feet, he ran straight towards the angry bellows of the hideous beasts ahead.

Wonderful, he thought. *Absolutely wonderful.*

Chapter 34

Gart guided Bessie along the trail, ducking his head every so often to avoid a low hanging branch. The road south wound through forested hills, and the birds sang their lovely songs all around him. The journey from Willowbranch had been uneventful thus far, but the farther he traveled, the more tense he became. He knew that he was drawing ever closer to the conflict described by Brunar. Although the message left by the Mage was months old, Gart knew that whatever had befallen the city of Laro would likely be happening all across the region, judging by the fate of his own home. The creatures that had destroyed his village had likely been on their way to join that force, since Tiller's Grove was to the East of Laro and Gart had pursued them west before they turned to attack him.

He had barely survived. Battered and knocked unconscious, a Weya had inexplicably carried him away from the road and thrown him into the Lake of Whispered Sorrows, where he was tended by the spirit of the lake, the Lady RaeLynn. She had helped him and set him on the path to the Choosing, the claiming of his Jidaan. It was his now, and although he was still learning its ways, he was prepared to do all he could to stop the evil that was spreading across the Realm. Killing Jor Dayne and Mordak would just be a bonus.

His thoughts wandered for a time as Bessie steadily plodded forward. She had been the only horse available in the little town where he had bought her, but she had been steadfast and dependable, even in combat, and Gart was well pleased with her. He patted her neck at the thought. "Good girl, Bessie. Keep it up, we might just survive all this."

Just then the sounds of voices reached Gart, and he sat up straight in his saddle, listening. The road twisted and turned, so he could not see anyone, but their voices were becoming clearer as he approached. There were at least two people, arguing noisily. An old woman's raspy tone was loud enough that he could hear her clearly.

"Mine! It's mine! You can't have it! Leave an old woman alone."

Coarse laughter was the immediate answer. Though Gart couldn't make out what was said in return, it was obviously a man, probably two of them. There was a muted thump and a cry of pain from the woman, followed by more laughter. Gart frowned and kicked Bessie into a trot. If it was anything like it sounded, then Gart was not happy. *Of course,* he mused, *it could be a trap.* He shrugged at the thought. He'd been through that before, and had come out just fine. A grim smile played at the corner of his lips as he rounded the next bend in the road. He'd had more than a full share of stress and frustration lately, and he found himself welcoming something as simple as a couple of road bandits.

He was not disappointed. As the owners of the voices came into view down the road, Gart saw an elderly woman crawling in the dirt, her wispy hair flying in several directions as she struggled towards the two men who stood just out of her reach. They were still chuckling as they rifled through a large rucksack, presumably belonging to the woman.

The two men looked up at Gart, their faces registering surprise. One man, slightly larger than the other, handed the rucksack to his companion. "This ain't none of your affair, so keep on riding, mister."

Gart silently glared at them from the shadows of his hat and reined Bessie to a halt. He sat there for a moment, unmoving, letting the silence grow. The old woman crawled closer to the men and reached one clawed hand towards the rucksack, mumbling as she did so. "Give it back. No right to take it. Mine." The nearest of the two bandits raised a boot to kick her.

"Stop." Gart said, his voice as icy as his piercing blue gaze. The man's boot hovered in the air for a moment, then he settled it back to the ground. Gart continued, "If you give the lady back her bag and move along, I'll let it go."

The two men looked at Gart, then at each other, then burst out laughing. The first man said, "Well sir, there are two of us and only one of you. I'd say the odds are in our favor, don't you think?" He pulled his sword out of its scabbard while the other man slung the stolen rucksack over one shoulder and produced a long, rusty dagger from his belt. They began to spread out, moving so that they could attack Gart from either side.

Gart watched them for a moment, then reached out with his magick. It had been roiling inside him, eager to be used, and he directed two tendrils of power at the men. For the first time, he noticed a subtle golden glow, almost invisible in the sunlight; he could actually see his magick manifested as he used it. The translucent, misty ropes of magick reached for the men and latched on to their weapons. Gart pushed more energy along the links he had created, and imagined the steel in the ruffians' hands becoming warm, then hot, and hotter still. The men screamed and dropped their weapons, holding and shaking their burned hands, and Gart smiled. He slid out of the saddle and unsheathed his Jidaan, its Weya-forged blade shining in the morning sun, its emerald blazing green fire in its pommel. He had no intention of using it on the two men, but they did not know that, and Gart was rewarded by their frightened stares. Gart laid the weapon nonchalantly on his shoulder and walked to the old woman. Keeping his eye on the two men, he knelt at her side, his voice calm and soothing.

"Are you all right, old mother?"

"They have my bag!" she cried, her voice as brittle as old parchment. Her breath rattled in her lungs and Gart thought she might pass out. "It's mine!"

"There now, it's all right. I'll get it for you; just calm down." He gently patted her on the shoulder and she clutched at his hand, murmuring her thanks. Gart stood and faced the men, who were still holding their burned hands in front of them. He tilted his hat back on his head to be sure that they got a good look at his scarred face. He saw their eyes widen at the sight of him. "Last chance. Leave the bag and go. I've had a rough week, and I'm nearing the end of my patience."

Without warning, an arrow embedded itself in Gart's thigh, the impact nearly knocking him down. He grunted in pain and clutched at the arrow. It was deep. Through the blinding haze of agony that engulfed him, Gart looked across the road to see a third man stepping out of the trees to join the others. He was lowering a short, curved bow and sneering beneath a set of long mustaches. The other men, still in pain and afraid, looked wide-eyed from him to Gart and back again.

His magick lashing like a whip, Gart reached out and grabbed the first ruffian's fallen sword. Before the archer could say a word, Gart whipped the sword at the man, embedding the blade in the center of his chest with a meaty *thunk*. A startled expression slowly dawned on his face and then he slumped to the ground, his face forever frozen in surprise. Gart reached down and wiggled the arrow enough that he could pull it out, though he nearly passed out from the pain. Taking deep breaths to steady himself, Gart discarded the bloody shaft and managed to stand up straight. He stared intensely at the two men, who peered fearfully back at him. Struggling to keep his voice even, he grated, "I have officially reached the end of my patience."

The two men bolted past Bessie, leaving the rucksack in a heap in the road. Gart listened intently and was satisfied to hear their running footsteps heading off into the distance without slowing. He shook his head. *Idiots.* He glanced at the body of the dead thug in the dirt nearby, the sword sticking up out of his chest. Using his magick again, he picked up the body and hurled it into the nearby woods, out of sight. Moving very deliberately, he sheathed his Jidaan in its scabbard at his back. Limping badly, he made his way to the rucksack and picked it up.

"Here," he grunted to the old woman, who had finally managed to regain her feet. He presented the rucksack to her and she snatched it out of his hands.

"Thank you, sir! Rowann's blessings upon you for helping an old woman. Thank you!" She opened up the sack and began to paw around inside it.

Gart's head had begun to pound and a rushing sound was in his ears. The pain in his thigh had spread and his entire leg was throbbing. "You're welcome, old mother." He stopped for a moment, his words starting to become jumbled in his mind. As he pondered what he was going to say next he suddenly realized that he had somehow ended up on the ground, looking up into a remarkably clear blue sky. Wispy clouds drifted by in their lazy travels overhead, and Gart felt a sense of peace as he watched them. Then a wrinkled face obscured his vision as the old woman leaned over him.

"Poison!" her rattling voice filtered through the fog in Gart's mind. "Must be. A filthy poisoned arrow!"

Poison, again, Gart thought to himself in disgust as the crone's words filtered through the deepening fog in his mind. *Wonderful.* And then the darkness claimed him completely.

Chapter 35

"He's gone!" Kiran blurted.

Layton stared at Nessar's empty saddle in shock. The old man had been riding right between them only a moment ago, and now he simply was not there.

"He could be using his Jidaan to cloak himself, but why?" Layton mused.

Kiran immediately pulled out her sword and swung the flat of it through the air where Nessar would have been. Layton winced, thinking Kiran would surely hit the old man, hidden beneath the magickal cloaking power of his Jidaan, but her blade passed through empty air. Grimacing, she slid it back into its sheath. "Nope. His Gift of Stealth makes him silent and unseen, but his body would still be there. He's not here anymore. Damn that old geezer, getting himself ganked off to who knows where..." Her eyes narrowed as she searched the empty plain for her old friend.

Layton spurred his horse forward and caught the reins of Nessar's mount. "I'll go tether his horse, then we can scout the area." He frowned as he looked out over the empty land before them. "Somehow, though, I don't think we'll find a whole lot of anything. This place is so flat and barren, we can practically see all of it from here." He led the riderless horse back to one of the stones that made up part of the ancient wall and dropped lightly down to the ground, tying off the reins so the beast would not wander off. Leading his own mount, he walked over to Kiran, who was still in her saddle. He looked up at her as he patted her horse's neck with his free hand. It leaned into him, obviously enjoying his attention. "Where do you think he went?"

Kiran scowled down at him. "I don't know, and that's got my dander up." She looked back at the huge plot of land, noting its oddly uniform, flat surface. "Hey, could you do that thing you do? To look down from up high with your Gates?"

Layton remounted his horse and nodded. "Sure. You want to do it?"

Kiran was surprised. "Me? What?"

Layton smiled. "Sure, it's easy. Look, when the Gate appears next to you, just lean into it. You can't fall; you'll still be sitting on your horse. Think of it as if you're looking out a window, and you'll be fine." The pommel of his Jidaan suddenly flared into life and a window-sized, opalescent square of energy appeared alongside Kiran, close enough for her to touch. She gasped in surprise, then coughed loudly in embarrassment to cover herself.

Kiran stared at the swirling colors in the Gate, its flat surface mere inches from her face. She took a deep breath and held it, then squeezed her eyes shut and leaned into the Gate. A cold breeze instantly caressed her face and blew her hair around. She opened her eyes and discovered that it was, indeed, like leaning out of a window...if the window was high in the air without a wall around it. She let out the breath she was holding as she recovered her composure. She scanned the area from her lofty vantage point, amazed at how much she could see.

Directly below, she could see the rest of herself, sitting on her horse with what appeared to be only half a body, the missing part seemingly cut away as if by a razor. She knew that was where the Gate existed, magickally transporting the rest of her elsewhere. Layton's upturned face revealed his wide grin, even from that distance, and Kiran reached out with one hand down below to smack him in the arm. Up in the clouds, she heard his exaggerated yelp of pain through the Gate as though he were right behind her. As concerned as she was about finding Nessar, she couldn't stifle a laugh.

"Yes, I know. It's exhilarating up there! Now look around and tell me what you see," Layton suggested, his words floating through the Gate to Kiran's ears. She scanned the land below for a full minute, then pulled her head back through the Gate. Layton allowed the magickal portal to disappear, and his Jidaan dimmed to quiescence. "Well? Anything?"

"As much as I hate to say so, that was amazing," Kiran grudgingly admitted.

Layton's boyish smile lit up his face. "I know, right?" He turned and surveyed the area yet again as he continued. "I'm still learning how to use the Gates. I feel like a baby compared to the rest of you, but some of the things I've figured out have been kind of exciting. Granted, we're all learning under fire, so I don't have much time to be thrilled about this stuff. I'm just happy it helps me stay alive so I can keep fighting."

Kiran cocked an eyebrow at him in irritation. She was surprised that he didn't sound more confident about his abilities. She thought it sounded like false modesty, which she hated. In her eyes, Layton's almost constant use of his Gates had set him far above her in terms of what he could do. Surely he knew that. "Seriously? A baby? You've been Gating around like crazy for weeks like you've been doing it all your life. You're the one who makes me look like a kid who just picked up a sword for the first time!"

Layton turned back to her with an expression so shocked she nearly laughed in surprise. "After that thing you did with the Ogres? And the wall that smashed Jor Dayne senseless and held the horde at bay until everyone could evacuate? Hey, that was incredible to watch. I'm basically just a hornet that stings a few here and a few there. What you did was really important! You saved hundreds of lives!"

Kiran searched his face for any signs that he was pulling her leg. She was certainly not used to anyone singing her praises. More often, every soldier, thug, guardsman, and idiot she met would question her abilities just because she was a woman. She'd spent the better part of her adult life proving herself again and again and again, and had initially thought that Layton was merely patronizing her. She was uncomfortable with his compliments, but could hear the ring of truth in his words. Moreover, she could feel his sincerity through her magickally enhanced senses. He was telling the truth.

"Well...thanks." Kiran looked away and abruptly changed the subject. "There's no sign of anyone other than ourselves. It's peculiar; I can see exactly where the city must have been. There's a big, circular patch of dead earth where it used to be. I could see other roads leading up to it, and fields farther out that looked like they might have been farmed long ago, but it's as though the whole thing was just scooped up and then...I don't know, *taken* somewhere. I don't know how you could do that to a whole city, but that's what it looks like to me."

Layton could feel her momentary agitation, but shrugged to himself. He highly respected Kiran, and if she wanted to focus on the task at hand, he was happy to do the same. "That's pretty much what it looks like from down here, too," he said, agreeing. "Brunar was pretty cryptic about the whole thing, but only because he didn't know that much himself. If I remember correctly, some wizard had made the amulet for the king, and thought the king might double cross him somehow. The other wizard who had received his letter apparently thought that something had happened, since there was no communication from Linbourne after that. Judging by this," the young warrior gestured at the barren site with one hand, "he was right."

Kiran cursed loudly, making Layton wince. She was frustrated and angry, not to mention concerned for her old friend's welfare. "Well, Nessar had to go *somewhere*. There's definitely magick at work. I can feel it; it's making me itch inside the longer we stay around here."

Layton nodded. "Yes, I feel it too. It took a while for me to realize that's what I felt, but whatever happened to the city a thousand years ago is either still happening or it was so powerful that echoes of it are still affecting this place. That's probably what happened to Nessar. He went wherever the city went, though I have no idea why it took him and not all three of us."

Kiran merely grunted in reply. "Well, let's walk the area and see if we can shake anything loose. I'm not sure what else we can do other than hope to Rowann that he reappears somehow."

"Fine by me. That's better than just sitting here, I guess." Layton gently nudged his horse forward and Kiran did the same. They angled off to their right and began following the border between the dead space that had formerly been occupied by the city and the green grass and shrubbery of the still-living land beyond.

As they rode, the crawling sensation within each of them became more and more noticeable. It was an uncomfortable feeling, but it leveled out after a while and did not affect them further. Kiran thought back to their entry to the city, when Nessar had immediately felt that something was off. She guessed he had simply been the most sensitive of the three of them, as he had felt the magickal resonance much more intensely.

After they had ridden a crisscross pattern over the entire area and found nothing, they wandered back to the broken archway where they had left Nessar's horse. The animal stood calmly, cropping grass on the far side of the city's border. Kiran and Layton got down and tied off their own horses, then sat down in the meager shade of the nearest tree. Layton wasted no time in pulling out some of his rations for a late lunch. He offered some to Kiran, but she refused with a curt shake of her head as she stood and began pacing anxiously, one hand toying with the hilt of her sword. Layton shrugged to himself, then started eating without her. He knew Kiran would eat when she was ready and decided not to push her.

Indeed, Kiran was quite worried about the old man. He had been more like a father to her than anyone she had ever known. Through all the rough times in her life, she could count on Nessar to be there to support her. He always had something wise to say, and had no problem saying it, even if he knew she would not want to listen. Sometimes, he irritated her beyond belief. Yet underneath it all, she could feel his love. The gnarled old man knew her better than anyone alive, and in her heart of hearts, she wished that he actually was her father. Now the damned fool had gotten himself into the thick of it, and there was nothing she could do to help. It was immensely frustrating. A tear slid down her face as years of memories crossed through her mind, and she angrily wiped it away before Layton saw it. She folded her arms tightly and stared out at the desolate area where Linbourne should have been, wracking her brain to think of a way to get Nessar back.

Layton saw her gazing at the empty land and spoke up. "All right, good. Keep a sharp eye out for Nessar in case he returns. I'm going to go catch us a rabbit or something."

Irritated, Kiran spoke over her shoulder at the young warrior. "Didn't you just eat?"

She didn't see his grin, but heard it in his voice. "Of course! That never stopped me from hunting before. Besides, I'd rather do it now before I'm all cranky from hunger after exhausting our supplies."

Kiran had to admit that he had a point. "All right then. I'll keep watch here. He might need me."

Layton could feel the anxiety behind her tightly controlled words. He wanted to comfort her, but by now he knew she would probably not welcome his attempts to do so. He sighed quietly, then awakened his Jidaan and stepped through a Gate, emerging at the edge of a nearby forest they had passed on their way into the valley.

He had always liked Kiran, though she had generally been standoffish with him. *She's been standoffish with pretty much everyone,* he thought. What little she had said of her past implied that she had scarcely any reason to be warm and friendly. He sighed again, wishing there was some way he could break through her walls, if only to let a little light in.

Back at camp, Kiran finally turned away from the barren patch of earth and dug through her pack. She looked around carefully to see that Layton was nowhere near before reaching into an inner pocket of her rucksack and pulling out a small flute. It was made of wood, and slightly shorter than her forearm. Its surface was smooth and unadorned, and the holes running along its length were carefully spaced.

Kiran looked around again to be sure that she was alone, then seated herself on a nearby rock that afforded her a clear view of the area. Frustration and worry had her mind all ajumble, and she did not like that feeling one bit. Carefully situating her fingers on the holes, she held the instrument up to her chin and played a single, clear note. The horses pricked up their ears at the sound, but calmed immediately as the music reached their hearts.

It had been a long time since she had played. Indeed, no one other than Nessar knew that she even owned a flute. She was embarrassed that she played and did not want anyone to find out, but she also had a desire to keep something for herself that was no one else's, just hers. Music was a deeply private thing for Kiran, and she guarded it with extreme care.

As always, the flute felt right in her hands and the music soothed her. She began a simple melody, her fingers expertly moving from note to note as she began to focus on the sensations of breathing and playing. The song started with sweet, low tones and gradually moved into a higher register. Soon, Kiran had lost herself in the music, an old and melancholy tune that both expressed her sorrow and brought her comfort. She had learned it from her mother when she was a little girl, and it had become part of her over the years. For long minutes she played, gaining confidence as she went, her hands and body remembering how to coax the stunningly beautiful music from the simple instrument. Finally, the song reached its end, and Kiran lowered the flute to her lap, her soul settled at last.

"That...that was beautiful," Layton said from behind her.

She stood with a gasp, immediately furious that he had snuck up on her. She instinctively hid the flute behind her back, though it was obvious that Layton had already seen it. She was about to launch into an angry tirade, intending to punish the young warrior for invading her privacy when she got a good look at his face. He was crying.

"Well, what's the matter with you? Never heard somebody play the flute before?" Her anger stopped in its tracks as she saw him standing there, holding a pair of rabbits in one hand, his Jidaan in the other, with tears still streaming down his face. He stood there for a few moments before he managed to regain his composure.

"I have...but not like that. Never like that." He slid his Jidaan into its scabbard at his back and used his sleeve to wipe his face, embarrassed. "I'm sorry. I didn't mean to sneak up on you. I just popped back here from the forest; I didn't know you would be sitting right there." Still visibly moved, Layton walked into the shade of the tree and squatted down to dress the rabbits. He drew his dagger and got to work. Shaking his head, he said, "That was...that was beautiful."

Kiran was angrily stowing the flute away in her backpack again, but his words stopped her. For a moment, she said nothing as her embarrassment at being caught battled with her curiousity. *Did he really think it was beautiful?* she thought. She had never allowed anyone to hear her, not since she was a child. Layton had never once lied to her about anything. Indeed, he had never been anything but supportive and good-natured towards her. She decided to take a chance for once.

"I don't play for anyone," she said, her eyes narrowed as she regarded the young man.

"I've never heard anything like that, Kiran, and I've been around. I've been a bodyguard for more than one pretentious noble, and I've heard minstrels and bards aplenty. Not one of them could touch what you just played. What was it called?" He deftly skinned the rabbits as he spoke.

Still wary, Kiran closed up her backpack and walked back to sit on the stone again, flute in hand. "Autumn's Lament," she answered. "I never learned the words. It's hard to play flute and sing at the same time."

"Ha!" Layton laughed briefly. "I bet it is, at that. I can't do either. I can't carry a tune in a bucket." He cleaned his knife and put the rabbit meat away, then sat back on his heels and looked at her. "Kiran, that was seriously the most enchanting thing I've ever heard. I'm honored that you shared it with me, even if it was by accident." He paused, as if to make up his mind, then he forged ahead. "Could you teach me to play?"

Kiran's mouth dropped open. Of all the things she thought Layton might say, this hadn't crossed her mind. She blurted the first thing she could think of, and then immediately regretted it. "What, you never tried? You're such a master of everything, I would have thought you'd be able to play anything."

For the first time, Layton actually looked hurt by her words, and Kiran suddenly felt ashamed. Layton's voice was small as he spoke. "I wanted to, very much. I love music, I really do. But it was deemed 'unnecessary' by my teachers. My talent lay in movement, not music, is what they said. Over the years, I tried to play the lute, the drums, even the flute a few times, but it was useless. It's a complete mystery to me. I don't understand any of it at all. It's like trying to hold water in my hands; I can't grasp it." His hands clenched in unaccustomed frustration as he spoke.

Kiran listened, and then sat quietly for a time. She wondered what that would be like, to be unable to play her music, to be denied the one magick that she had ever really felt before being Chosen by the Jidaan. Without her music, she just wasn't complete. Even if she did not play for weeks at a time, she knew it was there, always waiting to comfort her. Layton, however skilled in the art of fighting, had been denied the simple human pleasure of making music. Her heart finally softened towards him.

"Maybe...maybe I could teach you," Kiran steeled herself, just in case he said something stupid, but she need not have worried. Layton's face brightened as though he had just received the greatest gift, and hope shone through his glistening eyes.

"Oh, would you? I'd really like that! I promise I'll do my best, though I think you'll be ready to throw me in a lake before too long."

The thought of tossing the Weaponsmaster in a lake for being a poor music student finally made her laugh, and the sound lifted Layton's heart.

"Well, I'll try and keep my cool while you get through the basics. Here, come sit next to me and I'll show you how to hold the thing properly."

Layton quickly complied, and they began a slow study of music. Kiran discovered that Layton was, indeed, very slow to learn. As the sun made its lazy way across the sky, she gradually helped him move from wheezy toots and squeaks to a few sustained tones that were somewhat recognizable. Although Kiran kept a close eye on the spot where Nessar had disappeared, she finally calmed down. She reassured herself that the old man was wily, skilled, and aided by the magick of a powerful weapon. If anyone could make it back from wherever he had gone, Nessar could.

Chapter 36

"Ghaaaahhh!" Jor Dayne bellowed in fury and frustration as another Gholan fell dead, an arrow standing out from the back of its misshapen head. The big half-daemon turned to peer into the night in an attempt to find the unseen archers that had been harrying his Gholans over the last few days. The squad of creatures that Mordak had magickally lifted over to his side had been able to make little progress in clearing a path over Bjarke's earthen barrier. Both Morcats and Gholans were excellent climbers, but the newly fallen earth and rock was far too steep and unstable to be clambered over by so many. Entire squads had already been lost to rockslides and falling boulders, so they had decided to try installing a huge series of climbing ropes to help them reach the valley. The almost constant attacks of the archers from Alverton Falls slowed them considerably.

Frustrated, Jor Dayne drew his sword and spurred his horse towards the western slope, from whence the arrow had come, just as he had a number of times before. A hundred Gholans skittered alongside him, all lusting for the taste of human flesh. They reached the slope and churned up and into the forest beyond, furiously searching for those that had been sniping at them. But, as always, the archers had melted away as if by magick. The wooded hills were more dense the farther up they went, and yet again, Jor Dayne's squad was thwarted by the terrain.

Suddenly, an excited yowling off to his left caught Jor Dayne's attention. He wheeled his horse in that direction, picking his way through the thick forest until he found the source of the caterwauling. Standing near three Gholan corpses was another of the little beasts, jumping up and down and pointing at a large copse of shrubbery next to a particularly steep part of the slope. Jor Dayne slid from his horse and moved closer to take a look; a crowd of Gholans and a handful of Morcats converged quietly on their location.

Using his sword to probe at the leafy shrubs, the huge man-daemon suddenly felt a gentle gust of cool air. He pushed his sword farther into the limbs and leaves, expecting to meet solid stone at some point, but the blade vanished all the way up to the hilt. Using his other hand, he reached out and grabbed the nearest limbs and pulled. The bushes came out of the ground easily to reveal a man-sized hole in the side of the mountain, leading away and down into darkness.

An arrow suddenly winged from the opening, striking him high in the chest. It pierced his chestplate and lodged in the thick pectoral muscle beneath. As he turned away from the impact to deal with the arrow, another zinged past him from deep within the tunnel, and another right after. With a sharp, savage movement, he snapped the arrow off as close to his breastplate as he could and discarded the broken shaft. Without a word, he reached out and grabbed the nearest Gholan by the neck, instantly choking off its sudden cry of alarm.

Holding the struggling creature up in front of him as a living shield, he turned back to the tunnel's opening only to be rewarded with another arrow that slammed into the Gholan's exposed back. It squirmed a moment longer before falling limp. A sly grin crossed Jor Dayne's face and his eyes gleamed bright yellow in the darkness.

"Well, it looks like it's time to go exploring! We may have just found our way into the valley!"

Chapter 37

The darkness was cool and soothing. Fragrant summer breezes brought the scents of the nearby forest wafting into the little camp, and Kiran breathed deeply. Layton had already taken his turn at watch and was sleeping soundly beneath the tree, one hand curled around the handle of his Jidaan, his other arm tucked under his head as a makeshift pillow. There had been nothing to see so far, but Kiran kept a sharp eye out anyway in the hopes that she would see Nessar again. Shifting to find a more comfortable position on the rock, she tried to stay positive and avoid falling into despair at the thought that he was gone forever. Where magick was involved, anything could happen. It took great effort for her to hold on to the tiny shred of optimism that kept her going.

She just could not think of a world without Nessar in it. Even when they had gone months without seeing each other because she was traveling as a mercenary or a caravan guard, his presence always seemed to be close by. A much younger Kiran, an orphan well shy of ten years old, had been snatched from the market by two men who were up to no good. They had managed to get her into the shadows of an alley, where she fought them tooth and nail, bloodying them both. She had nearly escaped the pair when one of them finally clouted her on the back of the head with a sap. Her last thoughts were that she wished she were dead already; she knew what the likes of those men did with girls like her.

The next thing she remembered was Nessar's kindly face hovering over her with concern. His features had sported far fewer lines and creases back then, but to a little girl, he still seemed ancient. She tried to fight him too, but the pain in her head almost made her black out again. He had shushed her and calmed her before gently picking her up and carrying her to a place of warmth and safety. She vaguely remembered seeing her two kidnappers slumped in the shadows of the alley, unmoving. He had killed them, she had later discovered, though they had both been much larger than he.

Nessar had taken her in, but also allowed her to come and go as she pleased so that she never felt trapped. He had taught her how to fight, how to pick pockets as well as locks, and even some basic sleight of hand. She strove mightily to master those skills, but it was in combat that she excelled. He taught her what he could before introducing her to a handful of shady and dangerous men that owed Nessar favors. From them, she learned a thousand ways to win a fight, not all of them very sporting. With sword, daggers, even axes, Kiran learned to beat the best of them eventually, and Nessar was proud beyond words. As the only father she had ever known, making him proud was meaningful to her.

She eventually got her first job as a bouncer in a local tavern by thrashing the previous man while he was still on duty. That job led to others, some legitimate, and some less so, but all made good use of her hard-won fighting skills. Through it all, Nessar had been there with seemingly grudging encouragement or surly advice. Whatever his tone, his fatherly love for her was evident. The thought of not having him around was nearly inconceivable for her.

Lost in her memories, she let her gaze travel over the site of the ancient city, still seeing nothing under the pale moonlight. She was about to stand up and walk around the camp when she was struck by a wave of air, only slightly stronger than the breezes she had enjoyed earlier in the evening. It was there and gone in an instant, but Kiran felt the distinct tingle of magick in the passing wind. It had been faint, but strong enough to raise goosebumps on her skin. She quickly turned to find the source of the brief gust and saw dust settling all over the barren site of the absent city, falling gently back to earth in widening circles.

"Whuzzat? Whozzere?" Startled from sleep, Layton had smoothly rolled to his feet with his Jidaan at the ready, his body moving well in advance of his sleep-muddled mind. Though his eyes were still somewhat unfocused, his grip on the spear was sure and his footing perfectly balanced. He squinched his eyes shut and opened them a few times as he threw off the last traces of drowsiness.

"Shh!" Kiran hushed him before continuing more quietly. "I don't know. It was a wave of some kind, just a breeze, but it came from out there. And it felt like magick." She scowled into the darkness, searching for anything amiss.

"Yes, I felt that too. It's what woke me. It didn't feel good, either. It felt...I don't know, *bad*, somehow. Dark. Not like when Brunar throws his power around, but not like Mordak either."

Kiran nodded her agreement. She was not the most adept in the group at using her own personal magick and she wasn't overly sensitive to it, but even she had been able to tell the difference in the feel of the energy when it had touched her. It had been faint, but hinted at a vast and potent power.

"I think we should mount up. Better to be ready to move in a hurry if we need to." Keeping her eyes on the huge patch of empty earth, she quickly gathered up her pack and started stowing their few camp items for travel. Layton did the same without responding. They had been on the road together long enough to be comfortable in their trail duties, and striking the camp took only moments.

As they were loading up their horses, another wave struck them, stronger by far than the first. A faint rumble accompanied the wave and the leaves on the shrubs and scrubby trees rustled as the unknown force passed through. Hair stood up on the back of the Guardians' necks, and the horses whinnied nervously as the air settled in the wake of the unseen surge of power.

"Something's happening," Layton's voice was tense with concern.

"Wow, you figured that out all by yourself?" Kiran's voice was tight, her tone cutting. Layton heard the gibe, but he knew her well enough to let it slide off his back without an acknowledgement. He calmed his horse, then pulled himself lightly into the saddle.

"Grab hold of Nessar's horse. You'll have to bring her along; Nessar will need her when we find him."

Kiran grunted in frustration as she stepped over and snagged the horse's reins before mounting her own. "You think you know where he is?"

Another wave of power rolled over them, stronger and sooner than the last. They were increasing in speed and intensity. Layton grimaced. "No, not really. But something big is happening, and I have no doubt that Nessar is involved. I'm hoping we'll find him soon; we can't stay here much longer." The rumble of magick had quickly come to resemble a great thrumming heartbeat, and it was quickening moment by moment.

"We're not leaving him!" Kiran's voice was strained with anger and frustration. She had nearly drawn her sword on Layton at the least implication that they might have to leave her old friend behind. She would rather die. "He's got to be here somewhere!"

Before Layton could respond, a faint light flickered somewhere in the distance. It was a bright, intense purple, and it flashed for only a moment before it vanished. Seconds later, another rush of power washed over them, stronger again than the previous one. Layton pointed so that Kiran would see what he had seen, and she turned towards it as well.

Moments later the flash reappeared, but this time, it did not vanish. It twinkled and danced like a violet flame not far from the dusty ground, roughly in the center of the barren area. As the ripple of energy spread out from it, the shadowy outlines of buildings became visible as the wave rolled in an ever widening circle away from the epicenter. Domes and slanted roofs appeared as the power passed, then dimmed into shadow again only a moment later.

"I think we found the city," Layton said just before the wave hit. They squinted and leaned into the surge as it washed over them, and their horses shied and whinnied nervously. The waves were still getting stronger with each pulse, and the time between surges was getting even shorter. "I sure hope he's in there, 'cause it doesn't feel like this is going to end well."

Kiran didn't even hear him. The moment she saw the city, hope grew in her heart. He *had* to be in there somewhere, he just had to be! She spurred her horse forward without a backward glance at Layton, intent on guiding the beast towards the lone archway where they had last seen the old man. "Nessar!" she cried, even as another blast from the city slammed against her. "Where are you? NESSAR!"

"Kiran, wait! I can just...ugh!" Layton grunted in frustration as he watched her ride away. He knew that he could easily use his Gates to get Nessar out if he showed up, but Kiran was beyond listening. He spurred his own mount to follow her.

Waves of power were coming faster, buffeting the two warriors and their horses as they tried to keep their bearings. The ancient city was becoming clearer every second. Its squat buildings and lofty, domed towers shone in the ghostly purple light, seeming to solidify more as each wave passed through the deserted streets and empty alleys.

The city slowly took shape under the power of the ancient enchantment and other forms became visible in the dim, pulsating illumination. Tall, shambling forms that might once have been human staggered, apparently confused, from the alleys and open spaces between the buildings at the city's edge. Some of them collapsed in the dirt and lay still while others moaned loudly and crawled away from the beleaguered city of Linbourne. A few had their huge, misshapen hands over their ears as they stumbled aimlessly around. Some clawed at their own faces in agony. Their long talons left vicious wounds as though something was afflicting them. Out of the corner of her eye she saw three of them disappearing over the outer wall that had appeared along with the city.

Kiran's mind rebelled at the sight of the hideous creatures, but she forced herself to remain as calm as she could. The surges of power were now close enough together that they started to sound like a hum instead of a heartbeat. Kiran urged the horses to pick up speed as they headed towards the archway, leaning into the gale generated by the pulsating energy. She squinted into the rising wind, desperately searching for her old friend. She yelled his name again and again as she rode, the waves of energy crashing into her repeatedly and making the horses harder to control.

She crossed the border of the city and found herself on shifting cobblestones rather than bare earth; her horse's shoes rang on the stone. She reached the area where Nessar had vanished and stood in her stirrups as she searched, hoping to catch sight of him.

With a howling roar, one of the tall creatures lumbered out of the nearest alleyway and attacked, its long talons gleaming in the violet light. Instinctively, she threw up a Ward, and the powerful blow did not touch her, though she rocked in the saddle at the sheer strength of it. She released the reins of Nessar's mount and cursed furiously at it as it immediately bolted to safety. Her words were abruptly cut off as she saw the horse savagely ripped apart by more of the awful monsters. Their claws dripped blood that looked black in the violet light. Her Ward was nearly invisible, but still solid and strong. She righted herself and drew her Jidaan from its scabbard at her back, holding it near the middle.

The beast roared again and swiped at her, only to have its claws strike the Ward, breaking two of them near its misshapen hand. Kiran whirled her horse and began an attack of her own, swinging the blade of her Jidaan at the creature's neck with all her strength. Timing her move carefully, she let the Ward vanish just as her weapon reached it. The Jidaan moved smoothly through empty space, silencing the huge monster's yowls of pain and anger. Its body slumped clumsily to the ground, and Kiran spurred her horse away from it. Unfortunately, some of the beasts that had killed Nessar's horse decided to abandon the bloody carcass, their attention drawn to live prey. Four of them growled and spread out as they attempted to surround her, joined by others that had begun to pour out of the city. They came in singles and pairs, the crowd growing steadily.

Eying the creatures defiantly, Kiran stood up in the saddle and challenged them. "Bring it on, then!" Kiran shouted. "You'll get the same as the other one, each and every one of you! Come on!" She swung her Jidaan once over her head, its blazing sapphire overpowering the odd violet light of the city.

Suddenly, Layton was among the creatures. On foot now, he danced between them liked a ghost, cutting, stabbing, twirling, killing. Everywhere he moved the brutes fell. Kiran reached out with her own weapon and felled one beast that had gotten close, and then another.

There are far too many of them, Layton's voice echoed in Kiran's mind. *I'll engage as many as I can; you look for Nessar. Be ready to ride hard and I'll catch up soon enough.*

Kiran maneuvered her horse expertly around the monsters, striking at every opportunity. She strained to see past the tall, mutated brutes, hoping that Nessar would have sense enough to find his way out.

As it turns out, he did.

"Kiran! Over here!" His raspy voice was the most welcome sound Kiran thought she had ever heard. As she moved and fought, she craned her neck to see a dark figure standing on a nearby roof, waving his arms frantically in her direction. She could see his Jidaan strapped to his back alongside the old backpack he always had with him. He stood somewhat awkwardly, and Kiran noticed that there were dark stains on his pants and his shirt. Blood. His face and hands were tightly wrapped and blackened, effectively hiding his features, but Kiran knew him as well as she knew herself. Without hesitation, she kicked her heels into her horse and spurred it towards the old man's perch, breaking through the line of angry creatures that tried to bar her way.

The pulsating energy had quickened until it was a constant thrum of power and pressure. The light from the center of the city glowed brightly, reflected off the few low-hanging clouds overhead. The tension was nearly unbearable, and Kiran thought her head might break open at any moment. As she brought her horse under the ledge, she did her best to calm herself as Brunar had taught her. She always felt silly doing the Mage's exercises, but they had helped her more than once, and now was definitely a time to be focused and calm.

Nessar dropped lightly from the roof onto the horse behind her and wrapped his long arms around her waist. "Go! Go! I've got it!"

Kiran needed no more urging. She leaned over her horse's neck and spurred it away from the city, away from the pulsating light.

Layton, I've got him! Get out of there! Even as she finished sending the thought to the young warrior across the mindlink they all shared, Layton vanished in a flash of opalescent color, leaving a crowd of bewildered and angry creatures behind. She didn't know exactly where he had gone, but she knew he could take care of himself. Her horse's hooves thundered off the cobblestones as they passed through the ancient archway, galloping along the worn and grass-covered road that lay beyond it. Nessar gripped her tightly around the waist, and Kiran hoped the darkness would obscure the tears of relief she could not hold back. They rode like that for a few heartbeats more, hooves drumming beneath them as they made their escape.

Then they felt rather than heard the explosion behind them, a deep seated, muffled thump accompanied by a blinding purple flash of light. They did not turn to look at it, choosing wisely instead to stare straight ahead and Kiran pushed the horse harder. A great, howling roar reached their ears, the sounds of buildings being torn asunder and pulverized by the ancient magick. Their hearts filled with dread as the blast wave approached and they willed Kiran's brave mount to go faster, knowing they would never be able to get out of range in time. The massive shockwave spread out from the center of the city as Wendall's curse finally came to fruition. The blast had already laid waste to the entire city, and now was pursuing Kiran and Nessar as though it were alive and hungry for their blood.

The shockwave overtook them in moments, a colossal blast of energy that threw them forward in an overwhelming storm of howling wind and flying debris from the devastated city. Kiran's horse flailed frantically as its hooves left the road, and it whinnied piteously as it was carried aloft. Kiran fought to stay in the saddle, gripping the horse ferociously with her legs and struggling to right herself even as Nessar gripped harder from his precarious seat behind her.

Just as the most powerful part of the wave was about to pulverize them all, a bright square of swirling, opalescent colors appeared directly in her path. They flew into it, horse and all, and then the portal simply ceased to exist. The blast continued its destructive journey, scouring the land surrounding Linbourne down to the bare earth for miles around, killing everything within its reach.

Wendall finally had his revenge.

Chapter 38

Gart opened his eyes and saw a thatch roof overhead. He was lying on a soft bed that smelled somewhat musty, but was comfortable nonetheless. A deep ache throbbed in his head as he started to sit up, and a sharper pain made him look down at his leg. He saw that his trousers had been cut off above his arrow wound, which had been cleaned and bandaged. It hurt far less than he expected. *I've got to stop passing out. This is ridiculous,* he thought to himself as he rubbed his head. He looked around and saw that he was in a small, one-room cabin. A fire was burning in the fireplace and a pot was hanging over it. A wonderful smell emanated from the huge black cauldron, making his mouth water.

He glanced around the room and guessed that it likely belonged to the old woman he had aided. A few of the windows were open and the sun shone through, making big pools of light on the floor. Racks of herbs and potted plants were everywhere, as well as huge pots that were lined up carefully along one wall. In one corner sat a rickety table covered with tools and pieces of things Gart could not readily identify. His Jidaan and its leather shoulder harness leaned up against the table, as did his sword, backpack, and boots. His floppy hat was hung on the top of the nearest chair.

Moving slowly, Gart swung his legs over the side of the bed and gently put weight on his feet. The wound throbbed but the pain was bearable, and he finally tried to stand. He was balancing there, carefully putting more weight on his injured leg, when the woman pushed open the door and walked in carrying her rucksack. It bulged now with items unknown.

She was hunched over, wearing a thick shawl in spite of the heat, and she shuffled oddly when she walked. She muttered constantly in her raspy voice, talking to herself about everything she was doing as though clarifying it for her own benefit. She ambled over to the table and began pulling things out of her sack, then putting them on its flat surface. When she saw Gart standing, she smiled with what few teeth she had left.

"I see you're awake. Good, good! Nasty poison arrow, that was. It's ok now though, I cleaned your leg and put a poultice on it to draw out the poison. It'll be a while before you can walk right, but it'll be fine."

She hobbled over to the fireplace and used a poker to swing the kettle away from the fire. With one foot, she hooked a nearby stool and pulled it close enough that she could sit on it and still reach the kettle. Using practiced motions, she began pulling vegetables out of her bag and cutting them up with a knife she found somewhere, letting the pieces fall into the pot. "The stew will be ready in a bit. You should rest. That poison will make you weak for a while yet. I did what I could, but the wound is deep."

Gart sat back down on the bed, tired from standing as he had. Frustrated, he squeezed his fists tightly, then relaxed them as dark motes began to swim before his eyes from the exertion. He snorted quietly to himself. *I was poisoned before, but I got that stuff out of me somehow. How did I do that?* His memories from his time in the cave, shaking with fever from the bog monster's venom, were hazy and indistinct. He strongly recalled seeing his own body as though he were standing alongside it. But what had he done then? Gart closed his eyes and drifted into his memories, irritated that they were so fleeting and undefined. He wondered if his magick could help him at all. At the thought, his power leapt up inside him, filling his body with strength and vigor. Suddenly, his visions of his time in the cave came into sharp focus, replayed in his mind with stunning clarity.

He contemplated for a few moments, then sent his magick towards the wound in his thigh. He immediately sensed the oily corruption of the poison. It had not done any permanent damage yet, probably due to the gooey paste the woman had smeared underneath the bandage. Gart surrounded the intruding substance with his magick, and guided it carefully out of the wound and into the poultice. Soon, the toxin was completely purged from his body, and Gart set about gauging the severity of the wound itself. It had not gone all the way through, the arrow having been stopped by his thigh bone. There was a nick in the bone, and Gart gently probed it with his power. Unsure of what else to do, he began to imagine how the divot in his leg might look if it were whole, unmarked by the arrowhead. He focused on that picture and was startled to feel something happening. As he continued sending power to the area, he felt the nick in the bone filling with new growth. It become progressively stronger until it felt as though it had never been damaged.

He then turned to the puncture, a small tunnel that delved deep into the muscle of his thigh. Starting at the bottom, he imagined the flesh knitting together again, reconnecting, reestablishing its undamaged condition. He frowned in concentration as he stared at the bandage on his leg, not really seeing with his eyes anymore but focusing entirely on the sensations within him.

Finally, Gart let out a sigh. He was tired, but this was a good kind of tired. He slowly began to unwrap the bandage from his thigh.

"Here now, leave that alone! That wound will still take days to heal!" The old woman stood up from her chair with some difficulty and hobbled towards Gart just as he finished unwrapping his leg. He held the bandage and a gummy, foul lump of something that had once been a poultice.

"It's all right, old mother. I'm fine now, I think. Thank you for helping me." Gart handed her the bandages, careful not to drop any of the muck onto her floor. She accepted them with a look of shock on her wizened face. He carefully stood up again, this time putting weight equally on both feet. He bent his knees slightly, testing his handiwork, and was pleased to find that his leg felt good as new.

The old woman screwed up her face in a grimace. "Hmmm...healed it yourself, did you?"

Gart walked over to his backpack and pulled his spare pants out of it. He glanced at the old woman, shrugged, then stepped out of his one-legged pants so he could get into the other pair. "I guess I did." He took his hat off the chair and placed it on the table, then sat down to put on his boots. "To be honest, I don't know that I could explain how I did it. I'm learning as I go."

She nodded and walked away to dispose of Gart's bandages. "You've got the power in you. Felt it the moment you rode into sight. It's strong, your power is. To those who can see it, you shine like the sun."

"You can see it, then?" Gart said, surprised.

"Only if I *look*," she replied. "But then, with you, I didn't have to look that hard." She went back to the kettle and resumed work on the stew. She nodded sharply in the direction of Gart's weapon. "Where did you come by that, if I may ask?"

Gart sat quietly for a moment, his eyes on the emerald in the Jidaan's pommel. It glimmered there, a deep green fire in sparkling slumber. "It...it Chose me. I'm supposed to have it."

She turned a twinkling eye in his direction. "You're one of them, then. A Guardian."

Gart paused for a long while before he replied.

"Yes. I am."

She went back to cutting the vegetables into the pot. "Thought so. It's been a long time since the Guardians walked the land. A long time. Something bad must be going on. I've felt some things, dreamed some things. They must be true, then. Sorry to hear that. Yes, yes, very sorry." She cut the last carrot into the pot, then found a long wooden spoon. She began to stir the stew with it. "I know you're heading south, right into the worst of it. That bastard sorcerer has gathered all manner of foulness to himself and is laying waste to everything in his path. I tell you what, though," she turned and jabbed the dripping spoon at Gart. "Your comrades are fighting them, and doing well, too."

"My comrades?" Gart was confused for a moment, then recalled the empty rooms in the mountain Keep, the other brackets on the wall that had held weapons like his own. He remembered meeting the shade of Brunar on the road a lifetime ago. *A Guardian is a Protector of this land. There are six, one for each of the Jidaan created eons ago to ward against those who would use dark magick to overcome the world.* That's what the Mage had told him. There were five others who wielded weapons such as his, five other Jidaan. "Ah, yes. I don't know them. I was, ah, somewhat late in coming to the party."

The old woman let out a cackle. "Ha! Party, indeed! Ah, well. From what I've seen, you're a Guardian all right. And a powerful one, more powerful than any of the others. Oh, the big brutes are always stronger physically, but your strength is different from theirs." She paused for a moment, thinking. "Yes....you're different from the others." She pointed one long, gnarled finger at Gart. "Very different. They all have some of your powers, lad," she shook her head as she turned back to the stew, "but you've got far more power than you think, more than they will ever have. You're just made that way."

Gart eyed her warily. "What makes you such an expert, if you don't mind my asking?"

She cackled again, a ragged but amusing sound. "Well my boy, let's just say I've been around for a good long while. Long enough to know something of Brunar, the Guardians, and even that foul creature that calls himself Mordak." Her voice turned icy at the mention of his name. "I have some power myself. Nothing like yours, mind you, but some. I knew Brunar when he was just a young apprentice, wide-eyed and dying to learn everything there was to know about magick."

Gart raised an eyebrow. "I know he's older than me. Maybe by ten or fifteen years, I'd say."

"Ha! A hundred times that, boy! Twice over! Brunar has seen well over two thousand summers, as have I. Mordak is the same, roughly." She saw his doubt written plainly on his face. "It's the power keeps him alive. Same as me. He's mastered the

Sleep, though, and that keeps him young. Mordak was entombed as a shade for the last twenty centuries, so he must have stolen a body when he escaped, changed it into something that suited him." She shook her head sadly as she stirred the stew again.

Gart scratched his head. After all he had seen and endured, and the power that seemed to still be growing within him, he decided she was telling the truth. "I apologize for my lack of manners, old mother. My name is Gart. Might I have your name?"

The old woman turned a nearly toothless smile at the young man. "So polite! I am pleased to make your acquaintance, Gart. My name is Agatha." She looked back to her stew. "This is almost ready. You should eat up before you go. Your horse is outside; she's well-fed and happy. Bigger things await you."

Gart smiled. "Trying to get rid of me so soon? Do I smell?"

Agatha snorted. "Well, of course you smell! Been on the road for weeks! Yes, you smell like feet and dirty underwear. But that don't bother me none, not at all. No, I just know you're needed elsewhere, young man. And you know it too. That's why you're heading south."

Gart sighed. "Yes, I think you're right, Miss Agatha. I was told that the others like me were headed to Laro, but that was weeks ago. I don't know anything for certain. I've basically been following my nose ever since I picked up this thing." He waved a hand at the sheathed Jidaan nearby.

"The Jidaan of Storms, yes, I know what it is." Agatha answered as she ladled a generous portion of stew into a wooden bowl. She set it aside, quickly got one for herself, then picked them both up and ambled towards the table. She put the bowls down, then retrieved spoons for them before settling herself in the chair opposite Gart. "You'll need it before this thing is through. Mordak has gathered an army of nasty creatures to himself; Gholans, Morcats, Krell, and likely other fell creatures to do his bidding. He's using the dead as well, animating their corpses." She grunted in disgust at the thought.

Visions of Tiller's Grove flashed in Gart's mind before he could quell them, and his face grew stern. "Yes, I've seen some of Mordak's monsters at work."

Agatha ate some of her stew and nodded thoughtfully. "I'm sure you have, sonny. I'm sure you have." They ate in companionable silence for a short time. Soon, Gart's spoon was scraping the bottom of his bowl. Without a word, Agatha swept up the empty bowl, hobbled over to the kettle and refilled it. The stew was back in front of Gart before he could speak. Agatha sat back down and continued picking at her meal. "I'll tell you, there's something else about Mordak. He's evil to the core, y'see. Always has been. Crazy, too. But he's called on something very, very bad this time, and very powerful. I'm not sure what it is, but it doesn't feel right. Not right at all. Whatever it is, it's not from this world." She finished her bowl and moved to the basin where she used water from a pitcher to wash it out. She set it aside to dry and wiped her hands on her frayed apron before turning to face Gart again. "I have felt great disturbances from the south. Movement of dark energies, very evil magick. It feels to me like it's moving closer all the time, making its way north. I don't know more than that, I'm sorry."

Gart finished the last mouthful of stew, then walked over to the basin to wash his bowl out. "Well, that's not exactly a lot to go on. But thank you nonetheless. And again, thank you for helping me."

Agatha dismissed his thanks with a wave. "You helped me first, boy. Don't forget that. If I could help you more, I would." She hobbled over and picked up his Jidaan in its shoulder harness. Turning, she held it out to Gart, who accepted it and slipped it into place so that the weapon rode comfortably along his back. Next, she handed him his pack, which he quickly slung over one shoulder, and then his hat. He plucked it gently from her hand and twirled it once before settling it firmly on his head.

"Thank you," Gart said quietly. A warm feeling bloomed in his heart as he saw the old woman smile.

"You're welcome, lad," Agatha replied with a short bow. "Bessie's right out there. Just follow the road to your right. It will take you south the way you need to go. Alverton Falls is just a few more days that way...the waterfall, not the town. Town is just another day or so beyond that, but you can see it down below if you're standing atop the Falls. I can feel it in my bones; that's where the fighting will be. That's where the Guardians are, and that's where you are needed."

"Again, thank you Agatha. You've been most kind." He moved to the door.

"Wait, before you go," Agatha interrupted his exit. "Tell Brunar that Agatha...Aggie...is alive and well," she winked slyly at Gart, "and she still wants a piece of him." Gart's mouth dropped open in surprise. "And as for you, young lad," Agatha looked up into his scarred face, gazing into his piercing blue eyes with her old brown ones. "Should you ever need anything, just come see old Agatha. There's a lot about your power that I could teach you. In the meantime, just trust yourself, and believe in your power. Use it. Experiment with it. It can do things you haven't even dreamed of."

Gart paused for a moment. He assumed that Brunar would be the one to teach him about his weapon and his powers, but friends were good to have. "I'll keep that in mind, Agatha. Stay safe, and watch out for bandits in the road." A half-smile crawled up one side of his face as he showed himself out the door, leaving Agatha standing next to her kettle, absently wringing her hands.

Chapter 39

A week had passed since Brunar and Bjarke returned from Redleaf Valley, and naught had been heard from the brave warriors who had remained behind to harass Mordak's forces. Brunar had presented his plan to Count DeRoberds, and the tall ruler had agreed that, although dangerous, it was their best chance.

"A force that size will take this city easily if it actually makes it across the river. Fortunately, the current is swift and the rains have swollen it to the widest it's been in years. We can destroy the bridges if necessary to hold them off, and the earth and wood wall we've constructed along the south side of the river will help us as well. We must try to thin out the horde in the hills between Redleaf Valley and here." He pointed to a spot on the map that designated the vast killing ground south of the city. A grim smile appeared on the Count's face as he continued. "Our people are well-versed in hit-and-run tactics, and we know the land. They may well be surprised at how much damage we can inflict that way."

The Count leaned back in his chair and sighed. "Beyond that, we'll have to use the warren of trenches and pits we've dug to good effect, and draw back gradually to minimize casualties." He glanced at Brunar. "We will be depending on you and the Guardians for your magick at that point."

"If they do take the city?" Fiona asked quietly, concern plainly written on her face. Her blue eyes darted towards the Mage, only to find similar concern in his expression as well.

Brunar answered her. "We must be ready to move at speed, but we can escape north and west into the Shadowed Forest. If we can get far enough in, we may meet the Weya as they approach, and they will aid us." He tried to voice optimism he did not quite feel. ValElder Moihra had disappeared into the forest many days ago with the intent of bringing the Weya to their aid, but she had not been heard from since. Brunar did not want to assume that she had also run into Mordak's minions, but the possibility existed. And if she had, that meant the forest would not be safe for any of them. Brunar stayed calm, though the thought bothered him immensely. They would cross that bridge if they came to it.

Just then, the door burst open and a haggard, bloodied soldier stumbled in. He took a couple of halting steps and fell in a heap on the floor before he could say a word. Alyssa ran to him, her Jidaan already flaring in a brilliant, sparkling flash of light.

The man gasped as the power of the Jidaan of Healing raced through his body, scouring it clean of injuries and hurt. Alyssa's face was stern as she guided her magick through him, but then she sat back on her heels. The bright radiance of the ancient weapon dimmed and went out, leaving everyone in the room to blink away the sudden spots that yet danced in their vision.

Alyssa sighed, "He'll be all right. He was more exhausted than injured, though he did have some nasty gashes and a broken arm."

Even as she spoke, the soldier sat up with a very surprised look on his face. He had been sure he was going to die, but he pushed himself hard to get back to the city so he could alert them. Now, he felt physically better than ever, though his news still weighed heavily. Climbing to his feet, he bowed to Count DeRoberds and spoke.

"My lord, they are coming. We kept them from getting over the barrier for a while, but then they found the caves. They swarmed into them and overwhelmed us all." His breath caught in his throat for a moment before he continued. "Meliantha saved me. She killed the Gholans that had attacked me and held off the rest so I could escape. I'm fairly certain I was the only one to make it out alive."

The Count's face was ashen. "What happened next?"

"I managed to make it to the north end of the valley before coming above-ground again. I know they found the tunnels leading to the far side. The sun was just coming up and I could see a long stream of those horrid creatures pouring back down into the valley from where they attacked us, far more than had come in with that big yellow-eyed bastard. They had to have gone through the tunnels to get there, and last I saw, they were massing in the valley. Judging from the size of the force we saw on the other side, it would have taken at least a full day to get all of them into the valley, but they are most likely on their way here right now. I rode here as fast as I could."

Count DeRoberds took the news stoically, though his lips were pressed in a grim line. "How long before they reach our southernmost defenses?"

"Nightfall tomorrow would be my best guess, my lord. They had not yet begun their march when I escaped the valley."

As the soldier fell silent, the Count took a deep breath and let it out. "Well, ready or not, it's time to put our plan into action." He turned to Brunar. "Sir Mage, I must go and address the soldiers who will be fighting the hit-and-run battles south of our lands. If you receive word from your Guardians that are retrieving the artifact, please let me know. In the meantime, whatever you need of me, you have but to ask."

Brunar bowed slightly. "Thank you. We will keep you informed." He watched the Count and his advisers exit the chamber before turning to those who remained, Bjarke, Alyssa, Fiona, and Cohl. "I have heard nothing from Layton, Kiran, or Nessar. That does not mean anything, as they are too far away for me to hear them. We can only hope that they will be successful. In the meantime, we will do what we can here."

Cohl spoke up. "I have experience in the kind of fighting you have described. If you will excuse me, I would accompany the Count to offer advice."

"I'm sure it will be most welcome, Cohl. By all means, do so."

Alyssa frowned as they watched Cohl exit the same way the count had. "I feel helpless here. Is there anything else I can do?"

Brunar shrugged and nodded towards Bjarke. "You could go and see that this giant beast gets some food in him. I can hear his stomach growling from here, and I'm afraid he'll scare the locals." In spite of herself, Alyssa cracked a smile. Bjarke's prodigious stomach had, indeed, growled loudly during the meeting. Twice. The big man started to protest, but then sheepishly sighed.

"I will admit to feeling peckish, Brunar. If Alyssa will have me, I'll escort her to get some food before I go back to helping them finish the last of the wall they're building along the river." He looked down to find the diminutive healer beaming up at him and his heart leapt. Every time he had looked at Alyssa over the course of the last few eventful weeks, his heart had become something of an acrobat. Her lovely brown eyes twinkled as they looked up at him, and her smile made him weak in the knees.

"It will be my pleasure!" Alyssa replied, her tone light and happy. In spite of the knowledge of what was to come, being near Bjarke had always reassured her and made her all tingly inside. Her hand crept up into his enormous paw and gave it a squeeze, surprising him.

Brunar smiled as he saw the two discovering feelings for each other that he had recognized weeks ago. "Get along, you two. Eat something and rest a bit. Come find me at nightfall; I have some things to prepare first."

The pair turned without saying goodbye to the Mage, occupied as they were with each other. Bjarke politely opened the door for her and Alyssa glided through it, Bjarke following after. The door closed, and Brunar stared at it for a few quiet moments.

"They are cute together." Fiona's low voice was bright with amusement and her eyes twinkled as she spoke.

Brunar turned to her and sighed. "They are indeed. I pray to Rowann that this conflict will end soon, so that they and others like them can live out their lives in peace."

"And find love?"

Brunar smiled. "Yes. And find love. Though it looks like those two won't have very far to look."

Moving in front of him, Fiona reached out and gently placed a hand on Brunar's shoulder. "What about you, Sir Mage? Is there...someone?" She looked up into his stern grey eyes, searching for the story there.

Brunar was quiet for a moment. He put his hand on hers and squeezed it gently. "Not for a long time. Here and there over the years, but never anything lasting."

He looked into her eyes and found them to be a startling ocean blue. She was no young girl, but a strong woman in her middle years. Wisdom lined her face, but it enhanced rather than detracted from her beauty. Far more than her looks, though, Brunar had recognized in her a kindred spirit. She was a woman of intelligence and strength, not afraid to speak her mind and fight for the good of others. Brunar had to admit that he had been drawn to her ever since their initial meeting, though he had shied away from those feelings. He was The Mage, the leader of The Guardians, not a normal man. He was over two thousand years old. He was above such things.

Or so he thought.

Looking into her eyes, Brunar felt his heart warm to her presence, and he watched her smile widen in return. Suddenly he was no longer Brunar, the ancient and powerful Mage. In that moment he was a young man again, on his first outing with a girl he knew from his village, hundreds of years past. Everything was bright and shiny and new, and his heart was afire with youth and life and passion.

Fiona leaned closer and spoke, her eyes still on his. "Brunar, one of the very things that we fight for is love. Love of family, love of friends. Romantic love, as well. The right to spend time with those whom we love and enjoy our lives as we see fit."

She reached up and put her other hand on his cheek and smiled as he leaned into it. "I would spend some time with you, Brunar."

Brunar took her hand in both of his. Gently, he brought it to his lips and kissed it. For once, he just did not have the words.

Chapter 40

It had taken the rest of that night, the full of a day, and into the next night for Mordak to assemble the remainder of his horde in Redleaf Valley by way of the hidden caves and tunnels beneath the western slopes. Many of his creatures ate well then, feasting on the dead that Brunar and Bjarke had left behind, as well as those few brave warriors whom they had slain in the caves. Under the wavering light of the moon, Mordak gave the command to move northward. The vile and monstrous army swarmed over the land, befouling everything it touched.

Riding in a hastily constructed litter carried on the shoulders of six burly and fanatical Krell, Mordak schemed and planned. Displeased with the diminished size of his army, he reached out with his power, calling more of the vicious Gholans from the edges of the nearby Tanglewoods. The effort made his nose bleed and his head ache, but the sorcerer had deemed it necessary. Power he had in plenty, but his body could only handle the strain of Balroth's intense magick for so long. He wiped the black blood on his sleeve with a curse, shuddering as he felt the wriggling bumps on his arm even through the thick cloth. Using his power to calm himself, he quelled the incessantly writhing nodules on his body. When his skin finally stopped crawling, he sighed heavily and relaxed back into the cushions.

The creatures he had called were quickly making their way overland to join the horde. He could feel their approach, and estimated that they would arrive in another day at most. The thought made him smile. By the time they reached Alverton Falls, his army would be enormous again, and there would be no way for the townspeople to defend against it. He would add most of the populace to the ranks of his undead and then the march to the capitol city of Bos Aldas could begin. It was only a matter of time before Mordak would rule all. He laughed aloud at the thought of it and relaxed into the constant sway and roll of the litter as his Krell continued their determined march.

Chapter 41

The late afternoon sun lay behind purpling clouds that lazily made their way across the sky, shading them with pink and peach as the evening approached. Gentle breezes caressed the golden, waist-high grasses and the stately green-leafed trees that dotted the landscape, the soft susurration breaking the silence. The land rolled gently, leaving hills and hollows as far as the eye could see. The trees thickened to the west until they became dense enough to be a proper forest, while the hills gradually became steeper as they flowed into the lowest part of the Blackthorne Mountains to the east. It was a beautiful landscape, peaceful and idyllic.

One would never know that hundreds of deadly warriors lurked among the flowers, stalks, and clusters of trees, and indeed, in the trees themselves. They were steely-eyed men and women, each determined to defend their home and loved ones. Each would fight to the death if it meant life for those they protected, and they would not go down easily. All eyes turned towards the south, from whence they knew the enemy would emerge. Arrows were nocked, swords and daggers were honed and ready.

A lone warrior stood in the center of the meadow, a woman. Her brown hair was cut in a shoulder-length bob that the wind toyed with, and she shook her head to free a few loose strands from her eyes. Emmi had changed out of her priestess garb and donned tight-fitting clothing in an elusive grey-green color that seemed to shift depending upon whether she stood in grass or wood. She had fought this kind of battle before in the wayward days of her youth, and she knew it well. Her hand axe and a wicked dagger were firmly attached to her belt, and in her left hand she held a powerful longbow and a dozen arrows. A quiver rode on her back, tightly packed with more arrows, each razor-tipped and true. Her mouth curved in a crooked smile as she stared southward, awaiting the first sight of Mordak's horde.

They felt its approach before they saw anything, a faint rumbling in the ground that increased moment by moment. Flocks of birds, startled, scattered up into the sky as the yowling mass of hideous creatures drew near. Emmi held her ground. She fought for the Goddess Rowann, and for everyone on Talwynn. If she were to die today, then so be it.

The howls of the unruly Gholans reached their ears first, followed by the roars and snarls of their Morcat captains. The rumbling of so many feet, clawed, hooved, and booted, vibrated the earth below. At last, the front lines of the enemy came into view, stretching wide across the rolling grasslands, polluting it with every step. Jor Dayne rode in front, arrogance plain on his face. He was flanked by one of the largest of the Morcats on one side and a huge Krell warrior on the other, neither choosing to ride. The Krell's dark red skin seemed to absorb the sunlight, and a single plume of dark ebony hair stood out from the top of its shaven head. Its jet black eyes stared straight ahead, malevolence in its evil glare. Thin lips were skinned back from horridly pointed teeth, and the Krell warleader grunted harshly as it caught sight of the lone figure ahead. It slowly pulled a sturdy warclub from a strap on its back and hefted it with both hands in anticipation. The Morcat growled low in its throat before looking up to Jor Dayne for orders.

When Jor Dayne saw Emmi, alone in the middle of the meadow ahead, he raised one massive fist in the air. The horde came to a stumbling halt around him. For a few long moments he stared at the woman without saying a word. Then her voice drifted across the distance, melodic and lovely, but stern.

"Stop! You are not welcome here! Turn back, or face the consequences!"

Jor Dayne enjoyed the sound of the woman's voice. It pleased him greatly. He almost thought it a shame that he would have to kill her. A wide, toothy grin appeared on his face beneath his black mustache. The half-daemon had not kept it trimmed as had his host, the man Lucanos, but it still retained something of a jaunty look. Jor Dayne's glaring yellow eyes slowly scanned the whole of the meadow from left to right. He knew that there were likely others hidden in the tall grass and among the trees, but of them, he saw no sign at all. No matter. Their sheer numbers would overwhelm any resistance they could put up with so few. He cast his gaze once more upon the woman who stood opposite him.

"I doubt that, love. No matter how many you have brought with you, I have thousands with me. And they will feast on your flesh."

Across the distance that separated them, Jor Dayne saw her face erupt into a sly grin and a thrill of excitement went through him. Things were about to get interesting. He saw her raise her bow, and reflexively threw one huge arm up to protect his face.

Emmi's right hand was a blur, pulling arrows from her left hand one after another directly to the bowstring as each one flew towards its intended target. Before any of the creatures next to Jor Dayne even knew what she was doing, six arrows struck in the hearts and throats of the Krell captain and the huge Morcat, as well as others on either side of them. The powerful bow put one bolt through Jor Dayne's meaty forearm, the razor-tipped arrowhead punching completely through armor, bone, and muscle alike. The pain was intense and delightful. As much as he had come to hate doing Mordak's bidding, the excitement of combat was deeply enjoyable for the half-daemon. He reached down and broke off the feathered end of the arrow and pulled out the remainder of the shaft before tossing it aside. He fixed his eyes on the girl, still standing boldly with her chin held high in defiance. As he gathered breath to order a charge, she blew him a kiss and twiddled her fingers in a dainty wave, then sank down into the grass and disappeared from sight.

Right, he thought. *Try and lure us down the middle so you can hit us from the sides again, eh? Not this time, wench.*

Jor Dayne whistled loudly and caught the attention of Morcat and Krell captains farther down the lines. Through a quick series of hand gestures, he ordered a two pronged attack on either side. At his command, the bloodthirsty army surged forward like the horns on a bull, planning to encircle the entire area where they had seen the archer. They would flush out any hidden soldiers, driving the two wedges directly through the area their enemies would have lain in wait for a central charge. He smiled at the thought of the foolish humans scrambling to escape their own well-laid ambush. Bellowing over his shoulder, he called for the unruly Gholans to step aside and let the undead Riders through. Those, he would send up the middle to assail any who tried to escape that way. His horse snorted at the stench as the reanimated corpses made their way to the front of the horde and pressed forward to gather near Jor Dayne.

Gholans howled for blood and Morcats snarled loudly in their eagerness to kill as they loped across the prairie, flattening the tall grass as they went. Suddenly, their screams of bloodlust turned to yelps of pain and fear, and as Jor Dayne watched, creatures on both sides of the charge suddenly seemed to vanish beneath the swaying grass. More and more hideous soldiers raced after them, ready to slay anything they encountered, but they found nothing but blood, bodies, and more grass. They spread out, searching for the soldiers that had just been there, but found none. A Gholan shouted in surprise as he was suddenly yanked down and slaughtered within mere feet of his comrades, who found only the body and no enemy warriors to vent their wrath upon. Then another fell. And another.

On the east side, where the Krell were more prevalent, the same thing was happening. Arrows from unseen archers thunked home and dropped the Krell warriors in their tracks. Others fell with gaping wounds from weapons that flicked out from among the swaying grasses, only to vanish again once the damage was done. Frustrated, the Krell yelled war cries and plunged into the grass, swinging their swords in broad sweeping motions and stabbing frantically with their spears as they hunted for those who assailed them. They found naught but death.

"Forward!" Jor Dayne gestured furiously with his jagged blade, and the undead began lumbering ahead. Ahorse and on foot, the stinking corpsefolk with their glowing red eyes marched implacably into the grass, their weapons held in nerveless fingers.

The dead and decaying riders made their way forward until they had reached the rough center of the meadow where Emmi had been standing. They turned their heads left and right, searching for their prey, but found only the swaying grasses. After searching for a minute or so, they simply stopped moving, having reached the limit of what they had been commanded to do. Jor Dayne swore loudly as he scanned the countryside in the failing light, desperate to find a target.

"What's all this? Why have we stopped?" Mordak's voice startled Jor Dayne, and he turned towards the sound. The sorcerer's tone was rough with annoyance as he leaned outside his litter to see what was going on. His eyes gleamed scarlet with madness.

"They are striking from cover of the tall grass, Master. We are searching for them now, and we will skin them all alive when we find them!"

"HA!" Mordak barked his laughter at the big man. "It looks to me like they are painting you as the fool." He laughed again, though it was cut short by a fit of coughing. Jor Dayne smiled, showing wickedly pointed teeth as he clenched his fists in rage. "Advance the entire horde! A handful of sneaky townspeople won't be able to hide from all of these creatures marching shoulder-to-shoulder. We'll flush them out!"

Bowing slightly, Jor Dayne spoke in his deep, rich voice. "As you wish, Master." Then he turned and trotted his horse out before the front lines of the horde and prepared to order the advance.

As he raised his sword in the air and drew breath to give the order, he felt something impact his horse near its neck. The horse neighed in surprise then fell sideways, forcing Jor Dayne to dive out of the saddle lest he become pinned under the dying animal. He landed hard, but managed to avoid breaking anything. He shook his head to clear it and then stepped over to examine the beast. A tiny tufted dart was deeply embedded in the muscle of the horse's shoulder. He cast an appreciative glance at the grass-covered field and smiled at the warriors surely hidden therein. *Poison! This is certainly a clever bunch of monkeys.* Another dart hissed over his head, missing him by inches, and he hunched over as much as he could. Staying low, he quickly crawled behind the body of his massive horse and took cover.

Suddenly, the air was alive with hissing darts, thumping into the front line of Mordak's horde. The Gholans fell right away while others of their kind shrank back in fear. The frontmost Morcats took longer to die, but in the end, they, too, succumbed to the deadly poison brewed by the Sisters of Rowann. Adept in the ways of healing, they also knew the most effective ways of taking life, and they had equipped the stealthy warriors of Alverton Falls quite well. Hundreds of Mordak's vile soldiers fell dead and writhing to the grass.

With a gesture and a flex of his will, Mordak ordered the undead Riders back from the center of the field where Jor Dayne had sent them, as well as calling up another squad of them from the rear. He directed them to take position as the first three rows of the horde, protecting the living creatures behind them. Darts and arrows struck them from many hidden assassins, but those bolts simply stuck fast into their dead flesh and harmed them not. Mordak smirked at his own ingenuity.

"Now then," he sneered at Jor Dayne, "sound the advance, you idiot! I tire of these delays!" Mordak sat back in his litter and focused his energy inwards again, conserving it for the full-scale attack on the city ahead.

Jor Dayne crawled on his belly until he was behind the shielding ranks of undead, then stood once more. Gritting his teeth at the sound of Mordak's voice, he yelled for the horde to move forward again, trampling those who had already fallen.

Not half a mile away, in the shelter of a small cluster of oak trees, Emmi suddenly slithered out of the tall grass to stand next to Brunar, Bjarke, and the Count. From their vantage point, they could see the ranks of undead soldiers shambling forward, weapons held loosely before them. They were slow, but nearly unstoppable in combat, since normal wounds would not kill them. They could only be disabled by beheading or otherwise destroying their brains. Brunar grimaced as he took in the grisly sight of so many unfortunate souls, their bodies forced to do evil that their spirits would never abide.

"There are so many!" The Count's voice was barely a whisper. "I never dreamed..."

"Indeed, the horde has grown since they assailed Laro, in spite of the losses they took there," Brunar affirmed. "Many of the humans you see once fought bravely against the very vermin with whom they now march. At this point, killing them is a kindness." Adding a note of distaste, he continued, "And there seems to be no end to the Gholans. It looks like he's called every single one of them on Talwynn to fight for him, not to mention the Morcats and the Krell."

At the mention of the mutated cannibal warriors from the far East, Fiona turned to Brunar. "Yes, I was surprised to see them, too. They fought alongside Mordak before, but when he betrayed them somehow, they swore eternal vengeance if I remember correctly."

Keeping his eyes on the steadily advancing army, Brunar nodded. "Yes, you're right. They worship the evil god Balroth. This time, Mordak is cloaking himself in a glamour that makes the Krell think that he, himself, is Balroth. They are falling all over themselves to do his bidding." He cast a quick glance at Fiona and saw her looking at him. He could not hold back his smile, which was answered by the priestess, her blue eyes sparkling. He reached out and quickly squeezed her hand in reassurance before turning back to survey the battlefield once more.

The Count stared for a moment longer before seeming to come to grips with the size of the enemy army. Then he scanned the rolling grasslands for signs of the brave warriors that remained hidden in the field ahead of the horde. "Are they ready?"

Brunar sent a silent question to Alyssa and almost instantly got a response. He had tried to leave her back at the city in case either Kiran's group or Moihra arrived, but she would not hear of it. The other priestesses were already planning to take the fight directly to the enemy and she was determined to do the same. She had tired of merely healing the wounds presented to her and wished to deal out a little damage instead.

Yes, Brunar, we're ready. We had to scramble to find a way to deal with the undead shield they are using. Damn that evil Mordak! Alyssa could not hide her anger, and it came across loud and clear along the mindlink she shared with the Mage. *I think we can clear them out of the way enough to cause some trouble. Bjarke says he's ready too.* At the mention of the big Guardian, a sudden rush of warmth and happiness flowed along the mindlink. Brunar could not help but smile at Alyssa's feelings for the huge forester since they had been obvious to everyone but her. He turned to address the count.

"Yes, Count, they are. Just watch the first ranks of the enemy." Brunar pointed towards the middle of the approaching lines of undead that preceded the rest of Mordak's creatures.

They stared straight ahead, their eyes aflame with Mordak's unholy scarlet magick. The wind shifted, and the nauseating smell of decomposing flesh washed over the hills. The hidden defenders quickly covered their mouths and noses with sleeves and steeled themselves against the ghastly stench. Stiffening their resolve, they clutched their weapons and waited for the signal. The horde marched on, determined to trample anything or anyone in its path.

Without warning, the first rank of undead fell face-first into the long grass, immediately followed by the second, then the third as they tried to slow, but they were pushed forward by the creatures behind who had not seen the danger. The many tripwires laid across their path had worked flawlessly, leaving the living creatures vulnerable once again to the poisoned darts and deadly arrows of the defenders. The moment the way was clear, the air was suddenly buzzing with darts and arrows. The Gholans, Morcats, and Krell died screaming in pain and anger, and as they collapsed where they stood, bedlam erupted among those behind them.

After the initial volley, the unseen warriors in the grass began stealthily making their way back through the sheltering stalks, continuing to loose arrows in high arcing trajectories that fell into the midst of the mob, causing further confusion. They knew the charge would soon be ordered, and they had to be out of the way before then.

"Forward, you scum! Overwhelm the humans! Feast on their flesh! FORWARD!" Jor Dayne's voice thundered, cutting through the cacophony of yowling and screaming. Gradually, Jor Dayne brought order to the confused creatures around him. Brandishing his huge, jagged sword, he spurred his new horse over the slowly rising bodies of the undead soldiers and pressed forward to attack. Hundreds of angry Gholans and a handful of furious Morcats flanked him on either side while the Krell hung back, waiting to see the results of the charge.

Unseen in the fields ahead, warriors hurried to reach their next positions before the charge reached them. Led by the priestesses of Rowan, as well as Cohl, the Weya, most of the brave warriors of Alverton Falls disappeared like ghosts into the tall grass and headed for their rendezvous points. One squad got turned around somehow and quickly found themselves in brutal combat with the forerunners of the horde. The battle was short and bloody, and a score of brave warriors fell to the claws and fangs of Mordak's creatures. The vile Gholans crowed over their victory by waving grisly trophies, ripped from the dead and dying. Although they met a dire end, each member of the squad took the lives of three or four enemies before their deaths.

From their hiding place, Fiona made a quiet noise of anguish as she saw the bloody conflict. Brunar clenched his teeth in ire as he, too, saw the deaths of the brave warriors. Fortunately, Bjarke chose that moment to attack, and the sight of it filled those in the hidden command post with hope.

Bjarke emerged from the trees of the thick forest to the west, just a short distance from the westernmost ranks of the evil horde. His face was set in a stern, determined scowl. In one hand, he held his Jidaan high overhead. Its ruby pommelgem shone in the deepening dark, its power flaring brightly and drawing all eyes towards the burly warrior. He was dragging something in his other hand, but the tall grass made it all but impossible to see.

It took only moments for those foul creatures closest to Bjarke's light to break ranks and rush towards him, eager to vent their frustration on a single human. Their talons clicked and their jaws snapped in anticipation of tearing the huge bearded warrior to shreds as they scrambled towards him.

Bjarke jammed his Jidaan point-first into the soil so that its pure scarlet light shone brightly, holding the attention of the throng. With his other hand free, he bent down and laid hold of the thick chain that had been spiked into the end of a massive log. The timber was far thicker than a man, and nearly twice as long as a wagon. He took a couple of steps to gain momentum, then pulled the huge timber into a great circular swing. Round and round he went, gaining speed with each turn.

The first Gholans to reach him were utterly smashed by the whirling log, swatted away like broken insects. Bjarke made one more turn, then another, and then he released the bloodied log directly into the oncoming rush of inhuman warriors.

The effect was devastating. Hundreds of Mordak's creatures were crushed as they frantically tried to dodge the enormous, whirling missile. It wobbled and rolled and crashed into the mob, killing as it went. Before any of Mordak's vermin could recover, Bjarke had yanked his Jidaan out of the ground, extinguished its light, and vanished back into the forest. Somewhere on the battlefield, Jor Dayne howled in rage as he struggled to reestablish order among the ranks.

Back in the command post, Count DeRoberds turned to Brunar, an astonished look on his face. "That Bjarke of yours, he's, um...strong."

Brunar allowed himself a smile. "That he is, my lord. That he is." He looked out at the roiling horde as it scrambled to regain its composure. From far in the back, the Mage caught a glimpse of an oily scarlet radiance, a sickly burst of dark magick that could only come from Mordak. Even from that distance, Brunar felt the power of the evil sorcerer as he gathered his strength to counterattack. Brunar briefly hoped that Kiran, Layton, and Nessar had been successful in their quest and would arrive soon with the artifact. In the meantime, they could only fight with everything they had.

"Quickly. It's time to move to our next position. Stay low, I'll hide us as best I can." Brunar turned to find that Fiona had vanished. From somewhere nearby, he heard her quiet voice, a smile somehow evident in her words.

"Don't worry about me. You take care of yourself, old man."

Brunar was not used to smiling so much. Gesturing for the Count to follow, he began easing through the tall grass towards a stand of trees to the east. He was glad, at least, that Alyssa's healing had restored him to almost full strength. It was nearly time for him to place himself directly in the evil sorcerer's path.

Chapter 42

Gart pressed on, guiding Bessie along the lofty trail. He kept the river below to his left and the slope of the Blackthorne Mountains on his right as he headed south. The path followed along the side of the mountains, allowing Gart a breathtaking view to the west. Beyond the river, the land rolled and swayed for many miles before leveling out and becoming more gentle and flat. Trees dotted the landscape, gradually becoming a dense forest well before the horizon. The sun had already crawled beyond the peaks to Gart's right, leaving the sky above colored in beautiful purples and pinks. Its passage beyond the mountains had left him in shadow as he pressed forward, and he started looking for a likely spot to camp for the night.

A flash far to the west caught his attention, and he reined Bessie to a halt so he could get a better look. "Whoa there, girl. Did you see that?" Bessie huffed briefly but offered no further reply. Gart shifted in the saddle and peered out over the land, enjoying the cool breeze that washed over him. He had noticed it out of the corner of his eye, a momentary glint. It was like the reflection of the sun on the water, but somehow different, hinting at several colors at once. Although his eyes were keen, he saw nothing but the gently winding river below and the green of the distant trees.

As he was about to kick Bessie into action again, he caught sight of not one, but two bright spots of light in the distance. One was roughly where he thought the first had been, the other much closer. They shone for only a moment, then both disappeared again. Gart's hand drifted to his sword, but then he removed it. Whatever was out there was miles away, and could not possibly pose a danger no matter what it was.

Another pair of flashes arose, appearing to make a straight line towards the mountains Gart now rode through. If they continued moving in the same direction, whatever it was would cross the road not far ahead of Gart, although they would have an arduous climb to reach the path. That could take hours.

Fascinated, Gart watched as more flashes arose, always in pairs, and always moving along the land on a southwestern path. He wondered what it could be. *Magick. Has to be,* he silently answered his own question.

Soon, the bright flares had moved close enough that he could finally see something of their origin. Squinting into the distance, he saw the nearer of a pair of colorful bursts appear ahead of him on the far side of the river down below. He was astonished to see what looked like a rough square of brightness, swirling with all the colors he had ever seen, suddenly appear out of thin air. Even more surprising was the fact that two riders emerged from it, their horses unperturbed, as though their actions were commonplace. Gart peered more closely and noticed one horse had what looked like a body tied to it. The distance was great enough that he could see very little detail, but he got a strong impression that one of the riders was female.

As he contemplated this, he saw yet another bright square of light burst into being right in front of the pair far below, while another appeared on the road a stone's throw directly ahead of him. Before he could even take another breath, the riders walked into the bright square below and emerged on the same path as Gart. The two incredible doorways disappeared, just as they had before.

Definitely magick, he thought. They were still far enough away that they would not be able to hear him over the rush of the river, even if he yelled. Though they were out of earshot, he could finally see them well enough to know they had not seen him yet. There was a man and a woman, both garbed as warriors, in addition to the inert body on the woman's horse. They had a tired, dirty look to them, and Gart could see what he thought were bloodstains on their clothing. The female turned in her saddle to check on the body. She reached out and appeared to touch it briefly on the neck, then gave it a few pats on the shoulder. *Hmm. That one might be alive, then. A wounded ally, perhaps?*

Suddenly, Gart saw something that electrified him. The woman wore a shoulder harness similar to his own, and he could see the pommel of a short spear sticking up. The man, too, was carrying a spear in his hand that echoed Gart's. Before he could call out, a flare of scintillant brightness exploded from the pommelgem of the man's weapon, and another of the bright squares of light sprang to life in front of the trio, obviously a portal of some kind.

"Wait! WAIT!" Gart yelled, startling Bessie. He heeled her into action and burst into a gallop towards them. The two were already moving into the magickal doorway, the man having disappeared into it first. The woman turned and looked at Gart, her expression startled. She kicked her heels into her horse's flanks and hurried through the square of opalescent energy, keeping a wary eye on Gart as he rode towards her. Gart leaned over Bessie's neck and urged her to run faster, straining to catch up with them.

It was no use. In no more than two heartbeats, the pair disappeared into the portal and the magickal doorway blinked out of existence. Gart cursed in frustration as he pulled on the reins and eased Bessie to a walk. He knew there were others out there, others like him. Guardians. The pair he had seen must be such as well, on their way to the battle Agatha had described. He knew he had to be getting close. Somewhere nearby, the creatures that had destroyed his village and killed his wife and daughter were doing battle, and more innocents were dying. But this time, he had the power to help.

Gart kicked Bessie into a ground-eating trot, mindful of her growing weariness, yet desperate to make faster progress. The sight of the other Guardians had galvanized him. He had no idea who they were, but the fact that they had been moving southwest confirmed Alverton Falls as his goal rather than Laro. According to Agatha - *Aggie,* he corrected himself - the road he was on would take him directly to the city. But how long it would take, he was uncertain, and that was bothering him. The farther he got from the spot he had seen the other Guardians, the more itchy he became. They had been traveling in a straight line across the land, right into the side of the mountain where Gart had seen them. They had vanished from there, presumably to a point farther along the course they had plotted, which almost certainly led them to Alverton Falls to the west.

And he was riding farther and farther south.

Gart reined Bessie to a stop and gathered his thoughts. The full moon overhead showed the mountain path very clearly, and to Gart's eye, it continued to the south for at least another day's ride. Gart looked to the mountain on his right. At first, the steep slope looked impassable. Awakening his magick, he closed his eyes and reached out with it, searching for a way up. His senses came alive as his magick moved quickly over the rocks and ledges, caressing the mountainside with Gart's energy and sending information back to him.

As a picture began to emerge in Gart's mind, he opened up and sent even more magick out over the mountain. He sensed the presence of minute details, the positions of animals startled by the tingling touch of his power, the rough edges and slippery slopes that made up the Blackthorne Mountains. He opened his eyes and froze at the sight that greeted him.

The entire mountainside was glowing with a soft, golden light. It spread out in all directions only a few inches above the surface of the stone, a gentle, misty fog that Gart was surprised to see emanating from his own body. As he lost concentration, the sensations from the mountainside suddenly faded into nothingness, and the golden light likewise disappeared. He sat in Bessie's saddle for a few quiet moments, assimilating what had just happened.

I'm getting stronger, he realized. It had only been seconds, but he now knew every inch of the mountainside for nearly a mile around. He knew there were ground squirrels, a small herd of mountain goats, and a handful of snakes that he needed to avoid, and he knew right down to the inch where they were.

More importantly, he knew exactly how to get himself and Bessie over the mountain. It would not be easy, but he had not expected it to be.

Gart's scarred face split in a grin. However, had anyone been around to see him, they would have noticed that his eyes remained cold as blue ice.

Soon, he thought. *I'm coming for you, Jor Dayne. Mordak. I know I'm getting close. Your time is almost up.*

Chapter 43

Most of the warriors from Alverton Falls had survived the first battle, and hundreds of Mordak's evil soldiers had fallen to the Count's stealthy tactics. Brunar and the others had retreated nearly another mile to the north, allowing their forces time to regroup and prepare for the next attack. They were only a mile or so away from the open land just south of the river and city, so they knew they had to stop as many of them as possible. Brunar hoped it would be enough to push Mordak's forces into retreat, or else they would have to fall back into the trenches and fortifications they had prepared and hope to hold out as best they could. Still, Mordak's army numbered in the thousands, and it did not look good.

Brunar stood in the flattest part of the land, feeling the thrum of his magick flowing through him as he maintained his enchantment. He held his staff in his left hand, planted firmly in the soil at his feet. It glowed with an intense purple light that played over its length as his power suffused it, though no one could see it. His other hand was empty for now, so he could use it to gesture when he cast his spells. There he stood, unseen, a single man awaiting an army, while the others took their places nearby.

The Mage did not have long to wait. He felt their approach from far away, their collective evil energies grating on his awareness and making him vaguely ill. Brunar shook it off and mentally checked over the spell he had cast upon himself. Although not nearly as effective as Nessar's Jidaan, the enchantment rendered him invisible. As Mordak's army crawled over the terrain, looking from that distance like a swarm of army ants that covered the land as far as he could see, Brunar steeled himself for what he knew would come.

Step by clawfooted step they came, their very touch despoiling the land upon which they walked. Ranks of vile, slavering Gholans skittered along in the lead, bearing makeshift shields to protect them from the deadly arrows and darts of the allies. Morcats strode among the ranks, keeping order among the unruly Gholans. The undead had moved to the rear of the horde, and the Krell had been moved to the flanks to protect against another devastating attack from Bjarke. He had thrown three immense logs into the host, killing scores of the enemy each time, before being forced to make his escape from the savage cannibal warriors that surged into the forest to find him. Brunar allowed himself a grin as he saw that Jor Dayne had chosen to ride on that side of the horde, no doubt hoping for a chance to vent his frustration on the huge Guardian.

Under the pale light of the full moon that had risen over the Blackthorne Mountains to the east, Brunar allowed himself a grin as he surveyed the army that marched unknowingly towards his position. His spell was working perfectly, and they did not see him. Soon, they drew close enough that he could hear the guttural, slurring speech of the Gholans as they muttered to each other. He could even smell the rank, rotten odor that invariably accompanied the foul creatures. The Mage carefully covered his face with his sleeve to filter out the stench, if only for the short time that remained until he sprung his trap. He kept as still as possible as the front lines came closer.

Brunar finally moved when the first rank of Gholans was close enough to touch. He shifted slightly to his left so that two of them would pass on either side, then became still once more as he waited for the middle of the horde to reach his position. A Morcat walked by a mere arm's length away, and it suddenly stopped to sniff the air. Brunar tensed, one hand slowly inching closer to his sword. He could not yet risk a flare of magick to defend himself; that would alert Mordak to his presence, and his plan would certainly go awry.

Fortunately, the huge beast chuffed once as if clearing its nose of a foul smell and then stalked away. Brunar watched it go, then turned back to scan the remainder of the mob as it flowed past him. The moon's glow cast a silvery light over the enormous mass of dark bodies that quietly swarmed over the landscape, undulating like waves on a benighted ocean. As far as his eyes could see, the land was simply covered with Mordak's creatures. Dismay threatened Brunar's heart, but he held strong against it. He had seen odds like this before, and against this very adversary. Two thousand years ago, Brunar and his allies had been victorious, though it had come at a steep price.

Shaking off the memories and the pain that always followed them, Brunar took a deep breath and let it out, focusing his mind on the task at hand. It was almost time. Carefully, gradually, he called on his magick, increasing its magnitude in preparation for the spell he was about to cast.

High on a nearby hill, sheltered in a small grove of trees, Count DeRoberds and Captain Jeddah stoically watched the oncoming army.

"When will the Mage spring his trap?" the captain whispered.

Count DeRoberds kept his eyes on the massive flood of evil creatures that steadily advanced on his beloved city. The shorter but deadly Gholans were being urged along by their overseers, the burly Morcats. Ferocious Krell warriors traveled in small groups throughout the horde. No less than a dozen massive shamblebeasts were present, and Count DeRoberds' blood ran cold at the sight of the enormous, vine-covered beasts. In his heart, he was fervently praying to the Goddess Rowann that the Mage's plan would work. They were woefully outnumbered, and the only equalizer they had was the powers of the Mage and Guardians, only one of whom had any kind of destructive power. He replied to the captain without taking his eyes off the horde.

"Any moment now. Just be ready to give the command to loose arrows when you see it."

The captain was a bit confused. "See what, exactly? I'm not sure what he is going to do out there."

"You'll know it, Captain."

And at that moment, a massive thunderclap nearly scared the life out of them both, and an enormous flare of red and yellow brightness appeared above the ranks. Mordak's creatures flung themselves on the ground in fear as an immense dragon suddenly appeared overhead. It was easily three stories high, its scarlet and gold scales shimmering in the dark. Huge muscles bunched and flexed as it unfurled massive wings, spreading them wide as it confronted the army of tiny beings below. Its head was ridged and horned, with great golden eyes that stared down in disgust at the screaming Gholans as they scrambled madly to escape the beast's formidable fangs and claws. Throwing back its reptilian head, it bellowed a roar of challenge that shook the leaves from nearby trees and struck fear in the hearts of Mordak's fell legions.

"I'm...I'm pretty sure that's it." The Count's eyes were wide in disbelief as he took in the sight of the majestic beast that now menaced the horde. Turning to his captain, who was equally slack-jawed, he recovered his authority. "Signal the attack! Hit them from both sides, now!" The captain quickly stepped out into the open and unshuttered a small lantern he had prepared for that purpose. He swung it in a wide arc, back and forth, three times. Instantly, he saw an answering arc of lantern light from the trees on both sides of the beleaguered throng, and arrows immediately took flight.

As if to confirm that the battle had truly begun, the dragon filled its lungs and sent a sweeping blast of fiery breath down over the terrified soldiers of Mordak's vile army, incinerating them by the score. Those on either side who had escaped the intense flames ran right into a deadly hail of arrows from the hidden soldiers of Alverton Falls. In the middle of it all, Brunar struggled to control the illusion of the dragon, as well as the true fire that it breathed, all while maintaining the enchantment that kept him invisible to the frantic creatures that surrounded him on all sides. Thanks to Alyssa's healing, he was strong enough to manage it all, if only for a short time.

The battle raged on all sides. Jor Dayne led the Krell on the western flank in a hunt for the huge man that had harried them earlier with his enormous strength. Jor Dayne was furious that the red-bearded warrior did not appear, and he drove the Krell and vicious little Gholans into the forest to take the fight to the archers he knew were there. Finally, he was rewarded by the terrified screams of dying soldiers as the Krell crashed into their positions before they could retreat. Some tried to escape by running towards the battlefield, hoping to lose themselves in the chaos wrought by Brunar's dragon, but Jor Dayne swiftly cut down any that came close. Blood spattered his sword and his armor and he laughed as the joyous sounds of battle filled his ears.

At the rear of the horde, Mordak's raspy voice bellowed from inside the litter. "Put me down, you fools!" The Krell bearers carefully set down their lord, then stepped away to kneel and press their foreheads to the dirt, lest they offend him. Still cloaked in the guise of the young, blond-haired Balroth, Mordak stepped from his litter and stared at the massive dragon that was laying waste to his army. He knew it for what it was in an instant, an illusion combined with a flame spell. He immediately began searching for the Mage that had conjured it.

Intent as he was on the battle in front of him, Mordak failed to see a large pile of dirt suddenly rise up from the thoroughly trodden earth they had just crossed over. Had he looked, he might have seen that the dirt-covered figure held something shiny in its big hands, a short spear with a long blade and a ruby that suddenly flared to life at Bjarke's command.

Mordak caught sight of the ruby glint of power behind him and turned to look over his shoulder. "Eh?"

That's when Bjarke released a scathing blast of power from his Jidaan. The intense bolt of scarlet energy shattered Mordak's litter into kindling. The Krell bearers died as they lunged towards Bjarke, weapons and teeth bared, but their broken bodies were flung away like leaves on the wind in the face of the Guardian's power.

For just a moment, Bjarke allowed himself to believe that he had done it; he had killed Mordak. But then he saw the sickly crimson shine of Mordak's power from high overhead. He realized that the sorcerer had escaped on the wings of his unholy magick, somehow springing away before Bjarke's bolt could slay him. The huge forester cursed aloud as he watched the reddish blot glide up into the night sky, well out of his reach. He followed the path of Mordak's flight and saw that he was heading towards Brunar's illusory dragon, which was still throwing flame into the middle of the army.

The Vile One is in the air, Brunar. I'm sorry. I did my best to catch him unawares, but he escaped. Bjarke's frustration seeped across the mindlink he shared with the Mage, but if Brunar was discouraged with Bjarke's lack of success, the big forester could not tell.

It's all right, just make your way to the western flank and aid our allies there. Jor Dayne is on that side, and I think that Alyssa and the priestesses are giving him Hel. They could use you.

By then, the nearest ranks of the horde were upon him, glad to be fighting just one man rather than the dragon that lay ahead. Bjarke took a deep breath as he prepared to cut his way through each and every one of them, Gholan, Morcat, and undead warrior alike. He sent Brunar a brief affirmative and got to work. His power flared again, the ruby pommel of his Jidaan answering his call as he lashed out and killed the first Morcat that attacked with its vicious claws. Somewhere ahead, he knew that Alyssa waited, and if he fought hard enough, he could make his way back to her. As he began his grisly work, he prayed to Rowann that he would hold her in his arms again soon.

Chapter 44

From his high vantage point, Mordak looked down at the battlefield. Although momentarily routed by the dragon's flames and attacks from either flank, their superior numbers were starting to tell, just as he knew they would. A sharp pain worked its way through his magickal ward, and he knew that he would have to use his surprise guests soon. He focused a bit more energy on his internal barriers and the pain subsided.

That fool using Rhu's weapon almost had me, he thought. *But he's young yet. Inexperienced. Now it's time to show them all who they are up against.*

Casting several vision spells in rapid succession, he finally managed to locate Brunar on the battlefield below. He knew the Mage had to be close by to control the image of the dragon, as well as the intense flames that issued from its gaping maw. Cloaking himself so that his scarlet glow of power would not give him away, Mordak drifted slowly down out of the sky, careful to avoid the dragon's fiery breath.

To his augmented vision, Brunar appeared in shades of red, a stern expression on his face. He held a staff overhead in both hands, the length of it glowing white and orange to Mordak's eyes. The sorcerer smiled and allowed his glamour to fall away, revealing himself without the appearance of Balroth's youthful face. He wanted Brunar to see him.

Brunar's eyes widened in shock as Mordak appeared mere yards away, floating on a cloud of unholy power. Before he could draw breath to cast a spell of protection, Mordak raised his hands and Brunar's world vanished in a burst of red and white.

Mordak laughed as he blasted his old adversary, laughed as his fiery, crimson energy launched out of his outstretched arms to slam into the body of the Mage. Brunar flew backwards, the front of his robe already blackened and burnt, his body limp. He landed in a heap of tangled limbs, his staff broken nearby. He lay still.

"Finally!" Mordak yelled in triumph. "You've been a thorn in my side for two thousand years, you fool! And look what it's gotten you. DEAD, that's what! Now, I just need to finish off your little Guardians!"

Turning to survey the field, he saw the shamblebeasts acting as a living shield wall as they led a force of Gholans and Morcats into the trees to the east. Their roots and limbs formed a natural armor that protected them from the arrows and swords of the warriors there, and even now, Mordak could hear the screams of soldiers as they were ripped apart. Mordak smiled, knowing that his shamblers would lay waste to everything on that flank. To the west, he saw the flashing sword of Jor Dayne as he directed more Gholans to swarm the archers on that side.

Leaving the shamblebeasts to themselves, Mordak started towards his Champion. *That oversized fool is probably doing something wrong.* After taking a moment to be sure he still had control over the wriggling cargo he held within him, Mordak marched to the western flank to set things right.

Meanwhile, Jor Dayne was relishing the success of his squad of Krell and Gholans. They had spilled much blood among the trees, and were starting to edge towards the north, where another huge pocket of resistance was starting to make progress. A flash of sparkling white light caught the huge half-daemon's attention, and he stared into the darkness to make it out. It came again, and he realized that it was a small and nimble woman bearing the same kind of spear he had seen used at Laro. Whenever a nearby warrior would go down, its pommel would blaze brightly for a moment. Each time, the woman who wielded it would gesture towards the fallen warrior. Wherever she invoked whatever power was in the spear, those injured soldiers would suddenly regain their feet and fight with renewed vigor. They did not rise as Mordak's would, slow of gait and eyes glowing red as his power possessed and reanimated their bodies. No, they rose whole and sound, ready to fight even harder. Jor Dayne's interest was piqued. She was lovely.

"Well, well, this just won't do," Jor Dayne said aloud, his deep voice purring seductively in the night. "I'll just have to go and deal with this luscious little girl with a spear. She looks positively delicious!"

Just as he was about to move towards her, he felt a firm grip on his left arm. He looked down to see his master, Mordak, holding fast to his wrist.

"Where do you think you're going, lackey?" Mordak's voice dripped with contempt.

"A Guardian is over there, and that side is weakening. I will break her!" Jor Dayne's grin was wide, indeed. In a whisper, he added, "She is mine!"

"No!" Mordak replied curtly. "No, go deal with the big one. He is far more troubling than that little wench. Do it now!" He pointed one long-fingered hand towards the turmoil that Bjarke was causing, flares of bright crimson magick punctuating his powerful blows. Singlehandedly, he was working his way into the middle of the horde, and nothing, not even the shamblebeasts, had been able to stop him. Soon, he would join his allies at the front. If they turned and fought all together, it would be disastrous.

"But..." Jor Dayne scowled down at the sorcerer who had called his daemonic soul from the netherworld and bonded it into the body of a strong warrior, making it even stronger as a result. He was bound to do Mordak's bidding, but his limits were being reached.

Mordak looked up at him in outrage. "You will do as I SAY you humongous oaf! I summoned you! I created you! I OWN YOU!"

Something cracked inside Jor Dayne at long last as his final bonds fell away. The spell Mordak had used was ancient, and often mistranslated. Unbeknownst to Mordak, it had been written with an ironic release trigger, and those were the very three words that released Jor Dayne from bondage.

Jor Dayne barked a short, vicious laugh in disbelief at his new feeling of freedom. Then he raised his sword high in the air. Astonished, Mordak tried to shield himself, but he was too late. Jor Dayne's jagged sword slammed down into the sorcerer's collarbone and continued into his chest. The half-daemon yanked the gory weapon away, leaving Mordak to fall backwards to the bloody earth, his eyes wide with betrayal. He knew that the sorcerer would be able to heal himself. But it would hurt in the meantime. Oh, how it would hurt.

"Not anymore. Go handle the big one yourself! I am no longer your servant. Good riddance to you, filth! I fight for myself!" Jor Dayne turned and strode away, heading straight towards the flashing in the near distance, towards the female Guardian. A squad of warriors from Alverton Falls flowed into the gap between them as they engaged another group of Gholans and Krell, and he began cutting his way through them. Jor Dayne smiled his biggest smile as he stalked towards the object of his sudden desire.

Chapter 45

"That was close! Did you see that rider on the high road with us back there? Another few seconds, and he'd have caught up with us." Kiran shook her head, then looked back yet again to make sure that Nessar was still firmly tied to the saddle of the horse behind her.

Layton scanned their new surroundings and was pleased to see they had arrived exactly where he had intended. "Yes, I saw him." Then he grinned, his smile visible in the moonlight. "I'm pretty sure you could take him, Kiran."

Kiran scoffed at him. "Well, of course! He'd have been pretty surprised when I laid him out on the road with one punch."

"Exactly," Layton agreed with a tired chuckle. He had no idea what the stranger on the road had wanted, but he was certain that Kiran would have handled him accordingly. She'd have knocked him right out from under that battered hat he was wearing, and she'd have enjoyed it.

Layton scanned the rocks around them. The three Guardians had come out of his Gate on a ledge that surrounded Balroth's Abyss. The enormous crater sat right on the western edge of the Blackthorne Mountains, and the huge depression overlooked the Alvion River and the city of Alverton Falls beyond, all the way to the edges of the Shadowed Forest. The rushing sound of the waterfall on the far side of the crater confirmed that they were exactly where they needed to be. Satisfied that they were safe for the moment, he cast his gaze farther west to gauge the distance to the city, but movement to the south caught his eye.

What he saw chilled his blood.

The land was flat and open south of the city. Layton could see that the fortifications had been expanded since their departure, but that was not what concerned him. Farther south, where the land turned more hilly, the surface of the earth seemed to be moving. It appeared to be covered with a twitching blanket of darkness that slowly crawled northward towards the city.

Mordak's troops had arrived.

"Kiran, we've got to move! The enemy is marching on the city right this minute, look!" He pointed at the invading army in the distance, thousands strong.

Kiran's head snapped around, and she looked where the Weaponsmaster had indicated. It took her only a moment to see what he had seen.

"Great Theonas' balls!" she cursed. "Let's go, then! Nessar is still snoozing, but he's secure. Come on, come on!"

Just then, a great burst of crimson and gold exploded over the distant horde, and Layton watched the faraway creatures suddenly spread out, clearing away from the blast. The light boiled and seethed for a moment before coalescing into a mighty beast that immediately began bathing the mob in deadly fire. Several seconds later, the echoes of the initial explosion finally reached them.

"Sweet goddess above..." Layton's voice trailed off into silence as he watched the magnificent creature laying waste to the enemy in the distance. He knew Brunar was a powerful Mage, but this was truly impressive. Both he and Kiran paused for a moment, awestruck by the skill of their mentor. Their enhanced senses were tingling from the power Brunar had unleashed.

"Hey," a soft voice surprised them. "Hey, I think I'm gonna be sick. Could someone get me down from here?" Nessar's voice was rough and woozy.

"Not now!" Kiran's immediate reply surprised Layton, who gawked at her. "Look, we need to get down there right away! Ness is fine where he is. Now let's go!"

Layton shook his head ruefully. "All right, but he's going to be pretty upset."

"Yeah, yeah, now come on! They need us down there, and we've got to get this thing to Brunar!"

In a flash of brilliant opalescence, they entered another of Layton's Gates and exited to find themselves far below in the foothills. Another few Gates would take them to the fortifications just south of the city, where they were sure to find the others. Once there, they could unstrap a now constantly cursing Nessar from where he lay across his horse's rump.

They did not see Bessie just cresting the ridge above them, nor did they see the piercing blue eyes beneath the brim of Gart's floppy hat as he carefully guided her over the rocks.

He, too, had seen Brunar's dragon. And he, too, was determined to strike a blow at the enemy.

Chapter 46

Alyssa and Emmi fought side by side, whirling, dodging, and killing with almost effortless grace. Alyssa was glad to be on the front lines at last, rather than safely tucked away as she had been at Laro. She knew she was being selfish, but after seeing so many hurt by Mordak's vile creatures, she was ready to even the scales a bit. She took to healing the wounded right in the middle of the battle, using her incredible powers of focus and concentration to reach out and restore soldiers even as they took grievous wounds, their gashes and punctures gone before they could fall to the ground. It was exceedingly difficult, especially when hacking and slashing at the same time. However, Alyssa found that she could do it, and her Jidaan flashed its diamond brilliance repeatedly as she both fought and healed.

Her squad had met up with Emmi's, and the combined force had run roughshod over the Gholans that had assailed them. Suddenly, out of the dark, a pair of Morcats rose up and yowled ferociously. The first soldier they met was quickly clawed to death, as was the next. They were big, strong, and incredibly quick, and where they walked, warriors died.

"Alyssa!" Emmi yelled over the din of combat. "I'll take the one on the left!"

Before Alyssa could respond, Emmi had already burst into a sprint towards the beast, leaving her to face its companion. It focused bright, slitted eyes on her and growled in challenge as it flexed claws already dripping with the blood of brave warriors.

That made her angry.

Gathering her energy as Brunar had taught her, she lunged forward with her Jidaan, stabbing the huge creature in the leg before darting back out of reach of its bloody claws. It yowled in pain and clutched at the wound for a moment before focusing on her again. She feinted forward as though she were attacking the same way, but the Morcat was ready. It slashed ferociously at her, but she was not there. As the beast swung at her, she sprang high over its head and twisted so that she landed feet first on its burly shoulders. Using the momentum from her jump, she slammed the blade of her Jidaan deep into the juncture of its neck and back, severing its spine. The creature instantly went limp and collapsed, and Alyssa performed a diving roll, coming up with her Jidaan at the ready.

Her heart sank as she heard Emmi's scream. She whipped around to see her held tightly in the arms of the other

Morcat. It was crushing her, and even as Alyssa listened, she heard muffled cracks and pops along with Emmi's cries of agony. Before Alyssa could rush to her aid, she saw Emmi free the arm that held her dagger. As blood sprayed from her mouth from her internal injuries, she slammed the point of the dagger home into the creature's eye socket. It dropped as if poleaxed, and Emmi fell awkwardly to the ground with it, her broken body twisted.

Emmi was hurt too badly to heal on the fly, but killing the Morcats had left a momentary lull in the fighting. Alyssa rushed to her side and grabbed her by the collar. Within moments, she had dragged the woman into a nearby hollow. Two other wounded warriors crawled into the minimal shelter after her.

The moon bathed the inside of the improvised shelter in silvery light just bright enough for Alyssa to see her patient. She held her hands over Emmi's battered body, using her power to sense the extent of her injuries. They were grave, but she had healed worse. At her side, her Jidaan flared brilliantly as she focused on fixing the deep internal issues first. As her power repaired and energized Emmi's body, the injured priestess gasped and arched her back. Alyssa continued until Emmi was whole once again and they both relaxed.

Without warning, the young priestess sat up and planted a big kiss on Alyssa's cheek. "You are a gift from the Goddess, Alyssa! I feel like I could take them all on myself!" Without another word, Emmi stalked over to the edge of the hollow and then she was gone, presumably to continue her one-woman attack on the enemy.

Next, Alyssa focused intently on the two men who lay before her, and decided to try healing them both at once. Neither was fatally wounded, but time was of the essence, so she resolved to do her best. She grimaced as she channeled her weapon's energy into the two men, her brow furrowing in concentration. The healing took only moments, and the men both gasped and sat up in surprise, their wounds completely gone.

As her Jidaan darkened, she sat back with a relieved sigh. The double healing had worked.

Just then the eyes of both men flew wide, and one of them drew his dagger and scrambled forward. He roughly shoved Alyssa aside as he flung himself at a pair of Gholans that had climbed over the lip of the pit in which they had been hiding. The other man followed suit, only to be overcome by the half dozen creatures that skittered in to help their hideous brethren. The men's screams were short, but defiant to the end.

Alyssa regained her feet and whipped her Jidaan's shining blade through the throats of the first Gholans that came at her, then stabbed the next in rapid succession. Placing her foot directly on the fallen corpses of the beasts, she focused her energy into her legs and sprang high into the air, arcing up and out of her momentary refuge with a single graceful flip.

She landed deftly on the ground several yards away from the pit, right in the midst of a Gholan squad that had already been headed in her direction. She was eye-level with the hideous, bloodthirsty creatures, and they quickly moved to attack her, thinking her to be easy prey.

That, she was not.

Although she did not possess a lifetime of training such as Layton or Kiran, Alyssa had pushed herself mercilessly during her time in the mountains with Brunar. Using her natural ability to focus and a good dose of old-fashioned stubbornness, she had mastered the basics of fighting with fists and feet as well as with the shining spear she now wielded. She was terrified of each and every monster that lunged, clawed, and snapped at her, but her anger far outweighed her fear. She drove straight into their midst, hacking, dodging, stabbing, and whirling all the while. Everywhere she went, Gholans fell dead and screaming, none able to so much as put a claw on her.

Over the sounds of the melee, she heard a man bellow in rage and frustration. She recognized the voice of Jor Dayne, the huge leader of Mordak's forces. Even as she continued to fight anything that came within her reach, she looked toward the sound and saw the hulking warrior locked in battle with several men from Alverton Falls. He swung his great sword in vicious arcs, with a cruel smile on his lips and eyes that blazed yellow in the dimming light.

For the first time, Alyssa saw something more. It was fleeting, little better than a flash, but she saw a shape within the shape of the huge man. She focused her magick on him as she fought, struggling to make sense of what she saw.

As her power came to the fore, it displayed a surprising scene to her eyes. Within the silhouette of the enormous warrior was someone else, another being entirely. He was smaller, but not by much. As Alyssa stared, she watched his form become clearer to her magickal sight, and details emerged. He shared Jor Dayne's face, but gone was the evil glare in his eyes, the devilish grin. Instead, the man within wore an expression of desperation, of intense anguish. His body moved in time with Jor Dayne's, suffering with every blow that was struck, helpless to resist.

Alyssa watched Jor Dayne's sword run through another warrior from Alverton Falls, and although she heard his laughter, the man trapped within him recoiled in horror and shame at the act.

Her Gift opened her eyes to what Jor Dayne really was: a man. Just a man, but with a daemon latched onto his soul. Like so many others, his body had been hijacked against his will by the evil sorcerer. As Jor Dayne swung his enormous blade, Alyssa's healing magick showed her what needed to be done. With a few final slashes and stabs at the Gholans nearest her, Alyssa channeled her power into her legs and leapt high into the air. She landed a few yards away from the towering, grinning man-daemon just as he felled the last of the men that had been attacking him. He turned his reptilian smile directly on her. The power in his gaze sent a chill down her spine.

"Well, hello, my pet," he said in a sensual, slithering tone. "It's so sweet of you to come to me. I regret that I am far too busy at the moment to make proper use of you, my love." His slitted yellow eyes gleamed down into hers, their insidious power crawling over her, and she shuddered at the repellent feel of it.

"Oh, I'm not here for you, Jor Dayne." She shifted her stance a little as she surveyed the giant before her. Her Jidaan gleamed brightly in front of her, held firmly in her steady hands. Its blade shone as cleanly as if it were new, for Gholan blood could not stain its surface for long. Alyssa saw confusion dawn in his serpent's eyes at her words. "I'm here for the man whose body you've stolen. I'm setting him free."

A brief burst of surprise and unaccustomed fear flitted across Jor Dayne's face before rage found a home there. Gripping his huge, jagged blade with both hands, he raised it high and brought it down with all his might, intending to cleave Alyssa from crown to feet. It whistled through the air with astonishing power behind it, but she was not there. Knowing she could not match his force with her own, she deftly sidestepped as the terrible blow slammed into the earth where she had been. Steeling herself for what she knew she had to do, she whirled and brought the razor-sharp blade of her Jidaan down and neatly severed both of Jor Dayne's arms at the wrists. His hands remained where they were, firmly clutching the great and bloody sword's handle, and blood sprayed from his arms. Jor Dayne bellowed in agony and fell away from her. She had anticipated his movement, and swiftly hooked one booted foot behind his heel and swept him completely off balance. He landed flat on his back with a resounding thump, his cries of pain momentarily silenced as the wind left his lungs.

Alyssa jumped on his chest, holding her Jidaan in one hand and reaching for his throat with the other. She stared down and saw fear blossom in Jor Dayne's terrible, serpentine eyes.

"No! NO!" He struggled to get the words out, but Alyssa paid him no attention. Holding her weapon overhead so that all could see, she called to her Jidaan. It answered, blazing so brightly that none nearby could look at it. She gasped as its power coursed through her and slammed into the huge being on the ground. He struggled mightily and snarled like a trapped animal, but he could not throw Alyssa off of him, and the fire of the Jidaan was in him now. Finally, he opened his mouth and screamed, a long and mournful howl that echoed through the night. Even as he howled, the voice changed, softened, and slowly became more human than beast. When the Jidaan's light finally went out, the body beneath Alyssa's hands was smaller, and the fight was gone from him. Jor Dayne was gone, and only the man, Lucanos, remained.

Lucanos looked up at Alyssa, not trusting his ability to speak.

"Thank...thank you." Tears of relief and anguish trailed from the corners of his eyes, making tracks through the dust of battle. He murmured faintly, the sound a mere shadow of the deep and sonorous voice possessed by the daemon while in his body. "I tried to stop him, but I couldn't. Not strong enough. Thank you."

Alyssa's own tears fell and she quickly wiped a sleeve over her face. She did not know this man, only that he had been a pawn of Mordak. His mutated body had been nothing more than a vehicle for the daemon, Jor Dayne. The huge warrior had committed innumerable atrocities, leaving the devastated man before her to carry the guilt for each and every one. She leaned closer, sniffling, intending to ask his name. Before she could say a word, the light went out of his eyes, and he was gone. More tears fell as she reached out to close the man's eyes. For a moment, she knelt there in reverence and sorrow, staring at the still features of the man that had been Jor Dayne.

Without warning, Alyssa's Jidaan was ripped from her grasp by a snakelike tendril of scarlet magick. It floated in front of her, just out of her reach. She gasped and desperately lunged for it, but it eluded her, borne on misty coils of power. Before Alyssa could say another word, the serpentine arm lashed forward with the deadly weapon, slamming the blade into her chest and piercing her heart. The impact knocked her back several feet, and she stumbled clumsily until she fell on her back, her own weapon still embedded deeply in her body. Before she could reach up and pull it out, before she could call its power to heal herself, the crimson tendril yanked the spear out of her and then whipped it through the air. It sailed end over end in a high arc over the bloody combat that raged on the field nearby, flying so far away that Alyssa could not reach it, even with her magick. She lost sight of it in seconds as it disappeared somewhere on the battlefield. Although it was not far away, in her current state, it might as well have been on the far side of the moon.

She stared after it, hardly believing that it was gone. The agony in her chest was astonishing, and it was becoming increasingly difficult to breathe. She struggled to speak, her hands clutching at the wound in her chest as she lay there in the bloody dirt.

A face suddenly loomed over her. It was a young man with blond hair pulled back into a long braid that lay over his right shoulder. He was clad in a simple black robe trimmed in scarlet. His boyish face would have been handsome but for the cruelty that shone forth from his scarlet eyes. As she watched, his entire body blurred and shimmered, his image changing. A moment later, the façade of the Daemon-God Balroth was gone, and Mordak stood above her, with his mane of silver hair and hawk-like nose. The eyes had not changed a bit.

He leaned over her, studying her intently. "Fool! How poetic. Killed by the weapon you used to heal so many. How wonderful!" He laughed, madness and mirth combined. He planted a muddy boot on her body in triumph and laughed harder. It had taken quite a bit of energy to heal himself after Jor Dayne had nearly cleaved his body in two, but it had been worth it, both to see the huge half-daemon fall to this little girl, and then to kill her in turn.

Alyssa looked up at him, taking in the hideous bumps and bulges that covered every inch of exposed skin, the filth of his garments, the insanity of his gaze. She wished it had been different. She wished she could have done more to stop him. In the end, she wished for Bjarke.

With Mordak's boot on her bloody chest, Alyssa died.

From a stone's throw away, Bjarke had just dispatched another of the huge shamblebeasts with a vicious slash of his Jidaan that lopped off its misshapen head with a *CRACK*! He had just let it drop to the ground when he felt Alyssa call to him. Her voice was loud in his head, stopping him in his tracks.

"My love..." Her voice drifted away and she said nothing more.

Frantically, Bjarke turned and searched for her. It took only moments for him to spy Mordak standing nearby. The sorcerer was peering down at a body, one booted foot firmly planted on the small form.

Bjarke's eyes grew wide with horror and a chill ran through him. He could see a spill of auburn hair spread out on the bloody earth beneath the body, its limbs splayed like those of a discarded doll. Mordak was laughing with his head thrown back, as if her death was thoroughly amusing to him.

"No," Bjarke whispered. In that moment, he did not want to believe what he was seeing. It could not possibly be real. She was just in his arms, alive and warm and smiling, only hours ago. He remembered the feel of her, small, but strong. He remembered the smooth touch of her cheek, the smell of her hair.

Something broke inside him.

Bjarke's cry of rage made the very ground shake and struck fear into the hearts of every vile creature that heard it. They cowered and ran from the huge man whose Jidaan had suddenly ignited into a crimson flare of blinding, intense power, shining like a beacon. He held the weapon in both hands and raised it over his head, channeling all of his fury and anguish into it. Then he brought the unbreakable weapon down, slamming the pommel straight into the ground with all his might and emotion behind it.

The explosion was deafening. A scarlet shockwave rolled away from the blast in an ever-widening circle, vaporizing everything in its path. Mordak's creatures disintegrated as Bjarke's savage blast hit them, their bodies instantly pulverized to dust that scattered on the wind. Hundreds of Gholans, Morcats, and Krell died in an instant. When the dust settled, Bjarke stood alone, his body glowing with a pure ruby brilliance that churned and roiled. He had a clear path to the sorcerer, who had managed to shield himself with his own magick and was just recovering his balance.

"MURDERER!" Bjarke thundered. His voice was ragged, enraged, and it shook the leaves on the nearest trees. He started walking towards Mordak, blood trickling from one nostril unheeded. He took one step, then another. He held his Jidaan, almost forgotten, in one hand, while the other clenched and unclenched in mindless fury. Bjarke began to growl, low in his chest, as an animal rage overcame him. Every step brought him closer to his target, to the one who had murdered his love.

Mordak watched the enormous Guardian approach, and gathered his energy to attack.

"Idiot! You're no match for me!" Mordak hissed. He cast a deadly bolt of energy at Bjarke, meaning to incinerate him. The bolt merely bounced away, repelled by the power that Bjarke now wore like armor. Mordak redoubled his strength and threw intense gouts of flame from both hands, but none of it touched Bjarke. The big forester never slowed, never flinched, never wavered. Blood slowly oozed out of the corner of one eye, but onward he came.

For the first time since he had escaped two thousand years of imprisonment, Mordak was visited by doubt. The fury and unbridled rage that poured from the big man in waves unsettled the sorcerer. Quickly, he began to throw bolt after dark, crimson bolt of power at the oncoming giant, desperately trying to stop his inexorable advance. Nothing worked. He continued his relentless march.

When he was a few yards away, Bjarke unleashed a bestial snarl and flung himself at the sorcerer, who threw up his hands in an attempt to protect himself. An oily scarlet shield of magick sprang up around Mordak's upper body, but Bjarke ignored it. Instead, he gripped his Jidaan with both hands and plunged its blade down into Mordak's unprotected foot, impaling it and pinning it firmly to the earth. Mordak howled in agony and instinctively reached both hands towards the pain, his shield disintegrating as his concentration was broken.

Bjarke let go of his Jidaan and wrapped his massive hands around Mordak's neck and squeezed, the corded muscles of his burly forearms bulging mightily. He brought his face down close to the sorcerer's, staring into the Vile One's suddenly terrified eyes. He wanted to see Mordak's fear, see him suffer for all the pain he had caused. Even as he squeezed, Bjarke's heart broke again and again.

Mordak clawed ineffectually at Bjarke's vise-like grip. As his windpipe closed off, Mordak resorted to the only thing he could think of. He changed form. Enabling the shape-shifting spell he favored, he changed into a huge, winged thing. His arms lengthened into great, leathery wings that flapped at Bjarke and sent gusts of wind blowing away from them. His neck elongated and his snout stretched out to accommodate many sharp teeth. The creature snapped at the big man, but Bjarke held onto the slender neck of the beast and squeezed harder.

Changing again, the sorcerer turned into a yowling, struggling panther, scratching Bjarke mercilessly on his arms and body with razor-sharp claws. Great gashes appeared on the big man's face and body, but he paid them no mind whatsoever. His pupils had shrunken to scarlet pinpricks, his entire being focused on the thrashing sorcerer. Bjarke squeezed harder and growled in his fury.

Mordak changed into a huge, coiling serpent, its tongue lashing out at Bjarke as its fangs snapped in the air, questing for Bjarke's face. Thick ropy coils wrapped around Bjarke's legs and body, squeezing with unimaginable strength.

But Bjarke would not stop.

He was unmoveable, completely implacable. His power flowed through him and around him, and his body was as stone. He kept his wide eyes focused on those of the creature in his hands, his unfathomable fury driving him beyond the limits of his tortured body, beyond the limits of anything he had ever imagined. Harder and harder he squeezed, feeling his fingers sinking into the vulnerable flesh beneath.

At last, near death, Mordak was forced to do the one thing he had the least control over, the one thing that could either kill him or free him. Frantically calling upon an ancient spell that terrified even him, Mordak went completely limp and dissolved into a thick, oily mist.

Bjarke frantically clutched at the smoke, desperately trying to regain the advantage, but he could not. He could feel the mist like a dirty silken cloth that caressed his arms as it swirled about him, but he could not hold it.

Seizing the opportunity, Mordak's amorphous form darted into Bjarke's mouth, driving deep into his lungs. Bjarke's eyes went wide, this time from terror, and he clawed at his own throat as he began to suffocate on the cloying mist that forced the life-giving air out of his body. His face began to turn red, then purple, a mask of horrid despair. Bjarke dropped to one knee as he gasped for breath that would not come. He thought of Alyssa, his love, his heart. They had only just begun, and he had not even managed to put his feelings into words. His vision dimmed as despair slowly overcame his fury.

Suddenly there she was, standing before him. Her lovely face was clean and bright, and she smiled up at him with love. Bjarke swept her up in his arms and laughed with joy and he kissed her as he had always wanted to. She kissed him back.

The light went out of Bjarke's eyes and he toppled face-first to the bloody ground. His hands clutched at the earth as his life ebbed away, but then his massive body finally relaxed. The glimmer in the pommelgem of his Jidaan went out, leaving it dark and cold. Bjarke was gone.

The oily mist seeped quickly out of the body's nose and mouth, coiling upon itself until it gathered in a spot a few yards away from the fallen Guardian. Slowly, the mist coalesced into the bent form of the sorcerer, regaining solidity in fits and starts until finally, Mordak was whole once more. He coughed harshly and then threw up on the ground next to Bjarke's body. The spell had taken every ounce of his focus. He had very nearly lost control of his swirling molecules, nearly dissipated into the void of nothingness, but he had survived.

Wiping his mouth on his sleeve, Mordak drew himself up to his full height. He spat on the Guardian's back, sneering as he did so, then he walked over to the Jidaan that yet stood with its blade embedded in the earth where it had pinned his foot during the struggle. A sly smile crossed his face, and he reached for his prize.

Before he could lay a hand on it, a bright, swirling square of light appeared inches away from the weapon. As he watched, a slender, muscular arm extended from it, the grasping hand laying hold of its wooden handle. The instant it had a good grip, the hand yanked the Jidaan back through the square of energy, which then vanished. Mordak blinked in surprise. It was gone. Mordak clenched his fists in ire and turned away only to find that Bjarke's body, too, was being dragged through another one of the magickal portals, disappearing through it before he could do anything to stop it. Only a vague outline of his enormous form and marks showing where it had been dragged away remained on the dusty earth. A quick glance told him that Alyssa's body, too, was gone.

Disgusted, Mordak furiously kicked dirt at the spot where Bjarke had lain. When he had vented his anger, he finally turned back to the battle that raged around him, assessing the situation. It was most certainly time to release his surprise on the unsuspecting people of Alverton Falls. He sent out a mental call to all of his creatures to mass in the center of the battlefield, to converge on him so that he could release his next attack.

Chapter 47

Kiran could not stop the tears that rolled unbidden down her cheeks as she carried Alyssa's limp form away from the battle. Inside the small wooden structure that the Count's men had built as a command center, Layton had already pulled Bjarke's huge body through another of his Gates and laid him with care on the floor next to one wall. Kiran knelt to gently deposit Alyssa's body next to that of the huge forester. He was quiet now, his full-bodied, jovial laughter forever silenced. The carefully hooded lanterns made Kiran's tears glisten in the dim light.

"She loved him, Layton. She told me so." Kiran sniffed and angrily wiped a sleeve across her face to obliterate the evidence that she cared so much.

"Yes, I know," Layton replied. They all had known, except for Bjarke himself. He had not known until the night before when it had become abundantly clear. Layton kept his mouth clamped shut after that. Tears were close, and he felt that he might not be able to stop them once they started. He used an exercise that his old masters had taught him, a breathing technique that helped him focus on the tasks at hand. Carefully wrapping Alyssa and Bjarke's Jidaan in a cloth and laying the bundle alongside their bodies, he found a place of stillness once more.

Nessar stood in the opposite corner, pacing irritably, looking everywhere but at the lifeless bodies in the corner. He had seen death before, a thousand times over. These, however, cut too close to the bone. "Where is that bastard Mage? I want to give him this trinket so we can end this thing." The moon shone through the open roof and glinted off the amulet as Nessar stuffed it back into his belt pouch. He had checked it over carefully after Kiran had finally helped him down from her horse. It was intact, as was he, more or less. His dignity had suffered the most during the latter part of the journey from Linbourne, having had his unconscious body strapped to Kiran's horse like luggage. That embarrassment just didn't seem to matter, though, in the face of the deaths of two dear friends.

Count DeRoberds stumbled into the enclosure, flanked by two of his soldiers. His voice was low and shaky with despair. "Brunar went down a few minutes ago. He was frying those creatures with the dragon he had conjured." He paused to catch his breath. "He was supposed to be hidden by his magick, but I saw a burst of red light where Brunar was supposed to be and then the dragon disappeared. No one has seen him since."

Nessar swore. "So he might be out there somewhere?" Anger gave his voice strength.

The Count sighed as he replied. "His body has not yet been recovered, sir Guardian. The field has been swarming with all manner of evil creatures, and we are currently engaged on all fronts."

"Well, I haven't gone to Hel and back to get this thing just so that Brunar can lay around on the job. I'll be right back. Slacking son of a..." He picked up his Jidaan from where Kiran had leaned it against the wall.

"Ness, no! You've only been conscious for a short while; you can't possibly think that you can get him!"

By the flickering light of the lanterns, she could see a fire in Nessar's eyes that made him look thirty years younger.

"Just watch me, baby girl."

And he was gone. There was no transition as he ignited the power of his Jidaan and engaged the Gift of Stealth. It was as though he had never even been there.

A canteen flew through the spot where Nessar had been standing and slammed into the opposite wall. "Hel's Bells, old man! One day, I'm going to wring your neck for driving me crazy!"

"That's not a long trip, Kir," Layton quipped, happy to have something to joke about. Kiran merely glared at him.

Just then another soldier stuck his head into the enclosure, his voice urgent. "Something is happening! They are lining up in the middle of the field. That sorcerer is in front."

"Do we have any forces left on either flank?"

"No, my lord. Everyone has retreated to the first line of trenches. There are fewer than two thousand of us left."

Kiran looked at Layton. His dreamy smile was nowhere to be found. Although Kiran loved a good fight, four to one odds, maybe even five to one, did not sound good to her at all. Even so, she would not run. She wanted to give old Mordak a little payback for her friends. She blew a stray lock of hair out of her face and slid her Jidaan into place on her back as she spoke. "Let's take a look. There's got to be something we can do out there." With that, she ducked outside.

Layton slipped his Jidaan back into its shoulder harness and exited the enclosure right behind her, ducking low as he left the shelter of its walls. Kiran moved carefully but steadily, muttering curses under her breath as she went. She unconsciously touched each of her sheathed weapons in a pattern that always served to soothe her. Things were probably about to become very interesting, and she wanted to confirm each and every blade, sap, and dart that she had hidden on her person. Thus assured, she led Count DeRoberds and his escort to a new rampart where they could see the oncoming horde. Fiona was already there, tears still wet on her face. She greeted them with a terse nod and then turned to face the oncoming army.

From their new vantage point, they could see the remnants of Mordak's army, still several thousand strong. Standing in front, wreathed in a scarlet glow of power that made the air crackle with energy, was a single figure. He was clad in a red-trimmed black robe, once of high quality, but now ragged and torn. He was illuminated by his own power, though his countenance seemed to shift and change moment by moment. As Kiran watched, she saw a weathered face with a hooked nose and a mane of pale silvery hair disappear under the guise of a fresh-faced youth, his long blond hair braided into a single plait that hung over one shoulder. Like a reflection in a pool of water that had been disturbed, the image fluctuated and rippled. First one face, then the other.

"Is it my imagination, or is he having trouble with his face?" Kiran blurted.

Layton replied in a tone much less jovial than his usual banter. "It's probably a glamour of some kind, an illusion. I think it's how he's controlled the Krell. Brunar said they'd never knowingly follow Mordak. I'm not sure who the younger face might be, but the older one with the white hair, that's Mordak."

The line of horrendous creatures held steady, though there was much snapping of teeth and clicking of talons. A Morcat roared somewhere in the crowd and the call was picked up by others. The chilling howl sent icy fingers of dread into the hearts of the human soldiers that opposed them. Standing tall before his army, Mordak savored the moment. He knew he had them right where he wanted them.

His deep voice, amplified by stolen magick, echoed across the hills and flatlands, audible all the way into the city of Alverton Falls beyond.

"People of Alverton Falls! I was going to offer you terms of surrender, but I have changed my mind. I've decided to simply kill you all. Your worthless lives are of no consequence, and I can make better use of your bodies as soldiers in my army. Behold! I have brought you something!"

With that, he grabbed the front of his robe with both hands and ripped it open, baring the pale skin underneath. Shrugging his shoulders, he allowed the robe to fall to the ground, where it puddled around his feet. He spread his arms wide and prepared to release the cargo he had carried for days.

Kiran gagged as she saw the welts on Mordak's body, huge nodules that now seemed to move freely beneath the sorcerer's skin. "Oh, yeech! What in the name of the Goddess is that?"

Fiona gasped. "Sweet Rowann! Blood wasps! He's infested with blood wasps! If he has carried them long enough, they will obey his commands!"

The first boil burst on Mordak's body and he uttered an involuntary gasp of pain. An impossibly large chitinous creature crawled from the wound, still covered in its host's blood. It swelled in size and flexed its wings experimentally until they functioned, and then it buzzed itself into flight. It rose a few feet and hovered over Mordak's head, its wings vibrating fiercely. The moonlight gleamed on its wicked stinger, easily as long as a man's index finger. Other nodules began to burst on Mordak's legs and torso, and more overlarge wasps pulled themselves out of the bleeding holes. He cried out in ecstasy as the exquisite pain threatened to overwhelm him. One by one, they erupted from the sorcerer's skin. They crawled forth and took flight with their kin until a huge swarm of wasps hovered above Mordak. Their wings buzzed angrily as they awaited his commands. Bleeding heavily and nearly blinded with pain, Mordak fell to his hands and knees, temporarily stricken.

"Those things are bigger than my fist!" Kiran's comment was met with silence, though everyone agreed with her assessment.

Fiona's voice was barely above a whisper. "Those are some of the deadliest creatures in the Mire," she informed them all. "They don't just sting and fly away; they're far worse than that. Their stingers are hollow, and their venom is always fatal. Always. Each wasp is capable of completely draining a full-grown adult of blood. Somehow, they quickly digest it and can do it again within minutes. They are aggressive, quick, and their venom causes incredible pain before it kills you." A tear rolled down her cheek, though her face remained stern and determined. Her hands disappeared beneath her cloak and reemerged with a wicked dagger in each. No matter what her feelings, she would neither shy away nor go down without a fight.

As they watched, the kneeling sorcerer slowly regained his feet. His wounds were already closing as he shakily shrugged into his robe and stood silently for a few moments, using more of his stolen magick to repair his shredded body. The power he had tricked out of the Daemon-God Balroth coursed through him, hurting him almost as much as the wasps had. His breath hissed between clenched teeth as the magick did its work, but a few agonized heartbeats later, he was whole again. Smoothing back his hair, he stood, tall and regal, and a ruthless smile appeared on his face. He knew he was about to kill every soldier that still opposed him. Once deceased, their bodies would then be his to rule. His army would be unstoppable.

Reaching upwards with his power, he connected with the primitive brains of the blood wasps that hovered there. They were simple creatures, but their murderous bloodlust was astonishing. Mordak smiled. He liked these creatures. With a gesture, he sent them on their way.

As the swarm of enormous wasps hurtled through the air towards the allies, Kiran burst from hiding to stand defiantly in their path, holding her sapphire-pommeled weapon high in the air.

"Oh, HELS no!" She ran forward several steps so that she was clear of the first rampart. "No way am I going to let you get away with this! You can take those wasps and shove them up your arse!"

With that, she called upon her Jidaan's Gift. The sapphire in the weapon's pommel blazed like a miniature blue sun, its light shining brightly in the pre-dawn darkness. Its power made the front lines of Mordak's army flinch away, but the blood wasps flew on, heedless of its light.

Kiran felt the Jidaan's power merge with her own, and she focused her mind on what she wanted to create. As the wasps approached, a hazy, blue nimbus of energy appeared around the deadly swarm, completely enclosing it. With a thought, Kiran solidified the energy into an impassible membrane. It surrounded the flying insects, becoming a net of cerulean power, and then tightened. It drew the frustrated insects together, crushing them into a furiously buzzing, wriggling, squirming knot.

As she continued to tighten the net, they started to sting each other in their desperation. They were dying, victims of Kiran's expertise and their own viciousness. Kiran gave them one last ferocious squeeze and felt the exoskeletons of the huge insects buckle under the intense pulverising power of her Ward, killing the entire swarm. When she was certain that the life had been crushed from each and every blood wasp, she let the Ward vanish. The pulped bodies fell to the earth in a single oozing mass.

Spent, she fell to one knee and gasped in relief. A trickle of blood oozed from one nostril and her head began to throb with the effort she had just expended. Not bothering to wipe the blood away, she shot a triumphant grin at the sorcerer. "In your arse, Mordak."

"No! Nooooooo!" Mordak's normally deep voice had risen into a shrill scream as he saw the creatures he had borne through several days of agony destroyed like no more than common pests. His frustration was nearly more than he could bear. Taking care to strengthen his illusion of Balroth, he turned to his inhuman troops and floated upwards on a crimson glow of magick so that they could see him in command. "Kill them! Kill them all!"

His army was more than happy to oblige. Its creatures surged forward as though they had waited for this moment all their lives. They sprinted for the earthen ramparts, screaming their hatred of humankind the entire way. The remaining warriors of Alverton Falls readied themselves for the charge, weapons held ready in white-knuckled hands.

Something changed in the air, then. A breeze picked up, ruffling the clothes and pennants of the defenders as they prepared to meet the oncoming rush. It grew in strength until it became a gale, a strong wind that hurled dust and debris in the faces of the horrid creatures that came on. They slowed in the face of the wind, their progress becoming more difficult with each step. Still, they struggled forward, driven by their bloodlust.

Thunder rumbled across the sky, the sound rolling across the darkened land. An intense spiderweb of lightning snaked across the heavens, accompanied by an earth-shattering BOOM. Its power was so strong that many of Mordak's creatures flung themselves on the ground in fear. The defenders looked at each other in confusion and disbelief until one of them cried, "Look!" and pointed towards the mountains that hid the oncoming sunrise.

From the east, a brilliant glimmer of emerald green, a searing viridian flare, was rapidly approaching. Gart had come at last.

Chapter 48

Gart held his Jidaan high overhead as he rode, and Bessie's hooves pounded the earth as she galloped towards the battlefield. The power of the weapon was coursing through him, singing in his blood. The pommelgem was afire with emerald radiance, and as its power filled Gart's body, he, too, glowed like a green sun. As he rode, he focused his will, reaching into the sky over the battlefield with the Jidaan's magick.

As he drew alongside the defenders, firmly entrenched behind earthen ramparts and wooden stakes, he could more easily see the front lines of the horde. The sight of the hideous creatures brought back awful memories, but he set his jaw firmly against them. *This is where I avenge you, Gennie, Rheann. This is where I make things right.* He scanned the line and was pleased to find a sickly scarlet blot of energy floating above the crowd that could only be the sorcerer Mordak, himself. *Right where I hoped you'd be, front and center. Here I come, you bastard.*

Gart felt all of his rage, all of his frustration and pain, come pouring out of him in a ferocious battle cry. He pointed the glowing weapon into the sky and unleashed his power.

Mordak leaned into the howling wind, using his magick to stabilize himself in the gale. The last thunderclap had startled him, but he was still in control. He caught sight of the emerald flare from the east. "It can't be! No!" He threw a shield of glimmering scarlet around his body only an instant before a bolt of lightning as thick as a man's arm slammed into him, and the world went white.

Gart saw Mordak blasted out of the air and allowed himself the ghost of a smile. Still holding his Jidaan aloft, he slammed bolt after bolt into the terrified mob, gritting his teeth and grunting with effort as each jagged blast of lightning exploded into the earth. Creatures and body parts flew in all directions only to be buffeted about by the gale. It was chaos.

Kiran watched it all with wide eyes. They had retreated behind one of the ramparts with the Count and Fiona while the man with the emerald Jidaan wreaked havoc on the enemy. She remembered Brunar talking about the one man who had refused to join them, the Guardian of Storms.

Layton put a voice to her thoughts. "I...I think that's Gart. The one who wouldn't join us."

Although hard to hear over the wind, Nessar's voice seemed to come from nowhere. "That's right, lad. That's Gart. Brunar showed me his face back in the Heartstrong Mountains when we first got there, and that's definitely him. I recognize his scars."

Startled, they both turned to see Nessar suddenly appear before them, the limp body of Brunar slung over his shoulder. The old thief knelt and carefully laid the Mage on the ground. Fiona rushed to kneel at his side and placed her fingers on his throat.

"He's alive!" she choked back a sob of relief. "I'm not sure how, but he's alive. I'll do what I can to help him." She held her hands over him and began a quiet chant that was completely lost in the gale. A warm glow suffused her palms as she used what healing magick she had. He was battered, his robe burned, but he had escaped death somehow.

Kiran stepped over and slapped Nessar in the face. Then, before he could even register his shock, she grabbed him in a bear hug. He held her close for a long moment before pushing her away and admonishing her. "Hey, that hurt!"

"Yes. It did." Kiran locked gazes with him for a moment, then turned away.

Count DeRoberds cleared his throat, then spoke up. "We need to be ready to charge. It's too dangerous yet with the storm, but if that man's attack slows, we need to move right away to hit them while they're down."

Nessar leaned against the rampart and peeked over it to see Gart continuing the onslaught against Mordak's horde. "I agree. Don't worry about the west flank, though. I've got that covered."

Kiran looked at him and realized that he was breathing heavily, as though he were in the midst of lifting a great weight. She caught sight of his Jidaan. Its pommel was visible over Nessar's shoulder, held blade down in its harness, and she realized the onyx stone was alive. It was a seething little blot of darkness, its power fully engaged.

"Nessar, you old fool! What did you do?"

He turned to her, his face still red from her slap and from his exertion, and smiled. "You'll see."

Count DeRoberds turned and made hand signals to his captains, who passed the word along: Be ready to attack on my signal. Energized by the success of the newcomer with the blazing emerald weapon, they prepared to charge.

On the field, Gart had decimated the ranks of evil creatures that were arrayed before him. The winds kept them off-balance, and the bolts of lightning killed them by the score. He rode in their midst, finally allowing himself to engage the horrid beasts hand to hand. His Jidaan cut a bloody path through them as Bessie carried him like a born war-horse.

"Jor Dayne!" he yelled over the howl of the winds and the rumble of rolling thunder. "Where are you, murderer? I've come for you!"

That's when something hit Bessie. She whinnied in pain and crumpled, throwing Gart head over heels to the earth. He tried to roll with the impact, but still wrenched his right knee badly in the process. He hit with a hard, jarring thump that stunned him. Immediately, the winds began to die down and the lightning bolts stopped, though the thunder continued to roll overhead. He shook his head to clear it, and found that his Jidaan had fallen close enough for him to grab it. He collected it, then snatched his hat out of the dust with the other hand and jammed it firmly back on his head. He struggled to one knee, using the Jidaan to steady himself. Bessie lay nearby, and Gart was shocked to see that she was already dead, a gaping hole in her chest.

"Fool!" a raspy, harsh voice accused Gart. As he searched for the source of the voice, a blast of scarlet magick slammed into him, flinging him to his back on the dusty earth. "Jor Dayne, that idiot, got himself killed by one of you, a girl less than half his size. He was useless to me!"

Mordak stalked around Bessie's dead body. His robe was charred and bloody, and the right half of his face was blackened and burnt into a horrific mask. The other half was his true face, and his contemptuous sneer was still visible. He stalked closer to the stunned body of Gart, who was trying to assimilate the news that the murderer of his family was already dead.

"You've cost me dearly, *Guardian*," Mordak sneered the word. "You've left me with a tenth of my horde." Mordak leaned closer to Gart. "But that's still more than enough to make undead soldiers out of everyone in Alverton Falls!" The sorcerer raised his hands, which began to glow with vile energy. "And you'll be one of the first!" Mordak thrust both hands towards the injured man on the ground and a blast of foul magick boiled forth, enveloping the cowering figure, immersing it completely in crimson flames. The sorcerer laughed, exulting in the use of the power he had tricked out of Balroth, enjoying the feeling of sheer potency as he incinerated the Guardian before him. When he was sure the kneeling figure could be nothing more than ash, he reluctantly cut off the flow of power and lowered his hands.

Gart was still there. Mordak gasped in surprise before he could stop himself.

Piercing cobalt eyes blazed defiantly back at the sorcerer from beneath the brim of Gart's battered hat. His body was surrounded by a shimmering golden glow shot through with swirls of emerald, a shield of his magick. Its light flickered across his scarred face, illuminating his harsh features, the grim line of his mouth, and the hard set of his jaw. Gart was completely unfazed by Mordak's attack.

"Is that the best you can do?" Gart challenged. Outrage flickered across Mordak's face, and Gart used that moment to attack. Throwing out one hand, he sent a thick bolt of energy towards his enemy's head. Mordak flinched aside to dodge the blast just as Gart had expected, and it flowed past him. Even as he moved, Mordak's hands began to glow again in preparation for another strike.

With a grunt of effort and a yanking gesture, Gart called his power back to himself. The leading edge of the surge instantly turned in flight and hurtled straight towards the back of Mordak's head. It slammed right into the necromancer's unprotected skull, sending him facedown into the dirt, stunned.

Gart reached out with his magick once more, sending a thick tendril of glimmering power snaking through the air towards the prone sorcerer. It wrapped around Mordak's waist and instantly tightened into an unbreakable noose. Mordak weakly clutched at it, to no avail.

Mordak struggled to free himself as Gart's magick lifted him high into the air, higher than the tops of the tallest trees. Then, with a grunt, Gart slammed the sorcerer down into the hard-packed earth as hard as he could. Bones snapped, and he heard Mordak cry out in pain. Again, he lifted Mordak's limp body high into the sky, then once again slammed it to the ground with devastating force. He started to lift Mordak's body a third time, but exhaustion and pain finally overtook him. The golden glow of his magick faded and Gart pitched forward on his hands and knees, his chest heaving as he fought to catch his breath. Mordak's limp form fell bonelessly back to earth with a thump, his limbs splayed in all directions.

Gart stared at the body for a few moments, but it did not move. Mordak was completely silent, his body broken and still. Gart lowered himself to the ground, utterly spent. He prayed that Mordak was dead, that his job was done. Fatigue burned in every muscle and sweat dripped down into his eyes as he lay there, weary to the bone. The wind he had conjured had faded away, and Gart slowly became aware of scuttling noises nearby. Snarls and growls came soon after, and the sounds of claws and teeth clicking together. Gart slowly raised his head a fraction so that he could see, and suddenly wished he had not.

All around him, a ring of Gholans was closing in. A couple of Morcats towered over the little beasts, and they seemed just as eager to see Gart at their mercy. Fangs were bared, and throaty growls made Gart's skin crawl with revulsion as he saw the hideous creatures up close. His fatigue seemed overwhelming. Just for a moment, he thought about closing his eyes and letting it all end in a flurry of flashing, tearing, and ripping. He lowered his head and stared at the dusty ground mere inches from his nose as he pondered the oblivion that death would provide. He need do nothing more than wait until Mordak's creatures had finished him. He could rest at last.

Gennie's lovely face appeared in his mind's eye, matted with dirt and blood. He saw her fighting with nothing more than a pitchfork, not for herself, but to defend the others. She would not have stayed facedown in the dirt. She fought until she could fight no longer. How could he ever do less? And he had a lot more than just a pitchfork.

When his ice blue eyes rose again, they gleamed with rage. With a thought, he ignited the shining emerald in his Jidaan. Feeling the energy of his magick flowing within him and the answering flare from his Jidaan, Gart pushed himself to his feet. He raised his weapon high overhead, where it blazed brightly for all to see.

Mordak's creatures flinched away from the green brilliance as the wind around them gathered strength. It rose to a howling gale, swirling around Gart, who stood with his feet firmly planted on the ground. The creatures tried to run, but the wind lifted them into its churning embrace, slamming them into each other at every turn. A column of dust and earth reached upwards from the ground surrounding Gart, and soon the long, spinning column of a tornado reached high into the sky above. Gart limped through the wall of the powerful vortex, untouched by its enormous power. His Jidaan blazed brightly in the gloom as he channeled his rage and pain into the storm. The strain was enormous, yet he held his Jidaan overhead with both hands and swayed unsteadily as he guided the tempest.

The twister began to move enthusiastically around the battlefield, leaving a trail of devastation in its wake. The bodies of

Mordak's creatures were flung this way and that, like rag dolls that had been discarded on the bloody ground. Gart clenched the handle of the weapon harder, using the unyielding wood as an anchor as he struggled to stay upright. The strain of controlling the storm was nearly more than he could bear, yet he was determined to do as much damage to the horde as he could before he collapsed.

A blast of crimson energy hit him from behind, and Gart sprawled forward into the dirt, his Jidaan's light extinguished like a candle-flame. Instantly, the tornado began to dissipate, the howl of the wind fading quickly. Gart wearily spat the dirt from his mouth and clutched at his Jidaan with one hand. He laboriously pushed himself up onto one knee as he turned to search for Mordak, surely the source of the attack. It was taking all of his remaining strength to avoid lying back down on the ground. He tried to reach for his magick, but was too exhausted to use it.

Mordak stood, somewhat awkwardly, just a few yards away, looking like a broken scarecrow that had been badly reassembled. The madness that blazed in his eyes was unchanged, however, and his hands were glowing with power barely contained.

"Idiot!" Mordak spat the words. "Your feeble powers are nothing to me, spear-bearer!"

Exhausted, Gart replied evenly, "I don't know, looks to me like I gave you a good run for your money, ugly. And your army is definitely not what it was." He glared across the short distance between them and saw a nervous tic begin in Mordak's remaining eye. He almost smiled. "You're not going to conquer anything with what you've got left. People will fight. You'll lose."

Mordak's rage was plain to see; he clenched his glowing fists and ground his teeth in anger. Before he could reply, a hunting horn sounded somewhere in the south, three long blasts. Their heads both turned in that direction. Gradually, the sound of hoofbeats arose and echoed across the hills, accompanied by a long, barking howl. Gart's heart leapt in disbelief and he struggled to his feet to search for the source of the sound. The howl came again, louder, and Gart's heart nearly burst. Mordak saw the same thing Gart did, though his reaction was exactly the opposite.

A band of fifty riders was coming, swords and axes drawn and waving in the growing light of the oncoming dawn. At their head was an immense four-legged beast, running for all she was worth.

Beauty had come to find her master, and she had brought Ishabel with her.

The red-haired chieftain and her powerful horse were keeping pace right behind the massive dog, with Ishabel bellowing very unlady-like battle cries and waving a wicked-looking sword. She was ready to fight, and so was her entire clan.

They slammed into the rearmost survivors of Mordak's army, slaying them at every turn. Beauty was a blur of snarling ferocity, and her jaws were soon covered in blood, none of it her own. Gholans, Morcats, and Krell were all battered and exhausted, and even their utter hatred of all things good could not aid them against the newcomers. The walking undead fought woodenly, but they were too slow and many were cut down immediately.

"No!" Mordak cursed. "Shamblebeasts, go and aid them!" He uttered a few words in an odd, guttural language, and the three remaining hulks turned and began to make their way towards the rear.

Just then, the shadows on the west flank shimmered and roiled. Where naught had been before, ValElder Moihra stood with a full squad of five hundred Weya, ranks of archers in front with arrows already nocked. Behind them, a score of massive Augenan warriors waited for the command to attack, led by none other than the High Chieftain Ch'shok, who hefted his massive double-bitted battleaxe in one hand. Nessar's Jidaan had hidden them well.

With a wave of her hand, Moihra unleashed the archers. They loosed with deadly accuracy, every arrow finding a home in one of Mordak's fell creatures. Four lightning fast volleys were loosed before the Augenan sprinted into the fray, making straight for the shamblebeasts. The battle was ferocious, but the swamp creatures were no match for the immensely strong and mobile gorilla-people, each a born warrior. Following in their wake, hundreds of lithe Weya sprinted into the fray, wielding twin short swords that glinted in the pre-dawn light. They wove through the talons, teeth, and weapons of Mordak's army like ghosts, cleaving and riving as they went.

From the north, from behind a dozen earthen ramparts and out of many hidden trenches came the remainder of the Alverton Falls army. Few though they were, they were galvanized by the arrival of their allies and were howling their own brave war cries. It took them only moments to reach the nearest ranks of Mordak's undead riders and other creatures, and they mowed them down like wheat under a scythe.

Mordak watched his horde diminishing in utter shock and disbelief. It was all ruined. Everything he had suffered for, everything he had sacrificed, it had all come to nothing. Furious, he turned back to Gart and prepared to unleash a blast of unholy power that would completely vaporize him. The glow around his hands intensified and his face clenched in pain as he called up more of Balroth's power.

An opalescent Gate opened next to Gart, and Kiran leapt through, followed immediately by Layton. At her gesture, an intensely bright blue Ward appeared between Mordak and Gart, and the magickal blast that was meant to incinerate Gart bounced off in a fierce ricochet. Mordak tried to dodge the thick beam, but part of it slammed into his already damaged body. The impact flung his shattered form to the ground in a crumpled heap.

"Go, go!" Layton yelled to Kiran as he cut down the Gholans and Krell that had reached them. He twirled and dodged and lashed out with his Jidaan, killing anything that came close. He had found his dreamy half-smile again, and was reveling in the deadly dance.

Keeping a sharp eye out for attackers, Kiran got Gart's arm over her shoulder and helped him to stand. "Introductions later...come with me!" Gart nodded and allowed her to help him limp into the opalescent doorway as he craned his neck to see how Beauty and Ishabel were faring. Kiran ushered Gart through and they emerged back in the command enclosure. Gart blinked at the sudden transition and tried to get his bearings.

An older, tired looking man was leaning on the side of the roofless enclosure, a weapon like Gart's slung across his back. Its pommel was black as night. He turned to survey Gart as Kiran helped him sit down.

"Well, sonny, better late than never, I guess. Glad you could join us."

Chapter 49

Grunting in pain, Gart allowed the woman to help him sit down, but all he wanted to do was get back out and fight. Beauty was here! And Ishabel! His knee was definitely damaged, though. The pain was deep and intense and it was already starting to swell. Gart began work on it right away, probing the injury and carefully repairing it with his magick. He was startled to recognize Brunar, looking battered and worn, sitting nearby as a woman helped him drink from a tin cup.

"Brunar," he said with a nod of greeting to the Mage.

Brunar's eyes finally focused on him and he gasped in surprise. "Gart! You changed your mind! How...?"

"It's a long story, Mage, and an eventful one. Suffice to say that I," a brief pang of anguish crossed his scarred face as he recalled the loss of his family, "I ended up with nothing to lose and every reason to kill Jor Dayne and Mordak."

Kiran spoke up. "Jor Dayne, that arrogant bastard! Alyssa saved you the trouble," she nodded towards the tiny warrior's still body in the corner. "She killed him not long before you got here." Her voice quavered a bit as she spoke Alyssa's name, but she managed to hold her tears at bay.

"I see," Gart replied, his face blank. He had travelled hard for months, nearly dying several times, so he could face the man who had killed his family. Mordak was the ultimate source of the evil, but Jor Dayne had been the weapon that dealt the blow. He sighed heavily. It would be a difficult burden to lay by the side of the road, but apparently, that part of his quest was over.

"Well, Mordak is still out there. As I understand it, he's the cause of all this. He needs to be stopped as quickly as possible. I've got friends out there!"

Nessar looked away from the younger man as he answered. "As do we all, lad. As do we all. Old friends, new friends, and total strangers. All of us fighting that crazed madman." He turned and spat into the dust to one side. "Those riders from the south...friends of yours, I assume?"

Staying focused on repairing his knee, Gart replied softly. "Yes. My friend Ishabel and my dog, Beauty. I don't know the others, and I don't know how they found us." Gart was still in shock at seeing them. They had made their way across hundreds of miles only to risk their lives. *They came for me.* He tipped his head forward so the brim of his hat would hide the tears that welled in his eyes, then narrowed his focus so he could repair the torn ligaments in his knee.

Tactfully ignoring the young man's emotion, Ness continued. "Well, however they managed it, I'm glad they did. They're mopping up the nasties out there from what I can tell. We're happy to have them."

Kiran stepped into the conversation. "Ness, you've got some explaining to do," her voice was stern. "I assume you had something to do with the Weya and Augenan to the west?"

Nessar chuckled dryly. "Yes, Kiran, I was out scouting for Brunar," he crooked a thumb in the direction of the Mage. "I stayed hidden with the Gift of Stealth, so they couldn't see or hear me on the battlefield. When I found him, I managed to carry him to the trees on the west side. It turns out that I'm kind of sensitive to certain things, and I felt something familiar out in the woods not far from where we were hiding, like a tingling in my head. I investigated and discovered the Weya were nearby. ValElder Moihra told me they had run across the Augenan approaching from the south earlier in the night and they had joined forces. They were massing for a charge when I found them. I suggested the sneak attack instead, and they agreed. Took a lot out of me to cloak them for that long, but it worked."

Brunar finally stood up, his strength slowly returning. "Do you have it? The amulet?"

Nessar grinned and dipped a hand into his belt pouch. It came out holding a gold medallion the size of his palm, gemstones glinting in the hooded lanternlight. "Take it and good luck with it. I have no idea how it works, but I hope it's worth what we went through to get it."

Brunar took the medallion from Nessar's outstretched palm and felt the weight of it in his hand. He reached into it with his magick and was astonished to find that it was almost a complete void to his sight. Everything, alive or dead, had some form of presence. Living things practically gave off their own light; even stones and other objects gave an impression of solidity and strength. The amulet was a total blank. He canted a different spell and still found nothing. Wracking his brain, he finally recalled an obscure sensory spell that he had not used in nearly a thousand years. He cast it and the structure and workings of the amulet finally became plain to him. *Brilliant*, he acknowledged the work of its creator. *Such a simple twist on a common concept. I wish I had thought of it.* Turning his mind back to the here and now, a grim smile appeared on his face.

"Nessar, I believe it will be. Now, I just need to get close enough to..."

He was interrupted by a thunderclap so close it nearly knocked everyone off their feet, immediately followed by a great shuddering of the very earth they stood upon. A blazing red and orange light exploded from the battlefield, so bright it cast harsh shadows on the ground around the enclosure and forced everyone to shield their eyes.

Grabbing hold of the nearest wall to steady himself, Nessar said, "This can't be good. Nope. Not good at all."

Chapter 50

The pain was unbelievable. It was that, not the Krell warrior's incessant babbling, that woke him. It was transcendent, agony beyond anything he had ever felt. In answer to the pain, Balroth's stolen magick burned within him, and Mordak desperately tried to regain control of it to shut down the affected nerves so that he could function. Oddly, there were fewer of them than he thought there should be. A hand grabbed the front of his charred robe and roughly yanked him to a sitting position, causing more explosions of misery. Mordak quelled them and managed to open his left eye. The other simply would not respond. It was gone, though he did not know that. The ricochet of his own magick had incinerated what it had touched, and Mordak's right arm, upper torso, and the right side of his face had been seared to the bone.

Mordak's vision swam into focus, and he saw the furious face of a Krell Warleader only inches from his. Its black, bulbous eyes were wide with wrath, its sharpened teeth snapping and gnashing as it gibbered angrily at the sorcerer. It added a shake for emphasis, and Mordak finally realized that his charade was over. His glamour had dissipated after the lightning strike, and he had yet to re-engage it. The Krell knew he was the infamous Mordak rather than the manifestation of their god, Balroth, and he was not happy about it at all. The Krell yelled over his shoulder at another Krell warrior who screamed in rage, spit in Mordak's direction, and then ran off to tell the others.

Mordak grimaced and grasped Balroth's magick as it surged inside him. It burned, it hurt, and it was almost too strong for him to contain. Even though it seemed to have grown as he had used it during the last few days, using it now was almost impossible. His injured body could no longer handle the strain.

Suddenly, Mordak didn't care anymore. His horde was gone, and his hold over the Krell was broken. His body was shattered, nearly useless. He could feel it shutting down, and he knew there would be no coming back this time. But there was still something he could do; he could still destroy the Guardians. He could strike one last time at those who thought themselves his betters.

Mordak's single eye suddenly blazed a bright scarlet. His mangled face arranged itself in a hideous deathshead grin that stopped the angry ravings of the Krell Warleader. Embracing the intense agony of Balroth's magick, Mordak reached out with his left hand and incinerated the Krell where he stood, leaving nothing but a pile of ash. A mangled laugh escaped his teeth, garbled because most of his mouth was gone. The feeling of power was exquisitely painful, and he could feel it burning through him. Harnessing it, he built a barrier within himself to contain enough of the magick to keep his frail remains from being consumed until after he cast his final spell.

Struggling to his feet, he sent his senses down into the earth, questing beyond the topsoil and layers of rock and gravel beneath him. It took only moments to find what he needed. As he engaged the massive store of unholy magick for the last time, Mordak began to glow with a gruesome crimson light. His mutilated body began to drift upwards, his battered boots leaving the ground to dangle in midair several yards above the bloody ground below.

With a cry of ecstatic insanity, Mordak unleashed every bit of power at his disposal. The explosion was deafening, and the shockwave knocked every living thing within a quarter mile off its feet, as an unbearably intense beam of red-orange power plunged into the earth beneath him. Dirt and stone flew wide as Mordak's magick drilled downward, diving towards the heart of the world.

Chapter 51

In a great leap, the Augenan High Chieftain raised the double-bitted Tugan overhead and brought it down on the shamblebeast, splitting its head in two. No blood flowed from the wound, just a bit of oozy green sap, but the creature staggered to one side and fell heavily to the ground. Ch'shok roared in triumph as he thumped his huge chest with his left fist and raised the great battle-axe overhead. All around him, the battle was raging, and it was obvious to him that the tide had turned. Gholans were clustered together as they desperately fought losing battles against the graceful and deadly Weya, along with the overwhelming might of the Augenan warriors that had chosen to follow Ch'shok to the north.

After dealing with the small force that Mordak had sent to assail Laro, Ch'shok had offered his warriors a choice: go home with honor, or accompany him to the north to continue fighting for the humanfolk. A great many of them wished to continue fighting, more than Ch'shok had intended, in fact. When he explained that he did not want their city in the trees to remain largely undefended for so long, the great majority of them changed their minds. The smaller force that stayed with him were the hardest warriors of Clan N'atam, and they were reveling in the battle around him.

Nearby, ValElder Moihra danced and spun as she brought down a howling Morcat that was easily triple her size. As it tumbled, she expertly flicked its blood from her twin blades, then she spied Ch'shok. They had cleared their immediate area of the foe, so she stepped up to the big Aug.

"Ch'shok," she said, her grin coloring her voice. She was spattered with all manner of gore, but the thrill of battle was upon her, and she wore it as though it were a badge of office. "I'm so glad you chose to come north to join the fight again! It's always a pleasure to see you in action."

Ch'shok hooted in laughter. "Same, same, ValElder. Your people, fun to watch! Little, but fierce!" He lashed out and smote a Morcat that had gotten too close, then turned back to the diminutive Weya leader. "Also glad we meet sneaky old man. Guardian. His magick was good."

She tucked an errant lock of hair over one pointed ear and laughed, her voice like music on the battlefield. "Yes, Nessar's idea to hide us under the power of his Jidaan was definitely a good one."

Just then, Layton came trotting up to them, both his Jidaan and his clothes similarly splattered in Gholan gore. "We're winning! The warriors from Alverton Falls have attacked from the north and another band of fighters have come up from the south to aid us. I don't know who they are, but they're giving them Hel over there. Last I saw, Mordak was down as well!"

Before they could speak further, they were thrown off their feet by an earsplitting thunderclap that sounded like the world had exploded. The ground beneath them began to shudder as a bright orange-red light made them throw their arms over their eyes, lest they be blinded by it. A fierce wind began to blow away from the blaze as the air was pushed away by the flow of energy.

Moihra reached out with her senses, trying desperately to keep her bearings under the intense glare and gale. The air was thick with power, a strong and nauseating kind of dark magick that was not supposed to exist on Talwynn.

She was not surprised to find that Mordak was still alive, nor that he was the source of the evil power that had struck them all down. She was, however, surprised that he was directing his energy straight down into the earth, burrowing into the earth's mantle with an intensity of force that staggered her.

But why? She focused her energy beneath the surface in an attempt to find a reason for Mordak's change in tactics. It was not long before she found it, and she gasped in alarm and disbelief at her discovery. *Oh...oh, no.*

Layton crawled towards her, shielding his face with one hand, dragging his Jidaan along beside him with the other. "What is he doing?" he yelled over the noise.

Moihra leaned close to his ear and replied. "There is a pocket of magma along a fault line deep below us. If he reaches it and causes a reaction, he could obliterate the entire continent!"

Layton blinked at her, not fully comprehending her words. Then he set his jaw. "You mean, everyone dies."

She nodded. "Thousands upon thousands. The land will tear itself apart."

Layton struggled to one knee and prepared to intervene, though he had no idea what he could do against magick of that magnitude. He could not even stand up in the face of it.

Just then Moihra pointed to the north, just beyond Mordak's position. "Look!" she cried.

Barely visible against the overwhelming crimson and orange brightness that Mordak's magick emitted, there was an intense purple spot, a moving blot of writhing indigo energy that could only mean one thing: Brunar had reentered the fray.

Chapter 52

Brunar slipped the amulet around his neck. It felt cold and dead there, but it was not yet fully engaged. That was just as Brunar wished, for he still had spells to cast. From a small pouch on his belt, he pulled a thumb-sized amethyst, cut into a beautifully faceted purple gemstone. Moving quickly, he stepped over to Fiona and grabbed one of her wrists. Before she could protest, he placed the amethyst in her palm and closed her hand over it, then took her face in both of his hands and kissed her. Everything he had ever hoped and dreamed, all the love he possessed, was in that kiss. Fiona kissed him back with all her might. They broke apart, and he stared into her eyes for one brief moment, and he knew that she knew. Without another word, he ignited his power, armoring himself in a swirl of purple magick, and stepped out into the gale to face Mordak's assault.

This close to Mordak, the noise was deafening. A constant stream of energy three yards thick burned straight down into the ground. The heat of it was almost unbearable. Brunar steeled himself for what lay ahead. He used all of his discipline to strengthen his shield, forming it into a wedge before him, then he sprinted towards the crazed, dying necromancer.

When he was close enough, he leaped as high as he could, hurtling through the air until he collided with what was left of the ancient sorcerer. Brunar wrapped his arms around him, feeling charred bones break as he did so. Half of Mordak's face was simply gone, leaving behind a hideous half-skull that somehow still shone with evil power. Mordak's skin and muscle was slowly dissolving in the conflagration, but he never relented or wavered.

Dark and hateful power poured out of him as though there was no end to it. He turned his one good eye towards his ancient nemesis, and Brunar could see that his insanity was complete. The brilliant intelligence that had once resided in him was gone. All that remained was the singular desire to destroy everything, to burn himself into ashes and the world with him. He would never stop until he was dead, and he would be alive more than long enough to destroy everything that Brunar held dear.

Brunar took one last breath, then simultaneously dropped his shield and enabled the amulet.

The amulet instantly absorbed an astronomical amount of energy, far more than it had ever been designed to hold. In less than a second, it did the only thing it could have done - it exploded.

It vaporized everything within a quarter mile radius in a white hot blast that was heard and felt across the continent. Those on the field south of Alverton Falls were stunned, rendered momentarily blind and deaf, and blown away like leaves in the wind. When the echoes died away, thick tendrils of smoke oozed upwards from the scorched earth, and no one moved for long minutes. Beauty and Ishabel were thrown from their feet, knocked senseless by the power of the explosion along with every creature in their vicinity. The field was littered with bodies. Many would never move again.

When those sturdy enough to regain their feet did so, they were greeted by a very unexpected sight. Smoke from the small fires and smoldering embers that remained from the blast was flowing towards the epicenter of the explosion. The long, slender columns of smoke seemed to be converging on one spot several yards above the ground, as though they were being sucked into a void of some kind.

Fiona staggered out of the enclosure to behold this oddity and was immediately struck with a deep and intense feeling of *wrongness* that made her want to run screaming in the opposite direction. It made her feel nauseous, and she felt the edges of her sanity start to fray.

Gart stumbled out with her, followed quickly by the other Guardians and the Count. "What in the name of Rowann is that?"

Fiona stood quietly gazing at the focal point of the air influx, reluctantly using her magickal senses to find the source of her unease.

At that moment, a dark, spinning circle began to grow from the central point; it was a doorway of some kind. The smoke continued to pour into it, and a breeze picked up as air from the surrounding land flowed into the aperture. The circle grew and grew until it towered a hundred feet above the earth. It stood there, cold and forbidding, its interior an inky blackness that instantly reminded Nessar of his Jidaan. However, his weapon lacked the oily, nasty feel of this thing. Everyone felt dirty and sick as they stared at it.

Then the air changed. It became thick with crackling power, and a bolt of crimson lightning came out of the portal, followed by several more. An overwhelming sense of pressure arose on the battlefield, driving creatures and humans alike to their knees. An enormous boot of black leather, and a leg clad in midnight-black cloth, stepped through the circular opening. As it set foot upon the earth, a pervasive sense of wrongness set everyone's teeth on edge, and the thickening power pushed them harder into the bloody ground.

A pale hand grabbed the edge of the portal, and another appeared on the opposite side. The face of a young man, both beautiful and terrible, emerged from the opening. His eyes were as black as jet, soulless and cruel. The instant he appeared, the oppressive atmosphere increased tenfold. His hair was long and blond, and braided into a single thick rope that hung down over one shoulder. It was held together at the end by a human skull. He wore a simple tunic of black belted with a red cord, and he wore it well. He pulled himself forward and brought his other leg through the portal until both feet were planted firmly on the ground. He drew himself to his full height and took a deep breath, as though savoring the air, and surveyed the land that was now his. The sun illuminated him as it rose, though it was obvious his preference would be the dark of night. Turning away from the life-giving sun, he spoke, the power of his voice terrifying all who heard it.

"I AM BALROTH. KNEEL, PITIFUL CREATURES! THIS WORLD IS NOW MINE!"

When Mordak had come to petition him for a tiny sliver of his power, the merest drop of Balroth's mystical strength, he had lied and said he would pave the way for Balroth's return to the world of Talwynn. Balroth had seen through the lie immediately, but had made use of the opportunity. Mordak's very first use of Balroth's magick upon Talwynn had created a link directly to the Daemon-God, and every additional use of that unholy power had strengthened that link. The invisible tether that bound Mordak to Balroth had thickened and grown with every spell cast, every burst of magick that Mordak had used in his quest for domination. At the last, he finally expended enough energy to complete the connection, creating a direct gateway from Balroth's prison to Talwynn.

Ah, but it's good to be home again, he thought. *Now, this world will bow to me as it was meant to!*

Chapter 53

The sheer power of Balroth's presence overwhelmed every living being on the battlefield. Despair overcame the hearts of soldiers on both sides, falling over them all like a heavy cloak.

Except for Ch'shok. His people knew Balroth as Baulotha, the enemy of all upon Talwynn from time immemorial. For thousands of years, Ch'shok's people were brought up knowing that a day would come in which one of them would be able to strike a blow at the dark god. They had been given the Tugan, a great, double-bitted battle axe forged eons ago of an unknown metal, in order to strike that fabled blow.

On his hands and knees, the power of that evil Daemon-God pressed down on Ch'shok heavier than any boulder. Every fiber of his being screamed with anguish, begged him to give in and submit to Baulotha's evil power.

NO! I will FIGHT!

Ch'shok narrowed his eyes and grunted in defiance. His strong fingers clawed at the earth and he began to push himself away from the dusty ground. The Tugan lay only a few feet away, still stained with Gholan blood. Fighting the power of a Daemon-God a hundred feet tall, Ch'shok struggled to stand, his huge chest heaving as he caught his breath. Sweating with exertion, he got his feet underneath him. Then he flung himself towards the battle-axe, the totem of his people for millennia.

He landed in the dirt on his face, hard. For a moment, he thought he had failed. Then his fingers touched the familiar wood of the Tugan's handle, and he was free. The weight of Balroth's power was gone from him as though it had never existed.

He stood up, squared his shoulders, and raised the Tugan high in the air. He bellowed the hooting war cry of his ancestors, slamming his fist on his chest in challenge as he stared up into the face of evil.

Balroth raised an eyebrow at the sound. He turned to scan the field of prone bodies - most dead, but some alive - and was astonished to see one figure standing up in defiance.

Well, that just won't do. Not at all. Balroth knelt to get a better look, and almost snorted with laughter to see that it was an ape! An ape with an axe! *Does he really think I won't kill him for his audacity? Not that it matters what he thinks, anyway.* Balroth casually reached one hand towards the tiny creature and suddenly felt a searing pain, a fiery agony that he had never experienced before!

As the giant god recoiled in surprise and pain, Ch'shok urgently turned to Layton, who had struggled to one knee, Jidaan in hand. Layton had already guessed Ch'shok's intentions, and his Jidaan burst into opalescent brightness. A small window of energy appeared high in the air a few yards away from Balroth's face. At first, the gigantic Daemon-God did not notice it as he clutched at his bleeding hand. Then he caught sight of the tiny, glowing portal and shifted his gaze to it. He narrowed his jet black eyes in puzzlement.

The twin of that Gate appeared directly in front of Ch'shok, who held the great axe in both hands. He reared back and, with a mighty cry, threw the Tugan with every bit of power he possessed in his brawny frame. The shining battle-axe turned end over end as it went into one Gate and emerged from the other, striking the astonished Daemon-God full in the forehead. It was a perfect throw, and one huge blade embedded itself deeply in Balroth's enormous skull. A bright burst of light exploded from the axe, searing the inside of Balroth's skull.

Balroth started to scream, but the impact of the axe instantly froze him in place. For a moment, he was a hundred foot tall statue. The light from the axe grew brighter, and Balroth's entire form began to shimmer and shake, gradually becoming an enormous, vibrating blur. Pieces of his body began to detach themselves, becoming an inky black smoke as they disintegrated. More and more pieces broke away and the giant frozen figure began to dissolve, floating in the air like ash before coalescing into an oily fog. The smoke became thicker with each piece of Balroth that vanished until at last, his entire body had disintegrated into a seething black cloud that whirled and churned upon itself. Scarlet lightning began to play within its swirls and billows, but stayed contained within the intense thunderhead. The mass spun faster, and then faster still, and it tightened in upon itself as it spun. It became smaller as it whirled. It spun and spun and shrunk until finally, with a loud POP, the noxious mass vanished altogether. There was a quiet thump as the Tugan fell to earth, and a small puff of dust showed its landing site.

Silence settled on the battlefield. The sun was rising and the day was clear. Safe at last, the first bird finally sang its song, soon followed by others. The new day had dawned, and a gentle, cleansing breeze blew across the face of the land. Mordak and Balroth were no more. Talwynn was free.

Chapter 54

Beauty sniffed and snuffled her way around the battlefield, even as Ishabel called her name from somewhere behind her. She knew the woman was trying to catch up with her, but the dog continued on without a backward glance. She liked the woman well enough, but Beauty had important things to do. Her master had told her to find Ishabel, which she had. He had never said anything about staying away, though, and she was excited to find Gart again.

Occasionally, one of the bad creatures would come near, but she would snap at it and it would leave her alone. The wound in her side was still tight, but had healed well enough for her to deal with anything that accosted her. She kept moving, dodging startled soldiers as she headed north, following the gentle pull that had guided her here across the miles to be with her master. She barked every so often, calling out to him. She knew he was close, and her heart was already singing with joy.

Gart heard her bark and left the others behind as he stumbled back out onto the battlefield. "Beauty! I'm here! I'm here, girl!" The other Guardians stared at him wide-eyed as he lurched into a hitching run directly towards the biggest, most ferocious looking dog they had ever seen. When the beast saw him, she howled with glee and burst into a run as well, her long tongue lolling happily out of her still-bloodied muzzle. She seemed more like a pony than a dog as she thumped and thudded her way across the turf towards Gart, who could not hide the wide smile that had snuck onto his face.

Gart realized a little too late that his enthusiasm had overcome his good sense, and he ended up flat on his back with Beauty fiercely licking the tears of joy from his dirty face. He reached up to ruffle her fur and encircle her in as big a hug as he could manage.

"Well, I see she found ye, then," Ishabel's lilting highland accent contained more than a little laughter in it. "Ye know, she jumped off a boat so she could accompany me, the daft hound!" She reached a hand out and patted the animal's huge flank. "Me and me lads were coming down the River Blackthorne, and she jumped off another boat! The damndest thing, it was! I heard a howling, barking commotion from a passing boat, and then a big splash. We looked over and there she be, doggie-paddlin' for all she be worth. 'Twas quite the production gettin' her into the boat and all, but we managed."

"I'm sure Darryn was glad to be rid of her," Gart said, sitting up with a grin. "She was probably eating through their supplies like crazy."

Ishabel laughed, the sound of it lifting Gart's heart. "Aye! We had to dock a few extra times for more food once she was wi' us!"

Although happy to see her, he was confused. "How in the world did you come to be down here? You were headed to Tamaransett, last I heard.

"An old woman told me to come, that ye needed me, er, us. In a dream."

Gart looked at her in disbelief. "Agatha? She talked to you?"

Ishabel shook her head. "She ne'er told me her name, but she looked as old as dirt. I dinnae remember all of the dream, but when I woke, I kent that I had to gather the warriors of the clan and bring them here. Felt pretty strongly about it, ye ken? Once I'd rousted as many as would come, we boarded a handful of riverboats and headed down this way." With a smile, she reached over and scratched Beauty's head, making her moan with pleasure. "After Beauty leaped from his boat, we hauled up and I talked to yer buddy Darryn a wee bit. Boy, did he have some stories to tell about ye!"

Gart grimaced. "Yes, well, we went through some things together."

"That's what he said!" Ishabel agreed. "Anyway, he told me about ye wantin' to send Beauty to me for safekeeping, but she was having none of it. She must have smelt me or some such, and jumped off the *Goshawk* as soon as our wee ship came close enough! Once we got her onboard, she headed to the front o' the boat and wouldnae stop barkin' until we were headed south again. She missed ye something fierce, I'd say."

Tears welled up in Gart's eyes and he blinked them away. He leaned into the huge hound, hugging her tightly around her muscular neck, and she leaned into him as she panted happily.

Ishabel continued, "Took us forever to get down to the southern edge of the Blackthorne Mountains. We docked there and came west and then north as fast as we could. There was a huge blockage at RedLeaf Valley, but we found thousands of Gholan tracks that led to some caves. Whew! Those caves stank with Gholan muck, but they led us to the Valley. We knew we were on the right track when we saw all the dead beasties out there. We pushed north as fast as we could, and here we be!" She stood with her hands on her hips, smug as could be with a huge grin on her dirty face.

Gart carefully got to his feet, keeping one hand on Beauty so he could scratch her ears the way he knew she liked. She finally settled down and sat next to him, thrilled to her toes to be near Gart again. As far as she was concerned, all was right with the world.

He looked into Ishabel's jade green eyes and she looked into his of deep blue. His breath caught as he took in her rough-edged beauty, her sideways grin, and the morning sunlight shining in her fiery red hair. Before he could say another word, she wrapped her arms around him in a ferocious embrace.

"Ye gods, man, I'm glad yer all right. I..." her voice trailed off for a moment as she held him close, her heart beating loudly against his. Her voice dropped to a whisper. "I was worried we'd be too late. I thought I'd lost ye."

Gart's arms came up and he returned her embrace, relishing the feeling. Through his magick, he could feel her emotions, and they echoed his own: joy, relief, and a strong sense of affection. His face reddened as he also touched a core of desire. He was not ready for that, not yet. But maybe soon. He held her close and let himself enjoy their contact, their sharing.

After a moment she suddenly pushed away from him, still grinning. "Now that we found ye, would ye mind introducing yer friends? Or are ye still an unmannered clod?"

Gart looked up to see that a small crowd had gathered around them as soldiers had regained their feet. Gart recognized the old man he had spoken with earlier, as well as his female companion. Their weapons were sheathed, but he could see clearly how different their jeweled pommels were from his own emerald one. Yet, they were also very much the same. Another warrior, younger than himself, but moving with the ease and grace of a seasoned fighter, trotted up to the group. The young man had a beautiful opal in the pommel of his own weapon, also sheathed at his back. Gart recognized him from the road in the mountains. The man handed Gart's Jidaan to him, and he received it gratefully.

"Well met, sir! I'm Layton. You seemed in such a hurry to catch up with your friends that you left this behind back there." His boyish grin was completely at odds with the battered and bloody appearance of the rest of him. It looked like the lad knew his way around the battlefield, but his expression was that of a youth at his first SpringDay festival.

"Thank you, I...ye gods!" A shadow had been cast over Gart. He was startled to see a mighty gorilla warrior looming over him, its fur matted with blood and gore, its animal appearance somewhat belied by the copper ornaments that decorated its massive biceps and beard. When it merely stood there and raised an eyebrow, Gart recovered, embarrassed. Many people had reacted to the sight of him the same way over the years, and the creature before him was obviously quite intelligent. "I'm terribly sorry. I...um...well, you're a big fellow, aren't you?"

Ch'shok made a deep huffing sound that Gart eventually interpreted as laughter. "Little green Guardian funny!" The enormous warrior addressed the comment to someone at his side. A lovely, musical laugh was the reply. Gart saw his companion, a small and stunningly beautiful young woman, pale of skin, with long dark hair tucked behind her pointed ears. Her slightly tilted eyes sparkled like sapphires and Gart recognized her as a Weya. She wore fighting leathers and still had her slender swords in her hands. With a deft motion, she sheathed the blades and stepped forward to offer a hand to Gart.

"You are the missing Guardian," she stated simply.

"Yes, ma'am. I'm Gart."

"So I've been told," she replied with a smile. She proceeded to introduce him to the others. "You turned the tide, Gart. You wiped out a large part of Mordak's remaining army. Thank you."

Gart lowered his head in shame for a moment before meeting the eyes of the ValElder and the other Guardians. "Had I heeded Brunar's words in the first place, maybe some of this could have been prevented. I'm only one man, but this thing is powerful. I'm sorry I didn't come sooner, but my wife...my daughter..." His thoughts went back to Gennie and his daughter Rheann. He'd had time to think through it all again and again, and he still agonized over his decision. He had stayed, thinking he was protecting them, but they had died anyway. Even so, he had enjoyed a few more weeks with his beloved and his daughter. Selfish though he felt it to be, he would not have traded those days for anything.

Kiran spoke up. "Hey, you did what you thought was best. That's what we all do. You came and saved our bacon, and that's what matters to me." She sniffed and wiped blood from her forehead with her sleeve. "Now would someone tell me what we just saw? Was that who and what I thought it was?"

ValElder Moihra nodded. "Yes, Kiran, it was. It was the Daemon-God Balroth, in the flesh."

Many gasped in horror at the pronouncement. She continued, "Brunar and I had discussed the fact that Mordak was much, much stronger than he had ever been. We think he was somehow using Balroth's power as his own, at least, a tiny portion of it. That kind of power doesn't belong on this plane of existence. That's why it always felt *wrong* to us. When Mordak had released enough of it in our world, it acted as an anchor, one side of a bridge from Balroth's dimension to ours."

Fiona stepped forward. Her head was held high, but tears still stained her cheeks and her eyes had a hollow, faraway look. "Yes, that's exactly what happened. Balroth was cast out of our world by his mother, Rowann, thousands of years ago. It's been said he's been plotting his return ever since. Mordak thought he was using Balroth, but it was the other way around." The lump of amethyst Brunar had given her was cool and solid in her palm. She slid it into a pocket of her robe, then wiped the back of her hand across her face as she gathered strength.

Nessar was puzzled. "What happened to him? Most of us ended up facedown in the dirt under his power. Then there was a flash, and that pressure lifted. Next thing we knew, he was dissolving into a cloud of smoke and then," he made a *poof* gesture with his hands. "No more Balroth!"

The ValElder cast a glance up at the enormous red Augenan at her side, who bared his teeth in a rather shocking grin. "Ch'shok killed him. His axe was ancient and deeply infused with magick. It apparently had its own Destiny to fulfill. With a little help from Layton, he destroyed Balroth."

Ch'shok grunted and held up the Tugan. Where it had always been pristine, shiny, and razor-sharp, it was now dirty and pitted, an ordinary-looking weapon. "Augenan legend came true. Baulotha now dead!" The few remaining Augenan warriors had assembled behind their high chieftain, and they hooted with excitement in support of Ch'shok. Always respected, he had now earned a place among their greatest legends: the Aug who had killed Baulotha.

A rowdy cheer arose as the other soldiers joined in. Soon, the entire battlefield echoed with yells of triumph as the survivors waved their weapons in the air and cheered their victory, thrilled to be alive.

Amidst the celebration, Gart just smiled. He picked up his battered hat and secured it on his head. His heart was filled with gladness and relief, and it had been a long time since that had happened. He looked to Ishabel, who was jumping up and down and yelling herself hoarse with the rest of them, and admired her rough-hewn attractiveness. At his side, Beauty leaned hard on him, and he reassured her with a hearty pat on her side.

He had a strong sense of both ending and beginning. He had walked a hard and long road, yes, but he was just realizing that the road did not end here. Gart found himself wondering what he might find up ahead. Whatever it might be, he discovered he was looking forward to it.

Chapter 55

In the days that followed, there was great sadness and jubilation. The dead of Alverton Falls were rounded up and burned, as were the foul folk of Mordak's horde. One bonfire was far larger than the other, a fact for which the populace was grateful. Alyssa and Bjarke were laid to rest together in the forest nearby, and many tears were shed over their graves. A grateful Count DeRoberds commissioned a monument to the Guardians and all of the warriors who had fought so bravely against the forces of evil. Workers chiseled away at the majestic obelisk at all hours until the Count deemed it a fitting tribute to Brunar and those who had perished alongside him.

As the people came back to the city, they were overjoyed to find it was intact and that the threat to the Realm had been vanquished. A great celebration was held to commemorate the victory over Mordak and Balroth. Dancing, singing, and merriment went on for over a week before it finally started to wind down.

Gart had been there for it all, growing more and more uncomfortable as each day had passed. He and the others had, of course, been instant celebrities, and adoration was heaped upon them at every turn. The Guardians had been the center of attention at event after event, and Gart was most certainly not used to being around so many people, much less being the focus of their adulation. He was glad that, at least, Nessar, Layton, and Kiran seemed to feel the same way.

"If I have to get one more medal hung around my neck, I'm going to punch someone in the mouth!" Kiran tossed another gold-plated medallion on the desk in Nessar's room as she stormed in. "Blasted breakfast ceremonies! At this time of day, I should be training, not stuffing myself full of pastries and eggs."

Nessar clucked his tongue at her. "Now, now, baby girl. They're just grateful. It doesn't hurt anything. I, for one, am enjoying all the good food."

Kiran threw a pillow at him, which he deftly caught and laid down on his own bed. "You hate all this pompousness as much as I do, you old fool."

Leaning back in his chair with his boots on his desk, he quipped, "That's true, but the food is good, no?"

She sat on his bed in a huff, her arms folded tightly across her chest. "Well, yes. Yes it is," she grudgingly admitted.

She pulled a dagger from her boot and started cleaning her already spotless nails with it. "The raspberry pastries were tasty."

"After all we've been through, it's good for us to relax a little. I think we've earned it." Nessar leaned back a little farther, and Kiran thought he might hit the floor soon if he was not careful.

A knock interrupted her reply. She got up and opened the door to find Layton standing there. His face was alight with happiness, and he started talking the moment the door opened.

"Isn't this all just wonderful? I mean, the medals, the dancing, the food. It's amazing!" He came in and leaned his Jidaan against one wall as he sat in the other of Nessar's chairs. As he settled in, he sighed heavily. His expression shifted, losing something of its boyish joy. "As fun as it is, though, I admit I'm getting tired of it. Just a little."

"We were just saying something like that. Weren't we, Ness?" Kiran cocked an eyebrow at her old friend.

"No, *you* were saying that, baby girl. I'm still enjoying it."

Kiran rolled her eyes and moved to close the door when a hand pressed lightly against it from outside, holding it open.

"Excuse me. May I have a word?" It was Gart, and he was wearing his traveling clothes, complete with his battered hat. A heavy pack was on his back, and his gigantic canine companion was at his side. On his other side was the Highland woman, Ishabel. She, too, appeared to be dressed for the road.

Kiran opened the door and stepped aside to let them enter. Fortunately, the room was large enough for them all, but only just so. Beauty found a spot, turned in a circle and settled down on the floor. Gart and Ishabel stood.

Gart cleared his throat before speaking. "We wanted to stop in before we left."

Layton responded before he could continue. "You're leaving? But you just got here! We're just getting to know you." His disappointment was obvious.

Gart nodded as he spoke. "I know. Against my usual inclinations, I've enjoyed getting to know all of you, too. I'm not much for crowds, and this has pushed me to my limit of tolerance. I may never toast another glass again."

This garnered a chuckle from Nessar. "All right, all right, I admit it. I'm with you on that. I've had about as much hospitality as I can stand." Kiran thumped him on the arm and raised an I-told-you-so eyebrow at him. He shot her a lopsided grin and continued. "Where are you off to?"

Gart reached up and rubbed a hand across the scarred side of his face. "I met an old woman on my way here. Her name was Agatha, and she patched me up when I was hurt. She said she knew Brunar back in the day, and that she could help me with my powers. We're going to see her." He took his hat off, ran a hand through his shaggy blond hair, then replaced the battered old hat firmly on his head. "It feels like the right thing to do. We just wanted to say goodbye before we left."

Nessar was the first to respond. "All right, then. Godspeed to you, son. If you ever need me for anything, I'm good for it." He thumped his chair back onto the floor and walked over to shake Gart's hand briefly, and Ishabel's as well.

Kiran walked over and did the same, followed by Layton. Layton knelt to ruffle Beauty's fur and she licked his face for his efforts.

Gart looked relieved after having spoken, and he continued, "Where will you all be headed?"

Again, Nessar responded first. "I'm thinking of heading back to the Hall of Jidaana in the Heartstrong Mountains." Out of the corner of his eye, he registered Kiran's surprise.

"Ness, you never said anything about wanting to go back there. Why?"

Nessar scratched his snowy white scalp absently as he spoke. "Well, we're Guardians, all of us. That Keep was Brunar's home for centuries, and the home of the Guardians before us. It's our home now, if we want it. Seems like as good a place as any for an old man like me to retire. And I keep thinking that it needs one of us to keep an eye on it, anyway. Lots of special things up there. I'd hate for any of it to turn up missing on our watch." He cast a sideways glance at Alyssa and Bjarke's Jidaan, carefully wrapped in an oilskin in one corner of the room. He left unsaid the fact that he wanted to return their weapons to their resting places on the wall where they would be safe.

Layton stood up, his eagerness plain in his voice. "I'm in. The armory held some very rare and interesting weapons, and the library had some ancient manuals on hand-to-hand combat that I would love to research." He put a finger to his chin in mock contemplation. "I'll need a training partner, though. Hmmmm." His face suddenly brightened as though he had arrived at the best idea ever. "Kiran? What do you say?"

"What about your girlfriend, Bekah?" Kiran countered. "I thought you two had a...you know, a thing?"

Layton's hand automatically went to the bracelet on his wrist, made from braided locks of the young priestess's hair. His face reddened, but he responded. "We're just friends. Good friends." When Kiran raised an eyebrow in challenge, he capitulated. "Oh, fine. Yes, we had a thing. But she's going back to Alder Branch in the morning with the other priestesses. Continuing her education, she says. I'll not stand in the way of that." Then he grinned. "Come on, Kiran, I know you're dying to beat up on me. Let's go to the Keep! We can get in tons of trouble along the way; you'll see!"

Kiran threw up her hands. "Ugh! Fine! I guess it would be smart for someone to go along to keep an eye on you two. I'll pack my things and we can leave within the hour."

They all laughed together. Even Beauty joined in with a few good-natured barks, so loud they startled everyone.

An hour or so later, having quietly packed their things and borrowed a handful of horses, they met on the outskirts of town to say their goodbyes.

"When you're done with Agatha, come see us. There's a place for you there, too." Nessar clasped hands with the younger man, his pale grey eyes looking into Gart's intense, ice-blue gaze. Nessar felt Gart's power then, felt it deep in his bones. Nessar kept the smile on his face as he said goodbye.

"I don't know when that will be, sir," Gart had always been taught to respect his elders. "But I have a feeling you'll see me soon enough."

With one last round of waves and farewells, Gart and Ishabel turned their horses to the east and urged them to a trot. Beauty stretched her long legs into a lope alongside them, happy to be on the trail again, happy to be near her master.

Watching them go, Layton was puzzled at first. "They're heading straight into the Blackthorne Mountains. There's no trail through there; they won't be able to get through."

Keeping his eyes on the riders as they moved away, Nessar thought about what he had felt when he had shaken Gart's hand. It had shocked him deeply. Either Brunar had been able to mask his power better, or Gart was far, far stronger than the Mage had been. "Somehow, I don't think that will be a problem for him, lad. No problem at all."

Already several yards ahead of them, Kiran called over her shoulder. "Have you two finished gawping yet? We're burning daylight here! Let's move!"

Nessar and Layton shared a quick grin, then they, too, spurred their horses into motion. As they drew alongside Kiran, they kicked their mounts into a sudden gallop, blowing past her in a flurry of hooves and manes.

"You two scoundrels, I'll put a foot up both your arses! Come back here!" She lurched her horse into a gallop after them. In the center of the road ahead, an opalescent portal appeared, a huge doorway of swirling colors. Nessar and Layton disappeared into it. A few seconds later, Kiran followed, and then it vanished completely, leaving nothing but the echoes of their hoofbeats lingering on the air.

Epilogue

Rask looked out the window of his home and took a deep breath, filling his lungs with the smells of the forest. The freshness of the air soothed him as it always did, the rich aromas of vegetation and earth combined with the familiar fragrance of home. As he watched his neighbors go about their business, gliding along the path outside on their way to various errands, the Weya allowed himself to find peace at last. A lovely voice called out from farther inside the dwelling, and he turned quickly at the sound.

"Rask, love, she wants you!"

Rask instantly left his place at the window and moved towards his wife, who waited patiently in one doorway, a delighted smile turning up the corners of her mouth. Shrya stepped into Rask's embrace and he kissed her warmly.

"Is she feeling better?" Rask asked, just above a whisper.

"The healers have said that her wounds and burns are healed. Though the scars will remain, they should not hamper her at all. She still has nightmares sometimes." Shrya looked over her shoulder into the room, concern etched on her comely face.

Rask kissed her on the cheek, eliciting a bright smile, and then eased into the room. Carefully, he sat on the small bed and leaned towards the tiny figure bundled under the blankets, her face hidden, leaving only a mop of raven-dark hair visible on the soft pillows. Rask was struck by how tiny she seemed, curled up into a tight little ball as she so often was.

In a soft and playful voice he spoke, using the Common tongue, rather than the lilting, melodic Weya language.

"Who's that in my bed?" The bundle curled up tighter under the quilts, and didn't answer. Rask smiled and leaned in closer, speaking in tones of mock sternness. "I can see you in there, you know; I know someone's in my bed. Now who is that? Is it an intruder? Shall I call the Guard?"

A tiny voice answered at last. "It's just me!"

Rask laughed, trying to stay quiet and failing. "I knew it! I knew it was you!" He gently tickled her and her muffled laughter sparkled in the dim room. She squirmed, but did not try too hard to escape. The Weya Ranger smiled broadly at the wriggling bundle. He looked up to see Shrya smiling in the doorway, tears unabashedly rolling down her cheeks.

They had tried for decades to have children, but it had been for naught. They had remained childless, and no Weya healer had been able to discover a reason for it. But now, a child had come into their lives, and they could scarcely believe their good fortune.

"I have good news, my little nubbin!" The girl stopped squirming immediately and stayed still, listening. Rask leaned very close and whispered with as much drama as he could muster, "The Council has decreed that you should live with us, as our daughter. Would you like that?"

The little girl exploded from the bed, startling Rask with her enthusiasm. She leaped into his arms and wrapped her arms and legs around him in as big a bear hug as her little body could manage. Rask folded his arms around her and closed his eyes, overwhelmed by the wave of excitement and joy he felt from the little girl. An instant later, Shrya had joined them, her own slender, strong arms encircling them both. Even more tears flowed down her face as happiness overwhelmed her. The three of them would be a family now, at long last, a real family.

Rask hugged the little girl to his chest a few moments longer, then reluctantly handed her to Shrya, who started fussing over her and tickling her as well. He wiped the tears from his own eyes and gazed at his wife and new daughter as they played and talked. He reached out a hand to trace the scars on the girl's right arm, but she did not notice, so well healed were they. The burns had crawled all the way from her wrist to her shoulder, and across a small part of her upper back.

She had been in great pain and had nearly died, but Rask had brought her to the healers in his village as quickly as he had dared. It had taken them over a week to heal her enough that she could rest comfortably, but in time, they had worked wonders. Even so, they had been unable to take away the nightmares that had plagued the girl early on, and the poor thing had only spoken her first words to them a week ago. Only Rask and Shrya's love had been able to slowly push the dreams away and let the girl's resilient spirit find its way back to life. Now, she played and laughed happily with the Weya children, who had readily accepted her even though she was human. They did not even have a name for her, but that would be remedied soon enough.

Rask shared a look with Shrya and spoke to the girl again. "We've decided on a name for you, my little sweet. From now on, we will call you Reyanna. In our language, it means 'well-loved'. How does that sound, Reyanna?"

The girl turned to look at him, and cocked her head slightly. A slender trace of a burn ran along her jawline, only serving to accentuate her beauty. Rask thought she was the most perfect little girl he had ever seen, human or Weya.

"Reyann. That's my name!"

Rask shook his head and smiled. "No, it's Reyanna, my love," he corrected her gently. As he looked into her eyes, he caught his breath, startled. In the candle's flickering light, her eyes were absolutely stunning. They were the deepest blue, like icy sapphires. He gazed into them for a moment, then leaned over to kiss her gently on the forehead. "Get some sleep, my lovely little girl. We'll see you in the morning." He stood to leave.

Shrya tucked the little girl into her blankets and kissed her good night before joining Rask at the door. They gazed lovingly at her for a few silent moments, watching her immediately dozing off in spite of her desire to stay awake and play. It had been a busy day, and she was tired. Rask blew out the candle and silently closed the door. Hugging each other tightly as they walked, the couple moved down the hall toward their own room, satisfied that their little one was safe and sound.

In the dark of the room behind them, the girl's bright blue eyes opened again. She was unafraid of the darkness, but still felt somewhat nervous without the stuffed doll she had been given upon arriving at the village. It was a simple thing, button eyes and a plain dress sewn onto its cloth body, but she loved it dearly.

Casting her gaze around the shadows of the room, she at first could not see it. A heavy wooden chest occupied the center of the chamber. She thought her doll might lie on the floor beyond it, but the chest obstructed her view. She made a sideways gesture with one hand, but nothing happened. Frustrated, she sat up in bed and concentrated. A tickling sensation quickly grew in her belly, and she smiled at its comforting warmth.

Using both hands, she motioned at the heavy chest again as if to shove it out of the way. It instantly responded by scraping across the floor several feet to the right, allowing her a clear view of the room beyond. Sure enough, she spied the doll near where she had been playing earlier. She stretched out her arms and made beckoning gestures with her hands.

The doll smoothly rose into the air, then flew into her open arms. She caught it and hugged it fiercely. Suddenly tired, she snuggled herself deep into her pillow and blankets, feeling safe, happy, and warm. Her bright blue eyes closed at last, and she drifted into happy dreams.

THE END

Afterword

I started this story in 1994. At this point, that's 24 years. I'd like to thank everyone who ever encouraged me, who supported my work even if it might not have been the kind of thing they read. It's been a labor of love, to be sure, but it's also been hugely fulfilling and a ton of fun. I figure if folks reading have at least half as much fun as I did while writing it, then I've succeeded as an author. Thanks for your support.

For updates about new releases, exclusive promotions, & a complimentary short story, visit the author's website & sign up for the VIP mailing list at http://www.whitmcclendon.com

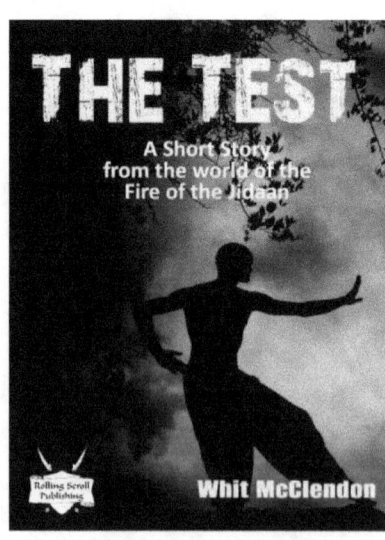

About The Author

Whit McClendon was born on October 31, 1969 in Freeport, Tx. He grew up in Angleton Texas and was active in martial arts, track and field, and playing the clarinet in band. One year at Texas A & M proved that lacrosse was far more fun than electrical engineering, and he eventually graduated with a degree in Engineering Design Graphics from Brazosport College. After working in the petrochemical field as a CAD drafter for many years, Whit finally realized his life's dream of becoming a full-time martial arts instructor. He now lives with his family in Katy, Texas, plays lacrosse as often as possible, and runs Jade Mountain Martial Arts. He laughs a lot more now than he did when he worked at the engineering firm.

whitmcc@jidaan.com
www.jidaan.com
www.jmma.org

www.ingramcontent.com/pod-product-compliance
Lightning Source LLC
Chambersburg PA
CBHW070532030726
47505CB00001B/11